RED EARTH
AND
POURING
RAIN

VIKRAM CHANDRA

RED EARTH AND POURING RAIN

a novel

LITTLE, BROWN AND COMPANY

BOSTON   NEW YORK   TORONTO   LONDON

First Edition

The characters and events in this book are fictitious.
Any similarity to real persons, living or dead,
is coincidental and not intended by the author.

Library of Congress Cataloging-in-Publication Data

Chandra, Vikram.
    Red earth and pouring rain : a novel / by Vikram Chandra.—1st ed.
        p.   cm.
    ISBN 0-316-13276-4
    1. East Indian students—Travel—United States—Fiction.   2. Human-
animal relationships—India—Fiction.   3. Young men—India—
Fiction.   4. Reincarnation—Fiction.   5. Storytelling—Fiction.
6. Monkeys—Fiction.   I. Title
PS3553.H27165R43   1995
813'.54 — dc20   94-48841

10 9 8 7 6 5 4 3 2 1

MV-NY

Published simultaneously in Canada
by Little Brown & Company (Canada) Limited

Printed in the United States of America

For my father and mother,
Navin and Kamna

Contents

Acknowledgments

FOR KIND WORDS, help, and inspiration, my thanks to Yogi Jain; Gilbert Bose; Roshna and Sudha Kapadia; Robert Mezey; Martha Andresen; Steve Erickson; Brad Dourif; Wendy James, friend and patron of the arts; John Barth; Donald Barthelme; Lynn Nesbit; Eric Simonoff; Alexis Quinlan; David Harvey; Amy Storrow; Leslie Richardson; David Davidar; Nicholas Pearson; Jordan Pavlin; Margo True, who made it possible, for whom each page was written; and my sisters, Tanuja and Anupama.

RED EARTH
AND
POURING
RAIN

. . . before.

THE DAY before Abhay shot the white-faced monkey, he awoke to find himself bathed in sweat, a headache already cutting its way into his skull in a razor-thin line across the middle of his forehead. He lay staring at the slowly-revolving ceiling fan that picked up dust with each revolution through the hot air, adding another layer to the black stains along the edges of its blades. Much later, he rose from the bed and stumbled to the door, rubbing his face with the flat of his palms. As he looked out at the sunlit court-yard with the slightly-dazed eyes of those who go away laughingly on journeys and return only to find themselves coming home from exile, his mother swayed across the red bricks, carrying a load of freshly-washed clothes on one hip, and vanished into the stairway leading up to the roof. In a room diagonally across the court-yard from where Abhay stood, his father's ancient typewriter beat out its eternal thik-thik, creating yet another urgent missive to a national newspaper about the state of democracy in India. A single crow cawed incessantly. Abhay forced himself out into the white, blinding square of heat, feeling the sun sear across the back of his neck, and hurried across it to the damp darkness of the bathroom. He stripped off his clothes and stood under the rusted shower head, twisting at knobs, waiting expectantly. A deep, subterranean gurgle shook the pipes, the shower head spat out a few tepid drops, and then there was silence.

'Abhay, is that you? The water stops at ten. Come and eat.'

When he emerged from the bathroom, having splashed water over his arms and his face from a bucket, his mother had breakfast laid out on the table next to the kitchen door, and his father was peering at an opened newspaper through steel-rimmed bifocals.

'We could still win the Test if Parikh bats well tomorrow,' said Mr Misra sagely, 'but he's been known to give out under pressure.'

'Who's Parikh?' Abhay said. He could see, in a head-line on the front page of the newspaper, the words 'terror threat.'

'One of the best of the new chaps. Haven't been keeping up with cricket much, have you?'

'They don't have much about it in the American press,' Abhay said. 'When does the water come back on?'

'Three-thirty,' said his mother as she emerged from the kitchen bearing hot parathas. 'I thought of waking you up, but you looked so tired last night.'

'Jet lag, Ma. It'll take a week or two to go away.'

'Maybe,' Mr Misra said, folding his newspaper. Abhay looked up, surprised at the sudden quietness in his father's voice, wondering how much change his father recognized in his eyes, in the way he carried himself. A quick movement on the roof caught his eye, and he craned his neck.

'It's that white-faced monkey!' he burst out. 'He's still here.'

'Oh, yes,' said Mr Misra. 'He's a member of the family now. Mrinalini feeds him every morning.'

The monkey hopped onto the roof from the branches of the peepul tree at the front of the house, loped up to the laundry line and, with a sweep of its arms, gathered up a sari, a shirt and two pieces of underwear, and raced back to the tree. It waited, firmly seated in the spreading branches, as Mrs Misra went up the stairs and laid two parathas on the wall that ran around the edge of the roof and stepped back some four or five paces. The monkey, moving with assurance, as one moves during the performance of a familiar ritual, swung back to the roof, dropped the clothes, seized the parathas, and clambered back into its familiar leafy territory, where, after it had seated itself comfortably on a suitable branch, it proceeded to eat the bread, cocking its head occasionally to watch Mrs Misra as she gathered up the clothes and put them back on the line.

'It's still terrorizing you after all these years,' said Abhay. 'You should do something about it.'

'It's just trying to make a living, like the rest of us,' Mr Misra said, 'and it's getting old. He's moving pretty slowly now, did you see? Forget him. Eat, eat.'

Abhay bent his head back to his meal, but straightened up every now and then to peer at the peepul tree, where the monkey was intently devouring its daily bread. Somehow, even as he savoured the strangely unfamiliar flavours of his mother's cooking, Abhay was unable to shake the conviction that the animal, secure in the cool shade of the peepul tree, was enjoying its meal more than he was, and that there was some secret irony, some occult meaning in their unwitting sharing of food. The monkey finished first and sat with its head cocked to the right, peering intently at the family below, a puzzled look on its face. It scratched at an armpit, turned and swung itself deeper into the recesses of the peepul, stopped and peered at the sparkling white house with its little square court-yard, and then abruptly slung itself away into the trees on the adjoining maidan.

That afternoon, in the course of his meanderings over the roof-tops of the city, the monkey found himself in a tree on the maidan again. More out of habit than from hunger, he negotiated his way to the peepul and vaulted onto the roof. Below, Abhay was seated at the kitchen table, sipping from a glass of cool nimbu pani, speaking haltingly and somewhat formally to his parents about his travels and times in a foreign land. As the monkey began his customary gathering of garments, he was surprised to see Abhay jump out of his chair and dash up the stairs to the roof. Moving as fast as his ageing limbs would permit, the monkey propelled himself off the roof and onto a branch, clutching just one piece of apparel. A moment later, a nasal howl of pain burst from his lips as a jagged piece of brick shattered into smaller fragments against his rump. Pausing only to bare his yellowed fangs in the general direction of the roof-top, the aged monkey disappeared into the trees on the other side of the expanse of open ground in front of the house.

'He got my jeans,' Abhay said. 'The son of a bitch has my jeans.'

'Well, what did you expect?' Mrs Misra said, a little stiffly, irritated by the sudden violence inflicted on a member of the tribe of Hanuman. 'You scared him away.'

'Will he bring them back? Cost forty dollars.'

'No, he'll probably drop them somewhere and forget all about it. You've lost those pants.'

She walked away, into her bedroom. As Abhay descended from the roof, suddenly aware of the perspiration streaming down his sides and his mother's displeasure, he felt an old adolescent anger awaken, sensed an old bitterness tinged with resentment and frustration leaping up again, ancient quarrels and terrors and reasons for leaving raising their heads, unquiet, undead, effortlessly resurrected.

When the trees extended serrated shadows across the maidan, under a few gaily-coloured kites that hung almost motionless in the air, tiny bits of red, green, yellow and orange against a vast blue, Abhay walked in a huge circle, over the tufts of grass and through the teams of barefoot boys engaged in interminable games of cricket. To the south, in the crowded lanes and bazaars of Janakpur, his past waited, eager to confront him with old friends and half-forgotten sounds and smells. But Abhay hesitated, nagged by a feeling that he had been away for several centuries, not four years, afraid of what he might find lurking in the shadows of bygone days, and suddenly he felt his soul drop away, felt it withdrawing, leaving him cold and abstracted. So he watched himself, as if from a great height, watched himself describe two great circles and then trudge back into the white house. In the same dream-like state, he watched himself converse with his parents and eat dinner. Much later, he calmly observed himself scrabbling in the recesses of a cupboard, throwing aside yellowed comic books and once-cherished novels, to emerge, then, finally, bearing a child's weapon, a child's toy, this: a rifle, bolt-action, calibre 0.22, a miniature weapon, yet sleek and deadly. Hands caress it, linger over its contours, feel the smooth blue-black steel, hands trace the lines of the heavy wood and test the action, snick-CLACK, these hands that belong to someone not familiar to the members of the Misra household, these hands that feed the slim golden rounds into the magazine, click-click-click, these hands belong to a stranger. This stranger sits in a chair next to a window, cradling the rifle, watching the roof. Far away, on the edge of wilderness, a jackal howls, and the dogs from the city retort, but there is no indication that the figure by the window hears any of this.

The monkey, propped securely in a fork high up on a banyan tree, was awakened by the first rays of the sun spreading warmth across his back and a sudden emptiness in the pit of his stomach. He recalled, fuzzily, having been hungry when the sun last set, but the encounter with the fragment of brick had already begun to fade into the undifferentiated grey mist that constituted his past. Ravenous, the monkey skimmed across the tree-tops and roof-tops of the city, to the white house at the edge of the maidan, where a substantial meal could usually be negotiated without too much trouble. The house, the top of its walls beginning to glow a rich pink, was silent, and the laundry line was bare. The monkey wandered disconsolately across the roof, pausing to sniff at the crumpled remnants of a kite. He squatted at the edge of the roof, above the court-yard, feeling faintly, tantalizingly, the lingering odours of cooking float up from the kitchen. Restless, he moves, and is momentarily silhouetted against the pink-white wall where the staircase emerges onto the roof, and then, abruptly, a thin line of white light blossoms from a dark window, and the monkey feels an impact against his chest, under his right shoulder, an instant before he hears the flat WHAP, before he registers, with a baring of fangs and an amazed growl, that something very bad has happened; he feels himself being spun around, sees suddenly the red sun, the pink-white wall splattered with red; the world spins and breaks into fragments, red and white, red and white, another wall a glowing yellow, staggering to the side, the edge, slipping and stumbling, a slow slide, a desperate grab at the edge of the roof, but already strength and balance are gone, and the monkey drops, turning, and in the drop, within the space of that turn, a wholly unfamiliar image, a completely un-monkey-like scene flashes into its mind, red and white, red and white, glowing yellow, three thousand lances, the thunder of hooves, and then the monkey hits the red brick with a thick thump, to lie silently at the edge of the court-yard.

Abhay walked out to the still lump of flesh and fur, carrying the rifle, and stood over it, staring down, blinking, at the neat round hole drilled into the fur, just beginning to fill with blood. A moment later, his parents burst out of the dark recesses of the house, rubbing their eyes.

'Abhay, what have you done?' Mrs Misra said.

'Abhay, you know there is a Hanuman temple not five minutes from here; if they find out they'll start a riot!'

'Is it still alive?'

'Yes, I think so; help me get it inside.'

Abhay watched, his pulse suddenly vibrating and strumming hoarsely in his ears, as his parents picked up the limp animal and carried it into his father's study. His mother came out, then hurried back past him, carrying a pot of steaming water, her eyes reproachfully averted, but he stood, paralysed, the stock of the rifle hard and heavy in his hand, staring with unbelieving, stunned eyes at the stains on the ground, red on red.

For nine days and nine nights the monkey lay unconscious, its chest swathed in cotton, eyes closed, while Mrs Misra held handkerchiefs soaked in milk to its lips, and Mr Misra paced up and down, hands clasped behind his back. The door to the room was kept closed to prevent visitors from catching a glimpse of the wounded monkey, but often Abhay stood outside the room, a puzzled look on his face, moving his head back and forth. On the ninth day the monkey opened his eyes and gazed uncomprehendingly at the ceiling. The Misras recoiled, a little frightened, but the monkey didn't seem to notice them. It lay, eyes glazed, lost in an internal fog in which pieces of a life long gone drifted together, images colliding and melding to form a self, a ragged, patchwork nothing, a dream, a person named Parasher. I know. I am he. I. I am the monkey. I am that diaphanous mechanism once encased in human flesh and known as Parasher, or Sanjay. I am he, come back from the phantasmagorical regions of death and the mists of animal unknowing.

I felt my soul settling into a shape, a form. Each day I remembered more, and each day I grew more conscious. At first, as I lay paralysed, I could barely see the man and woman who kept me alive. When my sight cleared, I saw that they were dressed in garb I could not put a name to but which seemed strangely familiar. There was a look of wariness on their faces that I could not quite understand, and I strained my throat to tell them that I was Sanjay, born of a good Brahmin family. I could, however, emit only sudden growls from the back of my throat, which caused them to retreat in fear. Then, you see, in my delirium and shock, I imagined I was still swathed in the human body I knew so well, with its two scars on the forehead, its flowing white hair and the missing finger on the left hand. So, I lay limp, seeing pictures coalesce in the motes of dust above my head, and I saw a face appear again and again, a broad, kindly face with sad eyes and a resolute jaw, greying whiskers, oh, my Sikander, those sad, sad eyes — I saw this and other things, tumbled together and indistinct. On the sixteenth day I found I could move my left arm. Slowly, straining, I raised my hand away from the soft cloth it had been resting on; slowly, my heart pounding — I believe I knew before I ever saw the fur and the brown-yellow flesh — I brought it up, closer to my immobile head until I could see it, and then my blood ran cold. In that instant, I remembered the last awful moments, I remembered my death, that terrible walk through the rain, and the dark figure that walked beside me. In that instant I knew what I had done and what had happened, what I had become. I brought the hand close to my eyes and looked at it, noting, in a wildly detached manner, the cracked skin of the palms, the matted fur and the small black fingernails. I ran my hand over the contours of my face, feeling the fur along the cheek-bones and the jutting jaw, the quickly receding forehead and the jagged teeth. Gathering all my strength, I raised my head and glanced around the room, seeing first a little ivory statuette on a table, a delicately sculptured chariot drawn by six horses, bearing a warrior and a driver under the banner of Hanuman, and seeing that familiar image I was momentarily relieved, but then I saw the rest of the room, the shelves brimming with books and the strange white sheen of the impossibly fast punkah that rotated overhead, the equally strange pictures on the wall, and I knew then that I was immeasurably far from home. Terrified, I tried to get up, scrabbling weakly at the sheets, whimpering. Somehow, I managed to turn my body; I felt myself drop and hit a hard, cool floor. Dimly, I sensed hands picking me up. My vision constricted, and I hurtled down a long, dark tunnel, and then, once again — darkness.

As my body regained its strength, I slipped increasingly into a hazy narcosis induced by fear, by the terror of the unfamiliar and unknown. Unable to speak to my benefactors, to produce the sounds of Hindi or English with my monkey-throat, I sat huddled in a little ball, paralysed, listening to the strange inflections in their language and the wonderful and incomprehensible things they spoke about. Consider, if you will, the hideousness of my situation. To be sure, I had once professed to despise the condition of being human, and had longed for a life confined simply and safely to the senses, but to be trapped in a furry, now-unknown body, fully self-conscious and aware yet unable to speak and unwilling to communicate for fear of causing terror — this is a terrible fate. To construct an elaborate simile in the manner of the ancients, my soul prowled about restlessly like a tiger caught between a forest fire and a raging river; I was now immeasurably grateful for the gift of self-awareness but was terrified of the trials and revelations that would undoubtedly follow in this strange new world. For a while, at least, I was content to sit in a corner and watch and listen. I learned, soon enough, that the woman's name was Mrinalini. With her greying hair, quick laughter, round face and effortless grace she reminded me of my mother. He, Ashok Misra, was tall, heavily-built, balding, gentle, with a wide, slow smile and a rolling gait. From their conversations I gathered that they had both been teachers, and now lived in retirement, in what passed for vanprastha-ashrama in this day and age, more or less free from the everyday tasks and mundane worries of the world. Apart from the natural respect one feels for gurus, for those who teach, I soon conceived a liking for this amicable, gentle pair. Even for one such as I, it is comforting to see people who have grown old in each other's company, who enjoy and depend on one another after long years of companionship. Perhaps, despite myself, I communicated some of this feeling to them, in the way I sat or the way I looked at them, for they grew less fearful of me. Soon, each of them thought nothing of being alone in the room with me, and went about their business as usual, regarding me, I suppose, as a sort of household pet.

On the twenty-ninth day, Ashok sat before his desk and pulled the cover off a peculiar black machine, which I was to later realize was a typewriter. Then, however, I watched curiously from a corner as he fed paper into it and proceeded to let his fingers fly over the keys, like a musician playing some strange species of instrument related vaguely to the tabla: Thik-thik, thik-thik, and the paper rolled up and curled over, revealing to me, even at that distance, a series of letters from the language I had paid so much to master. Intrigued, I lowered myself to the ground and walked over to the machine, causing Ashok to jump up from his chair and back away. Fascinated, I hopped up onto the table and circled the black machine, running my fingers over the keys with their embossed, golden letters. I touched a key lightly and waited expectantly.

Nothing happened, and I tried again. Smiling, Ashok edged closer and reached out with his right hand, index finger rigid, and stabbed at a key, and an *i* appeared on the paper. Without thinking, delighted by this strange toy, I pressed a key and an *a* magically appeared next to the *i*; intoxicated, I let my fingers dance over the keys, watching the following hieroglyphic manifest itself on the sheet: 'iamparasher.' Ashok watched this exhibition with growing uneasiness; clearly, my actions were too deliberate for a monkey. I learned much too fast. Bending over, he peered at the sheet of paper. Meanwhile, I was engaged in a frenzied search for the secret of spaces between letters, pressing keys and rocking back and forth in excitement. Finally, I sat back and tried to remember the manner of the movements of Ashok's hands over the keys. I looked up at him, and motioned at the machine, gesturing at him to type something again. He grew pale, but I was too excited to stop now. He leaned forward, and typed: 'What are you?' I hesitated now, but I had already stepped into the dangerous swirling waters of human intercourse, tempted once again by a certain kind of knowledge and the thrill of the unknown. There was no turning back. I leaned forward.

'i am parasher.'

When Ashok, his face pale, ran out of the room, I slumped to the hard wooden surface of the desk, suddenly exhausted. Drawing my knees up to my chest, I let my mind drift, filled with an aching nostalgia and afraid of what I would discover in the next few minutes, afraid of the bewildering depredations and convolutions that are the children of Kala, of Time. I let my mind fix itself on one image, and clung to it — red and white, red and white, three thousand pennants flutter at the ends of bamboo lances with twinkling, razor-sharp steel heads; the creaking of leather, the thunder of hooves; three thousand impossibly proud men dressed in yellow, the colour of renunciation and death; the earth throws up dust to salute their passing, and in front of them, dressed in the chain mail of a Rajput, the one they called 'Sikander,' after the rendered-into-story memory of a maniacal Greek who wandered the breadth of continents with his armies, looking for some unspeakable dream in the blood and mire of a thousand battle-fields; even the images we cling to give birth to other stories, there are only histories that generate other histories, and I am simultaneously seduced by and terrified by these multiplicities; I worship these thirty-three million three hundred and thirty-three thousand and three hundred and thirty-three gods, but I curse them for the abundance of their dance; I am forced to make sense out of this elaborate richness, and I revel in it but long for the animal simplicities of life pointed securely in one direction and uncomplicated by the past, but it is already too late, for Mrinalini and Ashok and a dark, thin face I seem to remember hover over me, filled with apprehension and awe and fear.

'Who are you, Parasher?'

I pushed myself up, and typed:

'who is he'

'My son, Abhay. But who are you?'

Abhay's eyes were filled with a terror I have seen before — it is the fear of madness, of insanity made palpable, of impossible events, the existence of which threaten to crack one's mind in two like a rotten pomegranate. He was very close to breaking, walking around me, rubbing his head. I hurriedly typed:

'do not fear me. i am sanjay, born of a good brahmin family. i delivered myself to yama in the year nineteen hundred and eleven, or, in the english way, eighteen hundred and eighty-nine after Christ. for the bad karma i accumulated during that life, no doubt, i have been reborn in this guise, and was awakened by the injury i suffered. i wish you no harm. i am very tired. i am no evil spirit. please help me to the bed.'

I lay exhausted on the bed, unable to shut my eyes, fascinated, you see, by the thought of the world that lay beyond the house. I gestured at Ashok to bring me the machine; as soon as it was set beside me on the white sheets I typed feverishly:

'where am i. what is this world. what year is this.'

The rest of the afternoon, as you may imagine, passed quickly as Ashok and Mrinalini, in hushed tones, told me of the wonders of this time, filling me with dread and amazement as they painted a picture of a world overflowing with the delights of a heaven and the terrors of a hell. Abhay listened silently, tensely watching his parents speak to an animal; he frequently looked away and around the room, as if to locate himself within a suddenly hostile universe. Finally, shadows stretched across the brick outside, and I lay stunned, my mind refusing to comprehend any more, refusing, now, to understand the very words that they spoke; drained, I was about to tell them to stop when a thin, piping voice interrupted:

'Misra Uncleji, my kite-string broke and my kite is stuck on the peepul tree and could you . . .'

The speaker, a girl of about nine or ten, dressed in a loose white kurta and black salwars, stepped through the doorway and stopped short, her face breaking into a delighted smile.

'A monkey! Is he yours, Abhay Bhai?'

'No,' snapped Abhay. 'He's not mine.'

'Come on, Saira,' Ashok said, trying to divert her, but Saira's interest had been aroused, and she was clearly a very intelligent girl with a very determined mien. Side-stepping Ashok, she stepped up to the bed, alert eyes instantly taking in the typewriter and the bandages.

'Is he hurt? I . . .'

She stopped suddenly, but I was unwillingly fascinated by the ball of kite-string she carried in her left hand. I reached out and touched the dangling, ragged end of the string; it dawned upon me gradually that a blanket of silence had descended upon the house — I could no longer hear the chirping of birds or the distant, hollow sound of cricket balls being struck; I let my eyes wander from the string and noticed, vaguely, the goose-bumps on Saira's forearm; I looked up at the doorway and knew then, stomach convulsing, knew, for the air outside had turned a deep blue with swirling currents of black, knew, for I felt my chest explode in pain, knew, for out of the densening air a huge green figure coalesced to stand in the doorway, knew then that Yama had come for me again. Yama, with the green skin and the jet-black hair, with the unmoving flashing dark eyes and the curling moustache, he of the invincible strength and the fearsome aspect, he who rides the terrible black buffalo, Yama, who walks in all three worlds and is feared by all.

'Sanjay,' said Yama, stepping in, banal as always, 'we meet again.'

I was silent, and noticed that the others in the room were looking at me curiously. Saira turned away and bent over the typewriter, reading my side of the strange conversation that had taken place earlier.

'They can't see me,' remarked Yama. 'Only you. The child felt something for a moment.'

'What do you want?' I snapped, and my friends, hearing only a monkey growl addressed seemingly to empty air, stirred uneasily. Saira tugged at Abhay's sleeve and began to whisper in his ear.

'What do I want? What do I want?' Yama gloated. 'Surely you joke. Surely you felt the pain in your chest, the convulsing of your stomach. You were an old monkey, Sanjay, and even though the bullet was small, it was enough. You'll notice I came for you myself. I, the very Lord of Death. No minions to be sent for you, an old and honoured adversary.'

'Already?'

'Already. You've had more than you should've already, this return to human consciousness. An accident which I must admit I don't understand completely myself.'

'To . . . to what?'

'You mean, what next?' he said, suddenly laughing uproariously, exposing great white teeth. 'Where on the wheel is the next time around? Is it to be up a ladder or down the slippery back of a past misdeed, suddenly fanged? I don't know, Sanjay. Karma and dharma, those are mechanical laws sewn into the great fabric of the cosmos, you understand, mysterious in their functioning; there's no predicting the results of those deadly calculations, each deed producing a little burst of karma to be weighed in those inscrutable balances; who knows, who can understand the subtle ways of dharma? — but you've undoubtedly been a bad monkey, Sanjay. Instead of attending to monkey dharma, you've haunted the dwellings of humans, begging to be captured, to be reintroduced, in one way or another, to the society of these clumsy but admittedly lovable creatures. In one life you allowed yourself to be captured by a princeling's hunters, and spent your time happily amusing spoilt young royalty, in another, you allied yourself with a blind holyman, thus adding to his reputation as a miracle worker and enabling him to carry on a life of debauchery and dissolution. In all your monkey-lives, you've ignored your natural relatives and hidden by ventilators and windows, listening to the speech of another species; haven't you noticed how easily you understood what these friends of yours were saying? Somewhere in your soul all those lives have left a sediment of the knowledge you acquired unknowingly, so now your speech is a curious mélange of living words, dead expressions and buried and forgotten phrases.'

As a rule, I am told by the ancient legends, Yama is shunned by inhabitants of the three worlds. It is hard to make light conversation with one who wears that deadly silver noose at the waist; consequently, when he gets a chance to talk, he tends to run on.

'A monkey again, at best,' he finished, frankly gloating (I had cheated him once too often). 'At worst, who knows? A shrew? A happy crab at the bottom of some turbulent sea? What do you think?'

I saw, then, clearly what lay ahead of me — life after life of scuttling through murky waters filled with danger, aeons of mute desperation divided equally between the twin demons of hunger and fear, and, worst of all, eternities of what I had once wished for: incomprehension, unself-consciousness; with the last of my strength, I rolled out of the bed and onto the floor and quickly dragged myself into the dark recesses underneath it. I lay there panting, watching Yama's gigantic gold-sandalled feet move closer to the bed to stand firm and immovable as pillars beside it; then, then a slim silver noose — so toy-like, you would think, so harmless — appeared to arc and weave like a living thing, nosing around under the bed, darting, snapping from side to side, seeking me, drawing closer, closer. I shut my eyes: Rama, help me; Vishnu, I seek your refuge; Shiva, Lord, I come to you with lowered head; I felt a swish of air across my cheek as the death-bringer snaked closer; Hanuman, best of monkeys, protector of poets, I am a member of your clan, bound to you by blood, help me; I felt a rough furry swipe across my right cheek, something long and thin — death, death, death. I awaited the beginning of the abstraction, the quick dropping-away from the flesh, but felt another rough furry slap across my left cheek. Rough? The noose is silver and soft, seductive in its silkiness, it comes to you gentle and pleasing like a lover; I opened my eyes.

An aged white monkey sat in front of me, swinging his tail back and forth. I moved my head just in time to avoid another encounter with his tail, and started to speak, but he held his finger to his lips. Reaching out towards the searching noose, he held his index finger out to it. Jumping forward eagerly, it wrapped itself around the skinny digit and tightened, already pulling back; I watched, appalled, and waited for the strange monkey to die. Nothing happened. I saw Yama's feet move closer to the bed — I could well imagine the puzzlement on his face, for who can resist the silver noose? — and then his heels dug in as he exerted his enormous strength on the cord. The monkey, holding Yama down effortlessly, holding, you understand, the Lord of Death as you or I would hold a child, turned his head back to gaze at me with glittering eyes, and winked at me, laughing, laughing, and it was then that I understood. O Hanuman, you are the best of monkeys, the most loyal of friends, the protector of the weak, the refuge of poets — you are eternal, undying, O Son of the Wind, strongest of the strong. I praise you.

A long time ago, in the second age of the world, when men could speak to animals and the great sages still walked among us, Lord Rama fought a great war against Ravana, the demon king, and Hanuman, Son of the Wind, fought by Rama's side. Long after the war was won, Rama felt the shadow of Kala sliding across his world, and bid good-bye to the grief-stricken citizens of Ayodhya. Hanuman too came to say good-bye, falling out of the sky like a thunderbolt, and it was then that Rama said to him: 'As long as men and women tell your story, you will live, indestructible and invincible.' And so Hanuman still lives on the green slopes of the Himalayas, his strength redoubling every decade as grandmothers while away long summer afternoons by telling children about his exploits, about Hanuman the loyal and the steadfast, this Hanuman who now leapt from beneath the bed, chattering with glee. He ripped the noose from his finger and jumped to the top of the doorway, down onto the desk, up again onto a bookshelf and then somersaulted down to squat on the ground, grinning.

'Oh,' said Yama, 'it's you.'

'Me,' answered Hanuman, and was lost in a fit of laughter. I crawled out to crouch behind him, still afraid of the moving silver circle swinging from Yama's waist-band.

'Not a very good jest,' said Yama primly. 'Stand aside. It is his time.'

'Not yet, great prince,' said Hanuman, lowering his head, suddenly obsequious. 'Grant him a little more time in this harsh world; he has unfinished business.'

'Can't be done. Stand aside.'

'He is my brother by blood.'

'Even monkeys are mine, at the last. Move.'

'He is a poet.'

'They especially are travellers to my kingdom.'

'He is a poet who called to me for protection.'

'A perpetrator of mere doggerel calling to an ancient tree-dweller,' snorted Yama. 'Stand aside.'

'Do you know who I am, Yama?' hissed Hanuman, rising, and suddenly he towered above the sorrowful god, his red lips pulling back to reveal yellowed teeth, muscles shifting like cables beneath the white fur. 'I am Hanuman; I live through the voices of men and women and the dreams of children; I defy you. I spit upon your clumsy ironies and your little indignities.'

Hanuman reached out, snarling, and Yama stepped back quickly. They faced each other silently for a moment, and I felt the very air come to a stand-still. Then Yama's face twisted into a smile.

'What, then?' he said. 'I can't just let him go. Can't be done.'

'Oh, he has something for you,' Hanuman said soothingly, small and amiable again. 'He's a poet. He was going to tell them what happened to him; a sort of story, you see.'

'I don't want to know what happened,' said Yama. 'I was there for parts of it. They all come to me. I know what happened.'

'I won't tell what happened,' I stammered eagerly. 'I'll make a lie. I will construct a finely-coloured dream, a thing of passion and joy, a huge lie that will entertain and instruct and enlighten. I'll make The Big Indian Lie.'

'Too easy,' said Yama. 'I'm an easy audience. It's no great trick to entertain me. Anything that will divert me from what I must do every day I'll take. No, that's too easy.'

'I'll entertain you and them,' I said, desperate, gesturing at Abhay, Ashok, Mrinalini and Saira. 'They're a fine audience, educated and discriminating, gentle and discerning. How's that for a wager? Suppose, suppose that in my telling I lose a part of them, then let me lose life. Suppose a part of them, say half, turn away, bored, then let it be the bottom of the sea.'

I must confess that I said this without sufficient thought. I was weak with fear, irrational and impulsive. Then, I would have bargained away kingdoms, gold, love, anything, for a minute of this precious awareness of life and living. Then, I didn't think about the monster that I was about to face, about this fearful adversary — an audience. Yama, however, seemed to realize what I had let myself in for. His lip twitched.

'Fine,' he said, 'fine. Let's say, half of the audience at any time, on pain of death. Let's say, for three hours an evening.'

'Hold it,' snapped Hanuman. 'That's too much. Let's negotiate.'

As they whispered, as proposals and counter-proposals circled each other like war chariots, I noticed my soon-to-be-audience, my jury, staring at me, bewildered. I pulled myself up onto the bed and typed a short synopsis of the events that had just occurred. I need not, I think, describe the expressions on their faces as the words and sentences appeared on the white paper; suffice it to say that Abhay walked around the room, reaching out into the air with trembling, searching fingers, finding, of course, nothing. Finally, he faced me, hands clenched.

'This is insane,' he whispered. 'Crazy. I can't be talking to you.'

'Why are you so afraid, Abhay Bhai?' said Saira, a little peevishly. 'Hanuman's here.'

Hanuman hopped over to me.

'Right,' he said. 'How's this? At least half of the audience is to be kept in a state of interest for a total of two hours each day. If, at any time, I judge that more than half of your audience is bored for more than five minutes, you will pay the forfeit. Boredom is to be defined as an internal state, externally recognizable through signs such as shifting restlessly, talking to neighbours, playing with shoe-laces or other items, drooping of eyelids and nodding of head, et cetera, et cetera. Do you accept me as judge?'

'You are Hanuman, the best of monkeys. I accept.'

'Fine,' Hanuman said, smiling. 'We'll start tomorrow. Our friend here will have his scribes draw up a contract, which we'll read carefully before signing.'

'Read it all you want,' said Yama. 'My scribes are faultless. I'll be back tomorrow at six. Be ready.'

He motioned with his arm, a great sweeping gesture that curved his limb like a striking snake, and a large black throne appeared in a corner, a throne with square corners and blunt contours and a blackness that is the colour of empty space, speckled lightly with the far-away glinting dust of stars. He stepped out of the room.

'Tricks,' sighed Hanuman, 'tricks and fancy dress, that's all he's good for. Well, sleep well. Think well. I'll be back tomorrow.'

'Thank you,' I said, bowing to Hanuman, my friend and my refuge.

'Ah, nothing, it's nothing,' Hanuman said. 'You're a poet and I'm your friend.'

And then he was gone, flashing out through a half-closed window.

I was tired and needed to think. Quickly, I told the rest about the story-telling that was to come the next day; again, Abhay reached out, trying to find solid tactile evidence of the presence of Yama's throne, and again his fingers, unfeeling, passed through the surfaces of what only I could see.

Later, I lay awake, listening to the crickets and the swish of wind through the plants outside the window, turning my head occasionally to peer at the black throne in the corner, a slab of greater darkness in darkness; faint diamond-points of light flickered deep within; I tried to cast my mind back and bring up memories that could be transmuted into stories, but could only think of the richness of the world, of its verdant profusion — the delightful perfume that issues from queen-of-the-night as its flowers slowly open, the croaking of frogs, the silver light of the moon and the mysterious shadows, the swaying of the tree-tops and the way voices carry at night, the way a soft hip fills the palm of a hand, solid and comforting. Overpowered, I thought: we are blessed, and how strange it is that we can learn to hate even this, that we forsake these gifts and seek release; the sheets are cool and smooth below me, and this I am grateful for, I can feel the breath slide in and out of me, and this I am grateful for; surely, this must be enough, to feel these things and to know that all this exists together, the earth and its seas, the sky and its suns.

THE BOOK
OF WAR
AND
ANCESTORS

. . . now . . .

THE CONTRACT WAS DRAWN on fine golden paper, smooth to the touch, in both Sanskrit and English. Hanuman and I pored over it, and, sure enough, there were no mistakes, no subtle clauses in fine print that would return to haunt us.

'Fair enough,' I said. 'Do I sign in blood, or what?'

'Don't be silly,' said Yama, holding out a quill. 'If that's the sort of thing your taste runs to, you won't last long.'

'We'll see,' I said, scribbling my name in red-inked English at the bottom of the scroll. I had sent Saira out to the maidan with instructions to bring back as many young friends as could be persuaded to abandon their games of cricket, swearing them to secrecy and promising a great story. If I was going to face an audience which could, at any moment, become my executioner, I wanted the odds stacked in my favour. I wanted an audience full of young faces eager for tales of adventure and passion and honour, full of young minds still susceptible to the lures of unearthly horrors and epic loves; even as Yama settled himself into his black throne and Hanuman found a perch on top of the doorway, I heard the murmur of young voices in the court-yard, speaking Hindi and English accented with the rhythms of Punjabi, Gujarati, Tamil, Bengali and a dozen other languages. The door opened and Saira walked in, looking pleased with herself.

'how many,' I typed.

'Four teams,' she said. 'Maybe fifty. It wasn't easy, I tell you.'

'The whole court-yard is filled,' said Mrinalini, opening the door a crack.

'thank you,' I said to (typed at) Saira, who was clearly not to be underestimated. 'what did you tell them.'

'What you said to tell: secret-secret, a story, nothing about you. Here,' she said, 'this is how you make capital letters. The shift key, you know.'

A, she typed, AB, ABC . . .

Hanuman swayed from the rafters, hanging by an arm and a tail. 'So,' he said. 'What's your narrative frame?'

'My what?' I said.

'Your frame story?' He looked hard at me, then dropped down to the bed. 'You don't have one, do you?'

'No,' I said, shame-faced. 'I was just going to tell it, straight-forwardly, you see.'

'Don't you know this yet? Straight-forwardness is the curse of your age, Sanjay. Be wily, be twisty, be elaborate. Forsake grim shortness and hustle. Let us luxuriate in your curlicues. Besides, you need a frame story for its peace, its quiet. You're too involved in the tale, your audience is harried by the world. No, a calm story-teller must tell the story to an audience of educated, discriminating listeners, in a setting of sylvan beauty and silence. Thus the story is perfect in itself, complete and whole. So it has always been, so it must be.'

'If you say so,' I said.

'I do, and who am I?'

'Hanuman, the most cunning of the dialecticians, the perfect aesthete.'

'And don't you forget it,' Hanuman said. 'I'm listening.' He rocketed up suddenly, into the rafters, round and around, laughing. Then he crouched in the corner between two beams, his red eyes twinkling at me, an enormous smile on his face.

'Enough,' Yama said. 'Begin.'

I looked around. Mrinalini was seated just outside the door, ready to read out the typed sheets to my little allies in the court-yard. Ashok and Abhay sat next to each other, behind the desk. Saira sat next to me, on the bed, holding sheets of paper and spare rolls of ribbon. I could hear the birds outside, in their thousands, and see the leaves on the hedge outside the window, turned gold by the setting sun.

'All right. Listen . . .'

The Strange Passion of Benoit de Boigne.

WHEN THE BLACK MONSOON CLOUDS began to appear on the horizon, Sandeep walked out of the forests at the foot-hills of the Himalayas and went, pausing often to breathe in the cooling air, to the ashram of Shanker. Here, he was received courteously by Shanker and the other sadhus, who brought good food and clear water. After he had eaten and enquired after the progress of their meditations, Sandeep sat back and said:

'I have heard a tale.'

Shanker rose to his feet and brought soothing tea and a cushion to Sandeep. Finally, when all were seated in a little circle around Sandeep, Shanker said, softly:

'We are eager to hear it, sir. Tell us.'

And Sandeep said:

'Listen . . .'

In my wanderings through the dense green forests of the foot-hills, I happened upon a clearing where soft grass grew under foot and sunlight hung in golden bars through the branches above. Weary, I sat on a smooth, black slab of stone and opened my bundle; as I raised my last apple to my lips I saw a form on the other side of the clearing, a dark form lost in the patchy shadows and in the green, black and brown of the trees behind. I rose to my feet and walked over, my feet sighing against the dense grass.

'Namaste, ji,' I said, folding my hands in greeting, for it was a thin, wiry, dark-skinned woman, dressed in bark, seated cross-legged on a deerskin, head bent over so that her shaggy black hair hung down to brush her shins. She was peering, unblinking, into her cupped hands.

'Namaste, ji,' I repeated, with no response forthcoming. I knelt down and saw that she was staring, with a wild intensity, into a little water that she held in the bowl made by her palms. Her face was emaciated. I looked around and noticed the grass growing over the edges of the deerskin, the dead leaves caught in the dark hair and the fingernails that had grown till they curled around, twisted and fantastic. Remembering, then, our first poet, who too had stared at a mystery in cupped hands and found poetry, I resolved to stay in the clearing and serve this woman who meditated upon water, probably seeing things I could not imagine. For a long time, I do not know how long, I attended to her needs, picking the twigs out of her hair and carefully cutting her nails with a sharp knife, while she sat like a statue, never once blinking or looking away from the secret in her hands. Every day, I laid wild fruit and a cup of fresh water by her side. About once a week, I woke to find the rough earthen cup empty and the fruit gone. I suppose I should have felt fear, but looking at her face, weathered and lined, not young or beautiful, I could feel only warmth. I could not imagine that she could do me any harm; I was, after all, her shishya, her disciple. One day, I knew, she would look up at me and smile.

The seasons passed, and still I stayed, and soon I grew so used to the routine of foraging, cutting grass and cleaning up that I expected nothing from her, no explanations, no gratitude, no smiles. In that clearing, in that world of sunlight and rain and night sounds, I felt that I should pass the rest of my days, perhaps the rest of time, serving my silent mistress. The wind moaned through the branches, and I felt as if we had both vanished into the light and dark of the forest, melting away until we were nothing but two particles in the huge surge of life that swirled around us, ebbing and flowing according to the rising of the sun and the rhythm of the rain.

So, one morning I came back to the clearing with a handful of ripe tamarind and two chikus. Putting the fruit on the deerskin, I picked up the cup and was about to walk away when I heard:

'Thank you.'

The voice was husky and deep. I sank to my haunches and peered through the thick black strands that hung down like a curtain. The cupped hands slowly rose and the water splashed over her face and chest; she looked up at me, then, large dark eyes twinkling, and smiled, smiled a happy child's smile that revealed a large gap between her front upper teeth.

'Thank you very much,' she said. I nodded, unable to speak. 'Have you been here for very long?'

I nodded again, and then burst out with all the questions that had accumulated over the long silent days. She shook her head, and would not tell me her name or where she came from. She did tell me, however, that she had fled from the world of men and women, disgusted with its inconstancy and the ephemeral nature of its pleasures. Fleeing, one day she had found herself in that clearing and had resolved to find the solution, the reason, the secret, or die. She had seated herself on the deerskin and had settled her gaze on something distant, neither near nor far, and had disciplined her breathing till she felt how it fuelled her body at each moment. Much, much later, a monsoon storm whipped around her, roaring and snapping, and she heard a voice cry out of the maelstrom — 'Your will is too harsh; your austerities burn the inhabitants of all three worlds; what is it you want?' And she replied — 'There is no completeness; nothing endures, nothing lives; there is only change, unreasoning, unreasonable; only birth and death repeating the same story each time, yet different; why?' The voice laughed — 'Why, you know already; look in your hands.' As she looked down into her hands, rain-water dripping from her forehead made a little pool that she held carefully, and in the pool she saw love, birth and death, poets and warriors, books and armies, the wheel turning, turning. When she awoke out of the dream, she saw me putting fruit at her side. When I would not be satisfied with this explanation, she laughed a little and told me of what she had seen, making, you see, a story of it. This is what she told me. Like Valmiki and Vyasa, who are our elders, incomparable and dazzling, she spoke of honour among men, and of true love long remembered, as in the stories of kings and demons that are told to children by old people, but do not think that this story is untrue, because it is itihasa — thus it was; let this story appear among you, as it happened long ago, and it will clear your heart and cleanse your soul, but beware, for it is no story for those with weak stomachs and nervous hearts — it has in it the heights of passion and the depths of loneliness, the tender wounds of love-making and the hideously cheerful, grinning death-faces of the battle-field. Remember, the players and the play, the song and the singers are the same, there is no difference, remember and listen. Listen . . .

'My life has been a dream,' Benoit de Boigne was often heard to say in Parisian drawing-rooms as his life drew to a close, and was understood, by the fashionable, secretly-contemptuous inhabitants of those rooms, to mean that his adventures in the far-away, unreal land of Hindustan now seemed fantastical and fictional. But when de Boigne, wiping his face and passing a hand over his eyes, muttered 'My life has been a dream,' he meant that he had encountered, in that far-away, unreal land called Hindustan, the unbearably real sensations and colours of a dream, had felt unknown forces moving him as if around a chess-board, had felt the touch of mysteries impelling him from one town to the next, from one field to another.

Even as he grew up in Chambéry, in that part of Europe known as Savoy, a hot wind whistled through the soul of Benoit La Borgne, later known as Benoit de Boigne, bringing with it fancies very much out of place in the simple priest's home that he was born in. In that quiet place of gentle candlelight and musty piety, La Borgne read, again and again, an ancient, tattered copy of a book called *The Romance of Alexander, with Stories of Aristotle,* by a Prussian officer named Blunt. La Borgne read, and dreamt of hidden treasures, turbaned warriors and princesses in distress; he played strange, wild music on an out-of-tune piano, took fencing lessons and surprised his master with the ferocity and determination of his thrusts. He spent much of his time at a stream that ran through the family's property, where a water-mill rotated endlessly, grinding, crushing; he liked to go inside, to sit on old wood and watch the wheels spin, driving the faithful machinery in predictable patterns. The workers in that mill grew used to the sight of Benoit La Borgne seated with his chin cupped in a hand, hypnotized by the regularity of the click-click-clicking gears. In that even, metronomic motion, the boy and then the man found a kind of peace; as the myriad grains, gritty and jostling against each other, descended into the hopper to emerge as finely-ground, white, even powder, La Borgne nurtured the other world within him, entertained and enthralled.

He was a somewhat listless and drowsy-looking boy who grew into a strapping young man with a large sloping forehead that belonged on a marble bust of one of the ancient Greek philosophers. His stature, his features, his remoteness, a habit of staring into the distance, as his heart stirred to inexplicable, abruptly-appearing internal images — all these things gave La Borgne an unintentional air of conscious superiority; it was this distant stare that inadvertently rested on a Sardinian officer in an inn in the European year of 1768.

The officer turned back to his food and felt La Borgne's grey eyes burn into the back of his neck. The food was rough and provincial, but good. The officer laid down his knife and turned slowly to look over his shoulder. La Borgne sat with an untouched glass of wine in front of him, his hands on the table; his glance, filled with something that could have been mistaken for hauteur, was unwavering. By making a physical effort, the officer was able to turn away again; he gestured to a waiter.

'Who is that? Behind me.'

'Benoit La Borgne. His father is a priest, and wants him to be a lawyer, but he does nothing.'

The Sardinian turned back to La Borgne, who was still lost in a waking dream, feeling vague unnameable tugs at his soul, pointing him in some unspecified direction.

'Why do you look at me, sir?'

La Borgne said nothing. The Sardinian pushed back his chair and stood up.

'Why are you looking at me?'

La Borgne gradually became aware of a dark, mustachioed face glowering at him. Unbidden, the words sprang to his lips:

'Your face: it reminds me of a pig's behind.'

A quiver of rage passed through the Sardinian's body; he patted his pockets, looking for his gloves. Remembering that he had put them on the chair beside him, he turned, but Benoit La Borgne, seized by a wild purpose, had already sprung up and moved around the table between them; the Sardinian felt a hand spin him around, and then he reeled back, his right cheek stinging.

'Outside,' said La Borgne, already turning away. Outside, behind the inn, the Sardinian attempted to suppress the bewilderment that threatened to turn into fear; taking off his coat, he clenched his teeth and looked at La Borgne, trying to hold on to his anger, but the other's cold, blank face and relaxed movements only served to increase his nervousness. The Sardinian had to look away, at the ground, at the yellow hay and brown soil, at the insects crawling across the little yard, at the dung and the cat staring back at him with unmoving, flashing dark eyes.

The Sardinian's uneasiness mounted; in a few minutes he was actually trembling, but by then it was too late because he was crossing swords with a stone-eyed La Borgne; panicking, the officer flung himself forward into a thrust at the other's eyes which was parried with a force that made his wrist numb, and then he was backing away, flinging up his blade to block a huge hacking slash at his neck; the Sardinian's fingers and forearm rang with the shock, and then his blood, deep red, spurted over bright steel which protruded from his belly; blood which spurted, then, over La Borgne's hand. As he slowly knelt (his sabre already rolling away over the rough reddened earth) the Sardinian looked up at La Borgne, and saw, for the first time, eyes blink and a lip twitch, and wanted to ask why, how, when, why, but the face was already lost in mist, unknown, unreal.

For La Borgne, then, there were witnesses, a furious magistrate and an outraged father. The magistrate threatened proceedings and prison, but was pacified by repeated visits by the good père and a promise from La Borgne to leave the province. Filled with a gratefully-felt sense of purpose, La Borgne set out for France and the famed mercenary ranks of the Irish Brigade.

He spent the next few years in Landrecies, Flanders and the Isle of France, learning the trade and craft of soldiering from men from every nation in Europe. For a while, in the tramp of close-order drill and the eager reconstruction of past victories, La Borgne's mind was clear, unvisited by the glisten of blood and the smell of fantastical animals; he kept *The Romance of Alexander* hidden and locked in his trunk. In barracks, however, he became aware of certain stories that were heard at the time of the setting of the sun, that perfumed the dreams of the rough, scarred men who slept, twitching, on wooden beds. There was a story about a huge diamond that glittered, waiting to be taken, in the forehead of a grotesque heathen idol. There was another story about a magical tree that, when shaken, showered rubies and pearls onto the ground. There were swarthy magicians whose curses bit and mangled like war-dogs, beautiful women who twined and twisted and teased and, always, wealth beyond imagining. These stories seduced La Borgne; despite himself, he found himself seeking out the best of the story-tellers, the ones who constructed the most enchanting and the most grotesque of fictions; caught, he struggled — he enjoyed the monotony of days defined by bugle calls and sweat-stained rule-books. For the first time in his life, he was free; he sensed danger in the titillations of the seemingly innocent tales that webbed the twilight air.

Sure enough, one bright crisp morning, La Borgne found himself telling the story of Alexander and a giant knot. 'Listen,' he said, to the circle of scarred men, and even as he told the story, as he invented and changed and caressed with his words, he felt the familiar, dangerous turbulence in his heart, like a storm of deep colours from a distant, unknown landscape. He understood that he had learnt enough, that his time of peace was over, that for him there was no deliverance from the tyranny of the future. The next day, he resigned his commission and began wandering through Europe until he was in Greece, where an Admiral Orloff was commanding a Russian force against the Turks, in a war that has already passed out of memory and myth into the deathly still of libraries.

Once again, La Borgne found time assuming a jagged, fragmented form, leaving him with sudden gasps of awareness and long periods that passed in a daze; and so one morning, before dawn, with the sea lightening from a deep black to an opaque grey, he found himself in a creaky boat crowded with Russian sailors and marines, moving slowly towards a dark mass called Tenedos. He clutched a pistol butt in one hand and a sheathed sabre in the other; listening to the slow groaning of the oars, feeling the way the brass arced smoothly across the polished wood of the pistol and the rough felt on the sheath that scraped across his thumb, La Borgne thought of what was to follow in a few minutes, but could feel no fear. Around him, the staccato hiss of whispered prayers rose to hang above the boat, but La Borgne could feel only an exhilarated wonder — the water lapped quietly against aged wood — and a white calm; he tried to imagine what was to come, the tearing boom of cannon fire and the blood. The wakening birds on shore twittered at the red tinge seeping over the horizon.

On shore, he crouched and ran, ahead of a line of men, towards the darkness massed under thickets of palm-trees and brush. Hearing a soft cough behind him, a curious cough with liquid in it, La Borgne turned his head to the right to look; his legs slid out and to the sides, his head seemed to slip back, sand swept up in a soft puff. He noticed that the sun had come up. There were feet, huge feet, black and awkward, soundless, running past his eyes. A sea-gull wheeled overhead. The sky is huge; it can swallow you up.

He woke in a creaking cart filled with blood and groaning, wounded Russians. He felt cord biting into his wrists, behind his back; a long, thin explosion of pain grew at the back of his head with each motion of the cart and drifted into his eyes. He raised his head, his cheeks brushing over wet cloth and stained flesh, then struggled to sit up. A bearded face bared teeth at him from the front of the cart, screaming invective in a foreign tongue; dizzy, his head rocking, La Borgne watched as an arm curled behind the face and swung back, as a black length of leather curved around and disappeared in a blur to crack, with a sound like dry wood breaking, along his temple. He fell back to the filthy bottom of the cart and wept.

A month later, La Borgne and the other survivors of the disastrous Russian attack on Tenedos were sold as slaves. Dressed in rags, ashamed of the manacles on their wrists and shamed by the vociferous bargaining, the prisoners avoided each other's eyes and did not care to say good-bye as they were led away. La Borgne was again possessed by an unnatural calm. The manacles around his wrists and his status as a draught animal had released him from his visions; he therefore took to the life of a slave with enthusiasm. In the household of a Turkish noble of middle rank, he hewed wood and drew water with relief and a kind of love; the children of the household soon clustered around the burly pale man and attempted to teach him their language, often scolding him and even cuffing him when he proved slow to learn. La Borgne smiled and shook his head like a bear, like a trapped animal glad to be in captivity and out of the jungle.

The Turk, meanwhile, conducted negotiations with La Borgne's father the priest through letters and couriers; two years after the battle of Tenedos fat sacks of gold arrived at the Turk's house on mules. Told that he was free, that he was supposed to leave, that he had to leave, La Borgne sat on his haunches in the fashion of the East and raised his hands to his face and wept, a nine-year-old Turkish boy by his right knee and a four-year-old girl to the left.

In Constantinople, then, he awaited a visitation, a direction, waited for some mad phantom poet to take hold of the strings again and fill him with purpose, with envy, lust, greed, anger and love. When nothing came, when no ghost horses wheeled about him and when no mysterious daggers beckoned, La Borgne felt a great disappointment grow within him. He stumbled through the crowded streets, pushing aside orange-sellers and potters and mullahs; slowly, he became aware that one word seemed to float on top of the buzzing murmur in the bazaars and cafés, a word that he heard even when it was spoken on the far side of a crowded room, a word that sounded like a distant drum in his ears: *Hindustan.*

La Borgne understood. Armed with letters of introduction from various European noblemen whom he had met in his wanderings, he made his way to St. Petersburg and presented himself at the court of Catherine. There was no reason, no reason that is comprehensible now, so many years later, no reason why that woman, that queen, should have agreed to finance a stranger's trip to Hindustan. It could have been that she remembered the czar Peter's greed, his intention of sending armies through the passes of the Hindu Kush and the Himalayas to acquire the fabled riches of Hindustan, to extend the borders of the monolith that he envisioned till they disappeared into the warm depths of the Indian Ocean. Or perhaps it was just that Catherine saw a kindred soul, another far-eyed face hiding internal hauntings. Or perhaps Catherine thought it inadvisable to detain one who strained towards the future, who was called by what-was-to-come as some men and women are beckoned by religion; a week after his first audience with the queen, La Borgne rode to the south.

In Aleppo, he found a caravan bound for Baghdad; harassed by wandering bands of horsemen from a Persian army scattered by the Turks, the long line of carts turned around a quarter of the way out and slowly made its way back. But La Borgne had seen his visions and heard voices speak to him; he found a ship bound for Alexandria. A storm picked up the boat near the delta of the Nile and flung it about like a toy, splitting it from end to end and scattering its passengers over the steel-grey water. La Borgne was found vomiting yellow and green bile onto a white beach by a group of Arab traders mounted on camels; the Arabs were bound by a code of honour bred in the desert, a code which forbade them from mistreating the weak and the sick. The Arabs picked up the unbeliever and tied him to a camel-saddle. Three days later, they dropped him, face down, into the mud on the outskirts of Cairo and disappeared into the heat-waves.

La Borgne recovered speedily from heat-stroke and starvation. Again, his stature and bearing and his air of mystery, the electric, dangerous smell of purpose that hovered around his body, assured that he was provided with money and letters of introduction; strangers reached into their pockets, strangers fed and clothed him. Armed and outfitted, La Borgne set sail for Madras over calm seas, the curved bow parting even, complaisant water at the Cape of Good Hope, then past Madagascar, through long, quiet days with a good wind behind. There were no more storms. La Borgne leaned against a bulkhead, at peace. The Hindustan that he was approaching was witnessing the decline of the Moghul empire and suffering the consequent fratricidal struggles. There would be place for a soldier.

Ten years after he had left his father's house, La Borgne smelt the odour of grass and mud and knew he was home; a skiff carried him to a flat, wide beach. He fell to his knees and scooped up handfuls of sand and flung them over his head. The sand clung to his hair, making him look older than his twenty-seven years. La Borgne laughed; he felt the sun on his face. He stripped off his jacket and flung it into the water. A few children, dark and curious, dressed in many folds of fine white cloth, emerged from the line of trees that ran around the beach. La Borgne laughed again.

In Madras he found Moulin, a tall, thin French officer with white hair and a scar that stretched from a corner of his forehead across an empty socket to just above his lip. Moulin read La Borgne's letters of introduction and took him back to his sprawling house in the middle of a thicket of trees and pointed him firmly towards the bathroom; when La Borgne emerged he found a new set of clothing laid out for him, a pair of closely-fitting cotton pants and a finely-embroidered, light coat that seemed to float against his skin. Moulin and La Borgne sat in a balcony, a breeze shifting their hair. Servants brought out plates of food.

'This is a pulau: rice and meat,' and La Borgne found himself leaning low over a dish, stuffing food into his mouth with both hands, the insides of his mouth dancing. 'I have a cook from Lucknow, and this is zarda, sweet rice with saffron and raisins, and this is kabab, ground beef, and this is paratha, bread,' and La Borgne was dizzy with the spices and the smells, rich and thick and heavy; later, the servants brought out hookahs that burbled gently, and La Borgne felt the quiet of the evening settle around him.

He was awakened from a deep dreamless sleep by the hollow click of hooves against stone. He sat up, and Moulin was looking away, to the west, where a line of horsemen drifted across the sun. 'Learn their languages,' Moulin said, and pointed to his scar. 'They can do this, but often they send a message to you on the evening before they attack, asking to be granted the honour of combat.' He shook his head. 'Somebody is going to take all this. On the field they fight each to himself, like it's a personal quarrel. I was a barber in Lyons, and now I eat like this.' He rubbed his face, and then said morosely: 'You're going to get dysentery soon. Diarrhoea.'

'No, I won't,' said La Borgne, and he didn't, and the days and then the years flashed by with an increasing velocity; fulfilled, he found a commission with the French forces stationed in Pondicherry; here, for the first time, he drilled Indian troops and encountered, irrespective of the age or religion of the men, that particular and peculiar mixture of pride, loyalty and anarchistic self-importance that distinguished these soldiers from any other martial caste in the world; La Borgne drilled, ordered and trained — he was at peace; then, predictably, he had to move on.

This time, there was a different kind of vision, a stirring of the flesh; he was found in the bed of another officer's wife; officers trained in the European way were scarce, and no duels were allowed, so La Borgne mounted a black horse and rode into the beckoning interior, into the boiling confusion of the clans and states and castes seeking to inherit the mantle of the Moghuls; let us say that he rode across dusty plains and swollen rivers, from Calcutta to Lucknow to Delhi (where the Moghul Shah Alam huddled in his palace and sought release from the misery of his life in piety) and down to the south again; let us say that finally he attracted the attention of a power-broker named Madhoji Sindhia, a man who ruled in the name of the Peshwa but insisted on being referred to as a Patel, a village head-man; let us say that La Borgne entered the service of this crafty Maratha whose armies circled the Deccan and sniffed at the outskirts of Delhi; let us say that La Borgne raised and trained two battalions of infantry for Madhoji, using all his skill, presence and sometimes his physical strength to transmute immensely skilled, courageous, individualistic and unruly men from every clan and class into a single mass, a thing of mechanics, a phalanx, a machine which finally turned and wheeled on order, coerced into synchronization by La Borgne's magical certitude (wheeling and turning while sometimes enduring the laughter and sneers of the proud wild cavalrymen who passed by, sniffing elegantly at roses); La Borgne persisted, driven, and was, finally, to a degree, successful.

Let us say, then, that La Borgne found himself one morning on a field near the village of Lalsot, near Jaipur, with his two battalions ranged to the left of the enfeebled imperial army of Shah Alam, in line with the Maratha cavalry of Madhoji Sindhia; let us say that these men were ranged against the armies of Jaipur and Jodhpur and the troops led by the Moghul nobles Muhammed Beg Hamadani and Ismail Beg; the particulars of this war are now confusing and dimmed by the years — as always, the causes could be said to include the lust for power, greed, fear, anger, ignorance and also courage, loyalty and love; let us just say that on this field of Lalsot, Benoit La Borgne became Benoit de Boigne, that years of wandering had pointed the boy who had been fascinated by the clock-work motion of the flour-mill towards this morning.

Horses danced uneasily as the whoosh of shells tore at the air, followed, a fraction of a moment later, by the dull thudding of the artillery pieces; Muhammed Hamadani was disintegrated by a cannon ball; his head spiralled through the air, sprinkling blood over his men, who moved back uneasily, muttering. Ismail Beg, sensing panic, spurred his horse to the forefront; shouting, he led the ranked squadrons against the Maratha cavalry ranged opposite him. The Marathas reeled; on their left, La Borgne saw a twinkling, silver mass beginning to move towards him. A convulsion seemed to pass through the ranks of his brigades, a whisper moving in quick waves, back and forth:

'Rathor.'

'Stand to!' La Borgne shouted, his voice breaking; ten thousand Rathor horsemen were coming against him, men dressed in chain mail and steel helmets, men from the Rathor clan of the Rajputs of the desert, ten thousand incredibly handsome men, the flower of the chivalry of Rajputana, ten thousand men who claimed descent from the sun, men of the clan which claimed to have forgotten the feeling of fear; sunlight glanced off their helmets as they broke into a trot. There was laughter as they swept down onto the infantry drawn into a hollow square, because no infantry had ever withstood the onslaught of the Rathor cavalry (there were songs that floated through the dry, wind-swept valleys of Rajputana, songs about the Rathor horsemen, the Rathor swordsmen); they broke into a gallop, coming steadily at La Borgne's lines; closer, closer, then the musket-men pulled back, revealing La Borgne's guns — the Rathors riding on, swords raised — then the hot yellow and red belch of grape-shot swept into the horsemen, spilling them over, and he thinks, I will henceforth be known as Benoit de Boigne; torn apart, they come on, keep coming, coming into the guns, slashing at the gunners, beyond, at de Boigne's line, closer, closer, then on command, a vast, long sheet of fire blossoms from two thousand muskets, tearing down the Rathors, spinning them down into the mud, sudden spurt of blood blackening the sand till it is too wet to rise into the air (horses fall into this, eyes rolling, with a wet slipping sound), the volleys ring out one after the other, regular, crack-crack-crack, and de Boigne's men stand elbow-to-elbow like figures made of rock, refusing to rise to the taunts that the baffled horsemen are screaming at them, the invitations to come out and test their skill. De Boigne's men are quiet; there is no cheering because no one has ever seen anything like this; the Rathors are trying to rally, eyes red, but de Boigne sounds the advance, and his battalions move forward, steady themselves, and again, precise and coordinated, the muskets swing up and spit. The Rathors flee.

The forces aligned with de Boigne's battalions won that morning, but that is of no consequence to us now. That evening, when other officers came to de Boigne's tent, bringing gifts, they found him seated outside, his gaze focused on the horizon. The officers laid their gifts around him and backed away, bowing, thinking that he was reliving the events of the morning, that facing the dreaded Rathors was an experience that needed to be faced again and again, till it faded away. They were wrong. De Boigne was seeing visions of the future, and was fighting them; he saw other villages, other fields where he would fulfil the destiny of his flesh and breeding and history, where he would be the instrument of the perverse gods who moulded events and decided the fate of soldiers and nations. De Boigne fought his private battles at night and in the morning, on horse-back and in the perfumed rooms of palaces, but to no avail. On other fields, near other quiet villages with names like Chaksana and Patan, his battalions, moving like clock-work, decimated other hosts. Again and again, the infuriated cavalrymen hurled themselves against de Boigne's unnatural unmoving ranks. At Patan, the Rathors broke and ran again, and a song was heard in the passes of the desert mountains:

> At Patan, the Rathors lost five things:
> Horse, shoes, turban,
> the upturned moustache of the warrior
> And the sword of Marwar . . .

Incensed at this shame, every Rathor capable of bearing a weapon made his way to Merta, near Ajmer. Eighty thousand Rathors collected in this dry brown valley, and awaited the arrival of de Boigne's battalions and their Maratha allies. The armies collected and formed their lines; on the night before the final battle, the Rathors slept well, glad for the chance to avenge themselves; they were awakened by what had never been heard of before — an attack before dawn, under cover of the last darkness. As shot and shell showered the camp, the Rathors awoke from an opiumed sleep to find the day already lost in confusion. Calmly, a certain Rana of Ahwa called twenty-two other chiefs to his side, and calmly they gathered four thousand horsemen; these four thousand prepared an opium draught, raised it to the sky and drank; they wrapped themselves in shawls of yellow silk, the colour of death; calmly, every last action prescribed by tradition was completed, and then the four thousand rode out to the field where de Boigne's battalions were advancing. The cry 'Remember Patan' was heard, and then the yellow horsemen dashed onto the ranks in front of them. Four bodies of men retreated before them, and then they faced de Boigne's main force, which was already settling into a hollow square. The Rathors split and enveloped the square and charged, to be faced by a wall of bayonets and muskets; again, the volleys tore through the mass of horsemen, again, the Rathors, the yellow-clad-ones, plunged madly forward; de Boigne watched, silenced, as they came back again and again; clenching his teeth, he looked up at the sky, looked away, then back, and they came on; finally, with grey smoke and the smell of powder and blood thickening the air and stinging his eyes, he understood that a man can become a general despite himself, that for some there is no escape from the siren call of the future; he looked about and saw with great clarity the frozen faces of his men as they reloaded, the gobulets of sweat on a soldier's forehead, a torn turban being blown about in the backwash from a cannon discharge, a horse on its side, kicking, and something wet and moving and red and white pulsing in a long tear in its neck, a shawl of yellow silk torn and floating and tugging with each volley, a hand poised, palm upward, as if begging, and they came again, and then again — there is no retreat in yellow — till there were only fifteen left.

There was a silence as the fifteen dismounted, a silence that is often heard in battle, when, incredibly, the chirping and twittering and flapping of birds can be heard in distant trees. De Boigne watched as the Rana of Ahwa dismounted and stood by his horse, stroking its forehead, between its eyes. The Rana looked up at the sky, then slapped the horse on its rump. He straightened his yellow shawl, then turned and walked towards de Boigne, the other Rathors following him. De Boigne looked at the Rana's face, noting the grey moustache and the bushy eyebrows, the bushy beard and the large, accepting grey eyes with bags beneath them. The Rathors walked, and there was no fire for them, no one to grant them the promise of their yellow silk; de Boigne opened his mouth but found that his lips were parched, that no words would emerge; in his great clearness, he felt an emptiness within him, a finishedness, and understood that there would be no more visions for him; looking into the Rana's calm grey eyes — so very close now — de Boigne understood that these eyes, clear and far-seeing, had freed him from private phantom sight; he knew that what he had to do now was the end of all romance; gathering all his strength in his throat, de Boigne shouted, and there were no words, no sense, only a howl was heard, a howl like that of an animal trapped by steel teeth, but every man in the line understood, and there was flame, and the grey eyes disappeared.

Sandeep raised a cup to his mouth and sipped. Something moved in the trees up on the mountain side, and a cicada called in alarm. Shanker wrapped a shawl around his shoulders. Sandeep began again:

Listen . . .

The years passed, and there were other victories for de Boigne; he amassed a fortune of three hundred thousand pounds and made Madhoji Sindhia the most powerful man in India. De Boigne's brigades were given the name of Chiria Fauj for their unmatched speed, for their propensity to appear unexpectedly on the horizon like a flight of predatory birds, for the headlong velocity of their marches. Armed with de Boigne's brigades, Madhoji ruthlessly pursued his dream of founding an independent Maratha dynasty; village cattle grazed on luxuriant blood-fed flowers; de Boigne, released from his phantasmic demons, discovered the boredom and banality of everyday life; he rode at the head of a corps, and was famous and rich, but found no release from the dreary everyday business of living, from the hot summer afternoons when the heat settles in the lungs and rises up the spine and turns into a humming in the head. He found no comfort, not in the sweat that gathers in that little hollow between deep breasts or in that heavy sleep that comes from opium. De Boigne prayed to the gods of his new home, but the stone idols did not move, did not speak; longing, soon enough, for the colours that once burned their way out of the darkness at the centre of his soul, he fell into a desultory affair with the daughter of one his Hindustani commanders, took her as a wife and fathered a son and a daughter, but even love and marriage and fatherhood felt like distant fictions, smokey dreams.

One day, unexpectedly, Madhoji Sindhia caught a fever, tossed and burned through the night and died before morning. De Boigne felt the touch of death hiss by him, for he understood now that there was no longer a special purpose to his life that protected him from the bullets of the battle-field or the fevers of the hot summer wind, that nothing but other men stood between him and charging horsemen. De Boigne thought of his three hundred thousand pounds, and the drawing-rooms of Paris, and the water-mill, and childhood, and the fact that if he stayed he would fight other battles not knowing why and when and how, not knowing anything for certain, not feeling anything but doubt, and then he decided to go home, to play the part of the hero, the soldier returned from magical, unreal lands. So he went home, without his Hindustani wife, who refused to leave her home and her relatives for what seemed a fantasy; de Boigne took his children and returned to Chambéry (with the slightly-dazed eyes of one who has journeyed far to find a home and has returned in self-exile) and played the part — he baptized his children and married a seventeen-year-old noblewoman who soon left him for the salons of Paris. He stumbled for a while through the wilderness of drawing-rooms and huge shining dances and noticed the smirks and the giggles that appeared when he did something provincial or unintentionally used a word of Urdu or Persian. So de Boigne lived in seclusion, ignoring summons from Napoleon Bonaparte, who too, it seems, dreamt of the riches and splendours of a faraway land called Hindustan; sometimes, especially when others who had served in Hindustan came to visit, de Boigne would speak of his past, but would always speak of himself as if of another, and would always end with the words 'My life has been a dream.' And the visitors would go away, unsatisfied and a little mystified, not knowing that de Boigne went to sleep every night longing to dream, but saw nothing, that as the years went by he wished that the past would return to him, that calm grey eyes would haunt his night hours, that something would reassure him that his life had been real, not just necessary, but no images came, and de Boigne discovered the horror of living solely in the present and for the future, knew that the present is not enough and the future can use and discard people, and one afternoon de Boigne called his lackeys and caused himself to be transported to the water-mill of his youth. Going inside, he found again his seat, and looked for a long time into the creaking gears and hoists. Finally, he said, in a choking voice, 'There was the start, and then the middle, and this must be my end.' He ordered the workers out and called for a torch; stumbling around, he caressed the old wood with the flame; finally, his attendants dragged him out.

He began then to walk round and around the fire, back and forth, and slowly the rage went out of his shoulders, and the despair from his heart, and after three hours he began to say aloud the names of his childhood friends, and the names of his first pets, and those of his nurses. It was something like a chant, this attempt to remember every man, woman and beast that he had ever touched or seen or heard, and as he went on his memory grew complete and rich, so that in the two days left to him he managed to work up only to the friends of his adolescence, with whom he had stolen apples from gardens and visited forbidden houses. He told his servants that even so it was not complete, that too much was left out, that he had not the strength to remember everyone and everything. He grew weak, but would not sleep, and from his bed he said to the attending priest, 'I have been enslaved by an idea, and this is my end, my climax. But I do not die.'

The priest, who was afraid of exotic blasphemies, crossed himself and said, 'You go to eternal rest, and eternal life.'

De Boigne shook his head. 'No, I die. But my life lives on, and I live, and live, and live.'

The priest said in a loud voice, 'You must believe that you are redeemed, that you go to perfect, eternal happiness.'

De Boigne laughed, and said cheerfully, 'We are not born to be happy.' Near the hour of his death, his eyes grew very bright, and he began to speak in languages that no one understood, and as he whispered in alien tongues, some thought he was asking for forgiveness, and others that he was giving it.

. . . now . . .

I LET MYSELF RELAX, pushing back from the typewriter and lying back.

'You said it was going to be a children's story,' Abhay said. 'What the hell was that?'

I was too tired to reply. I massaged my aching fingers and shook my head.

'Watch out with that martial stuff,' he continued, curiously concerned. 'These kids belong to a different world, they're a different generation. Too much more of that and they'll go back to cricket.'

A little irritated, I sat up. My muscles creaked. I tried to type on, but my fingers cramped.

'Better do something about that, Hanuman,' Yama said. 'Your friend still has an hour to go.'

'What?' I said.

'He's right. Fifty-five minutes, to be exact.' Hanuman dropped from above the door and came over to me. 'You've got to go on — and listen, be careful. You've got us hooked in here, but out there, they're getting a little restless; they're curious, but it's starting to wear off. Too much more in this mode and they're going to start pulling on pig-tails and making rubber-band-bows, and then what? You can rest for two more minutes, but then you've got to start up again.'

'I can't. Look at my fingers.'

'Yes, I know they hurt, but you must.'

'It's not even my fingers; I just don't have any more. Listen, do you think it's easy, doing this, making it all up so fast? Especially with that great black lump sitting there in the corner, even at night when he's gone.'

Hanuman looked at me, his red eyes shining.

'Listen, Son of the Wind,' I whispered. 'Negotiate with him some more; tell him about the wonders to come; make him see that the story will be grand and great. Tell my children out there not to abandon me, for there is much yet to come — Begum Sumroo, the Witch of Sardhana, and her lover, Jahaj Jung, who was once a sailor, and then Sikander himself: Sikander the brave, who led three thousand and was the friend of Parasher the poet, and the romance of their childhood and early manhood, their incredible adventures in Calcutta and in the embraces of the divine courtesans of Lucknow; tell them all this and tell them to come back tomorrow; please, I cannot go on. Look. Look at my fingers.'

'The young fellow was right,' Yama called from his corner. 'You're too old-fashioned; you haven't adapted. Too much more of this kind of heroic saga, distant and strangely impersonal, and I'll have to take you off. Shape up, Sanjay; I must admit I want to hear the rest of it, about Sikander particularly. But come on now; boredom must be reaching critical mass outside.' He laughed. 'Sometimes you outsmart yourself, Sanjay. Back to the typewriter.'

'Hanuman . . .' I began.

'He won't negotiate. The contract's signed. But don't worry, he's too dull for words. Don't let him scare you.' Hanuman turned to Yama. 'Prince, King, the story takes a different turn now. Sanjay cannot possibly give us another hour — look at his fingers. The cramp will not let up; however, the contract, as it stands . . .'

'No,' roared Yama, springing to his feet. 'No more cheating. A story. Now.'

'Exactly,' said Hanuman. 'A story is what the contract calls for; read it carefully — it doesn't say who is to do the telling. Read. "A story will be told. The audience must be kept entertained, or Parasher is to pay the forfeit." Somebody else could do the story-telling.'

'No. This is cheating.'

'Think about it, great Death-lord. Another story, for the price of one, with Sanjay sweating at the side-lines.'

Yama started to say something, then paused. I detected a faint glim-

mer of interest; I could sense his anger seeping away, blocked and
dammed by a delicious new nuance in his revenge.

'Who?' I said, nudging Hanuman.

'His future hanging on another's words, Death-lord. And him with
no choice.'

'Whose words?' I said.

'And a tale of strange lands and foreign folk . . .'

'Who, him, the boy?' I said. 'Look at him . . .'

'Done,' said Yama, 'I will be magnanimous. He has ten minutes to
prepare.'

'Hanuman,' I said, 'great Hanuman, you can't be serious, look at
his face: he can't tell a story; he hardly even knows where he is or who
he is.'

'A contract's a contract,' said Hanuman. 'Hurry up. You have ten
minutes to talk him into it.'

I started to speak, then thought better of it. Beckoning Abhay to my
side, I held my right wrist with my left hand and with a trembling
forefinger typed a summary of the conversation that had just taken
place.

'No,' said Abhay. 'I can't do it.'

'If you don't, he'll die,' said Saira, very ready to be furious.

'If you hadn't shot him, he wouldn't be in this situation,' said Mrinalini.

'You have a certain responsibility,' Ashok said.

Abhay looked around, then put his face in his hands. I gripped my
wrist again and typed; he looked up.

'Please.'

'It'll all be your fault,' Saira said, her lower lip jutting, now ready to
cry.

'I like her,' Hanuman whispered. 'I like her.'

'All right, all right,' Abhay said, his eyes sunken and shining. 'I'll do
my best. But I need more time. Fifteen minutes at least.'

I looked over at Yama. He was twirling his moustache, one knee
settled comfortably over the other, a foot swinging gently back and
forth. He nodded, looking smug. I nodded at Abhay. He rose and began
to pace around the room. The murmur outside began to grow. Mrinalini
opened the door and peered out.

'They're going to start leaving,' she said.

Saira rose from the bed. 'I'm going outside to tell them about you,' she said. 'It's the only way you'll keep them sitting. I'll tell them Yama's in here, too, and that he doesn't want any children inside, so they won't come rushing in when I tell them about a typing monkey; is that okay?'

Yama shrugged, smiling, and I nodded at Saira, bowing to a superior judge of the masses and leader of men; already, I seemed to have forgotten the reasons for wanting to keep my appearance a secret. Some last pride, I suppose, some final need to belong, to be thought of as part of the human whole, but already this vain hope had been crumpled and consigned to the rubbish heap; at last, I am going to be what I had fought against becoming, a freak, a fool, an exile, that most pitiable (forgive my romanticizing — I am conscious of it — but at this moment a pose is all I have left) and yet most generous of creatures: a monkey at a typewriter, a poet.

So Abhay paced up and down, and I hugged myself and massaged my arms. Again Yama called out to me: 'Listen, Sanjay, a bit of friendly advice. You're too attached to what-actually-happened. I recognized too much of what you told. You should be really going crazy, you know, twist your material inside out. Have fun with it.'

I had my own reasons for being attached to what-actually-happened, but I was in pain and in no mood to start explaining myself to this overgrown green idiot who reminded me of the villains from some of the worst melodramas that (in a long-ago life) my father and uncle ever wrote. So I snarled at him, a monkey growl that startled two boys who were sidling in through the door. They looked like brothers, maybe nine and ten, and they both wore strange caps with the bills pulled back over their necks, and loose white shirts with lettering on them, one that said 'Cowboys' and the other 'LA.' They glanced at me and then scuttled over eagerly to Abhay.

'Abhay Bhaiya,' the older one said. 'Did you bring back a video camera?'

'What?' Abhay said.

'Did you see any rock concerts?' the younger one said.

'What kind of car did you have?'

'Did you buy a house?'

'Does it have a swimming pool?'

'Why did you come back?'

'Where?' Abhay said.

'Here,' they said, both together.

Abhay shrugged, a look of confusion on his face.

'Were you happy there?' the younger boy said.

'What?'

'Happy.'

Abhay's face was blank, as if it had been wiped clean of sorrow, or joy. Then Saira came in, saw the two boys, collared them and had the both of them out of the door in a moment.

The little one called decisively through the doorway, even as it closed: 'You *were* happy there.'

Abhay looked after him. 'Happy?' he said.

Then he began to type.

A Thin Kind of Happiness.

ONE EVENING at the beginning of my senior year I was rewinding the second reel of *Lawrence of Arabia* when my friend Tom came into the projectionist's booth playing with his dark glasses. He had a sort of nervous habit with his glasses.

"Come on, effendi," he said. "Time to go to great oasis."

I was the work-study projectionist and he managed the student film series. I had known him for three years, and we liked the same movies. He was talking about the Wednesday night party in the Alpha Gamma frat house, which we never missed.

"Lead on," I said. "Lead on."

So Tom and I came down the stairs into the basement room, which smelled of decade-old layers of beer and sometimes piss and always grass. We pushed through the brothers and got a beer and then found our favorite spot, where we could watch people pushing through the door.

"They're here," Tom said.

"Who?"

"Freshwomen alert. Here they come."

I turned my head, and they were already past me.

"Go get one, bud," Tom said.

"There's only one way out of here," I said. There had been a glimpse of a face half-turned toward me. So we waited and drank a couple more beers and talked about Lawrence. The one in the movie, I mean, not the real one. The music suddenly got louder, and it was Echo and the Bunnymen doing "The Cutter."

Just as the song ended I saw them coming back.

"What should I try?" I said.

"Which one?" Tom said, leaning closer to me.

"In black. Red hair."

"Angst, baby. Be crazy but cool."

So when she was beside me, looking down and trying not to spill her beer, I leaned over and said, into her ear: "Elvis has *not* left the building."

She laughed. We introduced ourselves: she was Amanda James, Scripps freshman from Houston, Texas. Tom and I laughed at that and teased her about being from Houston and the soft southern twang in her voice. Then Tom, maybe noticing something, maybe the way I was looking at her, disappeared discreetly, and Amanda and I stood there looking at each other silently.

"They met in Los Angeles," she said, smiling.

"What?"

"They met in Los Angeles," she said, "at a party while Echo and the Bunnymen throbbed in the background."

"Feeling the cocaine rush through his brain," I went on, "he wondered if he had seen her before. In New York at the Palladium or in L.A. at Parachute. Then he realized it didn't matter."

"And then she — " Amanda stopped suddenly, and then asked: "Where are you from?"

"India."

"Oh." After a long pause: "Are you a Brahmin?"

"No."

"What are you?"

"Nothing."

She looked away, and then another girl tapped her on the arm. They whispered to each other.

To me: "I have to go."

"Why?"

"I'm here with the other girls on my floor," she said, "and they want to leave."

"You don't have to go with them."

"We're going to hate each other soon anyway. I should be nice and loyal for a while."

"Okay."

"I'll see you later."

"Okay."

I pushed through the crowd, nodding at people, looking for Tom. I felt a tap on my shoulder.

"Hey. Abhay." Kate was blond, beautiful in a kind of distant sculptured manner. We had slept together during our sophomore year, and still did sometimes, although we didn't need to be as drunk as we used to be and didn't hold on to each other as hard as we used to. That night she was dressed in a white sweater and looked like she was out of some purposely muted black-and-white picture from a fashion magazine.

"Katie."

She smiled. "How're you doing, Abi?"

I shrugged and smiled, and she moved closer to me, and I had to get my beer out of the way and we put our arms around each other's waist and we stood for a while. People pushed past us. Her hair was fresh, fine. I liked to touch it.

When I came up out of the frat room a bunch of the brothers were hauling a large plaster statue of somebody vaguely Oriental seated in the lotus position toward the staircase. I stopped and listened as they argued. Finally they left the statue at the top of the stairs and went down to get a beer. I went home to New Dorm, my feet scraping over the concrete, and let myself in.

I lay on my bed and peered at the pictures on the wall, darkened and indistinct in the silver light of the streetlight outside my window. Then I sat up and tried to unclench my jaw but couldn't without having the muscles on my face flutter. I went out and down and back to the frat room. Echo and the Bunnymen were still doing "The Cutter." Somebody really liked that song. I saw Kate talking to a girl I didn't know, and I walked up behind her and laid my face on the back of her shoulder, rubbing my nose across the smooth furriness of her sweater. She reached back, without turning to look, and began to rub my neck. "Spare us the cutter," said Echo and his Bunnymen.

When I woke up, my legs were under Kate's. She twitched suddenly and made a small sound at the back of her throat. I pulled my legs from under her and touched her hair and felt a slight sting in my fingertips and she turned to me, still asleep. After a while I let go of her and got out of bed. As I put on my clothes I could see pictures of her on a closet door, Kate with her mother, Kate at high school with friends, Kate with her horse, Kate in Paris with a boyfriend, Kate with various red-faced white-haired people.

Outside, the sky was graying. I walked across the Scripps lawns toward Pomona. A black German shepherd with a blue bandanna around his neck ran up to me and I sat down and rubbed his face, enjoying the warm panting breath on my face. I ran my fingers through the thick hair on his stomach, and he squirmed and reached up and licked my face, pushing me over. We lay happily on the grass laughing at each other and I realized it had been a long time since I had touched an animal. I got up, and he followed me for a moment and then veered off, running easily through the water arcing up from the sprinklers.

In the lounge the phone was off the hook. I picked up the receiver and laid it back in the cradle. There was a note on my door: "The phone's been ringing every ten minutes and it's somebody with a foreign accent." I went back out to the lounge and sat by the phone. The wall in front of me went from gray to orange and I felt heat spread across my neck. The phone rang, and I picked it up. An operator asked for me, fuzzy and distant, and then my father cleared his throat.

"Abhay."

"Yes, Pa."

"Abhay, your grandfather, he passed away yesterday."

I could hear birds far away, muffled by the door and the glass and the concrete.

"Abhay?"

"Yes, Pa."

"I'm going there tomorrow for the . . . He was in hospital with the old heart trouble. They said he was sleeping and then he seemed to wake up for a minute."

We were silent for a moment, and I could hear him breathing and I imagined the signal flashing up from land into space and bouncing off metal and then miles of space again until finally I could hear it.

"Pa."

"Yes?"

"Uh . . . I . . ."

"Yes. Listen, I'll call you again soon."

"Okay."

"Right."

"Tell Ma I'm okay."

"Yes."

I went outside and sat on the stairs and the sun sparked at me through the sprinkler sprays. I was feeling nothing and knew it would come later. I tried to remember my grandfather's face but could think only of his cupboard full of dusty medical books and homeopathic medicines. My father's father had been trained to be a lawyer but preferred to spend his time studying tattered old books and dispensing sweet white medicines to people who didn't trust the doctors with regular modern degrees or couldn't afford them. When I was very young we'd go to visit him in his old, old house, and I'd play chess with him, old Indian rules, and then there would be a knock at the door and he'd go away and I'd see a thin face, anxious and sometimes in pain, and my grandfather would scoop up thousands of little white balls in a glass vial and carry it carefully to the door and bring back some little white balls for my waiting mouth and he'd sprinkle them on my tongue, laughing his toothless clown's laugh. When I grew older he began to ask me when I was going to have my upnayana ceremony and be able to wear my sacred thread and become one of the twice-born, but I'd been to school in the meantime and had learned about the evils of the caste system, so we didn't play chess anymore. Just before I left for the States we went to visit him, and I spent most of that week up on the roof, reading and watching the kites weave in the sky. My mother came up and sat on the bed next to me and said he's getting old and you're going away and he worries, you know, you are the oldest son, he really worries, you could do it just for the old man; and for a moment I remembered the way his fingernails clicked against my teeth when he put the sweetness in my mouth and the innocence of his smile but I shook my head and went back to my book, and now I wondered what he'd thought of in that last moment of wakefulness.

The water stopped. I still couldn't feel anything.

In the slanting yellow light of early morning Mount Baldy looked closer than it really was, as if you could easily walk into the shallow dark gullies on its slopes, if you wanted to. I was still sitting on the steps when people started leaving for their first classes, and they stared at me curiously in passing, not saying anything. They were used to finding me asleep in the lounges or on the patch of grass outside, but I was, I suppose, especially ragged that morning. I pushed myself up and went back into the dorm, picking up my neighbor's copy of the *New York Times* on the way. I sat in the lounge, next to the phone, because he didn't like his paper disappearing, and read a front-page article about students marching in Beijing, raising slogans about freedom. In the Brazilian jungle, Catholics from New York were quarreling with evangelists from Texas about which was worse: frightening tribal Indians into conversion with sermons about hellfire and damnation or persuading them gently with lessons on agriculture. On the editorial page, under the headline "In India, Some Things Are More Important than Time," somebody named Krause complained about the thirty minutes and assorted forms it took him to get a taxi at Bombay International Airport and about the basic inefficiency of Indian methods of producing television sets under protective tariffs. "Some things should be more important than self-sufficiency," he said. On another page, the chief correspondent of the paper's New Delhi bureau had an article about a holiday he had taken in Darjeeling and the hotel he had stayed in, which was, he said, "full of the charm of the British Raj." This, I swear, was the *New York Times* the morning after my grandfather died, and as I sat there I felt as if I was in a film, and that I was expected to react somehow, but my head was pounding and I couldn't decide whether this was ironical or absurd or something else or anything at all, so I went into the bathroom and brushed from my mouth the accumulated bitterness of the night.

This feeling of being in a film hung over me even later, when I sat at the back of a classroom and listened to a fellow named Lin talk about Asian revolutions. The British, he was saying, changed India for the better with their efficient railroads and efficient administration and so on, and for a moment I felt that I should be saying something, but then, sensing my face flush, full, somehow, of the realization that whatever I said wouldn't make any sense, would sound crazy, I opened a notebook and doodled instead, and at the end of the period I found that I had drawn birds and airplanes soaring across the page.

Outside, the smog had moved in like a curtain and Baldy was invisible. I could feel my eyes stinging, and the acrid tickling moved slowly across my nostrils and into the back of my throat. Kate swung around a corner, laden with books. She snapped the hair out of her face with a quick jerk of her head.

"I have to be in class in three and a half minutes." She didn't smile.

"Okay. Talk to you later."

I stood there for a moment, stretching, watching her white skirt move on the back of finely muscled calves as she tip-tapped away with quick, little steps. Back at New Dorm, in the lounge, I sat and listened to the Talking Heads echo in the courtyard outside: "Psycho killer, qu'est-ce que c'est? Fa, fa, fa, fa; fa, fa, fa, fa fa fa." There was a torn newspaper under my foot, and a tank platoon ploughed through a field on the front page. The door opened in and Tom walked in, wearing silver-rimmed glasses with mirrored lenses. Again, I felt like I was in a film, and I liked it less and less, that feeling, I mean.

"What's up, buddy?" He sat down next to me. "You look like you dropped down a cliff. What's the matter, hungover?"

"No," I said, again unable to talk about Babuji, and so I pointed at the newspaper. "It's just geo-fucking-politics. Gets me down."

"You're not supposed to talk about it," he said, thumping me repeatedly on the back, just below the neck. "No, no, no, no. Very passé, Abhay. It's much better just to say it's angst. Everyone will understand."

"Right. Yeah. Let me wear those." I put on his glasses.

"Let's go see what Lawrence is up to."

So I sat in my booth and Lawrence went looking for whatever he was looking for across the burning desert. After the movie was over and I had put away the reels I was exhausted, drawn out like a string. I told Tom this.

"You're just susceptible to depression today, asshole," he said. "Or actually the last few days. Listen, let's go into town. Somebody's playing at Parachute. It's a bummer being around you when you're like this. Got to get you up again."

"I don't know."

"We'll get a ride. There's a whole bunch of people going."

"I don't know."

But there wasn't much else to do that evening, and I didn't want to be alone, so I sat in the backseat of somebody's car and listened to the tires humming on the freeway. The club was in a basement, very dark, and the music was loud, violent, the usual stuff. I bought a beer and walked around, scraping against the wall. I leaned on a round pillar and watched the band for a while, but then Tom found me and crooked his arm around my neck.

"Let's slam, Abs," he said.

"Isn't that passé?" I said.

"But it feels good," he said, and dragged me through the crowd, to where a circle of people, men and women, boys and girls, spun in a circle, bouncing off each other, impacting.

"Come on."

"Slam-dancing is passé."

"Come on, shithead." He pulled me into the circle, and instantly I was almost knocked off my feet. In a few moments I began to feel the rhythm of it and soon I was ricocheting from body to body, my eyes half-shut. It looked harsh, but it did feel good, and you could lose yourself in it. When I finally staggered out, my head spinning, my body was already starting to ache, but I could feel a smile on my face.

"Hello," she said.

She was dressed in black again, a skirt this time, with the ubiquitous T-shirt. The red hair was pulled back tightly into a braid, leaving her face exposed. She looked very young.

"Amanda."

"How are you?"

"Good," I said. "Good. And you?"

"Okay. The people I came with left."

"The girls from the hall?"

"They thought this place was gross." She shook her head. "Gross. Assholes."

"It is pretty seedy."

"Pretty seedy?"

"Something like that."

"You have a funny way of talking."

"I come from a funny place."

"Funny?"

Behind her, a bald head moved in the yellow light, perfectly spherical, with a curving scar caterpillaring up the lower hemisphere.

"How old are you?"

"Eighteen."

"You like this?"

"Do you?"

I shrugged. "Do they do this in Texas?"

"Everywhere."

I got another beer, and one for her, and we sat at a round metal table at the back, where it was so dark that all I could see was a flash when her eyes moved. There were black shapes around us, almost motionless. Listening to her voice in the darkness reminded me, for some reason, of being very young, of my friends and myself when we were at school together, of sitting up in bed, wrapped in blankets and telling each other ghost stories. I told her this and she laughed, and said that when she was very young she would lie alone in bed, eggs in both armpits, waiting for them to hatch.

"You what?"

"I thought I could make eggs hatch, so I took eggs out of the fridge and put them in my armpits when I slept, thinking maybe I'd wake and there'd be chickens. But they never did, and I guess after a while they would start to rot or something, my father would come and take them away, throw them away I guess. But I always thought I could make them hatch so I would get some more."

"That's a sad story."

"They never broke though."

"What does your father do?"

"He's a judge. He has white hair."

Tom came listing through the tables, leaning over bottles of beer and glasses and cigarettes, peering at the mannequin-still shapes.

"Tom." I raised my voice over the music. "Tom."

He slid into a chair, tilting to get a good view of Amanda's face.

"Amanda," he said. "Hey."

"Hi."

"Abhay, they're leaving. We have to go."

"Already?" I said, and saw the soft white of his teeth.

"You don't have to," Amanda said. "You can come with me later."

"You have a car?" Tom said.

"Yes."

"Perfect," he said, his head turning toward me, and I picked up a butt from the table and flicked it at him. It hit him somewhere around the chest and fell to the ground.

"Asshole," I said.

"Abhay doesn't drive," he said. "He wants to live in L.A. but he doesn't want to drive."

"Why?" she said.

"I don't know," I said. "I just don't like it. It's not like I can't. I learnt. But I don't like it."

"You're weird, boy," Tom said.

"Tom's a redneck from Ohio. His parents put him on one of those three-wheel motorcycle things before he could walk. Went tearing over the countryside chewing tobacco and drinking Jack Daniel's and chasing gals."

"Damn proud of it," he said. "Good ol' 'merican stuff, little Indian boy. What did you do?"

"Rode in horse-carriages, I guess. I don't know." A bubble, a little hard place of pain expanded in my chest then, and my voice changed, and I didn't want to talk anymore. I suppose they sensed it, because they began to talk about bands they had seen, in other cities and states.

We came up out of the club into the smell of piss. A black man with a speckled beard sat in a doorway, staring down at his feet, splayed before him on the sidewalk. He looked at us as we passed, then down again. Tom veered off to the left and staggered into the middle of the street. I ran after him and put an arm over his shoulders, pulling him back.

"What now?" he said.

"I don't know."

"Home?"

"Maybe."

"We'll think of something," Amanda said.

"It's early," Tom said.

A neon tube at the entrance to a parking lot buzzed and flashed as we passed under it. In the lot, Amanda dug in a pocket as we squeezed between vehicles. Tom ran his hand, on the side away from me, over windshields and roofs. Amanda stopped by a low-slung black car and put the key into the door.

"This is yours?" Tom said.

"Yes."

"This is yours?" he said again, pulling away from me and putting his hands on the car, leaning over it, stretching out on it.

"Uh-huh."

"This is yours?"

"She just said so, bonehead," I said.

"This," he said, turning to me, "is a Jaguar, bonehead."

"Oh," I said.

He bent and clambered into the car, uttering little sighs of ecstasy: "Smell that leather. Sweet. Sweet. I can't believe you drive this thing." Amanda shrugged: a nervous, awkward movement. I got into the front seat and buckled myself in, and then we were all quiet until we were on the freeway. Amanda pressed a button and the cabin — that's what it felt like, flying above the hunkering houses, separate — filled with music. I could feel the power of the machine in the way it kissed the road, lightly, smoothly, and in the way that Amanda drove, one hand on the stick shift, confident, veering from lane to lane.

"You're a good driver," I said.

"This is a good car to drive," she said. "You can really feel the road through it."

"You must learn young in Texas. I'd like to go there some day, just to see."

"What do you do?"

"What do I do?"

"What's your major?"

I smiled, realizing she hadn't wanted to ask the question in a way that would make her seem like a freshman.

"Anthropology," I said. "But I don't really know what I'm doing." "Who does?"

"Where are we going? — that is the question," Tom said.

"Go to sleep," I said. "We'll wake you up when we get there."

"Surprise me, surprise," he said. He twisted around for a moment or two, knocking knees against the back of my seat, and then was still. We drove on toward Claremont. Amanda and I talked now and then, but mostly there was just the music, and metal tearing at the wind.

We came off Exit 47 and turned north, toward the quiet dark mass of the mountains, sensed more than seen in the moonless night. "Let's go up Baldy," I said. Amanda nodded and we swung up past the colleges and into the lower slopes. Below us the city began to form itself into a checkerboard grid, into straight lines of light stretching on forever, into a cool Cartesian beauty that promised order and sanitation. Amanda drove off the road, onto a dirt track, and we stopped on an overhang looking out on the valley. She began to rummage through a purse.

"I wish we'd thought to bring beers," I said.

"Better," she said, holding up a little square of glassine. She pulled a rectangular mirror out of the bag.

"Oh, no," I said.

"You don't like it?" she said, raising her eyebrows.

"No, I like it too much," I said. She poured the white powder onto the mirror and began to cut it with an industrial razor. "Isn't coke supposed to be passé?"

"Who gives a shit?" she said.

"I suppose it doesn't matter." She cut the lines and gave me the mirror, and began to roll a five-dollar bill. I twisted in my seat and reached back to shake Tom awake. He came up with a look of terror on his face, with pupils dilated and lips pouting.

"What, what . . ."

"Easy," I said. "Want some candy, little boy?"

He rubbed his eyes, yawned, twisted his head from side to side. "It's so dark. I mean, up here." He took the mirror from my hand.

"There's no moon," Amanda said. "And it's cloudy." She gave him the rolled-up bill. We did the lines, passing the mirror around, and I was last. I let my head roll back and savored the clean, clean rush of it, the hard chemical taste and the buzzing numbness around the gums and lips.

"Hallelujah," Tom said, running a moistened finger over the mirror. He smiled and shook his head. "We are blessed." He put a hand on Amanda's shoulder. "Let me sit in the seat. If I can pretend I'm driving this thing I'll be in heaven."

She giggled. "Okay." So she got out of the car, and I went around the front and stood beside her, and we watched Tom wiggle into the front seat and take hold of the wheel. He made a low purring sound in his throat, turned the music up and started to dip his head forward and back, shoulders hunching up and down, in time to the beat. "Whoo-eee," he said. Amanda and I laughed.

After a while Amanda cut some more lines and we sat on the grass with our backs against the car. I reached up behind me and tapped on the door. "Tom," I said, "Tom."

"What?"

"Here. Turn the music down."

"No way. I'm having too much fun. Where's that bill?"

"Here. Roll up the windows."

He handed the mirror back to me and then I heard the quiet hiss of the windows as they slid up, cutting off the music. I shivered.

"Are you cold?"

"Feels like it's going to rain."

I lay back and put my arm under my head, and sure enough, in a few moments, I felt a drop on my forehead, in the middle, a little above my eyes.

I heard my voice say, "Let me read your hand," surprising myself, because this had been a well-known gambit even at fifteen, allowing you to hold and caress the other's hand, but Amanda responded enthusiastically.

"You can tell the future?" she said.

"Yes, Madame. Not only the future but also the past."

"But you can't see anything, the lines and stuff."

"Tell Tom to switch on the light inside."

She leaned across me and motioned at Tom. A weak illumination hit our bodies, and as she moved to lie down beside me, elbows on the ground, facing me, I felt the long coil of hair move across my chest.

"Here," she said, holding up her right hand. Her skin was cool and crisp, like paper. I ran my finger across the mound at the base of her thumb. "What?" she said.

"Nothing, nothing." I tried to remember the astrologers at home, the ones on the sidewalk who would let a parrot pick out your destiny from a pile of dirty pieces of paper. "You will have many children," I said, putting on a generic non-American accent. "I see in these excellent and clean lines in your palm much success and little pain, much joy and little sorrow."

She laughed. "Liar," she said. We kissed and her lips were supple, moving. I could taste the powder on both of us. She moved up and put an arm across me, smoothing away the water from my forehead. The bones of her shoulders were thin, fragile under my hands. She turned her head and began to kiss my neck, finding, instantly, a long bruise that curved downward. She said something indistinct and ran her tongue over it.

"That's a cliché," I said.

"What?"

"Kissing bruises or scars and that sort of thing," I said. "It's a cliché." I raised her chin back to me, to my lips.

"Oh, shut up," she said, and rolled on top of me, grabbing my head between flat hands, "shut up shut up shut up." I laughed, feeling her eyelashes whisper across my cheek, the warmth inside her mouth, her breasts touching softly, the tension in her thighs, I touched her waist and the muscles quivered away from me and then back again, taut, and then something moved, I don't know what, maybe something in the ground under me, and I pushed myself up, and in the valley below, I saw a light, a speck of fire that grew and brightened until there was nothing else and the horizon washed away. What is it? Amanda said. What is it? I waited for it to stop but I could see only a harsh brilliance, and it was endless, and my head fell back, and I was outraged. I was filled with disbelief. But it wouldn't stop, it was brighter than day, and it became still more radiant, the sky was a terrible burnished white, and now I could hear a roar, feel it in my legs. I began to tremble, to shake, with no thought now, no words, only a panic deeper than bone.

The sky went dark again and I found that I was screaming. Not loudly, but low in my throat. I was curled up on my side. I sat up, feeling pain shoot through the veins in my arms and legs.

"Can you believe it?" I said, and my voice broke and squeaked. "That was too fucking embarrassing. I thought it was the fucking bomb. Can you believe it?"

Amanda was a few feet away, around the front of the car, knees up to the chest. I crawled over to her on my hands and knees and put a hand on her shoulder. I tried to speak but my mouth felt like the inside would crack, like dry wood. I turned her head. She was crying, fisted hands held side by side in front of her lips, her eyes shut tightly so that they looked like stitched wounds.

"Amanda," I said, low and hoarse, "Amanda."

There was a trail of snot running out of a nostril.

"Amanda."

She raised her hands until her forearms covered her face and the hands curled, quivering very faintly, over her hair. My stomach squeezed and I turned away and vomited, trying to hold my head away from the grass with arms that shook and gave way and wouldn't lock at the elbows. When I could get up I stumbled over to the car. The music was still playing but I couldn't see Tom. I pulled at the door and the stench hit me before I saw him curled up, jammed into the space between the driver's seat and the pedals.

"Tom?" The window on the side away from me had a star growing from its center, a delicate foliage of crystalline lines that reached out to the chrome. "Tom?"

The inside of the car smelled of shit. I backed away from it a little, and as I did so his head whipped up, and he exploded past me in a quick scurry toward the bushes. I got in gingerly, looking around, but the smell had almost disappeared now, so I spun the knob on the radio from station to station, but all I could find was music, songs. Amanda walked up to the side of the car, wiping her mouth. I felt vaguely embarrassed.

"Um, the window, Tom must have thrashed around, maybe his foot hit it. Sorry."

"It doesn't matter."

I jacked myself over into the other seat so she could get in and sit down, but she stayed outside, looking down at the valley.

"There's parts down there that went dark," she said.

"Yes."

"Where's he?"

"Went back in there."

"Oh."

I couldn't stand the music anymore, but I couldn't find the button to make it stop. When I straightened up from the radio, into the sudden quietness of the rain, I heard the crunch of feet, and Tom appeared behind Amanda. He was completely naked. He pushed past her, as if he hadn't seen her, and clambered into the seat behind me.

"Tom? Are you okay?"

He seemed to be looking straight at me, but his eyes were focused on something over the valley, far away. We came down the hill, and nobody said a word until we were on campus.

"Where?" Amanda said.

"New Dorm."

When the car stopped I got out and turned, intending to tell Tom to stay in the car until I got him some clothes, but he pushed out after me and walked up the pathway without looking back. I ran after him.

"I'll see you later," I called back to Amanda.

She nodded and pulled away. On the stairs, John, the resident advisor, threw a rolled-up newspaper at Tom, saying: "What the fuck are you guys on now? Cover yourself up, you'll scare the little freshmen." Tom kept going, over the sheets of newspaper. John turned to me: "Are you okay? Get him inside his room, there's enough shit going on around here."

"What?" I said.

"Lightning struck a transformer and scared the hell out of everyone," he said. "Big white flash, of course everyone thought it was the fucking bomb. There's a girl, a freshman on the first floor, she's still hysterical. We had to call the paramedics, it looked like she was going to choke or something."

When I caught up with Tom he was struggling with the door to his room.

"Shit," I said. "You left your keys up there. John! JOHN!"

John came up and let us in with his master key, muttering to himself. Tom stood in the middle of the room, arms hanging limply. I pushed him down on the bed and found an almost full bottle of whiskey on the shelf above. I gave it to him and he drank, passed it back to me.

"Tom?"

His gaze didn't shift.

"Come on, Tom, cut out the thousand-yard stare crap, it was just lightning hitting a transformer or something like that. Electrical stuff, nothing else."

But nothing moved on his face, not a thing, so I put a bedspread over him, sat in the chair next to the bed and we passed the bottle back and forth. Then the silence started to bother me, that stuffy wet subduing absorption of sound by the air, so I switched on the television and we watched *Wheel of Fortune*. Soon, the flat colors on the screen began to blur into each other and the hysterical applause and laughter became a comfortable buzz. Tom began to change channels, flipping from an interview with Hugh Hefner to *Baywatch* to a shopping channel. I slumped back and let my head droop over a shoulder, drifting in and out of an uneasy doze, hearing, occasionally, the voices of policemen and the ranting of preachers, not dreaming, but whenever I slitted an eye, the air in the room seemed to vibrate, with the motes visible, and the walls changed somehow, bulging inward.

I jerked up and was on my feet, a thin, painful sliver of fear arcing through my chest, trying to remember what had pulled me out of sleep. I rubbed my eyes. Tom was kneeling in front of the television, palms on the screen, a sheet wrapped around his body, his nose almost touching the electric blue.

"Tom, did you say something?"

The image on the screen changed and his face took on a white tinge. "Look," he said. "It's so beautiful."

"What?"

I knelt next to him and pushed at his shoulder, trying to get a look at the screen. He moved a little, and I saw Mount Baldy, snowcapped, against a deep blue sky. The camera swept over the slopes, and they had some music playing, full of trumpets, and it was eternal and beautiful.

"It's perfect," Tom said, and his voice was full of longing and regret.

I lurched up and went across the room to the window. The plastic shade resisted as I tugged at it, and then something clicked and it snapped up on the roller, and there was Mount Baldy, golden in the first dawn, awesome and untouched and so very close.

"Tom," I said. "Look. Look."

He turned toward me, still holding the television set. I saw him blink, and then he stood up slowly and came to stand next to me at the window.

"Heaven," Tom said. "It's heaven."

Then he leaned out over the concrete and began to shout, in a quick chanting rhythm that I seemed to recognize but couldn't place: "Heaven, heaven, heaven." I thought of trying to stop him but couldn't stop laughing. I leaned out beside him, tasting the morning, and his elbow jogged against my side each time he bent forward to shout, then again as he came back with a long rasping intake of breath. It felt like a drumbeat. After a while I began to shout, too, softly at first, then louder as I discovered how good it felt: "Heaven, heaven, heaven."

"Will you jerks please shut up?" John's voice was sleepy, but it seemed to echo almost as much as ours. Maybe it was the air of that perfect morning, so rain-washed that I could see the trees on Baldy. "Please? Shut up?"

We stopped and turned into the center of the room, but the laughter wouldn't stop, and we whispered to each other, falling into a circling dance, feet rising and falling: "Heaven, heaven, heaven."

Outside, the edge of sunlight raced over the valley.

. . . now . . .

WHEN ABHAY FINISHED TYPING, he stood up, avoiding his parents' eyes, and walked slowly out the door. Saira ran through the court-yard, telling the children the story-telling was over for the evening, and then she went after him.

Yama stood up and bowed at me, then melted away. I could hear the rising hubbub outside as the children rose to their feet and left. I became aware of a steady ache in my jaw and realized I had been grinding my teeth against each other all evening; I bent over and huddled on the bed, feeling the muscles in my thighs and shoulder twitch.

'Wasn't that hard, no?' Hanuman said. 'Get rested. I'll see you tomorrow.'

'Thank you,' I said. 'Thanks to you all.'

'They can't hear you, but no matter. They're your friends.'

I rolled over and reached towards the typewriter, but someone extinguished the light and I felt my eyes close; when I awoke the moonlight made sharp patterns on the floor, and a cool breeze swept in through the window, smelling of jasmine. I pushed myself up. In a corner, a diffuse cloud of silver dust hung motionless; I climbed up to the window and craned my neck, but the hedge and heavy branches hid the stars. Slipping between the bars, I worked my way over the hedge and dropped to the ground.

As I swung through the trees I saw a lone figure on the maidan, walking slowly around the perimeter. It was Abhay: he was restless too. I watched him for a long time as I sat in a fork, as I tried to shape the past, to make something out of it. I suppose he was trying to do the same.

*   *   *

At precisely six o'clock the next evening Yama appeared in his black throne. The crowd outside was noisy and restless. I settled myself in front of the typewriter and cracked my knuckles.

'Wait,' Hanuman said. 'We can't start without Saira.'

I typed out an enquiry, and Ashok shook his head and shrugged: 'I don't know.'

'Who are all these people?' said Mrinalini, who had been peering out. 'They're not all children, you know.'

'One of them must have told a favourite uncle or something,' Abhay said, 'and then of course everyone must have found out.'

'What are we going to do?' Mrinalini said. 'It's getting packed out there.'

There was a determined knock on the door. Mrinalini opened the door and then stepped back. Saira came in, face tear-stained, her hand firmly clasped by a large, fleshy woman dressed in a green salwar-kameez, an older version of Saira herself.

'Sister,' she said to Mrinalini, 'what is this Saira is telling me? She came home so late last night and I said, where were you, but she wouldn't tell. Again this evening she was ready, very eager to go some-where, so I said unless she told me . . .' Then she saw me, sitting over the typewriter. 'Oh, Allah, it's true. A monkey. A typewriter.'

'She wasn't going to let me come,' Saira said, wiping her cheeks with the back of a hand. 'Mama, this is Sanjay. See, he types.'

Mama was staring at me, eyes bulging, caught half-way between horror and awe. So I typed: 'Namaste, ji. I am Parasher. Your daughter has helped me in my time of need.'

She backed away, moving her head from side to side.

'Mrinalini, what is this thing you have in your house?'

'Zahira,' Mrinalini said. 'It's all right. He's nothing bad.'

'How do you know? He could be anything.'

'Hanuman's here,' Saira said. 'Hanuman the Great.'

'Sanjay's done nothing bad yet,' said Mrinalini.

Zahira looked at both of them, perplexed. I started to type again, but stopped as three loud crashes rang out in the court-yard, one after the other.

'Mrinalini,' said Zahira, 'they're knocking over your flower-pots.' Glass crackled and splintered outside. 'That was your sliding window. Who are these people?'

'I don't know. I've never seen them before.'

'They're not even from this mohalla. They can't come into your house and do this. Come.'

Zahira left, followed by Mrinalini, and a moment later we heard Zahira's voice lash out, and the court-yard fell silent. Smiling, Saira peeked out the door.

'Saira, you stay in there.' Saira ducked back in.

'She'll have them organized in a minute,' Saira said.

'Too neat,' Yama said. 'Much too timely.'

'The three crashes,' Hanuman said, jumping down from his perch and stalking around the room, tail swinging restlessly, 'the three crashes like three drum-beats rising to a crescendo, completed by the glass breaking, just in time to distract that lady, to make her a participant. Much too neat.'

'Do you sense a hidden hand?' Yama said, standing up.

'A hidden something or other,' Hanuman said. 'But where? Where are you hidden, whoever you are?'

'Who?' I said. 'What are you talking about?'

'Someone who wants a story told,' Yama said.

'Someone who is bound to monkeys,' Hanuman said, 'but that's me, and I'm already here.'

'Judging by the timing and the rhythm of those crashes,' Yama said, 'an aesthete. A protector of poets.'

'Too vague still,' Hanuman said, 'but apply logic; Yama, ratiocinate. I feel something, someone here; look at the hair on the back of my neck. But my blood is rising, like on a hunt; you are the cold one, the icy thinker. Think. You know your own methods; apply them.'

'A protector of Parasher, and who is Parasher?' Yama said, sitting down. 'A sometime singer and poet, a lover, a fomenter of revolutions, a monkey. No. Nothing yet.'

'Nothing,' said Hanuman, leaping around the room, his tongue flicking in and out between his hard yellowed teeth. 'Something, something, I smell something. Why are you so much trouble, Sanjay? Why did you come to this house, singer?'

'Food,' I said. 'I was hungry. You can't blame me for that.'

'Food!' Yama cried. 'That's it! You're a thief, Parasher, a filcher of clothes, a robber, a pilferer, a rifler!'

'Listen, calm down,' I said. 'I was only making a living.'

'Thieves and poets,' Hanuman said, ricocheting from the walls, eyes dark, 'poets and thieves. And who is the fat patron of poets and thieves? All right, you fat snoot-face, where are you? Come on out, broken-tusk!'

There was a scraping behind the wall under the bookshelves, a rubbing of something over brick and wood, and Hanuman leapt at the wall, hand outstretched. His fist punched a hole in the wall (my friends watched the brick shatter, mouths open) and disappeared behind the plaster; for a moment, Hanuman struggled, pulling back, and then a nasal voice said: 'All right, all right. I'll come out.'

Hanuman eased away from the wall, and a small mouse backed out of the hole, its tail still gripped by the Wind-son's fingers. A small figure hopped off the mouse's back and took a few steps, growing larger with every step. My face curved in a ridiculous smile; I clapped my hands; I burst into laughter.

'O snoot-face!' I said. 'O marvellous excellent fat one!'

Ganesha picked daintily at his shawl with plump fingers, until it lay just so, and his trunk twisted about his head and neck, adjusting the brilliant necklaces of unearthly stones and the crown of gold.

'Do you have to be so rough, monkey?' he said. 'Uncouth.'

Hanuman was scratching the mouse between its ears, and he looked up, laughing. 'What were you doing skulking inside walls, han?' Hanuman said.

'There was a story to be told, and so, naturally, I came. Even though people around here seem to have forgotten who I am.'

'The remover of obstacles himself,' Yama growled. 'So it's been you all along. Did you interfere with my scribes? Have you been casting spells, making things easy for this monkey-man here?'

'Who, me?' said Ganesha, looking innocently at the Death-lord with his sunken elephant eyes. 'I haven't done anything at all. I've only been here for the last minute or so.'

'Thank you,' I said, bowing to the son of Shiva. 'Thank you.'

'I did nothing,' he said, his big grey head inscrutable, the ears flapping gently to and fro. 'Come, nearly time to start.'

He settled himself on the bed, next to the typewriter. Saira hopped up onto the sheets and sat on the other side of the machine. The door opened, and Zahira and Mrinalini came in. I could hear faint whispers circling the court-yard.

'I'm not sure about this still,' Zahira said, putting a protective arm around her daughter.

'Sister, it's all right,' Mrinalini said. 'My son's here too.'

'Yes, he is, isn't he?' Zahira said, looking at Abhay curiously. 'Well, Allah will protect. But only the children are in the house now; the rest of the crowd is outside, scattered on the maidan, and they want to listen to the story, too. Will you pass papers back and forth, from here to the court-yard, from there to outside? And it will be read here, and then there?'

'It'll never work,' Ashok said. 'You're asking for confusion.'

Ganesha nudged me and whispered in my ear, and I typed: 'Ganesha is here (we seek his blessing in our endeavours to attain wisdom and knowledge).' I received another nudge, none too gentle, in the ribs (just as Saira squealed, 'Ganapati baba moriya, Ganesha is here!'), and so I went on: 'Ganesha asks if you have a stereo speaker and if you do you should put it on the roof, never mind about the wires.'

Instructions were sent out to the willing children for this to be done, while I explained to the rest of my family (I think I can use that word now) what had happened. They looked a little concerned: one god in the house is fine, I could see them thinking, and two is better, but three in a room is a lot of divinity in a very small place, and what if this trend is to continue? Can we expect to see the whole immeasurable pantheon in the near future, the shining hosts? Should we also prepare for visitations from the big hitters themselves (Ashok's phrase), the heavy dudes (Abhay, edgy) and the boss ladies (Mrinalini, smiling) like Shiva and Parvati and Vishnu and Lakshmi and maybe even Brahma himself? That was a dizzying thought, and who can predict the actions of the mighty (Hanuman shrugged, Yama and Ganesha looked inscrutable), so I made reassuring noises and tried not to look nervous. The story-telling hour was drawing near.

Finally, the speaker was on the roof.

'Let the child say something,' Ganesha said.

'Saira, say something.'

'Say what?' Saira said, and the words rang out clear as the chimes of a fine bell from the speaker above. Saira jumped, a hand clapped over her mouth. 'One, two, three,' she said. 'Testing, testing, one, two, three.' Her voice went right to the edge of the maidan and maybe a little beyond.

'Obstacle removed,' said Ganesha.

'Don't be smug, youngster,' Yama said. 'All right, Sanjay. Where were we?'

Where we were, god, was with Benoit de Boigne, in his journey across the seas, in his search for a dream.

So, I began to type, and Mrinalini read it all out.

Listen . . .

George Thomas Goes Overboard.

ON A MAIDAN, within sight of green mountains, Uday Singh and George Thomas exchanged cuts, the sound of their clashing swords echoing among the banyan trees and the water-filled fields.

George Thomas watched Uday Singh's sleepy eyes and relaxed stance, listening to the other's easy breathing and waiting for an opening. They circled each other, moving always to the right; Thomas felt the world recede, distanced by their revolutions, and saw only Uday's white beard, the shimmering edge of his blade, the place where his tunic curled back to reveal the ridge of the collar-bone and the dimple at the base of the throat, and Thomas felt Uday's presence, his spirit, his courage, his old wounds, his loves, his disappointments, his fear, felt that old unspoken intimacy, that sometimes obscene knowledge between adversaries, and waited for a secret wavering, an internal retreating that would reveal itself as an opening.

Thomas saw Uday's eyes narrow, and suddenly saw a crack in his guard, felt Uday drop back, there it was; Thomas lunged forward, but even as his thighs clenched and his point reached out he knew it had been a mistake, because Uday moved lazily, slowly aside, avoiding the thrust easily and cutting from underneath in a scooping movement to tap Thomas gently on the stomach with smooth steel.

Thomas straightened up, panting.

'How do you do that?' he said. 'You knew I was coming before I did.'

'I could see you making up your mind,' Uday said. 'It's not so hard. It comes with age.' He thumped Thomas on the back. 'You're getting better. Your Urdu still needs work, though.'

As they walked back to the tents, they stripped off the heavy leather and chain mail armour that glinted in the late-afternoon sun. The grass under foot was wet with the first rains of the monsoon; in a red tent, Thomas ate, sitting cross-legged on the carpeted floor, and Uday watched.

'Eat something,' Thomas said. 'Nobody'll ever know.'

'The gods will know, and I will know,' Uday said, smiling. 'Eat, firangi.'

'Firangi? Me? I'm no foreigner, I'm Jahaj Jung, old man, or haven't you heard?'

'Jahaj Jung, the warrior from the seas,' Uday said, smiling.

'That very man,' Thomas said, 'but here comes a firangi.'

The man who entered, stooping a little, was tall and thin, with long, lank dark hair and a large nose.

'Reinhardt,' Thomas said. 'Sit. Eat.'

'Later,' Reinhardt said. 'I have an idea. A plan.' He lowered himself to the floor and poured wine into a cup.

'Get on with it,' Uday said.

'Of course,' Reinhardt said. 'The rains will set in soon, and we will languish in these muddy fields, no campaigning, no money to be earned. But not far away, there is a palace. There is a palace with a woman in it. A palace with a princess who needs officers for her brigades.'

'Sardhana,' Uday said. 'You're talking about Sardhana.'

'Of course,' Reinhardt said, grinning. 'A beautiful woman, they say, a tempestuous woman, a hungry woman, a passionate woman.'

'A witch,' Uday said. 'Zeb-ul-Nissa, the Witch of Sardhana. Daughter of a dancing woman. Married a general named Le Vassoult, who died. Now she rules his estate, with spells and terrors and a hand of steel.'

'Will you come?' Reinhardt said.

'Of course he will,' Uday said.

'A beautiful woman?' Thomas said.

'Unquestionably,' Reinhardt said.

'A passionate woman?'

'Undoubtedly.'

'A tempestuous woman?'

'Surely.'

'You're crazy to go near her,' Uday said. 'She has the magic of the Brahmins, the hidden magic. But of course you have to go.'

'A woman with an estate, a kingdom,' Thomas said. 'Too good to let go.'

'You have to go,' Uday said. 'You would have to.'

'Uday the fencer with the foresight,' Thomas said.

'Fencing or women, survival is the same thing,' Uday said. He smiled. 'Jahaj Jung. Be careful.'

'You aren't coming?'

'I have more sense than to go near a witch.'

'Children's stories,' Thomas said.

'Precisely the ones to be afraid of,' Uday said.

The next morning Reinhardt and Thomas rode out. Uday waved good-bye from a ridge of mud between two fields, his white tunic transparent in the low slanting sunlight, his beard shifting slowly across his broad chest in the wet breeze. Reinhardt began to sing a French song in a thin, piping voice; Thomas twisted in his saddle, watching the straight-backed figure get smaller and smaller until it was hidden by a grove of heavy-topped mango trees; then there was the distant singing of women in the fields, the heavy sticky fall of hooves in mud, the creaking of leather, the call of thousands of crickets, the busy chirping of birds, and the distant rumble of thunder, the rolling black and grey of the clouds above.

At noon they stopped in the ruins of a serai at a cross-roads and sat on crumbling stone, nibbling at cold chappatis and pickles. A group of Marwari merchants and their Pathan escorts huddled on the other side of the building and watched them curiously.

'How long have you been here?' Thomas asked.

'Here, in India? A year and eight months.'

'Why do you still wear that coat?'

'This coat? What's wrong with the coat? It's Parisian, I had it made in Paris, made for me.'

'Why not wear this? It's better here, more comfortable.'

'I like this coat. Do you find something wrong with it? What?'

'No, nothing.'

Thomas looked away, and said nothing about how the long tails of the coat flapped about the rump of the horse when Reinhardt rode, making rider and horse look like some monstrous bird of prey; that afternoon they cantered through a light drizzle. Reinhardt seemed to recover from his quick irritation and resumed his singing. The road grew steadily wider, and the traffic thickened: farmers with loads of hay on ancient two-wheeled carts drawn by magnificent white oxen, shepherds with flocks of thick-bodied goats, traders with covered carts, caravans escorted by lance-bearing Rajputs and Afghans; Reinhardt grinned and slapped his thigh.

'A rich place, this Sardhana,' he said.

'It's all rich,' Thomas said. 'If it weren't for the wars, what a thing this Hindustan would be.'

'If it weren't for the wars, where would we be?' Reinhardt shouted, spurring his horse. 'Come on, on to the Begum.'

At dusk they drew up to a large arched gate in a crenellated wall.

'We are officers,' Thomas said, 'come to see the Begum and serve her.'

The officer of the guard, a toothless, much-scarred campaigner from Bengal, hooked his thumbs into his belt, and walked in a half-circle around the horses.

'It is late,' he said, 'and the Begum gives audience in the morning. Go. Come tomorrow.'

'Send word to her now,' Thomas said.

'Go.'

'Tell her Jahaj Jung is here.'

'Jahaj who?'

'You know what, Bengali. Go, tell her.'

'Jahaj Jung is the one with the cannon?'

'Yes.'

'A fine soldier, they say?'

'Yes.'

'A good man?'

'A generous man, yes,' Thomas said, and a coin arced through the air and disappeared into the Bengali's belt.

The halls of the palace were dimly lit; tiger skins and swords and round shields gleamed in the flickering torchlight. Thomas and Reinhardt followed the Bengali officer through dark rooms and up staircases, their heels clicking on polished stone and wood, spurs clinking; higher and higher, and then Thomas heard, far away, low laughter, the laughter of girls, turning into long trails of giggles. The rain swept down suddenly, drumming against glass windows in three gusts, one after the other, and then the three men emerged onto a roof.

'Wait here,' said the Bengali.

Under a red-and-yellow canopy, a large silver swing creaked back and forth; the Bengali stepped over the moving, bejewelled forms seated on the carpeted floor and leaned close to the swing. Eddies of water skittered over the roof and scattered themselves on parapets and railings. Thomas wiped his face with a sleeve, smelling, faintly, the aroma of tobacco, the heaviness of rich perfume and the wetness of the earth itself; Reinhardt muttered under his breath and blew his nose.

The Bengali beckoned. 'Come,' he said.

The woman reclining on the swing raised an ivory mouth-piece to her lips and inhaled; a hookah murmured; Thomas bowed.

'Salaam walekum,' he said, echoed by Reinhardt.

'Walekum salaam,' she said. Her voice was rough, alternating between girlish highs and deep huskiness; a tiny white diamond perched on a nostril called attention to the perfection of the nose, to the sculptured length that stopped just short of the awkwardness of too-long; white smoke drifted up from full lips, shrouding large, dark, kohl-rimmed eyes. There was a fullness about the face, an almost-plumpness that hinted at soft fleshiness hidden below the dark blue silk of a loose kurta-garara.

'We heard you need officers, Highness,' Reinhardt said.

'Yes, but how well do you ride?' said the Begum.

'Well enough,' Thomas said, smiling.

'Good. Come. The Chiria Fauj marches nearby, I hear. I want to see it.'

She rose from the swing in one swift movement. The men followed her down the stairs, through the dim halls and corridors, out to the front gate where a company of mounted soldiers waited beside four saddled horses. They rode through the darkness, mud splashing, leaves and branches brushing their faces and arms; occasionally, when the clouds scattered, Thomas saw the Begum, riding far out in front, bent low over the mane of her white horse. He twisted in his saddle and slowed, letting Reinhardt come up to him.

'Crazy,' he shouted over the rolling beat of hooves. 'Mad.'

Reinhardt glanced at Thomas, his lips twisted back in a grimace that revealed uneven teeth, and said nothing. Thomas settled back in his saddle; soon, in the swaying back and forth, in the sounds of night and the hooves and saddlery and water, in the regular bunching and relaxation of the faithful muscles beneath him, Thomas lost track of the passing of time; when they halted near a grove of trees, he had to shake his head and breathe deeply, as if he was awakening from a deep sleep.

The Begum dismounted, beckoning to Thomas and Reinhardt.

'Put these on,' she said, throwing a bundle of black cloth at Thomas.

'A burqua,' Reinhardt said.

'I don't want to be recognized,' she said, pulling a voluminous length of cloth over her head; when she had finished every inch of her body was covered except her eyes. She arched an eyebrow at Thomas and Reinhardt. 'What delicate women you make.'

Thomas bowed, and Reinhardt muttered something in French; the two Europeans and the Bengali followed the Begum around the grove of trees and into the outskirts of a little town. The streets were crowded, even at that late hour of the night; little boys ran excitedly from one side of the street to the other, waving wooden swords and brightly-coloured bows. The Begum and her companions found a perch on the raised veranda of a halwai's shop; Thomas looked at the Begum through the fine netting that covered the burqua's eye-slit, trying to see her eyes. The fragrance of sweetmeats still lingered about the veranda, despite the closed doors, and Thomas was suddenly hungry, the back of his mouth aching for the taste of laddoos, jalebis, balushahis and imurtis; the Begum turned to him abruptly.

'Do you know why we are here?' she said.

Thomas shook his head.

'Because the world is old, and this is something new.'

'What?' Reinhardt said. 'What?'

'Hush,' the Begum said, as a steady tramp was heard from the head of the street. The boys scattered to the walls, and the Chiria Fauj marched through, in the numbing rhythm of the long march, faces blank, feet falling together, thrump-thrump-thrump, eyes fixed on the back of the neck of the next man in column, yet looking through the sweating flesh and hair at something maybe a thousand feet away; they marched determinedly, seemingly seeing and hearing nothing.

'Fine,' Reinhardt whispered under his breath, 'fine men.'

Thomas saw the Begum's head move, saw a quick little stiffening of the neck. The ranks passed by, steady and straight, and finally, preceded by a murmur of voices, a black horse pranced near, nervous, its flanks trembling, bearing a tall figure dressed in a green coat. The hand on the reins was still and very pale in the yellow light of the torches, the chest rose and fell evenly, the shoulders were thrown back and the head tilted up, eyes cast over the heads of the soldiers, over even the clustered houses, up at something lost in the black clouds and the night.

'He rides like a king, this de Boigne,' Thomas whispered.

The Begum's head moved again, and then she stumbled back, falling slowly, gracefully; Thomas reached out and caught her, clutching at her around the waist. The moon broke through the clouds then; with the Bengali shouting 'A lady has fainted,' Thomas and Reinhardt carried the Begum through the bazaar and out into the darkness of the fields. They stopped near the grove and laid her on the ground, her head cushioned on Thomas' knee; the Bengali raised the flap away from her face. Her eyes bulged, the breath whistled in and out of her taut nostrils, her lips convulsed. Even in the dim moonlight, Thomas could see that the Begum's skin was splotched with dark stains that chased each other over her face, like the massive black shapes of distantly-seen fish in deep water. The Bengali began to chant something under his breath; Thomas recognized the long resonant vowels of Sanskrit.

'Has this happened before?' Thomas asked.

'Never,' said the Bengali.

'She's saying something,' Reinhardt said.

A globule of saliva bubbled out of a corner of her mouth and slid down her chin.

'The thing,' she said.

'Begum,' the Bengali said, gently wiping the moisture from her face.

'The idea. The instrument,' she said, her jaw moving strangely from side to side. 'The thing. The idea. Everything will become red. Everything will become red.' She shuddered again, and tears broke from her eyes and raced down the sides of her face; her body relaxed, her eyes closed. They carried her to the horses, and took her home, riding slowly; the Begum seemed to be sunk in a deep sleep, impervious to the guttural calling of thousands of frogs and the incessant metallic twittering of the crickets.

The next morning a peacock spread its tail against the red and grey of a monsoon sky, tiptoeing back and forth along a garden wall in the palace. Thomas and Reinhardt sat in a canopied veranda, sipping at cups of lassi. The peacock spun slowly, carefully, arching its neck.

'Thomas,' Reinhardt said, 'do you know how old creation really is?'

'No.'

'A priest in England calculated it. I forget his name. He considered all available scriptural evidence and worked it out — four thousand six hundred and sixty-two years.'

'Wrong,' the Begum said, and the two men rose to their feet. She smiled, cheerful and relaxed.

'Wrong?' Reinhardt said.

'The Brahmins say creation is without beginning and without end. Three hundred and sixty of our years make one god-year; a Kali-yuga is one thousand and two hundred god-years, a Dvapar-yuga is two thousand and four hundred god-years, a Treta-yuga is three thousand and six hundred god-years, a Krta-yuga is four thousand and eight hundred god-years; one cycle of these four types of yugas makes one Great Interval; seventy-one Great Intervals make one Period — at the end of each Period the universe is destroyed and re-created — and fourteen Periods make one Kalpa, one Great Cycle; the Great Cycles follow each other, the smaller cycles within, wheels within wheels, creation, construction, chaos, destruction. Many universes exist beside each other, each with its own Brahma; this is the wheel, immense, beyond the grasp of conception.'

Thomas laughed. 'And up and down we go, back and round again, again and again.'

'Something like that,' the Begum said. 'So. It seems you have served me already. Officer my brigades.'

'As you wish,' Thomas said, bowing. Reinhardt sat silent, looking at the floor between his knees. 'Reinhardt?'

'What? Oh, yes. Thank you.'

And so Thomas and Reinhardt drilled the Begum's brigades. They spent long days with the motley collection of Europeans and Hindustanis that led Zeb-ul-Nissa's men, practising the quick controlled frenzy of the move from column into line, the almost-panic of the falling into square, bayonets bristling. In the evenings the officers drank in their bungalows or walked through the gardens of the palace, listening for the far-away laughter that drifted down from the roof. Sometimes the Begum held durbars; the officers would sit in long parallel lines in front of the Begum, offering flatteries and receiving gifts and khilluts; sometimes a dancer would whirl over the cool marble, filling the great hall with the jingling of her anklets, her hands curving and head swaying and eyes flashing; at such times, even Reinhardt was seen to sit with his head low, jaw working, calling often for wine.

At night, when the other officers visited their mistresses or gathered to tell stories of combat or seductions, Reinhardt was seen to lie spread-eagled on the floor of his bedroom, his hands clutching at the floor; at other times he took long walks through the country-side, striding across fields and fighting through hedges, returning dishevelled and sweaty and wild-eyed. Soon, for his downcast countenance and his silence, for the constant working of his throat and his sudden sighs that rang out even on parade, attracting curious looks from the soldiers, he was awarded the sobriquet of Reinhardt the Sombre. Finally, one evening, Thomas strolled past Reinhardt's bungalow and observed him squatting in the garden, writing something in the mud and wiping it out, over and over.

'Reinhardt,' Thomas said.

Reinhardt jerked up quickly to his feet, then slowly sank back to the ground.

'Reinhardt, what is it?' Thomas said. 'What has happened?'

Reinhardt shook his head.

'What is it?'

'Do you remember what she said?'

'Who said?'

'Her. The Begum.'

'Said about what?'

'How old it is.'

'What is?'

'This, this,' Reinhardt screamed, waving his hands about his head. 'All of it. This country. Just this. How many years?'

'Yes, I remember.'

'No, you don't. I worked it out. Do you know what it is? Look.' He scratched with a stick in the mud: 4,320,000,000. 'Look. Look.' His voice was a whisper, a whimper.

'Listen, so what?' Thomas said.

'So what? So what?' Reinhardt said, rubbing his upper lip with a knuckle. 'It weighs on me like a great stone. It crushes me.' He wrote again, digging in deep: 4,320,000,000. He sighed. 'It's endless.'

'Nothing dies. Surely that is good.'

Reinhardt turned away, a disgusted look on his face; he strode off, face thrust up at the sky, hands swinging limply near his thighs. Thomas knelt and looked at the numbers, at the long string of zeros; the mud was already beginning to seep back into the scratches, filling them up; he picked up a twig and traced the figures. A flight of pigeons wheeled overhead, their wings snapping and flapping, and a delicate shadow, full of shifting areas of light, like a lacy Lucknow shawl, moved over the ground. Thomas smiled, and picked up a clod of mud; he walked on, pressing it between his finger-tips, feeling its smoothness.

That evening, the Bengali officer knocked on Thomas' door.

'The Begum requests the pleasure of your presence at her unworthy abode,' he said.

'Of course,' Thomas said. 'One moment.' He pulled on his boots and put on a turban. The Bengali maintained a discreet silence as they rode through the darkness. Finally, as they drew up beside the outer walls of the palace, next to a little-used door set deep in the wall, Thomas asked, 'Why, what is it, Quasim Ali? Why does the Begum need to see me at this hour?'

'Why,' said the Bengali gravely, 'I imagine she wishes to discuss the weather.'

The Begum sat on the roof, in her swing, surrounded by her usual entourage of girls; Thomas sat on a low stool a few feet away, his feet on a cushion. A few minutes passed in the exchange of greetings and the passing to and fro of paan; Thomas peered through the dim lamplight, hearing the sleepy cooing of pigeons from the cote at the other end of the roof and the jingling and rustling of the girls.

'So,' the Begum said, 'Thomas Sahib, my little daughters here are curious: Where do these tall pink men come from, and why? Who are they, they ask, these brave warriors who come so far to our Hindustan?'

'Do they ask?' Thomas said.

'They do, indeed,' the Begum said.

'Then listen, and I will tell you,' Thomas said. 'I don't know about any of the others, but I will tell you about me. Listen . . .'

I was born in a place called Tipperary, in Ireland, where it is always cold and the fog drifts over moors. I lived well, and my family ate and drank to satisfaction, but always I felt a little empty, a little absent, as if something was missing; always, I thought of places I could go where everything would be new, and when I thought like this, for a while, that feeling would vanish; so one day, when I was very young, maybe ten or eleven or twelve, I walked away from my home and made my way to the coast and became a ship's boy, a cook's helper, and in time, a sailor.

I will tell you about how a gun made me a sailor. At the time I was a general-purpose scullion and helper in the gallery of an English two-masted brigantine named *Constant,* sailing in the waters north of Calais on blockade. One winter morning we engaged the French sloop *Ella* when she caught us unawares by coming out of a heavy bank of fog to the west. She had the advantage of us from the very start. As we came around slowly into the wind, with the beat to quarters sounding, we could see that she would pass us astern, raking us from head to stern without a shot fired in return.

That is the thing about a naval engagement: you can see it coming. I was carrying cartridges from the magazine up to the deck, laying them by the number two gun, and each time I went down and then up it was awful how she drew slowly closer, beautiful with the sails against the dark grey of the fog and the wake rising clean and white behind her. All this time there was not a word said, just the creaking of the timbers and the slow rise and fall of the deck under our feet, and then the side of the French ship was hidden by smoke and suddenly I was lying flat on my back wondering at the terrible, torn state of the sails above me.

When I pushed myself up I rose into a reeking mess of blood and fire; the marines on the quarter-deck above us had been cut up awfully and two of the guns on the starboard side were knocked over on their side, one with the wood of the carriage splintered away. Our number two gun was loose on the deck, bucking back and forth with every swell, running over and crushing the bodies that lay on the deck. As I stood it came at me, and I was dazed enough to be cool about the way I stepped aside, stooped down for a capstan which I jammed into the wheel, stopping the gun short in its wild career.

'Good lad,' said a blackened, grinning face to me as I stood, quite unable to know what to do next. I recognized the layer of the number one gun, which was now on its side and finished; he motioned at me and we worked like fiends to get the cannon back into harness. Now that I had someone showing me what to do I was myself again. I was always strong for my age, and between the two of us and another of his crew we had the gun ready when our sails took the wind and it came time to give reply. Even on that first day I had a feeling for the craft, and as the gun grew hot and leapt like a beast into the air when we fired, it took me not long to learn the rhythm of it, the quick scrape with the wet cloth inside, the cartridge, shot, running it up, the tap-tap as the layer took his sights and then waiting for the top of the wave, and then the roar. We were taken apart, though, that day, and we must have surrendered if a frigate hadn't come up to scare off the Frenchman, and when it was over my part was noted and I was made a part of the number one crew, which suited me very fine.

After that I served on many ships, most of them men-of-war heavy with cannon and shot and low in the water; we sailed many waters, and as the years passed I visited many countries, many cities in Europe and Africa and then Asia; I fought men of all races and colours and learned how to use the instruments of war. Then an English ship I served on docked at the port of Goa, and that evening for the first time I walked on the soil of this country which we call India; we traded with the Portuguese and two weeks later sailed again. I sat on deck whenever I could and watched the coast of Malabar slip by, green and dark, with fishing boats slipping in and out among the beaches and the palms and the swamps; we passed by many ships, some Portuguese and some Arab and some belonging to the kingdoms on the coast. One afternoon, a week or two before we rounded Comorin, I saw a tiger lying on a beach, stretching and yawning in the sun, and we all rushed to the rail, shouting and gesturing, and I remember thinking, I must remember this; and as we watched he stood up and stared at us; even at that distance I could see the yellow glare of his eyes; then he grunted (I felt my heart squeeze) and moved off into the darkness under the trees.

We docked at Calcutta, and I wandered through the streets, the bazaars full of fruit, muslin, silk, fish. I saw people dressed in every imaginable colour, turbans round and triangular, jewellery on every limb; there were traders, soldiers, scholars, priests, labourers, servants; there were dozens of languages, accents sibilant and staccato, long hovering vowels and strong decisive consonants. We stayed for a month, and I spent every moment I could walking, alone.

Finally, loaded with spices and silk, we set off. I watched the white beaches recede into a distant stain on the horizon, with the sails cracking and the mast creaking above me, a heaviness in my heart. For two days we headed due south-west, and then were seized by a dead calm; we drifted. The sea was a flat grey; a school of dolphins surrounded us and splashed through patches of seaweed, walking through the water on their tails, grinning up at us; on the tenth day we saw land to starboard, and slowly drifted closer to it. I could see huge trees, gnarled and twisted, branches reaching down, roots rising out of water; the air was very still, the sun sent us scurrying for whatever shadow we could find, and the pale blue of the sky hurt the eyes; I sat under a boat, fanning myself with a little straw punkah I had bought in Calcutta, dreaming, thinking of the stories I had heard of the kingdoms of the plains and the Deccan, the nawabs of Avadh, the broken Moghuls, the Sikhs, the Marathas, the Rajputs, the sultans of the south. Late that night, a slight breeze sprang up, and our captain came running out of his cabin, shouting orders; ropes creaked and wood groaned, and we began to move, slowly, hesitantly, and then out of the trees, from the dark forest, I heard a coughing grunt; I stood bolt upright, and then a tiger's roar boomed over the ship, a harsh fearful spitting sound, unbelievably loud; I felt warm liquid spill out of me and spread down my thighs, but even before the echoes had died away I was running towards the rail; I went over in a running dive and hit the water like a knife; racing towards the trees, I could hear shouts behind me, but I knew they couldn't stop to put out a boat after me — the wind was up, and they couldn't be bothered with one man; so I pulled myself through the darkness, weeping and laughing and talking to myself. Soon, I was able to pull myself up onto a thick root. The lights of the ship receded. I was alone, among the trees.

Thomas was quiet, then, for a moment, and looked dreamily into the dark.

'Why?' he went on. 'One might ask, why? Listen . . .'

As I stumbled and swam through the swamp, thirsty, starving, I asked myself again and again; but the roots of things are hidden, shrouded. The black trees towered above me, and I sprang from branch to branch, my skin covered with sores and bites and cuts. I lost my shoes in the bubbling ooze that rose and fell each day with the tide; I grew faint and lost all sense of direction, and often I collapsed, my limbs jerking and flopping about, dreaming, seeing impossible creatures rise out of the green water: chimeras, gryphons, phoenixes. Why? I asked, and all I can say even now is that for some the unfamiliar holds the promise of love, of perfection.

One morning, I lay on my back on a small island, a patch of brown soil in the middle of rushing water. With watery eyes I watched the sun climb through the leaves, and then I felt a hot rush of breath on my feet, a miasma that climbed up my thighs and over my chest, a rich rotting-meat smell that filled my nostrils. I looked up into golden eyes, calm eyes, eyes vacant in a natural ferocity quite without malice. I felt whiskers brush softly across my cheek, and then there was the sharp pain of a bite in my left shoulder, just below the neck; he picked me up and carried me easily through water and over trees and dry ground. The blood slipped out of me and over his jaws, dripping into the thick green scum; the sun followed us, moving over the patchwork canopy above; the light danced in my eyes and I knew I was going to die. Just before the last fragment of my awareness dropped away, I lost all control and smelt, in the mist that hung above the water, the odour of my own refuse.

I opened my eyes and there was a man standing above me, his bare brown legs straddling my body; he was shouting at the tiger, waving a spear. The tiger was crouched, its belly flat on the grass, its tail flicking to and fro; it snarled, jaws thrust forward, teeth stained pink from my shoulder. The man's voice dropped into a tone almost conversational — he spoke to the animal in a language full of grunts and clicks; the tiger seemed to listen, and then the man screamed, raising his hands high above his head. The tiger backed away, easing out of its crouch, and then turned and disappeared into the trees.

My saviour bent down and smiled, speaking to me in that gentle clicking language. He was an old man with a tiny wizened face painted in red and green and crowned with coloured feathers; around his neck and in his ears he wore jewellery made of bone and chiselled pieces of coloured stone; he wore animal skins, and carried a spear and a bow. All this I saw as he bent over me and brushed the salt-encrusted, matted hair away from my face. He clapped a palm on his dark, muscular chest.

'Guha,' he said, 'Guha.'

I tried to speak, but could produce only a thin scratching sound. Guha wiped the blood and mud away from my shoulder and picked me up effortlessly, draping my limp body over a shoulder. My head swayed with each stride, and my cheek slid back and forth across smooth brown skin; soon, the regular rhythm of our motion and the sound of the swamp, that twittering, grunting, humming, booming song, answered each other in a hypnotic antiphon that compelled a descent into the region of dreams and memory: already, the places and faces of my past had taken on that soft glow that hides, forever, the grotesqueries and sufferings of childhood and the desolate loneliness of first youth.

When I woke up Guha was rubbing my limbs with a wet tuft of soft grass, wiping away the caked dirt and sweat; later, he cradled my head in his lap and squeezed the juice of fruit into my mouth; and always, he spoke to me, chuckling and clucking softly, rolling his eyes, gesturing. Often, he left me in the little clearing where he made his camp and loped off beneath the heavy branches. He would return, hours later, bloody carcasses hanging from the belt at his waist. When I could walk, I hunted with him; I would crouch behind him; we stalked, and in the swamp where I had seen nothing, felt only hunger, I saw an abundance, life burgeoning, swimming, crawling, giving birth, clawing, biting, all the wonder and the filth. I killed, and each time Guha knelt over the still-warm body, murmuring under his breath, touching the bloody flesh with his long, thin fingers.

*   *   *

By the time the sun moved to the south and the days grew short, my clothes had disintegrated into fragments, and I dressed like Guha, even wearing feathers and stones. I learned some of his language, the words for leaves, insects, fruits and animals, for fear and danger, and we spoke to each other in fits and starts. Sometimes, in camp, at the end of the day, he would sing, raising his eyes towards the red glow between the trees; I understood some words, grasped some small fragments of what he offered to the sky, but even if I had understood nothing there would have been no mistaking the wonder in his voice, the awe and the good humour. In return, I sang him songs I remembered from my childhood. One night, under a full moon, I sang a ballad, an old clan favourite about knocking the English about in a battle long ago, and as I paused between verses Guha piped up in his quavery voice and let loose with a few lines of one of his little ditties, and soon we were swinging back and forth merrily, sending the birds whirling above the tree-tops in confusion; he bent over and thumped my knee, nodding his head, and then we both collapsed in laughter, roaring, infinitely pleased by our madness; our camp-fire crackled on, and perhaps even the watching moon smiled a little at our antics, because good friendship is hard to find, and life is long.

The next morning Guha walked around the camp picking up things, suddenly filled with purpose; he motioned to me to collect my meagre belongings. I followed him out of the clearing; that day we walked in a straight line, due west, with Guha slipping soundlessly through the bushes; at sunset we paused for a few minutes to eat, and then went on. Where are we going? I tried to ask, where? but he pressed on, silent.

That night we left the entangled trees and still water behind and moved across a rolling plain; walking across a raised dike, I saw the light from a distant lamp blinking in the dark, and realized we were in a place of cultivation, of irrigation and harvests. For a moment, I felt fear, and wished we were back in the damp recesses of the swamp, but I had crossed oceans to escape the strangling constrictions of home, to find a shining fiction called Adventure, so once again I licked my lips, grasped my weapons firmly, and we went on, never slowing or pausing. For twenty-four nights we journeyed, hiding during the days in groves of trees or fields dense with sugar-cane; several times people passed within a few feet of us, and sometimes packs of village dogs loped by, sniffing and restless, but Guha's skill was ancient and boundless. At the end of this time we reached a region where the ground rose up in wooded ridges, and as the sun rose on the twenty-fourth day we left the fields behind and climbed into the shade of the jungle.

Now we seemed to wander aimlessly, meandering in great arcs among the trees and the brush. Guha grew dreamy, reaching out with searching hands to touch leaves and bark. By a stream, at a place where the ground was dark and loamy, he turned back to me and pressed on my shoulders, making me sink to the ground. He arranged my limbs so that I sat cross-legged, pushed at my back until my spine was straight. With his spear, he etched a circle in the ground around me. Then he cupped my face in his palms and leaned closer until I could see the flecks of yellow in his eyes, and with the tenderness that one sees in a mother's face as she wipes her baby's bottom, with that awkward craning of the neck, with that defenceless love, he whispered slowly, so that I could understand: 'In the circle, stay, here it is.'

'What?' I said, but he stepped back and reached down to the muddy circumference that bound me in, his fingers bending and snapping out, and just when it seemed that he was about to touch the soil, a sheet of white flame rose up from the circle, smokeless and clean. I cringed in terror, then stood up and screamed, begging Guha to stop it, to let me out, but he smiled, shouldering his spear, and then the flames rose up and hid him, hid everything, until I could see only a round section of sky above me, and even that was soon wiped clean by the hot orb of the sun. I sank to my haunches, sobbing. For a while, I prayed to God, to the saviour of my childhood that I had forgotten in my travels, and his blessed mother, I begged to be delivered from this place of evil and witchcraft; I mumbled apologies for associating with the undelivered who had sold their souls to Satan; I asked for divine retribution to be visited upon the mage Guha, who had trapped me, no doubt to use my soul in some filthy ritual, in some bargain with unclean demons. I knelt, my face pushed into the mud, hands clasped, confessing every transgression, every sin, every craving that had ever sprung from my sweating, excreting, mucus-ridden flesh, every burst of anger, every last iota of greed, every afternoon lost in sloth, every evening given to the disgusting business of mastication, salivation, and digestion; I confessed everything, the sins multiplying, breeding on each other in a bloody, monotonous manner, like some species of low animal: murder, lechery, buggery, covetousness; I wept until my body hurt with each wrenching sob, and then I fell into an exhausted doze.

When I awoke the flames were gone, leaving only a glowing, deep red circle that moved and trembled, like the molten lava I had heard described by a traveller on one of my ships, long ago; the ground on which I crouched was covered with congealed yellow masses of vomit. I reached out towards the red border, feeling no heat, but the closer I came to it, the more I felt a dread that rose from the region of my belly; I cannot explain this now, cannot make you understand, I think — I could no more have touched that circumference than I could have caressed a blade fresh from an armourer's smithy, hissing and spitting; I certainly could not bring myself to step over Guha's magic line, out of my airy prison, so I stayed.

In the dim light of dawn, I watched a deer emerge apprehensively from the trees and tiptoe to the water. Feeling the pangs of hunger, I looked around my little patch of ground, finding only a few blades of grass; I plucked a green sliver and put it between my lips, and instantly a great rush of saliva filled my mouth, but even before I had finished chewing I felt satiated. Over the next few days I discovered that I seemed to somehow absorb nourishment from the air and the sunlight, from the fragrance that drifted up from the flowers that grew among the rocks on the banks of the stream; so I survived, watching the animals and the birds, who circled me warily at first but soon accepted me as one of the inhabitants of that world, as a spectator as silent and as unthreatening as the rocks or the trees. None of the predators attempted to enter the circle, so after a while I grew to trust the efficacy of Guha's magic, and watched the graceful lope of the leopard by day and the heavier, confident tread of the tiger by night.

I grew light-headed as the days passed; the dew lay thick on the leaves at dawn, and the white clouds moved imperceptibly against the sky; sometimes I slept and dreamt, and when I opened my eyes the dreams seemed to continue. Mist, the world is mist, terrible and lovely, and sometimes even as I dreamt I knew I sat still within the circle, my body growing translucent like imperfect glass, so that I could see the blades of grass through my fingers, and now the sun pierced my heart and my shadow grew faint and indistinct; finally, I could stay upright no longer; I curled up on my side, my knees drawn up to the chest.

When they found me they could see the earth through my thighs and my arms; for a while, they told me later, they watched me, believing that I was a piece of someone's dream, or a ghost grown weak from grief. Guha's red circle was gone, leaving only a faint dark stain; after a while I began thrashing about, and they saw how I scraped in the mud until I found a tiny sliver of green that had barely thrust itself into the air and raised it, trembling, to my lips; they knew then I was a human being. They picked me up, exclaiming how easily my body rose from the ground, and carried me to their village where an ojha shook dried leaves over me and an old woman fed some glutinous grey stuff into my mouth, her fingers rough and hard against my lips.

They called themselves the Vehi, and told me, later, that once a piece of the sun had fallen, circling end over end; an eagle, imagining it to be some kind of small hummingbird, had stood on one wing-tip and arced down to snap it up, and had fallen immediately groundward, rendered insensible by the heat within its gullet. As time passed the eagle's feathers and claws and beak had fallen to the ground one by one, until all that was left was a soft-skinned animal reshaped by the luminosity within, and this was the first human, the remote ancestor of the Vehi. I lived with them for many months, recovering from my ordeal, learning their language; I threw away my remaining ornaments, and learnt to dress like them, wearing about my loins a single piece of cloth, obtained in trade from the plains. At first I spent my time wandering among the trees, watching the women gather fruit and roots, but when I had regained my strength I went hunting with them, tracking animal and fowl of every description. Sometimes I told them of home, and of the other great cities I had seen, and they tapped their cheeks in wonder, but it all seemed distant to me now, colourless, flat, and I wondered how I could have lived like that; once I would have called these people savages, and even unsaved, but now I knew that but for them I would have vanished into the mud of the forest, become a dream or a ghost, because I understood now that this is what the forest can do. So I stayed with them and learnt their stories.

Now the days passed and I spent my time with the young men of my age-group; I learnt to use the weapons of the Vehi, and soon my forearms were covered with the curving white scars of the bow-string; at night, with the young of the tribe, I told stories, sang songs, and made love in the Gotul; at twelve years of age, the girls and boys of the Vehi began spending their nights at this school, under a thatched roof, where they learnt song, the telling of tales, and love, all the business of living; each chose one other, a sweetheart, a beloved, but often these pairs parted, and new ones formed, with little anger and jealousy. Outside, the older people married and saw to the governing of the settlement and the appeasement of the gods and spirits who lived in the trees, the streams, the sky; sometimes the monsoon arrived late, and when it came the rain was momentary and weak, not the furious drenching the parched and cracked ground seemed to call out for, and then there was drought, and hunger; the animals died quickly, pawing at the crumbling furrows on dry river-beds, and the Vehi grew thin and bright-eyed, eating leaves and fighting wild pigs and squirrels for pieces of roots; some of the older people sat in the shade staring into the distance while flies buzzed about their mouths, scuttling over corners of lips and settling near the nostrils; now, children died. But this passed, and it was easy and good to live with the Vehi, because their priests were merry and there was no money; I don't know how long I stayed with them, maybe a few years, maybe two or three or four, but I know my age-group had left the Gotul and my friends and I hunted far from the settlement, in places where I had never been.

One afternoon, we came up to a huge cliff where a plateau dropped down onto a plain, and on the plain there were coloured tents with flags, elephants, horses; as I watched, a troop of cavalry wheeled out of the camp and disappeared in a cloud of dust; the sun glanced off cannon and lance-heads; we sat and watched, and as the afternoon passed my friends told a story I had heard before: the Vehis had once been kings, and they had ruled the plains, vast and rich; they had lived in palaces, commanded armies like the one below, but one day a neighbouring king had surprised them, coming over the borders in the night, by little-known routes, and soon the Vehi were fighting in the streets of their own towns and villages. They were defeated, and they retreated into the jungles, their ancestral home, where they took up again the old ways of life, as if the palaces had been merely a dream. I listened, watching the elephants move ant-like below me, and thought of how it must be, with the French to the south, the Marathas and Rajputs to the west, the Sikhs in the north, the British in the east, and the Moghuls in the middle (shattered and haunted by memories), and all the others, all those kingdoms, the kings and princes and generals and soldiers, maharajas and sultans, queens and commoners, all uncertain, frightened and rapacious, the centre gone; long into that night, I watched the camp-fires below, and the next morning, when my friends gathered up their bows, I stopped them, and said: Wait, the Vehi will be kings again.

The swing creaked, soft and low, and then sharp; some of the lamps had flickered out, the oil gone, and when Thomas looked up, he could hardly see the Begum's face. He swallowed, tasting the bittersweet tang of the past, and went on.

I said, the Vehi will be kings again, and they all laughed at first, eager, caught up instantly in the thought, in the future, but when I explained what it would mean, spoke of the descent from the jungle, over the jagged sweeps of the cliff, and the striving that would follow, the struggle, the soldiering, they sat, sober, thoughtful. I saw it on each of their faces, as they pondered: the imaginings of palaces and power, and the smell of the cooking fires of the settlement in the evenings, and the distant singing from the Gotul at night, and even before they shook their heads I knew that I was the only madman who would take the plunge into the world below, into that chaos of ambition and greed we choose to call civilization.

So I said good-bye to the brothers of my age-group, holding each one close for a moment, and then began to work my way down; their voices soon faded away, and the steep slope hid the jungle above. By late afternoon I could see the leaves on the bushes below, and the camp's picquets had seen me: as I scrambled over the loose shale at the bottom of the precipice, three horsemen waited, their eyes searching the rocks above me, and I could see that they were nervous, not knowing what to expect; I could see that this was a time of war. I knew how strange I must have looked, carrying a tribesman's bow, with the blue eyes and pale skin of a firangi or a Pathan, so I smiled cheerfully and greeted them in my suddenly unfamiliar English and small French; they looked at each other, puzzled, not understanding the sense of it but clearly recognizing the rhythms, and then they herded me back into the camp, riding behind me, lances at rest.

They were well-built men, riding good horses, dressed, it seemed, each according to his whim, in a wild variety of colours; they were like no other horse soldiers I had ever seen: though each carried a lance, the length varied from six feet to about twelve feet, and only one lance had a pennant attached; all three carried tulwars, and each weapon had a different kind of hilt, one in particular being richly-chased in silver; two carried pistols, and all three had a number of dirks and daggers distributed about their belts; they were an altogether varied and dashing-looking trio, with their turbans and upturned moustaches and long locks, but decidedly, to my eyes, much too unsoldier-like in their accoutrements and demeanour, even for cavalrymen, who, as is well-known, make a fetish of dash and spirit.

By the time we reached the camp a crowd had gathered to drift behind us like a comet's tail; amidst shoving and exclamation I walked between what seemed to be merchants' booths, grocers, jewellers, cloth-sellers, sweetmeat-men, armourers, forming a regular bazaar, almost as well-stocked, from what I could see, as the crowded commercial streets of Calcutta, which, you will remember, I had seen briefly. Again, this was most curious: this army marched with a regular complement of traders and craftsmen and entertainers, a sort of moving city that allowed the soldier in the field the benefits and comforts of ordered life; I knew even at that moment, in that babel of foreign tongues, that this would bear some thinking upon, because although this system no doubt made for a more civilized mode of warfare than that practised where I came from, it would result in a loss of mobility, a fatal inability to move fast and strike first; already, you see, something had happened to me, already I was thinking, this I will do, these I will strike, that will be mine, I will be this, I will be that; I had told the Vehi that they would be kings again, but they had disappeared into their mansions of green, and I thought of them no more.

We walked up to a large red tent, and the horseman with the fancy sword hilt swung himself down and went in, nodding to the guards. The crowd arranged itself in a half-circle around the entrance, and as we waited some called out to me, and when I didn't react others poked at me, none too gently, with sticks and sheathed tulwars; I stepped back quickly, turning, unslinging my bow, and for a moment there was a tense silence, and I could hear the flags flapping in the wind, but then footsteps came closer, behind me, and the crowd seemed to subside into itself, the raised sticks being lowered and twitchy hands moving away from hilts. A stout man, perhaps of about thirty years — dressed in white silks with pearls at his throat, diamonds on his fingers and an emerald-laden ornament on his turban — circled me slowly, keeping a good ten feet away at all times; another man, broad-chested, white-haired, stepped up to me, peering down at my bow; he looked around quickly, then pointed to a spear stuck into the ground some fifty feet away. I notched an arrow, breathed a prayer, thought inexplicably of Guha for a moment and let fly; the spear shook, and I could hear the quick dying buzz of the vibration. Confident now, I pulled out another arrow and put it below the last one, and then another one above. The crowd babbled approvingly, and the white-haired man grinned.

This was how I came to the service of the Raja of Balrampur, for that was who the silk-clad man was; in the early mornings, Uday — the one with the white hair — and I walked out beyond the lines and skimmed arrows at trees, twigs, and finally leaves that fluttered unpredictably through the air; I taught him what I knew of the use of the Vehi bow, and he showed me exercises to strengthen my wrists, and the art of wielding the tulwar, the curving sabre of Hindustan; I learnt, too, the language of the camps, of soldiers from Rajasthan to the Deccan, that startlingly beautiful patois called Urdu. In those first days and weeks, as I learnt the ways of these people, these morning sessions were the only contact I had with soldiers, because they would, according to the rules of caste, not let me near their cooking fires, and I was a weird, ragged firangi, so the only people who would let me sit with them were the lowest of the low, the foragers and the sweepers, who, I suppose, enjoyed the thrill of having a genuine foreign-sounding firangi at their fires.

I was lonely then, more alone than I had ever been, even more sunk in solitude than during the early frightening days of my first voyage, when the sea was flat and still, and the slops that we threw overboard vanished with hardly a splash; I lay at night, grinding my teeth, an oppressive soreness pressing up in my chest, at the bottom of my throat; thrashing about, I wondered why I had to go on, from one unfa-miliar vista to another; I dreamt about the Vehi, about my lovers, my brothers, but already I knew there was no returning. For some of us there never is.

The Raja of Balrampur had succeeded to the throne a few months earlier, when his ageing father spit blood into his treasured rows of jasmine. When the old man died the nawab of the neighbouring principality of Amjan sent parties of raiders into the villages near the border, testing Balrampur's nerve; negotiations had taken place, and Brahmins had gone back and forth bearing queries and threats, but finally armies had taken the field, and we marched in long arcs, feinting and probing, looking for that one opening, that one chance. The two masses of men drew close to each other and then drifted apart, caught in a slow centrifugal dance, reluctant to come together but unable to escape those converging orbits.

From the periphery, dressed in Uday's cast-off clothing, I watched the everyday business of the camp: the mornings when men practised with their weapons, the haze of blue smoke in the air and the peppery smell from the cooking-fires, the elaborate etiquette of the durbars and the presentation of khilluts, the quick shouting matches over arrears in pay and the grand promises, the long jingling dances by famous courtesans on festival days and the ranks of abstracted eyes. I followed Uday as he strode about, growling orders, checking horses and guns, giving advice, and so on, fulfilling, it seemed to me, the duties and obligations of an officer of middle rank; soon, I was accepted as Uday's body-guard or major-domo, a position which, I was to understand later, was traditionally held by foreigners of one type or another, by Arabs, Abyssinians, Pathans, Afghans, Mongols, Turks, Persians, all the quick-handed adventurers who had come in turn to Hindustan seeking fortune. I began to speak, first the words of greeting and good manners, then the convoluted soldiers' curses of nature familial and anatomical that rang out of the dust in the chaos at the beginning of each march; so as we marched, I watched and learnt, and we seemed to march, as the saying goes, wherever the lizard runs and the tortoise crawls. Finally, the two armies confronted each other, next to a town, the name of which I have forgotten, and when the sun became a puddle of crimson and purple on the horizon, we could see their fires dotted about the plain to our north, like a nest of fire-flies, like cat-eyes in the dark.

I slept fitfully, and in the grey hours of morning, when only flat shadows exist, when it seems impossible that the clash of colours will follow, I sat on my haunches, shivering, listening to the beating of my heart; when the camp began to stir, I walked around, looking at the sleepy faces as they scrubbed their teeth with a dantun twig or performed their morning oblations for the sun, and I could see no fear, none of that frenzied scribbling of letters that I had witnessed on other mornings, before other battles, and so then I understood that I was amongst strangers, amidst soldiers who followed a foreign creed, born of an alien soil.

After a leisurely breakfast we formed up and took to the field. You may well imagine the scene: the flare of the sun off armour and weapons, the dust, the beating of drums, the shriek of conch-shells, the jingling and creaking of horse-furniture, the whinnying of the horses and the screams of the elephants, the rich stink of dung. Balrampur arranged his army thus: the front consisted of three regiments of infantry, interspersed with a motley collection of cannon from his gun-park; the left flank was covered by a rissalah of cavalry, mostly Afghans and Rajputs; our right flank was protected by the empty houses of that nameless town, where a brigade of infantry had dug in; behind the front line of infantry he positioned three rissalahs of cavalry and one of elephants, and finally, in the rear, at the centre, he sat, surrounded by his household cavalry, resplendent in white, on a richly caparisoned elephant, in a howdah with steel walls some three feet high, so only his eyes and head were exposed to attack.

Uday's rissalah was positioned behind Balrampur, held in reserve; I had no horse, so I had run beside Uday's black Arab, holding on grimly to my meagre Vehi weaponry, augmented by a tulwar given to me by him; he smiled at me, fingering the knob at the top of the hilt, and it rose away, turning on some sort of hinge, revealing a shallow compartment built into the hand-grip, full of little green balls. Uday lifted out one of these balls and put it into his mouth; seeing me watching, he flicked a ball at me, and I put up my hands to catch it, but lost it in the sun. I knelt and ran my fingers through the grass, looking for it, and when I brought it up to my lips my fingers were stained green with sap from the broken blades; I chewed, licking my fingers, watching Amjan's army spread over the field opposite, and a calm lassitude, an accepting quietude flowed through my veins, into my finger-tips.

The two forces were about equally-matched, though perhaps we had a little more infantry; they were deployed in a formation approximately the mirror image of ours, with cavalry on the flanks, and infantry and guns at the centre, their line being a little shorter than ours, with their left flank angling towards the town on our right. A little before noon, judging by the sun, I saw smoke puff across the field, and then the thud of the pieces echoed over us, followed by the whoosh of shot. Our guns replied with a cannonade, and instantly the firing became general, but the men around us seemed unconcerned; the blood thrilled through my limbs, and I remember feeling only a mad excitement, and seeing, un-expectedly, the cannon balls (little black dots against the blue) sus-pended at the top of their arcs before they plummeted down to raise fountains of mud. The firing seemed to create more noise and smoke than casualties, and was punctuated by the hiss and roar of rockets, fired by men who ran out between the lines carrying sticks and fuses; all this was new to me, then, you see, so even when a ball of flame, spitting sparks, meandered crazily through the air and spent itself against the ground near us, causing the horses to shift from leg to leg uneasily and toss their heads, I stood straight, my neck rigid, my eyes darting about, drinking it all in, eager young fool.

With a shout, Amjan's skirmishers at the centre started forward to-wards us, with little jets of flame springing out at our lines. Balrampur said something to one of his generals, and two horsemen raced away from us; moments later, one of the rissalahs in front of us galloped between our brigades of infantry and cut into the enemy, scattering them to and fro, but almost instantly they received a charge from Am-jan's cavalry, and then the horsemen wheeled around each other, dust eddying around the mêlée, and from where I was I could hear the shouts, the commands and the calls of recognition and the screams of pain, far away and brittle on the hot air; my head pounding, I thought then of what it must be like in there, in the whirlwind, and I cannot describe that feeling to you, pity and fear and eagerness and something else moving underneath, that obscene other thing, the moving of blood, and I was young, so I watched, lost in it, in the spectacle, and forgot to observe carefully, as I had planned in the calm of night, the tactics used by the generals, their feints and techniques and use of ground, so I cannot tell you exactly what transpired on that field as the sun moved above us, as our shadows shifted about us, but I remember a sudden commotion nearby, a craning of necks and moving.

I looked up at Uday, who was shading his eyes to peer at the town to our right, where smoke was rising above the roofs. To our front, our whole line was engaged, shrouded in dust; the sun was a glowing yellow patch above us, dimmed, but the air was searing hot in my nostrils, and the metal on the hilt of my sword burnt my fingers. It was clear what Amjan had done: some troops had been concealed, perhaps during the night, near the town, in a copse of trees or a fold in the ground, a nullah or such-like, and when our line was engaged, they had hurled themselves at the point where we least expected attack, in an attempt to roll up our flank; orders were shouted, and the horsemen around me began to move; I ran beside Uday, and he looked at me, thoughtful, calculating, and they began to trot — now I could barely keep up with them — and I lifted up my bow and gestured at him, not knowing myself what I meant, but something changed in his eyes, and maybe it was a squint against the dust, maybe something else, but in any case he reached down to grasp my arm, lifting, and a moment later I was seated behind him, bouncing as we galloped hell-for-leather towards the white houses.

We leapt over overturned carts and twisted bodies in the main street, at the other end of which two groaning masses of men strained and twisted against each other, but even as we drew near a shower of missiles enveloped us, coming from the roof-tops, whizzing past our heads and making sudden thudding sounds as they hit flesh. I felt the horse beneath us stumble, twist to the side and then we had to scramble as it went down; I tried to fight my way to the side of the street, something hit me on the nape of my neck, a boot or somebody's knee, and I tasted blood and my vision constricted, and when I came to myself I was on my knees, being dragged along by Uday, who had his sword out and was cursing, shouting about mothers and sisters, and I found myself wanting to laugh, and I could see thrashing horse limbs and a fine spray of blood, and I giggled a little and struggled to my feet.

In that narrow street, jammed together, the sowars had no chance to use their speed, mobility or weight; the arrows kept coming from the roofs, where another battle was being fought, and I could hear the whip-lash crack of jezails, and soon a pile of men and horses, bubbling and leaking, jammed together like drift-wood, became a dam against which the ranks behind milled and eddied, falling in their turn, helpless. A riderless horse squeezed past me, maddened with fear, and I thrust my hand into its mane, pulling myself into the saddle, then reached down for Uday; we hurled ourselves back down the street, away from the scything hail.

Uday shouted orders, and soon the whole rissalah burst out into the maidan at the end of the street. They wheeled around, clearly on the verge of another headlong charge, angry and spontaneous; again, Uday shouted, and they quieted down a little; meanwhile, I was thinking of the engagements I had been in, on the water, and the two ships tacking to come up alongside each other, and the broadsides, the grape punching holes in the sails and sweeping across decks.

'Cannon,' I said, in Urdu, somehow finding the word instantly, without effort, pointing to the centre of our line, and then back to the town, 'cannon.'

Uday seemed to understand, and on his order half the rissalah dismounted, some running down the street, others pulling themselves up onto the roofs; four followed us, still mounted, as we turned about and went into the dust. A regiment of infantry trotted out of the haze and vanished behind us; here and there, men sat looking down helplessly, death already making its presence known in the way in which their hands lay palm upwards, limp, on the ground. We swerved suddenly to avoid a collision with three horsemen who passed us in a whoosh of rolling eyes and bared teeth, gone before we could tell whether they were friend or foe. The soil looked as if it had been furrowed, chewed up, by a giant animal; a cannon lay on its side, wheels splintered. Some distance away, two men were loading another gun, a twenty-five-pounder, preparing to fire. As we rode up to them they rolled under the gun, expecting to be speared. Uday spoke to them, and they emerged, blinking; the fighting had surged over them and back again, I expect, and the bullock-teams that drew the guns were long gone, having fallen back to the rear or been killed. I could see no rope, so our horses were of no use, and time was short, so we jumped off and put our shoulders to the cannon. The gun moved slowly, stubbornly, in the loose mud, and my cheek lay against the hot metal as I sobbed for breath, feeling the blood rise to my temples; a little ditch that we had ridden over moments ago, barely noticing the momentary bunching of muscles be-low the saddle, now became a moat, an almost insurmountable obstacle that we cursed and reviled; I pushed, the world contracting into a little sphere filled with the wood under my hands, the heavy burnt odour of the metal, and then it went over, our gun, and we ran it towards the town, followed by the two artillery-men, who were laden with powder-bags and shot and leading our horses, similarly loaded. In the town street, the dismounted sowars had been pushed back almost to the end of the street, and within a spear's length of the combat we loaded and primed our gun.

I gestured at Uday, and we pushed our gun forward, pushed it for-ward, you understand, till we were in that first line, that extreme border where steel raised fire from other steel, and men gasped to see a twenty-five-pounder being manhandled and used like a short weapon for close fighting, but then I held a piece of smouldering rope to the touch hole — some stumbling back, now, holding up arms, still unwilling to comprehend the sudden appearance of that black muzzle — and then it jumped, leapt straight up in the air, both wheels clearing the ground by at least six inches, and when the smoke cleared a moment or two later I could see that the blast had knocked them down like dolls. For a mo-ment nobody moved, and then Uday and his sowars jumped forward with a shout, swinging and cutting down the dazed, the blinded, the deafened enemy like boys slashing at half-dead weeds with sticks. I reloaded, pushed forward, laid the gun, fired again; in that hour, on that day, fortune changed sides on that field, because we cleared that street in less time than it took to drag that gun to the town.

The momentum was now ours, and they could do nothing, and after I elevated the muzzle a couple of times, even on the roofs they fell back easily, demoralized, stunned; now when we lifted the gun over the clumps of bodies and debris that lay on the cobble-stones it seemed to weigh nothing. Now I could hear myself shouting, roaring, my face flushing, laughing with a mad fury born in horror; I don't know exactly how many times I fired that gun, how many times my comrades and I leap-frogged each other, but soon we were clear through to the other end of the street, where it opened out into an expanse of grass; Uday shouted orders to our rear, and now the other half of his rissalah — mounted, weapons at rest — rode up in a compact mass and past us.

Uday swung himself into a saddle, and they debouched into the field, riding through the fleeing enemy, gaining speed, lances lowered for the attack, and I sank to my haunches, conscious now that a band of pain encircled my brow, and watched as they launched a charge at the contingents of Amjan's cavalry which had been waiting some few hundred yards away. I felt the shock as the rissalah hurled itself onto the unprepared ranks of the enemy, I heard that indescribable, shattering groan as that combined weight of horses and men descended like a hammer; Amjan's cavalry wavered, broke and fled, and that lost him the day, because his entire left flank crumbled, like a wall shaken to the foundations by an earthquake, and it seemed marvellous to me then, that a small body of men could ride at and defeat a foe superior in numbers, but I have seen much since, many battles, and it seems to me now that numbers, the quality of weapons, the use of ground, the ability of men, all these things are to be valued, but there is a secret hand, a blind god of chance who decides victory and defeat, the sacking of cities and the fate of countries. Because of a memory from my past, because of a momentary collision between a remembered image and present need, I had thought of the gun, and it brought us victory; perhaps someone else would have thought of it a moment later, or maybe we would have beaten them anyway, but battle is like a haze, a chaos in which order is seen only after the fact; men tell themselves stories to comfort, to protect, but Kali dances on these fields, her face black, her tongue red, and she is mad.

Their left flank shook and began to scatter, but they were good soldiers, and could have held on, reformed, counter-attacked, but Amjan lost his nerve, and fled from the field on his elephant. Seeing him vanish, the entire army seemed to give up, and they fled helter-skelter, with our cavalry riding in among them, chopping them down. I sat, exhausted, watching the rout, and I realized now that at some time in the day I had lost my bow and quiver. On the cannon, which lay quiet now, close by, there was some writing in Urdu, in that script which looks like a flight of birds aimed at the horizon, and I ran my fingers over the swooping letters.

'Ghazi,' a voice said behind me. It was Uday, with his face and clothes splattered with rust-coloured blood and black powdery grime; he pointed at the writing on one side of the cannon, and repeated: 'Ghazi.'

I shook my head, and he pointed to the other side: 'Himmat-i-mardan, maddad-i-khuda.'

But I had to shake my head again; he thumped the rump of the horse, and I clambered up behind him; we rode back together, with men pointing me out to their friends, staring frankly at me; the street was covered with blood, tufts of hair, shoes, tulwars (some broken and shivered to pieces), entrails, severed limbs, bodies.

At the camp I was given a tent, a soft bed with silken pillows, and food was put before me in golden plates, but I could only drink water, cup after cup, and had to wave away the food, the smell of which filled my head and gullet, bringing up the bile, the nausea; I lay back, hardly able to move, but unable to sleep, reliving each moment of that day, and already the unbelievable richness of sight, sound and smell had begun to contract into a series of fragmented pictures.

The next morning, I bathed, and Uday gave me a new set of clothes. In open durbar that morning, I sat a little behind Uday, and tried to imitate his every movement, his every polite bow and gesture. Balrampur handed Uday a khillut, and then I was motioned forward; the maharaja held out a khillut, which I accepted with the same gestures and salutes that Uday had just performed, but then the maharaja began to speak, saying, I suppose, something statesman-like and inspiring, as good commanders should; he finished, and the rest looked expectantly at me. I stuttered for a moment, then without thinking, burst out with the formula I had heard recently: 'Himmat-i-mardan, maddad-i-khuda.'

The assembled nobles burst out in laughter, amused, no doubt, by my clumsy accent, but the sentiment seemed to meet with approval, and I knew instantly then that I had risen from the doubtful status of a strange firangi to that of a soldier, from being almost a pariah to being a kshatriya of dubious ancestry: the natives of Hindustan, I realized, are, despite their belief in caste, eminently practical, but I looked around at the broad smiles and understood I had said exactly the right thing, that they liked me now, that I could perhaps have fought ten battles without gaining the same degree of affection; as we left the maharaja's tent Uday smiled and draped his arm around my shoulders.

In my tent, I put on the robe of honour that Balrampur had given me and marvelled at its rich cloth, and at the stranger who peered at me from the mirror, the man with sun-burnt skin and careful eyes, so un-

like the boy who had jumped into unknown waters; from the distant
battle-field, I heard the howl of a jackal, and wondered what the words
on the smooth, black skin of my fortune, the gun, meant. Since that day
I have ridden far and have served many kings, I have fought and loved,
I have dreamed, and now I understand that phrase, those words, those
words which I uttered without comprehension, like a mantra, which
brought acceptance and so changed my life, and I can say them now in
knowledge and with pride: With the help of God and the courage of
men.

When Thomas finished, silence hung over the roof. His audience —
usually given much to giggling and whispering — was hushed by the
unexpected violence of his tale. Thomas himself rubbed his eyes, dislocated, dazed, but then the Begum briskly took charge, and asked that
musicians be brought up, saying: 'Come, come, girls, Thomas Bahadur
has told us his story, we must return the favour; Sangeeta, Rehana, you
dance.' So the flute, the tablas, the jingling anklets soon drowned out
the curious tug, the emptiness that Thomas felt, that aftermath of story-
telling. He watched as the two girls re-enacted a legendary love: the
longing of Radha for her lover, the intolerable hours of night, and then
Krishna the cow-herd, sweet-limbed and graceful, his maddening flute,
calling, the dance, ecstasy.
   The next evening, Thomas once again received a summons to the
roof-top; once again, he told a story; once again, he was rewarded with
a dance, this time by Sita and Nerou, and each night he told a story, and
each night pirouettes followed, side-steps, the mudras of love, fear, anger, warning, joy, the quick slap of feet against stone; he told stories of
his youth, his home, his parents, his journeys.

'Of course,' Sandeep said, 'when I heard this first, in the terai, from
my nameless story-teller, I asked: "What were these stories? How did
they go?"'
   'Of course,' murmured the sadhus. 'It is a question to be asked.'
   'But she said: "Don't be greedy. Something must be left for the future
interpolators." Still, I asked again, and she said: "All stories have in
them the seed of all other stories; any story, if continued long enough,
becomes other stories, and she is no true story-teller who would keep

this from you." Then she was quiet, and I imagined stories multiplying spontaneously, springing joyously out of a mother story, already whole but never complete, then giving birth themselves, becoming as numerous as the leaves on the trees, as the galaxies in the sky, all connected, no beginning, no end, and I grew dizzy, and then she went on. Listen . . .'

Every evening Thomas left his quarters and walked through the fields to the Begum's palace, seeing, sometimes, the distant forlorn figure of Reinhardt, fixed between the earth and the sky in a never-ending series of peregrinations that seemed to go nowhere, reduced now to drawing lines and series of zeros, just zeros, on walls, roofs, trees, ground.

On the roof, by listening to the Begum's criticisms and the spirited discussions among her disciples, Thomas grew intimate with the intricacies of the dances, their techniques and subtleties, the traditions that distinguished one style from another and the art or genius that touched some performances, like a gust of purifying, incendiary air from some other plane, that exalted some dancers, on some nights, into a state of perfected self-knowledge, so that the technique of the dance became invisible, and only the emotion remained, the naked soul. On these nights, when the disciples exhibited some special talent, Thomas wondered how she would dance, what levels of ability the teacher had mastered, what cries of admiration and sighs of satisfaction she would evoke from her audience, from him. He began to watch her across the space where the dancers performed; the intervening bodies, the whirl of embroidered cloth, the sharp glint of silver, all these became blurs, and it seemed that the music was created as an accompaniment for the fluctuations in her face, lit red by the lamps, reacting to every nuance of the dance. He watched the dark eyebrows, the fleshy mouth, the tiny diamond stud set in a nostril, and one evening, after the story-telling and the dancing was over, he realized he had seen every one of the disciples dance at least three times; the musicians were putting away their instruments, but it seemed he could hear, faintly, the last quivering note from the sitar as it slipped into silence, and he asked, dreamily, as if he had been hypnotized: 'When will you dance, Begum?'

'I don't dance,' she said, shortly, and then softened what had sounded like a rebuke by smiling brilliantly at him. 'Do you play shatranj?'

'I have played chess,' he said. A board was produced, and the girls left, filing out slowly, studiously refraining from glancing at Thomas. She taught him the rules of the game, as it had been played in Hindustan since antiquity, and now this too became part of the daily ritual, this matching of wits. In the beginning she won steadily, but soon he began to match her, to trap her, never quite sure whether he was really getting better or she was letting him beat her. When she check-mated him, he became obstinate, and she giggled to see him crouching by the board, his face angry and red, his eyes flickering rapidly from the pawns to the rooks to the queen; after finally tipping the surrounded king over on his side, he would pace about, jaw twitching, and once he burst out in curses, calling down damnation upon the inventors of the rules, because on the field a trapped king meant nothing, because battles should be fought to the end, and the last player with a piece on the board should be the winner, but she remarked laughingly that that would be a very stupid way of conducting business, to win but to be left with nothing but a desolation, and then he grew quiet, looked at her calculatingly, without knowing he was doing so, wondering at a people who so mistook games for real battle, who confused rules with reality. At that moment he felt a wave twist up in his belly, and wondered whether he should try to kiss her, but she suddenly had a small smile on her lips, and he blushed, stammered pleasantries and excused himself for the night.

When it grew cold, the evening meetings moved to a room in the palace, a large room next to a small garden full of plants with broad leaves, and flowers of many colours and scents; there were two beds in the room, built low on the floor and covered with cushions, round and square, big and small; the carpets on the floor were deep and took their patterns from flowers, creepers, and the intricate geometry of the imagination; musical instruments hung on the walls, their shapes functional and yet elegant. In this room the story-telling took on the cosiness of a family event, safe from the chill outside, and Thomas found himself spicing up his recollections with pieces of ghost stories he had heard on his travels, little dashes of fantasy complete with malignant spirits and good wizards. After the girls left, the Begum seemed to discard the formalities proper to her position and age, and became, herself, a laughing girl, mischievous and coquettish, but despite her flashing eyes, exotically lined with kajal, her elegant nose and the richness of her lips, or perhaps because of these, Thomas found himself unable to make that last move, to take that last initiative which would win everything.

He found his seriousness fading away, and when he became aware that she cheated, that she moved pieces on the board when he wasn't looking, that she distracted him with small talk and the jingle of bracelets while she stealthily resurrected dead pawns, he grew irrationally happy, and cared not a whit for winning or losing; he attempted to cheat himself, trying to keep a straight face: one night they crouched above the board, their heads close together, at the end of a hotly-contested game, the casualties of which littered the ground around the black-and-white battle-field, and he realized the only way to avoid immediate check-mate would be to move his queen one square to the left; deliberately casual, he glanced over her shoulder, behind her, exclaiming: 'Look, a parrot.' She turned, and he reached for his queen, but even as he did so her long, black hair spilt over her other shoulder and swept over the board like a wave, knocking over foot-soldiers, rooks, cavalry, artillery, queens, kings, wiping it clean, continuing like a dark cloud to hit Thomas in the face, perfumed, with the smooth texture of her dupatta somewhere in it, and he buried his hands in it (somewhere, his voice in an unbidden, anguished groan), holding it to his eyes, his lips, welcoming it like night.

Making love with her was like dancing; there was the same attention to choreography, to positions illustrated in brilliant colours in old palm-leaf books (the whole body used without shame), to technique that lasted for moments and minutes and hours of controlled breathing and formalized caresses, lost finally in the last blinding clutching heaves and the quietness afterwards; love was not merely love, it was something else always, a hidden language for a greater secret, and coming with her he felt a vanishing, a flowing that stretched from his tip buried inside her, back through the groin and up into his belly, his diaphragm, his heart. They made love every night, through the long dry winter, waking in the morning to find the marble patio outside the room strewn with rose petals; it began to grow warm, and one evening they sat cross-legged, face-to-face, joined, covered with a glistening sheen of perspiration, his hands tracing her spine. Her tongue flickered over his face, over the contours of his ears, around his nostrils. 'Marry me,' he gasped, 'marry me.'

She laughed, throwing back her head, and said: 'Find your own kingdom, this one is mine.' She laughed again, and he felt his face flush, his neck tense; he rose on his knees, pushing her to the ground, pushing with arched toes against the ground, his hands tangled in her hair, trying to hurt her, but she squirmed under him, flexing invisibly, and pleasure spread up his spine; she turned her head and bit at his wrist, then struck him in the small of the back with a clenched fist, stinging but not hurting, then again, along the flank, with a cupped hand, carefully controlled; they rolled across the room — sometimes her on top, thrusting, sometimes him — leaving a trail of moisture on the sheets and on the floor. When they lay still, side by side, panting, she touched a curved nail-mark on his thigh, a scratch, and said: 'Half-moon'; touching a reddish mark like an irregular circle, made with the teeth, on the soft underside of her breast, she said: 'Broken cloud'; he looked at her blankly, mouth slack, and she shook her head affectionately: 'O Jangli, didn't you learn anything in that jungle?'

'Are you really a witch?' he said, his anger gone. 'The Witch of Sardhana?'

She smiled, her pupils expanding like black moons until they filled the corneas, and the lamps in the room flared up, the leaves and petals outside swirled up, forming a momentary curtain of red and green behind the windows; he smiled uncertainly, then said: 'Whatever you are, you should get married. A widow alone in a place like this, is temptation to a thousand freebooters.'

'I must have a king, must I?'

'It would be safer.'

'Perhaps you're right; it might hold them off, and why ask for trouble? Who shall it be? A firangi, for survival's sake, because I know the thing that moves at our doors, I alone.'

'What do you mean?'

'Reinhardt, I think it shall be, if it must be.'

'Him? Him?'

'Who else? You'll do for a lover, but if I must have a foreign king, let it be him,' she said. He spluttered for a moment, insulted, but he thought of Reinhardt, of the Sombre (or in the Hindustani soldiers' twisted version of the English word, the Sumroo), grown thin and pale because of the infinite eons of creation, because of the unspeakable age of Hindustan and the burden of unending time, and, looking at her, at her breasts and her thighs, still wet from both of them, he understood how it would work, and saw the justice, the completeness, the complementary nature of it. He laughed, bent over and ran his tongue over the mark on her breast, down the crease below, where the flesh rose up from the chest, into her armpit, and they made love, slowly. 'Yes, I think I will,' she laughed, 'yes, I will become the Begum Sumroo.'

. . . . now . . .

'YOUR TIME'S NOT UP YET, MONKEY,' Yama said. 'Five minutes.'

He was always a stickler for the letter of the law, and the spirit be damned. This is why a visit to any babu's office in this land is like a little taste of death. So I made a place for Abhay at the typewriter and motioned at him to sit.

'What, me?' he said. 'I'm not ready yet. No, really, I'm not.'

'Somebody must have a story,' Hanuman said.

I looked around wildly. Ashok and Mrinalini were sitting next to each other. 'A matter of a few minutes,' I typed. 'Most urgent. Anything will do: the conditions must be fulfilled.'

'But us?' Ashok said.

'We don't have a tale to tell,' Mrinalini said.

'Of course they do,' Ganesha said. 'They're teachers. Tell them to tell the big story.'

'Which big story?' Ashok said, peering over my shoulder.

'Our story, of course,' Ganesha said. 'What really happened.'

What Really Happened.

LISTEN . . .

This is a what-really-happened, a remaking of the past, a reconstruction of the things that live on within us as they might have happened once upon a time. Suppose someone says, what really happened? Then say that once there were people who built cities in the valley of the Indus, large teeming cities with broad straight streets intersecting at ninety degrees, like a well-made grid. There are some things that have appeared out of the drifting sands to speak cryptically about these people; there is a statue of a sophisticated, gentle man with contemplative, inward-looking eyes. There is a figurine of a dancing girl, head proudly thrown back, hips carelessly and confidently thrust forward, hand on waist, ready to break impulsively into movement. There are thousands of lines of beautiful undecipherable writing on clay seals; on one of these seals Pashupati sits in meditation, the supreme Yogi, the Lord of animals, the wild king of the forest who holds the universe together with his dance, penis erect in gathered energy. There is the figure of the bull, dewlapped and powerful, repeated endlessly on the seals. There are the toys, the thousands of clay animals and carts like the ones we see on country roads today. There are the great baths, now empty; the wind shifts dust endlessly across the desert.

Where did this richness go? Is it true that a tribe riding chariots appeared out of the western passes, filled with the uncouth strength of the steppes, worshipping a rain-god soon to be called the Destroyer of Cities? Were there massacres and raids and despair? Or did the river change course and leave the long streets empty and silent? Or did the cities just grow old, very, very old, and collapse in on themselves like a stand of dying trees? Nobody knows, but we do know that Shiva still meditates endlessly among the awe-struck animals, that the legends of the chariot-riding Aryans speak of old dark-skinned Asuras, who imparted knowledge of secret sciences to chosen students, that brave adventurers fell in love with the daughters of their enemies, the ones from before, the ones who worshipped old gods, that the sounds of the languages of the south seem to fit the strokes of that undecipherable writing, that Urvashi and Menaka and the other Apsaras of Indra's heaven dance in ancient rhythms, hands curving in old, old gestures that hold oceans of meaning, that bulls stride pulsing with strength across landscapes imagined and invented aeons later, that thousands bathe and then sit in meditation every morning in Bombay and Calcutta and Madras and Delhi, calmly observing the breath, gathering energy.

What really happened? Suppose somebody says, what really happened? Say that Kala walks among us, in all our cities and villages and fields, awaiting his chance, patient, unnoticed and always triumphant; when he wins, finally, only names are lost, only names drift away, dry and hollow, to break up and mingle with sand, but something else is left that lives, that meditates and dances and walks. Say that the wheel turns. But say that there are things that even Kala cannot touch.

The Aryans moved west and south, clearing forests for their cattle, and Indra the thunder-god became Indra the Destroyer of Cities. But, though cities are often destroyed, sometimes they do not vanish, sometimes they become invisible and invade the hearts and minds of the destroyers, who then live forever changed.

So the newcomers and the old ones collided and metamorphosed into a thing wholly new and unutterably old, fell into new orbits around new centres of gravity. In this anomy, the ones newly in power quickly created a perception that promised order, flung out that oldest and most fundamental of definitive statements at the world: I and you, us and them, what I am and what I am not, white and black. More importantly, there was another perception, or rather an experience of some kind of truth, being born in lonely forest meditations, in the mathematical and musical rhythms of great sacrifices, or perhaps in the heightened awareness of the hunt, this: the universe is one, there is a unity that is the boundless mother of the world of this and not this, and this great harmony, this oneness, this Brahman, bursts into being as differentiation, is visible only by becoming non-unity, so that — Are you ready? Here it comes — unity is diversity, diversity is unity. And this diversity, every part of it, is sacred, because it is one — the sky and the fields, the summer and the rains, life feeding on life, the birds and the animals, each a part of some web: 'Everything is the eater and the eaten.'

So, it seemed, people must be different, and a story was told: human beings were born when Purusha, the primeval human, was dismembered in a great sacrifice; from his head were born the Brahmins, the scholars; from his arms, the Kshatriyas, the warriors; from his thighs, the Vaishyas, the farmers; from his feet, the Sudras, the labourers; and each had a different part to play, a different role in Leela, the great cosmic play; from each, it might be said, according to his ability, and to each, at least in principle, according to his need.

So the Brahmins made sacrifices and wrote hymns and the Kshatriyas fought wars, and the Vaishyas and the Sudras went about their tilling and labouring. Huge herds were seen in the fields, and cities of wood were built, shining cities with gardens and lovers and good houses. The years passed, then centuries, and the words of the ancient seers, those discoveries made in solitude, were compiled in the Vedas in the shape of formulae, of verse that reveals little to the uninitiated but nevertheless stirs the heart, because the power of the goddess Vac — speech — is immeasurable; it was she who brought forth both the seen and unseen from potentiality, the external from the immanent. The Vedas show little, and tell much. Those who can see will see. Sacred knowledge in the hands of fools destroys.

. . . now . . .

THE WIND moved through the branches of the peepul tree. I was sitting on the roof in the darkness, watching the moon move across the sleeping city. In that light it was possible to imagine that I was back among the roof-tops of my childhood. Yama had gone in his usual manner, disappearing as he bowed from his corner in the moment that Ashok and Mrinalini had finished their story. Sleep, sleep well, Hanuman had said, but I was still awake, and the story still turned within me, making itself.

'What comes after death?'

I turned and saw Abhay's face, his eyes hidden in shadow. I was not the only one unable to sleep. I looked around for something to write with, and Abhay held out a piece of paper and pen to me.

'After death?' I wrote (wondering at the smooth glide of the strange metal pen over the paper). 'Why, this, all this: life again.'

As he held the paper up to the moonlight I looked down at the pen, and clicked the knob on top back and forth. I was fascinated still, you see, by the smallest pieces of technology in this new world. Abhay watched me, finally with a very small smile on his face.

'Life after death,' he said. 'I never believed in that. Didn't sound reasonable. Always thought it was a local superstition.'

'What superstition is more local than reason?'

He laughed and sat down slowly beside me.

'But what do you remember?'

'About death? The sound of rushing water, and darkness.'

'And after that?'

'Life again.'

'Always life,' he said.

'Always.' But then I had a question for him, and sitting through the night he told me of the life of this terrible century, the hundred years of hope and terror I had escaped in my flight from humanity and myself. Past midnight and through the dawn I heard it all, reluctant and trembling but listening still as the sun rose and brought a new day upon us.

So I began to try and catch up. Abhay brought me books from the bazaar and the library, and when I asked Saira about the cinema (wondrous invention!) she said, 'No problem,' and took charge of my education. That same afternoon a video-player was installed in the room downstairs, and a stack of tapes arrived from the Kapoor Universal Video Centre down the street. And then of course the arguments started: it turned out that Yama was an enthusiast of the art cinema, while Ganesha was a fan of Manmohan Desai. There was some lively back-and-forth that first day, and after fidgeting through *Aparajito*, Ganesha whispered in my ear, glaring at Yama, 'That's the trouble with these *arriviste* pseudo-intellectuals. Not only are they so irritatingly *sincere* in their good intentions, they insist on boring the rest of us.'

Hanuman stretched, twitched his ears, and grinned at me. 'O wise one,' he said. 'Then what in your opinion is a good story?'

'What it's always been, monkey,' Ganesha said. 'One dhansu conflict. Some chaka-chak song and dance. Grief. Love. Love for the lover, love for the mother. Love for the land. Comedy. Terror. One tremendous villain whom we must love also. All the elements properly balanced and mixed together, item after item, like a perfect meal with a dance of tastes. There you have it.'

And so in the time left to us before the hour of story-telling we watched *Amar Akbar Anthony,* and a fine feast it was; replete and nourished, I leapt up to my typewriter, and typed, and laughed as the words echoed over the growing crowd on the maidan: 'All right, all right, bring them on, it's time for the brothers to be born.'

Ram Mohan Ties a Knot, and Sikander Is Born.

IN THE SPRING Zeb-ul-Nissa married Reinhardt the Sombre, but a week before the wedding, which was celebrated with fireworks and dances, George Thomas rode to the south alone. He had lost, he had been defeated, but he was oddly free of bitterness; he felt, in fact, a surge of freedom that seemed to find amplification in the plunging rhythm of the horse and even in the Holi bonfires that bloomed over the plains. As they had said good-bye in the meeting of seasons, the soon-to-be Begum Sumroo had told him about the fires of spring that celebrated the death of Holika, who had stepped into flames in response to a challenge from a holy man, and had been speedily immolated; the Begum smiled as she told the story, but Thomas had seen the flesh pooling and cindering, stripping away from clean white bone, and shivered.

'But, Thomas Sahib, or Jahaj Jung, I should say,' the Begum said, 'in the evening there are the fires marking her immolation, and when the morning comes, there is the throwing of coloured powders at each other, the drinking of bhang, singing of ribald ballads, teasing, cajolery, a harvest and then a planting. The one cannot be without the other; ask any village dotard and he will gravely scratch his beard, try to look wise and tell you this, and probably ask for money after.'

Nevertheless, at the beginning, as Thomas meandered he stayed away from the villages and towns, from the flickering red dots; later, when the celebrations were over and he ventured into settlements and camps, looking for service, because of his long dark hair, his sunburnt skin and his equipage — which included a ten-foot lance — he was taken for a Pathan, or a Persian, or sometimes even a Turk. On the road, in way-side serais and by wells, he heard the story of his encounter with the Witch of Sardhana, a hundred garbled versions of the affair in which the great Jahaj Jung always emerged the loser to Reinhardt the Sombre; embarrassed and shamed, Thomas accepted employment under a series of aliases. A succession of not-very-remunerative hirings as escort for traders' caravans brought him into Rajputana, where the ground sloped and hillocked endlessly, scrub-covered, every rise topped with a fortress or keep, every mile marked with a small steeple-like chattri recording the death of a hero: this was Rathor territory.

Here, Rajah Cheit Singh of Benares had come to marry off one of his sons, and Thomas was retained as part of a cavalry escort: he reconnoitred the gullies ahead as the baraat wound quickly along the road, the elephants ambling gracefully, the camels harrumphing at the dust. With each passing day, the heat collected among the rocks and sand, so that each night was a little warmer, and the summer and the road seemed endless, like hell rolling away into infinity, but this wasn't the only reason for the desperate hurry, for the tense urging by the rajah's senior commander, for the goading of bullocks and the cruel tugging at creases in elephant-skin with hook-like ankus; the rajah was threatened by his eastern neighbour, that profiteering, hungry amoeba-like being that had not yet metamorphosed into an empire, the East India Company. An old question of ascendancy and tribute had simmered for months, kept alive by border skirmishes and probing raids, and the enemy had taken advantage of the rajah's absence to escalate the level of conflict to open manoeuvring in preparation for war, for invasion and besieging and all the bloody business that settles the quarrels between nations.

So the elephants jogged along, snorting, and the bullocks were whipped into exhaustion (listening to them breathing through ringed nostrils, Thomas thought again about Holika), and one afternoon, at a turning above a small precipice, a heavy pachydermal step fell on an outcrop that crumbled, and with a shrill scream and a blur of grey, a howdah tumbled through the branches of babul below, spilling its previously-purdah-hidden load of princesses and ladies-in-waiting into the thorns. The road curved around as it descended, and far below, Thomas looked up to see the elephant dropping, bouncing bulkily off protruding grey rocks, turning end-over-end, trailed by splintered pieces of wood and doll-like bodies that clutched and screamed.

He wrenched the horse around and spurred up the slope; then, seeing a yellow-clad form struggling in the entangling branches, he slipped off his saddle. The woman, whose face was turned away, was bleeding in several places, slashed in long black-red lines across the arms and white back (the dupatta gone, stripped away by the modesty-outraging, veil-tearing, brute wood). Forgetting himself, Thomas leaned across her, pulling at a branch, and as his body touched hers, she jerked away, deeper into the embrace of the babul, glaring. Her face was thin, the nose narrow and long, ornamented with a gold ring; later, he remembered her eyes, very dark and large, lined with kajal, beautiful, but then they compelled him to back away apologetically. It was her eyes and her arms, thin — weighted down with thick gold bracelets — that he remembered even after she had freed herself and stalked past him, her gaze passing across him impersonally while the elephant's screams reverberated across the defile. Even afterwards, after the animal had been despatched and the sun had set, even after he had understood that she was a great Rajput lady who would look through him, who would confer upon him that metaphysical state which is the burden and boon of servants — invisibility — he could not forget her. Even among the stone turrets and battlements of Bejagarh, when the marriage party had reached its destination, he felt her eyes watching from the far-away pink walls of the Rani Mahal, the palace of the queens; even as he tried to tell himself that there was no reason for her to remember him, for her to stand, as he imagined, lonely at a filigreed window, searching the parapets below for a glimpse of him, he felt a caress on his skin, a rising of the follicles, a touch, a palpable response to being seen from afar: he was drawn inevitably towards the guard-ringed zenana palace.

Using influence, hints, bribery, cajolery, flattery and occasional veiled threats, he inveigled a series of appointments that led through the concentric layers of the fortress towards the central, protected sanctuary, where the high-born women sang their songs and constructed subtle intrigues designed to acquire influence over princes and heir-apparents. The angling towards the centre was slow, hard work; below, on the plain, the armies of the Company spread like a creeping ooze, meeting, blending and spreading until they ringed the fortress, settling in for the long business of attrition, for the heavy grinding and chewing that is the main ingredient of the restrained art of the siege, which precludes the quick passion of reduction.

Several times, while on sentry duty in the third watch, when the camp-fires below — carpeting the plain like a sudden growth of seasonal flowers — had ebbed to a dull glowing crimson, when the night brought that especially bitter taste of loneliness and clear-headed perception of failure that comes in the hours just before morning, Thomas thought of revealing himself, of declaring himself to be Jahaj Jung. He dreamt of being promoted despite the stories of defeat at the hands of Reinhardt the Sombre, of suddenly being talked about in the corridors of the Rani Mahal. Perhaps, then, there might follow some wild chance, some god-given opportunity to see her again, to talk to her; but Jahaj Jung would undoubtedly be sent to the outer parapets, where shells breached walls and besiegers flung themselves forwards in forlorn hopes, while an anonymous sentry could stay near the centre, near the unobtainable heart, and so he stayed quiet, and remained at his post, obsessed.

By the time Thomas had worked his way to the outermost gates of the Rani Mahal, the plains below were riddled with tunnels and trenches, zig-zagging towards the fortifications; by night, the besiegers pick-axed and spaded, mole-like, and the defenders on the walls listened to the sounds of metal biting into earth, the clinking of iron on stone, the rustling of scurrying feet, and they calculated distances and directions, and lobbed shells into the darkness. In the fortress the price of grain spiralled and cheekbones edged their way out, casting shadows onto paling skin, but Thomas became glowingly confident, because he now stood guard at a gate where the princesses' dolis passed by every morning and afternoon: it was impossible that she was not in one of them, that she did not see him. So every morning, he waited eagerly for the cry of the palanquin-bearers, 'huh-HAH-huh-HAH-huh-HAH-huh-HAH'; below, parties of defenders sallied out at dawn to surprise the parallels and siege batteries of the foe; at midnight, parties of sappers burrowed into each other's tunnels and killed with glacions, picket posts, hammers, spades and stones, tore at each other, cursed, strangled, pressed faces into mud; the earth grew rich with the return of its elements; in the fortress, arms and armour became exceedingly cheap.

One afternoon, Thomas bought a graceful steel sabre, chased with silver on both sides of the blade: two rampant lions on one aspect, the words 'The Red One,' in Urdu, on the other. The next morning, while standing watch, he fancied he saw a quick movement in one of the dolis, a rippling of a curtain that caused a momentary crack. That same night he bought a polished and tufted helmet, nose-guard still stained on the inside by the crusty black blood of its former owner, who no doubt had caught a sniper's ball through the eye, or a skirmisher's arrow in the forehead, or a digger's pick-axe under the chin. Thomas appeared on his next watch resplendent in his new helmet, equipped with the flashy sabre, studiously ignoring the sneers of his fellows, and this time, no doubt about it, there was an unmistakable flutter of feminine interest behind the brocade as the dolis swayed through (the dark-skinned doli-wallahs, sweating and white-eyed, maintaining their steady trotting gait and even chant, 'HAH-huh-HAH-huh-HAH-huh-HAH-huh').

Over the next week, Thomas enriched his equipage with a suit of chain mail that covered his whole torso, down to the thighs (with a barely-visible kinking, under the left arm, where there had been a hole); black plate armour that buckled around the body, covering both chest and back; grey steel plastrons that sat snugly over the forearms; dull-grey thigh-pieces with decorative engraving suggestive of leaves and creepers; red cavalry boots, sturdy but soft; a curving dagger with a green jade handle carved in the shape of a horse's head and neck; a pair of horse pistols minutely etched with gold in an abstract Turkish design; a fawn leather wrist-guard; a composite bow made of wood backed with strips of horn, sinew and leather, varnished and covered with red cloth and tied in the middle and ends with gold thread; a stiff leather quiver and arrows, some tipped with quadrangular or blunt points, others like razor-edged leaves or crescents, and still others in the shape of wolves' and tigers' heads that screamed as they flew through the air. At night, in his charpoy, in that border-line area between sleep and wakening, Thomas felt, still, the weight of the metal on his limbs; his dreams were invaded by other men's pasts, by the memories of things he had never seen or experienced, by languages so foreign that he had never heard the sounds in the words; in his sleep, he relived other men's agonies, rejoiced with them in the explosion of fertility when the first rains soaked the ground, tasted the ashes of bitterness when loved ones died, worshipped the goddesses of spring, knowledge and small-pox; in the morning, when he first put on his equipment, each piece seemed to speak to him through his finger-tips: the helmet hummed with the courage of a cavalryman born to the saddle, the chain mail reeked of the guilt-ridden rage of a rapist, the sabre buzzed with the white-hot, unreasoning rage of a berserker, the thigh-pieces tintinnabulated with the tenderness of a rissaldar well-loved by his men; at these times, Thomas thought he was being driven out of his mind, either by the strength of his infatuation with a girl he had seen only once, or by the anguish of the heat-maddened city. Nevertheless, he persisted; every day he was seen at his post, his huge body hung with the appliances of combat, like some over-equipped incarnation of Mars or — as he thought with his new-found knowledge — Kartikeya; the other men laughed, and one, an ancient Sikh, said, rubbing his stomach and grinning, 'Ohe, what is this pen-ance in this sun, this weight of metal? Why burn under that chain mail? They won't get here for weeks, to this den of exquisite delicacy — we're well-protected here, and this is what they — our fools down there — will fight like lunatics for, like madmen, when those out there come.' Thomas looked away, towards the dark windows over the Sikh's head, who went on, 'Ah, I understand, a private oath, a warrior's vow. What will you ask for then, when your god appears? Wealth? Love? No, look at you, it will be a soldier's demand: like Hiranakashyapu, you'll ask to be invulnerable; let me be deathless, you'll say, let no man or animal be able to kill me, by day or night, out-of-doors or in; make me, you'll say, hard as thunder.' Thomas pushed past him, hearing, far away, 'Huh-HAH-huh-HAH-huh-HAH-huh-HAH'; the dolis passed, leaving the air redolent with rose-perfume and sweat; Thomas turned, looking for the Sikh.

'Eh, Iqbal Singh-ji,' he called, 'what happened to Hiranakashyapu? In the end?'

The Sikh was standing spraddle-legged on a parapet, urinating, enjoying the sight of his water curving through the sunlight and splattering on the rocks a hundred feet below. 'He died,' he said. 'You don't know? He killed so many that he thought nobody should worship anyone but him. But his son was a Shiva-devotee, a most pious, priggish little brat, it sounds like. So Hiranakashyapu told his sister Holika to burn little Prahlad, and, holding him, she jumped into the fire, but she burnt instead. So then Hiranakashyapu drew his sword to kill the boy, and noticed Prahlad looking quite fearless, said, Are you mad, Prahlad said, My Lord is everywhere he will protect, and Hiranakashyapu thumped a pillar saying, Oh really is he here, and Shiva emerged from the pillar, half-man, half-lion, at the hour of twilight, carried Hiranakashyapu to the lintel, so that he was half indoors and half out, and tore him open.'

Thomas laughed, a small uncertain giggle, and then they both ducked to the ground as a dark object whistled down from the sky, its shadow skimming over them; Thomas landed awkwardly, his body twisted, and looked up into the snarling face of a small dog as it turned through the air, legs stiff and outstretched, it hit the ground and exploded, spraying black fluid and maggots.

'Sisterfuckers,' the Sikh growled, rubbing at a stain on his pantaloons. 'Motherfuckers.'

Thomas straightened up, clanking, and gingerly picked his way through the mess to where the dog lay, trailing entrails in which white worms moved slowly; its lips were twisted back from the teeth, the eyes very black and quite impenetrable. 'Very close,' he said. 'Too close.'

'They're closer than I thought. They'll be up here soon,' the Sikh said. 'It won't be long now.'

So, in the height of that summer, in the time near the summer solstice, the Company began catapulting long-dead animal carcasses into the fortress; rotting-skinned calves and evil-smelling goats dropped in long, high arcs, thumping into rocks and dry grass. Now, disease spread; plagues raced through the stronghold, whittling down the already-denuded garrison; now, when red-hot shot set fire to roofs, it fed unopposed, gulping down homes and shops. In his basement room,

Thomas was often awakened at night by the flat whump-whump-whump of mortars and confused shouting; he would twist on his charpoy, his legs hanging over the lower edge, mumble, glance sleepily at the armour and arms distributed around the bed in concentric circles (glinting, gleaming despite the darkness) and feeling a huge surge of satisfaction and confidence, fall back into a sleep delightfully burdened by palanquin-riding princesses.

One evening, Thomas swaggered through the bazaar, armed at all points, his long hair oiled, eyes outlined with kajal, a pink flower behind an ear; he walked past blackened gaps in the rows of shops, some still smoking, past empty houses, bedraggled courtesans calling without enthusiasm or hope from upper-storey windows, squeaking pigs feeding on corpses, groups of tea-drinking soldiers caught in that absolute silence that comes from absolute knowledge of impending disaster, streets clogged with debris, weeping children, families staggering under the weight of their quickly-bundled possessions, packs of sleek white dogs, threatening and feral.

'Sahib. O Sahib. Wait.'

Thomas turned, flicking his hair over a shoulder; it was one of the many arms-sellers he had dealt with recently, a thin, nervous man with Shaivite caste-marks on his forehead.

'I am going, Sahib,' he said. 'We will try to get out, tonight. But before I go, I thought, I must see the Sahib, only he will appreciate this. Look.' He held out a two-and-a-half-foot length of heavy steel, worked at the top into curving petal-like flanges, crowned with an octagonal spike at the top of the bud. 'Look. It is less a mace, more a thing a woman might love for its delicacy. Look at the workmanship of the handle. Look at the strength of the neck. One might be glad to fall under a blow from this, one might consider oneself blessed.'

'Indeed,' said Thomas. 'It is pleasing to the eyes, with the curve of these, the boss and then the heavy straight line of the spike.'

'I knew it. Only you could appreciate the worth of a piece like this. Call her Rose-of-the-Morning, Sahib. Bulbul-of-Heaven.'

'Princess-of-the-Heart.'

'Marvellous. Princess-of-the-Heart, indeed.'

'How much?'

After the obligatory bargaining, Thomas carried his new possession home, swinging it to and fro, listening to the faint but clear whistling of air between its blunt blades. That night, he slept with it by his head, rubbing his palm over the cross-hatching on the hilt, liking its comfortable chill, and later turning, in his sleep, to rest his head against it, to taste, inadvertently, the electric bitterness of the metal. He awoke, suddenly, with dirt in his nostrils and mouth, ears ringing; there were voices, raised and hysterical, nearby, muffled by the yellow haze of plaster and dust shaken loose from the walls; Thomas began to strap on his buckler.

'Come, brother. It is time.' Iqbal Singh emerged from the murk, tying the drawstring to his pants.

'What was it?'

'A mine under the East Gate. It vanished, I hear, the whole gate.'

'Of course.'

They ran up a narrow staircase; outside, the sky was coloured with the first hint of grey to the east, silhouetting the rush of figures, the faces of men, the rhythmic up-and-down of the battlements. 'We live,' Iqbal Singh said, 'in very bad times.'

Then they rushed into the mêlée; in the jostling, heaving mass it was impossible to tell friend or foe, and so blows were exchanged anonymously, randomly, and bodies moved under foot, writhing, suffocated; Thomas used his weight, pushing his way through the crowd, flanked by Iqbal Singh, noting, curiously, the queer high-pitched sound emitted by the throng, its heavy, not-unpleasant odour of perspiration and fear, and the momentary glimpses — in the jumping red light of flames, the quick hot white flashes of pistol discharges — of bulging eyes, gaping mouths, hands, lips, elbows, eyebrows. Finally, they gasped for breath at the gate of the Rani Mahal, at their accustomed post. Above them, a thick column of pitch-black smoke grew thicker at the base, piling billow upon billow; the gate itself stood open, and a dozen men from the guard crouched by it, nervous and indecisive; below, a dense, rippling line of flashes marked the enemy's advance party as it ascended, rolling up the defenders.

'Close it,' Iqbal Singh shouted. 'Close it, fools.'

They strained at the gate, which moved, creaking, slow; something rang against the arch above, sprinkling them with a stinging cloud of marble chips, and a man dropped behind Thomas, exhaling breath in a quick whine; the gate closed, they struggled with the huge rusted bolt, which squeaked and fought them, dropping large brown flakes on their feet, and just as it slid, protesting, through the first hasp, the gate sagged inward, reverberating like a gigantic diaphragm from ramming blows and shot.

'Leave it,' Iqbal Singh said. The echoing drum-beat sound chased them as they ran along a circular, rising passage-way, overlooked by balustrades and loopholed walls; then they were in the palace proper, racing through pillared halls and court-yards where red and green parrots squawked and flapped and fell out of branches; a figure appeared in a doorway, an obese, finely-dressed man holding a cavalry sabre awkwardly.

'We're your men,' Thomas said.

'Where are all the guards, all the rest?' Iqbal Singh said.

'No guards, it was all so sudden.' He began to cry. The tears left shiny tracks down his puffy cheeks. 'We didn't even have time to put by wood for jauhar, it was all so sudden, so they all went out to the balconies at the back.'

'Fool's errand we came on,' Iqbal Singh said. 'They can't char themselves, the great Rajput ladies, so they'll fly like little birdies. Nothing to protect here, brother, let's go home.'

But Thomas was already off, running, The Red One in his right hand and Princess-of-the-Heart in his left, and the others followed; they bolted through carpeted living rooms, under huge crystal chandeliers, and over silk-laden beds in apartments, up flights of stairs, past delicate stone screens, and then into a large hall — black-and-white tiles, Thomas saw in that first moment, and on the wall a painting, a large painting, a dancing woman, musicians — where on the other side a large group of women clustered about a series of balconies that opened out onto the valley below; he ran towards them, and seeing him come, one of them, an old woman, with white hair, pale skin, raised her foot, put it on the sandstone railing running around a balcony, and stepped, face quite without fear, into the air, and for a moment her yellow skirt, patterned with red, ballooned out around her, holding her up, it seemed, but then she dropped out of sight. Shouting, Thomas ran along the edge of the hall, herding them away from the balconies, away from the edge; he saw her and knew it was her, despite the voluminous ghunghat veiling her face: she was motionless, facing a balcony, back to a pillar, clutching it; he ran up to her, saw her head move beneath the cloth as she felt him approach, he reached up with the mace, notched a fold of the ghunghat with the spike, pulled it away, it was her, as the cloth fell away from her head her eyes were quite without expression, the pupils dilated, the blood rushed to her skin, reddening, the cloth fell, Thomas heard a roaring, smoke, masonry collapsed, the cloth fell.

'JAHAJ JUNG!'

Thomas turned, dazed, to see Uday Singh, his white beard blackened by soot, coming through a jagged hole in the wall in a crouching run, followed closely by a squat, ruddy-faced European in a green coat; oily smoke poured through the gap in the brick, sliding over the tiles; Uday moved sideways, crab-wise, relaxed but already stalking, presenting never more than a profile closely guarded by the oscillating point of a sword.

'A coincidence worthy of the old stories,' he said, chuckling. 'But I should have known I would find you in here, Jahaj Jung, among the pretties.'

The European had stopped in the middle of the hall, his jaw working back and forth, sweat running down his face, his chest pumping until it seemed he would burst out of his green coat.

'Damn' black nigger bastards,' he said in English tinged strongly with a Scottish accent. 'Get them away from the women, Uday Singh.'

'Yes, Skinner Sa'ab,' Uday said, in English, and then switching to Urdu: 'The firangi wants you away from the pretties.' Uday smiled. 'Will you go, Jahaj Jung? I serve the English now, and I must make you go.'

Thomas, his attention still focused on her, saw, at the edges of his field of vision, men hanging back, staring at him with fear and even awe, but even now he watched her, the mace lowered (the ghunghat dragged to the ground). She looked past him, her eyes lowered, at the drop, at the valley beyond, the scattered trees, the brown fields, haze, heavy cumulus clouds massing to the south.

'Will you go?'

Thomas turned and leapt, without a word, covering the distance to Uday in a stride, mace rising across body and splintering Uday's sword on his parry, sending him stumbling back, sprawling, Thomas was over him, a shoulder hit Skinner at the plexus, collapsed him like a sack, on, The Red One swung up, cut, men hesitated, retreated, jostling and pushing to get out of the way, a gap opened, Iqbal Singh and the others followed, swinging, through the hole in the wall, into a smoke-filled corridor, men falling rapidly as they ran, backs pierced and bloodied by swords, pikes, spears (a long-ago rissaldar's voice: 'Remember, children, it is when you break and run, when you can't see them, when you can't parry or thrust, that they'll massacre you, cut you down . . .'). Afterwards he could never remember that corridor, he only remembered stumbling into a stinking alley, and the sting of two long cuts on his torso, under his right arm, and a bloody gouge in his thigh. They ran in a single file down the lane, and he went first amongst them, guiding them away from the wider streets, and keeping to the close and narrow, but he did not know where he was going.

Then they heard horses screaming, a resonant blowing sound that hung among the houses. They found the stable easily enough, behind a white palace, but inside there was the steady cracking noise of burning, and smoke, and the horses flung themselves against wood, brick, stone. Thomas threw back a stall door, and around him men grabbed desperately at manes, and then he was up, smooth muscle underneath, sliding, falling, but no, out of the door; in front of Thomas and Iqbal, a man lost his grip, rolled on the horse's back, clutching, disappeared underneath, and hooves bore down and impacted with the sound of tearing cloth, and now they were racing downhill through back alleys and little-known lanes, and men threw themselves aside, no time for even a cut. Thomas leaned over the horse's neck, arm around it, Princess-of-the-Heart slung around his wrist by a leather thong, froth covered the horse's neck, flicked back into Thomas' face, he tasted, cherished the animal; now the houses petered out and the dusty slope ended in a bluff that dropped down a hundred feet into the moat, turn turn turn, and they rode along parallel to the precipice but lancers spurred out of the town, cutting them off, and Thomas shouted, where, pulled the horse's mane, turn, tugging to the right, turn. He could see the shiny points of the lances, turn, ten-foot lances, come around, boy, and the pursuers opened out into line, they were many, they rode outwards, flanking, a half-moon, a scythe, no escape, none, but: the drop.

Thomas could feel his heart racing: Oh, come my lovely, come my heart, old friend, we are for the cliff, the precipice, come my beautiful, turn again, quick quick quickly, and now nothing impedes us, the summer has expended its dry poisonous malice, the monsoon rumbles again in the clouds, now the sky waits for us. Thomas dropped his weapons, leaned over further and reached out and gently, as gently as he could, clapped his palms over the horse's eyes, no fear, and the edge raced up, swallowed them, unhesitating, and both man and animal screamed, full-throated. They fell, all the smooth-muscled equine grace gone from the animal: it huddled like a child, limbs crossing each other. The air pulled at them; Thomas opened his arms, extended his limbs, the wind stroked the hair away from his face and streamed it behind him, he stretched his fingers, and below, the sinuous green form of the moat rotated, readying to receive him, and, turning, Thomas fell close to the horse, and its huge brown eye watched him impassively, impartially, and he felt something break in his chest, felt the bubbling heat of new birth, it took him so that he curled and stretched, felt no pain, no fear, and still the calm golden eye, and he cried out I love you O I love you, and the water took them.

Coughing, Thomas pulled himself onto the crumbling slope on the outer side of the moat, while behind him, a groaning wreckage of men and horses shrieked and bubbled and settled quickly into the water. He tugged on weeds, scrabbling up the bank, which collapsed and gave way under him; behind him, stones and missiles hurled from the parapet above crashed down and exploded skulls, crushed bones already snapped by the fall. He turned his head for an instant, but his mount was lost in the spuming, offal-like mess settling quickly into the green water, so then he slithered out onto level ground, crawled frantically on his hands and knees for a yard or two, then tottered to his feet and meandered dizzily, arms held out at right angles from his body, towards the relative safety of a line of trees.

Once in the concealing shade of the copse, he paused, trembling, leant against a peepul tree, then clumsily folded into a half-reclining position. A moment later, Iqbal Singh flung himself to the ground beside him, inhaling with deep breaths and exhaling with little cries, 'Ah-ah-ah-ah,' and as they lay there, a dozen men, then two dozen, wet, leaving trails of sludge, groped their way into the darkness and sat shuddering. Above, the figures on the parapet seemed to lose interest and wheeled off; Thomas reached out for his tree and stood with quaking knees. He looked up at the wall, at the blank height of rock and masonry, which, because of the angle of his vision, cut off any sight of the town or buildings above; his mouth opened and a muscle jumped and fluttered in his jaw, and then he howled, wailed, spraying little pink balls of spittle that ruptured against leaves and mud, leaving quick stains and marks.

'Now, enough,' Iqbal Singh said. 'You did enough.'

But Thomas bawled again, this time moving his head back and forth and making a red shower that Iqbal ducked away from; Thomas' eyes were half-closed, and his teeth seemed to be rooted in masses of blackish blood.

'Now,' Iqbal said again. 'Now enough. These came with you, these men, over that thing, some blindly, some without wanting to, but all followed. They came unknowingly, following you, but now they are yours forever. Now they'll follow you anywhere, Jahaj Jung.'

Thomas swallowed, hiccupped, turned away, then back; he raised a hand to his face, and it came away gritty and black, with green snot curling over the wrist; he looked down at himself. Much of the plate armour was gone, and the chain mail was torn and slashed, and hung in tatters where he had taken thrusts he could not remember. He nodded, then again, and turned and began to walk through the trees, followed by the others; after a few minutes, he said, in a very conversational tone, without turning back, causing Iqbal to start: 'I wonder what happened to the eunuch?'

'He survived,' Iqbal said after a moment. 'He must have. His kind always do.'

'And so,' said Sandeep, 'Thomas attempted, briefly, to escape from his destiny, from the inertial velocity of his name, Jahaj Jung, which led him inevitably towards a certain jungle, a city, a wilderness peopled by a man and two lions, even as it beguiled him away from the virgin forests of the Vehi. Friends, friends, we struggle, we scream, we dream, but forms make us, metaphors break us, names are mantras (hide them) and the goddess Vac, queen of speech, is the hidden mistress of the world; but come, to work again.

Months pass, and in a town named Barrackpore in Bengal, two men — or let us be blunt — two Avadhi Brahmins, who just happen to be neighbours of the fellow Skinner we have just met, two Brahmins addicted to oration and given to sermonizing, are discussing the fate of poetry and the character of Alexander of Macedon — sometimes called the Great, and sometimes, by Indians, Sikander the Madman. They are gossiping about the intrigues at the court of their RajaSahib, a minor princeling controlled by the British; about their friend, the Daroga; their neighbour, John Hercules Skinner, who is the British resident at this court; and they are contemplating the role of this Alexander, Sikander, in history. Listen . . .

'He said, can you believe, that a thing should do what a thing is meant to do, nothing more, nothing less.'

'Barbarian,' Ram Mohan said, wrapping his arms around his knees and peering up at his brother-in-law.

'Quite. And the armourer turned pale and looked away.' Arun walked back and forth, forgetting for once, it seemed, his daily ritual disrobing, the casting aside of sweaty clothes. 'I was no more than three feet from him, and I distinctly saw his lip tremble.'

'And what of Daroga Sahib?'

'Well, since he had recommended this armourer, brought him to the city, given him money to set up a work-shop and presumed upon his relationship with the RajaSahib, you can imagine his state. He laughed, he blustered: "Iskinner Sahib," he said, "Iskinner Sahib, but you see . . . ," but before he had gotten out two sentences the firangi said, his lip turning, "My name is Skinner, Skinner." '

'Unbelievable. Absolutely unbelievable.'

'So now you can imagine the Daroga's state; he was incoherent. Finally I said, Arre Skinner Sahib, look at the workmanship, see how the lion howls around the muzzle of the thing, how cunningly the shape of the animal is made to conform to the necessary lines of the weapon, how beautiful it is, how the thing is made, but he said, all that is unnecessary, a thing should do what it is meant to do, no more and no less. And then he took his leave.'

'The man is unbearable.'

'But our RajaSahib is enamoured of him because the Company wins battles. The Company wins here, the Company wins there, the Company always, everywhere wins, and so we are judged by the Company. I tell you, brother, we live in ugly times; our lives are invaded by soldiers. We speak their language, we aggrandize them, we celebrate their virtues, our poetry is infected by their artifices, our ideas by their craft.'

Hoping to cool the other's anger, Ram Mohan held up a silver paan-box, and Arun grabbed up a leaf and chewed angrily, the crimson liquid spurting out of the corners of his lips. 'Skinner lives over the wall from us, but he has taken over our house, my brother; here we are, you and I, love-poets of the first order, reduced to writing about a homicidal madman because our majesty is fascinated by Skinner's bluff tales of first he went here and conquered this, then he went there and murdered those, and finally he ambled over and set so-and-so country on fire. Our name will die out with us.'

'Hideous.'

'Oh, we are slaves, and to work, to work; have you made the knot?'

'Yes, brother, it is in the back.'

They walked around the house, keeping to the outer verandas and porches, carefully avoiding the inner rooms; Arun began to shrug off his clothes, and Ram Mohan limped behind him, bending awkwardly to pick up the garments.

'I made the knot,' Ram Mohan said, hopping along. 'I made it of twine, string, leather thongs, strands of fibrous materials from plants, pieces of cloth, the guts of animals, lengths of steel and copper, fine meshes of gold, silver beaten thin into filament, cords from distant cities, women's hair, goats' beards; I used butter and oil; I slid things around each other and entangled them, I pressed them together until they knew each other so intimately that they forgot they were ever separate, and I tightened them against each other until they squealed and groaned in agony; and finally, when I had finished, I sat cross-legged next to the knot, sprinkled water in a circle around me and whispered the spells that make things enigmatic, the chants of profundity and intricacy. My brother, there has never been such a knot. Look at it.'

It hung between two branches of a peepul tree that grew near the boundary wall running around the unkempt garden, among mango trees and bushes of hibiscus, its suspending cables reaching up like untidy tentacles; as Arun strode up to it, now clad only in his dhoti, it rocked forwards and back, its shadow moved lightly over the ground below, and he stopped short.

'How did you get it so big?'

Ram Mohan smiled, pleased, and ducked under the ball, running a hand intimately over its rough surface and holding on to it as he bent down to the ground.

'Here's the sabre, freshly sharpened like you said.'

'Let the sabre drown in its own piss, Ram Mohan,' Arun said. 'Look at this thing, it's a monstrosity.'

'But you said you wanted a big one. You said it.'

'Yes, yes, but I meant big, not this.'

'I don't know; after a while, it took no effort — I'd bring something close to it, and it would attach itself, suck it up, it seemed.'

'All right. All right. Now. But there's no cutting this thing,' Arun said.

'You have to at least try.'

'It's clearly impossible.'

'Sikander did it.'

'He was a madman, with a lunatic's strength; sickness sometimes brings brawn; write that down.'

'Or he was a king of kings.'

'All right, all right. Here. Let me have it.' Arun took the sabre, unsheathed it, flexed his shoulder, looking all the while at the knot, at the riot of colour and texture that was almost as big around as Ram Mohan's torso. 'Even if he could cut it, if he did cut it, how could he bear to? Look at the thing. You said it yourself, it is a thing of profundity; think, a knot that nobody has been able to unravel for thousands of years, an undecoded mystery, an obscurity so deep that it becomes a pain and a pleasure at the same time, what I mean to say is: it is a monument, and along comes this bravo, this puling upstart given to melancholic fits and uncontrollable rages, and he rips it in two! Cuts it.'

'He was a brute. But Skinner calls him king of kings. The world calls him king of kings.'

'What a robbery! What a disregard for future generations; how many thousands of young people would have made the journey, hoping to solve it, to take it apart, strand by strand, but he reduced it to nothing, to nothing.'

'Nothing. But cut it, brother.'

'Step out from behind it. Away, I mean. Good.' Arun shuffled back and forth on the balls of his feet, settling into a wide stance, weight held low; he measured the distance to his target with a slow swing, and took a deep breath.

'You look like a warrior, like Arjuna,' Ram Mohan said.

Arun smiled. 'Like Parashurama, I hope. For the glory of our family.'

'For the good name of the Parashers.'

The blade shrilled through the air, and then Arun was rolling on the ground (the knot oscillated above him, barely dented, squeaking), holding his wrist, shouting and cursing; he called down maledictions on the knot, on Ram Mohan, on himself, on the sword, on Skinner, and finally he cursed Sikander himself for being a passion-ridden, syphilitic fool who disturbed the sleep of millions even centuries after worms had disposed of his flesh.

'Brother,' said Ram Mohan, 'look, look —'

'Look at what, you owl's spawn? Look at my wrist, it's swelling already; Oh, what a fool I was to do this, why did I do this, what do poets need of experiments? Go, what are you looking at, mud-head, find somebody, send someone to the bone-setter's, get him here, stop gaping.'

'But, brother —'

'What brother-brother? Get me the vaid.'

By now Arun had raised himself to his feet, cradling his wrist, turning as he twisted up, so when the voice spoke behind him he spun around and thumped into the knot, which swung back and hit Ram Mohan in the chest, knocking the wind out of him and causing a sudden state of breathless, heightened wonder, a moment of excruciatingly acute sensation in which he stared with astonishment at the tremendously pregnant woman who balanced on top of the garden wall, teetering, the sphere of her belly pulling her to the point of imbalance and then back. She spoke again:

'What was it he said about Sikander?'

The two men moved forward uncertainly, Ram Mohan holding out his hands, palms up; they had seen her before, had goggled at her narrow-nosed beauty, at the great Rajput lady who had inexplicably become Skinner's wife: she had passed them in the road before their houses, the curtains to her doli thrown back, as if she needed all the air she could get, and she had gazed out at the world with the sullen, inward-looking abstraction of those compelled to hate; always, she had looked through them, without hauteur, but with the distraction of somebody contemplating a past tragedy. Now, as Ram Mohan extended his arms upwards, stretching himself against the stone, her face glowed with something like hope.

'What about Sikander?'

'That he frightens us even after he is long-gone,' Ram Mohan said. 'But, please, be careful. Come down from there.'

'Tell me about him,' she said, swinging an arm imperiously, almost propelling herself from her perch.

'He was the scourge of the earth,' Arun said, finding his voice at last. 'When a city wouldn't surrender, he would deliver its inhabitants into a holocaust, till the name of their race was vanished from the world.'

'He wanted to be king of the world,' Ram Mohan said, 'and for this he destroyed it. Finally, when he came to our country, Bharat Varsha, he turned back, but the world remembers him, and for his slaughtering some think him a hero, and others a god.'

At this her eyes did a strange thing: they blazed; and after seeing this happen, after seeing a burst of cold white-blue light obscure her face, Ram Mohan was never again able to use that tired turn of phrase in his writing, because he understood how inadequate it was, how much it didn't catch, what it lost of the innocent ash-white destructiveness of that radiance (it reminded him not of death, but of something else entirely, something he couldn't quite remember), and finally and mainly because he knew then and forever that it was not a metaphor he was using, or perhaps that it was a metaphor and yet it was entirely descriptive of what happened, completely factual and true; all this he realized in a moment, and yet when it was over, when he could see her again, see her face, he could hardly believe that it had happened. So he rubbed his eyes and reached up again, trying to calculate how she would fall and stiffening his bad leg in anticipation of its giving way.

He turned his head then, as a woman's voice spoke authoritatively behind him: 'Oh, come down, child, you'll hurt yourself.' His sister swept along the narrow path-way among the trees, the pallu of her sari falling to her waist as she strained agitatedly towards the wall, buttocks and hips pumping massively. 'What are you doing just standing there, ji, go get the small couch from my veranda,' she snapped at her husband, who jerked himself out of a slack-lipped reverie and hurried off.

A few minutes later (meanwhile: 'Sikander! Tell me about Sikander!'), Arun appeared again, tussling with the awkward shape of the couch, which he placed under the wall; the two men stood on it, and with Shanti Devi hurling instructions and imprecations, they managed to reach up and pull her down, the firangi's wife, the protuberance at her front bumping into their arms and faces, and they seated her on the couch: she sat like a queen or a goddess, one leg drawn across her front, flat, and the other angled straight down, off the couch, planted firmly on the ground.

'Tell, tell, tell, about Sikander!'

'Why do you want to listen to their terrible stories, child?' Shanti Devi said. 'What is your name?'

'I am Janvi. He calls me Jenny.'

'How beautiful you are,' Shanti Devi said, raising a corner of her sari and wiping the sweat away from the girl's forehead. 'Did he really capture you in a battle?'

'I was a coward. I loved life too much. I couldn't jump.'

'What has he done to you, to make you like this?'

'He calls me Jenny,' she said, as if that explained everything.

'You should go back to your house,' Shanti Devi said. 'What will he think, what will he do if he finds out you've been going into a strange house, in front of strange men.'

'I want to hear about Sikander.'

'Really,' Arun said. 'This could cause unpleasantness. You should go back.'

'I want to hear about Sikander!'

'Brother, sister, listen,' Ram Mohan said. 'Listen. Sikander was a king, a king of a place far away. Driven by a motivation which we yet have to ascertain, he killed people until he was king of all Greece; he then decided to kill more people until he was king of the world. On the way he did many things, including cutting a knot which had resisted unravelling for eons, and this was what we were doing when you stumbled in on us, analysing that event, I mean. I think it couldn't be done. Brother here was of the opinion that a strong man could have cut such a knot. So we decided to try it, and you can see what happened.'

'Oh, my hand. Shanti, we need a doctor.'

'It's nothing much, I'll put some turmeric on it, it'll be all right.'

'So, I think Sikander saw this knot, tried to untangle it, lost his temper, tried to cut it, broke his wrist, fell to the floor, frothing at the mouth, and then screamed for his personal guards, who hacked away at it for an hour or two with axes until they finally managed to destroy it. How's that, brother?'

'That's not what RajaSahib wants to hear,' Arun said, massaging his arm. 'You want to get us exiled?'

'No, no, I suppose not,' Ram Mohan said. 'But what about the motivation? Why did he want to kill the world?'

'I don't know,' Arun said. 'How would I know about a thing like that?'

Shanti Devi shook her head wearily. 'Who can understand a man?'

'Revenge,' Janvi said, slowly and very clearly. 'Revenge.'

'Revenge?' Ram Mohan said. 'For what?'

'The world,' Janvi said, and raised a hand to her face, rubbing a cheek, faster and faster, until her lips twisted and rose away from the teeth.

'Oh, child, don't do that,' Shanti Devi said, catching hold of Janvi's wrist and pulling her close, smothering her in the expanse of sari that stretched across her front. 'You should take care of yourself. For the sake of your son, you understand.'

Janvi stiffened. 'It'll be a daughter.'

'A daughter?'

'A daughter.'

'How do you know?'

'I won't have his sons. Not *his* sons. I won't, I won't, I won't.'

'All right, all right. What are you waiting for, ji? Start the story.'

So Arun turned so that his profile was to Janvi, placed one foot in front of the other, raised an arm in a declamatory position, and began; Ram Mohan sat at the foot of the couch, looking up at Janvi's face, saying a word now and then, and the old story meandered along: Sikander was born (Ram Mohan made notes on a tablet — out-of-ordinary birth? evil omens? a prophet raving in the palace yard? a curse? family persecuted by the world? unfortunate events damaging the soul as it descended into flesh?), grew up, was tutored by a famous philosopher (who exactly was this teacher? pinched old man? frustrated soldier-turned-guru? school-yard tactician yearning for glory?

pederast?); Sikander tamed a stallion (fabulous birth for the stallion? symbolic value? did the horse have official status as friend-of-the-king, or minister? why horse? why friend? why do heroes/villains/butchers fall in love with horses?) and then began the bloody business of sub-jugating all the other Greeks (where are the victims' histories? how many died?), armed, of course, with the oldest rhetorical trick in the book: 'Unite, countrymen, the enemy looms at the gate'; unnerved by fear of the Persians (passionate speeches? the Persians as rapists/idolaters/beasts?), the Greeks regimented themselves behind Sikander, and then he plunged into Asia, disposed of the Persians, his clock-work battalions moving as one being (how can men do that? why were the Greeks able to do that better than others? is this a good thing?), and, having done this, of course they didn't stop (did they ever intend to? did they know all along? did they care? did they believe they owed it to the barbarian world? did they see themselves as bearers of light? did they dream of a Greek peace, even as they lopped off heads and exe-cuted villages? was the victims' pain invisible to them? did they not hear the screams? did they see a Greece that sat like a fat leech over the world? or were they just greedy? or did they like murder? are all cities and nations doomed to expansion? is murder our passion? is it? who are these filthy Greeks anyway? O my questions); like an arrow he came, an arrow aimed at the cities of gold, the streets paved with gems, the fabulous Pagoda tree, the Golden Bird (did the old tutor tell him, once, lips wet, about the wealth of the country beneath the towering Abode of Snow? did he hear, once, when he was so young that he barely even remembered the telling, about the richest country on earth, the source of spices and royal cloth and sandalwood?); and as he came down into the Punjab he met some naked sadhus (what did they say to him? did they laugh at him? or did they just ignore him and his armies? did they frighten him?); and finally the battle by the Indus, the ele-phants screaming, throwing men and trampling horses, but he wins again (why? why do some win? and others lose? such simple ques-tions), and brave king Porus stood in chains (who was this Porus? what was his story?), and Sikander asked, pompous and patronizing, how should we treat you? and Porus replied, like a king treats another king (well done, Porus, who are so full of the grand theatricality that is the best trait of our countrymen), and then Sikander, it is said, set him free and turned back (turned! retreated? withdrew? ran away? was it the vast armies waiting on the plains?); and then he died, of a fever. (Who was this Sikander? Why did he do what he did? This shall be our question.)

As Janvi listened, her face grew calm; she looked around at the Parashers, and it seemed that she really saw them now, and in the following days and weeks, as the story grew, as it accumulated flesh over the bare bones of that first day, as it collected characters, motivations, conflicts, thunderous scenes of battle, quiet moments of reflection, climaxes, beginnings, her small body seemed to accumulate energy and purpose, so that Ram Mohan marvelled at how she had been transformed into a paragon of motherly health: still quiet, but now it was as if she was gathering herself for something momentous. When her time came, she gave birth without any fuss, and appeared the next day at her usual seat, smiling.

'Child, child,' Shanti Devi said. 'You should be resting. Where's your new daughter?'

'He has her,' Janvi said. 'They are his, both daughters, I don't care. But now. I have to meet privately with Uday Singh. Will you tell him to come here?'

'Who?' Arun said.

'Uday Singh. His second-in-command. I want to talk to him without my husband knowing.'

'I can't go around whispering to soldiers about private meetings,' Arun said. 'If somebody finds out, they'll think I'm planning a regicide or a coup or something. I'll be lucky if they let me poison myself. No, no.'

Janvi turned to Ram Mohan, who was massaging his leg, seated cross-legged next to her couch. 'Will you?'

'Me? Me?' In his agitation, he relaxed his customary guard over his lips and tongue, resulting in a vaporous discharge of spittle. He covered his mouth quickly and tried to smile.

'Oh, don't you send him out there, to totter around, spraying secrets at anyone who has two minutes to listen,' Arun said. 'Don't do that. Then we shall certainly hang.'

'What is her choice if you don't, ji?' Shanti Devi said, raising her eyebrows. 'What but it?'

'You would do it too, wouldn't you, you smirking fool?' Arun pulled at the sacred cord that looped over his shoulder, sending it hissing around his body. 'No, no, enough. This I won't do. Already I've allowed danger to hang over my house. No more.'

'What danger are you talking about?' Shanti Devi hooted. 'You're always talking about danger that nobody else can see.'

'And you, you, you're always ready to do anything if she asks. Not a care in the world if your own family lives or dies or anything.' Arun turned, stopped to glare at Janvi, and then went striding off towards the house. Shanti Devi heaved up after him.

'Don't worry,' she said. 'I'll settle him in five minutes.'

They heard the fight as it drifted through the various rooms of the house; from a minor skirmish it developed speedily into a full-scale engagement: at first the shouting spoke mostly about the logic of the situation, about the probability of danger and the limits of obligation, but then soon the voices shrieked about wounds taken and given long ago, about years-old insults and ancient family feuds, and snatches of the quarrel echoed amongst the trees, frightening the birds into sudden flight: 'If it hadn't been for my father you would have still been back chanting slokas in that sleepy village of yours for a tenth-of-a-paisa a morning; all because of him you're here today wearing fine clothes and putting on courtier's airs.' 'And what airs do I put on now? What do I do but work day and night to support you and that brother of yours. For two dozen years I've supported that slobbering idiot brother of yours; in all this time he's never done a day's work.' 'Leave my brother out of it. Don't say a word about my brother.' 'Oho, so your family's sacred. We can't discuss your family, but you'll insult my poor mother day and night. I see, I see.'

Ram Mohan ducked his head between his knees and scratched aimless designs in the dust between his toes; he tried to shut out the familiar design of abuse that was forming in the house, the old repeated pattern of insult that circled around the one thing always finally unsaid, the one resentment that accumulated more bitterness, like a pus-filled canker, the one fatal accusation held close to the heart by both sides but left unused: 'You have given me no children.' But today the husband and wife scratched and tore at each other with unusual ferocity, probing and hurting until Ram Mohan could stand it no more: he flung himself prone and locked his arms over his head, pounding the ground with his feet; he felt a hand on his shoulder.

'Be quiet,' Janvi said calmly, gazing off at the house. 'They'll be finished with each other soon.'

'I wish I could go,' he said. He had never left the house alone. 'I wish.'

'Yes,' she said, and her eyes moved, and she watched as he pulled his feet up under him and crouched, hands resting palm up before him; then she sat back and waited. When the sun settled behind the house and the chattering of the birds became an unbroken clamouring, Shanti Devi walked out to the garden again, not exultant but with the certain, magnanimous tread of the victor.

'It's all right. Everything is all right.' she said. 'He'll go.'

So, two days later, in the grey of early morning, Uday Singh appeared at Arun's gate, his face hidden by a shawl wrapped around his shoulders and head; amongst the trees, he bowed low to Janvi and swept his palms together, saying 'Khama ghani, hukum'; after he had seated himself on a white sheet spread in front of her couch, she waved the others away, and they watched the two motionless figures as the garden filled with the clear light of first winter. Occasionally, under the call of cicadas, they heard the murmur of her voice, level and constant; finally, they heard Uday say something, and then he strode past them, flinging the shawl about his shoulders, his face held carefully impassive, and that afternoon the court was told that Uday Singh, commander in His Majesty's armies, had been given leave for compassionate reasons and had ridden north on personal business. Now, Janvi was quiet and gentle and fulfilled; she seemed to enjoy the warmth of the afternoon sun and the little bursts of wit that peppered the play about Sikander; every afternoon, when Arun read out their morning's work, becoming, in succession, Sikander, the teacher, the holy men at the edge of wilderness, and Porus, Ram Mohan watched her face carefully, trying not to blink, measuring her reactions and cutting and pruning the work accordingly.

One evening, when the worst of the winter was over, they had finished their reading and discussion, and were gathering their booklets and pens in the early twilight when a dark figure vaulted over a wall in a flapping of cloth. Ram Mohan dropped an ink-stand, stumbled back, tripped and sat joltingly, stammering in fear, 'Ah-ah-ah-ah.'

'Don't be frightened, boy, it's only me. If they knew I came back and brought something for you, Parasherji, they would suspect us both. There were questions enough when I left. I just got back, and I think they know. So I came in the dark.' Uday laid a bundle wrapped in white cloth before Janvi; he quickly untied the knot on top and peeled back layers of muslin, and a soft orange glow lit his face from below. Ram Mohan pulled himself closer, and reached out to touch, wonderingly, the little orange balls made of smaller spheres.

'Laddoos,' he said. 'You went away for three months to bring back laddoos.'

'From what confectioner?' Arun said. 'From what witch have you brought these things back into my house? Why do they glow like that?'

'Pretty,' Ram Mohan said.

'Don't touch them,' Arun said.

'Listen, hukum,' Uday said. 'Like you said, I went and spoke to him, but he is caught up in an extraordinary combat for a kingdom, or something greater than kingdoms. So he couldn't come, but he said "Take these to her. Tell her to eat them, one at a time, to put each one whole into her mouth. Tell her she will have sons. Tell her she will have sons worthy of their mother. Tell her she will have sons who will face the world. Tell her to have sons." So I have come back with these for you. Now I must go. They must be expecting me at the palace.' He hid himself in the folds of a grey blanket and clambered up the wall.

'O Rama, save us,' Arun said.

'Give me one,' Janvi said; she held out a hand, steady.

Ram Mohan picked up one of the laddoos with the tips of his fingers and held it in the hollow of his right hand; it felt heavy, like iron, and despite the warmth of its brilliance, it was cool against his skin; he held it out, his biceps twitching a little from the weight. Janvi took it, held it up, and it danced in her pupils like fire; her tongue flicked out, red, and then her cheeks puffed out and her eyes bulged; for a moment or two, her throat worked, and then she fell over onto her side and rolled off the couch, struggled across the tamped-down clay, hands reaching until they brushed against Ram Mohan's dhoti, and she held on, body arching. Ram Mohan touched her face and flinched at the clammy sweat that instantly coated his fingers; at last, she managed to get it all down, and her mouth opened and she gasped for breath: 'Aa-ha, aa-ha, aa-ha.'

'What is it, child?' Shanti Devi said.

'At first,' Janvi said, panting, 'a sweetness so sweet I thought it was ambrosia. Then a bitterness so complete that I thought my mouth was melting. Then it forced itself soft but insistent down my throat and I felt it in my belly and my bones and my blood, and I felt it settle in and harden like steel.'

'Oh, god, what is it, child? Where is it from?'

'Give,' Janvi said. 'Give me another one.'

'No,' Ram Mohan said.

'Give.'

'Please.'

'Give.'

'No, no more.'

'Mohan,' she said.

He picked up another laddoo and placed it on her mouth, feeling how soft her skin was just below, how the fullness of the lower lip curved away into the sweep of the chin; she swallowed, and again her body thrashed against him.

'Worse,' she said. 'That was worse.'

'Please,' Ram Mohan said.

'Sons,' she said. 'I must have sons.' And she swallowed another, and her hips lifted off the floor this time and smashed down, and he felt the tears break from his eyes; this time, when her throat had stopped working, she screamed, a quavering hiccup. 'I can't. No more.'

'Good,' Ram Mohan said, and reached out for the last laddoo.

'No, don't, don't do anything to it,' Janvi said, struggling to prop herself up on an elbow. 'Shanti Devi, you have done much for me. Take it. We will have sons together.'

'No,' Arun said. 'Don't you dare. Don't do it.'

'Who is it from?' Shanti Devi said.

'I can't tell you. Please take it,' Janvi said, taking the laddoo from Ram Mohan. 'I can't throw it away.'

'Shanti, you can't,' Arun said. 'Think of what it might be. Think of what evil we would do to our forefathers, giving them a son spawned of who-knows-what evil. Think.'

'Greater evil if we give them no sons,' Shanti Devi said, and extended a hand, in which Janvi placed the last laddoo. Shanti Devi hesitated for a moment, but Arun stepped forward, and that decided her, and the laddoo disappeared; it sent her rolling off into the darkness, groaning, and when Arun jumped to her aid, her body twitched him off like a mosquito and continued its thrashing alone. When it was over she crawled from under the murky shade of the trees to Janvi, and they held each other, heads close and hair hanging down like wet rope, tangled together, and the men watched quietly, still trembling a little from fright.

'Some poison, some poison you have taken,' Arun said, but shortly, both women ballooned, and both walked about with a smile of secret pleasure on their faces, feet angling out and hands on hips to support the weight. Both acquired a taste for bitter foods: karela, grapefruit, methi; and now both listened to the final versions of the Sikander play with a dream-like expression on their faces, and Ram Mohan wondered if they were listening to the story at all, or whether they were concocting some private tale of conquest and glory. Ram Mohan was hoping, with a sentimental poet's whimsy, that both children would be delivered on the same day, and that would be the day of the court presentation of the play — entitled, now, 'Sikander, Master of the Universe'; but the play's day in court came and went; and the two women went on as before, calm and other-worldly.

One night, Shanti Devi sat up in bed, and called out for her brother and husband. 'I heard a shriek,' she said, but nobody else had. They waited till morning, listening to the crickets and then the birds; as soon as it was light they went out to the wall, and the men paced nervously until they heard the scraping of foot-steps in the mud on the other side; Janvi's head appeared over the stone.

'I delivered last night,' she said with a smile.

'Oh, child, we heard you,' Shanti Devi said.

'No, that wasn't me,' Janvi said, climbing lightly over the wall. 'I didn't make a sound. It was nothing. That was the midwife. The fool, she said when she laid the boy out on the cloth she could see straight through him, the sheet and everything, and then he solidified slowly.'

'Hai Ram,' Shanti Devi said.

'No, it's all right. When they showed him to me, I knew he wasn't the one. He had pale skin, and thin limbs, and how long they were, with an awful stretch between the elbow and the wrist. I had always known that he would want the first son, and so he did. He took him, and I said nothing. Let him have him. The next one will be my Sikander.'

'Yes,' Shanti Devi said. 'Of course.'

'Yes,' Janvi said. 'But what about you now, sister? It's your turn.'

But it wasn't to be Shanti Devi's turn yet, not for another nine months. For nine months, during which Janvi's belly grew full again, they waited anxiously, hoping every day that the time had come, that Shanti Devi's child would at last descend into the world, but nothing happened. At first vaids and physicians and surgeons were summoned, but they retired baffled; then, as the pregnancy became ominously long, priests, sooth-sayers, astrologers and magicians were called, and they all looked appropriately troubled, practised their respective crafts and retreated. One morning, in the seventeenth month, Ram Mohan was shaken awake by Arun, who looked old and exhausted and grey.

'She's gone,' he said. 'She's not there.'

They stumbled through the house, waking the servants, and then ran into the garden, calling her name; hearing a soft thumping, Ram Mohan stopped, then tacked off to the right, crashing clumsily through the bushes, slipping often, and then almost falling into his sister, who ran past him, arms extended to her sides, the swelling of her belly held out like a weapon, ran slowly forward and crashed into a peepul tree; with every impact Sikander's huge knot, suspended nearby, swung backwards and forwards; Ram Mohan lunged at her, and they collapsed against the wood, her face against his chest; she put her hands together in front of her face and wept.

'What sort of monster will I breed? What lives in my belly? He kicks and shakes my whole body.'

'Hush, sister. It's nothing like that. He's just wary of this wicked world, he's too wise to come out yet. He's just waiting until he's strong enough.'

'No, he was right. I have something evil inside me.'

'Shhh. Shhh.'

'He will never come. He will take my life. He'll eat me up.'

He didn't take her life, but he did eat her up: by the time he was born, Shanti Devi had lost all her bulk, and resembled, post-natally, the slim girl Arun had married; one night in November, she screamed joyfully, an exuberant ululation mingling pain and relief: 'Oh, it's starting, it's starting.' And far away, on the other side of mango and peepul trees,

Janvi answered her wail for wail; Arun and Ram Mohan fled into the garden and sat side-by-side on a little ledge, among flower-pots and heaps of rich-smelling mulch; Ram Mohan flinched every second or so, as the women screeched at each other, and as Arun reached some particularly vehement passage in his incessant prayers (appealing to all the gods in heaven, and for good measure, to some not-so-savory characters who resided elsewhere), but even as he flinched Ram Mohan was thinking of aesthetics.

'This fellow,' he said with some satisfaction, 'was just waiting for his friend over there. They just wanted to be born together.'

Arun looked up, and thought for a while, his lips pursed. 'You're right. This thing started with Sikander, and so he was waiting for Sikander.'

'He must,' Ram Mohan said, smiling with satisfaction, 'be a poet.'

The sons were born in the morning, in the deepest silence of the hour that is simultaneously the latest and the earliest, that silence just before the explosion of the dawn; they were born not quite together, but almost, one emerging just as the other had finished, but afterwards, nobody could quite remember in which quarter the screams had subsided first, nobody could remember, nobody could tell which was the older. Just a little later, before the sun had risen too high, the mothers met out by the garden wall.

'It hurt,' Janvi said. 'It never had before.'

'It did, didn't it?' Shanti Devi said. 'But look at them.'

'How alike they look,' Arun said. 'How beautiful they are.' He looked adoringly at Shanti Devi, his eyes shining, and then back down at the boys, who lay wrapped in orange cloth on the couch, one asleep and the other awake, a little black kajal dot on their faces, for protection from the evil eye. Ram Mohan knelt by the babies, smiling so widely that his cheeks hurt.

'Look at him,' Arun said. 'After two years in his warm and comfortable residence, he graces us with his presence.'

'Look at his hair,' Ram Mohan said. 'How thick it is. He is strong; look at his arms; he is wise; look at that forehead.'

'We decided last night that he was a poet,' Arun said.

'Just like his father,' Shanti Devi said, cocking her head to one side and flashing her eyes at her husband. 'How quietly he sleeps. How long he sleeps. Since he came he has been sleeping.'

'Not all those who close their eyes are asleep,' Arun said.

'A poet, like his father,' Ram Mohan said. 'We should name him Sanjay, after one who closed his eyes and yet saw everything.'

'Yes,' Arun said. 'Sanjay.'

'Look at him,' Janvi said, watching her child. 'Look how he gazes at the world.'

'Calm and fearless,' Ram Mohan said. 'Fearless. Look at his chest; he will have the courage of a lion; look at his thighs; he will have the strength of ten men.'

'His father wants to call him James,' Janvi said.

'James?' Ram Mohan said.

Janvi picked up her son; Shanti Devi bent and raised her child to her shoulder; they smiled at each other.

'Oh, my child,' Shanti Devi sang softly, rocking from side to side, 'listen, listen to the world.'

'I will call him Sikander,' Janvi said, lifting her child above her shoulders, her hands under his armpits, so that his head wobbled back and his eyes (steady eyes, Ram Mohan remembered later, so steady) gazed into the sun. 'Look,' Janvi said. 'Look, Sikander, at your world.'

Nine months to the day after Sikander's birth, Janvi delivered the last of the laddoo-children, a boy who was christened Robert by his father but whose real, mother-given name was Chotta Sikander, and it was true: he was indeed a little replica of his brother.

The three boys grew up in that garden, clambering, as soon as they could walk, over the dividing wall, and dropping easily into each other's territory, or into the lap of Ram Mohan, who, when the mothers were absent due to household duties, deputized himself as looker-after, sending away maids and servants; 'Ohe, Sikander,' he would say, grinning lopsidedly, 'stop pulling on small Sikander's head like that, you'll detach it in a minute; and you, Sanjay Sa'ab, that's mud you're making a meal of, nothing wrong with that, but it'll spoil your appetite, and it's me your mother will chasten.' When the mothers finished with the ordering of servants and the planning of meals, they would come out to sit in the afternoon sun, and watch their boys climb over Ram Mohan, pulling at his hair and using his leg in their games of you-can't-see-me. Not too long after, he was frequently seen tottering about the garden, arms outstretched, an orange dupatta wrapped around his head, surrounded by three small leaping monkey-like forms, chanting 'Mamaji, here I am, there I am.'

One afternoon, five years after Sikander's birth, the boys slept on the couch (weathered and twisted by the sun and the rain) next to the wall, exhausted by a game of hide-and-seek; Ram Mohan dozed, seated on the ground next to them, his back against rough stone, dreaming. Then, feeling (not hearing) a quick movement to his left, he dragged his eyes open, fighting against the sluggish inertia of drowsiness; for an instant, the greens and browns of the world swam, rolling against each other: the sun had moved while they had slept, and Chotta and Sanjay flinched away from it, pushing their heads against Sikander, who slept in the middle. Sikander slept peacefully in the centre, his face and chest covered by a dark shadow, dense; the penumbra suggested a regular shape, a leaf perhaps, a big lotus, and Ram Mohan's eyes began to close again, but then a drop of liquid splattered against Sikander's chest and curved down a rib, into the armpit, and Ram Mohan jerked out of sleep and looked up into a pair of glittering red diamond-eyes, and his bowels spasmed, and his mouth began to shake, and he tried to speak, but the black head moved slightly, and a blaze seemed to race up and down the tiny golden flecks along the sides of the slim, black, powerful shape of the neck and the body, and Ram Mohan's body shrank, and again, then, a drop of liquid formed at the corner of a red eye and dropped through the air to make a silver streak on Sikander's body; as the shadows and areas of light shifted across the mud, the king-cobra moved, its huge opened hood, two hands across, held above Sikander always, shielding him from the sun, and its tears wet his body, and its twenty-foot length curled around the boys, holding them in. Much later, when Ram Mohan was finally able to make a sound, he tried to shout a servant's name, to call for help, but only a strangled yelp emerged, a sound like the last dying call of a fatally-shot gazelle, and, instantly, Chotta sat up, while on the other side, Sanjay began to stir and rub his eyes.

'What, Mamaji?' Chotta said, looking at his uncle's drawn face; he turned, and seeing the snake, jumped to his feet, drawing back his fist. The king-cobra arched its neck, lowering its hooded head closer to the ground, to Sikander, and opened its mouth, revealing milky-white, delicately-curved fangs, tapering two inches to the fatal points. They stayed like that for a moment, frozen, while Sanjay sat up, yawning, crossed his legs, leaned his elbows on his knees and propped his chin on cupped palms, and then Chotta laughed. Slowly, he reached over to the king-cobra, to its mouth, its jaws, a forefinger held out to touch a tooth, to run up and down its length. When Chotta pulled his hand back, a yellow bubble of venom glistened on his finger-tip; he held it up for a moment, twisting his finger this way and that, smiling, and then Ram Mohan scrambled forward on all fours, foreseeing exactly what was about to happen: Chotta's tongue flicked out and picked the liquid cleanly off his finger.

The king-cobra shivered along the length of its body and hissed a long fierce warning to stay away, stay back, and then its head darted forward, back again, to the side, its eyes shining, and Ram Mohan thought he must die, and cowered, but he heard another hiss, a softer one, to his right; the snake's hood folded up, it seemed to relax, and it hissed again, a short sound this time, somehow enquiring; Sanjay replied, his plump lips pulling back and his teeth clicking together, and what was clearly a conversation ensued, and then the snake curled around and whipped through the grass.

Sikander stretched, raising his body off the couch with his extended limbs. 'Oh, what a lovely dream I was having,' he said. 'Of lions, lions, and great cities.'

Shaking with excitement, Ram Mohan called for servants and instructed them to take the boys inside and to stay with them, to not leave them alone; then he hurried to his room and pulled a trunk from under his bed, from which he extracted his Diwali gifts, a silk kurta from Lucknow, a fine dhoti from Benares, and leather jootis from Jodhpur. He put on the clothes speedily, but by the time he managed to get his turban tied his fingers ached. He stepped into the crisp new shoes, threw an embroidered white cloth over his right shoulder, and walked out into the main hall at the front of the house.

When he asked for a closed palanquin and bearers, the servants stared and whispered to each other, and he had to look a little irritated and snap out reprimands before the vehicle arrived; he managed to sound confident as he gave instructions to the crew, but as soon as they had trotted out the front gate, into the road, he felt a sudden rush of bile at the back of his throat, which made him sink back into the cushions, pulling at the curtains to open up a crack, to let some air into the stifling darkness. The streets outside seemed strange and unfamiliar, the houses — with their shuttered and loopholed doors and walls — mysterious and forbidding; he realized, then, that he hadn't left his sister's home from the day he had arrived seventeen years ago. By the time they halted, in front of a red brick house surrounded by high walls, a vein which curved over his right temple throbbed painfully with each beat of his heart; he cupped his hands over his eyes for a minute, then pushed the curtains aside and stepped out onto a marble stairway lit by lanterns.

'I would like,' he enunciated clearly, painfully, to a mustachioed major-domo, 'to request the honourable commander to grant me the favour of an audience.' The man stepped back, and Ram Mohan realized that in his eagerness to say the right thing properly, he had forgotten not to spit on the plosive consonants. He went on: 'I realize it is highly informal of me to appear like this, without notice, but I hope the Commander Sahib will excuse my bad manners. I come on urgent business.'

The retainer disappeared, gesturing at a couch and nodding up bowls of water and paan-containers; a few minutes later, he reappeared.

'Come.'

Uday Singh was practising in a tiled court-yard, stripped to the waist, spinning a ten-foot lance slowly above his head; his shadow loomed above, dancing on the white walls.

'I'm sorry to receive you like this,' he said, moving the lance from hand to hand without interrupting the slow rhythm of his circles. 'But as you said, Sahib, you came without notice. So I presumed that you wouldn't take offence at my lack of courtesy.'

'No matter,' Ram Mohan said. 'No matter. No matter.' He forced himself to take a deep breath and look away from the black point of the weapon. 'I came, I came to ask you about the boys.'

'What boys?'

'Our boys. Skinner's boys, and my sister's boy.'

'Why would I know anything about them?'

'You brought the laddoos.'

'What laddoos?'

'You know. You brought them. I was there.'

'I must have forgotten.'

'You have to remember. How could you forget? You brought the laddoos that enabled their birth.'

'What a strange idea. Even if it were true, what then?'

'Where did they come from? Who was the man who sent them? What were they?'

'Too many questions. I haven't any answers.'

'You do.'

'I don't, really.'

'You must tell me. You must.'

Uday stopped moving and straightened up, and as if by chance the lance angled towards Ram Mohan's chest.

'Why must I?' Uday said.

'You must.' Ram Mohan stepped forward. 'You must. For her. For the sake of Sikander's mother.'

'Her? Is that why you came? For her?'

'I saw today, in the garden behind my brother-in-law's house, a king-cobra spread its hood above Sikander, shielding him from the sun and weeping at the same time. I saw today Chotta Sikander reach out and take poison from that same cobra's mouth like one takes water from a spout, and drink it like other children drink cow's milk. I saw today Sanjay speak to that cobra as if they were old friends exchanging greetings or a couple of versifiers comparing couplets. That's why you must tell me who and what these boys are.'

'A cobra?'

'A king-cobra, black and flecked with gold and with a hood as big as this.'

'You look after these boys?'

'I am with them day and night.'

'All right,' Uday Singh said, laying down the lance and sitting on a stool. 'Sit, please. You should know. I don't know how you'll feel about all this, but you should know. Listen . . .'

I first saw her (Uday Singh said), the woman who is now Skinner's wife and the mother of Sikander, during the siege of Bejagarh, when we had finally blown up the East Gate and were in the city, in the palaces. All around us the shells were still falling as we chopped up their defences. I served then, as I do now, under this Skinner, a careful, stolid man, without much in the way of dash or daring, but a soldier, nevertheless, in a monotonous, determined way. So we broke into the city at the first hint of light, and struggled up the hill, coming up against little knots of resistance every so often and taking casualties, but we were already certain that we had won, and finally, with whoops of joy we plunged into the palaces, eager for the rubies and gold inside that were ours for the taking.

And in a certain palace, a richly-appointed place, we saw, down a corridor, what seemed like a few men running, and we decided we had caught up with some stragglers, so we rushed on after them, losing sight of them, then spying them again, like jungle dogs after antelope; a shell landed then, tearing through the roofing, and wood and masonry flew everywhere, and I saw a gap open ahead of me, and without thinking, in my momentum, you understand, I ran through it, and saw instantly my old friend and once-comrade, George Thomas, known to the world as Jahaj Jung, and he was standing as if stupefied, in front of a woman of beauty.

Even as I ran towards them her loveliness began to work on me, and I felt the sounds of war fade away, and my breath left my body, and I wanted to weep, so it was as much to release myself from this as to warn him that I was coming that I shouted, 'JAHAJ JUNG!' and he turned, stiffly, still not seeing me, and me, I was trying not to look at her, trying to keep my attention on my weapon, and on him, because I knew I must face him. Then Skinner said something, with the arrogance he must have been born with, and I spoke to Thomas, but he jumped at me, came at me instantly, you see, without a word of greeting or recognition, as one expects from an old comrade, even if the circumstances of fate and combat should pit one against the other, and so he surprised me, surprised me not only by the quickness of his attack but with the mad strength of his blow, which threw him off balance and open to my thrusts, had it not splintered my sabre and sent me stumbling back. So I picked myself up and chased after him, angry beyond words at his rudeness and insensitivity — you see, after all, one does not expect such behaviour from friends — but in the crowd and confusion of fighting, I quite lost track of him, so on the street outside the palace, I was obliged to give up the chase.

I went back inside and found Skinner organizing a guard around the few women who were left, the few who were seated on the black-and-white floor of the great hall we had found them in, their heads bowed in shame, and I felt pity for them, because now, denied death, they had nothing left but dishonour; Skinner was strutting about, looking busy, and I noticed he was paying particular attention to one of the women: he knelt down, next to her, and said, in his abominable Urdu, his face ruddy, a smile on his lips, 'Don't worry. You're safe now,' and she said, her voice muffled by the dupatta, 'Just let me kill myself.' He said, 'No, no, nonsense. Nothing of the sort,' and she glanced up quickly, and the veil moved, and I saw her eyes flash with hatred, but again my heart moved for her loveliness and I cursed myself for not having the courage to kill her there, then. But she lived and Skinner took her in marriage, and what could she do? — her city was dead, her people were dead, her family was dead, her time was dead.

So I thought I would never see her again, but as you know, some years ago she summoned me, and I thought of the danger of going to your house, of the suspicions of plotting and treason floating in the air like poison, but I tried to remember her face and could only bring back the ache it caused me, and I thought I must go, even if it's only to see her again, once again before I die.

I came to your house in the early morning, to sit at her feet, and she was as beautiful as ever, only now she looked like a radiant young girl, eager and flushed; now there was no longer that ache. She smiled at me and said, 'You were there when Bejagarh fell, when that man tore off my dupatta? Yes? And you called him Jahaj Jung? Is he that one? The warrior from the seas? The one with the cannon? The conqueror of cities?' And I said, 'Yes, it was him, for some reason, in disguise, or at least incognito.' And she said, 'As long as it was him. Listen, Uday Singh. I have decided. I have been insulted, but that was in my fate. My karma is bad, so I must live. But if I must have children by a firangi, let it be that one. If I must have sons, let them be fathered by Jahaj Jung. Go to him. Find him, wherever he is. Tell him I said, if I must have sons, let it be you.'

I looked at her happy face, and I thought of the terrible anger that must have driven her into this madness; I cursed this age, when the cow of morality stands tottering on one leg, when the only love that stands between men and women is passion, when the only virtue is greed, where honour is forgotten, but I said, 'I will tell him.' I said this because then and now I would have done anything for her, because like all those who have seen her I too loved her.

What was it? Her beauty? That was there, but perhaps it was too fragile; was it her grace? That was there, but even that is an artificial, temporary thing, which excites only need; what was it? I will tell you: You and I, Ram Mohan Sahib, and the others, have loved her for her innocence, for that genuine thing, like a child's, which makes it seem that she comes to us from some earlier age, from a time when the use of power had not made us cynical, when there was no distance between what was said and what was felt, when all actions had consequences. Now there are only causes and results, but I said, 'Yes, I will tell him,' and I rose to go, and she smiled, saying, 'Tell him that he was the first to raise the veil.' I understood.

I bowed and left the same way I had come, and contrived to be released from my duties, even at the risk of being suspected of plotting; the same day, I rode out on my strongest horses, money stitched into my coat, my bamboo lance couched firmly beside my stirrup, repeating to myself, 'If I must have sons, let it be you.'

After several weeks of chasing rumours, of frustration in small villages and towns and nameless hamlets frequented by bandits, I found him. I found him in an abandoned town, to the north and somewhat to the west of Delhi, amidst walls shattered by the patient weight of trees, among crumbling wells; and when I found him he was dressed in women's clothes, and in the process of having his face painted by a cluster of giggling houris, while nearby, three badmashes — the sort, you understand, who carry a dagger in their belts, a smaller one in the top of a boot, a still smaller one behind the shoulder, and a tiny blade up a sleeve, and another one or two secreted elsewhere — three scoundrels heaped flowers before an image of a woman made of wood and mud and chanted:

> HRING, O destroyer of time!
> SHRING, O terrific one!
> KRING, You who are beneficent!
> Possessor of all the arts,
> You are Kamala,
> Destroyer of the pride of the Kali Age,
> Who are kind to him of the matted hair,
> Devourer of Him who devours

Mother of Time
You are brilliant as the fires of the final dissolution,
Spouse of Him of the matted hair.
O You of formidable countenance,
Ocean of the nectar of compassion,
Merciful,
Vessel of mercy,
Whose mercy is without limit,
Who are attainable alone by Your mercy
Who are fire,
Tawny,
Black of hue,
You who increase the joy of the Lord of creation,
You who are the mad mother of the world,
Night of darkness,
In the form of desire,
Yet liberator from the bonds of desire.

But before greeting Thomas, I went and sat by a couple of his men, including an old Sikh, and asked, 'What is he doing? I am an old friend of his, Uday Singh. What is this?' And the Sikh said, yes, they had heard him speaking of me; they told me that at Bejagarh they had, while following Thomas, plunged over a cliff and into a moat, and after the drop, the escape, they had ridden aimlessly this way and that, surviving on what little they had, drifting after the ragged figure of Jahaj Jung. Finally, as if by chance, they had come to the town of Sardhana, where Thomas had sought an audience with his old acquaintance, Zeb-ul-Nissa, now known universally as the Begum Sumroo. At her court, Thomas and his little crew had caused no little trepidation — it was not entirely the fact that each of them was armed as if he intended to carry on a war single-handed, no, not that; it wasn't, either, their obvious hunger, that wild bright-eyed tattered look of starvation; no, it was, rather, the way they moved together, fluid, yet always guarding each other's flanks, it was their casual display of that wordless understanding that exists between those born from the same mother, it was the lack of back-slapping and loud laughter and boisterous speech that frightened the courtiers and, indeed, Begum Sumroo.

Understanding that it is not advisable to keep a pack of wolves in one's house, she said to Thomas, forget whatever has happened, whatever makes you sad, what you and your brave fellows need is a kingdom, a place to plant your flag, a place, as they say, to call your own; there is, a little to the west of here, a place called Hansi. Once it was a thriving town, fat with produce and craft, but of late the wars have rolled over it again and again, and since we no longer pay heed to the ancient rules of war (we live in evil times), crops are destroyed and innocents are murdered, and towns are emptied, and Hansi is a ruin now, full of ghosts and memories. But the ground is still fertile, she said, the people are still farmers; go and rebuild this town, and police the region around it — execute thieves, levy taxes, and grow old and fat, in short, construct a kingdom. Thomas, who until now had seemed to be in the grips of some mild drug, now looked up, and we each of us saw this new fantasy take hold of him, saw the intoxication of the dream clear his eyes, straighten his back, and he smiled back at us and said, what of it, laddies.

When we finally saw the town (the two men said), spied this little dump of mud and rotting wood, we let out a great whoop of joy and broke into a gallop, coming down through that slope there and beside that thicket, into what once must have been the main street of Hansi; we went through it, jumping the horses over and through the remains of the town, when we suddenly saw a man, a small, naked man with long muscles and tangled hair like straw, and skin covered with red mud. He stood erect on one of the few remaining roofs, hands fisted and arms held curving out by his sides, head thrown back, eyes rolled back; we speeded on towards him, Thomas ahead of all of us, shouting run, old man, we are here, flee, you fool, and a few of us levelled our lances, when suddenly, very close by, a sound like blood, like death itself, shook us, and trembled our horses, sending them twisting and falling, out of control; pray to your gods, whoever they might be, brother (the men said), that if you have never heard the roaring of lions at close hand, your ears might never be hammered by this noise: no matter what you might have lived through (and we live in inauspicious times), no matter what battles you have seen, no matter what hopes you have felt turning dead within your breast, this sound will make you a child again, will terrify you, will fill your pants full of piss.

A pair of lions appeared then, jumping from wall to roof to tree-limb, roaring, watching us with their yellow eyes, their black manes fluffing with every step, their tails twitching. We made our preparations: some of us aimed muskets, while others planted the butts of their spears against rocks, and we waited, sweating, but suddenly the man, the old man on top of the roof, with the reddened skin, he looked down at us, and even those of us far away felt the power of his presence (and the lions quietened and sat down) as he shouted, 'Why are you here? What are you doing in my city?' And Thomas shouted, 'Your city? How is it your city?' 'It is mine because I claim it,' the other said; and Thomas shouted back, 'I claim it, too. Leave my city, old man. Leave with your mangy pets before I throw you out.' 'Throw me out?' the old man said. 'Come. Throw me out.'

So Thomas put down his lance and sword, and ran up to the roof, and we watched, laughing, but the old man moved without seeming to move, and without the slightest trace of exertion he pitched Thomas off the roof, to lie stunned in the dust below. We picked him up, and the old man watched as we carried him out of Hansi, to this place; we moistened a piece of cloth and applied it to his forehead, but as soon as he recovered he stormed down to Hansi again, this time carrying two pikes, and challenged the old man to single combat, and again we had to carry him back, this time with two deep wounds on his left side and thigh and a cut on the head.

A few days later, as soon as he thought he could fight again, he went running on down there, and ever since then it's been one weapon after another, Thomas attacking furiously, the old man fighting back, and the defeats have come just as steadily; it had, recently, become clear even to the most dense in the camp that the old man was some sort of master of arcanum, or perhaps a necromancer, and by this time Thomas had forgotten his pique, and had started to take a sort of detached delight in the contest, so we persuaded him, the last time he went down there, to bow to him, and ask politely, 'Sir, how may you be defeated?' The old man smiled, crossed his arms behind his back, and said, 'I'm glad you ask, or otherwise you could never have defeated me. Listen, then; it has been said, by somebody long ago, that only one who is a woman can attain this city; this is how you can defeat me.'

That same evening, he sent a message to the Begum Sumroo, who

arrived a week later with her entourage of girls, and her battalions led
by her husband, Reinhardt the Sombre. Well, Begum Sumroo heard
Thomas out, and she stood looking down at Hansi, wondering, no
doubt, who the old man was, what had happened to a city that she had
thought empty; then she prepared three of her most beautiful girls,
bathing them in fresh spring water and sprinkling them with expensive
perfumes from Lucknow, three of her pupils, the ones most skilled in
the science of erotics, one tall and slim, one short and richly built, one
with the body of a boy — she dressed them in filmy cloth embroidered
with gold thread, and spoke to them in a low voice on the other side of
the clearing, telling them, no doubt, that their mission was to distract
the old man from his meditations, to sap his strength, to impel him to
discharge the psychic energy he had built up with years of sacrifices and
mortification. They left that evening, walking down the path with their
hips swaying gently, their anklets speaking *chanuk-chanuk,* and all night
we heard their shrieks ringing out above the trees, so that when morning came we didn't know whether they were dead or alive; but later that
morning they came walking up, walking stiffly, bending forward a little
at the waist, their finery very bedraggled, distant half-smiles on their
faces, and the short one giggled and said, 'I don't think we sapped him
very much at all.' So there was confusion and despondency in the camp,
and some of us wanted to leave, but Thomas said, 'Wait, my friends. Put
a woman's clothes on me, and I will go down there again, for the last
time, to try my luck, and we will see what happens.' So here we are (the
two men said), waiting to see if the woman Thomas will fare better than
the man, and what will become of the old man and his lions.

Then (Uday Singh said) I got to my feet, thanked the Sikh and the
other man and walked up to Thomas, greeting him courteously; 'My
friend,' he said, and I sat beside him, and told him for what I had come,
referring to Skinner's wife as the lady from Bejagarh. 'I'm sorry,' he said,
'but as I'm sure you've understood, I'm otherwise occupied. I think I
understand about the sons, but I really can't do anything about it at this
moment.' So I leaned forward, and looked at him carefully, and said,
'The lady in question has been insulted enough. You might die down
there tonight, and what will I tell her then?' 'Look,' he said, 'I can't.'
'Then I'm afraid I must fight you,' I said. 'I can't fight you and him,' he
said. 'That's how it is,' I said. Then one of the girls who was dressing

him, the tall one who'd been down in Hansi the night before, said, 'Why
don't you ask the old man down there? I'm sure he'll come up with
something.' So when Thomas was ready, I walked with him down to
Hansi; as we left the camp, the boyish girl, whose face was still puffy
from sleep, smiled and said, 'Good luck, O pretty one.'

On the path, Thomas reached out and touched the flowers on the
bushes as we walked along; the bangles on his wrists clinked and jan-
gled; behind us, the fading chant: 'Hring, Shring, Kring'; the wind
pulled the dupatta away from his face, and he snapped it back with a
flick of his wrist and a slow graceful twist of the neck, looked back at
me, his nose and lips hidden by the cloth, looked at me slant-eyed, and
I marvelled at how he was already learning the strange cunning of the
defeated, those weapons that are not weapons, the dharma of survival.

In Hansi, the old man waited for us, his lions by his sides — I heard
their breathing long before I saw them — and as soon as he saw us, he
called, 'There you are. I was wondering what had happened to you.' 'I
have come again,' Thomas said, 'and for the last time. But before we try
it again, there is a problem.' He told the old man why I was there, upon
which the old one scratched one of his lions behind the ears and said,
'No problem, no problem. Bring me a little gram flour, sugar, oil.' And
he said, bring me all this, so we did; he set up a pan over a fire, made
little balls of the gram flour, and, sitting cross-legged, pressed the balls
together into globes and fried them in sugar syrup, while we sat, watching him with gratification, because his movements were easy and supple, embellished sometimes with little flourishes for our pleasure.
Finally, he ladled out five laddoos onto a muslin cloth and turned to
Thomas, saying, 'Now, my friend. Now we must have a piece of you in
each of these.' Muttering under his breath — some secret charm, some
ancient mantra — he gave Thomas the small kitchen spoon he had
been using to stir the syrup. 'Make a cut in each of the digits of your
right hand,' he said. 'With this?' Thomas said. 'Why not a knife?' 'Don't
argue.' Thomas struggled a bit but managed to make a scratch in each of
the fingers of his right hand, using a jagged piece of the spoon, where
the iron curved from the handle into the cup. 'Now a drop for each of
the laddoos, one by one, one by one.' One by one, the old man picks up
a laddoo and holds it up; Thomas poises his hand above and squeezes a
shining black-red globule of blood onto each globe, a finger for each

laddoo, and the dark liquid melts away instantly into the scores of smaller spheres the laddoos are made of, causing each laddoo, in turn, to glow, to gleam. I shivered, a short spasm, and then I heard something and looked up from the spheres — Thomas' face was contorted, as the blood dropped from him he wept, quietly, and I could not tell whether it was joy or sorrow.

So when they had finished the old man dropped the spoon into the cloth, took up the four corners of the muslin, and tied up a neat little bundle for me. 'Here,' he said, 'tell her to eat each of these one by one, to place them in her mouth whole, and she will have sons.' 'Yes,' I said. 'Yes,' Thomas said, 'tell her to eat them, and she will have sons worthy of her.' 'And you, Jahaj Jung?' I said. 'I will stay here,' he said. 'Then,' I said, 'I will sit here in a corner, with your sons in my lap, and I will watch the combat.'

They crouched and circled each other, pawing occasionally at each other, and I saw instantly that the old man had learnt at one of the flashier schools of Western Avadh — he hooked with the insteps and lunged no less than five or six feet without warning — very quick and very dangerous; Thomas hung back and defended, hesitant, unsettled by the absence of weapons, the smacking impact of flesh, and, no doubt, by the unfamiliar flapping of the clothes he wore; under the old man's attack, he retreated, giving ground quickly, never staying in one place, rolling under the blows, accepting the pain, and this I promise you — I saw him learn, I observed him taking each blow as a lesson, an instruction in the inevitable laws of skill and strength and power, of domination and subservience, in that hideous association of the ruler and the ruled.

The old man, losing his patience, lunged again, over-extending his forward leg, reaching; Thomas grasped his wrist and fell over backwards, pulling, taking the old man on top of him, and quick, quick, he whirled, slid, was up, the old man rolled onto his back and Thomas stamped with his foot, coming down just above the old man's groin, then took a step, a stride, and the other foot crunched into the chest; he stood there, for a moment, legs frozen in mid-pace, balanced on the other, and the old man laughed, wheezing, 'I think you have beaten me.'

Thomas stepped off him, stumbling a little, and the old man curled up, holding himself, trying to breathe. After a while, he pushed himself up and beckoned to the lions, and resting a hand on their shoulders, walked slowly towards the edge of the city. Thomas watched him go in silence.

'Who was he?' I said. But then we heard the lions roar, and Thomas was staring off into the wilderness, and he said nothing at all.

Thomas and I walked up back to camp, and seeing us coming, the rest broke into cheers and applause, because they knew that if he came back he must be victorious. 'Victory to Jahaj Jung,' they shouted. 'Jahaj Jung will live forever.' But Begum Sumroo came straight up to me and asked what the old man had done about my problem, and I told her about the laddoos. 'Let me see them,' she said; I told her what the old man had said about being careful, but she said, 'Let me see them.' Her husband was skulking around, with his soldiers not far away, so I gave her the laddoos. She lifted them from the muslin, one by one, and held them up, examining them very closely, sniffing at them, then laying them back. 'What is it?' I asked. 'How does it work?' 'I don't know,' she said. 'I don't.'

The next morning I put my bundle in a saddle-bag, and said good-bye to Thomas and his men, who were already preoccupied with their city, with reconstruction and habitation and immigration. So I rode off, bearing as nearly south as I could, keeping to the big roads, and joining caravans when I could find them, but one evening, in that region where the clustered green trees of Braj shade off into the brown scrub of Raj-putana, I was riding alone, trying to make it to the next serai before darkness fell, when I rode into an infantry column's out-lying cavalry picquets.

Yes, I admit I was careless, I should have heard them, I should have paid attention to the sudden alarmed chirping of birds, I should have known, but perhaps it was the moon, fat on the horizon, or the purple of the twilight; I was careless, I was dreaming, they caught me. When I saw them I thought it better not to run, and so there was no unpleasantness — they took me back to the column, and when I saw the infantrymen's faces, their regular synchronized marching stride, that empty look (straight ahead, always straight ahead), the speed with which they thumped across the country-side, I knew it was the Chiria Fauj, and sure enough, as we rode along the road-side, there was a call from a palanquin borne by six men on each side, and six walking behind, ready to relieve. One of the cavalrymen turned to me, and said, 'Be respectful, now, fool-who-rides-in-the-night. You are about to meet the general of generals, the conqueror of armies, the master of Hindustan: General de Boigne.'

I muttered under my breath, 'The puppet-master himself, and his straw-headed doll-soldiers' and the cavalryman half-turned in his saddle, and there might have been some unpleasantness after all, but the man in the palanquin called again, 'What is it?' The cavalrymen explained, and de Boigne — yes, it was him — said, check him, check his saddle-bags.

They found the bundle and opened it, and the laddoos shone. They handed up the bundle to de Boigne, holding the muslin by the edges, and he asked, 'What is this?' His face was swollen, and rolls of fat bulged out of his shirt as he lay in the palanquin, huge and slow-moving; I told him that it was blessed parsad from a sacrifice conducted by an old man, which I was taking back to my home-town for my friends and relatives. 'Holy food? Really? A holy old man?' I nodded. He reached in and picked up a laddoo. 'Don't touch them,' I blurted. He raised an eyebrow, then picked each one in turn, rolling it about the palm of his hand. 'Don't,' I said, and he smiled. 'I make kings,' he said, and tightened his fingers about the laddoo he was holding in his hand until it crumbled and fell piece by piece into the cloth, its glow dying swiftly.

I said nothing; he sat up, rubbing his fingers against each other, and looking at me he spat into the muslin, carefully, one tear-shaped glob of spittle for each of the laddoos. I stayed still. 'Let him go,' de Boigne said; 'they're obviously nothing important.' He threw the bundle to the ground just as somebody else dropped me to the ground with a single neat blow to the back of my neck; on my hands and knees I scrambled to the side of the road, over the deep ruts, dragging the bundle behind me. I knelt over the laddoos, trying to reform the broken one, pressing the little balls together, attempting to stick them together like clay, but nothing I did could bring the glow back, and — I tried to stop it, but I couldn't, and I too touched them — the tears of my rage fell on them, on the sons that were not yet born, and the infantry and the cavalry and the artillery and the engineers tramped on by, raising a fog of dust that covered everything. I threw the remains of the broken one by the road-side, tied up the bundle, and set off again. The days passed, and finally, I appeared again in that garden, and the rest you know.

'Yes. She and my sister ate the laddoos, and they were born.'

'Your sister too?'

'It hurt to eat them. She gave my sister one, and my nephew was born at the same time as Sikander, two years after the day he was conceived.'

'I heard about the two years.'

'And we all touched the laddoos, in one way or the other.'

'Yes. The old man, Thomas, Begum Sumroo, I, de Boigne, you, all of us. All of us except the fathers.'

'Yes.'

'I thought of this, after I had given her the laddoos,' Uday Singh said. 'And I suppose it was for this reason that I counted the days after that morning, and had my spies hovering about your house, disguised as fruit-wallahs and beggars and gipsy children. But despite all this I had no idea the first one had been born until Skinner announced it in court; later, my men got hold of the midwife, and I heard of how he had been delivered, and what he looked like. And again I counted days, and this time my servants heard the shrieks, and I disguised myself as a watchman, with a dog, and I went and listened outside your garden wall. The night passed in the screaming, but when the moment came I knew, and I couldn't understand why I thought I knew.

'Maybe it was the two years of your sister's pregnancy, and maybe it was the memory of the old man and Thomas, and everything that had happened, but I was expecting comets to fly across the sky, and the braying of donkeys, and wailing in the heavens; I thought cows would give birth to asses, and blood would drip from the air, and ghosts would clang shields and swords in the streets; but nothing happened. I knew it was the moment because the whole world died away, because there was not a sound to be heard anywhere, nothing; there was just the quietness; I knew it then but later I thought no, it was nothing, it was just that the screaming had stopped.'

'But I saw the king-cobra today.'

'You did.'

'I did.'

Uday looked away, then back at Ram Mohan. 'Do you really think,' he said, 'that Sikander will be a king, an emperor?'

'I don't know,' Ram Mohan said. 'I must go, back to them.'

'Yes.'

When the bearers had picked up the palanquin and were already jogging away, Ram Mohan poked his head out and looked back at Uday Singh. 'Why was the cobra weeping?' he said.

Uday shook his head; the bearers chanted 'Hu-hu-hu-hu-hu-hu' over the crickets; the moon skimmed low over the tree-tops above; Ram Mohan lay back on the wood, exhausted, feeling the hardness of the earth on each step in his hip, in the place where the bone fused and remained stubbornly still; and the sweat dripped from his chest, smothering him with its rankness, but despite everything he fought down a fierce exultation that made him want to shout, 'I have sons,' because now all pain seemed unreal, all insults would be avenged, all possibilities seemed to exist, renewed, all death was defeated: I am the father of Sikander, the king; I am the mother of Chotta Sikander, the prince; I am the parent of Sanjay, the poet; I will never die.

Sandeep called:

HERE ENDS THE FIRST BOOK,
THE BOOK OF WAR AND ANCESTORS.
SIKANDER IS BORN.

NOW BEGINS THE SECOND BOOK,
THE BOOK OF LEARNING AND DESOLATION.

THE BOOK OF
LEARNING
AND
DESOLATION

. . . now . . .

'SNAKES?' Abhay said. 'Cobras?' He raised an eyebrow, smiling.

'You be quiet, bhaiya,' Saira said, plopping herself down next to me. 'How can you have a big story without a snake in it?'

'Exactly,' I scribbled at Abhay.

'And they liked it out there,' Saira said, with a big sweep of her arm.

'They did?'

'Yes. And there's a lot of them there. I've never seen so many people on our maidan before,' she said, glowing with proprietary pride. 'Come see.'

We went up on the roof and looked, and indeed there were a lot of people, filling up maybe half the maidan. I could see peanut-vendors working the crowd, and one enterprising fellow had already started an ice-gola stand under a tree, and he was playing film songs on a recorder. There were families bustling to and fro, and young boys on bicycles swooping through the clusters of people.

'Come on,' Saira said. 'Interval's over.'

As we came down the stairs the children in the court-yard were chanting, 'Where were we? Where were we?' Abhay's two young friends with the questions about America were planted firmly in the front row.

'Where we were,' Abhay said, 'was at a party, and then grieving for a death. Our consolations on a mountain-side were lit by the unearthly light of a thousand suns, the destroyer of worlds, by the fear in our hearts.'

Abhay began to type.

I passed a note to Saira: 'Is that line his own or is he stealing from somewhere?'

She hissed at me in a loud whisper: 'Oof! Of course it's a quotation. Didn't they teach you anything at school?'

What We Learned at School.

KATE KILLED HERSELF that night. Sometime before the sun rose, she dissolved three bottlefuls of sleeping pills in water, in one of her two fluted champagne glasses, and sitting at her desk, took little sips, washing it down with bourbon. She wore a long black skirt, a white blouse, and a string of white pearls. The sergeant who questioned me at the Claremont police station told me they found her with her hands folded in front of her on the table, the smooth blond hair falling over her face like a curtain. The glasses and the bottles were arranged neatly in two lines to the left. Everything was in order, except for her stockinged left foot, which had slipped out of her black shoe. Under the foot, there was a sheet of heavy white paper, with a few words in her fountain-penned, curlicued writing: "Abhay, just another tiresome suicide note." And that was it; there was nothing else.

The sergeant who questioned me — I forget his name — was a big black man with heavy shoulders. They called me in and sat me down in a brightly lit room with brown carpets and plastic furniture. There was that sharp light that comes from fluorescence, and I squinted my eyes, feeling like I was peering through a porthole at the world. I sipped at a cup of bitter coffee and thought about what she could have wanted to put into that white space, what reasons for dying she could have possibly set down into the emptiness under my name, why she stopped

writing. I wondered if she had seen the flash outside, if that had silenced her before she could start explaining. Or if she had seen it, and
then brought out the bourbon and the glasses.

"What time did it happen?" I asked the sergeant when he walked in
and sat down, opening a manila folder.

"We don't know yet," he said. "They'll do an autopsy sometime tomorrow. Are you doing all right?"

Somewhere, not far away, smoke rises from her skull as a fine-
toothed electric hacksaw buzzes through the bone.

"Yes."

"When did you see her last?"

"A couple of days ago. Tuesday, no, Wednesday night. At a party." In
her room, she poured red wine and went off to put in her diaphragm.

"And?" the sergeant said.

"We went home. I mean I went home with her. To her room, I
mean." On the way up to Scripps she tucked her hand under my elbow.
I could feel her knuckles rubbing against my ribs, the softness of her
sweater. Neither of us said anything till later in her room, when she
said, I'll just be a minute.

"Did she say or do anything that would've indicated that she was
depressed? Unhappy?"

"No. I don't think so." I know that she had on a black bra. I know
that she liked the tips of my fingers, very softly, across her shoul-
derblades. I know how her neck felt, taut, against my cheek, and how
the sound that she made, finally, vibrated through my skin. I know I lay
unable to sleep, staring at her wall, at the jagged collage she had made
of pictures cut from fashion magazines, angular black-and-white people
with the same cheekbones, all of them. This I know.

"Do you have any idea why she did it?"

"No." No, I don't. I am a victim of that boringly common ailment, sir,
that malaise that cuts so many loose in a world overflowing with con-
nections. For everything, they assure me, there is a cause, but I feel like
I am floating, adrift. I don't believe the sun will rise tomorrow. I don't
understand why the sky is blue.

"You have no idea?"

"No."

"How often did you see her?"

"Once in a while. We weren't, you know, seeing each other or anything like that."

"What was the last thing she said to you?"

"She was on her way to class and she said she had three minutes left."

"Three minutes?"

"Three and a half minutes."

He stacked up his papers, laid his pen on top, and looked up at me. "Why did you come here? To this country?"

"For an education," I said. "Of course."

He nodded, and then he got up and walked down the hall. I sat alone in the room with its plastic chairs and tried to remember why I had come. I had lied: an education is how I had come, with scholarships and grants. What I had come for was something else. What was it? I tried to remember and all I could think of was one Saturday afternoon when we broke school bounds at Mayo to see the matinee at the Imperial. There were five of us who always went, crowded into the tonga and happy with the clip-clopping of the horse but terrified that there might be a master around the next corner. The darkness of the theatre was a relief, and then, just before the movie, the manager always played a scratched, scraping record: 'Tequila.' I liked the Westerns best. That afternoon we watched *The Magnificent Seven*. Afterwards in the tonga homewards we were quiet, stunned, as if we were still watching the movie. Now the town of Ajmer, with the old mosque and even more ancient fort on the hill above, looked dirty and unreal and the bright afternoon sunlight hurt our eyes.

At that time, in ninth class, we were breaking bounds every week, and sometimes even during the week. I used to long for 'Tequila.' It was like being in love. That afternoon we kept the tonga going past the Main Building, with the statue of the founding British viceroy in front, past Ajmer House and Rajasthan House to the break in the boundary wall. We went over one after the other and I came last, and it was only after we were all in that we noticed Katiyar waiting in the shadows for us.

'Well, well, gentlemen,' he said.

Katiyar was the school captain, and cricket captain, and a topper in his class as well. So later that night, after dinner and prep, he drilled us until we were dripping with sweat and hurting. He was wearing his blue blazer with his colours and his scarf and looked elegant as always.

'What a bunch of whining babies,' he said. His father had been at Oxford, so he had the same clipped accent. He had us sitting in the invisible chair, with our hands held straight out in front, and my thighs were fluttering so badly I was sure I was going to drop. 'And I'm being so nice to you.'

'Thanks, Katiyar,' I said. 'We're really grateful.'

'I could have taken you in,' he said. 'What would have happened then? Expulsion, don't you think? Ask me why I'm being so nice.'

So we chorused, 'Why, Katiyar, why?'

'Because I got an acceptance letter from Yale today. Full scholarship too.'

'Katiyar,' I said. 'You're a god.'

'I am,' he said. 'Aren't I?'

He was, really, and that night he finally let us go after having us each bend over and sending us through his door with a stinging whack, a single smacking blow across the rear with his fine imported English cricket bat, and somehow even in that sharp pain it seemed he was gifting us with possibility, with all the promise of America. So the news of his suicide, years later as we were finishing our own applications, came to us as a kind of impenetrable hieroglyphic, something we speculated endlessly about but never grasped. We were told he hanged himself in his room at Yale during Thanksgiving break. It was stunning and unbelievable and finally absurd. I never knew him very well but I refused to believe in his death. I was sure it was not suicide but something else, a plot of some sort, a lie. To think of Katiyar at Yale was to dream a kind of paradise, and, though I tried, I could never see clearly in my imagination the scene of his death: the room, the rope, the reason why.

When I stepped out of the police building, it was dark, and there was water on the ground, slick black, mirroring my steps. The Jaguar slid noiselessly across the parking lot, spraying white from its wheels. It stopped beside me and a door clicked open.

"Get in, Abhay," Tom said as I leaned over. "We're going on a road trip."

"A road trip?" I said, pulling the door to behind me, feeling safer almost instantly amid the dark, artificed surfaces of the interior, the comfortable soft hum of the machinery as we swept onto the metalled surface of the street.

"Uh-huh," Amanda said. "A trip."

"Where to?"

"We're going to go look for heaven," Tom said.

I turned my head to him. In the scrolling light from the street lights, I could see only fragments of his face, but it looked like he was smiling.

"Heaven?"

"Yeah. We will seek heaven," he said, in the voice of a television announcer. "Or at least a little piece of it."

"So we're going into the city?"

"No, no, no," he said, shaking his head from side to side. "If you'd paid any attention in English 101, Abhay, you would know that one doesn't look for heaven in the city. Quite the opposite."

"In the other direction," Amanda said.

"Exactly. Abhay, we will find heaven in the great open spaces," Tom said, waggling a finger in my face. "In the prairies and in the mountains."

"Go east, young man," Amanda said, giggling.

What about school? I started to say, but felt my stomach knot at the thought of it. So I said, "What about money? I don't have anything with me."

"Our young friend here has a stack of credit cards, supplied by dear old Pop. Stop trying to make trouble," Tom said. "Think of the adventure. Think of heaven."

"Heaven." I couldn't help laughing.

"See. You're feeling better already."

He leaned across my shoulder and switched on the radio. The Japanese are buying MGM, a voice said, Sony wants Universal. So we glided up onto a freeway and headed east, past the deep red and blue glow of neon, the facades of huge buildings like frozen black oil, with the comfortable, anonymous companionship of other drivers and, always, the music, the simple but satisfying beat of metal and electricity. We all lapsed into silence, taken, of course, by the slow curves of the freeway, by its loneliness, its giant sprawl, the glittering constellations above and below, the dark, the speed.

*   *   *

In a McDonald's, as I squirted out red sauce — ketchup, they called it — from a plastic bottle, onto a hamburger, I asked, "Where are we going, really?"

"Just going with the flow, man," Tom said, doing a mellow sixties voice.

"Really?"

"Really."

But Amanda, she reached out then and took hold of my wrist, made me put down the bottle, and pulled my hand into her lap, where she cradled it in both of hers, not letting go until we were out in the car again and she had to drive.

". . . it was just one of those high school things, but it drove me crazy and crazier than anything before or after, and I don't know, still, why." I had changed places with Tom, and was now jammed into the backseat, half asleep, my neck stretched back against the curve of the leather. We had bought a bottle of Jack Daniel's and passed it back and forth until my head had drooped to the seat. His words, slurred, came to me distant and distorted through the steady hum of the engine and the pulling swamp of my own sleep.

"A high school story," Amanda said.

"Sure," Tom said. "A silly adolescent-type thing. See, this was how it happened . . ."

I had known her, known of her for years, we had gone to the same school since fourth or fifth grade, and all that time I knew who she was and she knew who I was, but she went with her crowd and I did with mine, so we never really knew, never even talked with each other, I think. But senior year, second semester, we both ended up in advanced English, AP, you know, American Life through American Lit, with Mrs. Christiansen, and so all of a sudden she's sitting in front of me, all this blond hair falling over the back of the chair, I'm catching whiffs and gusts and zephyrs of her perfume, and she's throwing her head back, you know how girls with long hair do, and Ling's rolling her eyes at me.

Ling's my best friend since seventh grade. Taiwanese, her full Chinese name is Ling-Ling Lee, both her parents are doctors, and Ling's going to Stanford — early decision — and then medical school, then surgery. Ling even had her specialty, right, what she's going to do as a doctor, when she was a junior. She's incredible. She works harder than anyone else I know, and is pretty funny when she wants to be, and wears her hair cut short and wears round gold glasses, with her dark eyes behind. So Mercy — the blond — has her hair over the back of the chair and I'm leaning forward a bit to get a good look and Ling's got her lips together, like she's on the verge of a smile.

Now I guess you could smile at Mercy. Her full name is Mercy Fuller Cunningham and that's how she writes it on her books, she's got all this hair, teased and brushed and whatever till it falls like the proverbial cascade, and she's got blue eyes and pale skin and these breasts that gently swell the Saks shirts she wears, you get the idea. When she walks through the parking lot in front of the school all the little freshmen sitting on the back of cars fall silent and a hush follows her as they watch her legs working the back of her skirt. But in any case she twisted around in her chair and stuck her hand out at me, and gave me this big awful bruising smile and said, "Hi, Tom. I guess we've seen each other around but we've never really met, so I'm Mercy Cunningham."

So it takes me a minute before I can get up a smile and grab for her hand, because I'm so stunned and charmed that here's Mercy Cunningham actually introducing herself, as if anyone in the whole school doesn't know who she is. Then Mrs. Christiansen starts in, but I sit there and watch the hair for the whole hour, and miss whatever Mrs. Christiansen and the others say about poor old Rip Van Winkle, who had to go off into the mountains. So now you're thinking I'm already a goner, but actually I'm sitting there kind of admiring how Mercy Cunningham can be so perfect and yet so incredibly sweet, and I've heard other people say this at school — "She's nice, really, she is!" — but I never really believed it before, because she hung out with the really snotty crowd, the kids with the magazine good looks and the perfect green sweaters and the whatever-it-takes-to-wear-them and the parties you heard about after they happened. And Ling and I, we were always the ones on the edges, we did the theater club and we won the scholarships and we were going to go to great colleges, but in high school we walked around together and nobody really knew us except our friends. So when Mercy Cunningham shakes my hand I just sit there thinking it's true, it is, but I'm not imagining anything else, and anyway I don't like blonds. At this point I've had one girlfriend, Sarah Nussenbaum, and she's Ling's best girlfriend, and is dark and cute and small and very Jewish — Princeton, early decision. Sarah and I went together for six months, and we nearly did it twice, and the second time she jumped up from the couch (her parents' house), trying to rehook her bra and turning away, crying, saying we had to be friends. I said all right, okay, no really it's all right, very comforting and sensitive even though I was throbbing painfully inside my jeans, so Sarah and I are friends now.

Mrs. Christiansen is going on about Rip, and Mercy Cunningham is bent over her notebook, writing industriously. I notice Ling watching me watching the hair, and at this I feel a little embarrassed for Mercy. See, Mrs. Christiansen has a gift for stating the obvious, and most of the kids in AP have read *Poetics* about sixteen times, and some of them like to talk semiotics, so it's like a point of honor never to write down anything Mrs. Christiansen says. And now Mercy suddenly perks up and says, "So, you mean, like, Rip is an *artist?*"

Mrs. Christiansen flushes with pleasure and I hear a snicker or two, and Ling rolls her eyes. Then the class is over and I stop at the door to let Mercy by, and she says with another one of those smiles, "See you around, Tom," and reaches out and touches me very lightly on the wrist as she passes. This time that fleeting touch really paralyzes me, I'm left standing by the door staring, preferring brunettes but still feeling a hammer on my heart. Then Ling grabs me by the elbow and pulls me outside, along the corridor.

"She must shampoo that hair every single day," Ling says. "My grandmother, in Taiwan, says that modern shampoo destroys hair. All the chemicals, you know. She's going to lose it someday."

"Don't be bitchy, Ling," I say. "She's nice."

"Uh-huh, and one of these days she'll be doing one of those cheerleader leaps and it'll all fly off and she'll come down bald," Ling says, so I punch her on the arm, but I'm laughing, and all the way home we make up this story about a bald cheerleader who lives in the Appalachians and kills innocent hiking teenagers by strangling them with her incredibly muscular thighs.

We go to Ling's house, walking through the shady avenues — Elm, Green — standard American upper-middle-class suburbia, in this case a few miles from Cincinnati, but indistinguishable really from a thousand other places anywhere on the continent. In Ling's living room, her father is seated in front of the television, a just-opened bottle of Johnnie Walker Black by his side. When we come out later that night, he'll be sitting there, his wife next to him, and the bottle will be half empty. They both wear gray suits and tend to get quieter as the evening goes on.

So Ling and I walk past him, and he smiles politely at me, and we get ourselves some soda and some cheese stuff and go into Ling's room and settle down in front of the VCR. Now Ling and I, despite our grades and our good schools and our obvious precocious eighties sophistication, share a ravening taste for bad movies. We had our own grading system and we kept records — we would joke about writing a book someday — and according to our system some grindingly pretentious crap like *Paris, Texas* would get a 2, out of a possible 10, while our all-time high was a movie called *The Snow Beast*. The Snow Beast was this guy in a jazzed-up gorilla suit who terrorized a ski resort, only I guess they couldn't afford to hire a whole gorilla suit, so for the whole movie you saw what can only be described as Buxom Babes being massacred by a gorilla hand or a gorilla head that descended on them from out of frame. *The Snow Beast* also got two whole extra points because its blond Aryan hero was named "Yar." The first time somebody said, "Yar, there's a durn snow beast out there on that there mountain, Yar!" Ling and I fell off the couch and made ourselves almost sick laughing.

So now we load up *Afterwards* and Ling punches the right buttons and immediately we are in a post–nuclear-holocaust, post–ozone-depletion, post–polar-cap-meltdown, post–chemical-disaster, post–raging-sexual-disease shopping mall. Scabby radiation-burned zombies, hair falling from cracking scalps, fight over food and designer fashions and wigs and lipstick and base, while the normal leads, un-scarred and golden-fleshed, blow them away with full-automatic com-bat shotguns and worry if any of their small, trusty band is really a zombie in deep Elizabeth Arden disguise. It is quite calculatedly gory and awful, but we don't enjoy it as much as we'd thought we would, maybe because I sit there, a little absent and distracted, not laughing at the proper cues. I say good night and walk home, skipping a little in the darkness. That night I dream of thighs pressing my ears into my head, and my tongue dipping into gold and pink. I wake up laughing.

So now you're thinking I have a normal adolescent crush on the school sweetheart, but the truth is I find this ridiculous. The truth is that the woman is boring: in the next few days I talk to her and discover that she is "bright," which is to say that she is capable of putting a sentence together and that Mrs. Christiansen litters the margins of her papers with "Good!" and "Exactly!" which is all very well, but I have absolutely nothing to say to her after "How're you today?" and "What's the reading for Friday?" Worse, she thinks Third World poverty is "sad," that a strong defense posture is "necessary," and Hawthorne is a "depressing" writer, and me, I'm the kid who sits at the back of the History class and insists, *insists,* that we use the word *genocide* when we talk about the Dakota and the Cherokee. I write turgid poetry, after Svetayeva and Pavese, which the editors of the *Hilltop High Viewpoint* accept for publication in a sort of cowed, abject manner just reeking of incomprehension. When I was nine, my father gave me the facts on sex, then turned back, adjusted his gray English cardigan, and said, "And another thing. The three greatest monsters of this century have been Joseph Stalin, Joseph McCarthy, and Margaret Mitchell."

So, okay, you say, so she's not exactly Mercy Sontag Cunningham, but she never pretended to be, and what you really want is her sweet jaunty bottom, her breasts like taut young fruit, her — what other way to describe it? — her magnificent mane, her baby–Billy Budd eyes. And I, too, consider this, consider each item, the sum of, and the greater than the sum of, but am left mystified: qua bottoms, I like the full and rounded; of breasts, the generous; hair, dark and silky; the whole package — I know, I know, the sexist language, this whole odious analysis, but fuck that for now, let's be blunt — the whole object ripe, mysterious, and a little sulky.

Well, Sarah Nussenbaum, as head of the Hilltop English Society, had organized the first ever Annual Hilltop Poetry Reading, and of course Mrs. Christiansen required attendance by all APs. And me, I brush down my hair as well as I can, wear black and black, shirt open at the collar, think about a hat but decide against, wonder if I can grow a beard or at least a respectable stubble, stand next to the podium and shoot my hip to one side, one hand in pocket and the other carelessly on waist, and rip into my epic poem *Me, Her, Bosch Landscape, and I, and I.* I refuse to reveal any more of this poem on the grounds that it might incriminate me straight into some special hell reserved for bad poets. Anyway, after, I lean over in the hallway, gulping water from a fountain, still sweaty from my impassioned delivery. I am thinking, of course, of Mercy Fuller Cunningham and my incredibly stupid thing for her, and I think at this point I am resigned to letting it go, to accepting that it would never happen, to accepting who I am and who she is. I straighten up, my lips cool from the water, and then suddenly there are arms around my neck, breasts sliding across my back, and she is leaning over and there are lips, warm and wet, touching me briefly, her saying, "Oh, Tom, that was great. I really liked it." Then she is down the corridor, and I can still feel her breath in my ear. And I know I am lost.

So now, dear listener, begins the period, the day and season of my madness. I spend that whole night — by that I mean from dusk to dawn, and I swear this is true — writing down "Oh, Tom, that was great. I really liked it" on a thousand different pieces of paper, in a million different ways. I examine every nuance of those words, there is no linguist on the planet who knows those nine as I do, their texture and rhythms, their meaning and derivations, their abundant connotations, and by the time the sun rises I am convinced that Mercy Fuller Cunningham is in love with me. By nine I am crushed, despondent, and full of self-loathing — I see her in the parking lot with her hip buddies, her smart set, her jet-setters, her in-crowd, and with a bare "Hi, Tom" the bitch brushes past, and not a glance more. So then I'm in English, going, fine, Tom, all the poor girl wants to do is be friendly, be nice, platonic, and here you are in some weird woman-as-destructive-other frenzy, but then she dances in, bright and unbearably perky, leans over my desk and kisses me on the nose, the very end of my nose, "Hi, you incredible poet you." And then Mrs. Christiansen has started on *Moby Dick* and I am simultaneously, at the very same time, you understand, calling down on Mercy all the pain and hatred accumulated by every teased-and-tormented male in history, and am seeing again radiant visions of me and her and am appalled by my own anger, the wish-to-do-violence of my own reaction. Poor Ahab. Poor Claggart. Life sucks.

I spend the next few days learning up her schedule and dodging down hallways and up stairs, and then trying not to breathe hard, walk casually past her, pleasant smile, nod. Then one day she says, as I take the most intricate route to History the school has ever seen, "Oh, Tom, there you are again." It's said with a smile, but that night I spend two hours looking at myself in the mirror and decide to go cold turkey. I skip English three times in a row, spend every spare moment in the library, and hand in my History paper on the Cultural Revolution two weeks early. Now I feel disciplined and strong, scoured and empty, confident that nothing can break me, but right before English I get that same old dropping-helplessly feeling again. So I cut, and read Poe behind the gym, and that afternoon I withdraw four hundred ninety-eight dollars and twenty-three cents from my savings account. I call Sarah Nussenbaum, and pick her up that evening in a stretch limousine.

So I take Sarah Nussenbaum to L'Auberge, where she whispers that she feels underdressed and I suppress my urgent desire to tell her to stop whining and instead ply her freely with expensive red wine. After a while her cheeks get flushed and she starts talking about how it's great that Ling and she and I are friends, how much it means to her and we should always keep in touch. I murmur, "Anything for you, Sarah," and narrow my eyes at her above the rim of my glass. Then she talks about something else and I nod and feed her pastry from my plate. In the limo on the way home she turns eagerly to me when I put a hand on her neck, and she runs her hands over my forehead and ears as we kiss, and her mouth tastes of wine but I break away suddenly, saying "I don't think this is such a good idea, Sarah." She shrinks away to her corner, and I can see that she wants to ask, then why all this? but she's way too smart and proud. "I'm sorry," I say.

After I drop her off I let the limousine go and trudge through the empty streets, trying to remember the exact state of my body and brain as we kissed, but all I can remember is my usual unbounded excitement when I'm anywhere near Sarah and an equally strong anxiety, a nervousness that afflicts me so I shake. As I go from shadow into light, I seem to remember that my hands shook through her hair, but I'm almost certain I'm inventing this as I try to see it again. Suddenly I'm in front of her house, not Sarah's, I mean, but the abode of Mercy Fuller Cunningham. In some hazy hour of self-deception, I've casually asked and looked in phone books and maybe even followed her white Audi long enough to get a general idea of where she lives, and now I'm there: "CUNNINGHAM," a brass nameplate says. Nameplates are signs, I remember Ling saying, because they communicate one sort of information, while flags are symbols, because they stand for a host of things. What sort of flag would Mercy fly, I wonder, as I work my way around the large white concrete house, through hedges and over grass. At the back, I find a window, high above me and curtained, which I know instantly is hers. It is very late, and a few lights burn feverishly in the distance, throwing up halos. I roll in the mud under her window, crushing little yellow flowers, and when I kneel finally, my arms clutched around my belly, sweat and the liquid from plants pouring across my lips, I can feel the moon on my face. It hangs above me as I totter from tree to tree on my way home.

The next day at breakfast, I said to my parents: "What are we?"

"What?" my mother says, putting down her newspaper. They're both looking at me with a certain eagerness, we can deal with this, we're both psychiatrists. Existential questions are what they live for, and they're especially partial to teenage angst.

"I mean, what are we? Are we German, or English, or Dutch, or what? Wasn't Grandpa's father from Germany?"

"Your great-grandfather spoke German, but I think he was born in New England," my father says.

"Why this sudden interest?" my mother says.

They're both a little puzzled and intrigued. The place of the human in the cosmos they can talk about, it's how they make their bread and butter, but ethnic stuff is a touch primitive and makes them uncomfortable.

"Oh, nothing," I say, "I just wondered."

"Mostly German, a little English, some Dutch, some French, I should think," my father says.

"No Italian?" I ask.

"It's possible," my mother says. "My side spent a lot of time in New York."

"Have to go," I say. I walk to school feeling my body move, trying to see if there's a little strut in it. The truth is that in the sunshine of the day I'm a little ashamed and more than a little frightened by what I'd done the night before. Rolling in the bushes is extreme for anyone, but me? In tenth grade I wrote a paper on the invention of romantic love in the court of Eleanor of Aquitaine. So now I want a genetic reason for my behavior, some dimly remembered racial memory that had awakened and pushed me headlong into lunacy.

In English, Mercy Fuller Cunningham is talking, in a breathless tone of horror, about some weird animal that rolled around in her yard and smashed hedges.

"Be careful," I say, as I walk to my desk. "It could be the Snow Beast." Raising my hands over my head, back humped, fingers hooked: "Arrr-rrr. Ahhaarrr-aarrr."

She looks at me, puzzled. I drop the Snow Beast, walk around her and swing into my desk in one fluid movement. As Mrs. Christiansen walks in, Ling leans over to me. "*Why* are you walking like that?" I shrug.

That day, after class, I walk next to Mercy Fuller Cunningham in the hall, making conversation about movies. "*Risky Business,* yeah," I say, "that was *totally* cool, but I liked *Top Gun* better." I know, I know: I had an anxiety attack when I heard they were going to make a movie which featured jets, motorcycles, and Tom Cruise. Ling said that the average teenage boy could get his hormone level maladjusted just from looking at the ad. But now the situation was desperate, and I think I would have raved about John Wayne if Mercy Fuller Cunningham had given me half an opening. So we casually walked into the cafeteria and I casually kept up my stream of carefully middle-to-just-above-middle-brow, not-too-radical banter, and casually we stood in line and casually I got some milk and stuff, and we walked outside to the patio, and she said, want to sit here? and we sat on red-and-green concrete picnic tables, and I casually opened my milk, one-handed, and all around us heads turned.

See, I don't know what it was like at yours, but at Hilltop, there were the Punkers and the Trendies, the Lot Dead Stoners, the Ethnics, the Jocks and the Cheers, the Nerds, the Super Nerds, the Artos, the Jesus Gnomes, and the Nobodies. Sometimes a Punker would go out with a New-Wavish Trendy, and sometimes a Nerd would sneak a smoke with one of the Dead, but mostly the caste rules were maintained with slav-ish obedience and enforced by vicious ridicule. You were judged for everything and could be ostracized for anything, and I mean anything, the shoes you wore, your parents, your car, your religion, your clothes, especially if you were a woman. So when I sit down to lunch with Mercy Fuller Cunningham a ripple passes among the assembled multitudes — here is a confirmed Arto Super Nerd breaking bread with the most exalted and rosy-breasted of the Cheers: Damn, I say, old man, what is this modern world coming to? Jolly bad form, what?

But I ignore the giggles and the sniggers, and actually exult in them, because for my passion I am enduring the slings and gibes of unbelievable conformity. I am able to endure anything. During the next few weeks I spend all my money on clothes, and wearing only underwear, lift weights in front of the mirror. I practice saying "Yo!" I eat with Mercy often and try to make conversation with her friends, all of whom react to me with careful politeness. Mercy always introduces me: this is my smart friend Tom, he's a poet. I get the feeling that this just heightens their ineffable feeling of superiority. And sometimes I just cannot believe these people, and at these times I get the feeling that Mercy is embarrassed by them. Like there's this one time, lunch again, and Salma walks by, Salma is this Pakistani girl, a power at math, solves differential equations in her head, and she has black, amazingly beautiful hair, that she lets hang in a thick coil to below her knees, and Salma walks on by, and Mercy's friends Mary and Ellen and Bill and Steve, all of them bat their hands in front of their noses, smiling. "What?" I say, feeling this nervous smile on my lips.

"Don't you know?" Craig says. "They never wash it, the hair." Craig and John are these two handsome buzz-cut black guys, both football players, and now both of them are sitting there smiling at me. I have a mad impulse to lean over and grab them by the collars and shout, what the fuck are *you* laughing at? but Mercy puts a hand on my arm, under the table, and so I sit there and they start talking about something else.

I want to tell Ling about this, but instead I talk to her about end-of-term papers or some such nonsense. She wants to come over and pick up a reference book I have, and I try to put her off, I'll bring it tomorrow to school, and she says, what is your problem? so I say, all right. At my house, on the stairs up to my room, her nose begins to twitch, and a full three feet before she reaches the door she bursts out, "What *is* that smell? Incense?"

She walks into the room and stops short. The walls are covered with Italian madonnas, sad-eyed women with pure, spiritual expressions and incredible sexual potential.

"Oh, Tom," Ling says. "Oh, oh, Tom."

From the next day on, she starts to leave Xeroxed articles in my desk, articles with two-part titles like *The Making and Breaking of Marilyn Monroe: A Post-feminist Perspective* and *Men, Women, Sex, and War: Gender Politics and Violence among the Kikuyu* and *Complex Dream or Simple Need: Towards a Bio-genetic Understanding of the Male Sexual Impulse* (the last by a woman named Emmaline Shakti Sharpstown). I want to tell Ling, thanks, but I don't need these, I understand only too well the shoddy symbolisms of my psyche, the grunting subterfuges of my id, but I am too embarrassed to even talk about it.

So the days go by and my GPA plummets and Mrs. Christiansen gives back my papers with large contemptuous C's scrawled across the front, and pretty soon the whole world knows I'm going mad. I actually hear a pimply little freshman tell her equally pimply friend, "That's the guy whose obsessing over Mercy Fuller Cunningham — he's gone crazy." I walk down the halls in my new Reeboks and my new haircut like some grotesque marked by fire: people stop talking when I draw near, and will look anywhere but into my eyes. And while this is happening I get a sense of some weird empathy from the Ethnics — I turn around in the cafeteria one day and there's Muhammed Ziai, a sophomore, the only kid in school of Iranian descent, and he turns away quickly but not before I see this sad smile on his face. This keeps on happening to me, Pakistanis, Lebanese, Vietnamese, Cubans stare at me absently and then flick their eyes away. Meanwhile, I wonder if Mercy Fuller Cunningham is aware of all this, and surely she must be, but every time I make some feeble effort to break the spell she does something that pulls me right back in, all these little touches and smiles and I didn't see you today, Tommy, I missed you, all so innocent that then and now I waver between thinking of her as the proverbial cock-goading bitch and a poor misunderstood generous girl trapped by her beauty.

So on it goes. I cycle between depression and expansive happiness, and the sight of lovers, of any two people, arouses in me a morbid, hateful jealousy. Even the sight of a bleached blond *Sheena of the Jungle* swinging into the arms of her Great White Lover makes me sullen, even as Ling snorts: "If she actually rides that lion this thing gets an extra two points." Noting my brooding fanatic countenance, she quiets down and pretends to watch the movie for a minute or two, then says, "I'll bet you five bucks she gets tied to a stake by chanting tribesmen in the next thirty minutes." When even that fails to get a response out of me she bursts out — the first time she has said anything to me directly about this — she explodes, "If it's going to do this to you, why the fuck won't you talk to her?"

I look at her, startled, because this is the first time I have ever heard her use the word *fuck*. I want to tell her I can't, because how can anyone live without hope? but instead I shrug. I lean forward into the TV screen and she lets it drop and never says anything about it again. I can't tell her that I want it to happen all by itself, that I don't want to say anything. In my fantasies I make millions and buy up Manhattan. In my fantasies I bomb the hell out of Cambodia and sleek women raise their black dresses for me spontaneously, in the backs of Washington limousines.

Toward the end of the semester Mercy Fuller Cunningham throws a party, and this time I get invited. The invitation is embossed, and comes in a heavy cream-colored envelope which she leaves in my desk, on top of an article entitled *Ego and Transference: A Post-post-modern Perspective.* I spend the next two weeks planning, I study myself, I study the objective, and, so to speak, the ground. I consider my clothes and try to remember if I've ever heard Mercy saying anything about haberdashery. I try to think Tom Cruise. I watch her friends. I flip quickly between Oprah Winfrey and Geraldo Rivera: "Women Who Love Too Much" and "How to Get the Most out of Your Relationship." I borrow money.

So finally the day arrives, and I won't put you through a description of my immediate preparations. I arrive exactly one hour and fifteen minutes late, which delay, by my calculations, conveys the exact intensity of cool I desire. And, I shouldn't forget, I drive up in my mother's Volvo, for which I have negotiated and wheedled and pretended impending nervous breakdown. But nobody's outside on the patio, so nobody sees the car but that's all right, I knock, and Mercy opens the door, simple white dress, off elegant shoulders that have the exact and right degree of definition and bone, the light behind glows through the dress and highlights the hair, some kind of natural but wet lipstick, all perfect and framed by the natural proscenium of the door.

"Oh, Tom," she says, "your hair looks great."

I suppose I should confess that I had, as the final touch on ensemble that night, smeared some soft gray goop into my locks, and had combed it back gently, as the tube advised, to get that slick but elegant wet look. This was the moment for decisive action, I had thought.

"Thanks," I say. "You're, you're dazzling tonight." In the Volvo on the way up to the house I had practiced being worldly and poetic all at the same time. Think Cruise meets Byron, I'd said to myself, Donne genetically grafted onto a Don Johnson carcass.

She takes me in and I sense heads turning, and she introduces me to some of her friends, and I nod at others I've met before. I can see Craig dancing in the next room. Everyone's sort of golden in the gentle light from lamps, and they're all standing around leaning on things, hands touching, arms curled comfortably around each other, drinking things from iced glasses. There's no sign of Mercy's parents. I talk to her for a few minutes and then the doorbell chimes again and she goes. I listen to the group she's left me with for a few minutes and they're talking about people I don't know. So then I clear my throat and say, "I guess I'll go get a drink." They all turn to look at me.

I get my drink, gin and tonic, and stand by the bar. The room stretches away from me and everywhere there's people talking to each other. Craig brushes past me, "Hey, Dude!" I look at the print on the wall, some kind of birds in flight thing, and then I look at the next one. I finish my drink and go back to the bar for another one. I read the spines of the books on a shelf in the hall. Then I go up the stairs and wait in line for the bathroom. The two girls ahead of me are both in pink dresses, and are talking about going away in the summer. I try desperately to think of something to say but then the bathroom door opens and they go in together. After I finish I head down the stairs cradling my glass, and I hear Mercy's voice from directly below me.

"Oh, but he *is* sweet," she says.

I feel my face flush and I want to wind up and throw the glass across the room to shatter at the wall, but suddenly I'm down the stairs, through them all and past the bar and into the foyer and out of the door. I never see Mercy, and then I'm in the car heading home.

In my room I realize I still have her glass. I put it down on my dresser and peer through the darkness at me in the mirror, at my hair and my new white jacket with zippers, pastel shirt, thin black belt, and I back away to get all of me in the mirror, trip over my two dumbbells on the floor and sit down with a jarring shock that races from my tailbone up into my head, and in that moment of real pain, as I look at the top of my head in the mirror, I understand exactly why I am trapped: it is my arrogance, my wiseass secondhand pitiful literary smarminess, my ambition that entangles me. So I get up and get her glass and walk into my bathroom and switch on the light. I open a new pack of Bics and shake them out onto the sink, so that they lie in untidy echelon on the porcelain. Then I take up a pair of scissors and start to clip off my hair. It comes off in tidy swathes and I lay them one by one in the glass. When I've finished cutting I squirt lather onto my scalp and set to work with the Bics. My skull comes up blue and bumpy and innocent. The razors scrape and resound through my head, and I cut myself often. When I've finished I mop up the lather with a white towel and sprinkle after-shave into my hands. It stings my flesh intolerably and starts the tears from my eyes.

So I take up the glass and go outside, onto the road. I start walking. It is dark, and I am looking for a body of water. This is a gesture I want, one which I do not understand completely myself, but by now I have accepted the necessity of gestures. I walk for a long time. Near morning I find a small pond in somebody's yard. There are trees around me, and trucks are whistling by on a highway. I lean over a fence and under-handed toss the glass into the water, and even the small splash it makes scares a covey of ducks into the air. Then I start walking back.

When I turn down the road to school, my thighs are aching and it is mid-morning. I walk in through the main gate, then into the halls. People turn and look at me, and by the time I reach the cafeteria a string of kids trails behind me. Inside, the buzz falters and dies down and then there is silence. Mercy, as usual, is sitting in the middle and to the back. She is eating a sandwich, it's in her hand and there is a plate in front of her, her body is turned sideways and her back is straight, and there are people around her on the benches and at her feet are two of her acolytes, lacing up football boots. I walk up and slide onto the chair in front of her, and then say, in a very clear and proud voice, "I love you, Mercy Fuller Cunningham." Then I lean over and put my head in her plate.

When I straighten up she is looking at me, the sandwich still in the air, and in her eyes there is not love, not pity, not horror, not repulsion, not abhorrence — forgive the Jamesian flight, but it is appropriate —

not loathing, not contempt, not scorn, not derision, not ridicule, not jeers, not sarcasm, not concern, not empathy, not pain, not pleasure, not humor, not sympathy, not disappointment, not discouragement, not dismay, not disillusionment, not despondency, not dissatisfaction, not shock, not alarm, not fear, not anxiety, not dread, not anything but this and only this: embarrassment. And so, then, I am free.

So she gets up and rushes out, followed by her friends. I sit there. Leaning over has stretched my skin and opened up some of the cuts on my head, and so I sit there smiling, blood and mayonnaise dripping off my face. Then Ling and Sarah come rushing in and take me home.

So what else is left to tell? My parents were called in to talk to my teachers, and I spent a lot of my evenings getting counseled by their professional friends. I didn't need the counseling but it made them feel better, and I guess I got a sort of quick lab course in The Problems and Questions of Modern Psychiatric Science. Schoolwise I struggled to catch up and Mrs. Christiansen gave me back my gnarly term paper on *Ethan Brand* with what I think was an overly kind B+. My grades that last semester weren't so hot but Pomona had already accepted me and I didn't screw up really badly enough for them to go through the hassle of canning me at that late date. Sarah and I went to the senior prom together and slow-danced defiantly to each and every song. And the last time I saw Mercy Fuller Cunningham was at the end of the summer when Ling and I were doing our ritual good-bye to the video store at the mall. We wanted to do one last huge bad movie marathon, so here we are stacking up *Frantic* and *Conan the Barbarian* and *Barbarella,* and I have just had the incredible good luck to stumble on *Genghis Khan,* with John Wayne as Genghis, when Mercy walks in with some guy. Now at this point I haven't really seen her for a while, because I've been allowed to skip AP English. I guess they figured I might start attacking her or reciting sonnets at her, so they played it safe. So now Mercy freezes between DRAMA and HORROR, her mouth opens and closes a couple of times, and then I say, totally cool and nearly suave, "Looking for a movie, Mercy?"

"Yes," she says.

So I pick up a movie at random from my side of the aisle and hand it to her, and say, "Here, try this."

She takes it and looks even more uncomfortable, and the guy, who is handsome, I have to admit, who I haven't ever seen before, is starting to suss out that some weird vibrations are clanging about his head, and I can see he's trying to decide whether he should be bitterly funny or violently hostile, so I say, "Have fun. See you later."

Ling and I stroll off through the check-out gate and when we're outside in the mall she turns to me.

"Did you see what you gave her?" she says.

"No."

"The old *King Kong*."

We both start laughing even though it isn't that good, but we crack up and get caught by it until we start staggering from side to side, disrupting traffic and so on, and the security guys start to loom toward us, so we sit on a circular bench and hold our stomachs. I stop before she does, and I sit and watch her unhook her glasses from behind her ears and carefully wipe her eyes with a folded white handkerchief. All around us there is the glint of glass, polished stone, anonymous hordes of teenagers, concrete, I can feel a cold draft on the back of my neck. I see very clearly the thickness of her hair, the wideness of her cheek-bones and the small nose, the fold at her eyes. I ask: "Ling, how do you deal with all this shit?"

She shrugs, looking, without her glasses, more gentle than I have ever seen her. "Draw water, cut wood."

I have fallen in love again, after that, not once but more than once. I have, but now I've also learned the necessity of rakish irony. I cradle breasts in my hand, and tip them to my lips, but I do it with a certain dashing expertise. I've learned that what we know, and what we tell each other, and what we think we must believe doesn't make one damn bit of difference to anything. So I forgive people, or perhaps I pardon myself. When I hear, "Attempted Robbery at Kroger's," I forgive. I read, "Father Kills Son and then Self," I shudder and forgive. I forgive "Mother of Three in Death Pact, Councilman on Embezzlement Charges." When they, all of us, move in inadvertent weekend caravans across the country, wagon-training to there to get away from here, I forgive, when they roar past me in their Transam with its firebird on the hood, tires tearing the road, eyes fixed eternally on the horizon.

When I awoke, the Jaguar was squeezed between a pick-up truck and a large black motorcycle, in front of a low white building. I pulled myself out of the car and leaned against it, trying to work my muscles out of their night-long cramp. Tom was sitting on a low wall that ran round the parking lot, his knees drawn up, pulling on a cigarette.

"Oy, Majnoon," I called.

He turned toward me, the smoking hand in front of his face. "What the fuck?"

"Majnoon," I said, feeling embarrassed. The building hid us in deep shadow, but I could feel the heat from the sunlight a few feet away. "Majnoon. He was a Great Lover. Literally means 'mad.'"

"What the fuck?" But behind the hand he was smiling a little now.

Amanda came toward us, shielding her eyes. "Come on," she said.

I slammed a door on the Jaguar and we fell in behind her. In her right hand she held a wallet and in her left two keys on huge brass tags. Tom raised an eyebrow at me. The motel was laid in two half-circles, with a ragged lawn in between. We walked across the grass, and then Amanda stopped in front of a door marked "8" and tossed a key at Tom.

"See you later," she said to Tom, taking my hand.

"Bye, Majnoon," I said. He smiled.

Amanda and I walked down the row to nine. Inside, I went into the shower first, came out in a towel and lay on the bed, waiting for Amanda. By the time she slipped in beside me, close, her back against my chest and hair wet on my face, I had already gone in and out of a dream. She took my hand and pulled it around, laying it on her chest, over her heart, and held it there. We lay like that for a time and then we were asleep.

I awoke out of another dream, of what I do not remember, and we were already making love. I tugged off her T-shirt and she reached down and found me, then guided me into her, we moved frantically against each other, her nails in my shoulder and small exhalations at my ear. When we finished I rolled over and she moved with me, her knees still tight and hurting against my sides, we lay like that for a long time, and then like a knot coming apart we relaxed against each other. Still, there was a pulse in my chest that beat and raced painfully, and I looked about the room in the darkness, trying to remember where I was. We kissed now slowly and I rubbed her back, moving the muscles gently under my fingers, and she said, "Oh, that feels good." Finally we slept again and I didn't dream.

In the morning I sat outside on the steps, drinking Coke out of a red can. The sky turned colors over the buildings, and far down the street a lone woman in red, yellow hair, tottered over the sidewalks in high heels. Coming home, I thought, going home.

. . . now . . .

WE HAD A CHILDBIRTH during the story-telling last night. It is said that a woman, not even a listener, but a hugely-overdue passer-by on her way home from the hospital, paused to listen to the distant echo from the other end of the maidan, which at that distance was comprehensible only in part, and felt suddenly the twinging onset of labour. She was taken back to the hospital, where she gave birth to healthy triplets, three girls. Of course this woman's name is not known, nor the name of the hospital she was taken to, but everybody has an uncle who knows somebody who knows the family. Now the whole town is said to be ringing with this news, and tomorrow we are expecting expecting mothers from all over the district, and soon our maidan will be filled to overflowing with fecundity.

Meanwhile I have seen translations being sold, or rather re-tellings of our stories in other languages, written by hand and copied on cheap coloured paper by indigent clerks and retired bureaucrats. This money-making scheme bothers me not at all, but Abhay seemed to be a little upset by the extrapolations and additions that these re-tellers have sprinkled throughout the text, and he muttered darkly about copyright laws.

'There are whole new stories in here,' he said. 'It's not even our story anymore, what these fellows are peddling.'

'It ceased to be yours the minute you wrote it,' I suggested, and earned a glare for my trouble. We were watching the crowd come in, bigger than before, and I thought, is this profusion a burden or gift? This size?

Ashok came in through the door, bringing a stack of newspapers. 'We're in all the local papers,' he said. 'And I hear the police are concerned. It's a gathering without permission.'

'Spontaneous expression of inventiveness,' Abhay said. 'Surely there's no law against that.'

'Surely there is,' Ashok said.

'Quiet,' Yama said. 'It's time.'

Janvi Defends
Her Honour.

AS SIKANDER GREW UP, his father, whose name was Hercules, applied himself secretly to the task of saving the natives of Hindustan from the eternal damnation that he knew was their fate, his efforts manifesting themselves mainly as succour, hospitality and aid to the missionaries who passed through Barrackpore, disguised as Calcutta traders or scholars. The Company, wary of the unrest that was believed would result from proselytizing, of the disruption of profit-making activity that would result from offence to native sentiment, had banned all missionaries from Hindustan, and so Sikander, Chotta and Sanjay, intent on their games of hide-and-seek, often bumped into thin, pale, men who gave off a sour smell consisting equally of anger and pride as they fingered a strange idol consisting of a bleeding man nailed to two pieces of wood arranged crosswise. Sometimes, seeing the boys scampering about the house, one of Hercules' guests would bark exasperatedly at them in an incomprehensible tongue, and then the children would run to the safety of the garden across the wall, to the refuge of Ram Mohan's domain, where he would seat them around an old couch and relate some familiar story featuring comedic demons, poor Brahmins, and selfless, gentle heroes; sometimes, Chotta and Sikander's mother would appear over the wall, climbing through a well-worn depression in the stone. Although Hercules was barely cordial to Sanjay's father in court, and scarcely bothered to hide his contempt for Indian poets in general, he allowed his wife and sons this one contact with natives, as long as it was kept strictly unofficial, and was conducted only through the back gardens, over the wall.

So Sikander's mother would come, and take over the story-telling, and then, invariably, the tales became more robust, full of Rajput warriors exhibiting casual, towering bravery and matter-of-course chivalry. She and Ram Mohan alternated tales, smiling at each other: first, 'Once there was a poor Brahmin student who fell in love with a beautiful princess . . . ," and then, 'Once Rana Sanga, of the eighty-eight wounds, captured a Moghul noblewoman . . .'; in the late afternoon, Sanjay's father would appear, hot and sweaty, trailed by his mother, and they would seat Sanjay between them while the father recited a racy ballad composed for the Raja, 'There was once a courtesan of Lucknow / Who saw a soldier stringing his bow . . .'

But once, once when Sanjay was old enough for his parents to be thinking about his upanayana, when his head reached his father's navel, once Chotta and he scrambled through Hercules' house, hiding from Sikander; they crawled along the side of a balcony, listening for the occasional sounds of their pursuer's feet, hearing, instead, a voice in the distance, speaking in the familiar but mostly unintelligible language of the firangis, yet managing to convey, in its frequent descent into distorted yawl and its sheer volume, an impression of the most intense anger and disgust. Sanjay listened carefully, understanding nothing. Every morning, Sikander and Chotta disappeared for an hour and a half, into the front half of the house, for what they referred to as 'Angrezi with Hercules' — their father seated them on two identical stools and drilled them in the strange sounds and usages of his native tongue. They both seemed to regard these daily encounters with their father as one of the unpleasant but unavoidable trials of life, and much to Sanjay's chagrin, refused to discuss their lessons, much less pass on their knowledge of English, saying, we had enough of that this morning.

Sanjay sat up, to listen better, and the voice went on: 'The people of India do not require our aid to furnish them with a rule for their conduct, or a standard for their property. Indian theology has as elevated a conception of God as in Christianity, and equally lofty ethical conceptions.' Chotta pulled frantically at his arm — from the room beside the balcony, there was the unmistakable, almost imperceptible padding (except to Chotta, who had the ears and all the senses of an alert animal) of stealthy feet, careful, deliberate. Sanjay looked around frantically, but the only door out of the balcony led straight into the arms of the stalker, and it seemed that their fate must be capture and disgrace, but suddenly Chotta scrambled behind Sanjay, scrambling, and in the next moment he dropped over the railing of the balcony, onto the narrow ledge outside. Sanjay followed, swinging a leg over the railing, and then he stopped, looking down at the drop, the stone cold between his legs, rough between his buttocks, his limbs powerless; Chotta pulled at his toe, and he took a deep breath and moved out onto the ledge, crawling on all fours behind Chotta along the narrow shelf of stone, moving towards the voice, which had now ascended into a higher register, propelled by rage: 'Any account of India's high civilization, and of the wonderful progress of its inhabitants in elegant arts and useful science must have some influence upon the behaviour of Europeans towards that people. We must realize that if civilization were ever to become an article of trade between the two countries, it is England which would greatly benefit by the import cargo'; Chotta and Sanjay rounded a corner, and now the speaker became visible: a tall man in a black coat, red-haired, teeth curiously narrow and protruding, white and freckled skin, now mottled with blood-dark splotches, struggling for breath, holding in his left hand a sheaf of yellow paper.

Hercules stood by his side, portly, head held tilted back in a habitual demonstration of sniffy pride, and seated around them, in wicker garden chairs, other black-coated men listened respectfully, brows wrinkled with concern and thought, their fingers steepled before their faces; the red-haired man took a deep breath, seeming almost ready to speak, and Sanjay caught hold of Chotta's dhoti, preventing him from crawling any further. 'And, finally, my friends,' the red-haired man said; 'the scoundrel says — and I almost lack the courage, the sheer gall to read this out before an assembly of God-fearing men — but he said, he said . . .'; he looked down at the paper, clenched his teeth, threw his head back and looked up to the sky, as if for help, then snapped back to the writing on the paper, licked his lips, and then spoke, eyes bulging: 'He says this. I quote: "The people of India are a sober, quiet and industrious race, and the propagation of Christianity is neither desirable nor practicable." '

Hercules and the other men raised a chorus of unbelieving and disgusted gasps, and above them Chotta tremored and turned, alert as a mongoose: Sikander swung around the corner, upright, eyes fixed on Sanjay and Chotta, feet falling easily and instinctively at the centre of the parapet, his body relaxed, a quick smile of triumph on his face, right arm outstretched to make the tag; Sanjay had turned to follow Chotta's glance, and now Chotta's legs pistoned against his back (the heads below were beginning to turn up), and as Sanjay pushed himself away from the eager-to-touch hand (he knew its bruising strength), he managed, even in the midst of that furious activity, to find a moment to envy Sikander's easy stance, his grace, to curse his own plump, ineffectual legs, to wish for strength instead of an early and wholly unprofitable skill at writing (at two he knew the alphabet, and at four and a half the pleasure of a couplet that fell into rhyme almost by itself), but then he abruptly became aware of the lack of anything under his behind, the ponderous, unceasing demands of gravity; there was an expression of bemused concentration on his face, an indication of what-is-this-nothingness-under-my-arse as he toppled over backwards, ankles sliding across the stone, the world turning upside-down, the things of the soil — its leaves, the blades of grass, the grain of mud, and something else, two bumps — getting bigger, a moment of light:

> Yama is a happy god. Ruins seed the ground, the harvest is tendrils that burst out of the soil, through the soles of our feet. They occupy us without our knowledge.
>
> Kites float in sluggish circles for thousands of years, alert for the faintest ribbon of dust below. Everything is the eater and the eaten, rocks throb, expand, contract, until they burst. Snakes abandon their below-surface treasures to husk off their skins under the sun, leaving the figures of former selves, fragile histories that begin to disintegrate as soon as they are formed.
>
> The passing of the powerful causes noise, but rain deadens even this sound. Rivers swell, and the bloated carcasses of lions bob up like children's toys, softened and ready for the surgeon-skill of the vulture. Monuments are silted over, windows are plugged with clay and ash, when the waters recede the farmers reap good crops.
>
> Above, those who cannot see the spirits are the dead. The gravity of the cold sometimes-glimpsed glow of the cities on the ocean's

floor, the hiss of the guardians, impels us. Even the deniers are driven: in each mouthful they ingest a hundred years, a million deaths. What is sacred cannot be history, but memory (the grimace of the monkey, the shark's yawn) is divine.

When Sanjay gained consciousness, there were two holes in his head, spaced evenly on his forehead above his eyes, and people began to tell him secrets; later, he decided that perhaps it was the fact that the holes somehow suggested an extra pair of eyes, that it was this that compelled confessions, or perhaps it was his constantly pained expression, which suggested a precocious wisdom (which, of course, meant piety, holiness) but actually resulted from a perpetual case of double-vision, of seeing everything twice. Perhaps it was also the manner in which he had been injured. When Ram Mohan told him that he had fallen onto Shiva's trident, he had wondered if his uncle was making some elaborate metaphor, but this was entirely and literally a fact: the injuries were from two metal points protruding from the ground; upon investigation, and excavation, what was revealed was first a trident with the middle prong snapped off at the root, and then the god himself, dancing. When Sanjay was alone, he wondered how long Shiva had hidden under the soil, his right hand raised: ten years, a hundred, a thousand? But now he had emerged, and the manner of his coming made Sanjay famous, as the boy who brought the god, and so there was a stream of visitors who came to sympathize and marvel at his survival, at his resistance to the twin assault on his brain.

The first visitor that Sanjay remembered, that he was conscious enough to recognize, was Hercules — this was the first time, in all the years Hercules had been a neighbour of the Parashers, that Sikander's father had deigned to visit the Brahmin household; and when he came, he arrived in the full glory of his uniform, resplendent in red and green, trailed by his two sons. Sanjay recalled, much later, the fastidious, finicky curve of the wrist with which Hercules flicked the tails of his coat out of the way as he sat gingerly in the only Angrez-style chair in the Parasher household, that and his arched-eyebrowed stare at the paintings on the wall and the colourful design on the bedspread. He looked also, long and carefully, at Sanjay's father, who flinched a little under the scrutiny but stood his ground, standing at the foot of the small bed,

unwilling to leave his son with the soldier, but finally Hercules leaned
down to Sikander, who whispered to Arun, and the three — Arun and
Sikander and Chotta — backed out of the room. As they left, Hercules
spoke a few words in broken Urdu, stumbling over the consonants often enough to bring a slight twitch of amusement to Arun's face, at
which Hercules resolutely turned to English, speaking perhaps just a
little louder than necessary. Hearing the sounds of English, Sanjay tried
to raise his head, fighting off the nausea that resulted from the duplication of the world in his head, from the doubling — presently of
Hercules — that would plague him for much of his life.

'My sons were undoubtedly involved in the inception of your present condition, my boy,' Hercules was saying; he leaned forward and
clasped Sanjay's hand, 'but one might state with some certainty that it
was also your unhappy country which assaulted you, since it was one of
those old, false gods who have oppressed and humiliated your simple
people since time immemorial who thrust his way out of the soil to
thrust his weapon into your brow.'

'Wait a minute,' one of the sadhus said. 'Wait just a minute here.'

'You have a doubt?' Sandeep said.

'I do, I do. We can assume with certainty that at this point in his
development Sanjay doesn't speak English, no?'

'We don't have to assume. I asked my story-teller in the forest the
same question, and she said that Sanjay knew no English.'

'Then how is it that he seems to know what Hercules is saying? Why
is it that *we* hear what Hercules is saying?'

'Because Sanjay hears it.'

'But you just said . . .'

'Sanjay hears it, and it is his blessing, or power, that even though he
doesn't understand what is being said, he hears each word, each sound,
as a crystal-clear, separate entity. You might say that he is cursed with
the inability to hear noise, that he is gifted with the ability, or, rather,
the imperative task, of really listening to language. So when he heard
Hercules speak, he heard not the confused jumble of clatter that most of
us hear when we listen to a foreign tongue, but a set of distinct, polished, complete objects, devoid of meaning but possessed of inherent
completeness or beauty, and so, later, he was able to remember these

things, or words. On learning the meanings attached to these symbols, years later, he was able, then, to discern what Hercules had said that afternoon, or what he had said apart from what he had uttered.'

'That's all very well, but a little too clever, if you ask me,' the sadhu grumbled. 'But I suppose we must give our story-tellers a little room to work in.'

'Clever is hardly the word I'd use,' Sandeep said. 'It is structurally necessary — if Sikander is the brave, and Chotta can drink poison, then it is necessary that Sanjay be able to listen to language.'

'It is?' said the sadhu. 'To me it makes no sense.'

'Listen,' Sandeep said. 'In fact there is even more to Sanjay, because he knows what he has never been taught . . .'

'That's completely acceptable,' the sadhu said. 'We all know about Mozart and his symphonies at four and a half, but this other stuff, you know . . .'

'Can we get back to the story?' another sadhu said, a young man with the nervous habit of tapping the sole of his foot with a bent fore-finger. 'I want to know what Hercules wants.'

'All right, all right,' Sandeep said. 'Listen . . .

'One might state with some certainty that it was also your unhappy country which assaulted you, since it was one of those old gods who have oppressed and humiliated your simple people since time imme-morial who thrust his way out of the soil to aim his broken trident at your brow,' Hercules said. 'Ah, boy, it is a pity that you cannot under-stand, yet, the manner in which your accident may be an act of provi-dence, in that your story, in Reverend Sarthey's capable hands, will be an instrument, a persuasive balm, which will bring about an agreeable effect on the Christians of Europe, loosening purse strings and setting in motion political action designed to rectify the Company's unfortu-nate policies towards the great work of bringing the Word to your coun-trymen. The good reverend will take that horrifying demonic effigy, with its serpent necklace and tiger-cloth and cavorting pose, and will travel with it throughout England, from village to little town, exhibiting the depths of degradation that characterizes the so-called theology of the Hindoo, that collection of libertinism, oppression, superstition and folly that masquerades as a religion; he will tell your story, pointing to you as a symbol, and so you must not despair. Your suffering has a purpose, a meaning — through your injury you have exposed the rot that hides below the surface of what is called civilization here, the demons that live just below a patina of effete conversation and decadent arts. You are chosen. Rejoice.'

Abruptly, Hercules snapped out of his chair, and left the room (when he drew back the curtain at the door, the light filled Sanjay's head with painful, luminous circles); Sanjay let his head loll back, exhausted, and listened to the voices outside — Hercules', Sikander's, his father's — listened, frustrated by the distance and the intervening, muffling cloth, but still catching some of the guarded tension of the conversation in the voices, by the rhythms and the pitch. He shut his eyes to listen better, and sensed, further away, the presence of his mother (shuffling steps, nasal and slightly-liquid breathing), his uncle Ram Mohan (a click of bone against bone at a joint, frequent swallowing), and Sikander's mother (something almost unheard; what was it?); they entered through the door which led deeper into the house, huddling together, pushing aside the red curtain.

'Has he gone?' Sikander's mother whispered. 'Has he?'

'I can hear him outside,' Ram Mohan said.

'What did he want with you?' Sanjay's mother said to him, running a palm over his cheek. He squinted, trying to fuse the two parallel images of her, and tears rolled slowly down her cheeks. 'Oh, child. Oh, child.'

Sanjay grunted, a ball of muscle moving up and down his throat, trying to bring the words up, and he could see the words, the forms they would take, and feel them, the emotional weight each would carry, but for all the gasping concentration he could bring to bear on it, his tongue flopped about his mouth, reptilian and trapped, uncontrollable. He gathered himself and tried again — the others watched, mournful but encouraging — and drool ran down his chin. He swallowed (Ram Mohan reached forward to wipe), compressed his lips, focussed every last iota of his being at the front of his face (lips and nose, eyes and chin), then released, and one word emerged: 'Mmmmm-Mah.' His mother, kneeling beside the bed, let her head droop until it was leaning on his chest and wept, her shoulders shaking (but above, the other image hovers, miming her), and then Sanjay's father entered, followed by Sikander and Chotta.

'He wants me to give him the Vedas,' Arun said, flinging his hands about. 'That's what he really came for, the Vedas and the Geeta.'

'What do you mean, give him the Vedas?' Ram Mohan said. 'How can you just give anybody the Vedas?'

'That's what he said. There's a man staying in his house, some Englishman with red hair, some Sartha or Partha or something like that . . .'

'Sarthi,' Janvi said.

'That's the one,' Arun said. 'And he's supposed to be a scholar or teacher or something, isn't that what he said, Sikander?'

'That's right, Uncle,' Sikander said. 'He told me to translate. And he said that Sarthi was a scholar who wanted to study the Vedas — only he called them the Beds — so Uncle here should give them to him.'

'Don't you give anything to him,' Janvi said.

'But how?' Arun said. 'Oh, he came very politely, in sympathy with our child and all that, and when he spoke to me it was a request all right, but he knew and I knew that I was expected to give them what he wanted. "If you would be kind enough to supply my friend with the necessary . . . ," he said; no, Sikander? And how he looked at me. Standing with legs apart in my house as if he knew who was really master. How will we say no?'

'The Vedas are for the twice-born,' Janvi said. 'They are not twice-born.'

'In truth whoever has the power to take the Vedas takes them, never mind twice-born or thrice,' Arun said.

'Power has nothing to do with it,' Janvi said, her voice rising. 'You say no to them.'

'The powerful are the twice-born,' Ram Mohan said, very softly, 'and the powerful take everything.' Janvi glanced at him, startled, and then lowered her head.

'They are very powerful now,' Arun said. 'For everything, the Raja looks to him. Their agents, the men of the Company, control every article of trade that we send out, every commodity that comes in. On everything they have a monopoly. And so the Raja looks to him. And this man comes now to my house, and tells me he wants the Vedas, that he needs the Geeta, that I must give it to him. Will he listen to you?'

'No,' Janvi said. 'And I would say nothing to him.'

'Then we must find something to give him.'

'He already has my daughters. And he wants my sons. How much must we give him?'

'The question is how much taking he can be satisfied with,' Arun said. 'I don't know what to do.'

'Our son is like this, and he comes to our house demanding things,' Shanti Devi said. 'What kind of man is this?'

Sanjay had been concentrating his strength again, and this time he managed two whole, difficult syllables: 'Ve-dah . . . Ve-dah . . .'; he wanted to advise them to effect an exchange — the sacred books (if they must be given) for the sacred books of the firangi, one language for the other, secret for secret, a dialogue, but his injuries — raw, leaking — stifled the suggestion, and so what emerged was mistaken for a precocious desire for theological learning.

'I'll teach you,' Ram Mohan said. 'I'll teach you everything.'

'You'll teach him everything,' Arun said. 'Yes, in this room, among the women, everything is fine, but out there, in the court, he will be on my back. What will I do? I'll have to give him what he wants. And I don't even know where to get a copy of any of the Vedas.'

'Fight him,' Janvi said.

'How?'

'Oh, make something up, can't you?' Shanti Devi said, wiping her face with the end of her sari. 'You're good at that.'

'Tell him we've sent for it,' Ram Mohan said.

'Yes, I'll tell him that,' Arun said. 'But finally we'll have to give him something, at least something.'

'I remember,' Ram Mohan said. 'I can recite most of it, some of it, at least something.'

'You can?'

'I learned it from my father, and it was the one thing I could do well.'

'So you'll recite. Who'll write down?'

At this Sanjay let forth an incensed growl, and thrashed his limbs about on the bed; the others watched him, a little frightened, till Ram Mohan clapped a hand to his mouth and said, 'Of course, child, of course, you will write down. Who else but you?' He turned to the others. 'Who else? He has known how to write without being taught, and Sanskrit without a single lesson. How and why, we used to ask, and perhaps it was only for this. I will recite and he will write down.'

And so Sanjay wrote it down, but before that could happen, there was the matter of his initiation, because of course the Veda could be studied only by one twice-born; so even before he could get up from the bed his head was shaved, and Sikander and Chotta carried his cot about the court-yard, where he ritually begged alms from assembled Brahmins and relatives, and then he was wrapped in a deer-skin, enclosed in heat, darkness.

At first he lay quiet, rather enjoying the soft, finely-grained texture of the skin, but soon he noticed a faint luminosity skipping in and out of sight, dancing at the edges of vision; he turned his head slightly and it disappeared, only to re-form at the other periphery. This time, he carefully avoided looking at it directly, and soon it resolved itself, the borders shifting and hardening until he could make out the shape of a gigantic fish, its size signalled by the lazy back and forth of its body and slow movements; it seemed to be drawing closer, and he felt the beginnings of panic when suddenly its contours fell in on themselves, closing and expanding, and then it was a boar, white, bristly and pawing, and now Sanjay fought to get the hide off his head, coming out sputtering, scrambling, into the harsh sunlight which he welcomed even as his eyes teared, his relatives gathering round, Ram Mohan clucking, running his hand over the smooth bald skin, touching even the thin pearly membrane on Sanjay's forehead, soothing with a delicate touch.

When he calmed, Ram Mohan carried him to the sacred fire, cradling him against a chest loosened by age, and hurried the priests through the ceremony, finally dropping the seven-stranded loop over his neck and under a shoulder (the Brahmins chanting), saying, 'Now you enter this world, now the world is yours,' and Sanjay started at a sudden sputtering blaze of the fire caused by the ghee dropping from the priests' fingers; through the momentary sparks and the heat-warped air, he saw Chotta and Sikander, faces rapt, sweating slightly, fixed on the flame, on the crumbling of the wood, the complex evolving patterns of ember and blaze (like quick cities seen from afar), calculating, it seemed, the possibilities of demolition by fire: What do the gods eat? What is lost? What is purified?

> *He shines forth at dawn like the sunlight,*
> *transmuting the sacrifice in the manner of priests*
> *unfolding their meditations.*

Agni, the God who knows well all the generations, visits
the Gods as a messenger, most efficacious.

With this verse, Ram Mohan began his dictation of the Vedas, at first checking Sanjay's transcription often, but finding, with no little satisfaction, that his scribe demonstrated preternatural accuracy, he concentrated on recalling what he could of the scriptures, scraps from the Rig and the Yajur, fragments from the Sama, a sloka or two from the Katha Upanishad; a word or a phrase from the Vedas would remind him of a verse by Kalidasa, and so, more for the edification of his nephew than the benefit of the Englishman, he would recite a couplet or two about sweeping rain and the elephant-walk of the beloved.

Sanjay, head bent over the palm-leaf, flicking the wrist on his pen-hand, invented elaborate flourishes and ritualistic reachings for ink, curlicued stylistic embellishments to the characters, all to gain time for the faintest chance for reflection, of comprehension: Yajnavalkya? Svetaketu? Who were these young men? Nachiketas? But there was barely time to put down one line before Ram Mohan was ready with the next (with a smile of satisfaction), and at the end of the morning, Sikander and Chotta would appear to hover impatiently, tiring quickly of the verbiage.

The session's work, however, was not officially over until Sanjay's and Sikander's mothers appeared, bringing paan, attar, and other refreshments; then the boys escaped, the brothers supporting Sanjay between them as he tottered along, his balance still shaky, his progress (when alone) often impeded by his tendency to bump into things — in deciphering his double-world, he often made mistakes about placing the phantom image, about deciding what was real and what was not. In their games, he was usually the rich merchant, and they the robbers, or he the powerful but stationary king, and they the dashing cavalrymen; it was on one of these afternoons, the afternoon after Sanjay had transcribed the story of Nachiketas, that he was set to be the guard at a treasury, while they played the adventurers questing for the key. He sat under a tree, in the grove some distance from their homes, next to a nullah where animals knelt and scraped at the dry bed for water; he sat on a mound — which represented the entrance to the underground passage-way, walls encrusted with precious jewels, naga-kings hissing — wishing that his double-vision rendered, as a compensation, widened perspective, instead of two versions of the same visual event placed side-by-side. An ability to see both coming and going, forward and back, would have proved a vital asset in the games with Sikander and Chotta, who moved slowly and silently, floating over the crisp leaves and brittle branches of summer, appearing suddenly to aim a blow at the back of Sanjay's neck ('Oy, Sanjay, are you deaf as well as cross-eyed?' 'You'd never make a sentry at my father's regiment, buttons-instead-of-eyes!').

Sanjay started then, because Sikander and Chotta appeared, unexpectedly, where he could see them; noiseless, as usual, but undoubtedly, plainly visible when a good ten feet off. Sanjay rose to his knees, hands signalling I-see-you, but the others covered the intervening ground in a quick-flash instant (how do they do that?), thrust a forearm each under his shoulders, and lifted him off the ground, into the bushes. He started to struggle, but a warning, painful pinch stilled him, just in time to hear a steady shuffling through the trees, a familiar rhythm to it, attempted stealthiness with an unmistakable clumsiness underneath; a gait is like a man or a woman's script — attempts at masquerade fail because the disguise is usually so exaggerated, and who can hide that arrogance, that assumption of strength that demands of things to move aside when the foot is put down, that assumes all roads will be smoothened? — it was, of course, Hercules. But Hercules was skulking now, his furtiveness emphasized by his obvious eagerness, by the haste with which he angled through the bushes. He passed the boys by, and Sanjay saw Sikander and Chotta look curiously at each other, clearly puzzled by the jackal-in-the-bush demeanour of their father. Without a word, a decision was made — they pulled Sanjay to his feet, placed him between them, behind Sikander and in front of Chotta, and began to follow Hercules.

Sanjay had, for as long as he could remember, understood that Sikander and Chotta had somehow learnt the techniques of being invisible (or had they been born with the skill?), but on this day he watched them exercise their art — they placed their feet wide-toed and ball first, quickly and surely, but without suddenness, so that a dry leaf, instead of cracking and crackling, only moved and bent, and obligingly bore the weight. Sometimes Sikander and Chotta seemed to delight in following their quarry so closely that it seemed impossible that he not see them — and he did look back, often, with the quick uptilted nose of a sniffing feline — but when it seemed that he must see them, they froze, and were somehow camouflaged by the shadow and sunlight, the golden grass and earth. Sikander's right hand, held behind him and below the waist, signalled stops and starts, safety and urgency; they passed from a maidan to a cluster of huts, and here Hercules straightened up, pulled at his lapels, extracted a kerchief and wrapped it, brigand-fashion, around his face, and resumed his usual, stately walk; now Sikander and Chotta modified their strategy — they strolled along, keeping Hercules barely in sight, stopping to look at fruit baskets and chat-seller's wares.

Sanjay realized, with a quick rush of excitement at having penetrated a forbidden zone, that they were in a settlement of low-caste people; he looked about himself with the eager curiosity of a foreigner, half-expecting and wanting to be shocked, but all around them were the business and affairs of ordinary, familiar life — food, chores, children, animals, the washing of clothes, and perhaps the only extraordinary thing was a difference in the tie of a turban, or a particular way of wearing a dhoti. The presence of three unknown boys seemed to provoke no hostility, but rather a blank, level stare that said precisely nothing; Sanjay was beginning to be disappointed that nothing more strange had happened when Hercules turned left down a lane. The boys turned the corner just in time to see him ducking into a door, and tugging aside a ragged red curtain hanging over the lintel; there were some children playing by the open drain that ran along the side of the lane, pulling a little wooden cart to and fro.

'If we could get up on the roof,' Chotta said.

'Right,' Sikander said.

Sanjay pawed at Sikander's arm, shaking his head, but the two brothers were already stepping down the lane, jumping over the cart as it rattled along; they edged over close to the hut, stood with their backs to it, watching the game, and the moment no eyes were turned their way, they dashed off to the rear, pulling Sanjay along. Behind the hut, a cow raised its head to look at them, then swung back down to its feed; Sikander and Chotta found a chink in the mud wall, wedged their feet into it, and pulled themselves up to the thatch above. They reached down for Sanjay.

'Come,' Sikander said.

Sanjay shook his head.

'Come on, pumpkin-head,' Chotta whispered. 'You won't break again.'

'Come on, Sanju,' Sikander said. 'I'll hold on to you this time.'

Sanjay turned away, pulse quickened; the cow watched, its mouth moving.

'Sanju,' Sikander said, 'don't you want to *know*?'

He lifted both hands up to them, and they pulled him up effortlessly (he felt his feet leave the ground, ankles extend); they worked their way around the edge of the sloping roof, and Sanjay resolutely turned his face to the comfortable, musty smell of the thatch, and clamped a grip on Sikander's kurta.

'Here,' Sikander said, moving aside handfuls of coarse straw, and Sanjay reached in beside him, glad to be doing something. 'Quietly, quietly.' The stuff came away in easy tufts, slightly moist, and then they were through: a small ragged hole, an obscuring beam, and, beyond, very white in the grey interior light (outside, the sun blazed), at first an unnameable moving construction, a twisting rectangular patch and two spheres, speckled, then the image twisted on itself, resolved (altitude is dizzying), and became a back ridged by shoulder blades, and below, two contracting and expanding buttocks, a quick moment of vertigo, a strong dislocation, longing, longing, it can crush your bones, and below, Hercules moved faster (ragged rhythm) between the dark splayed thighs, and above his right shoulder a dark face, a woman, heavy face, passive, impassive, eyes marking the colourful figures on the shelf, the icons, images, then turning slightly to look at an empty corner (only dust floating like stars), time passed, time, and Hercules grunted, his fingers in her hair, pulling, twisting her face to his (her lip drawing back, pain), grunted again, long rattling sigh.

Sanjay turned his head toward Chotta, then Sikander, but found that he couldn't bear to look at them, and so his memory of that moment was always a confusion of straw, the base of a neck, hands, perhaps eyes; he looked back down at Hercules, who had rolled to a corner of the mat and was lying on his side, silent, his chest heaving. Around his belly a single shiny streak of wetness dripped to the ground; the woman moved — density, darkness between her thighs — and began to pull a piece of cloth about her.

'When I was very young,' Hercules said, then stopped, reaching forward to rest a palm, flat, on the smooth mud wall. The woman moved
about the room, paying no attention, tucking away strands of hair,
bending to move a pair of boots into a corner. 'When I was very young,'
Hercules began again, 'the only nightmare I remember from my childhood was this — I dreamt that I was walking through a street paved
with stones, flanked by white houses, when the grey sky opened up like
a funnel, sucked me up. The ground vanished from beneath my feet,
and I plummeted upwards, limp, terrified. In a moment it enfolded me,
sky stifling like a shroud, I was scattered, vanished, gone, not capable
then even of being scared. But then I awoke, shaking. Later that
morning — I must have been no more than nine or ten — my father,
my mother and I, with my other sisters, walked to our church. All was
well — there was not a cloud, I could hear birds, my brothers ran about
despite my mother's entreaties — but even then I was frightened. They
asked me what it was, but what child of nine could tell about what I had
felt, so I shook my head, went along, trying to keep between my parents. In the church, I clutched the wood of the pew, and tried to pull my
legs up onto the seat. My father reached around my mother and tapped
me sharply on the back of the head; when the tears cleared I found my
eyes fixed on the image of Christ: a simple representation in dark wood,
a certain heaviness about the figure, as if the agony dragged, pulled. I
wiped, snuffling, then looked closer. His muscles bulged. I followed the
strained curve of the arm to the taut tendons in the wrist, and then to
the nail, piercing straight and perpendicular through the flesh. I tried to
follow the line of the metal, through the flesh and into the wood, and I
saw how firmly fixed He was, how pinned. I wept with relief, and my
parents looked on me proudly, thinking that the sermon had moved me.
I knew I had been told something then, as firmly as if He had spoken to
me, moving his wooden lips: the mark of man is tragedy, and the world
must know this. I was nine, the years passed; I became a soldier, to take
the Word to the world. In this country there are many, most, who have
spent their lives without the Knowledge, so I have aided those who tell,
who speak. I have given them shelter, and food, and protection, and
tried to keep the memory of that hour alive, when I knew that He stood
between me and devastation. But comes now the hidden army of the
Other, the march of moments, the thousand things that are necessary,

that distract. All that must be done I do, I earn, I administer, I feed, I fight, but finally, in the pause, in reflection, I am brought to the comprehension that I have been consumed again, engulfed, the great task left undone. His Act is forgotten, that perfect culmination, everything stretches forever, behind and in front, like that endless, hideous pantheon. He died! Something changed! But weariness brings doubt, and then I come here, to be doubly devoured. Here, in this place, I am finally finished. Do you listen?'

Hercules sat up, and the woman glanced at him, then began to arrange the betel leaf and tobacco in her palm; he reached for a shirt, drew it over his shoulders, and stood, his thighs exposed between the tails. Sanjay watched him pulling on his clothes, still unsettled by the extreme sadness in Hercules' voice, so unlike his usual plummy confidence. Sanjay wanted to ask Sikander and Chotta what it was that Hercules had said, that had made his words so faint, what had compelled him to touch the wall as if testing its solidness, its physicality, but a glance on either side convinced him that it was wiser to wait: the two brothers were watching their father, below, with a concentration that seemed to reject the possibility of emotion, much less conversation. So Sanjay too watched Hercules as he dressed, straightened his hair, picked a few coins out of his purse to place on a mantelpiece built into the wall; Hercules left without a word to the woman, who sat chewing moodily on her paan — they seemed indifferent, now, to each other.

'Come on,' Sikander said. They dropped to the ground — this time not earning even a glance from the cow in the corner — came around the corner of the hut, and were halted by a rude phalanx of children.

'Who are they?' a small girl dragging the wooden cart said from the rear, rising up on her toes.

'What are these rich babas doing sulking behind our Amba's hut?'

'Stealing her cow.'

'Not even going out by the front door, like the others.'

The line pressed forward, and Sanjay stepped back, but Sikander and Chotta stood their ground, only moving a little closer to each other; Sikander seemed to be calm, almost dreamy, but Chotta was crouching, eager, hands held in front of his thighs, palms up.

'Why here, babas?'

'Motherfuckers,' Chotta said. 'Fuck your sisters too.'

'Enough,' Sikander said, but already there were three or four boys pushing through the press to get at Chotta, who for his part edged forward to meet them. The first of them had to step past Sikander, who reached out and put a hand on his shoulder. 'No,' Sikander said.

'Eh, don't you drop in the middle,' the boy said, moving his arm to brush Sikander off, and suddenly he flew through the air, landing jarringly on his buttocks in front of the little girl with the cart.

'I told you no, no?' Sikander said, smiling pleasantly. The others stopped, uncertain, as the boy picked himself up, eyes tearing, and then they all began to move forward in small jerks and starts, each waiting for another to lead the assault, cursing fervently in a kind of courage-building chant. Sikander moved his head in a funny rolling motion, and Sanjay, hearing the bones in his neck crackle, shivered.

'Oh, why are you fighting in the lane, you dirty children? Fighting outside my door, making bad noises. Go away. Go, run away, or I'll come after your heads with a rolling-pin.' It was the woman from inside, Hercules' woman; she stood at the door of her hut, hands on her hips, hair rolling over her shoulders, mouth red from the paan. 'And who are these? Why are you bothering these fine boys. Go away, leave them alone.'

'Are they your customers too, then, Amba?' a boy called from the rear, and at that she ran after them, swinging her arms, dealing out slaps and cuffs, and they scattered, laughing. Finally, she came back to them, huffing.

'Come inside,' she said. 'Wait for a while and the little oafs will go away. Then they won't bother you.'

Inside her hut, Sanjay tried resolutely not to look at the small puddle of light that gathered along the wall at the back, and concentrated instead on a minute inspection of the images of gods and goddesses that were arranged on the numerous ledges, crannies and shelves built into the walls.

'Are you lost? Why did you come here? Poor boys, this isn't a place for you. You are lost, aren't you?'

This was directed at Chotta, who was staring at her, lips puckered, eyes shining, as if he was about to burst into tears. She looked curiously at him for a moment or two, then Sikander turned to her.

'Yes, we're lost,' he said.

'How did it happen? Did you just pay no attention, and get lost in some game? Where do you live?'

'Char Bagh.'

'Ay, what a long way you've wandered. Don't these other two talk at all? I suppose they're scared. But don't be scared, this is a place you all would have found a way to, sooner or later. You three just got an early start all right. All of you from Char Bagh come here, no matter how high and mighty you act.' She laughed; the pink of the inside of her mouth was very bright against her dark skin, and again Sanjay felt his belly full of an incredible longing. 'They all come here, Brahmins and Rajputs and Company men. Here, touch-this-and-don't-touch-that and untouchability and your caste and my people and I-can't-eat-your-food is all forgotten; this is the place that the saints sang about, little men. Here, anybody can touch anybody else, nothing happens. When you are a little older, when you understand a little more, you too will come and touch, and maybe by then I will be an old woman, but remember me. Here you can forget the world, and be friends with every man. Do you see what I say? I have a friend, a little way down the lane, in a big house that she was brought to when she was just a child, but she remembers something from before, when she was home, far and far to the south; she sings it sometimes, and I ask her, What is this? What does it mean? Whose song is this? and she says, listen, sister, I don't know who wrote it, but it means this:

> *What could my mother be*
> *to yours? What kin is my father*
> *to yours anyway? And how*
> *did you and I meet ever?*
>
> *But in love*
>
> *our hearts have mingled*
> *like red earth and pouring rain.'*

She put her hands on her knees and leaned forward, raising her eyebrows. 'Do you understand, babies? That's what happens here.'

She smiled, exposing again the pink gums; Sanjay pulled at Sikander's arm: let's go.

'We have to go now,' Sikander said.

'Be careful.'

Outside, they stumbled through the streets, feet scraping through dust; Sanjay put up a forearm to shield his eyes from the light, squinting, and noticed, now, how many women sat in door-ways, clad only in petticoats, and how they looked bluntly at passers-by, sometimes calling out to them, 'Come, come to my house.' Now, he saw many smiling, oily men with flower-garlands around their wrists lounging between the shops, and other men who walked slowly through the lanes, stumbling a little, speaking in louder-than-necessary voices intended to project jocularity, fraternity, but Sanjay wondered at the underlying, unmistakable presence of fear and hope. He looked back at Chotta, who was dragging his feet, looking down at the ground; Sikander saw the glance, and looped an arm around both their shoulders.

'We're almost out,' he said.

Chotta's pout seemed to intensify, and Sanjay wanted to say, no, she said we'll be back, we'll come back like these others, like lost children, but instead he forced a smile, and they walked on.

In the dry nullah-bed, Sanjay's knees gave way, and he sat down, exhausted, on top of the curving channels carved by once-running water. He was covered with a film of cold perspiration, and once or twice he felt something hot and sticky rush up to the back of his throat. Sikander and Chotta squatted next to him, resigned to waiting; they scratched absently in the mud, making patterns, sometimes figures, mostly horses.

They heard the singing first, a high, cracked voice in a strange language, and then the man appeared — he was a tall man, a firangi, with pomaded, dirty white hair, a scar that stretched from his forehead across an empty eye-socket, a bottle in his hand; bits of blackened lace hung in little wisps off his blue coat. He stopped at the edge of the nullah, leaning down towards the boys.

'Ah, there you are,' he said in English. 'There you are, my little friends. I was thinking I had lost your trail. I introduce myself — I am Moulin, the would-be adventurer but most-times cook.' He paused to take a swig from his bottle. 'I shall climb down to you, boys. I shall, appropriately enough, descend into a sewer.' He slid down the side of the ravine, half-sitting, and then came up to them, weaving a little. 'What hostile little faces you have! But that is why I followed you, I saw you walking through the bazaar, and I thought, there are the three saddest boys I have ever seen. And what are they doing here? So I came after you, because, I, Moulin, am sad, too. I, gentlemen, am the saddest Frenchman you will ever see. But are you understanding anything I am saying?' He switched to rough Urdu: 'Do all you understanding English?'

Sikander and Chotta nodded, but Sanjay stared up apathetically, too drained to even shake his head.

'Then,' Moulin said, sitting down beside them, 'we will converse in English, my Urdu being but rudimentary, even after all these years.' He paused to devote his full attention to the bottle again, then wiped his mouth. 'Rudimentary Urdu. But how is it that you two speak English? And aren't frightened of me — I am, after all, that most fearsome of things, a white man. Doesn't your mother tell you, hush, baba, or the firangi will come and take away your little clay cart, and all your toys? And he'll take your father's land? And your mother's honour? No? Oh, you don't want to talk? No matter.'

He settled himself with some ceremony, spreading the tails of his coat around himself, like black wings. 'I will talk. I will advise you. How, then, about a story? I will tell you a story concerning myself, and something I did, with a friend, when I was younger. Like all good soldiers' stories, this one involves two cavalrymen, a beautiful woman, a good horse, a sword. In fact, even now I have this sword, look.' He pulled at his belt and slid it around till they saw a sword hilt, carved from white jade in the shape of a horse's head.

'Listen. Once, long ago, when I was young, almost as young as you, I met a man, a man named La Borgne, a Savoyard. In the rough-and-ready way of men meeting in a foreign land, I conceived an instant liking for him, and so I invited him to my home. At the time, my fortunes were good, I was a soldier serving a certain power (never mind which one; in the end they are all the same), my house was full of servants, and so I entertained my friend with a magnificent meal. He ate, and I watched and envied him the pleasure of discovering, for the first time, the delights of the Mughlai cuisine. After, he slept; his face relaxed, and I wondered at the look of peace on his face, for certainly he was a man free of dreams. I confess: after eating like that, I am susceptible to the chimeras that lurk within; my friends tell me that my eyes dart from side to side, my limbs twitch and sometimes I get up and wander under the top-heavy trees. So I watched him, and then, as he slept, I heard the quick rolling rattle of hooves, and far away, a party of horsemen cantered. La Borgne awoke, and we both watched the riders, and the setting sun; curious, I summoned my spies and sent them out after those far-away men.

'The same night, they returned, my seekers, one dressed as an old gipsy woman, another as a seller of perfumes. They told us — by this time La Borgne was privy to all my doings, for he was a fine young man — they told us that they had gone to the party's camp-fires, and had mixed with them, joking, advising them on the best wine and the most tender meats, and they had ascertained that the men, a varied bunch of Rajputs, Turks, Afghans, Sikhs, Marathas, Avadhi Brahmins, Bengalis, Kashmiris, Arabs, Germans, a lot of Germans, and a couple of English, were engaged in a quest, a search for a treasure which moved with the sun. And I said, how splendid, but my friend sneered.

'Nevertheless, the next morning, I pulled him out of bed, and we rode out and slipped up to their camp, taking advantage of the natural cover and the darkness. Just before the sun began to rise, the men arose and quickly moved into a circle. In the centre of this circle, they constructed a strange apparatus: a fire, above it a cooking pan full of water, and in the water a mirror, floating face up. As the lip of the sun appeared above the trees, the smoke from the fire curled above and around the pan, but then the mirror caught a ray and flashed it back, like an explosion, and we all moved our hands to our eyes.

'When I looked again, there was a woman standing in front of the fire, wrapped in smoke, a white sari, jet-black hair, and out of her mouth came a white horse, a horse of perfect proportions, and it pranced around the circle, raising its knees high, shaking its head from side to side, eyes rolling and flashing, screaming, and I was afraid. And then she asked each of the men in turn, do you want this horse, tell the truth, and each of them replied, yes, and she said, then you shall not have the treasure.

'She looked up at us, and she knew we were there, even though we were well-hidden, and she said, do you want this horse? and La Borgne stepped forward and said, no, kill it, and all the rest of us gasped with horror, because of all things that had ever lived it was too perfect to die. But she drew a sword — this one, this one with the white hilt in the shape of a horse's head — and the horse came to her, and she plunged it into his chest, in the place where two ridges of muscle sloped down into a valley. The horse threw its head back, then tumbled down, rear first, and the sword slipped from the yawning red wound, and all of us except La Borgne shouted in dismay. Then the woman said to him, you have the treasure, and she disappeared, and her sword clanged on the hard-packed earth.

'Now all the men cursed La Borgne, because he had caused the death of the horse for nothing, there was no treasure, and he laughed at them. They drew their swords, and I rushed them from the rear, and we fought them, over and around the corpse (even now beautiful!), and we killed them all. Then I said, I have helped you because you are my friend, but now I will fight you, because you have caused the death of the most perfect thing in the world. He laughed at me, and then I hated him; I ran at him, my point presented, but he parried easily and dealt me a great slashing blow across the forehead, taking my eye. I fell to the ground, and lay, my face in the horse's belly, crying with pain and anger, and I said, you have done all this for nothing. You fool, he sneered, you fool for thinking the treasure was gold, or this horse, or this sword, or the woman, and with this he threw the weapon to me. I had the treasure in the instant I spoke, he said, and walked away.

'I recovered from my wound, or at least it healed, and have had many other adventures. I have been rich, then powerful, then poor, and then rich again; finally, I am here. And while I was slowly climbing into the pit of poverty and old age, La Borgne was passing from victory to victory, always richer and more powerful, until he finally became de Boigne, the master of the Chiria Fauj. I thought of him often, or rather constantly, and each time I heard of another one of his triumphs, a sliver of pain shot up from my gut and transfixed my throat; if only I had realized, I would think, if only I had thought, I might have been the ruler of all Hindustan, if only. So, full of bitterness, I wandered about the country, from one bad situation to another worse, with no money to go home, and nothing to go home to, till finally the only employment I could find was as a cook for a procurer, a buyer and seller of half-castes, and it galled me, believe that it tasted bitter as rotted meat, but I never sold that sabre, I kept it with me always, although several coveted it and offered me sums of money.

'Today, a great noise ran through the bazaar, and groups of people hurried through the streets; children danced by, feinting at each other with wooden swords. What is it? I called, and they said, the great de

Boigne is passing by, he is sailing to Calcutta. So I put down my ladle and my spices and put on my best coat, strapped on the sabre, ran down the street to the river's edge, pushed through the throngs. After an hour, or maybe two, a group of boats floated down the waters, slowly, slowly, and I shaded my eyes from the sun, but the glare off the river dazzled and defeated me. So, I shouted, La Borgne, La Borgne, La Borgne, L-aaa Bo-ooooooo-rgne, and the people about me moved away, laughing, but I kept on; the people on the boat looked at me, and some shook their fists at me threateningly, be quiet, but then a man pushed aside the flaps of a canopy on the third boat, a tall man, a large, heavy man, and he levelled a glass at the banks. I jumped, waved, held up the sabre, L-aaa Bo-oooooo-rgne, and he put the glass down, Moulin, Moulin, is that you?

'Suddenly, I was happy, I ran down the bank, keeping up with the boat, and he shouted, Moulin, you were right, you were right, and his voice bounced off the water and echoed, I cannot dream, Moulin, I cannot dream, and even across the distance and the wrenching of my breath I could make out the sadness in him, the break in his voice; unable to run anymore, I stopped, and the boats began to quicken their pace around a slow curve, and he called to me again, for the last time — a tone of unbearable, shattering nostalgia — Moulin, Moulin, I am free, free.

'When I could get up, I came back into the town, sold everything I owned, not much, and with what I could get I bought half a dozen bottles of this miserable wine; French, it was, six bottles; now, I have only the last. When this is over, I shall be finished; the story is nearly over, gentlemen, and what is the moral? The meaning? I do not know, gentlemen; that you must calculate yourselves; but, you probably think, it is the story-teller's duty to give something, something at least. Very well, for my part, I will give you this sabre; I pass on to you, carefully and gratefully, my last illusion.'

Moulin pulled at a buckle, then arched his back to get the belt off; he threw it so it landed at Sikander's feet. Sikander bent, picked it up, ran a finger over the horse-head hilt, nodded at Moulin, whose face was now almost a caricature of sadness, with pouches below the eyes, drooping lips, tangled hair.

'Let's go,' Sikander said. Sanjay got to his feet, both hands pushing against his thighs, feeling like an old woman for doing so; as they walked towards the edge of the nullah, he quickened his pace, even though it hurt in the calves and knees, eager to be home, in the garden with the familiar chatter of his uncle, the friendly squabbling of his mother and father, the lofty story-telling of Sikander's mother. As they began to climb the bank, he heard Moulin again, the incomprehensible tongue of the foreigner:

'Come back, come back. In return, you must use it. Use it on me. Gentlemen, kill me. Dispatch.'

'Hurry,' Sikander said, but Sanjay couldn't help but turn to look — how can hope live in the same words as the most crushing despair? Seeing them continue their clambering, Moulin reached back and threw the bottle; it spun at them and hit the bank — they cringed away from it, expecting a shower of glass — but it stuck, head-first, at an impossible angle, in a patch of soft mud under an over-hang. At this Moulin howled like a dog, scrambled towards them on all fours, face distorted, then staggered up to his feet and ran at them; Sikander and Chotta went over the lip, then reached down for Sanjay. He reached up, placed fingers over a tuft of grass, pulled, feet feeling for a rest, other hand reaching up, Sikander's hand, then there was a rush of hot breath on the small of his back, a pressure around his chest, down, grass pulling out of earth, Moulin's face, eyes shining, pupils afloat in a lace-work of red, then a body flew overhead, wrapped around Moulin's head, and almost instantly, transmitted through Moulin's body, the shock as something else collided; they rolled down the slope, the world spinning, Moulin's clutch, an embrace, Chotta screaming, wordless, Sikander concentrated, single-minded, thoughtful, tufts and particles of mud, dead leaves spinning, flap of green cloth, thrashing, the panic of insufficient strength, then stillness.

Sanjay's right hand was under a knee, a body of unusual pressing weight that refused to budge; pushing against it with his other hand, he felt an inertia that was unquestionable, immutable, and then he realized what it meant. He felt his body cleave in the middle, letting something, his heart, his soul, drop into a vacuum; he looked up — Sikander sat cross-legged, his hands folded in his lap, fighting to control his breath, Chotta lay face-up, blinking, opening and closing his mouth, which was ringed with dark blood, and Moulin's face was pressed into the mud (which was darkening, a steady drip from somewhere), his back to the sky, hands turned at the wrist and palms upwards, one foot pointed in and the other out: he was quite dead.

'Come on,' Sikander said, tapping Chotta on the head; they pulled Sanjay's arm from under the body, and hoisted him up, between them, over the bank. 'Wipe your face.' Chotta rubbed at the stain while Sikander bent and picked up the sabre; without waiting for them, Sanjay began to walk towards the trees. Sikander caught up with him and put an arm over his shoulder. 'We mustn't tell anyone. Understand. No one at all. Mustn't tell anyone.' Sanjay nodded, feeling the weight of his friend's arm on the back of his neck, struggling against the urge to cry; in the grove of trees, they stopped to wrap the weapon in Sikander's kurta and hide it under a rock at the base of a banyan tree. Feeling a steady accumulation of moisture, Sanjay rubbed his right eye, and realized that out of the other eye he could now see normally — one perfectly resolved image of Sikander kneeling, pushing leaves around a rock, Chotta rocking forward onto the balls of his feet, then back onto his heels. Sanjay cupped a hand over the other eye, and again, there were the trees, a brown sky, grey squirrels and birds, without duplication; when he looked with both eyes there was the old doubling, but he was so excited by the return to monocular singularity that he spent the rest of the journey testing one eye and then the other, and almost forgot the stains on his clothes and the scratches on his limbs.

'Go in quietly and take a bath,' Sikander said. 'All right? And don't tell anyone anything. If they ask, tell them we were playing and you were Treasure-keeper, and we two jumped on you. Don't forget.'

Later, in an enclosure near the house-well, Sanjay sat on a wooden stool and poured water over himself from a bucket; under the cool stream of water, his skin felt smooth and resilient, his muscles relaxed, and a quiet drowsiness came over him. When the water was finished, he sat quietly, the wrinkled skin of his scrotum contracting and expanding against the cold wood; thousands of birds cheeped and swooped in their evening frenzy, and very faintly he could hear the tinkling of cowbells as the animals were led home; and it wasn't until the thread over his shoulder began to stiffen into dryness that he realized that his face was still wet, that he was crying.

The next morning, while transcribing the story of Yajnavalkya, who was born without a father, Sanjay looked up at his uncle — Ram Mohan was seated cross-legged as usual, wrists resting on knees, in the classical pose of the teacher or scholar, head tilted back a little, eyes fixed on something a little above the horizon; to his right, Sikander's mother sat with her head to one side, gravely regarding her toes, which protruded from under her full red skirt. In that moment, Sanjay saw quite clearly the chaste and desperate love between them, the years of need and public companionship, the mutual recognition of the impossibility of consummation, of the audacity of the possibility itself (the immensity of the barriers, social and physical), and yet, the quiet, relentless passion. Sanjay wondered why he had never seen it before — it was plain enough to see — why no one else had ever seen it; he wrote a few words, and then, as he reached for a dip in the ink, he shut one eye — in the utilitarian spareness of monoscopic vision, the scene took on the stillness of a tableau: the scholar and the noble lady, the poor Brahmin and the Princess, the yogi and the temptress. Seen with one eye, in singularity, their love seemed so fantastic, so idealized that it became unreal, and therefore did not exist, could not be allowed to exist; he opened his eye, and now, in the double-imaged richness of his handicap, what was real became indistinguishable from the unreal, and all that was fantastic was forced to exist, really and severally. Conscious, for the first time in his life, of power, he giggled, and they looked up at him, pleased; he smiled back at them, feeling ridiculously old and benevolent. He wanted to hug them, press their heads to his chest, say, go in love, be prosperous, but instead he giggled, purposely, in order to play the child, and bent again to his task.

They looked at him, surprised; he smiled, then handed them a note: 'Let us all go, when the moon is full, for a trip to the Ganga.' Ram Mohan read out the note to Sikander's mother, and then they handed it back and forth, unsettled by Sanjay's unusual loquaciousness — he had earned, in the weeks and months after his injury, a reputation for being dull and sullen. Sensing that the issue was still in doubt, he handed them another note: 'Often, I feel like I am eaten up by the sky. It will make me feel better, I think.' Ram Mohan perused the note, and from his puzzled look Sanjay concluded that the claim to terror or death was too alien, much too pathetic for a child. Another note followed: 'Uncle, Uncle, talk to Ma, she'll listen to you. My head hurts, and the water of the Ganga will cure it.'

Ram Mohan reached over and patted his knee. 'Don't worry, I'll talk to your mother. A trip to the Ganga will do us all good.' He squared his shoulders, and Sikander's mother looked away from him and resumed her inspection of her toes. 'The scriptures say that Gangaji is our mother, and he who bathes in her waters is washed of all karma.' He began to recite hymns to the Goddess Ganga, and then launched into a recitation of the story of Shantanu the king, who married a woman who killed her children, seven of them, one by one. 'Death,' Ram Mohan said, 'as Shantanu found out, can sometimes be a gift to the dearest ones. Also, it is advisable to learn how to recognize goddesses when one intends to marry, or risk being left ultimately wifeless, with only a child who will cause great wars.'

'Let me do it,' Sikander's mother said suddenly, without looking up. 'Let me — I will talk to whoever needs to be talked to, I will send for palanquins and elephants, and hire cooks and coolies and servants and bearers, I will arrange for guards, soldiers and cavalrymen, and we will proceed, over hills and through deserts, to the sacred river.'

'There are no hills here, and nothing like a desert,' Ram Mohan said, 'but if you wish it, of course you must do it.'

'Good,' Sikander's mother said, very stern-faced but exuding, all the same, an unusual air of eagerness and satisfaction; she stood up quickly, whipping her ghagra around her ankles, and walked off briskly, tucking the end of her chunni into her waist-band, as if she was about to start, at that very moment, the disposition of camels and the organization of food-stuffs. For the next few days, they saw her rarely, and even then always on the way to a kitchen or a store-house, trailed by three or four maids of various ages, a white-haired faithful retainer or two, and a sweating cook; Sikander and Chotta brought back reports of a break-down in the armed truce that existed between their parents — there were heated arguments about the possibility of a trip to the river, and then about the necessity of such a thing. Leaving his black-coated friends in the garden, Hercules had appeared at the doors of the women's apartments and had spoken (in English, translated by Sikander, Chotta and their sisters) about the lack of safety on the roads (thugs, not long banished from these provinces), the discomfort of travelling (dust, heat, unfamiliar faces), the change in the children's diets, the expense, but Sikander's mother went on with her preparations, saying merely, 'It will do them good.'

Finally, with the look of a man who has encountered an unfamiliar, immutable natural force, Hercules began to seek a compromise — the journey, he said, would be sanctioned if the party were escorted by a detachment of the Company's cavalry, which precaution would properly foster an atmosphere of official formality and strength likely to prevent criminal mishaps. My daughters must come with me, Sikander's mother said. Leave them out of this foolishness, you will endanger their health, the air in this country is foul always, but especially fecund for fevers at this time, and who knows what waters they will have to drink, and why not go to the river here, on the edge of the town, if you must, it's just as good, to my eye. There is only one holy river, they will drink what I have tasted first, Sikander's mother said, and whatever you want you have done with them, you have done with them as you Angrez do to your women, so that now I can hardly speak to them, but before I die I will see them bathe once in the river.

At this Hercules looked a little taken aback, even a little ashamed, and he said, perhaps if Mr. Sarthey and two of his companions could go along to chaperon the whole affair, maintaining, thus, a sense of propriety and so on. Fine, Sikander's mother said, but Sanjay's uncle will come, he must come to look after the boy's health. The cripple? Hercules said, I suppose it is all right if Mr. Sarthey is there too, but all in all this is a sorry piece of women's uselessness, and too damn close to the monsoons for comfort. But Sikander's mother was already gone, looking to packing of provisions; Hercules turned, nodded at his sons, and walked back to his part of the house, clearing his throat.

Nine days later, the party set out. In front of Sikander's house, elephants shook their heads, camels refused to get to their feet under their loads, horses balked and cantered about, servants ran about doing nothing, dogs barked, soldiers shouted orders and palanquin-bearers sat in groups, smoking sullenly. But finally, out of this swirling mass, a stream evolved and sluggishly headed off down the street — a party of cavalry went first, lance-heads sparking red from the first sun, and Sikander and Chotta, after much consultation and assurance, were allowed to go with them, seated in front of two grey-bearded officers; behind, their mother and sisters followed in two curtained palanquins (the bearers now chanting steadily, 'Hunh-HA, Hunh-HA, Hunh-HA'), surrounded by attendants on foot; then came an elephant named Gajnath, the largest elephant in the group, and on this elephant, behind the mahout, sat Sanjay, giddily happy, almost unaware of the slight pain in his right upper arm, caused by the bony grip exerted on it by his uncle, who sat bolt upright behind him, his face twitching in alarm each time Gajnath's back rolled and dipped in the course of a stride. As they wound through the streets, children ran out onto balconies and roofs to look at the horses, the soldiers, and Gajnath; Sanjay straightened up, concentrated on looking directly ahead, and wished they had a band of musicians to play some sprightly martial tune — he was a king on his way to survey his domains, he was a prince off to win a beautiful princess in spite of scheming rivals, he was commander of a small army headed into battle with a powerful invading tyrant.

'O Gajnath, Lord of Elephants, you are indeed mighty, O Expansive One,' Ram Mohan said. Finding that the pressure on his arm had ceased, Sanjay turned, his illusion broken, to his uncle, who was laughing at the way Gajnath had twisted his tail to one side and high, at the huge steaming circles of black dung he was depositing, one after another, in the middle of the street. Then Gajnath stopped, and began to mark the path with a dark, wet circle that soon spread at least twenty feet, and two soldiers who cantered past raised their right hands and said, 'Fine, fine, very good!' and the on-lookers applauded in wonder, and Sanjay wished he could get off and look at the prodigious stream, for surely it was something to be remembered. But just then, as Gajnath finally lowered his tail, three horsemen in black, their long coats flapping, rode up and past, their faces held carefully up, nostrils quivering, and then took positions around the red palanquin bearing Sikander's sisters. One of them, whom Sanjay recognized as the choleric foreign gentleman from the garden, the speaker with the book, leaned close to the curtains and spoke, then straightened up to peer about at the crowds with unmistakable hostility, or at least fear.

'I think that one, the one with the red face, is the one who wants our books, Sanju,' Ram Mohan said. 'What's the matter? Do you want to pee? No? Listen, if you want to, you must, keeping it in has the most undesirable results. We'll hold you here at the back of the howdah, and you can make a nice mark in the mud just like Gajnath. No?'

Sanjay shook his head violently, aghast at the loss of regal dignity such a procedure would entail; in fact he wasn't sure of the reason for his sudden uneasiness, at his inability to sit still. He shut one eye, and the three black horsemen rode steadily alongside the red palanquin; he repeated the same operation through the other eye, and still they trotted along, surrounding the palanquin like guards; he opened both eyes, and the three became six, a black circle.

'Listen,' Ram Mohan said. 'I'll tell you a story, all right? Did I ever tell you about the play that your father and I wrote once, long ago, when you weren't even with us, and the knot, and Sikander of Macedon, who wanted to kill the world? Did I tell you about that? Well, in it, we had a part, a scene which dealt with this very issue, a short scene that we took out before we performed it in court, because Skinner, yes, Sikander's father, in his capacity as resident, advised us such a thing was incompatible with the dignity of the court, that's what he said, 'the dignity of the court,' which he had himself degraded and humiliated until the Raja became like a nervous old camel, but in any case there was this scene, want to listen? Listen, then; it went something like this. This is the famous scene when Sikander comes upon some sadhus under a tree, and we thought we'd done a good job of it, but the Company man said that Sikander of Macedon deserved a more digni- fied treatment, more exalted dialogue, but in any case it went like this. Sikander, you understand, is speaking to the sadhus through a trans- lator.

TRANSLATOR

He wants to know why you're naked.

SADHU

Ask him why he's wearing clothes.

TRANSLATOR

He says he's asking the questions here.

SADHU

Questions give birth only to other questions.

TRANSLATOR

He says people who get funny with him get executed.

SADHU

Why?

TRANSLATOR

Because he's the King of Kings. And he wants you to stop asking questions.

SADHU

King of Kings?

TRANSLATOR

He came all the way from a place called Greece, killing other kings, so he's King of Kings, see.

SADHU

Fool of Fools. Master-Clown of Clowns. Maha-Idiot of idiots.

TRANSLATOR

You want me to tell him that?

SADHU

I said it, didn't I?

TRANSLATOR

You're crazier than he is. He says he'll kill you. Right here, right now.

SADHU

I'll have to die someday.

TRANSLATOR

Listen, don't do this. He's demented, he doesn't realize who you are, he thinks naked people are poor savages. He'll really kill you.

SADHU

I'll really have to die someday.

TRANSLATOR

He wants to know why you aren't scared of dying.

SADHU

That'd be silly.

TRANSLATOR

He says that's not a satisfactory answer.

SADHU

What sort of answer would he like?

TRANSLATOR

He says you should tell him exactly what mystic path you followed to reach this sublime state of indifference. And he wishes you would stop asking questions. Really, this is incredible, I think you've got him hooked.

SADHU

Mystic path?

TRANSLATOR

Mystic path. Literal translation.

SADHU

When I feel like shitting, I shit; when I feel like eating, I eat.

TRANSLATOR

I don't think I've ever seen him like this — he doesn't know whether to be upset or horribly fascinated. You're very good at this. He says that shitting when you feel like shitting is irresponsible, you should have some discipline in your life, instead of lounging about naked under a big tree. He says people who shit when they feel like shitting never do anything with their lives.

SADHU

Ask him how often he shits.

TRANSLATOR

You want to ask Sikander of Macedon how often he shits, in public?

SADHU

I said it, didn't I?

TRANSLATOR

You know, you're starting to get on my nerves with this answering-questions-with-questions dodge. All right, I'll ask him. I think he's speechless. I think he's upset.

SADHU

O-ho. I thought he looked constipated the moment I saw him.

TRANSLATOR

What? What? You want me to tell him that?

SADHU

Why not? Tell him that's probably why he's impelled to invade other nations and massacre tribes and all of that — any student of yoga will tell you that mistreating the body leads to mental disaster. Yogic science has shown that people who hold it in are inescapably driven to behaviour like running about slashing at people, besieging towns, and frivolous acts of bravery.

TRANSLATOR

Now you've done it. He has those fits when he gets angry, see, he's rolling about on the ground. Last time he did that he put a city of eighty thousand to the torch, no survivors.

SADHU

He'd be a lot better off if he shat more often. I wonder what his per week rate is.

TRANSLATOR

I'm not going to ask him, understand? He'll kill you and all your friends and probably all the rest of Sindh too. I refuse on the grounds of conscience. It's my job but I refuse for the well-being of all the population of this country.

SADHU

There's a yogic cure for constipation. Every morning, you take . . .

TRANSLATOR

Shut up. Shut up. You've caused enough trouble for one day.

SADHU

You'd be remembered as the man who saved the world from Sikander the butcher. Get this fellow shitting right and he'd probably go home, quiet as a lamb.

TRANSLATOR

No, no. You're lucky, he's decided killing you would be bad for his campaign at this moment, he'd look cruel, and then nobody would surrender. He's having his chroniclers strike this conversation from the record. Now history will state that Sikander the Great met some strange naked men under a tree, that's all.

SADHU

Well, well. Good luck, friend.

TRANSLATOR

Good luck to you too, or is that what one wishes people like you? Now I'm asking questions.

SADHU

Why don't you write this down, or at least the gist of it? Then this history will remember you as the originator of the world's only all-comprehensive theory of imperial conquest: the constipation hypothesis, or the shit-glory affinity.

TRANSLATOR

No, thanks. Even if I hated my children, I would wish other curses on them, not ridicule.

SADHU

You'd save the world from a lot of tight-assed murderers.

TRANSLATOR

No. No.

SADHU

You'll see. All the truly great liberators will admit this theory into their ruminations and calculations.

TRANSLATOR

No.

SADHU

And so the world dies, from a surfeit of surly sphincters. It is, after all, so very simple.

And so, that's how it went, and your father and I, we thought it one of our better efforts, but the Company man said that Sikander would have asked more penetrating questions about philosophy and metaphysics, so we had to take it out, our metaphysic of shit. And a very sorry day it was, when we had to do this, it seemed to take the centre out of our dramatic construction, or should I say, all the horseshit out of our Sikander.' Ram Mohan laughed, then shouted, 'Oh, you are truly magnificent and noble, sweet Gajnath,' for at that moment the animal blared out a huge, resounding, richly-odoured, indisputably-elephantine fart. Sanjay laughed in silent accompaniment to Ram Mohan's long cackle and the raucous guffaws of the servants and soldiers and attendants, but then he glanced ahead, and the angry man's face was very white under his wide black hat, and his mouth was drawn up tight like a purse with its strings pulled taut, the pink lips puckered, and in the middle of all the laughing, all the new smells of the country-side, the bantering of the soldiers and the maid-servants, Gajnath's easy rolling grace, all the anticipation of the river and the road ahead, amongst all of this a very cold fear took hold of Sanjay, and he compre-hended completely and without doubt that something very bad was about to happen.

But, as always, the sun came up, and the road now wound through fields and groves of trees, and behind Gajnath horses and camels and people on foot trailed out for two and a half miles; horsemen rode up and down importantly, their turban-tails floating behind them, metal clinking reassuringly, and Sanjay's dread receded. Sikander and Chotta rode back with their officers and tossed up half a dozen mangos, for-aged from a grove of trees by the road; Sikander had the reins now, and he was turning the horse confidently and sharply, causing his grey-beard to laugh with delight.

'Who knows where these came from, whose orchard?' Ram Mohan said. 'But on the other hand, it is the road, and in difficult circum-stances dharma permits the eating of unknown food. Eat, eat.'

They rolled the small green mangos between their palms, pulping them, then opened a small slit in one corner with their teeth; the cool, unbelievably sweet golden juice spurted into their mouths, thickened by long delicious strands. Gajnath slowed and extended his trunk above his head.

'He wants one,' his mahout said. 'Gajnath requests a mango. He is partial to them.'

Sanjay handed one forward, and Gajnath took it from his mahout's hand as delicately as a musician accepting a piece of paan from an admirer; a moment later, he put his questing, sniffing instrument above his forehead again.

'Gajnath wants more,' Sanjay scribbled on a slate.

'Gajnath the magnificent,' his uncle said.

'Gajnath always wants more,' his mahout said, rubbing a hand over the cracked grey skin between the two flapping ears; as if in gratitude, Gajnath quickened his pace, bringing them closer to the palanquins again. The three firangis had wrapped strips of white cloth around their faces, and rode with their heads down; leaning on the front of the howdah, Sanjay watched them slump further and lower in their saddles, and now as the heat mounted the shouting and chatter subsided, so there was only the repetitious creak of leather, the shuffling of feet through mud and dust, the officious blowing of horses and the wheezing of the elephants; the sky was a huge dome above, high, hard and totally blue. Now Sanjay's neck seemed to grow limp, and his head lolled; he felt his uncle pull him back, and he tried to utter a protest, no, I want to watch the road, watch them, but the dark was good (Had Ram Mohan drawn the curtains on the howdah?), and Gajnath rocked him, up, down and around, is this the sea, mother, will I dream, can I? The dream came, a ship, a black, viscous sea, water lapping, endless days, eternal sky, and a feeling of resignation, the same quietness hour after hour, years passing; Sanjay awoke abruptly, eagerly, glad to discover again Gajnath's tireless stride, to find Ram Mohan's familiar wheezing as he slept with his head against the side of the howdah. Sanjay moved a sequined curtain aside, then squinted against the glare; the horses were plodding, necks craning low, but far ahead there was a glint of red, lost now and then in the green. Sanjay settled down to wait, impatient now, because he had seen the tents being folded and loaded onto camels, and had been told that a party of servants would leave early, in the darkness of the early morning, and knew that hot food awaited, a chance to stretch cramped limbs, and of course an opportunity to examine, at close hand, the behaviour and appurtenances of the firangis. His earlier feeling returned now, undiminished, but now the apprehension was spiced with the anticipation of an encounter with the unknown: he promised himself he would listen carefully to the language of the firangis, would note its inflections and tones, and that he would badger Sikander and Chotta to teach him the meanings of the words that he remembered distinctly, *di-gra-did, si-vil-iz-a-shun, prau-gres, di-cay.* Happily, he knelt and poked his head out between the curtains, then shook his uncle awake, handing him a note. Ram Mohan cleared his throat, then called, 'Come on, Gajnath, faster, faster, Sanjay says they have mangos waiting for us at the tents, and sherbet, and barfi.'

'Careful, master,' the mahout said nervously. 'If you say all that you're going to have to give him all that. He doesn't like it when people promise and don't give. It puts him in a bad mood, and he likes you, I can tell.'

'I'll give him, Sanjay says,' Ram Mohan said, reading again. 'Gajnath, don't worry, we have all that and more. Come on, Gajnath.'

In the camp, Gajnath knelt ponderously. Ram Mohan clambered down, with an attendant at each side, and hobbled away towards a tent. Sanjay mouthed at Gajnath, wait, wait (in the grey flesh, that old, knowing eye, with the tracks of tears underneath), and hurried off to look for familiar faces. At the peripheries of the camp, amongst piles of baggage, he found a harried-looking bawarchi shouting at his underlings. When he came back to the centre, he found Gajnath seated exactly as he had left him, legs bent at the knee before the huge body, ears flapping forward and back, trunk moving from side to side.

'He wouldn't move,' the mahout said, exasperated. 'What did you tell him? Have you taught him how to read now? He'll be even more of an impossible fellow than he already is.'

Gajnath lifted the mangos from Sanjay's hands, and the pink, soft tip of the trunk stroked his wrist for a moment, like a finger; the bawarchi says we'll have to wait for the barfi and the sherbet — Sanjay moved his lips — he says this is a camp on the road, not a palace, but we'll get some sooner or later. Gajnath swung up, looming, and Sanjay laughed in delight; watching Gajnath walk away (the little mahout beside, scolding), Sanjay understood all the various allusions in Ram Mohan's dictation to beautiful women with elephant-walks: there was that unhurried, graceful placing of one foot, then the other, the body swaying above, that delicacy. Sensing somebody behind him, Sanjay turned; the chief firangi stood a little distance away, his arms behind his back, leaning forward a little, flanked by his younger compatriots, watching Sanjay.

'Charles, if you please,' the leader said, and one of the others pulled out a notebook handsomely bound in fawn-coloured leather. 'The Indian, no, no, start again, the native of India is singular in his inability to make the natural and godly distinction between man and the other creatures. They are apt to treat of the lesser species as if they were separate and equal nations, instead of beasts lacking in the powers of comprehension that are gifted solely to Man by his just and good God. The natives further display the capriciousness of children, which is to say that while they display a sentimental and sometimes blasphemously

religious attachment to the lower animals, such as the grimacing monkey, the chewing, placid cow, and the elephant, they are capable of
displaying the most callous cruelty towards these very same species.' He
paused. 'What d'you think of that, Charles?'

'Er, enlightening,' said the young man. 'To the readers, it will be, I
mean, sir.'

'Properly so,' his elder replied. 'Heavens, why does he look at us so?
Is he trying to speak, d'you think?'

Sanjay was trying, silently, the taste of a new sound, 'crool-ti'; it felt
like ashes.

'This is the one that fell, the boy from the neighbouring house.'

'Er, yes, sir. I see the scars.'

The older man bent, and squatted on his heels; close up, his pupils
were pale blue, the eyes rimmed a distinct and startling red from the
dust; a white collar pressed up against the loose and raw-looking flesh
of his neck.

'Hallo,' he said, smiling. Sanjay was examining the blackness of the
stubble against the white skin, and was startled by the smile. 'I'm the
Reverend Sarthey,' the man said, smiling again, this time with rather
conspicuous effort, and putting his hand on his chest.

Sanjay pulled out his sheaf of paper, scribbled, and handed him a
note, causing considerable surprise. 'He writes! And not scared of us,
either. Charles, see if you can make something of this.'

'I'm afraid not, sir, it's rather a fluent sort of vernacular, I should
imagine, and colloquial, too. I can just about tell some of the letters
from the others.'

'Well, no matter. We will try to decipher your missive, young sir, and
will return with an answer on the morrow. Meanwhile, adieu.' He extended a hand, palm held perpendicular to the ground, thumb up, and
for a moment Sanjay tried to decipher the significance of this strange
sign (a one-handed namaste? did he want a mango?), then scrawled out
another rapid note and inserted it between two fingers. The men all
smiled together, then strode off; Sanjay walked slowly through the
camp, running over the various nuances of the recent meeting — how
much had they understood? What had they said? He wondered what
they would do with his two notes: the first one asked, 'What is *si-vil-iz-
a-shun?*' and the second one queried, 'What is the meaning of *di-cay?*'

Sikander's mother owned a very large tent, a crimson shamiana that was surrounded by a red quanat screen and seemed to spread endlessly in all eight directions, compartmented and partitioned so that there was always a new nook to be discovered; the textile itself was lined with chintz embroidered and painted in abstract designs taken from the flowers and vines of some imaginary, perfect garden and from the regular, hypnotic geometry of mathematics; there were yellow flags that flew from the tent-posts at regular intervals, and striped curtains hung over the entrances and narrow windows; the floor was covered with light dhurries, and folding furniture had been assembled and laid out with cushions. After walking through the arched main entrance (painted and cut to look like stone), where two soldiers stood guard, Sanjay made his way through the maze of corridors and rooms inside, all the way to the back; hearing Sikander's voice, he looked around for the entrance to the large zenana sitting-room, but there was only a blank white wall of cloth. He walked along parallel to it, running a hand over the smooth, heavy material, listening to Sikander's mother telling her boys that a whole day of riding was enough, especially in this rotting heat, they were on no account to venture outside; finding a break in the wall, a place where two sections came together and were secured to a bamboo pole, Sanjay worked on a couple of knots, pulling at them with his teeth, and then squeezed himself through the resulting slit. He strained for a moment, his head turned around, shoulder and knee scraping uncomfortably on the bamboo, and then he fell through, onto a providential pile of cushions, causing Sikander's sisters to scream and jump; he straightened up, rolling over, and sat cross-legged on the cushions, examining them unashamedly: they were a secretive, inseparable pair who constantly confided in each other, whispering mouth-to-ear in their father's language, interspersed with a few words in Hindi or Urdu. Sikander and Chotta seemed to treat the both of them with the same formal cordiality that they extended to their father, with that careful concern that one usually reserved for guests in one's home; on their part, the two girls — named Ai-mee-lee and Jain — seemed to prefer their father's rooms and friends to the apartments and intimates of their mother. Sanjay saw them infrequently, had never exchanged a word with either of them, but found them both utterly fascinating: their clothes were cut to a foreign pattern, presumably native to their father's country; they seemed to cultivate an air of generalized distaste for everything around them; and when they used a language that he could understand they unfailingly mispronounced vowels and misplaced accents in a manner that he found devastatingly charming. He smiled at them sheepishly, sticking out his tongue between his teeth involuntarily, and they tossed their heads and resumed their murmured conversation.

'No, Chotta,' Sikander's mother said, 'you cannot go out again. I want you to stay here, you've already burnt yourself black in that sun, by the time we get home again I don't know what you'll look like. Now where is that woman with the fruits? Has everyone died somewhere?' Two women hurried in, carrying trays of pakoras and sherbet, and Sikander's mother took a plate and held it out towards the girls, saying, 'Eat, eat. Take one more.'

'Try this,' Ram Mohan said, offering a plate of barfi; he was sitting on a low couch, shifting uncomfortably, and there was something in his voice that attracted Sanjay's attention. Ram Mohan noticed his quick glance, and smiled awkwardly, saying, 'And how are you, maharaj? My limbs are breaking; that elephant friend of yours tossed me about like a doll till everything ached and ached.'

'But I want to be outside with the *men*,' Chotta said.

'What I'll be like after a week or two of this I don't know,' Ram Mohan said, smiling again, looking not in the least bit apprehensive.

'No, you can't go outside, Chotta,' Sikander's mother said. Chotta, still sitting, kicked moodily at a cushion on his mattress. 'You're stuck in here with all of us, in the zenana.' At this, Chotta kicked again, and the cushion rolled over slowly and fell on a tray, knocking over glasses and spilling pakoras across the carpet; everyone jumped, and so did Sanjay, but as he jerked towards the tumbling glasses, his bad eye (the other vision) jumped to the periphery, zigzagged involuntarily (which was the bad eye, right or left?), and so inadvertently took in the bright blush that coursed from Ram Mohan's neck up to his face and bald pate, a blush so conspicuous and luminous that it caused him to change directions in mid-start and attempt to refocus; at this, of course, he lost control completely and fragmented images flashed about his head: Ram Mohan, Sikander's mother, Sikander, Chotta, the two sisters, the water spilling across the floor and carpet, the dulled glow of the sun on the roof.

When everything had settled down again, when the vertigo had ceased, Sanjay studiously avoided Ram Mohan's eyes; Sikander seated himself behind Sanjay and leaned against him.

'What is it, little brother?' Sikander said softly. 'You have that green stuffed look on your face again, like you're bursting with pressure, which usually means you're thinking and thinking and thinking.' Sanjay shook his head. 'One day you'll think too much,' Sikander went on, 'and you'll quite explode, like a cracker. Always thinking.'

Like a cracker, like a cracker: the words stayed in Sanjay's head that night, after the card game which Sikander's mother insisted on; everyone played except the two girls, who watched with an expression mingling disdain and fascination as Chotta plunked down his winning cards, whooping, and as Ram Mohan dithered and agonized over his moves, as he apologized to Sikander's mother, who accepted with affectionate indulgence. Years later, far away in Delhi, in the dismal palaces of Bahadur Shah II (who was born an emperor, made a poet by his misfortunes, and created an emperor again by his people), Sanjay would see a party of English who had come to look at the last of the Moghuls, and on their faces he would recognize that same look, that smugness and impatience that is given only to those who are travellers, who are powerful because of their ultimate indifference, that faintly-smiling detachment of the tourist; but that night it was still an incomprehensible gaze that excited his curiosity and raised his stick, hard and quivering, so that he had to tuck the end of his jama under his knees and make a tent, so that he played an utterly serious and ruthless game while the others laughed and carelessly flung away essential viziers and valuable kings.

They slept that night in a row, Sikander between Chotta and Sanjay, and still Sanjay felt himself throbbing, with now and then a lancing twinge of pain, and he twisted to put a flat pillow between his knees, holding himself, thinking for some reason of a snake raising its head to hiss, ffffff-fffffftt.

'How you won every game tonight, Sanju,' Sikander whispered quietly, 'how you played. That was clever, very clever.' Sanjay raised his head and nodded, then reached back with his free hand and traced out, on Sikander's arm, the words *king* and *minister*, meaning that the others had been careless with their court cards. 'Is that what you think, Sanjay? I think sometime we will be soldiers, we will raise armies, we will be kings. Can you imagine? We will get ourselves a fortress somewhere, and we'll defeat everyone who comes against us, and I'll lead out the cavalry, and you can be minister and send out spies, and advise.' Sanjay sat up; on Sikander's other side, Chotta slept face-down, limbs splayed and palms exposed, as if he had been dropped from a great height. 'We'll rule from the valley of Kashmir to the straits of Lanka, to the end, and Chotta will be my general, and you, Sanju, send out messages, tell them our horse is coming, our white horse, accept and give tribute, or fight.' Sikander sat up suddenly, and they peered at each other through the darkness, sinking in shadows; suddenly, Sikander got to his feet.

'Stay here,' he said, in such a voice of command, low and casual, yet expecting obedience so naturally and completely that Sanjay lay back down immediately and tucked the pillow between his knees. 'Go to sleep,' Sikander said. 'I'm going out. I'll come back later.'

He pushed aside a hanging and disappeared; Sanjay pressed his arms around the pillow and lowered his face to the sweet-smelling cloth. Much later, he turned in his sleep and was awakened by a not-unpleasant but bitter taste in his mouth; he was aware instantly that Sikander had returned and lay again in the middle, and also that he smelt of sweat. Sanjay pushed away the pillow and lay flat on the sheets, which now felt uncomfortably rough, and pressed down as hard as he could, crushing the unbearable, alien organ between himself and the bed; he opened his mouth and bit the cloth, felt his teeth grind, but there was no relief.

The next morning they drank milk out of large brass tumblers, sitting on a porch at the back of the tent. The chintz that lined the inside of the encircling quanat screen had large lotuses painted on it; beyond, they could hear, faintly, the animals humphing and calling as they woke up to the sun. Sanjay scribbled a note and handed it to Sikander: Where did you go?

'How did you ever learn to write without being taught?' Sikander said.

Thinking about it, Sanjay could recall no moment of movement from not-knowing to knowledge; conversation in the form of writing seemed more natural to him than speech — when you handled pen and paper, what was said was visible and solid, and could be handed back and forth, but words from the mouth, despite the pleasure one could take in their taste and form, were ephemeral, apt to vanish like life. He answered: Who taught you to prowl in the dark?

'I went where I went,' Sikander said, thumping Chotta on the shoulder. 'Come on. Maybe they'll let us ride by ourselves today.' Chotta had been paying no attention to them, being intent on getting the last drop of milk out of the glass, stretching out a tongue for the last white bubble. 'You have milk on your eyebrows, Chotta.' At the door Sikander turned back. 'And you, you have a white moustache. You look like an old man.'

But Sanjay was imagining a moving patch of white in darkness, a woman's face above a shoulder, calm beyond pain or even resignation; he sat for a long time with the white on his lip, looking down at the writing on the paper: when he thought with concentration and exactitude about that scene, that image that tended to dominate his memory and being, about the scratching against his chest from the thatch, the light catching a muscle flexing across the back of a thigh and rolling into a buttock, the small smacking sounds of movement, the lettering on the paper became black scratches, the familiar shapes of his own handwriting awkward and alien, the words themselves foreign. The sun had edged up to his toes, where he felt the heat gather at the skin; it was going to be a very hot day, a bad day for travel, but a cow lowed beyond the screen, and Sanjay felt an unaccountable, all-comprehensive tenderness, a softness of feeling that took in all the world with its horses and women and screens and mountains and dust and armies and poems and Gajnath and gods and sun.

The days passed; their party trailed along the roads, and every evening the tents awaited them. Sometimes they passed carts piled impossibly high with hay, with the drivers dozing; often they saw farmers bending over the meadows, and women with baskets on their heads walking along the high embankments between the fields. Everyone and everything moved slowly, as if things had settled into a test of endurance, of durability until the rains descended again; everything, that is, except the caravans and convoys that passed frequently in either direction: commerce alone seemed indestructible and unmindful of the dictates of the season. Watching them drive by, sweating, Ram Mohan settled down in the howdah and grew anxious.

'What are they doing now, Sanju?' he said every time they heard the crack of a whip. 'Are they twisting their tails?'

'Why are they in such a hurry?' Sanjay asked.

'I don't know, Sanju,' Ram Mohan said. 'It's the way traders are, and nowadays these seem to be in even more of a hurry than they were thirty years ago, when I first came to your parents' house.

'My father died in his sleep one night; I was the last one of the children, all the sisters had married, the brothers had moved to different towns. I had stayed in that house, had never gone out, but now the relatives and brothers told me I must choose somewhere to live, because it was finished, and I couldn't live alone, not in those bad times. So I said, I'll go and live with her — your mother — the eldest one of them all, and I was the youngest, perhaps that's why she had such affection for me. So for the first time I travelled, in a cart drawn by two painted bullocks, and everywhere we heard the same thing — the Angrez are coming, the Angrez are coming. They were still fighting then with all the nawabs, as they are doing now still more to the west and the north. And the caravans were few, but those we saw ran through the blackened and blasted country-side, cursing and fearful, towards the towns which themselves were not much better. Everywhere I saw empty villages; sometimes when we stopped some maddened skeleton of a man or woman would creep out of the fields and beg food from us. Now the same thing happens elsewhere, and the Angrez say they have made this country-side safe again, but I remember how much of the chaos came from their guns, and their threats, and their presence, how at that time you only had to go to a village and say, an army in red is coming, or even just that the tax-collector was coming, and the whole village would tie up little bundles and run away. But finally I got to your mother's house, and she sat and looked at me for a long time, and then she cried. Now the caravans and columns come and go, but these farmers, look at them, they're not much better; the country-side is safer for going from here to there, and we are off to the river, but all roads start here and end in London, remember that, these carts with their silks, and these other heavier ones with their metals, they will build some London nawab's palaces, and feed some pale family with a strange name.'

Sanjay had listened to his uncle's quiet monologue for a minute or two, and then, finding it fairly incomprehensible and largely boring, had concentrated on a brightly-coloured and fragmented fantasy in which he walked into a hut (a cow is visible somewhere, chewing quietly) and met a woman (her breasts are dark and bulge over her blouse, the smell of her armpits is overpowering) and did some business with money and somehow then they were unclothed, rubbing stomachs, but on hearing mention of the mythical city, London, he jerked back to reality.

'Lon-don?' he wrote. 'Have you ever been to London?'

'No,' Ram Mohan said. 'Maybe you will.'

'Maybe Gajnath and I will just keep on going,' Sanjay wrote, 'all the way to London.'

'I wouldn't advise it,' Ram Mohan said. 'I don't know if Gajnath would be welcome in London. In any case you have to take a ship, and go over the waters.'

'Maybe Sikander's big brother will take me,' Sanjay wrote. Sikander had an elder brother, a youth whom Sanjay remembered extremely vaguely as tall and thin, who had gone to sea and had not been heard from ever since.

'From what I heard of Sikander's big brother before he left,' Ram Mohan said, 'I don't think he could have taken even himself to anywhere. He was always in some dream, in some other place.'

Recalling the nature of his own dream, Sanjay turned away towards the mahout, sure that the fierce stream of excitement that swept up from his groin was visible to others.

'I'll have to take a ship and leave Gajnath behind,' he wrote.

'Even that is dangerous,' Ram Mohan said. 'You lose caste by going over the water. When you come back nobody from your brotherhood will even share a pipe with you.'

'Why?' Sanjay wrote.

'I don't know. That's what happens.'

'I don't care,' Sanjay wrote. 'I don't care if everybody sets me aside, I'll go to London, where the silks and the metals are.'

'All right,' Ram Mohan said. 'But say it quietly. Don't let your mother hear you, or Sikander's mother, or they'll make sure you never even get to Calcutta.'

For the rest of the trip, Sanjay made believe he was on his way to London: the procession was his royal train, the cavalry was his elite body-guard, the covered palanquins carried his queens (each with long, dark hair), Gajnath was the carrier of the imperial howdah, the country-side was a desert (surely a desert lay between him and

London); on the way, he fought many battles, out-smarted a succession of evil rakshasas and riddlers, rescued several princesses, all with the help of various befriending humans, spirits and animals. Towards the end of his trip, when they were nearing the river, Sanjay attempted to engineer a corresponding arrival at London, but found that his imagination populated the city entirely with shouting, red-faced men; try as he might, he was unable to conjure up a suitable London-princess (his dashing light cavalry, ranging far ahead, reported a city full of dark corners and terrified women), and so he resolutely turned his armies around and marched them to warmer climes: the London of his desire, he realized, was an ephemeral place that would skip forever slightly beyond his grasp.

The river itself seemed like any other river: the water was a rich silted brown, the surface sparked and threw up thousands of tiny ripples which danced up and died without suggesting any lateral movement, the huge curves of the course had left muddy beaches here and there, and in other places sticky banks riven by roots fell to the water, while above, trees leaned precariously. Long before they had seen the water, Gajnath had snorted and become impatient, and now he barely waited to have the saddlery taken off before rushing in, head down, stopping for a moment to squirt a trunk-full over his forehead, then collapsing ponderously on one side in the shallows. He stretched luxuriously and moved his trunk slowly through the water, occasionally throwing up fountains over his sides.

'He loves a good bath like nothing else,' the mahout said to Sanjay, 'so he rushes in without even looking around. But we small people, we have to look for maggars.' He peered at the river, shading his eyes. 'They hide under bushes just inside the water, and behind sand-banks, with only their eyes showing. Even in holy waters. But this place looks all right.'

Sanjay had been watching Gajnath at his ablutions, but now he noticed a boat gliding towards them, about half-way across the river. He could see the black figure of the boatman leaning over his oar at the back, but in front, near the bow, there were a group of white figures that he couldn't quite make out. Further down the bank to his right, the old Englishman, the one the soldiers called Sarthi, stood with his two companions flanking him as usual; the Angrez stood with his legs apart and his hands clutched behind his back, his dark coat fluttering around his legs because of the slight breeze that came off the water. The posture was one of anticipation, so even as Sanjay waded out and scratched Gajnath's back, he kept an eye on the English and the boat.

As the craft came closer, the people in it began to call out to the ones on the shore; there were four of them, two women and two men, all dressed in black. 'Reverend,' one of the women boomed, causing Gajnath to raise his head inquiringly. 'Reverend!' Even when they were still thirty feet off, it was clear to Sanjay that this was the biggest woman he had ever seen; sitting down, she cleared the others in the boat by a head and more, and she had a voice to match. The Angrez, on his part, seemed displeased by her shouting, and when she saw this — moving a huge white parasol to see better — she ducked her head and was silent until the boat scraped up the bank. 'Reverend Sarthey,' she said then, 'how good to see you again. And what a raffish bunch you've been travelling with. I'm so glad I brought my brushes and paints.'

'It has been rather a trip,' the Angrez said, 'but all for a good cause. Come.' They moved off together, into the camp, and Sanjay turned to the altogether absorbing task of scrubbing Gajnath's back with a pumice stone. He was jerked out of his reverie by a sudden hubbub from the camp; now, abruptly, he remembered his premonitions of calamity and ran up the beach, his bare feet throwing up gouts of sand, into the half-constructed camp-site. The English stood in a little knot just outside Sikander's mother's red tent, faced by Sikander and Chotta.

'What is it?' Sanjay wrote.

'They want to take the girls,' Chotta said, his face red.

'What girls?' Sanjay wrote. 'What do you mean, take them?'

'Our sisters, our sisters. Who else?' Chotta said. 'They said that he said they could take them.'

'Who, he?'

'Him. Our father. Hercules.'

'Be quiet, you two,' Sikander said. Both he and Chotta were dressed in patch-work chain mail that had been obtained for them by their adoring cavalrymen friends from some passing armourer, and Sikander was carrying the horse-hilted sabre.

One of the Angrez that had come in on the boat leaned down to them and said in passable Urdu, 'Did you tell your mother we have a letter from your father authorizing the Reverend to take the girls to Calcutta?'

'She doesn't want any letters,' Sikander said.

There was something about the way they both spoke, about the Englishman's contrived patience and attempts at a smile, about Sikander's quiet, adult anger that frightened Sanjay, and he turned and ran into the tent. He raced through the cool, flapping corridors and found Sikander's mother seated on a low couch, her daughters seated on either side of her, their wrists firmly grasped in her hands. The girls looked frightened, and the younger one was crying freely, the tears streaming unwiped down her cheeks and throat.

'If I hadn't sent for them at that very moment, to come and sit with their brothers,' Sikander's mother said, 'he would have had them. He would have taken them across, and there's not a thing I could have done about it. Tell the guards to chase them away. Tell them to whip them away.'

'They won't do it,' Ram Mohan said. 'They are after all not our men, they are his. They have to think of where their next meal's coming from.'

'Tell them to go away,' Sikander's mother said. 'Tell them I won't give up my daughters. You. Sanjay. You tell them.'

Her narrow face was wrinkled and tight, and at the end her voice cracked, and so Sanjay turned around and fled back up the cloth passage-ways. The Englishman-who-had-come-across-the-river was still squatting, his face earnest.

'Don't you want your sisters to be educated?' he was saying. 'Don't you want to send them to Calcutta so they can go to a big school and become ladies? They'll become mem sahibs and ride around in a big carriage. Wouldn't you like that? Then you could come and ride with them in their carriage. Wouldn't that be fine?'

Sanjay handed a note to Sikander, who turned to the Englishman. 'Go away,' he said. 'Nobody's going with you.'

Sarthi stepped closer, put a hand on the squatting Englishman's shoulder, and drew him up. 'Enough,' Sarthi said, in English, 'enough. Come. We'll send in some men, they'll get the girls, and that will be that. Come, where's the subedar? I will speak to him.'

'Reverend,' the Englishman said. 'Reverend, that's a respectable lady's zenana, not one of your men will go in there. That, to them, is unthinkable.'

'We will see,' Sarthi said. 'Come, let us not stand in the middle of a bazaar and banter with these, these children.'

They walked away, the men surrounding the women, but when the large one turned and looked back she stared straight over their heads.

'Good,' Chotta said. 'None of the cavalry will agree to come in here.'

'Yes,' Sikander said. 'But they won't let us move from here either — after all he must have told them that the Angrez was in command.'

They went inside, deputizing a maid to watch, through a net-lace curtain, for a possible return by the English.

'Are they gone?' Sikander's mother said.

'Yes, Ma,' Sikander said. 'They are. But he told the cavalry to follow what Sarthi said, and I think they won't do anything to us but they'll hold us here. We're surrounded.'

'No matter,' Sikander's mother said, straightening her back, and instantly her face took on a translucent, purified glow that Sanjay would see again, years and ages later, on the faces of certain cavalrymen in yellow robes. For now, however, he was consumed by curiosity, and inflamed by impatience that he could not be everywhere at once, listening to and watching all men and women everywhere, participating on all sides of a battle at once. Remembering, however, the tall woman, he got to his feet and ran outside, sprinted between the tents towards the river. He found the English on the sand-bank, climbing into their boat, with Sarthi hanging back, reluctant.

'Ask them,' Sarthi said to the Englishman with the Urdu. 'Ask them if they understand that they were told to follow my instructions, and that my instructions are that the girls are to be delivered to us. Ask them if they realize that they are disregarding a direct instruction from one who has a mandate from their supreme commander. Ask them if they understand that this is tantamount to mutiny.'

The ones being asked were three impassive cavalrymen, three subedars, all men with grey beards down to their stomachs, who looked as if they had between them at least three half-centuries of service, if not more, and the trio, arms folded, looked steadily at the English, not even deigning to shrug. Exasperated, Sarthi got into the boat and found a seat, his hands clutched in front of him.

'Those who ask impossibilities,' the oldest of the grey-beards murmured as the boat pulled away, 'can accuse no one of mutiny.'

'Yes, yes, subedar sahib,' the others said with much nodding, 'never heard anything like it.'

And with this the cavalry retired from the field.

Sanjay walked back through the camp, where everybody had adopted the quiet voices and significant tones of crisis. Sikander's mother had taken her daughters into the remotest nook of the tent, with two old women-servants set to guard them. As soon as Chotta saw him, he pulled him aside.

'We're holding a war council, you have to come and sit with us.'

Sanjay let Chotta pull him to a seat on the carpet, but his attention was on his uncle, who was sitting with his knees drawn up to his chest and his hands clasped in front of his shins; Ram Mohan's eyes were barely visible above the white cloth that could not conceal the knobbed, pitiful shapes of his extremities.

'The best defence, as everybody knows, is an effective offence,' Sikander said. 'We will raid them tonight.'

'Good,' Chotta said. 'A night raid. Evil spirits and ghouls will crunch the bones of those we kill. We'll make a feast of it.'

'It is against what used to be the rules of war,' Sikander said, 'but this is Kal-yug, and all rules are forgotten. We will go in the dark.'

Sanjay scribbled: 'All right. You plan it.' With this he got up quickly and walked across the room to Ram Mohan, ignoring their unconcealed disapproval; what interested him more at this moment was the absolute immobility of his uncle, the stone-like, yogic quality of his concentration (and again he regretted not being able to be everywhere at once, the stolid, physical existence of his body that reduced all the simultaneous potentialities of his life to a single, inescapable monster-strong narrative).

'What will happen?' He handed a note to Ram Mohan. 'What is the future here? What are the possibilities?'

'You ask too many questions,' Ram Mohan said. 'That's a bad habit I am responsible for.' He looked down at the paper, smoothening it on his knee. 'It isn't the future I am thinking about; the future is simple: there are those who could look within, into their souls, and up at the conjunctions of the planets, who could calculate the shape and form of the world and tell you thus exactly what is going to happen. The future is simple. The future is simple, I can hold it in the palm of my hand; and the present is just a matter of endurance, detachment, and a sense of humour. What frightens me is the past. What-is-to-happen is just a matter of talent and mathematics; what-has-already-happened is the slippery many-headed changing demon that eludes all our blows, defeats all our attempts at geometry.'

He looked down at Sanjay. 'I didn't mean to scare you; I feel, today, very old, for the first time. It is just that long ago, before you were born, there was another siege; there were other women who were taken from their families; there was one woman who was taken furthest. Now, today, I understand one thing: some will tell you that the secret of Maya is desire, and others will convince you that the key is knowledge, but in the end it is only one horribly old, dusty god called Time. A man once told me a story about laddoos, and if I choose to believe that story then the future is exactly clear to me, solid and perceptible, and I must prepare myself for it.' He laughed. 'I am babbling, I am, and pompously so. But forgive me; I am feeling very old and am very sure I know what is going to happen. That is simple enough, but I do not have the strength to battle Time: I am too weak to change the past, and this is why I will lose everything I love and everyone I love.'

He pushed himself up, smiled at Sanjay, then left the room, not lifting his feet from the carpet as he walked, very slow and halting.

'There are no boats at night,' Sikander said. 'We'll have to see if that elephant friend of yours will take us across. We'll ask the mahout.'

Sanjay handed him a note: 'I don't think so, why would the mahout risk his animal, and his job?'

The truth was that despite all his cravings and his curiosity, Sanjay did not want to go across the river; his uncle's words, inexplicable and muddled, had frightened him like the mutterings of some unknown animal in the dark. He wanted to stay in the tents, in some brightly-lit space, on secure land and amongst as many people as possible, but now Sikander and Chotta looked thoughtfully at him, as if it were incredible that someone might not want to go paddling over dark water, into the encampment of the English, who had a universal reputation for bloodthirstiness and disregard for life.

'We'll see,' Sikander said. 'We'll have to ask the mahout, and maybe offer some money or something.'

Clearly, the two were determined and not to be put off by mere logistical quibbles, and so Sanjay wrote: What exactly is the purpose of the expedition? Are we going to burn down their tents?

'If you knew anything about cavalry operations,' Chotta said, adopting the scornful tone he took when faced by Brahmin muddle-headedness, 'you'd know that the first duty of light cavalry is to recon-noitre. We have to know what they're doing.'

The only way to get out of it was going to be a bare-faced refusal, which Sanjay could not bring himself to stoop to; somehow, as he had grown up, he had unquestioningly accepted the exaltation of Kshatriya virtues: speed, courage, strength, dash, chivalry, aggressiveness, and to now reject those clear-faced verities, to question all those hundreds of stories told by Sikander's mother, was unthinkable — it would be a re-treat into the brilliantly-illuminated realm inhabited by his uncle, his parents, thousands of curving-limbed pandits with their endless con-versations and effeminate graces and impossible philosophies ('Form is emptiness, and emptiness is form'), a falling-back into stifling safety, or at least into the grip of very-subtle dangers that threatened only by insinuation and metaphor, through history and language. So Sanjay struggled against the tyranny of his flesh and his upbringing, and at-tempted to imitate the careless insouciance of his friends, the prideful, slightly swaggering honour-consciousness of Kshatriya dharma: all right, let's go find Gajnath.

The mahout, surprisingly, agreed to the trip without question or reservation; perhaps he too had succumbed a little to the common sol-diers' infatuation with Sikander's and Chotta's imperiousness, their ab-solute assurance and their obvious, amazing skill with animals and weapons. In any case, when they stole out of the tent at midnight and squeezed under the quanat screen, under the lotuses and out to the river-bank, they found him waiting with Gajnath.

'Gajnath's creeping about like a mouse,' the mahout said quietly. 'He's been noiseless all the way from the camp to here.'

'Good,' Sikander said. 'Come on.'

They clambered up to the howdah, and then Gajnath waded out into the water, and soon the voices of the crickets faded under the steady lapping. Sanjay was lost in the darkest black he had ever experienced — there was nothing, not the slightest glimmer of star-light and not the faintest suggestion of a distant lamp or candle. In the complete absence of light his mind produced whorls and spirals of red and green that floated about him, twisting and changing shape, always on the verge of metamorphosing into something, some thing; afraid, he shut his eyes, but they followed, spinning edgewise at him; he opened his eyes, but nothing changed, and after a series of rapid blinks he found it hard to tell whether his eyes were open or not.

He scribbled with his forefinger on Sikander's arm: 'Can you see anything?'

'No,' Sikander said.

'Gajnath can see, even in the dark,' the mahout said. 'When I was a child, my widowed father would go out at night, leaving me to sleep between Gajnath's feet. He would guard me, and nothing came near.'

'How old is Gajnath?' Chotta's voice was slightly disembodied, seeming to rattle in the stillness.

'Be quiet,' Sikander said. 'Voice carries over water, they'll hear us coming and that will be the end of it."

Sanjay settled in to wait, tucking his hands into his sleeves: after the dry heat of the day, the chill of the water lifted the hair on his forearms and thighs. Beside him, the mahout began to pray under his breath, making a staccato whistling noise that seemed somehow familiar, and now the complete and utter dangerousness of the expedition enveloped Sanjay: ahead, in the bushes that overhung the river, he could see, very clearly, a tribe of guards all equipped with huge moustaches and matchlocks, and underneath a long lizard-like creature detached itself from a cave at the bottom and sculled upwards through the water, its tail lashing powerfully.

Sanjay wondered how it was that in the presence of such fleshly dangers, such solid and potentially bone-cracking hazards, one could be frightened of abstractions; feeling Gajnath's rocking below, Sanjay conceived a certain contempt for his uncle, who tilted his metaphorical weapons at imaginary foes, and accepted defeat with very real despair (or so it seemed) before any battle was joined or could be. On the river (what river is this? he thought suddenly, unable to remember its name), with his friends the Rajputs (why do they wear yellow?), next to a man who prayed (who is his god? his goddess?), riding an animal who served without question (why does he love us?), Sanjay clutched his forearms, feeling the muscle slide over the bone, cherishing it, and the wind curling the hair at the base of his neck, and he swore: I will never let Death take me.

'Be alert,' Sikander whispered. 'We're almost there.'

They left Gajnath and the mahout squatting by a clump of bushes, both chewing on blades of grass; as they crept up the rise of the bank, the moon showed itself above the trees, yellow and pushing through racing wisps of black. There were many camp-fires clustered about the plain, among wagons and animals, and Sikander and Chotta worked their way between the flickering circles of light, looking always for the shadows; in the middle of the camp, they found a shallow depression in the narrow alley between two tents, and Sikander pressed Sanjay down into it.

'Stay here,' Sikander whispered. 'We'll split up and look around. Don't move.'

They crouched beside him for a moment, then vanished abruptly, without the faintest scraping of mud or rubbing of cloth on cloth. Sanjay crouched close to the ground, wondering what his role was supposed to be in the expedition, given his constitutional and possibly hereditary incapability of moving without sound, of possessing the skills or aptitude for combat, for by-night skulduggery and dare-deviltry. They seemed to include him in their plans as a matter of course, perhaps as a means of demonstrating their regret for his fall, his loss of speech, but their plans, their attempts at conciliation and affection — if they were such — inevitably seemed to lead to yet greater and more sustained exposures of life and limb to destruction; Sanjay's uncle, his intimate familial circle, seemed to be haunted by the cosmic, imperceptible manoeuvres of Kala, while his friends, his world, his public existence, were always the potential domain, the breakfast, the eatery of Kali; hugging himself in the dark, thinking of Kala and his sister Kali, Sanjay realized that life was attempting to tell him something, as surely as if the Earth had opened a muddy mouth under his belly and spoken in rumbling, bass tones: there is no escape from life, except — recalling his uncle's happy face when he told the story of Sikander — perhaps just a little by becoming a poet, by being in-all-places-at-once. So he resolved to be more attentive when his uncle dictated the next half-remembered instalment of the Shilpa-Sutra or the commentaries of Patanjali, told himself to commit to memory and every-single-day meditate on the principles of dramatics as enunciated by Bharata, to look upon the battle-field of the world with the aesthetic detachment of a poet, but even as he did this he heard a woman's voice, a husky voice speaking in English.

English, when one hears it surrounded by night, in the paralysis of fear, is an exotic and enticing thing: the syllables fall, short and regular, in a drum-beat cadence dum-DAH dum-DAH dum-DAH, the sense is lost, but the rhythm offers assurance and a certain confidence, the consonants clip along, sprightly and altogether ignorant of the darkness; so Sanjay worked his way out of his refuge and crawled along, raising his head to hear better, drawn by a completely unreasonable and unthinking curiosity.

'I hope it is not completely and unforgivably prideful to see in these events, the hand of Providence,' the woman was saying.

'No, indeed not.' It was Sarthi's voice. 'It is logical that He should aid us in the execution of His plan. While you must, of course, wear black for the proper year, it would not be improper to adduce that your father did far more for his country and faith by passing than by living.'

Sanjay crawled under a wagon, squeezed between some sacks.

'I'm glad he's . . .'

'Hush, dear. His money will aid in good works; it does us no good to mock the dead.'

'All the same I'm happy, Francis.'

'Yes.'

By now Sanjay was huddled behind a wheel, and through the spokes he could see Sarthi and the woman seated on cloth chairs, close together, glasses in their hands. The woman had changed her bonnet for one of white, fine cloth, and Sarthi's hair hung like a red cloud around his head, illumined by a hissing paraffin lantern.

'We will go to England,' Sarthi said. 'I have a title for my book: *The Manners, Customs and Rituals of the Natives of Hindustan; Being Chiefly an Account of the Journeys of a Christian Through the Lands of the Hindoo, and His Appeal to . . .'*

Suddenly, Sanjay felt an enormous pain: he was lifted up by his left ear, away from the wheel and into the light; he was dropped, unceremoniously and with a great deal of volition, in front of the chairs, and he bent over, quite blinded by tears, both hands pressed to his head.

'Rotten little thief.'

'No, look. I've seen him before. He's one of the boys from the front of the tent.'

'Ah, surely,' Sarthi said. 'He's an old acquaintance, from the Brahminical family whose estates border Captain Skinner's. Come,

come.' He bent down to Sanjay, smiling. 'This is a gentleman of some education and no little curiosity. He questioned us once, on matters of civilization and culture.'

'Really?'

'Believe me, they teach their abominable Brahmin sophistry at the earliest opportunity, so that the young soon become hardened debaters, ready to split hairs and question all that is sacred.'

Sanjay looked up, blinking. The woman's face was square, framed by brownish curls, her eyes were a clear, frightening blue, and her shirt buttoned all the way up her neck and at her wrists. He blinked again, then put one hand over his left eye to get rid of the phantom image (the same woman, somewhat smaller and sickly-looking) which hung over her; she put her hand over her heart.

'You little devil,' she said. 'How you startled me. For a minute I thought I was going to swoon.' Sanjay looked at her out of the other eye. 'What is he doing here, Tom?'

The Englishman with the pincer-like fingers asked the question in Urdu, to which Sanjay responded with a nervous shake of the head.

'He can't speak,' the Englishman said to the woman. 'And he's too scared to write, I think.'

'I do believe the lad was drawn over by, by, dare I say, a thirst for knowledge,' Sarthi said.

'How did he get over the river?'

'I wonder,' Sarthi said. 'Swam, boated, braved it somehow.'

'My word,' the woman said. 'What a brave little fellow. Look at those little jammies, that top-knot, he is so delightfully quaint, I simply must sketch him. Tell him, Tom. Tell him I'm going to draw him, there's nothing to be afraid of.'

So they seated Sanjay on a low stool, set some food before him, and the woman sat in front of him with a large white tablet on her knees, and her pencils and carbons scratched over the paper as Sarthi and the other Englishman attempted to converse with him, telling him not to be frightened; he shrank away from the food, and for a few minutes was interested in the woman's drawing implements, but then the two men gave up trying to make conversation with him, and sat looking at him, and in their appraising eyes, in the woman's quick, calculating glances at him, in the double, oscillating images of the lantern, in the lines that spread over the page, crossing and intertwining (a sort of net, a knot), he felt a curious emotion, indescribable, something like hunger, anger, grief, something imperceptible that entered his body and lifted his soul away from his bones, held it and squeezed gently but incontestably till it, his heart, became a contracted and shrunken orb, dead and cold, so that when the tears began to run down his cheeks he watched impassively, as if from some great height, as if it were happening to someone else.

'Oh, do tell him not to be frightened, there's nothing to be frightened of,' the woman said, and the Englishman reassured him repeatedly. He shook his head once, then again, to show that he was not frightened, that it was quite something else, not fear, but the tears continued uncontrollably, his body like a sudden stranger, and he thought then of his uncle pulling his leg after him, his spittle-spray, his ugliness, his poetry, his — what other word could there be for it? — doomed, doomed love, and felt hatred for him: he should have been a killer, a whirling, stoney, drunken-eyed assassin, who could and would have saved them all, raised his blood-layered arms in a call of triumph, a wail, a smoke-coarsened howl.

With a quick *chunk*, the glass on the paraffin lantern disappeared, the flame sizzled, then flickered out, and Sanjay thankfully recognized the arms that lifted him from his seat — he was being rescued; placing him again between them, Sikander and Chotta spirited him out of the camp, dodging shouts and exploratory torches. At the river, Gajnath was already in the water, with his mahout beside him.

'The moon's up,' Sikander said. 'They'll see us now for sure.'

Behind them, people were calling to each other, drawing nearer.

'Don't worry, Sahib,' the mahout said. He spoke to Gajnath, using a mixture of Hindi, some other northern languages, and a medley of cheeps, growls, and various sounds that Sanjay concluded were some elephant tongue. Gajnath immediately opened his mouth and squirted some water in, then ducked his head and went under until only the very tip of his trunk protruded above the water; behind him, the top of the howdah broke the surface here and there.

'Hang on to the wood,' the mahout said, 'and stay as low as you can.'

Don't be silly, Sanjay wanted to say, but Sikander and Chotta each put a strong fist on his waist-band and lifted him into the water; he found himself clutching a bar too wide for his grasp, still feeling detached.

'Go,' Sikander said.

The mahout ducked his head under and a moment later they moved off. Sanjay occupied himself trying to keep his face above water, fighting Sikander, who kept a hand on him to prevent him from exposing too much. A few moments later, they heard voices on the shore, and Sikander pulled him down till every choppy motion sent a rush of water lancing up his nose; Sanjay fought him, then fought the water, and even that receded and he was flying, strength gone, effortlessly, in a grey sky. Then there was gravel scraping across his shins and hands, and he was dragging himself through shallow water, spitting and hacking, crying; he lay face-down, his fingers spread apart so that the grainy pebbles popped between them, hurting just a little.

'Look at him, bathing again,' the mahout said. He was sitting cross-legged, running a wet cloth over his arms and chest. 'As if he hasn't just swum a river twice.'

Gajnath was lying on his side in the shallows, pumping water over himself; in the moonlight his skin seemed luminous, almost silver.

'O Sanju,' Sikander said. 'What were you doing sitting up there? Did she like you or something, that she was making a picture?'

'Are you going to run away and marry her?' Chotta said. 'And leave us poor men behind?'

They were quietly jovial, pleased with the adventure, especially the close escape, but he was too exhausted even to be angry at them. He wondered instead at Gajnath, who had the strength to kill them all with one blow of his trunk — why did he indulge them? Why risk his life? Why obey?

Sikander and Chotta lifted him up, and he let them walk him slowly towards the tents; behind them, standing now on the bank, Gajnath sprayed clouds of dust over himself, catching the light in a thousand whirling motes, which, for a moment, hid the firm lines of his body, dissolving them into the shifting vapour of some enormous phantom. Sanjay shivered, and Sikander put an arm around him and his brother.

'We found out something — he is coming,' he said. 'We heard them talk in the camp. They've sent for him, and they'll just sit there and wait. They won't do anything.'

Sanjay looked up: he was shivering feverishly, and he felt as if he was learning to walk anew — with every step his knees slid and buckled, and his body teetered. The words passed him by, without meaning, as if they had been spoken in a foreign language; he looked at them with the frank, unembarrassed blankness of an infant.

'Oh, idiot,' Chotta said. 'He is coming. He. Hercules.'

The two parties settled down to wait for the arrival of Hercules, and as the days passed servants and soldiers from both sides criss-crossed the river to play cards, to smoke a hookah, to exchange gossip, or to greet a distant relative; every evening, the day ended with the lapping of oars as the last boat-load of people were brought back across the river, inevitably talking about what would happen when Hercules did arrive.

Meanwhile, Ram Mohan seemed to realize that whatever the outcome of the struggle between the English and Sikander's mother, he was expected to have a manuscript ready by the time Sarthi was ready to leave, and so he began to dictate again; but now he did not, as before, blithely skip from scripture to poem to fragment of play, as prompted by memory and enticed by old association — now he recited, almost without pausing to take breath, leaf after leaf of axioms, propositions, clauses, sub-clauses and commentaries from the six major schools of philosophy.

Shining with sweat, his eyes fixed on some imaginary point over Sanjay's head, Ram Mohan went from the close examination of knowledge peculiar to Gautama's Nyaya ('If, against an argument based on the co-presence of the reason and the predicate or on the mutual absence of them, one offers an opposition based on the same kind of co-presence or mutual absence, the opposition will, on account of the reason being non-distinguished or being non-conducive to the predicate, be called "balancing the co-presence" or "balancing the mutual absence" '); to the metaphysic of particularity and classification embodied by Kanada in his Vaisesika school ('The means of direct sensuous cognition may be defined as any and every true and undefinable cognition of all objects, following from four-fold contact; substance and other categories are the recognizables; the self is the cognizer; and the recognition of the good, bad and indifferent character of the things perceived is the cognition'); to the causal evolutionism of Kapila's Samkhya ('Without the "subjective," there would be no "objective," and without the "objective," there would be no "subjective." Therefore, there proceeds two-fold evolution, the "objective" and the "subjective" '); to the methodical internal and external engineering of Patanjali's Yoga ('To him who recognizes the distinction between consciousness and pure objective existence comes supremacy over all states of being and omniscience'); to the investigations of right action by the adherents of Jaimini's Purva Mimasa ('Dharma is that which is indicated — by means of the Veda — as conducive to the highest good'); and to the confident idealism of the Vedanta ('The highest Self exists in the condition of the individual self').

As Sanjay wrote down these things, most of which he did not understand, he wondered what it felt like to have a hip that refused to bend, a mouth that spat involuntarily. The morning after the excursion over the river, he had woken up early, and looking around the tent, at his friends sleeping, their faces washed orange by the light from the roof, he had been conscious that nothing would be the same again. He had looked at them, noting Sikander's long nose (just like his mother's), his curving eyelashes, Chotta's round face and his nervous grip on the sheet even as he slept, and Sanjay wondered for the first time what it would be like to be them. For all his strength, his natural assumption of leadership, did Sikander ever feel fear? Did he wake up in the dark? What was it like to be murderously angry, to have that blank rage that Chotta found so easily? Or what was it like to be anyone else, to graze sheep, to carry baskets of rice across watered fields, to ride a horse and love it or, for that matter, to shit fifty-pound cylinders of steaming green dung?

Sanjay realized that something had happened to him, that until now he had been content to let people enter his life and act upon him, and he had accepted their presence and their actions as natural phenomena, as stimuli to be reacted to spontaneously; but now he doubted everything: he considered himself curiously, examined his own emotions and sensations, listened to his own breathing, and the simplest action — drinking a glass of milk, sitting at dinner with the others — became an event difficult to get through because of his acute sense of himself, because everywhere there was an irony inseparable from existence.

So in the afternoons, when it was too hot for dictation, Sanjay eagerly ran down to the river, where he found the one chore he could lose himself in: he scrubbed and washed Gajnath with the one-pointedness of a meditation, lifting aside folds of skin and getting into the most hidden cracks, where minuscule creatures lived and fed. Sometimes Sikander and Chotta wandered by and sat at the water's edge, quiet; their unusual stillness, without fail, broke Sanjay's concentration, so that he felt he had to make conversation to relieve the awful burden of mounting silence. So he made flourishes with his pumice stone, and great splashes of water, and finally one day — anything was better than nobody saying anything — he was reduced to offering a note to Sikander to read to the mahout: 'If Gajnath is the king of elephants, why does he serve us?'

'Ah, Gajnath,' said the mahout. 'He is not only the king, he is the descendant of kings. Listen, in the great Akbar's court, there were many elephants who were declared khacah, that is, they were to carry only the emperor. There was Koh-shikan, the Mountain-Destroyer; Uttam, the Amorous; Madan Mohan, the Heart-Ravisher; Sarila, the Polished; Maimun Mubarak, the Highly-Sedate; and many, many others, but of all these the captain-elephant was Aurang-Gaj. Aurang-Gaj was the beloved of Akbar, for his excellent proportions, for his courage and his loyalty, and he was given ten servants to serve him, and every day one hundred and sixty pounds of good foods. And so Aurang-Gaj carried his emperor at the most auspicious of occasions . . .'

'Yes,' Sikander said, reading from a note. 'But all the same the great Aurang-Gaj could have squashed the emperor Akbar like a peanut, so why carry him?'

'Because Akbar captured him.'

'But how did Akbar capture him?'

'By cornering him in a valley, then having other tame elephants box him in and lead him in.'

'But why did these other elephants begin to serve Akbar?'

'Because Akbar tied them to trees, and lashed them or starved them or anything else until the pain became unbearable, and then they decided that it was better to serve Akbar than suffer endlessly or die.'

'And so they all gave up?'

'They gave up nothing, they just decided to go on living. And so they served Akbar, but even the strong must grow weak, so that now Akbar's descendants huddle in their peeling palaces in Delhi, and the children of Aurang-Gaj are scattered over Hindustan.'

'But ever, did ever any of the elephants just say no, enough, no more?'

'In a thousand ways, every day. They serve us, we are their masters, that much is obvious. But if you live with them long enough, you know they understand that in reality they are the stronger, but to openly refuse would result in destruction. So they are endlessly patient, and they endure, and when you want them to go fast they go just a little slower than necessary, and when you want them to do something, they pretend they don't understand, oh, no, master, we are just dumb animals, we don't understand anything. Their rebellion is in little things, because they understand that it is better to endure and survive than to say no and die.'

'But Akbar loved Aurang-Gaj, and Aurang-Gaj loved Akbar?'

'In a way, in a manner of speaking, and that is the strangest thing of all.'

Sikander and Chotta stood up then to watch the Englishwoman as she walked to her boat, which stood ready to take her back across the river; every afternoon, she came across with one of the younger Englishmen, to make her way to Sikander's mother's tent. Then, when Sikander's mother refused her an audience, she sat on a folding chair, under an umbrella, sending in servant after servant with arguments and appeals to what she called 'common sense': the girls will be educated, they will be schooled in the best of environments, they will become polished mems and will marry the most eligible and powerful of men, surely you must consider what is best for them, for their futures. Receiving no replies, the Englishwoman would fold her chair, click shut her umbrella, and retreat over the river for the night, to return the next day. In the red tent, Sanjay would find Sikander's mother in a rage, snapping at Ram Mohan as if he were the one who was trying to take her daughters away; even though she refused to meet the Englishwoman, she listened to each of her messengers avidly, her eyes downcast.

'What does she think?' she would burst out after the messengers left. 'What does she think, a mother doesn't worry about her daughters' future? I know too well the sort of education they will give.' A pause as another messenger came in. 'I will not have them be made into something else.'

The two girls watched and listened quietly, their haughtiness quite broken by the experience of being at the centre of a struggle which caused such anger and grief; in fact it now seemed to Sanjay that they treated their mother with not a little affection as she plied them with food and encircled them with the watchful ferocity of a lioness. He was unable, ever, to find them alone, and was too shy to attempt a conversation in front of other people, but was content to watch as they played games of cards and parchesi with Sikander and Chotta, giggling and whispering to each other. They obeyed their mother instantly, without question, and seemed to enjoy their sessions with a local tailor and a jeweller, who outfitted them with bright ghagras and fine wrought-silver bangles and necklaces, so that they looked like little replicas of their mother. All this ended abruptly and without ceremony one hot afternoon, when everyone was dozing — Hercules strode into the tent, found the chamber where the girls were sleeping next to their mother, kicked aside two maids, lifted the children up by their arms with one hand, and when his wife pulled at the girls he hit her back-handed and knocked her over the bed. By the time Sanjay, Ram Mohan, Sikander and Chotta woke up he was already outside, handing the girls to two red-coated English cavalrymen who, escorted by English infantry, made their way to the river and across it. Hercules came back into the tent, brushing past his sons without a glance.

'Have I not treated you well?' he said to Sikander's mother in his accented Urdu. 'Have I not given you everything you needed? Have I not given you a house, servants, money? Have I not let you have your sons, as you wanted?'

She looked at him very directly, a small red mark on her right cheek, and said nothing.

'The girls I wanted to look to, and I have been a good father to them. I want them to be educated, and to grow up as Englishwomen. That is the best thing for them, and that is what I have wanted for them. Do you understand that? I will go now to Calcutta with them, and leave them there in the care of friends. If you want you can come, be with them until we come back.'

She said nothing, and he turned smartly on a heel and walked out; she sat without moving, on the floor beside the bed, and the evening came with its slow loss of shape and outline, its smell of flowers and water, and then the night. Sanjay and the others sat beside Sikander's mother through the dark, and Sanjay found that he did not need sleep, or even day-dreams: to watch her face, her eyes, as the shadows moved slowly, was enough. In the morning, when the birds began to call, she said in a very clear voice, suddenly:

'Bring sandalwood.'

Ram Mohan pushed himself up from a half-reclining position, next to Sanjay. 'What?'

But Sanjay knew already, somehow, what she wanted; some muscle or nerve, some single clear stream of emotion that stretched from his groin to the base of his neck tightened and convulsed.

'To make a pyre,' she said.

The word spread through the camp like a quick wind; within minutes the tent was crowded with maid-servants who crouched on their haunches, staring at the slim figure in the middle.

'Bring wood,' she said again. When nobody moved she got to her feet, quickly and energetically, and walked between them, calling them by name, pleading, and no one moved. She then kicked them, raging, reminding them of the years they had eaten her salt, but they only wrapped their arms around their legs and lowered their heads to their knees, and finally she turned to Ram Mohan.

'No,' he said.

'I have been insulted,' she said.

'No.'

'You know everything,' she said. 'I only do what I should have done long ago.'

'Not this. This is a crime.'

'I am a Rajput. Padmini did it, with all her princesses. The scriptures advise it.'

'What scriptures?' he said, face red. 'Which ones? The ones that do are lies and inventions.' Ram Mohan went on for some ten minutes, quoting commentators and citing precedents, demolishing the authority of every text which could possibly support what she planned, ending with, 'For a Hindu, all scriptures are without meaning anyway, and tradition itself is against it.'

'Very good,' she said. 'Then I choose it, I alone. Bring wood.'

'Think of your sons,' he said.

Sanjay looked at her sons, and saw that Sikander was weeping; Chotta was staring at his mother with a stunned look on his face, but Sikander was gazing up blindly at the roof, at the place on the cloth where the sun appeared as a clouded glow, and was crying. His mother said quickly:

'My sons are Rajputs. They will understand. Bring wood.'

'No,' Ram Mohan said.

Slowly, she stepped forward, four or five strides, hesitated, then reached out to him and put a hand on his shoulder; feeling Ram Mohan shudder, Sanjay looked at him for a moment, then back at her. She suddenly seemed younger, and a blush spread from her shoulders; she took her hand from Ram Mohan, and stood with her arms folded across her chest, like some girl in a painting. Abruptly, Ram Mohan struggled to his feet and left the tent.

They built the pyre — a platform of short lengths of wood stacked some three feet high and soaked with ghee — by the water. In the tent, Sanjay and Sikander and Chotta watched the maids dress her; they draped her in the red of a bride, and put thick gold bracelets on her arms. She seemed relaxed, and raised her arms away from herself often, in order to admire the gold against her skin.

'Bring me some kheer, will you?' she said, now soft and smiling at the servants. A black-skinned khansamah came, his fat legs shaking, bearing a common kitchen pot and an old iron spoon. While she ate the sweet rice-pudding, a crowd of thousands gathered outside, from the surrounding villages and fields: their murmuring swept over the tent like a breaking wave, and Sanjay's vision oscillated crazily, doubled by his old injury and multiplied by dizziness and sweat. 'Come sit by me,' she said. 'All of you.'

She had used a Lucknow attar of jasmine, and the light smell lifted Sanjay's head, ridding it of the soft hum from outside. He blinked and looked around: Sikander was still crying, Chotta was looking at his mother's face, his mouth open.

'Don't cry,' she said. 'Remember who you are. Always remember who you are.' She looked at Sanjay. 'And you. You with your dreams.' She spooned a mouthful. 'Come. It's time to go.'

She leaned on Chotta's shoulder, and he put an arm around her; Sikander and Sanjay walked behind. Outside, the crowd fell silent, and only the flags fluttered and the river moved slowly in the sunlight.

'Will you chant something?' she said to Ram Mohan.

'What?'

'Whatever is supposed to be said.'

'I don't know what is supposed to be said.'

'Chant anything.'

'All right. It is the only thing I can do.'

'From the first moment,' she said, stepping up to him, 'from the first moment, you forgave everything I was and did. And this, this is nothing, because you will be here always.' She turned to her sons, 'Remember. Death is nothing.' In three quick steps she crossed from the ground to the top of the pyre, and a single huge shout lifted from the crowd, leaving a silence hard as stone. She sat, still licking the iron spoon. 'It is very sweet,' she said, smiling, and then she put the spoon in her lap, folded her hands in front of her, and slowly her eyelids sank. She took a deep breath.

'You are the eldest son,' Ram Mohan said to Sikander, and from an earthen pot lifted a piece of wood, blackened and flickering at one end. Sikander looked down at the torch, then at the sky, always away from his mother. 'Now,' Ram Mohan said, 'please.' But Sikander let his arms fall to his sides, and sobbed helplessly, his chest rising and falling. With a shout (what did he say?), Chotta spun and snatched the torch from Sikander, paused for a single lost moment (how long?), then bent to the wood, reaching, and with a single gasp it ignited all over. Sanjay ran, but found his hand grasped by Sikander, five nails pressing into his skin (he felt it break, instantly, in five separate places).

'Look,' Sikander said, turning his head away. 'Look.'

For one quick convulsion of muscles Sanjay fought, but as always he was unable to budge Sikander, and then Ram Mohan began to chant, and Sanjay looked, and the flames had risen, she sat not moving, her head high, a dark figure. With his hand still in Sikander's (he feels his blood trickle), Sanjay looked, and Ram Mohan had begun to chant an ancient song in Sanskrit,

> Dhritarasthra uvacha —
> Dharmakshetre kurukshetre samaveta yuyutsavah
> Mamakah pandavasraiva kim akurvata Sanjay . . .
>
> *Dhritarashtra said —*
> *Gathered on the dharma plain of Kurukshetra*
> *O Sanjay, what did my sons and the sons of Pandu do?*

while on the burning wood, a blue vapour races over the dark outlines of the naked body (all coverings burnt away?), and then the wood collapses and they are all driven back by a shower of glowing-red, stinging embers, all except Chotta, who stands alone, welcoming the wounds, and Sikander, still holding his friend, still looking away, follows the sun, which roars and consumes, and nothing can be seen, Ram Mohan breaks and cannot sing, and Sanjay shuts his eyes, but still sees the pyre, clearly and not in imagination, the precise flames, the faces of those watching, the arrangement of utensils on the ground, the flick of a woman's chunni in the wind, an old man, bearded, unfamiliar, walking around the pyre, and Sanjay understands that whatever he does he cannot refuse to see, and he opens his eyes, looks fully into the fire, remembers that she asked for a chant, and quite naturally and without thinking begins to sing,

> Nainam chindanti sastrani nainam dahati pavakah
> Nacainam kledayanty apo na sosayati marutah . . .

> *Weapons do not cut it, fire does not burn it,*
> *Water does not moisten it, wind does not dry it.*

They waited for three days and nights for the remains of the holocaust to cool; on the last of these nights, when the grey ashes could almost be touched, Sanjay talked to the old man who had appeared beside the pyre. This old man, who was invisible to everybody but Sanjay, came and sat beside him and put a hand on his shoulder. The old man had straight hair held by a circular band over his forehead, a clipped beard, eyes half-closed as if in meditation, dark skin, a shawl with a flower pattern draped over one shoulder.

'I am Yama,' the old man said. 'The Lord of Death.'

Sanjay looked at him, and the old man's face was calm and refined, his demeanour that of an aesthete.

'There will be more of this, won't there?' Sanjay said.

'Yes,' the old man said, and just then Sanjay fluttered his left eye (the wind lifted the ashes), and for a moment the other disappeared, his voice lost. '. . . *sab lal ho jayega* — everything will become red.'

'More of this,' Sanjay said, and began tearing a strip off his dhoti.

'Wait,' said the old man, reaching out to him. 'Listen, you must listen . . .'

But Sanjay had already closed his left eye, and he then wrapped the cloth around his head so that it was firmly held shut: the old man disappeared.

'You go to hell,' Sanjay said.

After the ashes were thrown into the water, they stayed by the river, the whole party seemingly paralysed, no one willing or able to give the order to move one way or another. Sikander and Chotta rode all over the plain, leaving early and returning in the late evening, exhausted and blackened by dust; Ram Mohan sat by the river, his feet in the water, refusing umbrellas and cushions; and Sanjay spent the days with Gajnath. On the sixth morning Hercules came rushing back across the river, pale and incredulous, accompanied by the woman and Sarthi. As Hercules raged through the camp, kicking and shouting and interrogating, Ram Mohan said to Sikander and Chotta and Sanjay, 'Wait. I wish to tell you a story.'

He told them a story: Once a woman named Janvi was captured as a citadel fell, and a man called Jahaj Jung — who loved her — escaped from the burning city; Janvi's captor, Hercules, made a marriage with her, but by sheer force of will she produced only daughters, and one day she sent to Jahaj Jung, asking for sons; he sent back shining laddoos, and all who touched them became a part of the story, and Janvi and her neighbour Shanti Devi ate the laddoos; and when the sons were born a cobra held them.

'And so each of you was born,' Ram Mohan said. 'Born, she said, for revenge. But all of us who touched are your fathers, you are made for much more than that, and you are made of the dust from marching feet, the tears of men, spittle, hope.'

Hercules marched up to them, flanked by soldiers. 'Arrest that man,' he said. 'Aiding and abetting and materially enabling a suicide.'

The soldiers lifted Ram Mohan up and walked him towards the camp, and Hercules wiped tears from his face.

'There is much work to be done, sir,' Sarthi said, 'much work indeed.'

'Yes,' Hercules said.

*   *   *

Sandeep paused and rubbed his eyes. 'They put irons on Ram Mohan,' he said, 'on his arms and legs and put him in the back of a baggage cart. When they stopped after the first day's journey he was dead, sitting with his head resting on his knees.' Sandeep rose to his feet, gathering the folds of a loose shawl about his shoulders. 'In the first two months after Janvi's death, the Company annexed two small territories and one major one. Six rajas and two nawabs signed treaties with the Company, allowing the British to maintain garrisons within their territories and acceding certain rights, pertaining to politics and economics, in perpetuity. In the six months after Janvi's death, three hundred and four women were burnt to death on the pyres of their husbands. Some climbed onto the pyres of their own accord, proud and unheeding of all entreaties; others were forced screaming into the flames by their relatives. All these deaths were widely written about in newspapers in India and in Europe. They became the focal point of many sermons and editorials, and the campaign to allow missionaries into India gained momentum.' Sandeep swirled the shawl about him and stepped away into the darkness, then turned back. He called:

HERE ENDS THE SECOND BOOK,
THE BOOK OF LEARNING AND DESOLATION.
SIKANDER'S CHILDHOOD IS PAST.

NOW BEGINS THE THIRD BOOK,
THE BOOK OF BLOOD AND JOURNEYS.

THE BOOK OF BLOOD AND JOURNEYS

. . . now . . .

NOW THERE WAS a fierce debate raging on the maidan, sparked off somehow in the middle of the story-telling. The antagonists were the retired head of the Sanskrit Department at Janakpur University and a visiting biologist from Calcutta, and the question of course was consciousness and the body and the nature of the mind. Emotions were running high, and voices even higher, and Ganesha and Hanuman were laying wagers.

'Easy win, monkey,' Ganesha said. 'The old fellow's education is so much deeper.'

'Ah, yes, but the Bengali's reading is so much wider,' Hanuman said. 'He has an M.A. in colonial literature.'

'True, true, but that will apply only peripherally, if at all.'

'Wait and see,' Hanuman said. 'Wait and see.'

Now there was a noise at the door, and a man entered the room, bearing a box. He was a large, fat man with a round face and thinning hair oiled straight back, and the box he held in front of him was covered with iridescent paper, blue and green and gold.

'Gulati uncle,' Saira squeaked, jumping up.

He opened the box for her, and inside there were rows and arrays of sweets, gulab jamuns and jalebis and barfi. Over her lowered head he nodded at me. 'Myself Gulati,' he said. 'Proprietor of Gulati Sweet Emporium. Sweets for the story-teller. Please try.'

'You know,' Saira said, biting down into a gulab jamun. 'You're not supposed to be in here.'

'I'm going,' he said. 'Only to bring a small token of my appreciation, I came. Enjoy.'

As he manoeuvred his bulk past the chairs and to the door, Abhay scowled at Saira. 'How did he get in here, past all your security?'

'He probably bribed everyone with Gulati sweets,' Saira said. 'Who can resist?'

'Now he'll go and tell everyone he's official sweet supplier to the miraculous monkey,' Abhay said. 'What a greasy fatso.'

'You, Abhay bhaiya,' Saira said, gulab jamun juice running down her chin, 'have developed the deplorable habit of not believing anybody or anything.'

'Don't be rude to your elders, Saira,' her mother said, gesturing with a jalebi.

'It's true,' Saira said. 'It's a very bad habit.'

Meanwhile, I was trying a bit of the barfi, and I found it to be a very truthful barfi, full of the sincere and light essence of almond, and satisfying to both intellect and heart. I pushed the box towards Abhay. He shook his head.

Ashok and Mrinalini were at their place by the typewriter. 'We're ready,' Mrinalini said, wiping her fingers.

'Tell them to be quiet outside,' Yama said. 'Minds and bodies both. Or they'll have to deal with me.'

What Really Happened.

THE YEARS PASSED, and city nations collided with each other, and out of this churning came empires, with their monuments and epic poetry and sciences of assassination and power. There were some battles that passed into time, and others that became memory and gathered the dreams of whole peoples about them, like a speck of dust accumulates a pearl about itself, and these accumulated stories became the stories of stories, the stories of a nation made up of many nations, the collective dream of many peoples who were one people.

Even as the emperors and kings studied the land and sent out their spies, marshalled their armies, there were those who farmed the rich land, others who made things, served people, and then those who created the beautiful, in stone and wood, in words, in cloth. Traders traversed the seas, and took out and sent in, and gold filled their coffers. There were, as always, the rich and the poor, the suffering and the murderous, the kind and the patient and the bilious, but it was all in the wonderful richness of the world, the wheel turning, and in the end these men and women lived lives of wholeness. There was time enough for the philosophers to argue, and pandits everywhere debated the compulsions of ritual and the limits of reason, the existence of an after-life and the necessity of karma in moral action. And there were pandits who were women, and women who ruled families and more. There were women of the world who plied their trade, but they were renowned for their skill in the sixty-four arts, and famous for their wit. It was an innocent time when dharma was forgotten sometimes but still sought after, when the curse of a poor farmer could lower the head of a king, when the pride of a courtesan could turn back a river.

But ritual feeds on itself and grows like a wild hedge, until it makes all movement impossible and clogs the streets of crumbling cities. So men and women lost sight of the good and the true, and the past was made a time of innocence, but then came those who broke the beam of the world. Sakyamuni sat in meditation, and Mahavira walked alone and naked. And they and others emptied the cup, and then filled it again.

There was news of a madman named Alexander, a butcher who had cut his way through the world, who came now towards the realm. He destroyed many tribes, and then fought a pitched battle on the Jhelum, and then disappeared again into the depths of the continent. He went, but was not entirely forgotten. Some said he would come again.

Then there was a time of riches. A king named Ashoka did that rarest of things — he gave up aggressive conquest and ruled for the good of all creatures. Traders went to the empires of the west, taking goods and bringing back gold. Political parties rose and fell, and the hungry tribes waited beyond the Khyber, but still Bharat was peaceful, the wonder of the world.

In the court of Vikramaditya (long may his memory live) those perfect men, the nine jewels, perfected the arts and sciences. Outside, the city awoke, and one heard the songs of devotion from the temples. Crowds of people filled the street, going about their business. One heard the cries of the shopkeepers, offering wares from the world over. Old women walked from house to house, selling flowers. Noblemen drove past arrogantly, their gold-sheathed swords flashing in the sun, watched by perfumed women from their balconies. Young men-about-town woke wearily but contentedly from their night's carousing, and began the business of bathing and beautification, in preparation for a garden-meeting with their lovers. Their barbers, setting their hair in elaborate styles, whispered to them passages from the manuals on love. One could hear, far away, the banging of anvils and the rattling of looms.

In the evenings the streets were filled with music, the singing of courtesans. Villagers, drunken on city wine, reeled through the streets, laughing. Women hurried through the dusk with their families, laden with flowers for the gods. When the city slept the bold thieves came out to practice their science, but the watchmen were vigilant.

. . . now . . .

THE GREAT MIND-BODY debate went on through the night, and ceased only when both the participants simultaneously fell asleep. 'They're both snoring away now,' Saira said. 'As loud as train engines.' She had come over early in the morning, dressed in her school uniform, to eat Mrinalini's aloo-parathas. Now she smacked her lips loudly and started on her third paratha.

'What a little hog you are, Saira,' Abhay said, and tugged at her pig-tail.

'Oh, let her eat,' Ashok said, over his newspaper.

Saira made a face at Abhay. 'It's all right, Ashok uncle. I don't mind. But anybody who won't eat all they can of Gulati mithai and Auntyji's aloo-parathas, well, there's something wrong with them, I can tell you.' And she looked darkly at Abhay, and took a huge bite of her paratha.

'Well, I suppose there is, guruji,' Abhay said, laughing.

Now there was an uproar outside, and people stamping to and fro: news had arrived that the police had decided to disallow the daily gatherings.

'Why?' Saira said.

'Because no permission was taken,' Ashok said.

'We'll see about that,' Saira said, and stamped off in her uniform with her blue tie. Ashok and Mrinalini went off together to see the collector, who had once been a student of theirs.

'Permission!' Abhay said. 'Who do they think they are?'

I answered: 'The exercise of power is a great joy. Even when it's done in very little ways.' We had perfected a system where I wrote on little pads and he looked over my shoulder. It was possible now for us to have a conversation at an almost normal rate.

'You were powerful, were you?' he said.

'I knew a little about it,' I wrote, and was suddenly afraid of what I would have to write in the days to come. 'There are some things I wish had remained forgotten, out of memory.'

'Let memory come when it must,' he said. 'But for now, as I've been reminded, there is pleasure.' So we watched *Kagaz ke Phool,* and then *Sholay,* and about half-way through the movie, Saira came swinging through the door, pulling off her tie and skipping a little.

'All right, brat,' Abhay said. 'What great thing have you done?'

'Hah,' she said. 'In the very first period, we told our civics teacher we weren't going to study. Then the police commissioner's kids, sixth and seventh standard they're in, sent lunch back to their house without taking a bite. Then after classes were over and we all left and went home, somehow there was a spontaneous bandh in the bazaar, even the mithai shops closed.'

'Hah, indeed,' Abhay said. 'So now?'

'So now suddenly there's police permission, and they will even provide crowd control, and a lost-and-found booth.' She laughed, throwing her head back, with that deep and infectious giggle that shook her whole body. She grinned at us, and spun the tie around her head like a whip. 'Isn't democracy wonderful?'

Sanjay Eats His Words.

LISTEN . . .

A year and six months after the death of Sikander's mother, Hercules sent him to Calcutta to become a printer's apprentice. Chotta was now given to week-long silences and sudden laughs, agonized fetal crouching and long horseback rides, and so was kept back in Barrackpore as erratic and possibly self-injurious, but to Sikander, Hercules said: 'The world is changing. You are suspended in the middle, neither English nor one of the others, and no one will let you in, not one side and not the other. So learn a new trade, start at the bottom, learn something that will survive in the world.'

So Sikander, when he went quietly that evening, avoiding the main roads and staying in the twisting alleys, to Sanjay's house, brought this news of imminent departure; after Ram Mohan's death, Sanjay's parents had moved away, to a smaller house in the heart of the city (on the eve of their departure, Sikander's knot had vanished, leaving only a few strands and cables to sway in the winds). Arun, in the months after the episode, had been quietly but smoothly shifted from favour and prominence in the court, from the sight of the British resident, and had accepted his coming fate of obscurity with a calm resignation that had surprised his friends; in fact he now seemed content to turn to his writing, to write romances and have them read by a small circle of intimates. Sanjay's mother, meanwhile, had suddenly and in a great bout of pain lost all her teeth, and now it seemed that the death of her brother and her friend had crumpled her face, halved it in size and doubled its age. And so Sikander came to a household much reduced in munificence, still enveloped in grief. Sanjay greeted him at the door: 'I have chosen a pen-name.'

In the days after the fire, after regaining his voice, Sanjay had rediscovered his great love for language, for words and the way they rattled and rung and swaggered, for the lilt of a ghazal and the grandiloquence of an epic; he had begun to compose frequent but disconnected shers, finding the coupling rhyme easily but unable to concentrate long enough on any one theme to produce a whole lyric.

'Oh, so, great poet,' Sikander said, 'how are we to know you now?' Sanjay said, drawing himself upright, 'Listen to this —

> *The secret nature of all things, it springs forth at the call of its lover,*
>   *the wind.*
> *Says* Aag: *he sighs for me, my beloved, and consuming each other, we*
>   *will light the universe.*

What do you think?'

'A middling effort,' Sikander said, 'and an ominous name. Find another, Sanju.'

'It is fixed,' Sanjay said.

'You've become very obstinate,' Sikander said.

'It is a time for strength,' Sanjay said, and then his voice rose, 'in case you haven't noticed.' Even as he said it, the anger apparent in his tone, he regretted it, but in the months following the deaths Sikander had become, inexplicably, gentle and slow-moving and pliable, as if his grief had only sapped his passions, detached him somehow. So even now he just shook his head and smiled.

'Don't quarrel, fiery Aag-Sanjay. I came to tell you I am going. I am to go to Calcutta to learn the printer's trade, letters and ink.'

Immediately, Sanjay was full of anger: 'You? Calcutta? Printing?' Another thought struck him. 'Printing in English?'

'I suppose,' Sikander said. 'The press belongs to a friend of Hercules.'

'But what do you know of words?' Sanjay said. 'You're a damn Rajput, fit for horses and sweat. Brass-head!'

'O Brahmin cow-shit-poet, be not jealous,' and Sikander reached out and tugged at Sanjay's top-knot; in the next moment they were wrestling. Sanjay tried his best, but for all his arm-flapping and straining he was face-down in a moment, caught in some exotic wrestling grip which paralysed him at the edge of agony.

'Oh, let me up, bastard,' he said. 'My eye-band's coming off.'

'Who is the strongest of the strong?' Sikander said.

'You, you,' Sanjay squealed. 'The Great Sikander, warrior, emperor.'

Sikander stepped off him, and Sanjay worked at the knot on his eye-band, tightening it; every day, he moved the band from one eye to the other, taking care never to have both open at the same time — it was better to see nothing than to encounter things one could not control.

'Why not just come with me? I'll talk to Hercules,' Sikander said.

Sanjay stopped in mid-tie, mouth open at the audacity, the possibilities of the possibility, then he shook his head. 'No, they'd never let me. Even when I wake up in the mornings, she's always there looking at me. Only this morning my father said, "Now you're all we have." '

'You're such a player with words,' Sikander said. 'Talk them into it. Give them reasons, dazzle them with lucidity. Debate.'

But words are no match for love, Sanjay discovered; his mother wept and his father began to cough and spit incessantly, holding his chest. That night, Sanjay read by the light of the moon and a surreptitious candle; he was reading a half-paisa Urdu pamphlet published from Calcutta on coarse yellow paper, full of salacious couplets and gossip about the most famous courtesans of Lucknow, Renu and Banno, and scurrilous, punning stories about the English that referred to their principals only in sobriquets: 'It is reliably heard that the most revered RED ONE is given to joy-driving in his phaeton with the wife of the BIG FISH . . .' Hearing his mother stir in the next room, Sanjay waved out the light and tucked the pamphlet under his mattress in a single motion, unwilling to face her smothering concern about the perilous state of his eyesight. Everything was still again, but Sanjay lay quietly on his back, thinking about the vibrant streets of Calcutta, the loaded carts, the traders, the painters and the poets, and somehow through this laughing throng moved the gold-bangled and scented figure of Renu of Lucknow, whose beauty maddened nawabs and stripped young men-about-town of their fortunes. Renu laughed, her anklets jingled, and

Sanjay turned on his side and began to move slowly against a round pillow, uncomfortable against its unwieldy, bulky softness and yet unable to stop. Renu whirled through the crowd but still it was possible to see the delicate sheen of moisture on her neck, and Sanjay was sitting upright, rigid, the pulse expanding painfully in his chest, both eyes open and the band lost somewhere in the darkness. He groped with both hands, trying to remember the quality of the sound he had heard, or thought he had heard — had it been a voice, a whisper that somehow had the clarity and suddenness of a shout, or was it just a bird calling, or the movement of wood at night? A door threw a silver rectangle of light across the floor, and outside lay a court-yard with a tulsi plant at the centre, and Sanjay knew whatever had spoken waited there. He squeezed his palms against his eyes, feeling the liquid below the skin, and then lay again on his side, pulling a sheet over himself, over his head, but now each moment came slow and brought with it a new rush of curiosity.

Finally he stood up and walked slowly to the door, holding his left eye shut; the court-yard was paved with bricks, was surrounded by white arches and walls, and the tulsi moved slightly. Finally Sanjay let his hand drop away, opened his eye, and a beautiful young man dressed in a long white dhoti smiled at him, his eyes lined darkly, jewels on his arms, chest bare in an unfamiliar fashion.

'Who are you?' Sanjay said.

'I knew you would come,' the young man said.

'Are you Yama?' Sanjay said.

'I knew you would come to me. I am Kala.'

Sanjay clapped his eye shut, and now there was only the yard and its plant; he moved back into the room, then out. Slowly, he doubled his vision and let Kala form again: 'What do you want from me?'

Kala shrugged, his lips full and his hips curving forward to the waistline. 'To give you our love.'

'If you want worship from me,' Sanjay said, 'you'll have none. No gifts, nothing. For none of you, not you, not that fool Yama.'

'We don't . . .'

'I'll give you nothing,' Sanjay said, 'because you give us nothing, you cannot save us, you cannot protect us.'

'We ask nothing from you,' Kala said. 'But remember the stories you have been told, see that we are also your fathers, participants in your birth, and so we love you . . .'

'Go,' Sanjay screamed, his voice echoing in the court-yard. 'Go from my house. I expel you. I forbid you entry. GO.'

'I will go,' Kala said, and he was very lovely in the moonlight, with his black hair falling over his face, and his smell of jasmine water. 'I go, all the world is my home. Stay here in yours, look after your father and mother, grow to be a house-holder in the heart of your city.'

'May you suffer as you make us suffer, Kala,' Sanjay said, the tears starting from his eyes. 'I curse you. I will defeat you.'

'I am already and always beaten, my love,' Kala said, with a gentle inclination of his head and a dancer's folding of the hands, and then he was gone.

'What is it?' Sanjay's father said. 'What is it?' He rushed out of the house, closely followed by his wife. Shanti Devi stumbled over to Sanjay, pressed his shoulders with her hands and wiped his face with the end of her sari.

'What is it, son?' she said. 'Who were you shouting at? A bad dream?'

'I heard a voice in the darkness,' Sanjay said. 'It was no dream, it was a real voice.'

'Rama protect us.'

'It was a voice, and it told me I must go. It said to me I must go to the city and learn printing, and that is where my destiny lies, where they want me to go.'

'They?' said Arun.

'The gods.'

'Who knows what it was?' Shanti Devi said. 'A ghoul, a witch. And what is this printing-shinting, is this a job fit for you? For a Brahmin? For our son?'

'No, forget all that,' Sanjay said. 'I must go. They have told me.'

'If we try to stop you, you will go,' Arun said. 'Now you think it is your fate.'

'It is no such thing,' Shanti Devi said.

'He will go, Sanjay's mother,' Arun said. 'You do not know your son. I do not know your son. Perhaps even he knows little of himself. You think of him as injured and fragile, but he moves things in ways we cannot imagine, so he will go. Tomorrow or the day after. Come, let us sleep.' He led her away, then turned back to Sanjay. 'You think you are wiser than us, and certainly you know more already. But let me tell you something, before you go travelling. I have learnt one thing in my life, and it is this, that there is no such thing as fate, and freedom does not exist. So go, and I bless you, and I wish you well.'

So, three weeks later, Sanjay hardened his heart and turned his face away as a cart pulled away from his home and from his father and mother, a cart that was to meet Sikander's party at his house; Arun and Shanti Devi walked behind the cart, unwilling to give up the sight of their son; they walked through the bazaars of the city, where the cart moved slowly, Shanti Devi leaning on her husband's arm. When the congested core of the town was left behind, as the road straightened out and smoothened, they fell behind, and Shanti Devi called, 'Write every day,' and Arun waved clumsily; Sanjay looked once and then faced forward, his face burning, lips desperately compressed, and soon the road dipped into a hollow and behind some trees. Sanjay settled into the packets of food and apparel that his mother had prepared for him; under his left arm was a rough cloth bag containing his father's last gift to him: a complete, hand-lettered manuscript of the works of Mir. Sanjay pulled out a leaf at random and read:

> One day I walked into the shops of the glass-blowers
> And asked: O makers of the cup, have you perhaps a glass
> Shaped like a heart?
> They laughed and said: You wander in vain.
> O Mir, each cup you see, round or oval, every glass
> Was once a heart that we melted on the fire and blew
> Into a cup.
> That's all you see here, there is no glass.

Ashutosh Sorkar was a man shaped like an up-ended drum; when he stood in the midst of the various segments of his instrument, a printing press, wearing only a langot, his stomach bulged hugely from his chest, balanced nicely by a pair of large but high-riding buttocks, and all the time his already-pudgy cheeks were swelled by a large gout of paan. His hair lay flat and receded, but his eyes darted, and in consequence of his long-held post of printing-master at the Markline Orient Press he moved with a slow majesty that Sanjay instantly associated with his once-friend, Gajnath, the king of elephants. Besides this there was something else that Sanjay could not place, a refinement of tone despite his minuscule habiliments, a delicacy in the way he spoke and handled things, but Sanjay put that down to the sophistication common among Calcutta-folk, for which they were famous.

'So,' Sorkar said in Bengali-accented Urdu, 'you will call me Sorkar Chacha, or Chacha, no need for Sorkar Sahib or Sorkar Moshai or any of that. And I am told that you are Sanjay and you are James.'

'Sikander.'

'Sikander? Ah, grand name, good name. You, of course, are apprenticed to be shop manager, so you will sit at the front, in the little alcove, and will deal mostly with customers and their requirements and accounts. And you, Sanjay, will work in here with me, composing the page, setting the type, making the book. In our endeavours we will be ably assisted by our friends Kokhun and Chottun, who are old-hand ink-ball-rollers and master press-pullers.'

Kokhun and Chottun were brothers, two almost-identical men with the same black skin and wiry stick-limbs; they smiled together, rubbing their hands over the fine trace-work of muscle on their bellies.

'I feed them and feed them,' Sorkar said, 'and they stay the same. You two are frail in the body too, we'll have to put some Calcutta flesh on you, rosogullas and fish and curds. Gentlemen, you are going to discover the cuisine of the gods, I congratulate you.'

So Sikander and Sanjay set to work in the press. The machine itself was scattered over a large area: the type was picked with swift fingers from an inclining case against the wall and dropped into a composing stick, which in turn was securely locked into a forme; this forme of type ('Or chase of type,' Sorkar said. 'Say it after me: stick, forme, chase'), after the compositor had finished with it, was taken to another table by Kokhun and inked with ink-balls, then passed to Chottun, who set it on the press and pulled the bar to press the platen down, pulled again to raise the platen, and Sanjay gazed in awe at the letters which appeared, mechanically and magically, clean and regular, on the white paper. Pull and pull, two pulls for each impression, verso and recto according to Sorkar's mysterious calculations, the pages piled on each other, were folded over and became suddenly a book ready to be stitched and bound.

That night, Sanjay shook Sikander awake, amidst the reams of paper and the smell of ink; they were sleeping on thin mattresses spread out on the raised walk that circled the press building. 'Listen, Sikander,' Sanjay said. 'Think of what happens here. Did you see the pages fall, one after the other? Before, when people made a book, the writing went on for weeks and months, or even if it was from a block it had to be recarved after a while, mistakes everywhere, the carver interfering, the words diluted with all the errors and emotion in the middle, all clumsy. But now, something is written, the type's put in place, you check it, then khata-khat, khata-khat, page after page, book after book, the words multiplying, all the same, all exactly and blessedly identical, becoming millions from thousands, filling the world, khata-khat.'

'Khata-khat,' Sikander snorted. 'Go to sleep, idiot.'

'Sleep? Oh, you Rajput, don't you understand? Everything's changed now, horses and swords are finished, I speak a word here, tomorrow it's a book, the day after that the world is changed, khata-khat.'

'Poor world,' Sikander said, turning away onto his side and settling into his pillow.

'Think, think, some poor fool, some priest or poet or something is grinding away at his desk, making something, and in the time he takes to write a chapter and have it copied, two copies, a dozen, I've unloaded twenty thousand of my book at his door-step, he's done, he's drowned, he's finished. Think.'

Without turning or looking, Sikander swung his arm back and thumped Sanjay on the chest with the heel of his hand: 'Sleep, or I'll finish you now.'

So Sanjay quietened and lay back, but thoughts of a fame beyond imagining kept him awake; let Sikander have the kingdom, but in the households they'll speak my words, obey me. He got up and went inside, found his pack, groped inside for the Mir manuscript, and sat touching it in the darkness, overwhelmed by tenderness for his father's innocence; the paper was fragile under his fingers, and San- jay wondered how many copies of his father's plays existed, how many had read the writings of his uncle, how long it would be before their works would be forgotten, before they themselves would vanish forever.

The next morning Sanjay stood by Sorkar, by the case of type; as each letter was required, Sorkar would point to the appropriate compartment and call: 'Big Aay! Triangle with two legs, from the upper part of the case! Up, Sanjay, up! Aif! Soldier with two arms behind! El! Soldier with one trailing leg! Aay! Tee! Soldier with an English hat! Au! Circle with emptiness! Au! Endless potentiality! En! Soldier, then down, then soldier!' In three days Sanjay knew the whole alphabet, and in a burst of ambition attempted to read a sentence, or at least voice it phonetically; he leaned over a stack of pages that Chottun had just pressed. It sunk in then that he had learnt to recognize mirror images, that the letters he now knew were the wrong way around, that under Sorkar's tutelage he had learnt an upside-down language of iron; he twisted his neck, moving his head as he tried to see the letters on the page as their other, reversed metal ancestors, and instantly felt a burst of nausea, his head swim.

'Tired?' Chottun said, steadying him. 'Don't worry, you'll get used to it.'

'No, not tired,' Sanjay said. 'It's this English, hard to read.'

'Funny language,' Kokhun said. 'I gave up on it a long time ago, now I just look at it, all the letters sitting apart from each other.'

'Cowards!' Sorkar yelled from the other end of the shop, where he was leaning over Sikander and a ledger. 'Fear-mongers. Don't infect him.'

'Sorkar Sahib has mastered it,' Kokhun said.

'Defeated it,' Chottun said.

'Indeed,' Sorkar said, striding to the centre of the room and hooking his thumbs in his waist-band. 'Listen, Sanju, at first I was as scared as you. It snarled like a lion, this English, and I was afraid to go near it.'

'How did you learn it?' Sikander said, getting up from his seat. 'Did you have a teacher?'

'No, no teacher for Sorkar Sahib,' Kokhun said.

'He mastered the animal himself,' Chottun said. 'In fair and equal competition. He —'

'Be quiet, you two,' Sorkar said, with a quick glance at Sikander.

'Tell us, sir,' Sanjay said. 'Is it a secret method?'

'Please,' Sikander said.

'No, no,' Sorkar said. 'Enough talk. Get back to work.'

Sikander returned to his desk, and Sanjay went back to his reversed letters. Later that afternoon, Chottun pressed a stack of impressions and sat beside the machine, wiping his forearms and chest with a rag; Sikander stepped from his niche, taking off his shirt, and took the bar.

'It's all right,' Sikander said when Chottun and Kokhun twittered about propriety. 'Never mind all that.'

'What they mean exactly is that this work is not for you,' Sorkar said. 'After all, you're a Sahib . . .'

'I'm a Rajput,' Sikander said. He took the bar and set to work, and soon Kokhun and Chottun were scurrying to keep up with him; Sikander's body was smooth, built squarely and dense, gleaming dark brown, ceaseless and regular in motion, his face blank and eyes un-focussed and internal. The bar moved khata-khat, khata-khat, while the impressions piled up, ream upon ream. The next day, and the day after, Sikander worked, and they all watched him, awed by his stamina and strength; on the third evening Sorkar stopped him, offering a glass of sweet lassi.

'Enough work,' Sorkar said. 'Enough, O magnificent Sikander, or we will be finished with our job before the end of the week, and this hasn't happened ever in Calcutta. Here, drink.'

'How did you learn English?' Sikander said, his hands still on the bar, his chest heaving.

'I'll show you, I'll tell you,' Sorkar said. 'Drink, drink.'

Sikander took the steel tumbler, and he and Sanjay sat on the ground and drank while Sorkar disappeared into a store-room. Kokhun and Chottun squatted opposite, and then Sorkar came back out and put a parcel in the middle of the circle, a rectangular object wrapped in red cloth. He wiped his hands on his dhoti, and with an air of great cere-mony he untied the fat knot on top of the package. Kokhun and Chot-tun smiled knowingly; Sorkar peeled back four flaps, revealing a thick book bound in leather and embossed in gold. He lifted the cover, open-ing to the frontispiece, a dreamy-eyed man with a beard.

'Can you make it out?' Sorkar said to Sanjay, pointing to the title on the facing page. 'No, never mind, I was like that at first, I stole the book' — smiling at Sikander — 'and I could read not a word. It was a long time ago. It was when this press was first set up, and Mr Markline himself worked here, and I was a boy doing the chores and the clean-ing, and many an evening Mr Markline lay in this very place, drinking out of a black bottle, cuffing me whenever I passed within reach. It was a long time ago, he was young then, just come here from over the seas, his eyes as pale blue as today, his hair flat brown over his head. He was thin, always crisp and tense, always unpredictable. Everything he wanted exactly so, anything not just as he wanted it would throw him into a rage, red-faced in a language none of us understood. I would shake my head, sometimes without wanting to, break into a smile, and this would infuriate him, tears in his eyes, and he would hit me. Once he beat me with a cane, with a cane because there was dust where there shouldn't have been, the ink-balls weren't in their proper place, something, I've forgotten what. Afterwards he lay drunken in the court-yard, in the heat, and I sat feeling the sting of the cuts on my shoulders, weeping. I was young but I had already a wife and three children in my village, my mother, a small plot of land. I sat and cursed and wondered. When I heard his snores I went in and stood over him, looking at the length of him, his legs hanging off the sagging cot, his thick arms with their strong muscles, his pink lips, thinking I could kill him now, poison his drink, put a krait in his bath. But by his bed lay this book, one of a few he had brought with him, beautiful books he'd look at sometimes, examples, I suppose, of the English printer's art. I picked up the book and carried it outside, out of the house, and hid it in the banyan tree, lowering it into a hollow. Then I opened a window, but went back in through the door, closing it behind me, waited for a few moments, then shouted, thief, master, thief. He staggered up and we rushed around, lighting lanterns, checking locks. Finally he found the open window; discovered that the only thing missing was the book. I heard feet, I said, saw a form leaning over your bed, I said. He looked at me, raised the lantern to my face, but I held up my eyes to him, and what could he do? Well, we went back to sleep, and the days and months passed, we got business, we printed, things got better. I started to help in the composing, and a day came when he left the press to me, he started other things, other businesses, made money, and he let me take care of it, coming in once a day to read the proofs, once in two days, then even less. One night when I hadn't seen him in weeks, I went out and brought the book back in, out of the tree and into the house. It was weathered now, the leather stiff and faded, the paper curled. I opened it up and saw this picture, this bearded man with his ear-ring, and I thought of the scars on my back, and I said, I must read this. You understand, at that time I knew only the letters, separate and by themselves, and maybe a few familiar words, here and there. But I said, I must read this. So I read the first page, this title, can you see it, Sanjay, try it.'

'T-h-e,' Sanjay said. 'C-o-m-p-l-e-t-e . . .'

'Say it,' Sorkar said.

'T-hee?'

'The,' Sikander said, smiling.

'Com . . . ,' Sanjay said.

Sikander helped him along: 'plete.'

After a great deal of hesitation and fits and starts Sanjay said it: 'The Com-plete Works of Wil-liam Shakes-peare.'

'And so I began to read,' Sorkar said. 'And at first the complete works were like a jungle, the language was quicksand. Metaphors turned beneath my feet and became biting snakes, similes fled from my grasp like frightened deer, taking all meaning with them. All was alien, and amidst the hanging, entangling creepers of this foreign grammar, all sound became a cacophony. I feared for myself, for my health and sanity, but then I thought of my purpose, of where I was and who I was, of pain, and I pressed on.'

'Oh, brave,' said Kokhun.

'Fearless,' said Chottun.

'And so day by day I read through to the end, not understanding much but learning. The next year I read through again. And then again the next year. And so I have traversed the complete works thirty-four times, and from a foreign jungle I have made it my own garden. Every part of this terrain I have faced with my body, this earth is my earth, Willy is my boy. Ask me anything, and I will respond as he would have. Ask. Give me a word.'

'Heart,' Sikander said.

Sorkar smiled, then declaimed in English:

> The eleven-fold shield of Sikander cannot keep
> The battery from my heart.

'What does that mean?' Sanjay said.

'You'll learn, you'll learn, but give me a word.'

'Power.'

A greater power than we can contradict
Hath buried our intents.

'But what does it mean?' Sanjay said, his voice rising.
'It'll come to you presently, my son,' Sorkar said. 'But listen:

Time shall unfold what plaited cunning hides;
Who cover strengths, at last honour them abides.

'I wish you'd tell me what it means,' Sanjay said sullenly, but instead Sorkar began to instruct him in the language. Now, as they composed, he pronounced whole words and provided meanings, paraphrases, glosses; as he did this Sanjay became aware of the incontrovertible fact that Sorkar stole industriously and hugely from the Englishman: reams of paper were pronounced exhausted when there was a good quarter of an inch left, for every vat of ink that was mixed and used, a tenth part was secreted away by Kokhun and Chottun, perfectly good formes were thrown into a pile in a back room. And of course everyone except Sikander worked at a determinedly leisurely pace, pausing often to drink, rest, or merely reflect; in addition Sorkar was given to musing halts during which he would scratch his head, squint through narrowed eyes at his composing stick, and appear to calculate, after which, instead of calling to Sanjay for a letter, he would extract one from a case he kept under his stool, covered with a red cloth. Inserting this special letter into his stick, he would smile at Sanjay with a simper that would pull in his face towards its centre, making him look like a bullfrog with something in its gullet. 'Ooo yais,' he would say, delighting in his role of teacher, in what Sanjay already recognized as fatally Bengali-accented English, 'next please: letter v, making already half of "river," which is to say a flow, flood, or plentiful stream of anything.'

Yes, and I bow to you, O mine guru, Sanjay wanted to say, but why i from under your magnificent buttocks, what language is that a part of, but already it was clear that Sorkar revealed only as much as he wanted to, rewarded knowledge according to some secret reckoning, let one through his many-layered, soft defences to his innermost secrets only after a mysterious judgement quite beyond flattery or influence. So Sanjay waited, attempted to please, concentrated on the language, and sounded Sikander on the mystery.

'What do you think he's doing?' Sanjay said. 'I looked at the letters after you pressed them, the *i* in river, and it looks exactly the same.'

'I don't know,' said Sikander, and turned over and went to sleep. He had become strangely dull and incurious; every day he worked at the press, making impressions, heaving the bar to and fro until he seemed stunned with fatigue and monotony. In the evenings Sikander dropped into his bed and slept twisted in the sheets, insensible to the sounds and smells of Calcutta that drifted in over the walls and kept Sanjay awake till late: Sanjay lay thinking about the courtesans of the pamphlets, but was unable to bring himself to face the city by himself. After the voices quietened, and the wheels stopped creaking outside, the smell still tormented Sanjay with its wood-smoke bitterness, rot, its syrupy heaviness, so that he whispered 'Kali-katta, Kali-katta' even as he fell into sleep, dreaming of secrets.

One morning, Sorkar woke them up early, saying, 'Come, come, you two, it is accounting-day and Markline Sahib wants to see you, he has asked for you.' He instructed them to wear their best clothes — Sikander's black coat and Sanjay's silk kurta — and supervised their baths, then put them in a rickshaw, one on either side of himself, placed a roll of paper in his lap, and set off. The city slid past them, and then they had to get in a ferry to cross the Hooghly; the morning sun came off the water, the single sweep creaked in the lock, and the boatman sang an incomprehensible Bengali song full of longing. Then, while Sanjay was still unsteady from the motion of the water, they were at the house, a bungalow set far back behind a white wall, amongst clipped hedges and walks. They waited in an ante-chamber, sitting uncomfortably on thick couches, amidst small brown tables laden with silver, an elephant's leg umbrella-stand, paintings of pastoral landscapes from some cool clime, and under a series of mounted heads. A tall domestic, dressed in white, came in and motioned them forward, towards a large double door. 'Come.'

At the lintel Sorkar laid a hand on Sanjay's shoulder. 'Your shoes,' he said.

'What?'

'You have to take them off.'

Sanjay felt anger bubbling up from his stomach, and knew his face was flushing, but Sikander was already bending to his boots.

'Not you, baba,' the servant said to Sikander.

But the boots were already off, and then Sanjay had to hurry to get his sandals off as Sikander pushed through the door, animated for the first time in weeks.

The Englishman was seated on a long cane armchair, his feet up on its extended arms. Sanjay, finding it hard to look directly into the blue eyes, stared instead at the white shirt, the brown pants and boots splattered with mud, the long muscular length of arm under the rolled-up cuff; the marble was icy under Sanjay's feet.

'Are you James?' Markline said, and Sanjay surprised himself by understanding every word, despite the accent — he felt a sudden surge of confidence, and looked up: the man's hair was blond and fine, falling across his forehead, his skin red and a little wrinkled, but healthy, his teeth yellowed and clamped firmly around a long brown cigarette.

'Sikander.'

'I see,' Markline said, leaning forward, heels clicking on the floor. 'I see.' Sikander met his gaze without fear, and Sanjay thought, pridefully, for the first time in his life, my brother. Markline suppressed a smile and turned his head towards him: 'And this is the boy from the other family?'

'Yes, sir,' Sorkar said.

'Very interesting,' Markline said. 'Cheeky-looking fellow.' He turned back to Sikander. 'I knew your father well. We were young men together in Calcutta. You must do proud by him, work hard.' He lowered his head a little to peer at Sikander, who had by now regained his customary indifference to the world; Markline looked up at Sorkar, his eyebrows raised, then towards Sanjay. 'And this fellow? What does he want to be?'

'Writer, sir,' Sanjay said, surprising himself, because he had meant to say poet.

'You speak English, do you?'

'Little, sir.'

'How long have you been learning?'

'Little weeks, sir.'

'Good, damn good. That's the sort of work we want to see around here.' Saying this, Markline extended his feet to his man-servant, who, kneeling, pulled off the boots and put forward a pair of soft-looking

black shoes, and with this the interview was over: Sikander and Sanjay
were herded out to the other room, where they were told to wait again.
The animals on the wall — a few antlered deer, two boars, a nilgai —
stared down with what seemed to be a black-eyed, blunt contempt, and
so Sanjay tried once again to engage Sikander in conversation: 'I
wonder how he hunts.'

But Sikander was staring, head outthrust, at the elephant's leg, cut
level with the knee and scooped empty inside, and then Sorkar came
through the door. 'Come, come,' Sorkar said. 'Let's go home.'

They stopped, however, at a halwai's, where Sorkar bought three
seers of white rosogullas, which he handed to them one by one as they
walked down the lanes. Sanjay swallowed them and licked the syrup
from his hands, then asked: 'Why was he muddy?'

'They play polo,' Sorkar said. 'But he likes you, he said there should
be more like you, eager to learn, avid to change was the phrase he used
I think.'

'He did?' Sanjay said. 'He said that?'

'Surely he did.'

Sanjay walked on, his tongue slippery between his lips. 'He must be
very strong, no?'

'He is,' Sorkar said, and then picked the last rosogulla off the leaves
and held it, suspended between two finger-tips, towards Sanjay's lips.
Sanjay stopped, opened his mouth, closed his eyes as the ball rolled in
with a fleeting touch of Sorkar's fingers, bringing with it some vague,
half-formed childhood memory of things being slipped between his
teeth, but then Sorkar went on: 'He is strong, no doubt, but let me tell
you a story.' Sanjay looked again and Sorkar was flicking his fingers, a
thoughtful expression on his face. 'He is strong, of course, but consider
this, and see how it amuses you. You're a quiet boy, and a watchful one,
alternately one-eyed and all, but you see things all right, and I've seen
you looking at the case I keep under my stool, and how I take out
letters from it sometimes, and you wonder why but are smart enough
not to ask. But what do you think about it? You must have tried some
deduction, some elementary inferences, something? What?'

'The letters aren't different,' Sanjay said.

'If they were, then what?'

'Then I'd have to look at the letters.'

'With what purpose?'

'To see if they spelt something, but then it might be a code, like kings use in their secret missives, a spy's cipher.'

'You've read your Chanakya, haven't you? But why would I put a cipher in the things we print? Government pamphlets and Company reports? What would I say? Who would I be saying it to? Whose spy would I be?'

'I don't know,' Sanjay said.

'Ah,' said Sorkar. 'See, deduction has its limits. One must know the other half of the world.' He motioned them on down the road, and they walked through a vegetable market. 'Let me tell you a story. Suppose there is this man who loves Shakespeare, adores the sweet Willy, and suppose this man works in a printing shop. And suppose this man is called in one day by his master, the owner of the shop, who gives him a very special job, a sixty-four-page pamphlet to be done on heavy paper and bound in soft fawn leather, a booklet for private distribution. And suppose our man takes the manuscript to the shop and starts setting it, only to discover it is an attack on Willy, an assertion that some unlettered, mean, drunken and rustic farm lout, sunk in the superstitions and vulgarities of country-folk, could never have produced the divine plays, that splendid body of work. But that, rather, it was another man, an urban sophisticate, a courtier and noble and above all a scientist, who had penned these magnificent dreams and given them to the world under a pseudonym, out of fear of political repercussions; that this man, the true author, was a rationalist, an observer of human nature, a philosopher, a possessor of great learning, *glorius mundi*, Francis Bacon, Lord Verulam himself. Proof, you might ask, where in damn hell is the proof? All this, this robbing of poor Willy, all this was based on some wishful thinking, a refusal to accept that one who was not one of theirs could create something as excellent and as good, and finally some slipshod unbelievable discovery of mechanical proof in the text, which is to say this owner-master said there were ciphers in the text, sonnets which spelt out, acrostically, "Bacono" in reverse and "Francisco" on the diagonal, unbelievable bright-green horseshit the likes of which you'd never heard. So suppose our friend the printer, who considers Willy a personal friend, maybe perhaps his only and best friend, sits with this manuscript, this thing in his hand, thinking I have to do this, I'm going to have to do this, and he looks at the picture of poor Willy, balding head and huge eyes, that expression of reserve, that look of hurts taken and forgiven, and the printer thinks, the pompous stew-brained *knaves,* if they want ciphers, I'll give them ciphers. So that week instead of giving the left-overs from the shop, or to put it openly, the stolen materials from the press, to a struggling Bengali or Urdu newspaper, he sold them. He then found a master type-cutter, a wizened old Bengali man from Dhaka, a jewellery maker and sometimes gravestone-cutter and type-cutter, and commissioned him to cut a number of new sets of type. These characters were almost identical but not quite with the ones that were to be used to set the Bacon book, and so our friend built a cipher: calculating and calculating, he replaced certain characters in the book with ones from his near-duplicate fonts, so that only someone amazingly keen, with a trained and searching eye, could see them — they blended with the ordinary characters almost perfectly; then, if an alert reader saw these odd characters, depending on the positions of the characters in the line and relative to one another, and depending on his mathematical skills and ability at deciphering, he could uncover a hidden message. The code is based on the number of odd characters between —'

'Yes, but what was this message?' said Sikander.

'Well,' said Sorkar, 'for Markline's pamphlet, which he called *Was Sir Francis Bacon the True Author of the Stratford Plays?*, the enciphered message ran "Did the mother of this author lick pig pricks by the light of the full Stratford moon?" The week after that, the press printed a Company report entitled *A Physical and Economic Survey of the Territories of East India, with Special Attention to Bengal,* and our friend secreted the following message: "The Company makes widows and famines, and calls it peace." And so, in *The Religions and Peoples of India: Travels of a Rationalist,* "This writer is neither a true traveller nor a rationalist"; in *Britain and India: Reflections on Civilizational Decay and Progress,* "Britain is the pus from the cancer of Europe"; and in *Statistics Pertaining to the Growth of Rice and Wheat in the Bengal During the Year 18-something-something,* simply and clearly, "Fuck you." '

Sorkar stopped because Sikander was laughing: he was doubled over in the middle of the lane, and he whooped and guffawed and yelled, hitting his sides with his hands, helplessly. People stopped to stare, and then began to smile themselves, and two little boys fell into giggles, because Sikander's laughter was good, a laugh like water cold from a clay pot in the summer, a sound of release and gratitude.

'That's good,' Sikander said finally, his face flushed darkly red under the brown skin, and he reached out and took Sorkar's hand, so that they walked together, side by side. 'Tell me more.'

So Sorkar regaled them with a decade's worth of accumulated messages that he had camouflaged skilfully into the alien territory of the Markline's books: the content of these hidden slogans, by Sanjay's estimation, ranged mostly from the sentimentally puerile to the frankly inane. Sikander, however, enjoyed them with a gusto that seemed to gratify Sorkar and inspire him to further feats of memory — he had in caution kept no written record of these messages or codes — and what had to be invention: what sane and thinking adult would insert into a book called *A Comparative Meditation on the Metaphysics of Christianity and Hinduism* the message 'English food is the worst in the world, fit only to be eaten by donkeys and anthropomorpha'? Sanjay listened to Sikander's laughter with outward and quite sincere joy, which hid a deeper and shameful agitation; he had hidden, as long as he could remember, in some remote-even-from-himself part of his soul, an envy of Sikander's ease with people, of his easy and unforced banter, of his ability to converse with any and all stations without self-consciousness or effort, and so Sanjay for a while had derived some strange satisfaction from the other's retreat into silence and introspection. It was as if Sikander's quietness, his interiority, had brought to his Rajput carelessness and physicality that curse that had always lain heavily on Sanjay: the curse of a life inside that competed for attention and defeated the world outside, dreams that refused to be quieted, that unwanted double-vision that brought encounters with gods and half-knowledge of things to come. But now Sikander blossomed again, and he shared bidis with Kokhun and Chottun, and sat sweat-covered with his arms around their shoulders, and addressed Sorkar as 'Chacha' and affected familial chaffing, and now all the three printer-people slid joyfully down the valley of his charm into an affection both deep and boundless, much as the soldiers of their childhood had. So Sanjay, attempting to hide the small bone of resentment that poked painfully somewhere in his chest, retreated into the books that were stacked untidily from floor to ceiling, and was horrified to find that even those were not safe; as he read he could not help trying to find hidden messages according to Sorkar's cipher, but his eyes skittered painfully as he peered at the letters, trying to find the infinitesimal difference that would distinguish the disguised from the real, and his head spun with numbers as he tried to calculate the numerical relationships between cipher-letters according to Sorkar's elaborate rules, so that finally the messages that appeared were strange and incomprehensible. 'Fry the fish,' said *Calcinates and Sulphates,* and *McNally History Primer for Tots* remarked politely, 'Can you come over tomorrow and look at it?'

At first Sanjay believed firmly that these curious communications issued from these books because he was misreading the type, failing to see Sorkar's characters where they really appeared, and because he was making errors in his calculations, but one evening as he closed *Astronomer's Almanac,* a quite distinct voice said in Punjabi-accented Urdu, 'After his retirement he was quite happy.' Sanjay jumped, looked around, but he was alone in the room and the door was shut; he picked up the *Almanac* and flipped through it, and when nothing happened he swallowed, smiling at himself in relief, but when he flipped through it the other way a woman's voice spoke in some staccato southern language, incomprehensible but clear as a mynah on a spring night. Sanjay flung the book away, and it flew in a flutter of white pages and slid down the wall to lie face down, silent at last; he fled the room, and went outside to find Sikander and the others, who were sitting on a charpoy eating after-dinner paan and burping happily.

'What's the matter?' Sorkar asked. 'You're jumping about the place like a gazelle.'

'Nothing,' Sanjay said, and sat down beside them and tried to burp harder than any of them, because he was afraid that he might start to hear whispers emanating from all the paper and print scattered around the house.

'Good effort,' Sorkar said after one of Sanjay's burps. 'Sturdy of will but lacking in stamina. Try again.'

But all of Sanjay's efforts were defeated by Sikander's mighty and eruptive exhalations, which seemed to vibrate through his whole body before they burst from his mouth and sang through the air like a long blast from a sea-shell.

'Astonishing,' Kokhun and Chottun chorused. 'Tremendous.'

Sanjay stifled his resentment and a new-found distaste for gastric games, and applauded with the rest, and that night insisted on sleeping on the roof of the house, despite a slight chill in the air and the possibility of rain. After that evening he tried to avoid books, but was unable to keep away for more than a day: he sneaked peeks at the pages Sikander pressed, and the next afternoon guiltily picked up a text on gunnery, put it down again, then snatched it up and read ten pages, producing a perfect rattle and clatter of voices around his head as he blissfully consumed, from the paper, sentences he couldn't understand. In a mood of self-disgust, he walked around the house with a fierce expression of determination on his face, prompting jibes from Sikander and attempts at purgative medication from Sorkar; this time his abnegation lasted all of three days, and then late one night he jumped from his bed, ran to the loading area where books and pamphlets waited, stacked and tied, for the delivery carts, and read all night by the light of a sputtering, clandestine lantern, until his head spun and his eyes ached, and when morning came he knew he was ensnared, trapped forever by words, and in the instant he realized this, as a flight of sparrows manoeuvred dizzily through the court-yard, he remembered his uncle Ram Mohan, and cursed heavily and vilely with new-found Calcutta sophistication: you cannot choose what you are made of, whether it is spittle or dust from the still-blowing winds of another generation, but what is worse is that one morning you come to know that your bones have ineluctably bred the same impermanences that should have died with your ancestors, the same hopes and despairs and loves and weaknesses, that you are forever trapped by their knotty lusts and ideals.

So Sanjay learnt this early lesson of karma, and lived in Calcutta surrounded by voices from near and far; there were Punjabi women, Sindhi crones, Gujarati businessmen, Kashmiri intellectuals, and a myriad others in tongues he couldn't understand, some that he had never heard before, and some that he was sure could issue from no subcontinental mouth, clicking and clacking phonemes and nasal syllables completely and utterly foreign. But since these voices — or secondary articulations, as he now thought of them — issued from books, from novels and chronicles and documents and manuals that provided a steady stream of coherent and seemingly relevant information, Sanjay decided that the bargain was an even one. To listen to the clear music of logic, he told himself, one must tolerate and acknowledge the noise of muddy chaos; white palaces must be built, unfortunately but necessarily, on stinking mud, he told himself, and went on with his reading.

One day soon after, Sorkar waddled up to him, his hands held carefully over his stomach, exuding a kind of lardy politeness that made him difficult to see. 'Sanjay, child, he wants you,' he said.

'Who?' Sanjay said. The others, Sikander and Chottun and Kokhun, were drying their sweat or picking lint from their navels with an exactitude that suddenly reminded Sanjay of his father's description of courtiers as he finished reading a new poem: as hugely courteous as great ladies with an unexpected harlot. So Sanjay burst out: 'Why are you looking at me like that?'

'Mr Markline has sent for you,' Sorkar said.

'Why?'

'I don't really know,' Sorkar said. 'The message just says that he expects to see you tomorrow morning at eleven at his house. You are to present yourself punctually, et cetera.'

'Why me, what does he want from me?' Sanjay said vehemently, conscious from the first instant that he was dissembling, because ever since the visit to the bungalow he had expected something of the sort, and indeed he had paraded his precocious English in the hopes of impressing the Englishman. The others shrugged and turned back to their work, leaving Sanjay to think about the impending encounter, and even more about the meeting in the past — when he reconstructed the event carefully, peeling aside onion-skin–layers of memory's self-serving deceits, he seemed to remember straightening his back and neck, an attempt to imitate Markline's erect posture and meet his blue eyes. All that night Sanjay tried to imagine himself in beautiful mirror-shined boots and a white shirt, the slim hard figure of a dark rider on some imaginary landscape; but in the morning he put on, eagerly and nervously, without needing Sorkar's prompting, his white achkan and his best dhoti. He left early, and was at the Hooghly ghat a full half hour before he needed to be, but still the chattering of the boatmen and their slow luxurious passage across the river worked on his nerves like the long-nailed fingers of a sitar-player, until he finally snapped out a command to hurry, hurry.

The boatman said something to the other passengers in Bengali, and they all laughed, while Sanjay looked down, his face burning; there was no change in the speed of the boat, but the lazy splash of the pole now kept time with a song sung by the boatman. The people on the boat hummed along quietly, settling back into their seats, and several of them still smiled as their glances drifted over Sanjay. One of them leaned forward: 'It is a very famous song,' he said, 'about a young man driven mad by love, who hurries to his beloved's side, facing immeasurable and unimaginable hardships.'

'Why did he hurry?' Sanjay said instantly, in spite of himself.

'Because the beloved, after a lifetime of evincing distaste and rejection and harshness, was dying. And she called for him. And our young man loved her truly.'

'What nonsense,' Sanjay said, and turned away pointedly. He tried to fall back into his previous state of anticipation and excitement, but for the second time in a few hours he thought of his father and his uncle, annoyed at the mixture of guilt and mild aversion this recollection squeezed from some unknown part of his soul: he realized suddenly that he had not seen his father-gifted Mir manuscript in weeks, and hadn't the slightest conception of where it might lie, in the welter of paper and scrap that lined the press. What, what sensationalism, he thought, all this Mirism, why should love always be an agony, and then recognized with a pronounced internal lurch that he hadn't written to his mother since when, one month surely and maybe two, so then he turned his attention outward, to the water and the sun above. Observe, he told himself, observe and remember, for this shall be a momentous day in your life; but the water was flat and brown, the sky a huge washed-out blue, and the others on the boat were the usual collection of rustics, traders and nondescript types, squatting and jabbering, in short not at all the ilk of co-travellers that one wished for on a journey into the future. At the shore, the boat swayed away from Sanjay just as he leaped off, causing him to drop into a good three inches of water; dark, muddy stains stretched up his white dhoti, almost to his knees. All his angry wiping was useless, and so he walked up the slope, almost in tears, towards the green of the trees, the cotton sticking to his legs.

At the house, this time, he was taken in straightaway to Markline, who was eating some brown object with a flashing knife and fork; as

Markline sawed methodically at the meat on his plate, dividing it into identical brown squares, Sanjay stifled a quick upsurge of nausea.

'Good morning,' he said, as he had learnt from *Etiquette for the Young Child.*

'Morning,' Markline said. 'Why do you wear that thing on your eye?'

'I see doubly,' Sanjay said.

'Double. Have you seen a doctor?'

Dak-tah? Daak-ter? Sanjay shifted, and felt water drip from his knees onto his feet.

'Doctor,' Markline said. 'Have you seen a doctor?' He swallowed, then said slowly, 'Doctor?'

'O doctor, doctor,' Sanjay said in delight, finally understanding. 'Yes, yes, but they did nothing. Many hakims and vaids came.'

'I meant a real doctor,' Markline said. 'Come on.'

A closed carriage was waiting outside; Sanjay was motioned up, to sit between the driver and Markline's major-domo, the tall, thin man who soon revealed his name to be Ardeshir, and then sat silently, his hands held together tightly in his lap. The driver too was quiet, and it occurred to Sanjay that all of Markline's attendants were curiously un-speaking, but then he forgot all about this as they rumbled through the streets, causing people to break off conversations and gawk. Sanjay threw back his shoulders and affected a stare at something floating in the air perhaps a hundred feet away; the attention pleased him, but all too soon they were at a maidan surrounded by carriages. Markline leaped from the carriage, followed by Ardeshir, and was instantly lost in the crowds of firangis that eddied around the vehicle, filling the air with English too speedy and coloured by accents to decipher. Sanjay fol-lowed the driver to the other side of the maidan, where they squatted amidst others whom Sanjay recognized instantly as servants; he experi-enced a brief twitch of anger and shame, for a very quick moment thought of his mother, but then a bunched group of horses exploded onto the maidan, and the air was filled with cheers and shouts.

The dust boiled off the ground, and the riders materialized and van-ished into the yellow haze, slashing with sticks at a ball that ricocheted from one end of the maidan to the other; sometimes the whirling knot of men and horses followed the ball close to where Sanjay sat, and then for a few moments it seemed as if he was surrounded by screams and huge rolling black eyes, iron-taut horse muscle, yellow teeth, hooves, sticks hissing through the air and cracking against each other, shouts. Then all this would subside and they would vanish into the dust, leaving his heart thudding and thudding as if it wanted to crack his ribs, the wind whipping away the veil for a moment so that he could see, very far away across the expanse of pitted ground, the carriages in which the firangi women stood and waved handkerchiefs, hurrahing in voices that came to him subdued and yet sharpened by the distance, so that he was filled with a not-unpleasant but unfocussed nostalgia, as if he was longing for a memory he had never known.

When it was over Markline came to the carriage caked with dirt, climbed in without a word and they were off; Sanjay realized that in all the time of the match he had never managed to make Markline out among the riders, that the sport accorded a strange anonymity to the players. At the house Markline pointed a finger at Sanjay: 'Wait.' He went into the house, came striding out a few moments later and without pausing threw a small rectangular object at Sanjay, saying 'Here!'

Sanjay flung up his arms, wanting for once in his life to make the catch, but the thing of course spiralled through and hit him on the chest painfully, so that his eyes teared and he had to scrabble in the twilight dust for it.

'Read it,' Markline said, already turning around and walking away. 'And come back next week.'

It was a book, and Sanjay peered at the title page, bringing the paper very close to his nose; it smelt like smoke, and the title was arranged very symmetrically in simple black letters: *The Poetics of Aristotle.*

That week, Sanjay studied the book: the sense was clear enough, if limiting for the maker of art; there seemed to be an insistence on emotional sameness, on evoking one feeling from the beginning to the end of the construction, as if unity could be said to be defined as homogeneity or identity; there seemed to be a peculiar notion of emotion as something to be expelled, to be emptied out, to be, in fact, evacuated, as if the end purpose of art was a sort of bowel movement of the soul; but all this was reasonable, somehow, understandable, even if it violated all of the rules Sanjay had attempted to learn from Ram Mohan's fragmented discourses; even as it was, it was comprehensible as an intellectual exercise, a system of belief, one darshana of the world. What was unearthly and frightening about the book was a voice that whispered from its pages, a voice that whispered and yet silenced all others, that left a silence in the printery-shop, in which it alone remained and spoke, spoke again and again one phrase: 'Katharos dei einai ho kosmos.' And even in the evenings when the book was shut, or at dinner, Sanjay could hear the repeated syllables drifting through the court-yards and flying over the walls, under the wind and the rubbing of branches; it went on, gentle and reasonable at first but then maniacal in its insistence, morning and night, katharos, katharos, until Sanjay pounded at his ears and pressed his head between his fists, unmindful of the pain.

One morning, later that week, Sikander dressed and went to meet his sisters; he returned late at night looking exhausted. Sorkar sat him down to a large dinner and then herded him into bed, but as Sanjay lay awake long into the morning, listening to the constant whisper outside, he also heard Sikander breathing and knew he too couldn't sleep.

'How were they?' Sanjay said finally.

'Who?'

'Your sisters.'

'Fine. They were fine.' He paused for a moment. 'Tonight I keep on remembering them.'

'Of course,' Sanjay said. 'You just saw them.'

'No,' Sikander said. 'Not Emily and Jane. Them. Ma.'

'And my uncle?' Sanjay said.

'Yes.'

'Listen, Sikander,' Sanjay said suddenly, then stopped, embarrassed.

'What?'

'You know that book I've been reading?'

'Yes.'

'It's a book by a Greek.'

'Yes?'

'And when I read it I hear a voice.'

Sikander turned towards him. 'A voice? You mean a voice that says something?'

'Yes.'

'Poor Sanjay.'

'What poor Sanjay? I knew I shouldn't have told you. Damn Rajput.' Sanjay jumped from his bed and stood in the darkness, trembling.

'I didn't mean that way poor Sanjay,' Sikander said, infuriatingly calm. 'Sit. Sit, Sanju.' Sanjay found himself soothed, as susceptible to the charm as always. 'What does it say?'

'I don't know, it speaks in some other language, must be Greek. "Katharos dei einai ho kosmos," it says. Katharos, katharos, all the time.'

'A ghost, you think? A spirit bound to the book?'

'No, something else. But that's not the thing, not what scares me. What it is is that I think I know who it is, I don't know why, but I recognize it, the voice.'

'Who?'

'It's Alexander,' Sanjay said. 'You know, the Great.'

'Alexander the madman? The butcher?'

'Yes, him.'

'Did he write this book?'

'No. I don't know why I think it's him.'

They lay silent, then Sanjay said: 'Where was she from, Ma?'

'I don't really know,' Sikander said. 'She never spoke about it. But she used to talk sometimes about a place called Ahwa.' They could hear, now, from outside, the occasional call of a bird. 'Sanjay, what were we made for?'

But Sanjay had no answer to that; just before they dropped off to sleep, as the sun came up, Sikander said in a voice barely audible: 'Find out what Alexander says, Sanju.'

At the end of the week, Sanjay visited Markline again, and again he was taken to the polo match and its concealing haze, and then afterwards, at the mansion, on the porch, was engaged in conversation by the Englishman.

'Did you read the book?' Markline said.

'Yes,' said Sanjay. 'Cover to back.'

'Good boy. Keep it and read it again carefully,' Markline said. 'Study it well if you want to be any kind of writer.' He was sitting on a cane chair, drinking a whitish concoction from a glass, and now he leaned forward and jabbed Sanjay lightly on the chest with a stiff forefinger, just below the place where the ribs met. 'There is much in here,' he said, jabbing again, 'we need to get rid of, much stuff we need to scoop out and throw away. If you're to amount to anything. You're riding with a handicap, do you understand? All the weight of centuries of superstition and plain ignorance. I've read your great books, all the great wisdom of the East. And such a mass and morass of darkness, confusion, necromancy, stupidity, avarice, I've never seen. Plots meander, veering from grief to burlesque in a minute. Unrelated narratives entwine and break into each other. Whole huge battles, millions of men a side, stop short so that some dying patriarch can give a speech about duty, a speech that goes on for fifties of pages. Metaphors that call attention to themselves, strings of similes that go from line to line. Characters fall in love or murder, only to have their actions explained away as the results of past births. Characters die, only to be reborn again. Beginnings are not really beginnings, middles are unendurably long and convoluted, nothing ever ends. Tragedy is *impossible* here!'

Markline seemed to become aware of his raised voice, his flushed face, and now he sat back abruptly in his chair, gulped down his drink. 'Study it carefully,' he said. 'This book is the origin of all that is good in literature. It applies the principles of science to the art of the poet, and thus brings the realm of imagination under the clear light of natural logic. It enunciates principles that have been tested by time and have been approved by philosophy. This slim volume is worth whole libraries of the so-called great books of India. Keep it, young fellow, and study it.'

He closed his eyes, and the interview seemed at an end; Sanjay rose to his feet and walked away, only to be stopped by Ardeshir, who handed him a stack of books. 'For this coming week,' Ardeshir said.

Sanjay took the books and stumbled off, light-headed and dizzy, still feeling on his chest, near his heart, the Englishman's finger; he heard Markline's voice, calling: 'Remember!' Sanjay turned back and stood on the garden path, among the carefully arranged roses, his eye dazzled by the setting sun above the bungalow. 'Remember,' Markline shouted, 'if you want to progress, you must cut yourself off from your past! Amputate it!'

Not knowing why, Sanjay called back: 'Katharos dei einai ho kosmos.'

'Very good,' Markline shouted. 'Good boy. Greek too?'

'I don't know. I learnt it from somewhere. What does it mean?'

'It means, son, that the world must be clean.' Markline raised his empty glass to Sanjay. 'The world must be clean!'

Sanjay did not tell Sikander what Alexander was whispering in the dusty printery court-yard; instead, he shrugged when asked and retreated into an even more obsessive study of every book he could find, starting with Markline's books and extending into what the shop had to offer, not excepting those that merely listed the tonnage of wheat shipped from Bengal in a certain year or the minutes of a committee meeting in the Chittagong district. His reading was omnivorous — as his diet was not — and he consumed impartially and massively. 'Catharsis, catharsis,' Sanjay mumbled in reply to Alexander's incessant katharos, katharos, feeling that he was on the verge of uncovering a great secret, but also that he was hounded and harried at the same time by a steadily growing and slavering fear. Fear of what, Sanjay could not have said, but fear it was, a horror that lurked shadow-like in the long still afternoons and almost prompted him into removing his eye-band and calling for the gods he had already cursed; but he thought of his pride and told himself that the things he saw and heard were unreal, the results of damage to the body and remnants of an old insanity better forgotten. So he sought refuge in letters instead, plunged into them with desperation, slept with books under his head and draped over his limbs, one always open on his chest, several near his face where he could smell them; each morning he woke up thinking, if I can truly understand this catharsis, if I can hold it in my head and heart and hand, I will defeat this fear, make it irrelevant, banish it from my court-yard, then, Alexander, go and scream in some desert, amongst lizards and whited bones, whisper your sanitation and urgency to the winds, and we will laugh at you and forget you.

But the fear only mounted with each session at Markline's house, with each new book, while the Englishman's liking for Sanjay seemed to grow with each new word he learnt: when, in conversation, Sanjay used the word *gigantic,* Markline smiled; at *discontent* he threw back his head and laughed; and *perspicacious* impelled him to reach out and pat Sanjay on the shoulder. After *ratiocination* he began, spontaneously, to tell Sanjay about himself, gazing away over the trees and sipping at his drink: he was the youngest son of many in the house of a lord, who after an education at the great universities of the land, had left his family and his country because the laws of inheritance had relegated him to a life of idleness without responsibility, an existence of frivolity and empty carnality; in India he had refused the opportunities offered to one of his birth in commerce and polity, instead directing his activities towards the realm of ideas, since after all it was ideas, immaterial and seemingly impermanent, that determined the course of history and the actions of nations. And now the Markline Press and related enterprises supplied books to all of India and indeed the East, and profits and monies were Markline's proper reward, and Home his dream, but he had resolved to remain in Calcutta, to become a vital element in and contributor to that great task, the opening of the Orient.

'And so I am here, my friend,' Markline said, 'for that is how I regard you, and as we come to share a language you must begin to look upon me as a benevolent ally, an older benefactor concerned above all with your welfare, bodily, spiritual and otherwise. Agreed?'

'Yes,' Sanjay said.

'I will have, next time, someone here to look at your eye,' said Markline. 'A doctor, to see if we can cure the double-sight.'

'Yes,' said Sanjay, smiling. He smiled all the way home, not minding at all now the casual glances his eye-band attracted, had attracted for what seemed now his whole conscious life; but back at the shop when he told the others about his healing they reacted with what could only be described as mistrustful small-mindedness.

'Be careful,' Sorkar said. 'Be careful of Englishmen. Their generosity is poisonous, their love is destruction, their cures are robberies.'

'Poison and destruction,' said Kokhun and Chottun.

'Death,' said Sikander.

'You?' Sanjay said. 'You too? How? You, with your father, and all the others, you, you are an Englishman!'

And suddenly, he never saw Sikander move, but his hand gripped his throat, lifted him up and shook him, fingers settling like a collar of iron, Sikander's face red through a wash of tears in Sanjay's eyes, a fist raised. Sikander shouted, each word louder than the last: 'I am a Rajput,' and Sanjay was unable to see him now, a cracking sound erupted from the back of his head and flashed white across his eyes but then he found himself on the ground fingering at his throat and coughing.

'He wanted to kill you,' Sorkar said, squatting over Sanjay, in a voice wholly conversational, and then walked away, followed by Kokhun and Chottun. Sanjay sat up and rubbed the back of his skull, which Sikander had impacted against the wall, aware that he had crossed an unseen line into something unspeakably intimate, because in all their years together Sikander had never hit him; but after a full half hour of thought Sanjay could find no regret within himself and could only think, how *provincial.* This opinion was only strengthened during the following week when Sikander refused to say anything to him beyond pass me that forme and have you the second page ready yet and are you going to set this one solid or add lead; the others were now polite and courteous and therefore unbearable, so Sanjay worked in silence, furiously picking the type from the case with an efficient speed he had never found before. No one told him to go slow, so that when on the third day of the week a new manuscript arrived, wrapped in black paper and marked in a pen-hand that Sanjay recognized from the fly-leafs of Markline's books (tightly curled descenders, the letters so small and squeezed together that they looked like some foreign language, alien twice over), he had finished his whole weekly quota and was able to claim the job as his own.

'Special,' he said to nobody in particular, 'that's what it says on this. I'll see to it.' Of course there was no reply, and he tore away the paper to find a small black book. 'A reprint,' Sanjay said, but his throat clenched painfully, because in neat gold letters it said on the cover: *The Manners, Customs and Rituals of the Natives of Hindustan; Being Chiefly an Account of the Journeys of a Christian Through the Lands of the Hindoo, and His Appeal to all Concerned Believers;* and the author, of course, was the Reverend Francis M. A. Sarthey.

Markline's note talked about 'highest priority and care,' and besides, Sanjay was himself consumed with curiosity, so without a word to the others he set to work; he propped open the book at the centre of his case and steadied a stick in his left hand, and was soon so absorbed in the text that the letters flew into line and set into words as if by themselves: Sanjay had never worked so fast or hard. The narrative plodded forward in prose that was thick with ecclesiastical exhortations and self-congratulatory hindsight, but Sanjay followed Sarthey's progress from a Middlebury grammar school to priesthood with unswerving concentration, with a dreadful knowledge of the final collision that all the childhood fumblings and punishments and piousness were leading towards. In the middle of a sentence that began 'But luckily through the workings of Divine Grace I . . .' Sanjay flung away the stick, scattering a rain of language that stung the others metallically and resounded over the machines, then picked up the black book and riffled backwards from the back cover, searching for familiar names and fire and ashes. What, what, Sorkar said, but Sanjay finally found his page, and read aloud in a steadily rising voice: 'In the summer of that year a strange tragedy overtook a friend and benefactor, a certain captain whom we shall leave unnamed in consideration of his privacy and feelings. This gentleman had married, in an act of Christian compassion and protec-tion, an Indian lady of high Rajpoot caste who had become bereft of family and future in a bloody siege. The union produced five children, but it was two of this progeny, the daughters, who became the cause of a quarrel that led to a senseless act of self-destruction. The captain de-sired to educate his daughters in accordance with the norms of civilized society, to deliver them from the dark pit of ignorance, but their mother, seeing in this breach of the ancient sanctity of *purdah* a violation of her own overly-proud and sensitive Rajpoot honour, took her own life by immolation. Thus the interior darkness of India, that centuries-old bar-barism, took yet another life . . .' At this Sanjay flung the book across the room, and the force of the swing seemed to crack the spine so that the pages exploded outwards and fell swinging to the floor like a white fog. 'It's not true, it's not true, it's not *true*,' Sanjay shouted, his voice cracking, sweeping his arms from side to side and reddening his face until Sorkar caught hold of him and Sikander lifted him off his feet and lowered him onto a charpoy brought out by Kokhun and Chottun. They held him down, all clutching with one hand and stroking with the other until he quieted, heaving with hacking noises reminiscent of sobs but without tears.

'Shhh,' said Sikander.

'But it's not true,' Sanjay said. 'They're lying about her.'

'I know they are. We all know it wasn't like that.'

'What does it matter what we know? What they'll tell the world is this.'

'Yes.'

'What do you mean, yes? We've got to do something about it. Let me *up*.' He sat up, his arms around his body. 'What can we do? Let's burn the damn book.'

'What use?' Sorkar said. 'It's from one of these machines, remember, a lakh more in a second, more than enough to flood the world.'

'Break the mother-humping machines.'

'Even more pointless — they make more of themselves than you can break.'

'Speak against it. Write something,' Sanjay said.

They all looked at him and even he understood how ridiculous that sounded, but he heard from somewhere in the court-yard, katharos, katharos, felt suddenly his body becoming lighter, sensed that he was about to float off the bed and into space, and he knew that he had to keep speaking, that if he stopped now, that if silence took him now he would be lost forever, his dead betrayed, his parents — all of them — dishonoured, his memory nothing more than a lie, and half the world, half the world with its animals and trees and festivals and gods and philosophies and books and wars and loves, more than half the world made insubstantial and nothing. So Sanjay took a deep breath, and in the manner of a chant began to speak, in English: 'Did not happen like that, did not happen like that, did not happen like that . . .'

Sikander and Sorkar looked at each other, then Sorkar said, quiet, child, quiet, but Sanjay went on; they sat by his bedside and rubbed his limbs, while Chottun ran for a glass of water and Kokhun whispered bribes of rosogullas if he would only stop, but he went on; after two hours of this Sikander clamped a hand over his mouth, but Sanjay struggled not at all and went on, the words becoming a muffled hum in his cheeks. After a while they let him alone and went about their tasks, and he went on in an even, unhurried tone that matched the other invisible voice in the court-yard; when night came still he went on, pausing once to drink water but mumbling even through that in a frothy cloud of bubbles, and the first night was easy, his voice held out and his body regained strength as the morning drew near. But by the late afternoon on the second day his throat began to hurt and the wall in front of him swelled up and subsided in waves; the others watched him and now neighbours began to crowd through the door to look at him. On the third day, by noon, he was reduced to saying the single word *not* over and over again, mouthing the monosyllabic negative in a voice cracked and tasting of blood and sputum; he could feel his limbs now only if he pinched his flesh hard, till his fingernails left bluish marks on the skin. That evening he looked up from the bed and saw, floating above the onlookers like a bunch of string-cut kites, brightly-coloured and diaphanous and beautiful, saw flying above what he instantly thought of as a gaggle of gods: Ganesha, Hanuman, and of course Yama, besides others; he fumbled at his eye-band, found it secure, shut his eyes but still felt their nearness, their presence in the air making it fragrant and cool. Sanjay opened his eyes and looked up, trying to decipher their expressions, but they remained divinely inscrutable, and so he made an obscene gesture at them, to which they reacted not a whit, and he went on with his mantra: 'Not, not, not, not . . .'

Now there was a great whispering and going-to-and-fro amongst the watchers, and when they brought him a glass of hot milk he understood that out of concern for his sanity they had decided to silence him; he shook his head and when they laid hands on him he struggled and fought, all the time screaming, not not not not not, but finally they grip his head and force open his mouth shut his nose, Sanjay tastes warm iron-tinged milk seeping between his teeth, the warm metal pressing against his lips, voices murmuring and clucking, the sweep of god's clothes overhead, they fly around him and their silks fan over his forehead, enfolding him in red, gold and blue, then he can't speak, sleeps.

When he awoke two full nights and days later it was time again to go to Markline's house, and he eagerly set forth despite the others' entreaties.

'Don't go, don't go,' Sorkar said. 'You've had a shock, who knows what you might do?'

'Listen, Sanju,' Sikander said. 'You don't have to go. We can say something, anything. We'll tell him you're sick.'

Sanjay shook his head: he wanted to visit Markline and he didn't know why; when he thought of him, of his red face and shiny boots and precise manner, he was filled with a stupendous rage, but he still wanted to go. He made his preparations, and dressed with even more care than usual, leafing through his kurtas until he found one stiff and bluish with starch. The others came with him as far as the river, and as he was getting into the boat Sikander said, 'We'll wait for you here.'

On the water he dreamt about what was going to happen: in one minute he saw himself arguing with Markline, persuading the Englishman that the book was false, dazzling him with the subtlety of his arguments and demolishing his counter-contentions with terrible force; in the next minute he was slitting open Markline's throat from side to side as if it were paper, the black blood gushing like thick printer's ink. All these images became increasingly vague and insubstantial as they drew closer to the shore, and by the time Sanjay was trudging up the beach he was wholly unable to use any of them to ward off the fear that blew up with the sand and whistled into his nostrils; as he went through the gate all he was aware of was Markline's presence in the house, everything else was gone, the trees vanished, the birds silenced, everything illogically but incontestably reduced to nothing by the terrific and invisible power of the man inside, by Sanjay's terror. When he took his next step both his feet left the ground and he felt himself float, carried forward some twenty feet by momentum, until he cycled his legs and stretched for the gravel; both feet down again, Sanjay looked around guiltily to see if anyone had seen, and then took small shuffling steps all the way inside.

Remember, Sanjay thought, remember, but these words were all that came to him as he was led through the rooms of the white house by servants, he could not remember the face of his mother, the smell of his father; when he finally stood in front of Markline he could not hear anything but the thudding of his own heart.

'Hello, young fellow,' Markline said. 'You look well today, flushed.'

No, I'm not well, Sanjay wanted to say, but found himself looking at the thing Markline was eating: a brown slab that spurted black-red whenever Markline cut into it; the Englishman was using a thin silver knife that he moved in small sawing motions, a four-tined fork with which he speared the stuff, each time causing four reddish bubbles which soon disappeared into his mouth. Sanjay moved his head, shut his eye, tried to speak but found his throat blocked tightly by something as hard as metal; he did not know what he wanted to say but knew that he couldn't, what was possible to say he couldn't say in English, how can in English one say roses, doomed love, chaste passion, my father my mother, their love which never spoke, pride, honour, what a man can live for and what a woman should die for, can you in

English say the cows' slow distant tinkle at sunset, the green weight of the trees after monsoon, dust of winnowing and women's songs, elegant shadow of a minar creeping across white marble, the patient goodness of people met at way-side, the enfolding trust of aunts and uncles and cousins, winter bonfires and fresh chappatis, in English all this, the true shape and contour of a nation's heart, all this is left unsaid and unspeakable and invisible, and so all Sanjay could say after all was: 'Not.'

'What might you mean, not?' Markline said, leaning forward. He looked at Sanjay intently for a moment, a deep vertical line between his eyebrows, then said abruptly: 'Never mind. The doctor's coming.' He smiled. 'He'll be here in a few minutes.'

Sanjay nodded, feeling a steady wave of nausea: he had seen plenty of meat before, at Sikander's house they ate it curried every other day, but the thing on Markline's plate seemed pitiful and distorted; try as he might he could not imagine it as part of some animal.

'I notice you're looking at my food,' Markline said. 'And that is no wonder. Your present condition might well be a result of lack of proper nutrition, or at least it is probably exacerbated by your diet.' He leaned back in his chair. 'Let us make a secret covenant: I will do everything in my power to cure you, but you must in return do something for me. Agreed?'

'What?'

'You must break with these customs that make you weak. Let us be frank — one of us here has power, the other has not. We English rule in your country because we are sustained on a scientific diet, both bodily and intellectual. If you hope to follow in our footsteps, you must abandon superstition. I know you want to, but let there be some sign between us that you have made your decision, have made the first and most important step.' With quick squaring motions, he sliced a rectangular portion of the meat on his plate, then held it out on his fork. 'Eat.'

Sanjay swayed back and forth, looked around for help: he saw that the table-top was of veined marble, the legs of dark teak; there were two small side-tables, each bearing a brass cannon; there was a painting on a wall, a white-gowned woman and a hovering swan; a gold clock on a mantel-piece, its hands moving in regular and mechanical jumps.

'Eat,' Markline said, and this time the last consonant was hard and explosive; the rank smell filled Sanjay's head, he felt it pressing on his lips, then he felt it in his mouth, he swallowed as the four steel points scraped, retreating over his lower lip, felt his throat expand over the gristly mass, contract, but his mouth was full of blood, and he screamed, screamed once for his mother and fell.

Sanjay awoke to a piercing bright light and probing fingers; the light was near and white and overpowering, the fingers kneading his forehead and holding his eyes open. He turned his head against the fingers and pulled at the hands, moaning; his mouth tasted sour and he could smell his breath.

'Quiet, boy, quiet.' The voice was unfamiliar, but then Markline spoke from above him.

'It's the doctor, Sanjay. Be still.'

Sanjay pulled himself away and sat up; at first all he could see was spinning and intersecting diamonds of light, then the flashing subsided into a double-image of Markline holding a dark lantern which sent forth a single beam of intense, focussed light. The doctor walked around Sanjay and stood bending over him, hands on hips.

'Look,' he said. 'No sign of crossing. The damage is internal, as I thought.'

Sanjay clapped a hand over his right eye, jumped off the bed and ran to the door.

'Wait,' Markline said. 'Sanjay . . .'

'What did I eat?'

'Sanjay . . .'

'What was it?'

'Beef.'

Sanjay ran from the house; the ground outside was hot and stung his feet, but he did not stop. On the beach, next to the water, he knelt and tried to vomit, first one finger down his throat and then two, but all that resulted was a series of heaves that wracked his belly and prostrated him, his face in the water. He drank, huge gulps, and finally the taste went from his mouth, but his stomach remained hard, knotted and unyielding. The boat came and he found himself a place at the stern, tried not to look at anyone, hid his face between his knees.

'What did the fucker do to you?' Sikander said as soon as he got off the boat.

'You're so pale,' Sorkar said.

'White,' said Chottun and Kokhun.

But Sanjay refused to say a word and walked home barefoot, through the streets of Calcutta. The next morning he set to work as usual, but he set the type slowly now, putting each character into the stick with deliberate care, constructing Sarthey's book with passionless exactitude. At noon he said to Sorkar: 'Where does the man live, the one from Dhaka, the type-cutter?'

'What will you do?' Sorkar said.

'What you have done all along: put in my words under his.'

'Use my types.'

'No. This is personal.'

'What will you give the cutter?'

'I'll find something.'

Sorkar was hesitant, but in the end he drew Sanjay a map on the back of a hand-bill; with this in his pocket Sanjay walked alone into the city that evening. He slipped away from the shop quietly, avoiding Sikander's offer to accompany; he walked quickly, making precise turns at corners and anticipating twists in the lane: the thin lines of the map were clear in his memory, he found no need to look at it. In a poor Muslim quarter he stopped and spoke to a group of men sitting on charpoys: 'I am looking for Kabir the cutter.'

'I am Kabir,' said a thin man with a grey beard that reached his waist.

'I work for Sorkar Moshai at Markline. I need a type to be cut and cast.'

'Come in,' said Kabir the cutter, and led him into a tiny room, barely more than a niche in the wall; the walls were lined with racks filled with jewellery and type.

'Sorkar Moshai wants this type?'

'No, I do.'

'You?'

'Yes, I. As you did for Sorkar Moshai, a duplication of the ten-point Baskerville.'

'The same modifications on the font?'

'No. For me, just make the serifs thicker, so that on the page it looks like it could be an ink smudge if it is noticed casually.'

'Ink smudge? That much thicker?'

'That's what I want.'

'You know the money?'

'I have no money.'

'What do you have?'

'The complete works of Mir. Hand-lettered on fine paper.'

'You would give that away?'

'It is worth it to me.'

'Why?'

'I have been insulted.'

Outside, the sun had set and the men's hookahs burbled quietly in the dusk; the bazaars were lit up and crowded with people. Sanjay smelt food all over, the dense smell of mithai mingled with the spices from the chat-wallahs; now that the thing was started, the deed set in motion, he felt quiet and alone, no anger or bitterness, no fear. He felt no hunger, and the darkness and yellow light somehow distanced him from those around him, so that they looked curiously flattened and far; when he reached the shop he refused dinner and lay awake on his bed all night, listening to Alexander.

Three days later Kabir the cutter sent word that the font was ready; in the meantime Sanjay had looked for and found the Mir in a stack of books, jammed between *Principles of Physics* and loose pages from a work on animal husbandry. On receiving Kabir's call Sanjay dusted off the book and went forth eagerly; he had not worked on the Sarthey job for three days, and had spent the time thinking about what he would put in, what he would code into the language. At Kabir's house, the cutter handed him the font wrapped into small paper packets, then sat looking down at the Mir, lifting the pages and gently setting them to the side one by one.

'Listen,' Kabir said. 'This is a big thing to give.'

'Take it,' Sanjay said. He had opened one of the packets and was examining the letters *m* and *x*. 'For cutting such as this you deserve it.'

'It is still a big thing to give. Pick a number at random and you shall have that page. To keep.'

'No. It is yours. Thank you.' With this Sanjay closed his packets and walked out into the street; as he hurried away Kabir came running after him.

'Take this,' Kabir said, his voice rough as he stuffed a page down the open neck of Sanjay's kurta. 'Take it.'

Looking at his face, and sensing behind him the young men in lungis beginning to move, Sanjay nodded and nodded again, then backed out of the lane and started to run, the balled-up paper scratching against his chest. Once the lanes came into a wider street, he stopped and groped inside his kurta, found the Mir page and threw it hard across the road, into a puddle; the rest of the way to the shop passed quickly in anticipation as he moved his fingers over the packages, feeling their heaviness and the hard little shapes of the letters underneath the wrapping. He went immediately to his table and spilled the type onto the wood; without pausing to put it in a case he began to set, starting where he had stopped days earlier; now instead of the frantic speed there was a deliberate even motion, regular and without breaks or faltering. When the others stopped for the day they came to watch him, for a while, then left him to his task without arguing; he worked through the night by the light of a lantern, and the next morning he felt no fatigue, and knew for certain that this was no illusion, that he was making no errors, that the endurance of his body and mind was a gift from his anger, like the ceaseless flame that burns above cracks in the earth. He worked all day, refusing food and water, at which Sorkar muttered under his breath,

> Why, he has no tears to shed:
> To him this sorrow is an enemy
> And would usurp upon his ashy eyes,
> And make them clean with tributary tears:
> But he will grope the way to Revenge's cave.

The setting and pressing of the book was finished in three days, and Sanjay did not eat or sleep for all that time; when the galleys were finished he folded them into a red envelope and gave them to Sorkar to take to Markline. 'I will not go there anymore.' The galleys came back marked 'Not one mistake — excellent!'; they ran off a print, which took twenty-one days, and still Sanjay did not eat or sleep; to all queries he replied with a shrug, and did not tell anyone, even Sikander, about the thing that sat brick-like in his belly. When the print run was over Sanjay broke up the formes; he separated and wrapped Kabir's type again, put the bundles beneath his pillow and slept for eleven days, dreaming one long single dream in which he wandered amidst spare grey monolithic shapes rising out of mist.

*   *   *

'Wake up, wake up.' When he awoke it was dusk outside, Sikander was shaking him, and he could hear Markline's voice outside. 'Get up, he caught your damn type,' Sikander said. 'He saw the letters were thick and the thickened letters appeared regularly but he can't fig- ure out your code, so Sorkar told him it was just bad ink, runny, but he's got his people outside searching for a hidden type, where is it? He's red in the face and looks ready to kill. They found Sorkar's type under his stool but they couldn't tell for sure that it was different, he told them it was just a spare set. But if they find yours you know what he'll do.'

Sanjay gestured at his pillow and got up to peer outside, where he could make out dim shapes running about and hear things being thrown around, and under everything the whisper, katharos, katharos.

'Listen,' Sikander said. 'We can't hide it in here. Our retreat's cut off, there's no way out except through the court-yard, there's four of them besides Markline, but if you create a distraction I could maybe —'

'No need,' Sanjay said. 'Here, give them to me.'

'What? What for?'

'Give. I'm hungry.'

'Listen, you're dreaming or something still.'

'No, I'm not dreaming, I see very clearly now. Look, I'll even take the band off and look at you double-eyed and say clearly, give them to me, I'm hungry. I see now this has to happen whether we want it to or not.'

'What? What are you talking about? What are you going to do?'

'Give.'

Sanjay took a packet and opened one corner of it, raised his chin and opened his mouth until his jaw cracked, and then poured the letters in, in a single continuous stream, hard-edged, rattling, he felt his gullet expand and his tongue lacerate and his mouth filled with blood but they went in one by one and together and then the paper was empty.

'More.'

'O my mother, how did you do that?'

'I am our mother's son. I can do anything. More. Italics next, if you please.' He could feel a ghastly grin stetching his face; one by one Sanjay opened the packets and felt the type descend, felt it in his throat and chest, felt it reach his stomach; he felt it weigh his body and harden his skin.

'Come,' he said, when it was finished, spitting blood. 'Let's go and see the tamasha. Have they searched the roof?'

'First place they looked.'

'We'll sit up there.'

'Your throat, I saw them in your throat, it bulged like a python's belly. It's black.'

'What?'

'Your throat.'

'Come on.'

They went through the court-yard, raising their arms away from their bodies when Markline's servants came towards them, look, we have nothing. Sorkar was crouched on the ground in front of Markline, his head down, with Kokhun and Chottun just next to him; Sanjay stared fearlessly at the Englishman and walked past him without a word. On the roof, as he lowered himself into a squat, in an area of shadow where he could look into the court-yard below without being seen, he felt something sticky running down the backs of his thighs; he sat and opened his mouth and let the blood flow down his chin.

'We have to get you a vaid,' Sikander said.

'Nothing's going to happen to me, be still.'

Below, there was a shout, and a few moments later a red-wrapped package was laid at Markline's feet. 'Could this be it?' he said. 'Looks too small to me, and besides I wonder if you'd really have the audacity to use Bacon's code in a book you knew I was going to read. But this was kept like a secret, tucked away behind clothes and such, was it not? Let's see what it is.' He lifted away a flap and the pale yellow leather shone through the twilight. 'I'll be damned! Here it is! My stolen book!' He threw himself back in his chair, then leaned forward to put his forearms on his knees, his face close to Sorkar's. 'Look at me. Why did you keep it for so long?' Sorkar shrugged. 'What are we to do with you? I come to investigate one sin and find no evidence of it only to find another grown pale and cracked with age. Shall we send you home? Shall we have you jailed? Shall we have you whipped? How shall the punishment suit the crime? How will you bear up? Why, you seem sullen, do you blame me if I punish you? Do remember, dear fellow, the words of the great poet, *glorius mundi* himself, "To punish me for what you make me do, Seems much unequal —" '

'Willy,' Sorkar said.

'What?'

'It was Shakespeare, not the other.'

'What have we here? A Stratfordian? A Stratfordian who speaks out despite the threat of violence, the possibility of a whipping, the sack and forced return to the ancestral village, perhaps jail and a starving family! I see now what must happen, what we must have: a public burning, a demonstration of the eventual destruction of all error and misbelief, a dissipation of rank superstition and blind trust. A torch, bring that torch here. Now, my dear fellow, this is how it will be: you will take that tome, and page by page, starting with that atrocious portrait of the imposter, burn it, thereby admitting the error of your ways and the giving up of your claims.'

Above, Sikander had to get up and move away from Sanjay, because a black pool had formed on the roof, a sluggish puddle an inch thick and widening every moment; despite the flow from his body, from his mouth and anus, Sanjay felt himself getting stronger: his body was becoming heavier and heavier, and now he noticed that his double vision was ebbing, that his two images of the world were slowly but unmistakably converging. He watched the scene below with detachment, feeling anger in some remote, alien part of himself, hidden by an inevitable crust of calm and acceptance; and below, Sorkar looked up quickly at Markline, his dark face and white eyes in a flickering pool of light, no anger or pain, and without protest he took the torch, opened the book and ripped off, cleanly, the picture of the earringed man with sad eyes. In the clear gold liquid of the fire the Stratford man's face blackened and blackened and then disappeared. The pages hardly whispered, a quick crackle, before they disappeared in the leaping convection of the flame; when it was all finished there was an infinitesimally thin layer of black ash over the court-yard, a touch of bitterness in the air, the sky black overhead, and Markline left without another word.

When Sanjay descended from the roof, his body was encrusted by a black layer of blood from his mouth to his toes; it covered him like a new skin and cracked as he moved. He felt each step he took as a metallic impact that started at his heel and vibrated throughout his body; his flesh was now so dense that he was afraid he would leave imprints on the brick of the court-yard.

'I can see you clearly,' he said to Sorkar. 'The doubleness is gone.'

'What happened to you?' Sorkar said.

'He ate his type,' Sikander said. 'Swallowed it.'

Sorkar uncrossed his legs and leaned forward in the darkness: 'And he is still alive.'

'I feel strong,' Sanjay said. 'Stronger than ever in my life.'

'So he cured you after all,' Sorkar said, laughing shortly.

'I have to wash myself,' Sanjay said, taking Sikander's arm as he walked past him and leading him away. 'Alexander's voice is gone too. I wish to be gone from here,' he whispered into Sikander's ear. 'Away from Englishmen.'

'Wait,' Sorkar called after him. 'What was it that you hid in his book?'

'We have a right to know,' Kokhun said.

'What was the message? What was the code?' Chottun said.

'Just read it,' Sanjay said.

'There was no code?' Sorkar said.

'No mathematical code. Just pick the letters with the thickened serifs.'

'Why couldn't Markline read it?'

'It's in Hindi. He must have thought it was gibberish.'

'You took a risk.'

'No risk. If he lived in this country for two hundred years he wouldn't gain a word of Hindi, and he's too proud to ask.'

'What was the message?'

'It was this: "This book destroys completely, this book is the true murderer." Just that, repeated again and again. Excuse me. I must wash myself.'

'Yes,' Sorkar said. 'We must get back to work.'

'Work? After all this? After what he did?'

'I must work.'

'He insulted you.'

'Yes.' Sorkar struggled to his feet and walked heavily towards the press, followed by Kokhun and Chottun.

In the bath Sanjay poured bucket after bucket of cold water over his head, holding up his face to the purifying stream. The blackish layer on him dissolved and vanished, vanished down the drain in a thick stream clouded by black particles, and it seemed to him that the skin revealed underneath was more pale than he remembered; soon he was clean again, all the colour gone, except what looked like a purple-bluish bruise which encircled his throat like a collar. He took up his eye-band, shook it out, folded it over into a wide strip and wrapped it around his throat; as he did this Sikander appeared at the door.

'I wish to be gone from here,' Sanjay said.

'Yes,' Sikander said.

'Away from here, away from Englishmen. They have a monotonous tendency to come into my life and make it uncomfortable.'

'I see that.'

'I wish to be delivered of their judgements. Let's go tonight. Now.'

'Yes.'

'Quietly.'

'You won't say good-bye to Sorkar Moshai?'

'I don't want to.'

'Why?'

'He is a coward without honour.'

'You are a fool. He is the bravest man you will ever meet.'

'You say good-bye to him.'

'I will. I will touch his feet.'

As Sikander turned away, Sanjay called out to him: 'Let us go to Lucknow.'

'Why Lucknow?'

'I wish to be a writer. I wish to have women.'

'You wish a lot of things tonight.'

'I see things very clearly now.'

He waited in the lane outside for Sikander; the night was broken by lonely barking, and a breeze fluttered sheets and beds and set windows creaking. Sanjay imagined it springing from the sea, whistling from the dunes into the continent, unknowing and impervious to those it whipped over; he felt it pressing at his throat, close about his neck like a vice.

Sikander stepped from the darkness, soundless as always: 'Let's go.' They walked into the whole and unbroken black. 'Sorkar said to tell you good-bye, he sends his blessing. He said not to be angry like that, and said, Willy is my boy, tell you, to tell you, Willy is my boy. He said, tell him, tell him about the Englishman:

> It is himself, his own self's better part,
> His eye's clear eye, his dear heart's dearer heart,
> His food, his fortune, and his sweet hope's aim,
> His sole earth's heaven, and his heaven's claim.

He also said something else about the Englishman.'

'What?' said Sanjay.

'He said Markline is the most generous of men: he gives to charities, he sets up hospitals for the poor, he is angered and maddened by injustice and tyranny, he works harder than any man.'

'Is that why Sorkar chooses to stay with him?'

'No. Sorkar Chacha said it is this generosity which makes Markline dangerous.'

'Yes.'

'He said to be well.'

'Yes.'

Then they were both quiet, and they walked on, their faces set towards the sunrise, night their sanctuary: in this fragile darkness, delivered of the malignant judgements of reason, the past and present are the same, and the future is lit by the radiant light of hope, and the spirits of your ancestors walk beside you; in the trembling of the earth underneath and the movements of indistinct animals is all the pain of the mother, who loves the universe and makes it well.

In Lucknow they found a city mad with poetry. They reached the town one morning many days later at sunrise, and were stunned into silence by a song that lifted off the waters of the Gomti like the sun's fire and that dazzled them with its need to live; they sat on the river-bank and watched the egret and the heron curve against the darkness of the water, the morning mist vanish slowly, the distant minarets and cupolas of the city appear pink and then white as the muezzins called to prayer. The song vanished finally, seeming not to stop but to recede into the silence from which it had come, and afterwards neither Sanjay nor Sikander could remember what the lyrics had been, and they were left only with a memory of longing.

'Who was that singing?' Sanjay called out to a bazaar boy who was walking to the bridge nearby, carrying a pot on his head.

'Whoever has sung a song, ever?' sang the boy. 'It is the song that sings the players.' He walked on, swinging one arm jauntily, humming.

'These Lucknow types are mad,' Sanjay said.

How mad they were became even more evident as the sun came up: a kulfi-seller set up his cart near the bridge, and a crowd, mostly of young boys, formed around him; the boys shouted insults at him, and he replied to each in verse, never at a loss for an answer: he was, it seemed, a kulfi-seller famous for his wit and erudition. Sanjay and Sikander watched him sell his kulfis to people who came more for his verses than his confections, and as afternoon drew on they heard tablas burp questioningly and sitars quaver; voices tested hesitatingly: sa-re-ga-ma-pa, sa-re-ga.

'We're in the fast section of town,' Sikander said.

'Good,' said Sanjay. 'Where I want to be. But are you hungry?'

'Very. And you?'

'Yes.' But there was no money left; they had survived for the last two days of the journey on the kindness of peasants and an occasional charitable serai established for the help of travellers. 'What to do?'

Sikander shrugged; it was becoming clear to Sanjay that they were going to have to steal, and the only question was whether they were going to try it in daylight, when the food-stuffs were laid out for the taking, or whether they had the patience to wait for night. In either case he was not scared of being caught: to go filching with Sikander, the natural master of stealth and skill, was surely to go hunting with a ghostly and swift-stepping assassin — the quarry would not even know it had been cut clean, its fat flesh stripped away.

'When d'you want to do it?' Sanjay said, but Sikander looked at him stupidly, innocent as a tit-sucking babe; when Sanjay told him he, amazingly enough, reacted as if he had been insulted.

'I'm a Rajput,' he said. 'I don't go skulking around sneaking a chappati here and a couple of pice there.'

'And what's your plan then?' Sanjay said hotly. 'A day's honest labour in the field? Or is gold going to drop out of the sky?'

Sikander hardly seemed to hear the jibes; he wandered slowly through the streets, looking at things, taking an enormous, patient delight in everything from clay toys to the silver foil on top of sweetmeats, and all the while Sanjay felt a headache mount at the back of his head, not so much from the hunger but from his irritation at his friend's placid patience, and even more from something he could barely admit to himself: he was a stranger in Lucknow. During the journey he had imagined a city that looked very much like the one before him now, except for a few particulars, and had thought of it with relief and eagerness; he had wanted to come home. Calcutta had jolted him, with its black machinery and noise, and so he had imagined himself seated among polite, gentlemanly Lucknow courtiers, exchanging a quip here and there and bowing, he had seen himself by some river in the moonlight, leaning forward to stroke black hair; but now there was something about Lucknow that made him anxious, maybe the narrowness of the lanes and their twists, the undoubtedly old-fashioned caps the men wore, strange and box-like, perhaps the leisurely way the shop-keepers flicked at their wares with fly-sweeps. It was a city most unlike Calcutta, and he felt a foreigner in it.

'I'm hungry,' he said, and felt himself flush as he heard the whine in his voice. Sikander raised an eyebrow, in a manner that had his mother in it, and Sanjay turned away; he walked now with his arms rigid, his body angular with shame. A heavy-scented wave of spice stopped him short; he stood very still in front of a halwai's shop, and felt the smell of kulchas and chole work up his nose and tongue, disappear somewhere into his throat and wrap around his throbbing brain; he swayed from side to side, mouth aching, then without decision reached out and grabbed a kulcha, turned and ran. He ran with his chest out, head thrown back, but the sound of shouting behind drew inevitably closer; he scrabbled at a white wall taller than him, was lifted over by Sikander and dropped unceremoniously on the other side, he scooped at the ground desperately for his lost kulcha, felt himself being pulled along the ground by his collar, and then heard a voice: 'In here.'

A door clicked behind them and they were in a garden surrounded by tall brick walls. Their rescuer motioned them away from the door and deeper into the garden — it was the singing boy from the bazaar. He was about their age, but with a prematurely balding, round head that sat on his shoulders like a smooth ball; he smiled at them and walked backwards, shaking his head as if at some great joke. When they were out of sight of the wall, deep amongst green peepuls and mango trees, he squatted down by a fountain, snapping the thread that ran over his shoulder and around his body.

'So what was it?' he said. 'What did you do?'

'Took some food,' Sanjay said. The branches above were thick and intertwined, so that despite the afternoon sun it was dark under the trees, and his skin was suddenly cool from the sweat drying off.

'When I saw you in the morning I knew it was a matter of time. Where are you from? Listen, this is Lucknow, there is no need to take like that, Lucknow will give you what you want. Don't believe? Ask. What did you come here to be? I came here to be a cook, and I am already an apprentice at a halwai's, and soon I'll be a regular understudy to a great chef. So say — what do you want to do?'

'Soldier,' Sikander said. 'I want to be a soldier.'

'I don't want to be anything,' Sanjay said, leaning over to the side and curling up on the soft grass. 'Nothing at all.' He could feel the mud under the grass, damp and fresh-smelling.

'Listen,' Sikander said. 'Can we get something to eat?'

'My name's Sunil. Surely.'

'You stay here, Sanjay,' Sikander said.

Sanjay heard them walking away, and then there was only the occasional rustle of wind through the leaves, a regular cheeping as he sank gratefully into a deep sleep. When he woke somebody was shaking him, and the swaying trees above stretched fantastically high and curved to a dark violet sky, as if he was under water; he fought against the motion, trying to retreat into the calm emptiness, heard a voice saying Sanju what do you want to be, but resisted, and then his stomach knotted and a painful rush of saliva jerked him awake, because there was the hot smell of food, promising satisfaction. He sat up dizzily, and the black shapes of the trees loomed towards him and then away, and again there was the question what do you want to be, and for a moment he didn't know where he was or who.

'Poet,' he said automatically, and began to eat, scooping up scalding handfuls of rice and dal from the plantain-leaf wrappers. The food smeared over his face and dropped onto his chest, and once he put in such a large handful that he choked and struggled, but finally with a violent convolution got it all down. He ate and ate, until it was all gone; at the fountain he drank with his head lowered to the water like an animal. Finally he stopped and looked up at the sky, at the terrible distances and size of the clouds and the strange, alien shapes of the trees against them. 'Poet,' he said helplessly.

'You've come to the right place to be a poet,' Sunil said.

'Yes,' said Sikander excitedly. 'Listen, Sanjay, you'll never know who I saw. We went from shop to shop, talking to people that Sunil here knows, getting a little bit of food here and there, and then we went round to the back of the great houses, and Sunil talked to cooks and maids, and we were coming around the corner of one of these houses, and I saw a man on a horse, riding away from us. There was something about him, about the way he held his back, the throw of his head, so I pulled Sunil back around the wall, and peered out carefully, and you know who it was?'

Sanjay shook his head.

'As soon as I looked,' said Sikander, 'he knew he was being watched. He held back the horse, then turned him slowly, shading his eyes with his hand, and so I flung my head back and held myself close to the wall.'

'It was Uday,' said Sanjay.

'Himself. I knew if we stayed a moment longer he would find us, and finding us I don't know what he would do, take us back or not, so I drew Sunil away. He serves a great lady in that house, Sunil says. What do you think?'

'Stay away from him,' Sanjay said. 'He'll make us go back.'

'What to do then?'

'Stay here,' said Sanjay. After the food he was quite content to remain in the grove, and it seemed to him a fine situation, to write poetry in a clump of trees; Lucknow outside, with all its blandishments, was preferable at a distance, where its slight imperfections, its puzzling deviations from symmetry and elegance were diffused and hidden. But its food was good, and he said so to Sunil, who instantly started to tell tales of famous cooks and large-hearted gourmands:

Once (said Sunil) there was a cook named Mashooq Ali, who was famous for his mastery of food-disguise, and the tales of his prowess reached the renowned connoisseur Ajwad Raza. Ajwad Raza made a boast, in front of his friends, that no cook could fool him, and so the delighted young gentlemen set up a contest. On the proclaimed day Ajwad Raza sat down to one of Mashooq Ali's meals, took a mouthful of rice and was chagrined to discover that each grain was an artfully polished sliver of almond; then Ajwad Raza thought to clear his palate by taking a bite of pomegranate, but the fruit was a confection of sugar, the seeds were pear juice, and the seed-kernels were almonds. And so each thing he ate was something else, until finally he accepted defeat, and said the world had never seen such an artist, and Mashooq Ali said, bowing, Allah is generous and his ways are mysterious.

One other time (said Sunil) there was a wrestler named Abu Khan, a most monstrous being who consumed at one sitting twenty seers of milk, two and a half seers of dried nuts and fruit, six large loaves of bread and — we have it on good authority — an ordinary-sized goat. Of his greed he made a virtue and swaggered with his enormous body through the streets, until becoming annoyed, a certain learned munshi, a Pandit Jayaram, a physician of the body and fancier of pigeons, invited the behemoth to dine. The wrestler sat at the mat, twirling his moustache and rubbing his hands over his chest, and when no food came he snapped at the servants and waxed sarcastic at the munshi's expense. Then he began to shout, and made as if to leave, but the servants bowed and delayed, saying just another minute, please be patient. By the time the food came the wrestler was sweating freely, and his face was red, and when he lifted the cover off the plate his eyes bulged and he could hardly speak, because on the plate was a single small round ball of rice. So he threw it into his mouth with barely a glance, and called for more, but the servants said, that was all, great man. Abu Khan cursed and started to rise, thinking of where he would go to fill his belly, but suddenly he sat back down as if struck — his stomach was full, and his limbs filled with heaviness, as if he had eaten a granary, and a brood of hens besides. Now the servants brought out sweet savories, and said, here is dessert, maharaj, but Abu Khan could not eat; they brought out sherbet, and wine, but Abu Khan could not drink. Then the munshi appeared in the door-way, with a plate of the rice Abu Khan had consumed, and ate it all, easily and with delight; afterwards he drank some water, and threw the remaining grains of rice to the pigeons that fluttered about him. Abu Khan understood his lesson, and said, truly pride is the downfall of man. And the munshi said, eat not lustfully and indiscriminately, but with knowledge and humbleness, because the heart of a thing is a mystery, and what is big is small, and what is small, indeed, is big.

While Sikander and Sunil searched for food, every day, Sanjay sat in his grove and wrote poetry: he meant his lines to be precise, elegant and steely, but inevitably a touch of Mirism revealed itself, like a faint spice, remembered rather than tasted; after a day of this he gave in and decided to write a love poem full of gentle longing and sadness, but now the words drifted about and finally settled into an edge so hard and keen that it drew blood from his tongue, and the birds shrieked in alarm at the sudden dark burst of bitterness. So when he wanted a feeling as diaphanous as incense smoke, as slowly sliding, what came out instead was:

> The moon wafts across the sky not knowing its own
>   pain:
> What it leaves behind, the heaviness of the dark after
>   the unearthly light.
>
> O Aag, you are the debris in the invisible tide, twisted
>   and monstrous,
> Never known, much less forgotten.

And when what was required was a knife, a twisting thin blade that damaged without the penetration even being felt, he got this:

> What is the consummation I want from you, says Aag?
> I am angered that you don't come, that I am left with
>   the aching pieces of myself.

*But you know not that you are beautiful, or that you
    are loved.*
*When you appear, your innocence breathes softly on
    my flames, and I am helpless again.*

It was impossible for him to be one-thing-or-the-other, pure and with
the integrity of hate or the clarity of love, and it was this being in the
middle, or some other place altogether, that puzzled his audience:
'Doesn't sound like any ghazal I ever heard,' said Sunil, 'but it's good,
good,' and Sikander lay back amongst the roots of a tree, nodding his
head to the lines but saying nothing. So Sanjay tried again, and in two
weeks wrote seven poems, each half a ghazal and half something else,
and then in frustration he lapsed into silence; he spent his days now
walking the perimeter of the garden, running his hands along the small
bricks of the wall. One night he dreamt that he was ringed by fire, by a
circle that moved heavily with the sound of grinding bones, and then
the ground under his feet dropped and he was falling, tumbling towards
an expanse of black water that took even the orb of the moon and gave
nothing back. Then he knew that he would have to leave the grove of
trees, that the world offers no respite from its ambiguities, and worse,
no shelter from its prizes.

So he said to Sikander: 'Let us go and pay our respects to Uday.'

'I thought you wanted to stay here.'

'I did, but you are no more a soldier than when we first arrived, and I
must be a poet.'

So that evening, with Sunil, they left the copse of trees and went to
the house — it seemed more a palace — and Sikander said to the soldier at the gate, 'Tell the commander that his sons are here.'

The guards looked at them warily, not quite certain what specificity
of meaning to attach to that allegation of relationship, and there was a
great deal of scurrying about inside, but when they took the boys in, it
was not to the soldier, but to a woman. She was clearly a woman of
some age, but she sat on a low couch cracking walnuts between her
fingers, and her attendants and servants were brisk and efficient about
her; when she spoke her voice was lilting and also a little cracked, like
that of a practised singer, and yet laden with such authority, so sharp-
edged that Sanjay wished momentarily for his grove of trees.

'Sons?' she said. 'How sons? Where sons? Not inconvenient sons?'

'We have known the commander sahib for a long time,' Sikander said.

'Not as long as I have, nor as little as I have, judging by the looks of it,' she said. 'But are you his sons?'

'It was just a manner of speaking,' Sanjay said. 'We are not from this place.'

'But he is a strange and overly-quiet man,' she said. 'Who could know? In any case, you are not related by blood?'

'Not,' said Sanjay.

'By affection only, I am sure you are going to say. But, listen, who are your fathers then? You, with the bald head, I've seen you skulking around here, you look like a normal boy, but these two, look at them, who knows where they've come from, what they are, even if they are boys or what? Could be boys, could be demons, thieves, or anything else.'

'We didn't come here to —,' began Sanjay, but Sikander pulled at his arm.

'Let's go,' said Sikander. 'You will excuse us.'

'Stop,' she said, and her voice boomed so that her attendants came jerking through the doors, and Sikander dropped Sanjay's arm and widened his stance. She laughed, showing white teeth and reddened gums: 'Such proud *men* you are.'

Sanjay turned away from the door and back towards her, excited suddenly by a sure knowledge that he knew who she was, or at least had once known her; he walked towards her until he was impolitely close, then stood absolutely still and looked into her face: he was certain that she had been beautiful, but the comeliness was quite irrelevant; it was, he thought, a confident and quite ruthless nimbus of power, an air that took nothing away from her old washerwoman's laugh, her raucous and easy bawdiness. As he stared into her eyes he saw himself quite clearly in her pupils, which seemed huge; he grew dizzy, and felt himself grow from the top of his own head, like a flower, and before he could remark to himself on this unprecedented feeling, he shouted, quite unable to stop himself, like a child: 'I know, I know who you are.'

'And I don't know who you are,' she said, laughing again.

'You are the Begum Sumroo,' Sanjay said.

'Maybe I am,' she said. 'But who and what are you?'

'I am Sikander, come to be a soldier.'

'I am Sanjay, wanting somehow to be a poet. But you, you are the Witch of Sardhana.'

The fire had burnt so low that it was only a vague red glow in the night, and none of the sadhus could see Sandeep's face. Out of the dark his voice came:

HERE ENDS THE THIRD BOOK,
THE BOOK OF BLOOD AND JOURNEYS.

NOW BEGINS THE FOURTH BOOK,
THE BOOK OF REVENGE AND MADNESS.

THE BOOK
OF REVENGE,
AND
MADNESS

. . . now . . .

'THAT'S WHERE they're all falling in love,' Saira said. We were taking our customary interval break on the roof, exclaiming at the audience, which now filled the entire maidan and spilled over onto the roofs of the houses at the furthest edge. At the west end of the maidan there had sprung up a bazaar of thela-wallahs selling fruits, ice-cream, kulfi, film magazines, chat and kitchen appliances. At the east end, under the row of trees, where Saira was pointing, were the shadows where boys were undoubtedly meeting girls who had stolen away from their parents.

'Scandalous,' Mrinalini said, smiling. 'Which reminds me, Abhay, I met my friend Mrs Khanna this morning. Her daughter's finishing her B.A. next month. She was asking me when I was going to bring my U.S.A.-returned son for tea.'

'Oh, Mother,' Abhay said.

'What?' Mrinalini said. 'Why not?'

'It can't be that simple,' Abhay said.

'We'll have to see,' Hanuman said. 'If she's worthy of our Abhay.'

'Educated, charming, shy and yet somehow slightly naughty,' Ganesha said. 'Wilful and loyal, and beautiful. For our Abhay.'

I passed this on a note to Saira, who burst out laughing. 'You might as well get your suits stitched, bhaiya,' she said, handing him the note. 'With interested relatives like Hanuman and Ganesha, your life's going to get very complicated very soon.'

At which point Abhay muttered, 'I have a story to tell,' and fled down the stairs.

'We had heard a story of love,' he was typing a few minutes later as I swung up on the bed next to him. 'An encounter with an ideal in an American high school, that crucible in which the world's most weightless and alluring myths are perfected. We were on the road, you remember, looking for the good life, life free of gravity, for a light-filled paradise on earth.'

Sex and the Judge.

WHEN I FINISHED my Coke I squeezed the can so that it crumpled and made a sharp edge, which I pressed into my thigh until it hurt. The sky was already a washed blue, but still the road was empty, the fast-food restaurants closed and the video stores barred and shut. Very suddenly I began to cry, surprising myself and unable to stop. I could feel the tears, but inside myself I could find no pain, nothing that would make me weep, and so I started to shake my head. The more I shook the more ridiculous I felt, and so finally I stopped even that and sat there scrubbing at my face.

Then a smell came up around me, a good smell but so rich that I gagged and jerked my head away from the paper cup in front of me.

"Shake?" It was a woman in a red dress, holding out to me what looked like a small bucket. "Chocolate."

"God, no. That's big."

"It is. It'll cut whatever it is. Blow?"

"No."

"Booze?"

"No. Actually nothing at all."

"One of those."

We sat there looking at each other, and she was a very beautiful woman, with long straight blond hair caught up in a high ponytail, clear blue eyes, and the fairest skin I had ever seen. The dress was made of a material shot through with something petrochemical, so it clung and stretched, and as she moved I had to look at the freckled crease between her breasts and then away.

"I've seen you somewhere before," I said.

"Probably have," she said, grinning complicity at me. Her face was very finely wrinkled, and at the elbows I could see the roughing of age.

"Yes? So what d'you do besides offering balm to lost souls?"

"Well, actually, really," she said, "I'm an actress. A performer. Movies."

"Right. So what did I see you in?"

"Something you weren't supposed to see."

"Again?"

"I make dirty movies."

"Shit, now I know, you're the one on television, I mean regular television. You were in a committee or something."

"Testifying, not in. Drink the shake."

"Kyrie," I said, between slurps. "Kyrie, that's you. What're you doing here?"

"That's a long story. I'm not really here, anyway, just going somewhere."

"Where?"

"Why should I tell you?"

"You gave me a shake."

"Well, I guess so. But I don't have time. I have to get away from here."

"Are you running from something?"

"You could say that. You'll see it in the news today. No, I didn't kill somebody or anything like that. Not that kind of dangerous shit, just weird."

"You're going to walk?"

"I don't know. My car died somewhere out there."

So I walked her to the car, which Tom and Amanda were emptying of wrappers and plastic bottles and crumpled cigarette packets. Amanda said, all right, with a shrug and a toss of her head, while Tom leaned back up against the Jaguar and smiled.

"Pretty dusty, this thing," he said. So we took it through a car wash, and for a few minutes we were comfortably eggshelled in a wash of white, then we were out on the road. In a while we were out on the high desert, and the low sunlight filled the inside of the car until it felt like we were sending out a burst of light at every curve. I upended the glass over my head to lick out the last of the chocolate milk, and came out with it on my eyebrows and in my hair, and Amanda looked over and giggled. In the morning when we had woken up together we had said very little, but now I smiled at her and settled myself against the door, and after a while, without being asked, in a low voice, Kyrie told us about what she was running from, and what to.

So (she said), so, I suppose it all started with my mother. My mother — and that's how she liked to be called, "Mother" — when she was seventeen she was the best student and pastry-baker at the St. Jude's School for Girls in Houston. The nuns, who were mostly Texans of Irish descent, told her more than once how they had rescued her from her ragged, street-dusty father, a drunken Apache who couldn't rouse himself to find a soup line, much less look after a child as quiet, as inward, and as thoughtful as her. "But you," they told her in their lilting voices, their lovely broad accents, "but *you* will be something." So she grew up compact and contained, very short, dark, not pretty, but very strong, with a capacity for work, physical and other, that delighted the nuns and impelled them to write imploring letters to Ivy League colleges. There was a seriousness about her, a purpose: when the other girls, confident and careless with the beginnings of beauty, dared to steal the left-to-dry host from the back of the chapel, she not only refused, but disregarded their mocking with an indifference much worse than contempt. What she silenced them with was a moral assurance that made them feel petty, and it was this essential goodness, this refusal to smile, nervously, ecstatically, or otherwise, that the nuns loved and were a little scared by. So they teased her about boyfriends, and finally when she was seventeen and a half, almost out of their care, they decided that she absolutely must have some fun, and one Saturday they sent her to the matinee at the Rialto with two girls they trusted.

These two were Janine Alcott and Carol Ann Mayberry, clean, whippet-smart, and pretty, the first the captain of the debating team and the other a star hockey player. Despite their obvious healthiness, their basic straightforwardness that had won over the nuns, they were tormented by their share of repressed late-nineteen-forties horniness, so that as soon as they reached the theater they hurried to the john and set about remaking themselves with all the desperate art of seventeen. As they colored and pulled and tucked away, Mother watched them in the mirror with the impartial interest of an anthropologist: they didn't or couldn't think of offering her lipstick, or even advice, she was that damned objective. Outside, they shared a glance over her head, a moment of sympathy for her, because she was walking her quick little efficient walk, her shoulders squared under her absurd dress with its round collar, completely indifferent to the gigantic wave of concupiscence that billowed out at them from the darkened pit of the movie hall.

The next day, when the afternoon newspapers announced "Girl School Heist — Star Pupil Suspect" and "Valedictorian Vamooses with Catholic Cash," Janine and Carol Ann twisted and basked in the warm light of flashbulbs like a couple of trained seals, and said they always thought there was something a little hard about her, but nobody ever really knew what it was. Nobody knew what happened to Mother in the darkness, not them, not the nuns, not me, and maybe not even her. She never talked about it, not once, but I went back and dug up the papers, the police reports, all that, and I still don't know what made her do it. The movie that afternoon was *Top Hat,* in which Fred and Ginger float weightless above the rooftops of Manhattan, but in the Rialto that afternoon the audience ignored them completely, trapped joyfully in the fetid, fragrant gravity of each other's body, in the terrific incense of popcorn, Coke, chewing gum, sweat, exchanged saliva, and, very faint but incontestably there, the sweet smell of come seeping slowly into starched jeans. All of them ignored the angel lightness of Fred and Ginger, all, that is, except Mother, who sat bolt upright in her chair, her hands clenched before her chest, staring raptly at the glowing screen. What did she see? I don't know, but I think she must have seen spirit freed from body, love leaping away from fornication, joy uncoupled from suffering, and — pardon my high-flown bullshit, but you see, don't you see? — time emancipated of history. She looked up, her face stained with tears (Janine and Carol Ann tell us this, in yellowed newspapers), at the white stream of light above her head, and I know she must have felt the firm weight of her muscles weighing her down, the brown skin, the dark nipples, the flat nose, the hair. And I know she must have felt something so great, a conviction so real, that it shattered her and made her into something else, because that night she walked away from Janine's Studebaker without looking back, and later she broke into the sacristy, jimmied open the donations box, and emptied it of every last cent. She took the petty cash from the principal's office, and the day's take in the bakery, and when a Sister Carmina stumbled out of a hallway door in a pink nightgown, Mother punched her so hard between the eyes that the poor sister was knocked, raccoon-faced, back into her bedroom and into a sick-bed for two weeks.

In Manhattan Mother took a job as typist in a medical insurance company, where there was some hesitation at first about hiring her, but once they had seen the relentless regularity of her fingers against the typewriter keys, her amazing speed, they engaged her quickly and soon began to depend on her. She worked without breaks, except the regulation hour to eat lunch, and showed, even at the end of the day, no signs of exhaustion. The other workers, mostly stiletto-heeled Hispanic girls, started to call her "La Machina," and spent many coffee breaks making up horrifying stories about what Mother did after work. But what she did was simple enough — with her first paycheck she bought a set of dumbbells, and with the next another, and she spent her evenings alone in her small, yellowed room, lifting weights. This was long before the health boom, but I remember her very clearly, standing before a cracked mirror, regarding her body with a distant hostility, paying intelligent and unswerving attention to each small part, working on it, bit by bit, bit by bit, sweating and groaning until each curve, each dip, was firmly sculpted, until it all shone in the dim light like a brown statue tortured and polished by a thousand years of sea.

How do I enter this picture, you ask? Where did I come from? I think I was necessary because she never herself believed that she could fly, and so every Saturday she put on a loose green dress that flattered her skin and walked the bars, protected by that seriousness that had marked her from the start. It took her a long time to find what she was looking for, because in those days it was hard for a woman like her to meet a man, say a Yalie, down to Manhattan for the weekend, weightless and windswept in white flannels, perhaps a navy sweater, fine blond hair a sweep over a thin forehead, long delicate hands and half-mooned fingernails. That's what she wanted, and after a year and a half she found him in a jazz club on Amsterdam in the upper nineties. She seduced him not by feminine simpers or coy fluttering, but by looking at him very directly for half an hour, and then walking up to him: 'Come home with me.' He went, winking over her head at his friends, and was confident all the way into her apartment, until she turned to him and pushed him onto her bed, straddled him, and whipped off his belt in one movement. She refused to kiss him, and what frightened him more than the rocky strength in her biceps and shoulders was the way she looked at him in the darkness. After he had fled, she took a long shower, and slept a very deep sleep.

So I grew within her, cell by cell, washed in her blood, a body of her body. For the most part, she ignored the fact that she was pregnant, and worked just as ceaselessly, acknowledging all the half-snide inquiries with a curt nod. She typed, "On the afternoon of February 3, Mr. Hardin was struck in the facial area with a baseball bat, resulting in avulsion of three permanent teeth from the upper jaw," and I think I heard, some-how — I know it sounds crazy, but it's the only way to explain what happened later, what I did. "Mr. James stepped into a hole at a construction site and fell onto his left hand. He sustained a rotary subluxation of the scaphoid, and soft tissue damage of the left wrist and hand, including the metaphalangeal joint of the thumb. He subsequently developed de Quervain's disease and carpal tunnel syndrome." "There are small areas of increased signal intensity posterior to the C4–5 and C5–6 intervertebral spaces, with mild extradural impressions upon the thecal sac and the anterior aspect of the spinal cord at these levels — representing possible bulging or herniated intervertebral discs, or degenerative posterior osteophytes." "Mrs. Quevado was struck by small pieces of glass from the windshield, resulting in lacerations of both corneas." I grew with this knowledge of the fragility of the body, of its brittleness, of how it breaks and where it mends, of how it twists and mortifies, its strange humors and expulsions, its stenches and its ugliness, its suffering, and yet after all I was unable to regard it as she did, with such fascination and with such grief.

As I learned this, inside her, she exerted her will on me: by clenching her insides, by looking, for an hour every evening, at thousands of postcards of pearly eyed infants and at the society pages of *Harper's Bazaar* and the *New York Times* and *Look,* she made me pink-skinned, blue-eyed, blond. As I formed inside her, Mother erased herself from me. Believe me, it happened, it can happen, more powerful than science, the strongest magic in the world is the will, it makes miracles. After she made me she spit me from her like a peanut and never touched me again except to wipe the insides of my ears or tie my hair back in a ponytail. The nurse said, it's a daughter, look, such lovely hair, and she said, yes, I know, and turned over and went to sleep. I never cried, either.

So I grew, and she took a second job, night accountant in a hotel, then a third, weekend organizer and tax-consultant for truck stops and small restaurants. All this so I could have eighteen-dollar haircuts in Second Avenue salons, little peacoats from Charivari's, ballet lessons and perfect shoes from Stein's to go with, so that people could exclaim as I emerged from some dark glass door, letting a cool breath of luxury and just, how to talk about it, just rightness out onto the sidewalk, so people could say how lovely, how darling she is. At these moments Mother would stand a modest two paces behind me, and people would take her for a starched and blessedly efficient maid. They would look at her brown, blunt face, her hands clasped in front of her, her flat shoes, and with a trace of covetousness they would ask who she worked for, and she, with a quick, tight smile of delight would shake her head and whisk me off. On those evenings she would mix me an extra teaspoonful of Ovaltine, and would take my hundred-stroke brush and pinch away coiled hairs, looking at me now and then, that secret smile on her face.

I grew up and never thought we were strange. I knew Mother worked hard for me, and so I worked back for her, and the other things I accepted naturally and thought nothing of them. I was vain, I understood why mother was vain of me, and I pitied her a little for the way she looked, and this made me even more eager to bring home those perfect report cards, to be more buoyant in my jetés. But when I was twelve I came home one afternoon and found Mother, in her between-jobs housecoat, watching, on her new twelve-inch television, a feathery puff of white smoke that trailed away into the sky. I sat next to her and watched with her as she flipped channels, moving from image to image of a thin sliver of white riding a huge column of vapor, finally leaving a drifting stain in the sky and a memory of a roar drumming against the ears.

"Look at it," she said. "Just look at it."

"Neat-o," I said shortly, dismissing it with my too-usual and too-casual accolade. I started to flip through a copy of *Life*, a little scared and yet a little pleased to see the quick snap of her eyes in my direction. She had gotten angry at me before, but always about things I had done or neglected to do, it was always me, but now it seemed she cared about this other thing enough to be hurt about it. So now, in the weeks and months afterwards, I pretended that there was nothing weird going on, but there was: she collected every picture, every scrap of print she could find about those rockets that tore themselves free of the earth. I had to pick my way over stacks of *Popular Mechanics* and cheesy plastic models of *Gemini II,* clear my sofa bed of NASA publicity flyers at night, and stumble over paperback biographies of John Glenn in the bath-room in the morning. In the bathroom, on the pot, sleepy-eyed and fuzzy-mouthed, I abandoned my act and studied this John Glenn, his hopeful upturned face and clear blue eyes, and tried to figure out the connection. But I was young, and too attached to scientific fact myself, and so, unable to come up with a coherent explanation, I was forced to face the idea that my mother was strange. Always, my contempla-tions — made somehow comfortable by the smells of my body — were interrupted by Mother, who pounded rapidly on the door, saying, "I don't understand how you can spend all that time in there."

I did, though, more and more. As she followed her elegant ma-chines, I unearthed my body in the darkness of the bathroom, the only place in our apartment where I could be alone. In the shower, under the rosy sting of water, I fingered and excavated, discovered springs of fluid, smells salty and sweet, expanses. Sure, I sent myself off with the joyous discovering enthusiasm of adolescence, I masturbated under the faucet, on the floor, bent over the sink, but it was more than that, the thing was that as I pressed against the wall, lips on the cool tile, or as I bounced around on the floor or stretched against the roughness of the towel, I knew it was there, I mean the world, its roughness, power, itself, I could feel it. What, you say, what the hell are you talking about? but you have to understand that outside, with Mother, I some-times felt like everything was papery, flat, like light through stained glass, I felt myself floating sometimes, far away inside myself, and far away, everything, the exhalations of a ghost. When I felt like that I got breathless, but cool, like a stony calm chick, you know, a killer, or maybe a catatonic in a white hospital ward, so I'd lock myself away in the john and tear off my skirt, and mouth my forefinger, middle finger, thumb, then into myself, my radiant labia, my cunny (yes I'd started reading too, what did you think?), ringed pucker, silky curve of belly, tongue and teeth on shoulder, and I planted myself firmly again.

So it went on. Me in the bathroom, Mother outside, me humping and hunching across the cold tiled floor, me at school, serious and nervous. The boys chased me for a bit and then told ugly stories about me. I think I was pretty, but I hesitated, because in spite of everything I wanted to be right for Mother, I tried, I bore the pulping weight of her expectations and tried to become the thing she dreamed for me. All those years we lived together, not saying much to each other, I knew her pride in me, and I felt something else grow like a thorn in my chest, a tight place of resentment that I was ashamed of during the day. But I think I would have done it, I would have let her make me what she wanted to, if she hadn't cut me.

She cut me, I mean literally. She scalpeled into my flesh, chiseled away at my bone, and so then I hated her. But before I hated her I had wanted to fly for her, I had thought about it and thought and finally I decided that I would become an astronaut for her. The decade had passed me with all its anger and its distant jungle war, and I still knew I had to repay her. I knew she expected something from me, something that was a lot, but she never said anything and so I never knew. In my senior year I saw a movie at school, for a science class, ships silently curving toward each other against a deep black, people turning slowly, connected by silvery umbilical cords, and I thought, that's what she wants. She wants me to do this, and so I said, quite suddenly, out very loudly, "I want to be an astronaut." The kids laughed at me, but the teacher, a spiky old Irishwoman, smiled, and I smiled on the bus home, but on the kitchen table Mother had a brown manila folder open, full of glossy brochures and copied pages from medical journals. I could see cross section drawings in black and white, bone and cartilage neatly laid out and explained.

"What's all this?" I said.

"For you," she said. "This is the one we'll go with."

"For me? For me, a nose job?"

Well, it seemed she had watched it for years, my nose. I looked at it now in a mirror, and it seemed to me all right, but she said it was too broad and flat.

"Too broad and flat for what?" I said, my voice rising. "I like it just fine."

"Not for anything," she said. "It just is."

In the mirror it was a good nose, straightforward and blunt, not disfigured or ugly in any manner that I knew, but she had this thing in mind, she drew it for me on a yellow pad: it was supposed to start from the brow cleanly and well defined, on the thin side but not too thin, then proceed like a blade to the tilted and diamondlike tip, over nostrils sharp and hidden. She had worked on this concept for years, it was the distillation of years of research, and this is what she wanted from me and for me, and again I wailed: "For what? I don't need a new fucking nose."

"Don't curse," she said, not even angry. She had been putting money together for years, and I was now old enough, so the question of not doing it was not even real.

"Next Thursday," she said, straightening away her folders. "You'll have Thanksgiving break to recover."

She was smiling a little and I understood now that I was supposed to be grateful, this was a gift to me.

"Mother," I said. "Let me ask you. What do you think I should be?"

"Anything, dear," she said. "You can be anything."

I guess it was that stupid damn tale of hope she was trying to feed me, but then it also occurred to me that she didn't really care what I became, as long as I rose, escaped from her grimy prison of separateness and fit in, got the goddamned nose of belonging. So she cut me. Sure, it was a guy called Schwartz who held a cold chisel to it and in a single tap cracked away the cartilage from the bone, sure, but it was her hands I felt on me. Me, I sat there shuddering at the sound of it, feeling nothing, numb at least locally, I shut my eyes and felt the front of my face freeze. He talked to me, okay, honey, you might feel something now, nothing to worry about, all right, here it comes, and then far away, like an earthquake on the other side of the earth, crack, he broke it. I thought, bitch.

So I lay in my bed, my eyes black-ringed, a white bandage taped across my face. I guess I could say that of the Thanksgiving turkey I tasted only bitterness: the capsules Schwartz gave me filled my mouth with a sour taste that stayed for days. I went to school with the swelling nearly gone, but with a big white strip still across my face, and I found that I was already a heroine. They liked me even before they saw the new nose — I guess it was the effort they appreciated. The nose, after Schwartz had removed the stitches, settled slowly into its new shape. Every morning I got up and found a new configuration, and Mother said, it takes a while to get into its normal shape. Truth was that I didn't really care what it finally looked like, I couldn't care, it was raw enough just to watch it move, just to see this new thing on me. I mean, this is obvious but it looked the hell like somebody else, now and then I touched it tenderly and my fingers felt for the old, now-invisible contours. I felt done, I felt like I had been fitted.

What about Mother, you say, but I kept quiet and was carefully thankful, biding my time for I don't know what. I was waiting. I didn't know what I was going to do but I knew my reply would have to be momentous. Anyway, I knew my NASA plans were off, because even the thought of getting on a plane to go to Texas or someplace like that made me pukey. On the weekends I got up early to go to the park, where I watched the morning workers sweep up the leaves and work with the water and manure. Also I read a lot, mostly, why I don't know, but mostly folktales, German and Indian, Icelandic sagas, stuff like that. I guess it made me feel better. I talked to no one.

After a while I started to go to the park in the evenings too. I told Mother it was boys, dates, parties, and eagerly she believed me. I sat on the grass and waited as darkness came in, then I got on the last bus and went home. I should have been scared but I wasn't. One day, I fell asleep and woke up to the sound of sprinklers, a soft shushing sound repeating itself, I felt the water float onto my skin and bead and make it cool, and as I tried to raise my head I couldn't, it was as if my muscles had given way. I thought then that if I let myself go I would disappear into the earth, become mud and soil, and I sat up and came to myself with my heart pounding. Holding my chest, I scrambled up and started to walk. I went outside the park and walked on, and I walked past many things. First, near the park, were the houses of the rich, big and glowing, the windows like precious soft bits of hot metal, like barriers which hid a whole world. Then I walked past the houses of the ordinary people, past the orderly rows of boxlike, dark bulks. Then came a festive, noisy mall, the lots filled with cars. Then I saw scrubby grass lots, factory buildings, tin sheds. Then I walked past the homes of the poor, rows and rows of apartment houses, stoops, rotting vehicles. Then there was a huge empty place, gray and abandoned, strands of wire here and there, a white animal skull and barking in the darkness, here and there the scattered fragments of a building. Then a long moment of nothing, complete darkness, not even a road. Then, finally, a red glow in the darkness, a circle of neon, a jagged script with lost letters in it, spelling "Joyland."

When I went into Joyland they assumed I was looking for a job, and I didn't say no. Because I was so young they were nervous and yet obviously they wanted me, so I let them go through their moves, bargain and slick and wheel and deal, I knew as soon as I walked in. They took me behind and I waited in the wings until it was my turn. Then I walked onto the stage, ignored the music, sat on the edge and slowly pulled off my clothes. I mean it wasn't a show or anything, I didn't even try to dance, I just took off my clothes, but they seemed to love it because after a while I called for the lights to come up and I looked them in the face and met their eyes and just sat there and took them all off and then I sat there some more and stretched back a little and that was it. I mean it wasn't much and I've often wondered why there was that sudden quiet and the other girls stopped moving around on the floor and everyone just watched. I sure as hell don't believe that I have the kind of looks that stop people from drinking and buying stuff and going on just because I take my goddamned clothes off, so I wonder what it was that first night. I don't know. Maybe it was just that I looked everyone in the eye and I wasn't trying to sell anything.

So I started there. I don't want to tell you that it was all pleasant: there was booze on the floor, women working to feed kids and others, drunks in the bathrooms, all those men sitting in the darkness, their eyes, knifings now and then, cruising cops, bad money from the Families, all that. But three nights a week I told Mother I was off to see Eddie and Barbara and Pennel, and instead I went down to Joyland and did my thing. Why, you ask, who knows, it did good for me. I would have done it anywhere, I think, on the street or on a bus, but at Joyland it was all set up and I could do it, so I did.

Some of the women despised me, and others took care of me. The men circled and watched, not at all sure what to think, and all kinds of rumors flew. But still, you want to know, what did I get out of it, what did I feel, didn't I feel cheap and used or something? No, what I felt, under the sharp moon of the spotlight, was just me, the sweat on my skin. I think for sure there were others who danced there who despised those who watched and themselves, but to me that wasn't even important, that, or money, wasn't why I walked to the edge of town. It was that it anchored me. In there I was free of the knives of progress, at least for a while. And it was truly for me very innocent: I went straight home afterwards, ignoring all the invitations, the sad and hopeful queries.

Time went: I graduated, and did what I did, and one hot July night I walked home, and everywhere small groups of people gathered in front of store windows, watching a gray, rocky surface, a small white craft floating in black. When I got home Mother was sitting upright at her table, and in the back the television spoke softly, urgently. She was looking at me.

"You know?" I said.

"I know." It was no use to ask how, there were a hundred men who came to my shows, and so somehow she knew. She had her hands flat on the table in front of her, her face was in the darkness, but flashes of light danced over her head from behind.

"You filthy creature," she said, in a voice more full of wonder than anger. "You could have been anything, you could have done anything. But instead you —" and now her voice cracked, "you chose SHIT." Her gesture as she held out the world to me, my future, took in the small kitchen, the *Saturday Evening Post* covers framed on the wall, and especially the image on the screen behind her. She stopped, turned away from me, looked deeply into the television, then dismissed me: "You barbarian."

So I left. I walked down the street, and you know what I saw on the hundreds of brightly lit squares on both sides of the streets, in shop windows and in living rooms, you know whose voice followed me, repeating again and again, metallic and hissy from thousands of miles of space: "That's one small step for a man, but a giant leap for mankind." You know what I watched: a white form, light and clean, pushing a flag into the moon. So I found a telephone, and I called. There had been people asking me things, to do things, so now I called, and in a few hours it was all ready: a creaky metal bed in a faraway, smelly house, a torn mattress covered with a cheap but brand new cotton sheet, two small baby spots on metal stands, an ancient and scratched but working sixteen-millimeter camera, a photographer, and a man. At first the man, long-haired but cowboy-booted, thirtyish, and drinking from a small bottle, at first he smiled at me, baby don't worry I'll take care of you, but I didn't say a word and he shut up. I mean I was calm. In a minute I had everything off and I said, let's go, and he looked over behind the camera, surprised, I think he thought, maybe wanted, that I'd be scared. He sat on the bed and I rolled over him, skimming and struggling off his shirt, and then there was the bumpy skin on his shoulders, the slight sourness of his underarms, neck and pulses, sharp taste in the mouth, bourbon, smoothness of the inside of the lip, eyes darting under closed eyelids, each hair on the chest distinct, goose-pimpled nipples, my tongue like a dart, a swallow, teeth pinching skin, the trembling breath in the stomach and the twitching muscles, blessed solidity and the warmth, welcome hint of a pungent bouquet underneath, nose nuzzling and burrowing, wrinkled skin, so soft, and sliding and precious underneath, mouth opens and comes up to welcome: cock is good, and then visiting the knees, the poky and scarred childhood knees, extended ankles and curled toes. I swing up, and he moves kiss by kiss over my back, the side of me, arms and neck and ears, small wet animal, warm and nipping, vibration along breasts, nipples alert, scoots down and I hunch over his face, smell of myself, lips over me, each movement a long lightening into my heart, labia luxuriant and thick, ballooned, circling tip searching clit and finding and losing, hands spread on cheeks, my fingers on myself: sweet inexhaustible goodness of cunt. The camera whirs, I lean back and reach under, take him, now bouncy against my hand and muscled, move my hips until I hold him, then settle back, the sting takes a scream from me, but I can see my body shining and wet and above his, holding him inside the reach of him feels so strange, the thought of it — I have him in — so unexpected and wonderful that I laugh, he trembles and laughs too, and for some reason the giggling takes us, and we laugh and laugh until I slump and still laugh and the camera stops and all I can hear is the three of us laughing.

So we ran out of film and had to come back the next day to get the come shot. Then we sat up stickily in bed and ate doughnuts. When I asked why the come shot (this one in slow motion, luxuriant sprays of liquid), they both shrugged, said that's the way it's done, babe, it's the money shot. Weird, I thought, but I didn't really care, because I really was okay. People don't believe me when I tell them this, straights, I mean, squares, good folk, Mom and Pop with their two-point-oh-five kids. They look at me with pity and horror alternating over their faces, and when I insist, they try to pretend I don't exist. You're just deluded, Mom says, you're crazy, you don't really know what's happening to you, you don't know what's being done to you. When I still say, no, no, this is me, they snarl "slut," and try to forget about me. But, hey, I've been all over. After that first day, with the money I got, I bought a beat-up Packard, got in it and drove. I've been to every small town from Albany to Zanesville, every city, and when you get in, when you start seeing the shopping malls, you swing past the stores, you avoid the commercial streets where the suits live, you angle away from the suburbs and the lawns, and look for ruined buildings, bums, police cars, rain, and there you find it. I went from town to town and did strip. Then I came back up east and I did loops, grainy black-and-white stuff, badly lit, the guys sometimes with their shoes on for fear of cop raids. Then suddenly it was the seventies and we were doing film, with credits, music, and everything, and people, even women, started to know who I was. I never went home.

I guess to put it bluntly you would have to say I became a star, but what I want you to know is what I do is work, and it is a craft. Think about it — you show up in the morning, and maybe the person — him or her — the person you're working with, if you're unlucky, isn't into it, they hate it, hate themselves, or they're just bored or tired, so now you have to carry the scene. Then there are the lights, hot and headache-making. If they're going to move the camera you sit there and then you have to start again, maybe the guy's losing his hard, the fluff girl's working away on him but it's going, so then you have to revive him. After all this it's got to work, at least for me it does, I take pride in my art, and it does work, after all there's the flesh, shiny and soft under the arcs, the room fading away, a still, lovely concentration even with the director's voice from behind the camera.

So I did it for years. The first real film I did, credits and all, the producer said, honey do you want to use your real name. I told him I'd think about it. That night I sat in my apartment and thought about it.

My real name — never mind what it was — didn't seem real to me anymore, and maybe it never had. I thought of myself hiding in a bathroom, skin damp from steam, and outside the thin atmosphere of Mother's house, the climate of temperate reason we lived in, and I knew my name had never been mine. So I cast about for another one, I flipped through the books on my walls, walked about from window to window. Finally I threw on a coat and went outside, north — I lived in Manhattan then, on Columbus. It was late now, winter, and the streets glittered with ice. I walked, and I could hear the voices of carolers, clear and sharp as blades in the crisp air. I turned a corner, and St. John's loomed, I stood facing the huge black shell. As it hung over me I waited, waited for it to tell me something, waited to ask a question that trembled half-formed in me. But finally I turned away, nothing said, nothing remembered.

The next morning I had a call from a doctor at Bishop's: Mother had been brought into the emergency room after a collapse at work. The symptoms were of acute starvation. When I got to the hospital, the doctor (after his moment of startled recognition, I was getting used to those) told me that she had been suffering from long and unrelenting constipation, and it seemed that rather than suffer the abdominal pain, the headaches, the mixtures and pills, the indignity of straining morning after morning, she had stopped eating. She was asleep, and I looked through the glass window on the door of the room, preferring not to go in, scared of waking her up. They had an IV in her arm, a tube in her nose.

"We're feeding her," the doctor said.

Her hands were curled up in two tiny fists on her chest.

"How long didn't she eat?"

"Two weeks, it looks like."

"How long is she going to be in here?"

"A week, maybe ten days. Her insurance should cover it, don't worry. At least this time."

"That's not what I meant."

It wasn't. What I was thinking of was how dark her body looked against the white of the hospital sheets, her rage when she would awaken and find herself defeated. In the parking lot the tears froze quickly on my face, and my head was filled with a single word, a memory perhaps from some late late movie of childhood, or perhaps I had heard it lifting toward me from the hospital chapel. That afternoon, I paused from tonguing a breast, from sucking its perfect nipple, and I raised up and said to nobody in particular, "Kyrie. That's my new name, Kyrie."

They kept Mother in the hospital for three weeks, for treatment and psychiatric observation. She refused to answer the shrink's questions, and refused to see me: "I don't want any of her filthy money either." They released her on Christmas eve, and I watched her from my car as she strode out confidently into the haze of snow that hung over the city. She walked away and I watched, for a long time, the lights glowing dimly and far away, listened to the silence. They had her back at Emergency the next morning, throwing up violently and in pain — she had gone home and gorged on food, on thick slabs of ham, whole cakes of butter, game hens, pie. When they took off her clothes her stomach bulged, its circumference weirdly translucent and webbed with black veins. This time they kept her for a month, and had her looked at by teams of nutritionists and psychologists. Hesitating but reluctant to keep her in the hospital — she seemed so damn healthy — they released her to the care of a live-in nurse and a smart young doctor out of Harvard. But now, even though she ate regularly and carefully, under the eye of the nurse, her body seemed to starve. The food disappeared into her, and then vanished altogether — she grew weaker and weaker until she couldn't get out of bed. Her hair fell out, and she took on the appearance of a famine-ridden child, the swollen belly, the huge hurt eyes. She slipped silently in and out of sleep, then into a coma, but then suddenly she awoke and asked for steak. They gave her some sort of soft gray nutritive slop instead, but by next morning she was sitting up in bed eating huge quantities of scrambled eggs and asking for more. They swore, afterwards, that they had seen her flesh fill up with muscle minute by minute. So she lived for the next few years in alternative two-month cycles of hunger and gluttony, of control and terror, surrounded by her models of *Voyager I* and, later, the space shuttle.

Meanwhile, I lived. I made a deal with her insurance company, so I could pay most of her bills without her knowing about it. I was working almost every day — at first I made five hundred a day, then eight, then a grand, then two, then more. I became known, and I was able to buy a house on Long Island. I filled it with books, old ones, mostly, and, for

348 / THE BOOK OF REVENGE AND MADNESS

some reason, rocks. I don't know why, but to see an octavo of *The Recuyell of the Histories of Troy* in full limp vellum, next to a cracked and jagged piece of gneiss, gave me pleasure. I had a television for a while but finally I had to throw it out, because watching it late at night, seeing all those beautiful people, those beer commercials and ads for jeans in which they wafted toward each other, never quite fucking but always with a hint of it, all this gave me a quite unbearable feeling of loneliness, I mean the kind of loneliness which makes you hate yourself and talks to you about death, which makes your own home unfamiliar and waking up tomorrow impossible. So I threw it out. But mostly my life was ordinary and very good. I worked, I had friends, I had lovers. I came home in the evenings and made myself a cup of hot chocolate, and sat on my porch and read. When it grew dark I ate, usually healthy stuff, salad and artichokes and things. I invested in General Motors, two startup agricultural products companies, a bank, and so on. I had a live-in boyfriend for a while, for five years actually, a porno actor too, his name was George. We broke up because of the usual couple stuff, grow-ing apart and all that, but not jealousy as you might think. I've had other girlfriends and boyfriends after that, some for longer than others, and a couple of times I've thought of marriage but didn't really do it. I mean all in all my life was quite average and almost boring, except I went and sexed people for a living, which is good. It was good. But I've also seen people flame and crash, flame on some drug or some furious anger that drove them to the life, to the desperate affair with guilt and rejection that was mostly the meaning of Joyland. I saw some flirt with the hard guys and chicks who appeared like hyenas on the edge of the particular ghetto that I lived in, and these friends disappeared into the long black maw of justice. Some of these appeared later on talk shows to participate in the daily circuses of guilt and victimhood, to play the preening lambs who owned up to transgression, who bore the holy anger of America, and then returned gratefully, weeping and sometimes clutching a book contract, to the fold of righteousness.

Meanwhile Mother puked, starved, and ate. And so we went into the eighties, and quite suddenly, one morning, Reagan was in the White House, my once-boyfriend George was dead of AIDS, and entire battal-ions of wild-eyed, stiff-moving robots descended on us, various scrip-tures in hand, eager to have their revenge on sex. I avoided all of the early extravaganzas, but when my town council moved to have the local fornication emporium — Wonderland — expelled from the body civic, I called them and told them I wanted to talk to the committee, that I'd give evidence or whatever they wanted. When I explained who I was and what I did and why I was qualified to speak, at first the woman on the phone didn't believe me, she kept on saying, "*You* live here?" I told her to look up the tax records and hung up. So they had to let me in. On the morning I went in, the local NBC station had a van at the council house, and the room, a big auditorium with a mural of great American inventors (the Wright brothers, Edison, Henry Ford) on one end, was packed wall to wall. The panel was composed of these: a Catholic priest; a mother of three (that's how she described herself) who worked as an assistant editor in a publishing house in Manhattan; the minister from the local Methodist congregation (which was at the time just starting a two-million-dollar renovation on its church); a feminist writer of some repute and angry notoriety; and a couple, young and very clean and energetic, the wife a real estate broker and power in the P.T.A., the husband a lawyer. As these people arranged themselves on the podium, and as I waited, a reporter leaned over a pew and stage-whispered to me: "Hey, Kyrie, what about the Nero film?"

"No comment," I said, a little sharply, because that was supposed to be a secret. The thing was that I'd been negotiating for months with a major studio, which, with an already Oscared director, was trying to put together that elusive thing — a mainstream fuck film, you know, big budget, cast of thousands, maybe some real stars. I'd talked to a couple of the executives, and they were slick-haired and blown-dry, but I could tell they were desperate: their studio was dying. So they were seeing big bucks, they were hot for the four billion dollars on the other side of the tracks in Joyland, I could see the numbers ticking by in their eyes as they described the flames over Rome, they wanted to do decadence and lust and destruction and the final gory death of Nero. They'd gotten a couple of major male stars interested in Nero, and they wanted me to do his mother.

But now the loudspeakers crackled in the hall, and we were ready to start. I sat in front of the podium and faced them over a battery of microphones, and the scene had that strange flat look that comes from too many video lights. I'd worn a gray suit and pulled back my hair, so that I looked more like a mid-level executive than the wild half-broken slut they wanted, but soon they got over their slight confusion and the questions came hard and fast.

- Sex is a private act. It is a beautiful thing between two people. It is secret. Why do you degrade yourself and the holy gift of love by doing it like animals in front of the whole world?

- What you do dehumanizes human beings. What happens between two people is complex, mysterious. What you put on the screen is a caricature of human relations, and encourages people to treat each others like caricatures. Why do you do it?

- To any sane person this obsession with the nuts and bolts of the act, this unredeemed and unredeeming gaze at the mere body, this filth is sickening. The sexual act is a gift of God, to be engaged in with all seriousness and humbleness and spiritual consciousness. Don't you understand that what you are doing is sinful, that it is the enshrinement of sin?

- Pornography is violence against women. It is the colonization of their souls and bodies. It is enslavement. Don't you agree? How can you be a woman and not agree?

- Can't men and women just be friends?

I answered as best I could. I walked out of there weary, and was chased by cameras out of the building and to my car. At home, the phone was buzzing as I opened the door.

"Hi, babe. You were sensational." It was one of my executives from the coast. "Just keep on doing it. Every minute on the air is ten thousand tickets in the door. So here's the deal — I've been talking to the money people and it's a go situation. Almost."

"So what's the hitch?" I said.

"They're very impressed with the names we've mentioned for Nero, and they see you as the big Mama, I mean they can completely see you, you are her. Specially after your appearance on the tube today. But one thing. See, when you're talking Agrippina, you're talking a complete full-blown woman. You're seeing, I don't know, you get it, a luxurious woman, almost *zaftig*."

"What am I, a matchstick? I mean, am I bones?"

"No, no, you're it. Put you in a toga and you're it. All except for one thing. Or maybe two."

"A tit job! A greedy slimy Hollywood tit job. You want me to have a tit job."

"Why're you so mad? Everyone has one, you know."

So I hung up on him, and he was smart enough not to call right back. I sat by the phone holding my boobs, comfortable friends in my hands, not of spectacular DeMille proportions, but there and a little saggy and beautiful. I'd seen friends who'd done it, and I recalled the black bruises, the aching tenderness that held their arms tight to their sides, the bright purple flush of blood around the teats, the whole chest looking as if some maniac had swung a two-by-four to land smack across it, and as I remembered I twinged all the way from my nipples to the base of my spine. I sat there awhile, and then tried to eat, but my throat was tight and fear made my heart bigger and painful in me, so finally I sat down to a bottle of wine.

The phone brought me out of a fuzzy, drunken sleep, and for a few seconds I blinked, forgetting completely where I was.

"You'd better come," the voice said, and for one strange moment, in my dizzy state, it sounded not at all human, but as if it came out of the wires themselves, out of the huge network of coils and transistors and dishes and cables. The ground was icy and hard and in the hospital lot my boots rang on it like hammers. They had Mother laid out on this bed with railings around it, covered with a white sheet. The sheet went all the way up to her neck, and what surprised me was that her hair had turned an iron gray. I was afraid to lift the sheet away, but a doctor stood behind me and very softly began to tell me what had happened. He said that her eating disorder had been under control, it seemed to them, and she had appeared even more calm than usual lately. So all was going well, but that day the nurse found the bathroom door locked, and when they beat it down they found Mother in the tub. The skin around her stomach and her ankles was covered with small cuts, deep and deliberately made with a carpet knife, which she was still holding in her right hand. There was a fresh cut on her right ankle, and she had the foot propped up under the hot water tap. The insides of the drain were caked black — it looked like she'd been doing it for weeks, the doctor said, like she'd been trying to drain all the blood from her body. I don't know, why didn't she do it all at once, the doctor said, I can't figure it, but I don't think she wanted to, you know, go, she had a piece of chocolate cake on a plate by the tub, it was just the blood, I think she thought she could live without it.

They left me alone with her for a while and I touched her face, and the skin was cold but soft. Finally I turned away from her, but from the door I came back to her and lifted the sheet off. Her body lay with that opened up limpness that the dead achieve for a bit, an absolute absence of tension, hands gently curved, knees out. Her pubic hair was white, and above it at regular intervals, were one-inch up-and-down lines, slightly reddish. Around her ankles were rings, bracelets of the same lines. I looked at her neck, the deep creases at its base, the curve of the ribs just under the skin, the confident thickness of the thighs.

- A close-up. Full-color, outsized, magnified. A penis penetrating a vagina. The frame is so tight we can't see anything else. The focus is so sharp we can see each wrinkle, each bump, each hair. The human genitals are not beautiful. There is something ugly about this. There is something very ugly about this.

- We as a society are a hair's breadth away from collapse.

- A thick, musky light like clotted syrup; sidewalks and teenage hookers; bourbon and the tight ropy muscles of heroin addicts. This is the world you live in.

I listened to all this. The tips of my fingers grew cold and I shivered under my business gray. On the wall opposite, in the mural, a rickety plane teetered into the sky.

- We abhor, execrate, despise.

- Why does it have to be the thing, why must it be the thing, it shouldn't be this important.

- This is not the jungle.

- Just stop it.

So finally I shoved my chair back and stood up, and at the scrape of the wood they all looked at me, mouths open, their faces white splashes in the bluish light. I unbuttoned my coat, moving not hurriedly but deliberately, and shrugged it off. Nobody reacted until I had my blouse half off, and then a huge hubbub of voices rose, somebody shouting for a stretcher, I heard the reporters behind me scrambling over the railing, curses as a camera light crunched into somebody's head, then my bra was off and somebody screams, I step out of my skirt, the panties peel in a single movement, two cops are reaching over heads, I stand skin goose-bumped by the cold, hands by my sides, I cry: "No fear, no fear," but a woman is fighting her way through the roiling crowd, her face is so deeply red that it looks like a kumquat, she shouts, spraying spit, I haven't ever seen so much spit coming out of a person's mouth before, "Whore, whore!" and I think I know her, I've seen her before, an assistant D.A. or something, one of the cops shoves her aside and she swings at him with a pocketbook, he reels holding an eye, a small spot of blood appears on a white shirt, the cop's partner backhands with a nightstick and blood sprays from the woman's head, it spurts in a powerful, jerky stream that spatters everyone and everything. For a moment the screen freezes and I run.

I don't know how I got out of there. I remember running down a yellow hallway and into somebody's office, finding this dress in a closet, and then out onto the street and into a cab. I found some money at home, but I had barely finished paying the cabbie when the TV vans began to screech around the corner. So I grabbed a handbag, threw some stuff into it and climbed over the back wall. I caught another cab to La Guardia, and took the first plane I could get a ticket for. It dropped me off in Burbank, and from there I found a Greyhound, then I bought a car on one of my credit cards, and here I am.

When Kyrie paused, I turned to look at her. Listening to her I had slid down in my seat until I was as nearly flat as I could be. Now she smiled at me, her chin on her knees.

"I don't know why I tell you this," she said. "It isn't even perhaps a part of the story. But for some reason it sticks in my mind. You remember those two girls who went to the movie with Mother, the debater and the hockey player. Well, both of them died bad deaths. Janine Alcott, in 'seventy-four they found her dead by a highway near Pasadena, Texas. She had been stabbed seventeen times. They never found who did it, or even had any ideas. Carol Ann Mayberry, who got married and moved to California and got divorced, in 'eighty-one she tried to stab a lover with an eight-inch carving knife, and he shot her in the head. She died right there."

She looked away from me, out of the window. The only sound was the circular buzz of the tires. Overhead, two white trails slowly disintegrated into the blue.

"Bombers," Tom said. "Bombers from the air base at Edwards."

"I don't know why I tell you this," Kyrie said, stretching lazily and lighting a cigarette. "I don't know why."

Amanda and I kept a silence with each other as we skimmed across the country in the Jaguar. In motel rooms, under my fingers she opened to pleasure but in it went even further into some privateness that I could not follow into or penetrate. In spite of all the talk in the car she told me nothing about herself, and the only thing I knew was the sometimes strange look of inwardness that came over her when she thought nobody was watching her, a heaviness that she turned away from with a quick shake of her shoulders. When she was driving she was beautiful: we flew across the desert under the elegant skill of her hands, and sometimes the dust behind us, illumined by the sun, followed us like a contrail, and the car banked smoothly and turned to the contours of the road. That she took pride in her driving I could see, and there was a joy in it, as if she had forgotten herself, but I didn't know enough about the skill to praise, and so I watched her instead.

We went by the towns so fast that all I saw was a general, anonymous rush of storefronts and billboards. Once I woke from a deep sleep to see the same fragments of light in the dark, the same facades that I had seen a few hours ago. Where are we going so fast? I said, and I saw her shoulders shrug, outlined by a rapid red light that whipped past us with a distant howl of wind. I went back to sleep and awoke again to the same speed.

We stopped at a small town for food, on a scrubby main street surrounded by brown hills. I tried to eat at a diner, but I felt sick and finally the only thing I could have was a McDonald's milk shake.

*   *   *

I awoke startled to the sound of Gujarati, children's voices, catch it, get the ball, here to me. For one confused moment I thought I was back at high school in India, and felt a surge of panic: oh, God, I'm late for breakfast. Then I felt Amanda's leg against my own. She slept on her back, legs straight and hands folded on her stomach, never moving. I touched her shoulder and she came awake immediately, and in the quick moment between sleep and her smile at me there was an unguarded look of fear, a childlike glance of terror at the white ceiling and beyond. But it passed so quickly that I thought I must have imagined it. She turned over on her side and stretched slowly.

"What's this?" I said. High up on her left shoulder was a small smooth patch, an infinitesimal shade lighter than the surrounding skin, so subtle that it would have been invisible but for my fingers, which felt the change in texture.

"Oh, that," she said. "It was a birthmark. My mother had it removed when I was a kid."

"Why?" I called to her as she went into the bathroom.

"You can't wear off-the-shoulder gowns with a thing on your shoulder."

"A thing? Was it ugly?"

"I don't know. It must have been."

"Was it red?"

When she came back in she was laughing. "I don't know."

She sat on the bed, and I pulled her over until I could look at her shoulder. "Must have been red," I said.

"I don't know. You're so weird."

I kissed her shoulder. Making love with Amanda was slow and tense and tight and full of unexpected fierceness, and she held and held and relaxed only with a sob.

The children outside, boys and girls of nine and ten, were playing a game of Kings. I sat and watched them as they threw a tennis ball at each other, dodging and shouting. Then Kyrie and Tom walked past me.

"See you in a while," Kyrie said. "We're going to find a haircut."

They strolled away, and as they turned a corner Tom swung around and waved at me. I wondered what the sleeping arrangements had been in their room, but really he didn't seem cocky. Maybe just relaxed. But I was too lazy to think about it, and I put my chin on my knees and drowsed, the children and their game vague gray figures behind my eyes.

"Let's go." It was Amanda, buttoned up and packed and ready to move. I told her about the haircut and she turned about without a word and went back into the room. After a while the children broke for lunch, and when I went back in she was sitting upright on the bed watching television. I went past her into the shower, and when I came out she was still there, straight and concentrated.

"What's the matter?"

I could've sworn the look on her face was hatred, but she said, merely: "I'm bored."

"Change the channel," I said. "They'll be back soon."

A group of buffalo rumbled across the screen. We watched them move from right to left in an endless stream.

"I'm bored. I'm bored. I'm bored."

"So tell me a story."

"No."

I was annoyed by her now, and so I went outside again. I went around to the lobby, which was green all over and had bright pictures of fruit on the wall. The owner was a small Gujarati man wearing gold-rimmed spectacles who introduced himself to me straightaway as Desai. Desai's equally small but plump wife came out a little while later and gave us a cup of tea, and Desai said, "Is that your wife?" I shook my head, and he said, "Get married, young man. Get married."

I went back to our room and Amanda was curled up on the bed. The television was blaring but I thought she was asleep. She turned over and I saw that she was wide awake, trembling and holding herself tightly, her fists clenched between her knees. When I lay next to her and touched her forearm the muscle twitched away and back.

"Are you still bored?" I said.

She said nothing but her eyes had the blank glaze of panic now.

"Tell me something," I said. "Tell me a story."

"No," she said, and started to get up. I slapped a hand around her waist and held her back.

"No. Tell me something."

She twisted against me and the sheer force of her quick struggle almost had her away from me. We fought each other in a silent but completely serious tussle, and she was very strong. Finally I had her hands twisted above her head in her T-shirt and my knees on either side of her chest. We stared at each other, panting, and I felt my sudden, causeless anger collapse inside me. I started to get up, and she hissed, "No," and hooked a leg over mine, and she turned her head and bit my wrist. My hands left marks on her sides.

When we got into the car I had a comfortable kind of emptiness inside me. I was tired, and was anticipating the rush of the freeways. Amanda started the car, and as she backed the car out of the motel parking lot she smiled at me, a small tight smile empty of happiness. Behind us, Tom put his head on Kyrie's lap and dozed. They had strolled in lazily in the late afternoon, their heads shining and fragrant. Kyrie's hair was now a deep brown, and the change from the startling white-blond of the morning made her look younger. Tom had his hair very short, in what I thought of as a child's haircut, spiky on top. Both of them looked new. So we drove into the setting sun, and Amanda put on round, silver-rimmed shades that gave her a face from another, younger decade.

"Let's go to Texas," I said.

"Why?" said Amanda, and I could see that putting a direction on her flight displeased her.

"I want to go to NASA," I said. "Maybe we can see a rocket taking off."

Kyrie leaned forward. "Maybe I'll find my grandfather," she said, grinning, I suppose, at the absurdity of the thought.

"Maybe," I said.

"Want to see a rocket," mumbled Tom.

"All right," Amanda said. "We'll go."

So she wheeled us about in an enormous arc from one freeway to another, somewhere in the middle of that huge American night, and we went south. I sat back, wide awake, and for some reason, I kept on remembering Mayo, and a boy named Shanker, older than us, a prefect who every afternoon sat on the patio in front of his room wearing an enormous Stetson, and read avidly and thirstily one out of his almost complete collection of Louis L'Amour, while we threw stones at a tamarind tree to knock down clumps of the sour fruit. When we annoyed him too much with our shouting he would look up out of his dream, eyes glazed, point a forefinger at us, and cock a thumb back. So, Shanker, at last the real Texas.

"Real Texas?" Amanda said.

I must have mumbled it aloud, but the story was too long ago and seemed somehow too absurd to tell in that car, in that place, and so I shrugged. "Real Texas," I said decisively, and she cocked an eyebrow but asked no more. In real Texas I will find you. In real Texas we will see what it is. In real Texas we will come to the heart of it.

When we actually crossed into Texas I was asleep. What woke me up was the radio buzzing about Hindu-Muslim riots in Ahmedabad, and I fumbled with it until it clicked off. It bothered me not because of what it was about but because it seemed too messy, it had too much of the stink of belief and the squalor of passion. I wanted the blade-edge feeling I had, the keenness of my senses and the rush of speed.

"We're in Texas," Amanda said.

We flew in a long floating curve, the road smooth and the yellow line perfect and steady under us. I leaned low over the dash and peered ahead, straining as if I would see instantly the long white trail of a rocket far to the south. I looked at Amanda, and I said, "Cool!" and I felt my lips pulling back from my teeth. She laughed, her hair a dark red and flying, I could see her eyes shining, and it was something like love.

We came into Houston on a hot afternoon, and the road passed through dense, swampy land, where nothing moved. Then suddenly the city sprang up in front of us, as abruptly as if it had nothing to do with the wetlands around it, as if it had been created complete and whole out of a foreign imagination. The buildings ahead were huge and fantastically beautiful, so symmetrical and straight-edged that it frightened me to look at them. It was like a city on another planet. I glanced at Amanda, and she had a remote expression on her face, a look of concentration and resolve, like a soldier scanning a terrain for lines of fire and dead ground.

She stopped at a motel called The Hokaido, with exposed fake-wood beams and a rock garden in the front. The floor in the rooms was covered with a dense brown carpet colored to look fibrous and grainy. I sat rubbing my feet over it, waiting for Amanda to emerge from her endless shower. When she finally did come out, she was pink as a baby and as defenseless, and I held her in my lap and kissed the top of her head, which smelled fresh and wet and of innocence. I began to hum a song, a song from some half-forgotten black-and-white matinee, "*Too kahan ye bata,*" and she couldn't have known it or understood but she must have felt it in my chest, so she made small noises of contentment and wrapped her soft white towel tightly around her; for a moment the Japanese were at bay and mad India was far away and Amanda's hungry velocity was ceased and Houston was gone, the only sound was falling waters, and we were quiet with each other.

That night we drifted from bar to bar, and Amanda drank vodka steadily, the only change in her being a translucent look about the skin, so that in the humid night she had the appearance of a marble statue. The city itself was hot, huge, with a feeling of danger that puffed up from the exhausts of the cars and the blowing of the air conditioners on the sidewalks. I tried to imagine Amanda on the streets as a child, happy and skipping, but the picture faded away amid the clinking of the glasses and the slow waves of conversation.

"How will you find one man in a city?" I said to Kyrie.

"I don't know," she said. "He was a drunk. He's probably dead long ago."

"We'll look," said Tom.

"What, police stations, public records?"

"No, just around here. We'll ask."

So they got up and started working the bar from one end to the other, leaning down to people's ears, over the music. Every now and then somebody would stare after Kyrie, as if they were trying to remember her, identify her among the vague memories of childhood.

"They're crazy," I said. "It's impossible."

"Yes," Amanda said.

I took a deep breath, and said, looking at my glass, "When are you going to call your parents?"

"My parents?"

"They're here, right? In Houston?"

"Yes."

"You're not going to go, visit them, I mean?"

"No."

"Amanda, they'll know you're here. When the credit card bill gets there, at least."

"So?"

"So? So you've got to go there."

"Why?"

"Pay your respects."

She blinked, looking at me as if I was speaking a language she didn't understand. The words felt foreign and strange even to me, in the light from the red plastic–encased candle between us.

"You have to," I said. "You really do." I kept on saying this, and we gaped at each other until finally both of us burst into laughter. But I kept on at her, while Kyrie and Tom went from bar to bar, and finally at some hour of the night so late that it was actually cool, she broke and drawled, "All right, all right, we'll go," and I slept in a strange happiness, as if I was to meet somebody I'd been looking for a long time.

We went the next morning, leaving Kyrie and Tom at the motel with Amanda's credit card. It was a Sunday morning, and the roads were empty and quiet. The car turned a corner, and it seemed all at once that we had left behind the malls and the condos and the straightforward seediness of motels. Now the houses were two-storied and lawned, ivied and crenelated, the street was suddenly smooth and was no longer a street but an oak-lined boulevard.

"Amazing," I said. "Where are we?"

"River Oaks," Amanda said.

"Where's the river?" I said, but she didn't reply. She was spinning the wheel, and in a quick turn we faced a very large building, built on a slight rise at the center of the plot, that was unmistakably the same house I remembered from dozens of Classic Comics set in another-century England. "Wow," I said. "Wuthering Heights, man."

Amanda opened the door with a gold key on a chain. Stepping inside, I had the sensation of being transported to another time: the parlor was full of fussy Victorian chairs, all curlicues and massive feet, hunting prints, a quizzical deer head on the wall. Inside, the corridors were white and high-ceilinged, and the rooms were as gleaming and brown and perfect as film sets. Amanda walked ahead of me to the kitchen, and it was only here the dizzying illusion was broken, because she picked a sparkling glass from the shelf and held it under a tap inset into the fridge, which was enormous and white.

"Wow," I said. "Running cold water." That tap in the fridge fascinated me, and I gulped down my water quickly just so that I could stick my glass in and watch it fill under the gleaming tap. "This is so amazing." She looked at me, a faint grin on her face. "No, really, it's like really so damned elegant because it works." I drank another glass of water. It was funny tasting, clean and flat but impeccably cold. I took another glass and now I had to sip it. "You know when I got obsessed with America? It was a damn long time ago. It was when I was really little. This was when I was so little I hadn't even gone away to boarding school. I must have been five or six or maybe at the most seven. From somewhere or other there showed up in our house a nineteen-sixty-seven Sears catalog. It was quite thick and big and I used both hands to pick it up. I think one of our neighbors brought it over to show my mother dress patterns for her daughters. But I found it one winter day in the drawing room when I came home from school, when my mother was asleep, and I carried it up on the roof, where I sat and started to go through it page by page. I started with the men's wear, with all the blond, blue-eyed guys wearing checkered shirts tapering to their bodies. Then the men's underwear, then the women's dresses, then the women's underwear, then the whole family groups, the mothers and daughters wearing the same dress and same bell-shaped hair, then the garden tools, all these slick hedge cutters and long lengths of green pipe, and, amazing and unbelievable, drivable grass cutters, little too-much too-deadly tractors that you drove around the lawn and the grass came out packed in bags. But best of all, at the back, saved for last, whole working and usable and immaculate swimming pools! Swimming pools you could order through the mail, that would come to your house in boxes, that could be assembled, on your large and expansive back lawn, into what it said, into goddamn amazing swimming pools, so that your pretty daughters, your crewcutted sons, your bloody stunning wife could paddle and float gently under the best sun in this best of all worlds. I mean it felt as if the top of my seven-year-old head had come off, that I had seen heaven, no, not that exactly, but that this, this in front of me was what life must be. This was bloody it. So when my mother called for me I jerked up and hated her, felt instantly angry at the un-neatness of our house, how weathered and cracking all over it was, old and old in everything. I wanted to chop down the old peepul tree that hung its branches over the roof and scattered its leaves in our court-yard. I was so desolate with the feeling of who I was and where I was and how stuck I was in the whole untidy clutter that I started down the stairs with the catalog still in my hand, and only when I was halfway down did I think to go back up and hide it under the water tank. I kept it there for years and years until it fell apart. I used to go up there all the time to look at it. I kept it for years, until all the pages were curling and some of them had fallen out and blown away, and the families were faded, but still the pictures, the idea of them, were bright in my mind."

So Amanda took me out back to the swimming pool, which looked like a highland grotto, with a waterfall, and artificial picturesque rocks, or maybe real picturesque rocks artfully fitted and arranged to look like a scene from *Lorna Doone*, complete with a gnarled oak tree on a knoll.

"Who made this house? I mean who designed it?"

"My parents," she said. "Who else?"

"Where are they?"

"They must be at church."

For a moment I tried to imagine the church, but my mind swung wildly from one thing to another, from French Gothic to rural English, and realizing it could be anything, anything at all, I gave up. I sat eagerly by the pool, my mind a blank, waiting for Amanda's parents. We took off our shoes and dangled our feet in the water and waited.

"Are you bored?" said Amanda.

"I'm bored," I said. So she brought out a little color TV, and some vodka, and we drank Bloody Marys by the pool and watched *Star Trek*. Drinking Bloody Marys, I felt witty and cold, and Amanda and I talked back to Kirk and Spock, we made cutting, ironic remarks, and laughed at our own cleverness.

"TV is so fucking stupid," Amanda said.

"Bloody right," I said. "Stupid as all hell."

Amanda's mother was the most beautiful woman I had ever seen: she had curly blond hair, green eyes, broad shoulders, and taut legs. She strode in through the sliding doors like a vision out of a glossy magazine and the sight of her daughter and me floating around in her pool didn't pause her for a second.

"Hello, Amanda," she said.

I was on a red plastic raft in the middle of the pool, my feet in the water, a glass in one hand. Eager for the shouting to start, I paddled with my free hand toward shore, but managed only to set myself revolving madly, so that I saw only spinning glimpses of them.

"Hello, Mother," Amanda said, climbing out of the water. They puckered their lips a good inch away from each other's cheeks, and then the mother sat on a beach chair, her legs elegantly crossed and dangling a foot in a streamlined black shoe with a needle-sharp heel. Her dress was some kind of black lace and she was wearing a large black hat with a curving rim.

"Mother," Amanda said. "This is Abhay. He's at school with me. Abhay, this is Candy, my mother."

"Hello," I said. The raft was finally still.

"Hello."

Then we sat and waited. Amanda sipped her drink calmly, in what I thought was a kind of hushed anticipation of her father's huge patriarchal anger. But he was a tall, square-jawed man, William James, with absolutely white hair and brilliant blue eyes, who came in and said hello politely and then poured himself a drink. And this went on until the mother said, "Shall we go in for lunch?"

As we went in I whispered to Amanda, "They'll shout at you when you're alone with them?" I could see I had puzzled her again, but then we were pulling out the chairs around a large oak table, so I sat down and we ate, and the mother talked about state politics, film, and Jerry Hall. The lunch was served by a young Taiwanese woman named Annie. So we ate carefully, the cutlery click-clicking and Candy's calm voice a gentle music, but meanwhile Amanda had her bare foot up my trouser leg and was tracing circles and hoops of unmistakable lewdness on my shinbone. And over the table was a life-sized painting of two puffed-up people in formal clothes, whose names came to me from some unspeakable depth in my memory: Prince Albert and Princess Alexandrina. And while the prince and the princess gazed at me with a grand condescension that took no notice of time and history, I had the certain feeling that I had seen Candy somewhere before. It was a confusing lunch, and by the time it was over I was dizzy, more giddy now than curious about Amanda, and I very badly wanted to sleep. "Amanda," I said, putting down my coffee spoon. "Do you think I could take a nap?" I really was very tired, and I stumbled as I followed Amanda down a long wood-paneled corridor. I sank gratefully into the cool white pillow, and just as I began to breathe deeply I had the sensation I was falling from a great height, that I was floating, but then I was asleep.

I woke up and thought I was in another world. I mean I had no idea where I was and all I could see was the dim gleam of light on wood and darkness. The wind moved outside the window, gauzy curtains drifted and for a long moment I thought I was in some city of horse carriages and gas lamps, and my mouth was bitter and my breath heavy, but then slowly everything righted itself and I knew where I was. I stood up and walked slowly down the corridor, eager now to see what I could. But the house was still and silent, the lights all dimmed, and I found no sign of Candy, or William James, or Annie. From the kitchen I got a glass of water and walked back through the house again, and as I was going through a late Edwardian study I saw the outline of a head, and with a start I spilled the water on the ground.

"Abhay." It was Amanda. She was sitting in the darkness with a drink in her hand. I sat next to her and took up her hand, full of sympathy.

"Did it go all right?" I said. "Did they get real mean?"

"Abhay, you're so off. They're used to it."

"They're used to you just taking off from school and showing up with strange people? Strange men? Strange brown men?"

She said nothing, and emptied her glass. I watched as she poured from a bottle.

"You know," I said. "I think I've seen your mother somewhere before."

"Probably have," she said. "Everyone has."

"Everyone?"

"She was a centerfold."

"*Playboy?*" I asked, with a sudden shock of recognition.

"Yes."

And suddenly I was back in a seventh-grade dormitory, outside a windy desert night, inside Karan and Mich and I with a flashlight, bent over a magazine passed down from class to class like an heirloom, repaired and preserved with yellowing tape, now finally ours. Suppressed laughter, groans, oh, man, look at that, and finally when with a soft flick the gatefold fell open and the pool of light moved over unreal legs and breasts and blond hair so perfect, then only awe and silence. After years and years, remembering again the slow graceful fall of the page, the revelation of the paragon, I felt again the same mingled feeling of joy and sickness, the wonder and the bitterness of looking at the splendid goddess and wondering will I ever have that? So my stomach hurt a little but I laughed and said, "You'll never believe this but your mother and I go way back."

"I bet." She laughed as she said this.

"She got me in trouble." What happened was that there was a girl who lived across the maidan named Vibha, a second-year medical student. I knew only vaguely of her, but one summer when I came back for the holidays she was famous. People would turn around and elbow each other when she walked by, and she seemed to pass in a small circle of silence rimmed by whispers. When I asked, my mother shrugged and changed the subject, embarrassed. But others were eager to tell me: what she had done was fall in love. There was a boy named Ramesh who lived next door, two years younger than her. They talked to each other, it was told, in the early morning when Vibha went up to the roof to study. In that quiet hour before dawn they sat together and talked. They were, of course, discovered, and Ramesh was sent away to his grandfather's village and Vibha was suddenly infamous. But it wasn't the sordid stories I heard that made me sick and angry, not the ugly jokes told by men on street corners, it was Vibha's courage, her superb dignity, the way she held her head and walked down the street, her books held close to her chest, her clear eyes and her calm face, it was this that made me furious. I wanted to do something, to tear down the little houses huddled together in their own smugness, to free myself of the

heavy and unchanging air that settled in the narrow lanes and suffocated me. Yet there was nothing I could do.

I had the magazine with me, a Thanksgiving issue of *Playboy* from
six years ago, the pages a little yellow but still with a distinctive smell
that I had grown to like. The magazine had been entrusted to me for the
holidays, to keep carefully and bring back to school for the delectation
of all and the education of our juniors. I used to leaf through it at night
with my door closed, with a strong feeling of longing rather than excitement. Late one evening I was sitting by a tree on the maidan, my chin
on my knees, when in the darkness I saw a lone figure moving through
the dust. It was late, and everyone had gone in, so there were no cat-
calls, no lewd remarks, but by the gait I knew it was Vibha. She walked
by me without turning her head, and it was only after she had gone
through her gate, let the latch down with a sudden clang, that I heard a
single, soft sob. I stood up but I could see nothing in the shadows, and I
only heard a door open and close gently. I shook in the darkness as if
with a fever, and the next morning I left the *Playboy* open on my bed,
the centerfold opened over the pillow. My mother found it of course,
and then she and my father talked to me with sadness and concern.
Even then I knew how paltry the gesture was, how little, and that it was
somehow unfair to aim it at my parents, but it was all I had. I looked at
them, at my mother with her puzzled eyes, and at my father with his
gentleness, and my anger only grew. I tried to improve on my badness
by coming home late, by not speaking to anyone, and even went on a
search for serious evil, but I didn't know where to find a brothel, and
nobody would sell me a drink, and anyway I didn't have the money.
Anyhow, I felt a kinship with Vibha as I slouched through the streets,
and at the end of that summer I made my final declaration of war. Every
year my mother held a puja, a week-long prayer in which the pandit
told the story of Krishna, from his ancestry to his birth and his adventures, including his dalliances with the beautiful gopis, finally through
to his death. When I was a child I used to sit rapt, listening to the
repeated story, anticipating every turn and twist and finding pleasure in
all of it, especially in the mentions of Ganesha and Hanuman, whom I
loved most because they were animals before they were gods. Now I
stayed in my room, and when my mother came and said, come, come,
it's starting, we must start, I said, I'm not coming, I don't believe any of

it. All she could say was why, why? I shook my head, hypocrisy, hypocrisy, I said, that's all it is, Krishna's love, while outside . . . I finished with a shrug, and she left looking helpless. It seemed unbearably tawdry to me, the little black image of Krishna with its cheap little doll's clothes of pink and silver, the smell of the burning ghee, the fat priest and his smugness and his droning voice, all of it unthinking and by rote. For a week I left the house early and came back late, and after it was all over I found it hard to say anything to my parents, and the rest of the holidays slipped by in silence. I thought unceasingly of the woman in the magazine, and passed long hot afternoons dreaming of her, trying to conjure up the details of her life, her car, her perfume, her house, her dog, her family.

As I was telling Amanda this the lights flashed on. It was Amanda's parents, but now all my attention was focused on Candy. I like horses and nature, the text had said under a picture of her in a waterfall, rear toward the camera. Now she walked past me to the bar and I couldn't resist gazing after her, or actually after her silk-sheathed bottom as it sailed across the room.

"I take a keen interest in India," said William James suddenly, startling me into spilling my drink into my lap. "Colonial India, actually," he went on as I mopped at my lap. Amanda was looking at my hands, her lips tight in a suppressed smile. I looked down, and undeniably I had a bump in my pants, a straightforward and unabashed erection. I crossed my legs. "Mutiny," said William James, "is my specialty." Candy returned with a glass of red wine, and settled, fell gracefully onto a red sofa, one arm along the back, one hip cocked into the air. "I have a pretty fair collection of contemporary accounts," said William James. As he talked about leather-bound books and yellowed newspaper clippings, Amanda came and sat next to me. She bent close to brush at my shoulder.

"Want to prong dear old mum, do you?" she whispered in a passable English accent.

William James talked about Hodson's Horse, Kanpur, and Nana Saheb, and I tried urgently to keep my attention on him. Candy got up to refill our glasses, and Amanda hissed in my ear: "She's had her arse lifted. Surgical intervention." Her father went on with his catalog of

1857 reports, and Amanda confided body parts into my ear: "Stomach tuck. Rib removal. Breast lift. Breast implant. Lip injections. Tooth caps. Skin peel. Nose reconstruction. Face-lift." Candy stayed quiet and watched us impassively over the rim of her glass, and her eyes were great and green. Finally I realized that William James had finished, and was looking at me expectantly.

"Um, I'd love to see all that," I said. "Sometime."

"Tomorrow, perhaps," he said. "Meanwhile . . ." He got crisply to his feet. "Good night."

"Good night."

After they were gone, I turned to Amanda. "I do not want to prong your mother."

"Really?" She was smiling. "Come on."

"Where?"

"To bed."

"With you?"

"What did you think?" She paused. "Do you want to?" She had her chin tucked in, and was looking up at me appraisingly.

"Yes, but I thought, I thought I'd be down the corridor from you or something."

Her face cleared. "You wanted to sneak into my room?" Now she was delighted. "What fun!"

She leaned against me until I let myself be pushed out on the porch. When I came through her window she was lying on her bed, her hands folded on her chest. "I'm a virginal British maiden in the exotic Indian night," she giggled. "Mutiny me." I sat next to her, stroking her hair, and she felt my sadness, she sat up and put her arms over my shoulders. I held her and we lay back, and long after she had fallen asleep I saw moonlight move across the wall opposite, and shadows.

William James had grown up in Ohio, in rural country near Columbus. His father was a farmer and an insurance agent, a man who cultivated the land and sold assurance against the disasters of life. But William James had always wanted to move to Texas, even before he got a degree in history from Kent State and long before he started law school in Austin. The brightly covered novels of his childhood were still preserved in plastic sleeves on the shelves of his Victorian library. When his schooling was over, he went back to Ohio, found it somehow suffocating, even though the same sky came down to the cornfields. After exactly ten days, William James left and never went back. In Texas he practiced corporate law for oil companies, bought a house and ranch on which he bred Brahma bulls, and was contented with his life, except for a short stint in Korea in a supply battalion, during which he was mortared once. Mortaring, he found, was about a medium-stressful experience, worse than traffic jams but better than the time in court a drugged-out crazy grabbed a policeman's .38 and deliberately shot three people in the head. He came back happy that he was who he was and that he lived in Texas, and never again felt the urge to travel. It pleased him, though, that he had the military service behind him, and it served him well in his steady climb toward his judgeship. He believed in God and the legal system. He had a daguerreotype of Sherlock Holmes on the wall of his study, and he collected books about Victoria's life and wars. All in all he was a happy man, a man who had gotten in life what he expected from it. He met Candy at a Superbowl party to which he had gone reluctantly, a party thrown by a councilman, and William James had recognized in her the woman he wanted on his ranch. She was taut, healthy, and wore blue jeans tucked into green boots and a red bandanna. She looked clean. He said to her, "Do you like Brahma bulls?" They married four months later at a chapel that was designed to look like a huge ship.

This was what I was told about William James by Amanda, and some of it William James told me. He began to take an interest in me. I went into his library and found him reading the India entry in the *Encyclopedia Britannica*. "That's a huge country," he said with a tinge of disapproval. Then he began to talk to me. He told me pretty bluntly that the British Raj had been good for India: unification, railroads, the political system of democracy, the custom of tea drinking, and cricket, all these benefits accruing to the benevolently governed. Awakening was the word he used. I listened, not having to say much because he rarely paused, and I think because of my silence he began to approve of me. I know this because that evening, after pre-dinner cocktails, after during-dinner wine, and after after-dinner brandy, he grew confidential and leaned across to me: "Amanda's boyfriends have always been such cads."

"Bounders?" I asked.

"Absolutely." Then he thumped me on the back. Later that night while Amanda and I were fucking, she on her knees in front of me, I bit her so hard on the shoulder she screamed. When we were finished I lay on her, my face in the curve of her neck. I whispered, tell me about your boyfriends.

She did: "The first was when I was thirteen. He was a dropout, a scraggly drug dealer who I met behind the school building, black sleeveless moto-cross T-shirt, a dangling silver earring, dirty blond hair and a receding chin. Pale blue eyes. Then there was a trumpet player from a rock band. He wore black cowboy boots with pointy silvered toes, a bolero tie, and a belt with a big buckle in the shape of a W. I don't know why. He drank a lot and drove a jeep. That was at fifteen. There were others in between but that was the next important one. I mean he was thirty so it seemed like he knew a lot. He got me into all the big backstage parties. I met Jagger once. Jagger said, that's a cool necklace you're wearing. It was a jade necklace with a pendant in the shape of a horse. My boyfriend said yeah, she's pretty cool, Mick, and then he put his hand on the back of my neck. Then there was —"

"Thirteen?" I said.

"Uh-huh."

"Where were your parents?"

"Right here. Then —"

"Shut up."

"You're the one who's always asking questions."

"Shut up." I turned her over to me and held her and pulled her hair back from her face. "Shut up." She giggled into my chest, and I don't know why, but I felt this thing go through my body, this feeling, a pang, a bitterness like a wave. We were in a four-poster bed, a real antique. William James had found it at an auction in a little Texas town called New Brunswick. He had bought it for practically nothing. It was two hundred years old. He told me this.

The next morning Kyrie called. "We've found my grandfather."

"No!"

"Yeah. Or actually he found us. He heard from somebody at a bar that we were looking and called us."

We met them at a bar downtown, under the massive lengths of the buildings. Kyrie's grandfather was a short man in a worn denim jacket, shapeless pants torn at the knee, and yellow sneakers. He had thick white hair, and his hands were so seamed they looked like implements wrapped around the glass he was drinking rapidly from. His nose was thick and prominent and cracked. He put down his glass, looked at me for a long moment, then said, "I am White Eagle."

I took Kyrie by the elbow, and we walked away from the table, to the bar. "Look," I said. "You don't really think this guy is your grandfather?"

"He says he is."

"He's looking for a drink, that's about all. Really. 'I am White Eagle?' "

She shrugged and smiled, a little puzzled. We went back to the table, where Tom was laughing and patting White Eagle on the back. "You hunted buffalo once?" said Tom.

"I am a hundred and twenty two and a half years old," White Eagle said.

Amanda giggled. His eyes were sharp and black and set deep behind an enormous nose. I knew I was supposed to enjoy his air of cunning and the picturesque blue bandanna around his neck, but I felt only resentment. "Tell it to the tourists," I said into my drink, and Tom punched me lightly in the ribs.

"Listen to the man." He turned to White Eagle. "Tell us about it. Tell us about the hunt."

So the man starting telling a story about a buffalo hunt, complete with thundering hooves and blue-coated soldiers. I listened, and it all sounded vaguely familiar, and I wondered why. Then I remembered the Saturday night movies at Mayo, all of us sitting on the rising steps of the cricket pavilion, the canvas screen planted on the boundary line, the beam of light from the projector piercing the darkness, the desert breeze across our faces, the Indians on the screen, and us cheering for the cowboys.

Amanda and I left them still buying White Eagle drinks. He was drinking bourbon and water, and Kyrie was wearing his hat, which was brown and had a leather thong around it. When we got home I sat on the bed and had started to take off my shoes when I noticed a note on the pillow with my name on it. The name was written in a flowing black script inked with a fountain pen, and under it was a little flourish and a dot. The paper was heavy and dense, and inside it had William James's letterhead in gold, under which he said, "The Cricket League plays a one-day match tomorrow. Would you like to bat for us, or the other side?"

. . . now . . .

TODAY THE TELEVISION CAMERAS CAME, and also the death threats. We have been warned by several organizations that the story-telling must stop. The groups on the very far right — of several religions — object to the 'careless use of religious symbology, and the ceaseless insults to the sensitivities of the devout.' The far-left parties object to the 'sensationalization and falsification of history, and the pernicious Western influences on our young.' Everyone objects to the sex, except the audience.

We have become a national issue. Questions have been raised in parliament. Sir Patanjali Abhishek Vardarajan, the grand old man of Indian science, has offered a reward of fifty thousand rupees to 'anyone who can demonstrate the existence of a typing monkey under laboratory conditions.' We are besieged by reporters and photographers trying to climb over the walls into the house, so now guards are posted on the perimeter of the roof and in the garden behind the house.

And in the maidan, during the story-telling, and before it and after, Janakpur goes about its business: there have been marriages arranged, love-affairs sabotaged, fights started and simmered down, money made, deals struck and deaths from old age.

'We will not be bullied,' Saira said. 'Type on.'

'Brave child,' Hanuman said. 'Fearless.' When I told Saira that he had said this she had a question for him.

'Ask him why there are hypocrites in the world.'

'Because it is hard to bear the happiness of others.'

'When are we happy?'

'When we desire nothing and realize that possession is only momentary, and so are forever playing.'

'What is regret?'

'To realize that one has spent one's life worrying about the future.'

'What is sorrow?'

'To long for the past.'

'What is the highest pleasure?'

'To hear a good story.'

'Good answers, Hanuman,' Saira said, and tossed up an apple, which disappeared somewhere between her hand and the rafters.

'Go on,' Hanuman said, dropping down to sit beside me with a smile on his face. I could feel his monkey-heart beating against my side. Saira sat on the other side, an arm over my shoulders, eating an apple.

'Don't be afraid of what you have to tell,' Hanuman said. 'Tell the story.'

And so I began again. Listen . . .

Sikander Learns the Art of War.

AFTER BEGUM SUMROO WELCOMED Sikander and Sanjay to her house in Lucknow, she had them put straightaway to work. The Begum, although elegant, was not a woman for coddling guests, young ones in particular; 'What are you?' she asked, and the same afternoon she found a soldier's berth for Sikander, and a poet's apprenticeship for Sanjay. 'I believe in application,' she said. 'Be what you are, young men, be what you are. This is the important thing.' In spite of her love for travel incognita, her taste for intrigue, the reputation for poison-use and seductions that followed her around the country (the *wicked* Begum Sumroo), she was obviously a woman who knew what she was; it was her comfortableness that impressed Sanjay, her certainty that whatever she did was right. She screamed at her girls and it was imperial, she arrowed paan juice into a spittoon, pth-oooo, and it was somehow carelessly urbane. Meanwhile, it was as if he were made up wholly of doubts: the cut of his pajamas was obviously wrong, his hair crudely tied, his speech unutterably provincial; so when she told them that she had found positions for them Sanjay was completely unable to speak the delicate formula of gratitude he had been thinking up, and instead he blushed brightly.

They were given a small room to the back of the house, far from the women's quarters; from where they were they could hear the long bellows of the milch-buffalos somewhere to the rear, and the games of the servants' children.

'This is strange,' Sanjay said. 'Are we her sons?'

'I don't know,' Sikander said. 'Sleep. It'll be a long day tomorrow.'

But Sanjay gazed into the darkness for a long time, and he knew from Sikander's breathing that he was awake too; there was now in Sanjay's heart an eagerness he had not felt for a long time, a desire to see the morning, a gratitude for what the day would bring. He lay with his eyes open and thought of fame.

In the morning they were awakened early to a simple breakfast of parathas and milk, after which Sikander was led off by an armed guard; Sanjay sat in front of the room and waited. Finally, at noon he was beckoned by one of the minor servants and led on a twisting course through the lanes of the city; they emerged by the Gomti, and walked along a sandy beach, and turning a promontory of the river they were confronted suddenly by a huge white palace that sat improbably poised over the water. It was a fantastic place, overladen with red turrets, arches, battlements that went from nowhere to nowhere, vast sweeps of walls that cut each other at odd angles, and, here and there, a gold dome shining, and everywhere there were traditions mixed, architectures mingled. The servant motioned Sanjay through a huge gate (topped with a sunburst of steel spikes), and turned to go.

'Wait, wait,' Sanjay said. 'What am I supposed to do here?'

The servant shrugged without looking around, and went on; behind Sanjay, his voice echoed in a sort of large open antechamber lined by vaults, and when that died down all he could hear was the soft, monotonous calling of pigeons. Sanjay stood there for a long time, and then called out, are you there, are you there, louder and louder until he was shouting on tiptoe; after recovering from this he made up his mind and strode resolutely in. Inside, the light moved strangely against artfully arranged shadows, so that at every step Sanjay felt he was moving from one atmosphere to another, and quite soon he was disoriented and very lost; staircases took him into corridors which deposited him exactly where he had started from; for a long while he wandered around a huge, long room, capped by an unsupported cupola, and the sound of his feet leaped crisply from one wall to the other. Then he heard a voice, hardly more than a humming, but completely clear, and he spun restlessly, trying to follow it, but it appeared completely and causelessly above his head; he stopped, crouched, now surprised by the silence, the world waiting and paused. He found a door and rushed into darkness, around a corner and into dazzling light and out again, again until he stumbled into a garden, through a hedge, then he saw, very far away, framed by leaves, a tableau: two men, both white-bearded, leaned back against round pillows, pulling gently on bubbling hookahs; their angarkhas were very white, almost blue, against the deep red of the carpet they sat on; a woman sat between them, dressed in gold; her head was bent to one side, and she turned it slowly in luxurious ennui, her eyes were closed, she sang; Sanjay shivered, and then everything was quiet but for the hubble-hubble of the hookahs.

Finally Sanjay forced himself forward; as he walked down the path, the two men turned to look at him, but the woman kept her eyes closed even as Sanjay raised his hand to his bent head.

'Ah, good, you found your way in here,' said the thinner of the men. He was a tall man, long in every respect, a close beard, a shiny bald head above a long face.

'And your name is Parasher, is it not?' said the other, and his slight but unmistakable English accent caused Sanjay to take a step back: at once he felt as if the black band around his throat had constricted.

'Yes, it is,' Sanjay finally managed. 'I'm sorry to come in like this, but there was no one . . .'

'No matter,' said the long man. 'We are perhaps to be your ustads in the matter of poetry. I am Pandit Hari Ram Sharma, better known as Muraffa. This gentleman is Thomas Hart Bentford, once of Nottingham, England, now resident in these precincts and known familiarly to us as Hart Sahib.'

'So you have decided to be a poet, and must therefore have chosen a takhallus,' said the Englishman. His Urdu was perfect in all but a slight broadness about the vowels. 'May you tell us what it is?'

'It's Aag,' said Sanjay, and at this the woman abruptly raised her eyelids, shocking him again into silence: her eyes were a clear and distinct golden, the pupils a dark brown, and looking into them Sanjay felt quite small and foreign, unable to guess at what she was thinking, or feeling, as if she were of another species.

'A startling sobriquet,' said the Pandit.

'Yes,' said the Englishman, pulling his fingers through a white beard that left his upper lip bare. 'Yes. What shall the lesson for today be?'

'Observance, I think,' said the Pandit. 'Observe, my Aag. Through that door is a secret garden. In that garden are a thousand birds, perhaps more, I shall not tell you the exact number. You shall go in there, and will attempt to note carefully each song, and at the end of the day which five are most beautiful, and why.'

Sanjay bowed, and backed himself towards the door, still bowing and feeling ridiculous; when he was finally in the huge bird cage, ducking low-flying birds, he felt even more foolish — he had read all the stories about young poets and the tasks their masters set them, tasks designed to test the young disciples' zeal more than their talent or ability, but had somehow believed that these examinations happened only in legend, not to actual and real people in the harsh world of today.

'And the mother-jumping birds kept shitting on me all day,' he told Sikander that evening. 'What was I supposed to learn?'

'Maybe that beauty shits,' Sikander said, laughing. 'But did you get the right five ones?'

'No,' Sanjay said. 'They just said, wrong, and that was it. I don't even get a second chance; there's a different task tomorrow. What a couple of old dullards, I'm supposed to learn from them.'

'Don't go then.'

'Have to go. Begum Sumroo will be offended.' But that wasn't it: he had to go because the woman in gold hadn't said a word to him, even though he had looked directly into her eyes as he did his last salute; she had looked upon him with a gaze worse than indifference, one that was absolutely impenetrable and unknown. 'Got to go.'

'I don't believe you,' Sikander said.

'What's there not to believe?'

'You're looking crafty, I know you too well.'

'All right. There was a woman there.'

'A wife or a daughter?'

'No, I don't think so.'

'What?'

'She was singing. Dressed in all gold.'

'And?'

'She had golden eyes.'

'Oh, idiot. Forget her.'

'Why?'

'She's not for you or me.'

'Why? She's not that much older, maybe two or three or five years.'

'Still, she was there for them, not for you.'

At this Sanjay felt so angry that his eyes teared, and his throat began to hurt again; he pushed his fingers under the scarf and began to rub. 'Well, shit on that.'

'Listen, Sanju,' said Sikander. 'Listen. There's a girl here, I think a washer-woman's daughter. This morning she came by carrying a basket of clothes. She's got shiny black hair, a round face, huge round eyes, and breasts like apples. I saw her looking at you.'

'I didn't see her.'

'That's your trouble, you never see what's around you, and instead you've got your eyes on some stupid other thing or the other. Listen to me, young fool, and hear the wisdom of life: pay attention to washer-women's daughters.'

'I don't *want* her.'

'There, in a very small nutshell, is your problem: you're an idealist.'

Whatever the problem was, Sanjay was quite unable to forget the woman in gold, whose name, as he soon discovered, was Gul Jahaan; she was the love of Lucknow, the courtesan of the moment, and her likeness appeared on match-boxes and was sold in pamphlets, and the songs she sang became the rage of all the dashing young noblemen. Every day, Sanjay went to the White Palace, where he was engaged in an endless series of futile tasks: finding undiscoverable flowers, washing unending dishes, and so on; even though he knew this was supposed to test his fortitude and ascertain his hunger for poetry, he chafed and cursed, and only one thing made his travails bearable: the memory of Gul Jahaan's eyes. At times these eyes seemed his strength, and when he grew tired and his mouth filled with the bitterness of defeat, this image put a new vigour into his failing limbs; but at other times, especially in the bizarre hours of twilight when he awoke from exhausted naps, Gul Jahaan tormented him with her distance, and the height of her orbit, untouchable like the moon's, put him into such a frenzy of loneliness that he pulled at his hair and squeezed his head, trying not to give in to the urge to drum it on the ground. At these times, Sikander — apparently recognizing the madness in Sanjay's eyes — took him by the arm and walked him around the Begum's estate and told him stories of what he had learnt that day.

'Listen,' he would say. 'Listen. Today I met the ustad Kaliharan, who is this country's greatest living maestro of archery. Because of his friendship with my master, Uday Singhji, he agreed to teach me. Today, as the sun rose and we sat in the forest with our bows, he said to me, aim your arrow at that bird. I did, and he said, what do you see? I said, the bird. He said, anything else? I said no, the bird only, nothing else. He said, shoot, and I missed. You missed because you don't see the whole tree, its thousand leaves, the whole forest, he said, and still looking at me he shot, and the bird flew away. Go look, he said, and you will find one feather from its head pinned by the arrow, and it was so. When you look, he said, see the bird, see the sky above, the earth below, see everything, and you won't miss then because you cannot miss.'

'What is that supposed to mean?' Sanjay said.

'I don't know,' Sikander said. 'But he didn't miss. He never misses.'

The weeks passed and every other fortnight, it seemed, Uday took Sikander to a new teacher, and Sikander's skill and natural aptitude gained him the admiration of all; now people turned to look at him as he passed, and sometimes, at his lessons, it was clear that some people, mostly soldiers, contrived to be present. Meanwhile, Sanjay laboured; he was allowed, now and then, to be present at the soirées organized almost nightly at the White Palace. At these events he was constrained to stand quietly to the rear and watch, and fetch and carry for the Pandit and Hart Sahib; when Gul Jahaan was present he was transported by his passion and unable to see anything else, but on other occasions he watched and learnt; he found that the world of poetry is like any other field of action, it has its factions, its own manoeuvrings, its long drawn-out battles and all-destroying defeats. By the time six months had passed Sanjay had already seen: an old gentleman who conceived a passion for a handsome young poet and was therefore persuaded to forward large sums of money and much support, receiving nothing in exchange but little attention and occasional humiliation; the exact moment in which a poet who had done his best — who had once been considered promising — the second in which this poet discovered that he had gone from being promising to being merely old, that his literary worth had been judged and amounted to not even a footnote in somebody else's biography; also, a literally bloody battle over the proper use of a Persian word in Urdu poetry, the quarrel starting with carefully casual remarks, escalating to whispers and strained looks at readings, and ending in an unpremeditated but sincerely-fought duel with unripe cane-stalks after a picnic in a sugar-cane field. Sanjay saw that the fruit of poetry is sweet, but in order to be allowed to speak the language one must learn other things, that one must know how to get along in the world, to be thought of well, and, quite simply, one must know the right people, and having realized this he applied himself to the tasks set before him, exuding sincerity.

Sikander, meanwhile, came home every night with different stories about his numerous teachers; he learnt the art of wood-swordsmanship from Lale Khan, the patta-man, who could with his wooden blade beat any five Delhi sharp-sabres, knocking them around like so many drunks; there was Ilahi Baksh, the master of the straight-dagger, who was small and ugly, but who cut so fast and so subtle that many men had died still laughing at him; Arvind Khakka, the hand-fighting artist who placing three fast pigeons under a bed would sit on the bed and keep the pigeons underneath only by spinning and moving his feet, hour after hour after hour, until all the spectators became dizzy watching him and begged him to stop.

'And all this is true,' Sikander said every evening. 'If you don't believe me then come and look any day. What a place of artists this Lucknow is, what heaven.'

Sanjay had his doubts, but in the evenings preferred to keep his scepticism to himself, because now, when they were together, after bathing, was the time when they were invited to pay their respects to the Begum; every evening they followed the butler through the torch-lit corridors to the roof, where a flute showered nostalgia into the dusk and the Begum sat amongst her women. Her conversation was unpredictable, veering from the metaphysical to the questions of cooking and pickle-making; she had become informal with them, intimate and teasing, and one evening, she asked: 'What are they like, your teachers, Sanjay? Tell me the truth.'

'They are fine teachers, generous and —'

'No nonsense.'

'Really, they are good.'

'Yes, but what are they like?'

This time her voice tightened and cracked a little at the end, and so Sanjay said: 'They are strange. They live in apartments on opposite ends of the White Palace, and most of the day they stay apart, attending to business. Then in the evenings they have tea together. But it is dinner that is important; every night it is held at one place or the other, the English or the Indian, with the appropriate foods and drinks and wines, and so one day the English dresses in an angarkha and speaks Urdu, so the next the Hindu puts on a grey coat, tight shoes and flings English about. It is a curious business; they go from one to the other, and for what I do not know.'

'How are they with each other?'

'Formal and very correct. Each night, after the guests have departed, they bow and shake hands or salute each other, depending upon whether it was an English or Indian night. Then they retire, each to his own side. It is a very strange thing.'

'It is a very good thing,' the Begum said. 'But you are disturbed? Why?'

Sanjay shrugged, but the Begum waited; to distract her he said: 'May I ask you a question?'

'Maybe.'

'An impertinent question.'

'Well?'

'When we last heard a story about you — our genesis story, so to speak — there was a Mister Sumroo in it too. And now we hear certain things about him, and so we wonder.'

'Impertinent indeed!' But she was smiling.

'Although, you will allow,' Sanjay said, 'a natural wonder.'

'All right, I'll tell you.' She settled herself in her seat; they were on the roof, and far above them floated a constellation of lantern-kites. 'I'll tell, but in short, because quickness is the order of the day, every-thing is quick-quick short, getting quicker, no time or place for the long old stories, there's something in the air. So hear about Sumroo. Listen . . .

You know he was a sad man, taciturn and of lugubrious expression;

he moved through the world as if he bore some weight on his shoulders. Why he was this way he never told me, but even what we think of as pleasures he took with a sort of weariness; I could never tell whether one kind of food pleased him more than the other, or whether one dance meant more than some. He lived, as far as I could see, in a grey world where everything was dimly-lit and therefore devoid of colour; I have heard that far enough under water all things appear black. In a way this was convenient for me, because I did as I needed, and to all things he shrugged and said, well, that's all right. But one summer a certain section of malcontents in my brigades mutinied, and I was compelled to leave my Sardhana, but as I fled, with Sumroo, we saw the rising sun flash on something far behind, and we knew they were coming for us: we had been betrayed. I knew well what they would do to me, freed from shame as they were, so I drew a dagger, poised it over my chest and drove it down, and it seemed to me that the flesh parted, it penetrated, but when I looked down there was not a spot of blood, the muslin of my dupatta was whole. My hands were firm, not shaking, and I tried again, deliberately and calmly, but though for a moment I grew dizzy, nothing happened. Now I set it against the wood of the carriage and tried again, and again the momentary loss of self, and then me again sitting there, whole and quite unscratched; meanwhile, seeing the dagger out, its sharp curved length of brightness, one of my servants, a girl wholly vain and flighty, took it upon herself to run down the length of the convoy, to shout to Sumroo in ringing tones, the Begum is dead, the Begum has brought death to herself. Sumroo reigned his horse about, said, oh, really, in a voice mingling, I was told, mild interest and relief; quickly, he drew his pistol, a huge and ponderous dragoon affair, especially constructed for him. He placed the barrel under his chin, raised his eyebrows a little, and then with a boom his whole body rose three feet into the air, and — they swear to this — hung motionless and light there for an eternity till it crashed down to the earth, spraying matter.

So the mutineers came down on us, and capturing me — I was with bemusement regarding the matter of my unpricking blade — they took me back to Sardhana, where following injuries and abuses they chained me to a cannon in the court-yard of my own palace. Here, let me tell you, I had much time and motive to ponder the mysteries of existence:

why did I live, and how? Filthy, my head uncovered and my hair caked with mud and blood, my clothes torn, I sat, no water or food for days, calling for death. I should tell you I had no dignity: the sun takes that out of you, the burning metal, the dust, the unquenchable hungers of the body; I screamed, I cursed them and their mothers and told them what I would do to their sisters. I struggled till my arms and ankles were raw, and still I did not die. On the eleventh day I leaned against the cannon, and reached a period of extraordinary lucidity, the sky was a blue like a deep-ocean shell, the smell of dung from the quarter-guard's horses in the air, and it became very clear to me: for some people there is the luxury of honour and the benediction of a quick death, but for me there is only life. I live, and live, and will live, because life is good, and living is necessary. So I stopped screaming and waited, waited two days before rescue came. They taunted me, and I said nothing; so they whipped me. I waited, waited. Do you know who came? Do you? Of course you do. Who is the warrior who came looking for a kingdom, for himself? Who is a true friend, chivalrous paladin? You know because he too is a part of you: Jahaj Jung.

On the thirteenth day, just before dawn, over the walls came George Thomas and his band of madmen; what a massacre there was then, a fine bloodiness. They put the mutineers down, freed me; he had heard, in his Georgegarh, so he came. We spent a heavenly few days together, and back he went, to his dream. A happy ending, you think? Wait, wait, the story is not over. I was back in my seat, but I could feel it shake under me, and sure enough, a few months later, it happened. Two of my servants, my girls — they had been with me since they were this small, now these fell in love, and decided they must be free of my service, and not only that, they must steal from me enough to live in sloth. So, no, they do not ask me for my blessing or my gifts, but instead steal money, and not only money, but also three of my books, rare and secret, magic, if you must know, and not only my books, they decide they must try to hide the theft, and distract from their escape, so they set fire to my library. We lost much, but rescued some, at the cost of burnt flesh and two dead men, and we captured the girls easily, trapped them against a river, killed the paramours in combat and brought the girls back, and the books. I sat looking at them, these children I had known since they were innocent of all love, looked at their plump, tear-stained faces,

listened to their lamentations, and all the while I could feel the expecta-
tion in the air, the slowly-gathering contempt, the future rebellions and
thefts already present in the eyes around me. So I kissed the two of
them, gave my instructions. First they were stripped and whipped until
they were senseless, and then a deep hole was dug next to the library.
Then they were revived, and flung into the hole; after the mud had been
tamped down again I had my seat laid over it, and that evening I
smoked my hookah there. Now everything was quiet. When I rose to go
to my bed I felt my feet sink into the ground, and it seemed that my
flesh had settled into itself and become a little heavier. But do you
understand? I live.

Instead of frightening Sanjay, this story inspired in him a sense of trust
towards the Begum Sumroo: he felt, now, safe and taken care of, so
much so that the next evening he entrusted the affair of his love to her,
asking her for instructions for his future conduct. 'I want her,' he said,
plaintively.

'Well, I've never met her, but from what I know of her, and of all
women, the way is this: become a great poet and a great lover, and
perhaps you will get what you want.'

Of the two, the first goal was something he could pursue naturally:
pay attention at the lessons in the White Palace, complete all tasks,
look, listen, read. It was the second that he found inexplicably hard,
although all around him was the panorama of love, a constant and
unending theatre of passion and artfully-displayed opportunity: the
head steward was in love with the oldest of the Begum's ladies, and their
secret assignations on the highest terrace a cause of smiles for the whole
community; there were the gentle attachments between certain of the
ladies themselves, the hidden shuffle and the clink of bangles at night;
the fierce afternoon gropings of a soldier and his married-to-another
sweeper paramour near the stables; of course, the visits of a certain
middle-aged nobleman were awaited eagerly because of the fine couplets that came from his passion for a boy cousin he had grown up with;
and every evening, people ran to see the unhappy young man who
wandered though the lane at front, desperately in love with the youngest wife of the merchant who lived in the mansion opposite: he
had glimpsed her eyes once during a Moharram procession. All around

Sanjay, it seemed, along with the other business of life, there was a constant and unrelenting fever of infatuations, sighs, betrayals, and flesh, but he found himself withdrawing from it, even as Sikander pointed out chances and not-so-subtle invitations; finally, this became so obvious that the Begum remarked upon it.

'Why,' she said, 'are you like a pent-up balloon? Looking always like you're about to burst? Not delicate of me to put it this way, of course, but I gave up delicacy some years ago. Especially where my intimates are concerned. Now, out with it.'

'Well,' said Sanjay, a little petulantly because he knew people thought him odd. 'Well, because I don't want anyone else, I want her.'

'What an absurd idea,' laughed the Begum. 'What does one have to do with the other? You think when you're a great poet she's going to dream about you because you're still an unschooled, clumsy boy? Where does this go, Gul Jahaan, what do I do with that? Idiot. She'll want you because of the qualities of your earlier loves, the, the, let us say, depth of your knowledge.'

'But I don't feel like it with anyone else.'

'Where, in God's name, do you get these absurd ideas? I command you: find a woman and bump and hump. It's not such a big matter. Or is it?'

He shrugged; he could do little else, because he did not understand well himself why he felt this way; the feeling sprang full-formed and despotic out of some corner of his soul; it offered no explanations and brooked no resistance, and he gave in to it inevitably and with a feeling of relief. Ever since he had fallen in love with Gul Jahaan he had noticed strange white patches that appeared on his body, regular white marks in the shape of certain characters from the English alphabet, the first an inverted, upper-case A that materialized above his groin the same afternoon he saw Gul Jahaan in the garden, that came suddenly and remained for a few days before vanishing quietly and without pain. At first he had dismissed the marks as a skin condition, a minor ailment mystified by his imagination, but after he had endured visitations from a B and a C in regular and unceasing succession, he had been forced to admit to himself that what he had eaten was still in his body; the D that he expected next came on his right hand, on the back of it, and so for a few days he wrapped a bandage around it and pretended a sprain. Except for the Pandit, Hart Sahib and Sikander, he knew nobody who could recognize these alien marks on his body, but he preferred to wear loose and large clothes that hid and protected; it was enough that he felt himself strange and marked, that he be perhaps treated as a foreign oddity in a city that he had dreamed of as home would be more than he could endure. So Sanjay kept his silence, despite the jokes and questions, and held his mad love to himself, and tried to learn poetry.

The writing, for Sanjay, came hard; he had heard of poets of sweep and large imagination who dashed off whole elegies before breakfast, and a minor couplet during, a ghazal afterwards, but for him each word was placed laboriously like a brick, each phrase required mortaring and levelling and sometimes repair, and so whole afternoons and weeks passed in solitary labour. It was always so exhausting that afterwards he felt virtuous and worthy of Gul Jahaan, and in addition superior to Sikander, who came in sun-blackened and dusty from the field. Yet, in the end, there was something about his poetry, when it was finished, that he found bizarre and unfamiliar; this eccentricity wasn't in the language, or even in the mundane details of everyday life that kept on appearing, worming themselves into the text, but somehow in the pose, in the attitude. He was unable to place this voice until one evening when he was reading his latest couplet to Sikander; after it was over Sikander said: 'Have you written to your parents lately?'

'Why did you ask that?'

'I don't know. Just thought of it. Are you angry?'

Sanjay shook his head, but he was annoyed at being caught: when he had heard the question it had become clear to him that his poetry was a rejection, that where his father and uncle had been sentimental, he wanted to be cerebral; scientific instead of mystical; cool and dry instead of ecstatic; short instead of long. For a while this seemed so simple, so automatic and stupid that he stopped writing and tried to find another way to speak, but then for the first time he was allowed to bring in his work and read it in the White Palace; it was a spring day, and the two ustads met with their students outside, in the garden. The other two students were boys from the city, whom Sanjay had avoided instinctively; they reeked of oil and perfume, and now, as they read their poetry, he was quite unable to hear it, because of the roaring of his pulse in his own ears. Finally, they stopped, and he was allowed to read; when he finished, the first thing that he noticed was their open mouths, the insides coloured a dark red by paan.

'Very peculiar,' said the Pandit.

'Yes,' said Hart Sahib. 'A little too personal, I think.'

Sanjay watched them huddled over the sheets, going through his lines, marking and scratching and correcting, and amazingly, instead of apprehension or nervousness, he felt a little pity at the sight of the two white heads close together; he looked up directly at his fellow-students, and scandalized them with a smile, and forever after thought of them as mournful sheep. When his poems were given back to him, he bowed, bending over deep and stopping a hair's breadth away from mockery; outside the house, he tucked them inside his long overcoat without looking at the corrections and swaggered his way home.

When Sikander came home, he sat on the floor and tiredly peeled off his soiled puttees, and began his usual story-telling about his masters. Jettu was famous throughout Hindustan for his spear-fighting; Mirak Jan, the king of jal-bank, was unmatched for knowledge of under-water fighting techniques; Mahadeo Sharma, binaut-adept, secretive and swift, always unarmed but so knowledgeable that in his hands a rosary became an instrument of death.

'Why are you learning all this useless stuff?' Sanjay said suddenly.

'Useless?'

'All this is finished: combat now is masses of men with quick-loading muskets, moving like huge machines. Don't you read the papers? Who cares if you have all these skills? Even if you know all these things it makes no difference.'

'So what should we do with it all?'

'Obvious — if it doesn't work, throw it away.'

Sikander shrugged, then turned away, picking up his clothes; a while later, his hair wet from a bath, he asked: 'Do you want to come with me tonight?' Every evening, after the audience with the Begum, he went, with friends, into the city, to walk the bustling streets of the markets; sometimes they ate, and sometimes visited women, but mostly they strolled, making jokes, saluting acquaintances.

'No,' said Sanjay. 'I have to go to the Pandit's.' The truth was that he didn't really have to go to the palace, but wanted to; Sikander, leaving, smiled, but it wasn't even for Gul Jahaan that Sanjay went in the dusk to the White Palace. It was a pull much stronger, a secret more absurd: in the evenings, when he had no tasks, Sanjay liked to go to a certain room in the palace, exactly between the two wings, and in this room, in huge, untidy piles and stacks and shelves, were thousands of books, reams of papers, innumerable pamphlets. The servants referred to this room as the library, but nothing in that polite appellation prepared the visitor for the confusion of paper; the tall, dusty shelves disappearing overhead into darkness, the fizzing lanterns; the indiscriminate and promiscuous mingling of subjects and themes and nationalities; the unexpected treasures thrown carelessly everywhere. Here, Sanjay gratefully gave in to gluttony: he lay luxuriously on a bed of old copies of newspapers from every part of the world, and ravished himself with narrative, what happened, what happened next, and then what, and then; his appetite wasn't only for stories or novels (that were there in abundance), but also for the small fragments that appeared in letters to the editors, in historical footnotes, in introductions to scientific tomes, in the advertisements for hair liniment that appeared on the end-papers of books. He read and read, and only went home when he was chased out by sleepy housekeepers anxious to douse the lanterns and close up; on the way home his mind twitched from one image to another, uncontrollable, and often he was unable to sleep until early morning.

Many months later, on a hazy winter evening, Sanjay sat in the library, flipping absent-mindedly through a pile of London *Times;* the quick succession of names and agonies and distant political debates reduced Gul Jahaan to a remote ache, a persistent absence felt through a screen, and so Sanjay was comfortable. Very slowly, he became aware of another person in the room, and reluctantly he looked up; it was Hart Sahib, who, it being an Indian day, was dressed in a long purple choga and a turban. As Sanjay rose to his feet, he noticed with some irritation that Hart carried the garment with no little elegance; the turban was perfect, and the posture easy.

'Sit, sit,' Hart said (Urdu faultless), waving at him. 'Just wanted to chat with you about this morning's session.' Sanjay had brought in another three poems, had shocked the sheep, and had reacted sullenly and without regret when the Pandit had spoken of unnecessary attacks on tradition, posturing, unremarkable and indeed mundane language, and unsuitable subject matter. Now Hart Sahib found a stool, and sat on it with a sweep of the hand to collect the choga in regular folds about his ankles. 'What you are doing is natural and essential,' he said, 'but it seems to me the way you are doing it is too easy. You have the natural intolerance and impatience of the young, and you are acquiring something of a reputation, young fire-brand and so on.'

At this Sanjay felt a sudden surge of blood, a painful leap of victory in the pulse, and Gul Jahaan was all around, her perfume aphrodisiac and enticing. 'Will you, will you, if I study the poetry of Europe, will you help me? Can you teach me?'

The look on Hart's face was quizzical, a little sad instead of the gladness Sanjay had expected; he smiled and said: 'Listen. Let me tell you something, something I probably shouldn't tell you. The Pandit will be angry with me, but let me tell you: you have a great talent. Don't waste it in fighting. Don't expend it in making war on yourself.'

'Will you teach me?'

Hart was silent, his face pale in a dusty shaft of light from the door. 'If you ask, I must give. What will you start with? Shakespeare?'

'That's old,' Sanjay said. 'What are they reading now, over there? What's new?'

And so Sanjay began his study of English, and his writing of a new, unprecedented poetry, his pursuit of fame and perfection.

Six months later, almost at the same time, both Sikander and the Begum proclaimed an intention to leave Lucknow; the Begum's subterfuge-ridden diplomacy was over, her talks finished, and she longed for Sardhana, while Sikander, it seemed, had finished his apprenticeship and longed for the realities of service. All this, Sanjay thought, was normal: these were the inevitable partings of adult life, the diverging paths that led away from the common ground of childhood; it was all somehow too natural to grieve over, and meanwhile he was filled with the exhilaration of a rapidly growing packet of poetry, some interest from a publisher, the hope of youthful fame. And so the morning of parting caught him with neither fear nor sorrow, but with a self-reliant sort of confidence; the Begum left with the rising of the sun, and all would have gone quietly but for her unexpected announcement as her palanquin was lifted from the ground: 'I plan to become a Christian.'

At this remark Sanjay ran up beside the swaying carriage ('Huh-ha-ha-huh') and tried to look through the brocade curtains.

'You might as well be the first to know,' she said. 'After all my discussions with various rulers, and my understandings of politics, and divinings of the future, I know one thing: we are going to lose; everything will become red. If you want to live, think about this.'

Even with the weight of the palanquin on their shoulders, the bearers now began to outdistance Sanjay, and finally he stopped, his thighs shaking; after a while he turned and walked back to Sikander. 'And you,' Sanjay said. 'What will you become?'

'I'm going back to Calcutta, and I'll arrange for somebody to catch me, some friend of my father's. After I'm grabbed and back in custody I'll ask for an introduction, a few letters. I'm going to seek de Boigne; he's still around, you've heard the stories about him, every day there's a new one. He'll give me a job.'

But Sanjay was looking at him helplessly, becalmed, his carelessness shredded and made useless by these dangerous thoughts of becoming, these cannonades of elemental change; of what use were these brittle ideas of soldier, poet, if all the time, underneath, some sinister conversion happened, leaving you like an inverted snake, same on outside, changed within? After a while, he was able to move again, and that evening say good-bye to Sikander with self-possession, even elegance, but it was several days before he was able to write with his customary vehemence and live up to his pen-name; soon, he was shocking the sheep, just as before, but there were several nights when his project of innovation seemed distant and even repulsive. On these nights the darkness was filled with memories and voices, I have been insulted, what is the eater and the eaten, Nachiketas, grant me death, and even further, a puzzling memory of a tiger's roar echoing across sun-dappled water, a walk into the mountains, the snow awaiting. But this disquiet dimmed, and the days passed, the work continued, generally small successes followed minor disappointments, the weeks that were unremarkable in every way, and the months faded into each other, the years passed and Sanjay could remember nothing about them. Nothing, that is, except the legend of Sikander the soldier, which grew by the telling, and Sanjay heard incredible stories about his friend: his troop of cavalry was so fast that it could be in two places at the same time, it was seen one evening in one place and the next morning it appeared at a foe's campfire a hundred miles away, ready with lance; Sikander was bravest of the brave, in a duel with six horsemen he lanced two with one thrust, fatally butted a third with the heel of the lance on the withdraw, and cut off the heads of two more with a single flashing cut of a horse-hilted sabre, and spared the last; yes, he was generous, more so with his enemies than his friends, because that is true honour; he was wise, he sat at the durbar of his regiment and let the veterans rule, and there was love among the men, and the regiment was one; it was the best unit of irregular horse in Hindustan; they were fearless, they were bold and dashing, they were beautiful. Listening to all of this, Sanjay thought, maybe he will be a king after all, and the glory of Sikander's legend made him aware of the slow boredom of his own life, and he wondered about his own ambitions, thinking, is this all, is there no more, is this life?

'But,' said Sandeep, 'always, in the future, glorious and perfect, was Gul Jahaan. When boredom pressed, when Sanjay was crushed by nostalgia for childhood, she stood in front of him, recalled in complete and dazzling detail. So he went on.'

'But,' said a monk, 'what really happened to Sikander?'

'And what about Chotta?'

'What about Jahaj Jung?'

'Yes, yes, wait,' said Sandeep, looking a little harried. 'It's all coming. So listen; in these years, during them, infrequently and unpredictably, Sanjay received letters from Sikander. Sometimes they were brought by soldiers, sometimes by traders, but whenever they came the course of Sanjay's life was broken, and he was cast always into a sort of panic, his own life suddenly seemed strange to him. The first letter, for instance, came just after his first collection of poetry was published, and because of the letter Sanjay felt strangely lonely at his own celebrations, and looked at his poetry, thinking how odd it was, words on a page, so fragile and artificial, black on white.'

'But what did the letter say?'

'So, listen,' said Sandeep. 'Listen . . .'

This was the letter.

> My brother,
> I observed long ago your reluctance to put pen to paper in pursuit of anything other than poetry, and so am reluctant to send you

anything in the epistolary mode: how exacting must be the standards of one who refuses to use words in anything but song! But I am resolved unshakably not to be parted from my childhood, and will cling to you despite all fear and all disapproval, therefore I will pen something, however poor and undeserving of praise. So, begging excuse for the roughness of a soldier's language, indulgence for the blunt-facedness of a man of hands, forgiveness for natural clumsiness, I plunge now headlong into the customary opening: With the fervent hope this letter finds you in happiness, best of health, etc., etc.

What shall I tell you? I am not wise in narrative, and the actuality of a soldiering life is full of trivia, endless details, long waits, boredom; but I shall attempt to tell you. I will cut away all the baggage, and hope that what I give you will entertain. Now attend: I left you with grief, I was full of grief, these separations are too final, feel like dividings and tearings; then I felt for the first time mortality, felt for the first time that life is not endless. Did we believe that once, together? I left, and came safely to Calcutta; here I contrived to be discovered in a bazaar by a servant of Colonel Burns (my godfather, you may remember): I was taken back to his house, and thence to tears, sisterly recriminations (they remembered you), hasty messages to my father, you may imagine it all. I bore it all patiently, and when things calmed a little, I was finally asked, well, since you refuse to be a printer, what would you like to do? I said only, I will go for a soldier, and this occasioned another barrage of tears, dissuasions and the like, coming finally to the objection, the British will have no use for you, a country-born. Well, I said, quietly, I will serve the Marathas; again, refusals and arguments, but I stuck it out and after all I had my way, a letter of introduction to de Boigne was procured and I was off.

I will take you now hurtlingly forward, to my meeting with de Boigne — is this allowed in narrative? — sparing you the journey, minor adventures, all the long pleasureful days of travel in the winter. I met him in the heart of his camp, where he lives surrounded by his brigades; they are, Sanju, strange men, silent, disciplined, you could see they'd be good to have in a fight, but all the same there's something about them, something missing, a lack, of what I don't know. And him, sitting in his durbar, very grand, a sparkling green uniform, surrounded by bowing and fawning, you can feel his power every moment you are in his presence, but there's something dead about him. I'm sure you could catch it in a line or two, a single line from your expert brush would hold it forever, this thing about him, it's in the size of him, in the flesh around his chin, which looks very heavy and red, the way he sits in his chair, completely at ease, limp, the breath moving his huge chest up and down, very slowly. I'm not sure you'll know what I mean, but you'll recall that he's supposed to be one of our progenitors, and as I talked to him I remembered that strange story and shuddered. If it's true, I fear for us somehow; not fear for his power but of whatever made him what he is.

He didn't say much to me, barely glanced at my letter, but he gave me the job, and so as I left him I was a soldier, or at least I could call myself that. So I was a very junior officer, and the old soldiers who were supposedly in my charge took care of me, pointing me in this direction and that; but, after all, you want to know not the boring details of training, and logistics, and fodder for the horses, but about the heart of it. Yes, I have been in combat; I have been bloodied, and also I have killed. What was it like? It is impossible to say it in words. The first action came in the War of the Aunts, the details of which shameful civil war you must know: a war between factions of the Marathas; the cause being a new ruler neglecting the widowed wives of his uncle, the old king, or at least neglecting two of them while supposedly paying unusual attentions to the youngest and most beautiful; so now all the old rivalries crystallized around this new family quarrel, and people took sides, and there it was. Somehow it struck me as appropriate that my introduction to wars was through Aunts, but anyway we campaigned up and down the Deccan, and one day, during a retreat from a losing battle, I was ordered to hold a pass with two guns and two companies. Well, we did it, perhaps even in Lucknow you heard about it; they charged, we fired, we held, and finally we charged, scattered them, and that was it. How quickly it passes in the telling; what was it like? It was long, very long; we stood, and men fell around us, and we held; the bullets whistled, sprays of blood, the sound when bullets hit, all this, and what was it I felt, I can't tell, I was calm, not scared as a mouse is scared of a snake, unable to move, but frightened all the time, and yet giving orders, moving about; not enjoying (what a word) but like a diver who has given himself up to the leap. What was it? It was the surfeit of the world, its enormous weight, its madness, and also its life and its appetites; I have been to wars, and I have married, not once, but twice, and I shall again, I know. I think sometimes about what I am, Sanju, and look down at my hands, noticing how they hold things, while around me is this enormous whirl, the huge sky, the mountains. I am a soldier, soldier is not merely what I do, it is what I am, I am a soldier in this world I do not understand; is this what they mean by dharma? The world is hungry for me, and I am hungry for the world.

But enough philosophizing; I shall entertain you with my further adventures: hear, then, how I fought against the Rajputs. We fought against Jaipur, and I saw the charge of the Rathors, and no one can imagine this thing who has not seen it. Imagine a field, the scrubby desert, armies ranged in line, and suddenly a shifting of light, a slow thunder, a cloud of silvery flashing light that turns into a host of lances; I saw them fall, Sanju, vanish under the guns of a brigade, but they came on and rode over the brigade, rode down the whole unit into the dust, it vanished, and they went on laughing to attack another fleeing formation of cavalry. They careened from the battle-field, completely fearless, and in their absence their side lost; never mind how it happened, but by the time they came back, in confident twos and fours, the tide had turned, and we — that is to say de Boigne's brigades — cut them down easily. I turned away from this, and rode ahead, through the blackened heaps that marked Jaipur's lines, and there was not a thing moving; no one shot at me, and there was not a sound to be heard, far ahead of me the red sun fell silently into the dunes. We floated through the black smoke, broken here and there by the grotesque claw-like reaching of a tree; huge black rocks bulged and loomed above me, and for a moment a crow flapped around me, making no sound with its wings but exuding an overpowering miasma of rot. I don't know how long I rode, but finally I emerged upon a small rise, and found myself in Jaipur's camp, and everywhere there were empty tents, scattered shoes, not a whisper. I went on, and came to a large tent in the centre of the camp, an enormous tent, red, with fluttering flags overhead; the walls inside were painted to resemble a garden. The carpets cushioned my feet, there were large pillows, covered with gold cloth, fruit on the ground, as if everyone had just left; all these riches affected me strangely: for no reason I could place I began to weep. My face damp, I pushed aside silk curtains, went from room to room, until, finally, at the very centre, a flash of gold attracted my eye: it was a curious fish, brass, fallen to the ground. I picked it up, clutched at it, stumbled outside, and pulled myself onto my horse; on the way back I began to pass our soldiers, and all of them laughed and said my name, Sikander, Sikander, until it was almost a chorus, and when I asked, they said, that fish is the sign of a sovereign, it was Jaipur's emblem of kingship. Sikander, Sikander, that ghastly field whispered at me as I tried to find my way home.

The winner of that field, de Boigne, left for Europe soon after: the caravan that carried his riches was three miles long, I saw it. No one really knows why he left, why now, but I watched him go; he saluted us all, but I had the impression he saw none of us. He seemed to me a man who passed through the world, who ruled it but knew nothing of it; remembering those childhood stories I leaned close to him as he passed, and his eyes had the opacity of mirrors.

What is this narrative, Sanju? I don't know why I pick these moments for you, can you see a connection? I will soon be promoted, I think. Sanjay, I, Sikander, ask you: is this it, is this dharma?

Your friend, Sikander

The next letter came two years later, the morning after Sanjay first made love to Gul Jahaan; it was handed to Sanjay by a travelling Buddhist monk, who whispered, *om mani padme hum,* and left Sanjay to puzzle over what had happened the night before. The letter, as Sikander's other letter had, would impel him to evaluate his own life, to weigh and measure, and this he did not want to do.

On this morning he felt delicate and shaky, as if a slight push would cause him to crumble; now, after the event, all his plottings and manoeuvrings to win Gul Jahaan seemed trivial and nonsensical: what had once consumed him now evoked only self-contempt. The pleasure had been more than he expected (he had stared, amazed, at her breasts bared suddenly in the moonlight), but there had been something else; afterwards, he watched her sleep, curled into a quiet ball, small and tired-looking, and felt so lonely that he thought he would weep. The next day he busied himself as much as he could, carrying Sikander's letter in his waist-band, and in the evening he went to a feast organized by his friends. His passion for Gul Jahaan was well-known, and they had all watched his movement towards her, his increasing eminence as a poet of fiery sentiments and as an iconoclast, her recognition of this fact and then the final episode, and so they now greeted him fervently, the congratulations unspoken but apparent in the wide smiles. But none of them, as they raised their cups, knew about Sanjay's strange unhappiness, his inexplicable hidden gloom; and there was a deeper disappointment that he was unwilling to admit even to himself. He tried not to think about this, and it moved about him like a stalking presence in a forest, felt but not recognized; he smiled, laughed at their jokes, and it was only at the end of the evening, when they all fell silent and looked expectantly at him, that he knew what it was: he recited two of his poems, and they were full of delight and praise, and as they applauded the full weight of his realization swung against his chest, he struggled suddenly with the absolute knowledge that his poems were trivial, that they were clever and incendiary but only sensational, that they had gained him fame and therefore Gul Jahaan and that this was why and how he had written them, all his revolutionism was merely a leap into nothing, a pose, that he had wasted himself and his language. So, in the hour of what should have been his greatest triumph, Sanjay stretched a bitter smile on his face and secretly cried a shameful elegy for himself, for his once-innocent talent. And when he was finally alone, the shouting and felicitations still alive in his ears, he read the letter.

My brother,
    You remain still, it seems, wary of the written word; I hear of
you but not from you. I have followed your career and have even,

in the dusty outposts which are my usual habitation, been privileged to read some of your lines. Although these well-polished phrases convey anger, their wide use and familiarity all over the country promise that you are well. So I shall not wish you the usual advantages; I am confident you prosper. I shall tell you, directly, of my further adventures, which involve you also, and perhaps you will extract some greater meaning from these events. You will grant me, at least, that they were exceeding strange.

You know, perhaps, that Chotta has joined me; he followed me as a soldier, and served for a while with Begum Sumroo, and she treated him well, but he decided he must be with me. When he came from the Begum, my master, Uday, came with him, and now he serves with us, which is altogether an advantage I am glad of. I am glad, too, that Chotta is here; he is quiet, as always, and maybe a little quieter than before, and I am glad to keep an eye on him. As soon as he arrived I took him to the greybeards of my brigade, hoary old subedars, and said, fathers, this is my brother, to be an officer like me, and I present him to you, and beg you to take care of him as you have cared for me, look upon him as a younger son. And they gravely inclined their heads, and I felt a little better for him; there is something about Chotta that worries me. But this is by and by, and I must get to the main of my adventure (I am writing between marches): I shall tell you the story of my war with George Thomas.

You know that we struggle against the British, and the Sikhs wait to the north-west, and the prize is Delhi: who rules Delhi rules India; the Moghul is exhausted, weak, but the throne is all important, it has the authority of centuries. Thomas is poised just to the north of Delhi, within easy reach, and everybody knew that one day he would be removed, some day before the final reckoning with the English. The Marathas said, if we turn our attention to Calcutta, and Thomas leaps down to Delhi, then it is all lost; the English thought the same thing; and so it was resolved to remove Thomas, and nobody came to help him because he was inconvenient to all: in this game of states everything is prey. So we campaigned against him, he retreated towards his city of Hansi, and we caught up with him at a place called Georgegarh, a post his men

had built and named for him; we attacked, he defended, and they
stood well — by nightfall we had lost the slight weight in numbers
that we had the advantage of, and if it were not for the loss of light
it would have been bad for us. But, the greater fortunes of the day
apart, there was something else: I faced him on the battle-field. At
the end of the day, I led a charge against their rally (they would've
had us), and in a mêlée on an escarpment I found myself face-to-
face with him: unmistakably it was him, a gigantic man in archaic
armour, his cut on my parry numbed my wrist, so that I stumbled
back, fell, and he let me go, we were carried away from each other.
His face was covered by the nose-piece of his helmet and the chain
cheek-guards, but his eyes were a radiant blue, and it seemed he
looked after me through the dust.

Later that evening, when I came back to our camp, a number of
my fellow-officers regarded me curiously, and when I stopped they
told me Chotta was lost: several of them had seen him fall to a cut
from Thomas himself. So I ran back to the field, and in the shifting,
clouded moonlight I stumbled through the huddles of corpses,
looking for my brother; in that unsteady but unequivocal light it
seemed that the dead lay unto the horizon and beyond, and all of it
had an air of unreality, as if they were players, as if that catastrophe
were a stage, a scene set for the aftermath of a gigantic battle. I felt I
floated through this illusion for hours, my heart on fire, and then
suddenly I saw another bent shadow, another man bowed over the
ground and its burden: it was Chotta, intent on the same errand
that I was, looking for me, who he thought dead, victim to a cut
from Jahaj Jung himself. We embraced each other joyfully, and he
showed me the broken links in his chain mail, where the cut had
landed; he told me frankly that he had run from Thomas, unable to
face the roaring strength of the man. So we held each other by the
shoulders, and laughed into each other's faces, but then something
made me still, my back contract; I turned away from Chotta, and
saw above us a dark figure, silhouetted and silent, a spiked helmet,
winged shoulder-armour, armed at all points, angular against the
racing clouds, jagged and fearsome, and I thought some avenging
spirit of the battle-field had taken form in front of us, I stood frozen, couldn't move, and it said: 'I came looking for you.'

It was Thomas: after the day was over, he was unable to forget two encounters, those being his two cuts at either of us, and he had been unable to sleep, or think of anything else. So he had come out and found us, and now he asked, who are you; I told him our names, and that brought no recognition, and he stared at us, puzzled and confounded. Are you country-born, he asked then, and I said, yes, our mother is a Rajput lady, and at this he took on the strangest expression, and he said, you are *her* sons! So there is something to those old stories after all, Sanju, and he seemed to believe it all without question, and treated us henceforth in all respects as if we were his sons. This led, as you will see, to the strangest of situations, because that night on the field he embraced us, and afterwards absolutely refused to fight us; what I mean by this is that the next morning we all waited in trepidation for his attack, which was surely going to finish us. He had us at a disadvantage, and if he had come we would have been finished, and by all rules of combat he should have come, this was clear to every officer and soldier on that field. But he didn't come, and every minute and hour brought our reinforcements near, and we waited on that bloody sand, the day declined, and he did nothing; that night Chotta and I went out again, and he was waiting for us. I asked, what stopped you today, why didn't you attack, and he said, quite simply, I will not fight you. Now I didn't want to say, come, surely you must know this is your last chance, you have to attack, because that would have been disloyalty, after all every moment he was inactive was a grant from heaven for those I served, but I asked, why? The question seemed strange to him, and he just shrugged, and repeated, I will not fight you; and so for fifteen days our two armies looked at each other across the dunes, and there was much discussion in our mess about why Thomas, the dashing Jahaj Jung himself, why he was paralysed, why he waited, and Chotta and I said nothing. On the fifteenth night finally Chotta burst out, if you do not come tomorrow you are lost, the reinforcements are a day's march away, and again Thomas shook his head.

I must say that by now Chotta and I had conceived a great liking for this man: he was strong, he was honourable, and he was gentle with us, he stroked our heads in greeting and in good-bye. Why, said Chotta angrily, why? But Thomas shrugged, and then despite my attempts, Chotta shouted at him, you will vanish from the face of this earth, and nobody will remember you, you will disappear like a dream, even if we are your sons you must fight us. Is that what will happen, Thomas said; I jumped from a ship to escape that story; and then he would say nothing more. Only when he left us on that final night, he turned back and called to us, I will not fight you, I am an Indian, but what are you?

I never found out what he meant by that question, because that afternoon our reinforcements arrived, and then he was completely and finally trapped. What did he mean by that question, Sanju? Why did he ask me that? I thought of it all the time that we were going between camps, arranging for his surrender, talking terms, I thought of it; finally, it ended as well as it could have: he was deposed, stripped of his lands, exiled from Hindustan forever, but was allowed to take his fortune with him. He agreed to this, didn't have much choice, and before he left we invited him to dine with us in our mess, and he came, and it was not good: on the face of our commander, Perron, there was a smirk of disdain, and his favourites, following him, cut a haughty air, and Thomas leaned back in his chair, and drank. Finally, Perron raised his glass and chuckled, a toast to the defeat of all our enemies, and Thomas roared, I was *not* defeated, and his sword flashed over his head, and Perron ran like a frightened pig; we calmed Thomas down and took him home. As we walked beside his palanquin in the dark, he lay looking at the stars, mumbling some story about an old man in a forest, and another man in a ruined city, and he told us how lovely his Hansi was, how he had built it and populated it. I tried to say something, but what could I say to a man who had just lost his kingdom, lost his kingdom for love? At the last gate, there was a sentry, one of those insufferable men full of their own strength, and this sentry challenged us, who goes there? And Thomas' men said, it is Jahaj Jung, the Sahib Bahadur, and so this fellow, who I think must have heard already of the quarrel and was eager to curry Perron's favour, levelled his blade and said, I know of no Sahib Bahadur, I see only a drunk, who goes there? And, I swear to you, I had seen Thomas put down three bottles of wine that evening, but before I could even think of stopping him the sentry was sitting in the middle of the road, holding his wrist and watching the jet from its stump, and Thomas was turning back to me, jerking the blood from his sword. He leaned up to me, and said, I could have won, and I said yes, but I wish you a happy life over there; he smiled, and said, I will find my happiness, but not over there, not with all this wealth, an old man will come for me, and we will walk together into the hills. Then he went, and the next morning he was escorted to Delhi, and hence towards Calcutta. I never saw him again; I wonder now what he meant by any of it, whether he chose not to win, which old man he spoke of, and why, and I don't know what to think of it. But I know one thing: after he was gone, we told his men (and a hard lot they were) to join us, we offered them service on good terms, but all of them to a man said, we have ridden with Jahaj Jung, and we will serve no other, and then they all tore their clothes off, and each of those soldiers became a sadhu. This I saw. What was this man, Sanju? What was he, that could inspire this from soldiers? I think we shall never know, but I know that Chotta wept for him, that Thomas never went over there to Europe, as he had promised us; on the way to Calcutta, they told us, in sight of some green jungles, he died — they found him one morning smiling in his sleep. I think we shall not see the like again: he gave up a kingdom, and his men became monks in his memory.

I am growing older, Sanjay; I am married again, not once but five times more, in all seven now. I am happy, I have work, I know what my ambitions are and I move unceasingly forward, but there are some times, some evenings when it rains, some sudden wakings in the night, when some other apprehension lurks just outside my ken, I feel some other understanding. I cannot say it, I don't know what it is, but the road is not straight, nothing is clear, it is all branchings, circles, and journeys of strange destinations; I have confidently told you the story of George Thomas, Jahaj Jung, but I feel I have grasped neither it, nor him: the meaning is all around, in the dust of Hansi and in that forest, neither to be grasped nor said.

Your friend, Sikander

As the years passed, Sanjay found himself writing less; the act of putting words on paper became more and more a lie, an oppressive betrayal of life itself, and therefore one day Sanjay found himself unable to write at all. Taking up his pen, sitting at his desk, he felt like an actor; even as he scratched some flourishes onto the white sheet he floated above himself, watching, and the minutes ticked away, but there was not a word in him. He sat through the morning, and into the afternoon, scratching at his soul, worrying memories here and there, pulling and searching, but finally he had to admit to himself that nothing was left, nothing, and even as he realized this there was a huge, attendant relief. He put the paper away, closed the box over his pens, and swiftly got up and went into the evening; the lanes were unusually quiet, and as he walked he took pleasure in the twilight rush of the birds, the cool air, the heavy green masses of trees.

'You were walking very fast today,' Gul Jahaan said as they sat down. 'I watched you come up the garden.'

'I am happy today,' Sanjay said.

She looked steadily at him for a moment, and he at her; her face was well-known to him now, which once had seemed so exotic.

'I'm happy too,' she said quite seriously, and then paused for a long moment. 'I'm happy.'

'What is it?'

She regarded him still, her hands palms up in her lap, and then she smiled brilliantly, her eyes filling with tears. 'You will be a father.'

Sitting with her, her back solidly against him and the scent of her hair all around him, Sanjay thought about this person who sat within his arms, a whole identity, complicated and difficult; he turned her face gently to his, and said, 'How did you come to this Lucknow? Where were you born?'

'You've never asked me that, all these years.'

'Tell me.'

As she spoke of uncles and long-lost brothers, a mother, a village, he considered the face in front of him: a complete history of trauma and hope, quite different from the dream of his childhood, and yet it was the gentle, lined source of hope, unbearably beautiful; its warmth stabbed him, and he stopped her recital by kissing her eyelids, and she broke against him in laughter. Finally she stopped, and whispered, 'You look tired. Are you tired?'

'Yes,' he said. 'I'm a little tired.'

The child was a boy, still-born, perfectly-formed and with a golden complexion, tiny fists curled shut; the next one was dark, almost blue, again with no cry to announce his arrival to the world; there were three others born dead. By the time Gul Jahaan was pregnant for the sixth time, they had exhausted all the vaids, munshis, gurus and pilgrimages in Avadh; finally there was nothing left to do but wait. This time they couldn't even tell each other stories of hope, and were too spent to grieve; they awaited the birth with the grim acceptance usually given to inevitable death, where a certain horrible impatience wishes the event to be over and done with. Now, they hardly touched each other, and lived in a sort of quiet companionship; Sanjay received the proceeds from his former writings, but in the absence of any new work there was a slow but perceptible slide towards poverty, which again was accepted as inescapable. Sanjay found that the melancholy of his life was not as unpleasant as he might have thought it would be; there was a certain peace in the descent, and so he felt no pain, except on certain afternoons when he fell asleep, and awoke with a start and a great terror of age, thinking I am growing older, I am old.

All this lassitude was swept away instantly by a single report of a travelling English doctor, a man who moved through the country-side, giving aid to all at his nightly camps, without regard to position, age, or gender. He had acquired, in the short time of his voyages through Avadh, a reputation for the greatest skill, saving those ill with fever and given up for dead, rescuing from unbearable pain those maimed by accidents, and even, it was said, restoring sight to some blind from childhood; and so this man was the object of petitions from many, and even those most orthodox and wary of foreigners put aside their fears and sought his advice.

It was Gul Jahaan who first heard of this man, and she began instantly to plan with the passion of a slowly-drowning creature seeing a chance at redemption; she sold some of her jewellery, had new clothes made, and all this referring to him only as the English doctor. Sanjay proceeded slowly, wary and full of memory, but unable to keep hope suppressed, feeling it like a rolling but unstoppable wave; in the matter of the English, he told himself, he had learnt automatic distrust and watchfulness, and so he wrote letters to acquaintances, sent messen-

gers, and waited for information regarding this too-generous Englishman. Sanjay waited in a curious fever, half hope and half spite, so that
finally when he learnt the name of the doctor he laughed hysterically
and long; life, it seemed to him, had its own curious and juvenile sense
of aesthetics, because the name, was, of course: Sarthey.

He knew the rest without having to ask, that this was the son of the
man he had once known, and that the son was now a precocious and
well-known practitioner; that he was brilliant, having published two
books on the treatment of infectious diseases; that he was now travelling in Hindustan with the stated purpose of gathering material for a
third on tropical maladies. It was understood, of course, that he was
handsome, that he was tall, that his hair was long — for an Englishman — and that his eyes were blue; all this Sanjay knew, and he tried to
explain all this to Gul Jahaan, intending to say, we shouldn't go, I know
we shouldn't. But even as he started he saw the new light in her eyes,
the way her chest rose and fell quickly in joy, the half-smile that flickered on her face as she looked at him with love, not listening to him at
all; he shook his head in defeat, and said, 'Well, I suppose we'll go.'

'Of course we'll go,' she said.

They joined the doctor's camp when he came close to Lucknow, to a
small and unheard-of village, five miles away on the other side of the
Gomti. They crossed the river in a hired boat, and Sanjay sat in the bow,
looking back, watching the familiar city recede in the dusk, become
shadows, then herald itself in a blaze of diminutive lights that grew
small and smaller. The English camp was angled in straight lines
around the doctor's simple grey tent; the first things that Sanjay noted
were the swept, gravelled pathways that had been laid through even
this temporary camp, which fell neatly around these bisecting lines like
a chequer-board. The sufferers waited patiently in the darkness, organized into ranks by the doctor's servants; Sanjay spoke to one of these
attendants, and then came back to Gul Jahaan.

'We have to wait,' he said, shrugging.

'We'll wait.' Her voice was muffled by her burqua. 'Wait.'

Suffering has its own equality: in the darkness Sanjay sat next to
village labourers, farmers, and thought about this; every now and then
there was a muffled sound, a distant groan, a shifting of cloth as somebody got laboriously up and shuffled a few steps. When the call came,

the light in the doctor's tent was painful, white and sharp from some new kind of lantern that burnt with an unprecedented blue flame; Sanjay squinted, and the icy quality of the light was such that he first missed the speaker who addressed a question to him.

'Is he blind?' This was someone else, speaking in English.

'No, I am not,' Sanjay said in English. 'The patient is outside.'

'You speak English?' This time Sanjay saw him: he was dressed in black, in a formal English suit of the type Sanjay had only seen in woodcuts, a black cravat, so that at first Sanjay could only think, he must be warm in that.

'Yes,' Sanjay said, finally. 'I speak English. My name is Parasher.'

'Pleased. I am Doctor Sarthey. And the patient?'

'She is outside.'

'Well, I am sure you understand that I must speak to her, to the patient herself.' The smile on the doctor's face was small and intimate, asserting a common, shared knowledge.

'Of course,' Sanjay said, feeling foolish despite himself. 'I will go and call her.'

Outside, Gul Jahaan raised the purdah from her face, the better to speak to him; she listened to him gravely, then asked: 'Will I have to expose my face to him?'

'It is likely.'

'I have done worse,' she said. 'And this is for our sons and daughters.' She rose and walked rapidly past him; inside, she spoke strongly and directly, and without hesitation extended her wrist to the doctor. He, in turn, seated on an iron chair, prescribed rest, broth of fowl, some medicine he would provide, and finally advised, when the child was born, the presence of a good doctor.

'Tell him that we have no other doctor,' Gul Jahaan said. 'Tell him that we will come with him.'

'Travel with me?' the doctor said when Sanjay translated. 'It is hard, and also . . .' But he stopped, looking at Gul Jahaan's small face, framed by her black burqua, very serious and attentive as she looked at him unwaveringly.

'Yes,' Sanjay said. 'She is very determined.'

'Yes,' he said. 'I suppose it is all right, then.'

They had come prepared for this; Sunil, his bald head now shiny with the gravity and importance of a renowned cook, headed Gul Ja-haan's entourage. They had come with carts, beds, mosquito nets, and so they settled themselves a little distance from the English tents, adopting naturally the orderly rows and arrangements of the other set-tlement. That night she turned to Sanjay joyfully: her pleasure was al-ways slow, unhurried, completely conscious, but tonight it seemed like a form of knowledge itself; they sat in front of each other, joined, still except for secret movements and fluctuations, looking into each other's eyes, and it went on until passion gave way to a greater lucidity, it was dark but he could see her perfectly, as if her dark hair, the roundness of her breasts, all were radiant with some inward light, he laughed sud-denly because the air was so clear, every touch of her fingers carried inward along his body like a word, his head floating and transfixed and transformed by her, her smell, her presence which was everywhere.

The next day, it became clear to them that they were in a foreign camp: the young doctor forbade any sort of performance by Gul Jahaan; she was known of all over Avadh, and so there were more visitors, villagers and townsmen, and some of them asked the pleasure of hear-ing her sing. Sarthey forbade it, without anger or sternness, but nev-ertheless he said, 'That is impossible.' In all other respects he was courteous, and Gul Jahaan accepted his wishes as a condition of being a part of his camp; every day, he examined her, and kept a close watch over her diet, sometimes sending delicacies to her kitchen. Sanjay, for his part, often spoke to him, and Sarthey seemed delighted with his English, his interest in things English, poetry especially; soon the doc-tor took to bringing books to Sanjay, treatments of history, discussions of currencies and trades, practical discussions of geography and prog-ress, the vast potential of the future. At first their conversation con-sisted of these things; then they began to have silences between them, as they rode along in the early morning, and Sanjay recognized these incredulously as the natural quietness between friends. These mo-ments, as the sun washed a thin line of red on the furthest clouds, had the unmistakable taste of intimacy, and despite himself Sanjay could not dislike the Englishman: he was curious about everything, and wanted to know the names of plants; his hair pulled back from his forehead tightly, but his face, thin and serious as it was, had the habit of suddenly smiling, at which times he would bunch over in his saddle, hold an embarrassed hand over his mouth, and giggle. Although Sanjay knew they were the same age, he felt incomparably older, as if he was already tasting the time of ashes and compromise, while the other, yet, knew not even the complete and unbroken hopes of youth. And above all, further and more valuable than anything, was Sarthey's intelligence, not wit, but a slow circling watchfulness that approached and prodded and tested and finally held; to discover this in the Englishman was shocking, because all his life Sanjay had secreted a prideful loneliness, a certain belief in his precocity and understanding, the like of which he had recognized in no one else except this one, this man. So Sanjay reminded himself of the past, and predicted without doubt a future of disaster, but there it was, this companionship, unbidden and without reason; despite everything, at those times in the mornings Sanjay found no humiliation in asking question after question, what is it you do in the morning in England when you get up, how is breakfast made, and without pause came answers and then questions in return.

Gul Jahaan seemed to regard their meetings with the amused toleration of a woman for men's things, and she took to referring to Sarthey as 'your Englishman,' and professed a fear of him, of his blue eyes and ascetic air. But Sanjay, standing by to translate, watched sometimes in the evenings as he dispensed treatment: his precise fingers on the bandages, the knots square and neat, the clear gaze as he laved out wounds and boils, the doctor's eye that detached itself from the pain, the twitching faces, and yet was actively compassionate; all these things Sanjay found gentle.

At this time another letter came from Sikander. It was delivered by a seller of sweets who left the little packet of paper tucked between two rosogullas.

Sanjay,
   I am wounded.
   Another war, another combat: I will not weary you with the unfortunate details of a soldier's life. Enough to say that the struggle for supremacy over Hindustan rages on, the alliances shift, soldiers die. This time we were caught in the open in an unequal fight, no support and no hope, we fell back as best we could but they broke our square. Then it was cavalry all over us and terror; I

slashed about, and there was a moment, as I ran, of suddenly thinking about my wives, my children, and then I cut a man down, easily. I was shouting something, I don't know what, I couldn't tell you, leaping forward, and they fell back from me, frightened; then out of the corner of my eye I saw a rider spurring at me, turned to face him, saw him raise a pistol, felt a thick blow against my thigh, as if someone had taken an iron rod and swung it about at my abdomen, a blow blunt and numb, saw the flash at his hand, and I floated to the ground, and it seemed to me as I hit that the sound of the shot boomed forever in my head.

When I awoke, Sanjay, it was night, and I was pinned to the earth by a huge shaft of pain through my belly. The pain had its strictures about my body, its paths carved from my groin everywhere so that at each movement it tightened about me. At first I was afraid, but finally I forced my hand down and felt, but all I fingered were the raw edges of a wound, the shapelessness of the body when it is burst in some way. As I touched this rupture I felt that chaos reeled over me, and I cried out, not from pain, but in fear of this derangement that wanted to eat me, grind me all up into an obscene mixture. Mother, I shouted, Mother, Mother. Do you know what I feared, Sanjay? It was that battle-field aftermath, the parts of men scattered like refuse, everything pulped together, not anymore this and that, one and another, but all gone into the great whirl of fire and filth — it was this great loss, this anarchy that strangled the breath from me. I let my fear take my senses from me, gratefully I let it all go, but the moon came up and I saw it and could not hide anymore: Mother, Mother, Mother. I whispered with others beside me, we wept all of us like a chorus in the darkness, and in the flat white light everything became a sharp blackness, shadows and the edge of steel like fire, blood is black at night. Then I heard a woman's voice: Sikander, I am here. Mother, I said, but I saw her, a lovely tall woman in white, her skin illuminated from within, a red mouth, it was Kali. She came to me, Sanjay, and in horror and awe I shook, tranced and unaware, the night fell apart in fragments, the moon trembled and slid into the earth. When I came back to myself, could see again, think, I heard a voice, Sikander, is that you, is that you? It was Uday: I could hear the pain in his voice, the agony from an anonymous cannon shot that shivered his leg; he told me, he saw it coming a moment before it hit, and then it shattered him. Learn a lesson, young Sikander, he said, in this war skill can only take you so far, when it wants to find you, the bullet will, no honour, nothing keeps it from you. So we talked, and the pain ebbed but I felt it come again, the spinning of the sky, a chariot wheel spinning and spinning and flying apart, myself in a hundred places and pieces, Uday's voice, now hold on, youngster, hold on, steady, but I was gone, the darkness parted and from far away I saw the mound of crushed bodies, the spears broken and impaled, heard the ravings of the wounded, water, water, please water. It seemed then that Kali was holding me in her arms, cradling me in her arms, my head on her breast, and I looked up into her wild eyes and said, Mother; then she was above me, seated cross-legged on my groin: Sikander, why do you fear? She laughed, her dark hair floating about her face, and now she was dancing on my body, from head to toe her feet pressed me, and she said, Sikander, you were not made to be happy. Finally she lay beside me, stroked my forehead, and said, don't be afraid, there's nothing to be afraid of, and I knew she told the truth, the pain fell away, I smiled and fell asleep.

When I awoke I knew somehow that it was past midnight, I knew where I was, and now there was no longer that vertigo, that terror of before. I tried to sit up as best I could, to see my men and what could be done for them, and they were in the torments of a special soldier's hell, where time is forever, your blood flows, you cannot move, and there is no water. All around me I heard the cry for it, weak, desperate, hopeful, mad, as the condition of the man might be; over this there was Uday's voice, talking, encouraging, but even there I could hear the way his lips were sticking, the tongue moving like a leathery beast in the dry cavern of the palate. Is it very bad, O master, I asked, and he said, it is not so bad that it will not pass, and his words burdened me with grief, because suddenly I knew he was talking, not without hope, of his own death.

And so the night passed; in the morning came two old people, I saw them walk towards us from far, a man and a woman, very old and from their dress peasants, bearing water-skins. They were wrinkled and thin, blackened by a life of brutal work, but their eyes had the compassion of a thousand years. They passed from man to man, giving water and comfort and hope; the woman came to me, and I drank gratefully, and she folded a coat and put it under my head. She smiled, toothless, and said, we are farmers. But Uday would not take their water: he said, thank you, but I cannot, it would break my caste. I said, take it, Father, because even the scriptures hold that caste rules do not apply in times of disaster; but he said, it may be so, and I hold no man weak for taking water now, but I will not do it. So I began to speak to him about rationalism, science (remembering the conversations I had heard in my father's house), religion; we had, in short, a theological and philosophical debate, lying there in the tall grass with our bodies holed. We touched upon every question of belief and doubt you can think of, and even the other wounded grew quiet and listened; and finally I demonstrated to him the error of his thinking, and that it was not only possible but his duty to drink. But he said, I am an old man, I have lived too long and I have seen too much change, you are no doubt right, I am in error, I am sorry I upset you, but I have lived a long time in this dharma, and I will die in a few hours, I will keep to it. But your suffering — I could not help bursting out — but how you must suffer! He said, this is my dharma.

So all through the long day I watched him, and he lay pierced in a thousand places, steadfast; in the evening our opponents came back, having broken off the engagement, and they gathered us up and took us to shelter, to good doctors. But Uday was dead. As they lifted me up the old woman said to me, do not weep, do not weep for death. Uday was dead, and I could not remember the moment in which his voice stopped. As they lifted me up the pain flared and brought a cry from me, but in the sound was something of relief, of release; somehow in the confusion there was a sense, there was the sky above me, fringed with black birds, the eyes of the old woman and her husband, their kindness, the unbreakable dharma of Uday, the dead around me, and life which opened to me once more, and I said to the water-bringers: I vow by the pain I have suffered that beyond right and wrong, this and that, us and they, I will build a temple, a mosque and a church, all of these in honour of my mother and my father, in honour of these men who have ridden with me, and in honour of what is to come. I was half-mad by now, but the old ones said, this is good. I will do it; even though, now, in tranquil recollection, I do not know what I meant, cannot recall exactly what it was I saw on the field, I will do it.

I am permanently wounded; to be blunt, the ball took one of mine. I am healed, but I suppose I am halved. Mistake me not, I am as capable as before, let us say; but before I lived carelessly, I asked the world for victory, and that was all I asked. Now I am not so sure; now I am somehow unable to sleep, and victory, when it comes, is not all sweet. I am rambling, ahead to my further adventures.

I healed, was released by our foes, and took again command of my troops, but the misfortune which had threatened for long was finally against us, as you well know. The Marathas fight the English: the moment of decision is here. We waited for this so long, Sanjay, and we all knew it was coming, but after all, I fight not for the Marathas. What happened was this: a few days after the campaign started, Perron — you remember him, the posing Frenchman who ran from Thomas at Georgegarh — well, this Perron called all the country-born officers in his command to his tent. None of us could think why, but we went, and Perron, seated in state, told us our fates: while he did not doubt any of us individually, he said, it had been decided that those officers who were of partial English descent could not be wholly relied upon in the war to come. And in this supremely important war no doubts could be entertained, and therefore we were to be released from our services, and were free to do as we liked, with assurances of safe-conduct, etc., etc. At this there was a wild howl from those assembled, and a movement forward, and Perron blanched a little and his guards hitched their pieces; I stepped forward, and spoke: I am a Rajput, and my loyalty is unquestioned, you insult me. No insult is intended, he said, but there was a particular satisfaction in his voice, a faint gloating when he made his announcements; he hated the English, you see, and so he hated us. I am a Rajput, I said again. Undoubtedly, he said, but you are also something else. At this Chotta started forward, and by instinct I reached out to check him, and the sight of his face, blotched with angry red marks, a thousand of them, shocked me into self-possession: Chotta would have killed him. So I nodded my head, unable for anything to bow, and led them out, into the bright sun outside, and we walked through the military bustle we had known all our lives, suddenly foreign.

The road we took then, Sanjay, was the longest of our lives; we said good-bye to our men, stanched their weeping and their talk of mutiny and left the camp. The direction we took was the only one open to us — we travelled towards the British; what I am is a sol-dier, and that was the only service available then, and now. But before we had gone far, distance hid our comrades from us, and the road narrowed between fields and groves of trees, and all was peace; I bid my friends to go on ahead, told them I would catch up shortly. I left the road, found a shade of mango trees, and leaned up against one of them; my legs gave, and I sat, my legs apart like a child, and then I dropped forward and wept, smearing my face with the dust of my country.

So we went on towards the English. We had not gone far, the next morning, when disorganized groups of Maratha horsemen began to stream past us, replying to our shouts with only the cry that the English were coming, the English were coming. Then we saw Per-ron, hatless, fleeing down the road on a blown horse, and I ran out and caught his reins. It is all over, he said, all over, the English surprised us, flee, flee, and he was delirious with panic, his big yellow eyes rolling. But you haven't fought them, I shouted, look, none of your weapons have been discharged, you have done noth-ing, and he would say only that they had come upon the camp unseen and unsuspected, it was all over. Come, we will help you, I said, make a stand here, rally your men, we will beat them, but he began to weep, it is over, it is over. So I let him go, and said to the others, come, we will go and rally, and we will stop the English, and I began to saddle my horse, and Chotta followed me, but the others looked on grimly, and by the time I had finished tightening the cinch-grips I was weary with hopelessness and rage: if we had been with our men that night perhaps there would have been no carelessness, no surprise, no panic, no unfought defeat. The bigotry of this European and his fellows lost the Marathas this battle, maybe this war, maybe their kingdom; he had looked at me and had not seen the soldier's salt, the Rajput's vow. What men are these, Sanjay? Truly we are in Kalyug. In the dust of that road, when everything fell apart, and I was alone under the great sky, far from my men, what I felt most was the meanness of an enormous trap closing slowly about me, its oily hinges and its power that somehow was crushing me flat. I am fearful.

When we reached the English they kept us honourably, but more or less as prisoners; finally, a few days later, we were asked if we would serve with them. There was nowhere else to go, Sanjay, but still I hesitated, and then they said to me, your men, your old regiment, are here too, and will serve us. I said, let me see them, and they took me to my soldiers; in front of me, the English asked, will you serve with us, and there was no reply, only a muttering. Then the English said, we will let you choose your own commander, who will you have in command, and in a single voice they shouted, Sikander, Sikander, and in my ears it had the clang of a falling sword. Sikander, Sikander, my boys called, their lance-heads flashing in the sun, and I said, without thinking, it came from somewhere inside me, all right, we will wear yellow, and our motto will be, *Himmat-i-mardan, maddad-i-khuda.* And they called my name, Sikander, Sikander. And I said to the English, I will serve you. I will serve you, but not against my former master, Holkar, and they accepted; so now I take my regiment north to the doab, to pacify, to police, to guard Delhi. So I serve the English, Sanjay. Was I betrayed, or did I betray? As I sit here writing, it is the hour of cow-dust, and all around me I can hear the tinkling of bells; I am alone in my tent, inside its red walls, and I can hear the water of a stream close by. I remain, as always, your friend,

Sikander

As the days of Gul Jahaan's pregnancy went by, her face became round, and Sanjay was busy bringing her the sweet things she wanted to eat: ras mallai, gulab jamuns, jalebis, and all the time the countryside was quickened into unease by rumours of war. When Sanjay told Sarthey that perhaps they should stay closer to towns, should even consider halting for a period, the Englishman only shook his head, saying that the work must go on. This work, which was not to be interrupted by the English war, was more than medicine; it included also the planting of certain iron rods in the ground, and their measurement with an instrument that Sarthey peered through, all this being duly noted on large sheets of paper. This systematic sketching, which paid particular attention to elevations, declensions, and water-courses, was sometimes interrupted by the sighting of a new species of animal or bird, which unfortunate creatures Sarthey invariably shot and pictured in yet another sketch-book. All this curiosity Sanjay regarded with admiration, with wonder at the Englishman's voraciousness, his appetite for detail, but when Sarthey's delving pierced through the surface, when it undertook to prick and slice open, Sanjay was unable to watch. The first time that Sarthey took a squirrel and spread it out on a flat board, Sanjay watched not knowing what was coming next: angle-pointed scissors that snipped an opening from the groin to the chest, metal pincers that peeled back the layers of fat to the packed organs in the belly, and a skilful extraction of a grey sac that contained white, half-formed shapes. At this Sanjay turned away, and afterwards, although he would carry the ruled rods, the measuring instruments, the sketch-books, and even the black leather bag with its rows of knives, he preferred to be excused when the cutting started. This Sarthey agreed to always with a patient shrug, as if to imply an adult toleration of childish squeamishness: 'You are sentimental, my dear fellow' was the usual comment, with which verdict Sanjay agreed wholeheartedly, but still he was unable to make his body acquiesce, to make his stomach understand what he could perceive to be the intellectual and whole truth.

Seated away from the cutting table, Sanjay was given to thinking about his strange relation with the Englishman; should he confess — if that was the word — his true identity and his old encounter with the elder Sarthey? But more importantly, he was mystified by the friendship he felt for the Englishman: Sanjay, you who once cursed the race, why are you attracted to this man, why do you seek his company and inquire after his opinions? For this there was no answer; at night, lying by Gul Jahaan, his head pushed up to her stomach, it was difficult to think past his soon-to-be son, and the future was so powerfully illuminated by the impending birth that he thought it impossible to look beyond.

Finally, the hour itself came near; it was summer, and even outside, under a mosquito net, the air was close, lying like a blanket over the face. Sanjay thrashed about on his bed, moving first one way and then the other, and finally he pulled off every piece of clothing except his neck-band; still, he found no sleep. So, getting up and pulling on his loose cotton pajamas, he walked some distance to a water-matka, and dipped his hand in the cool, clay-smelling surface, noticing how the moon swam in it, and for several moments he was preoccupied by the fragrance of the water and its cold, but then he turned around suddenly. There had been no sound, and there was as yet nothing to see, but he knew something was there; Sanjay stepped back into a shadow and waited. When he saw the dark figure he laughed silently: he recalled the posture from long ago — that it was Sarthey was clear from the height, but the furtiveness, somehow feline, was what he had seen in his child-hood. Laughing, Sanjay began to follow the Englishman, wondering what sort of lover Sarthey had: a woman from among the maids, the servants? Or was it one of the hired soldiers from the escort? But it seemed a long way to go in the dark, and then Sarthey left the camp behind, and made his way along the little rivulet they had camped by; it seemed too much walking for a bath. Finally, Sarthey descended into the ravine cut by the water, and scrambled all the way to the bottom, where the reduced flow trickled along; and Sanjay lay on the bank above and watched while the other stripped off his suit and crouched in the course.

In the white light Sarthey's hair was black, and lay like a solid streak between the thin bones of his shoulders; Sanjay could see the narrow back and the delicate, descending chain of the spine. Sarthey was still, and then it became clear to Sanjay that he was holding himself with great force, so that beneath the rigidity there was a minute but rapid trembling. He rose from the water, then knelt by the dark puddle of clothes, and drew something from it; Sanjay was unable to make it out until it spun above Sarthey in a dark line and fell with a crack. For a very long time Sanjay watched as the belt curved and made a sound like a thick piece of wood swinging into wet cloth, again and again, again and again, and when Sarthey's back went black, when it glistened black, Sanjay crawled away and stumbled back to Gul Jahaan, and lay with a hand on her hip till daybreak.

In the morning there was hardly a pause between the grey coolness and the white heat of the sun, and Gul Jahaan began to have her baby. Sanjay sat outside the doctor's tent, cringing at every moan, but finally the screams subsided, and now the tent was glowing a rich orange, as if a fire were burning inside. A woman threw aside a flap and beckoned: 'Come.' Inside, Gul Jahaan lay in a sopping wet pile of sheets, her face a bright red and her eyes turned back, breathing in a rapid succession of pants, and over her leaned Sarthey, his face so vital with curiosity and inquisitiveness that he seemed happy.

'I've never seen anything like it,' he said without looking up. 'There.'

His gesture was towards a cradle (once made to order in Lucknow) that stood in a corner, now blackened and charred but barely visible because of a yellow-white effulgence that made it hard to see; shielding his face with his fingers and half-turning from the burning light, Sanjay leaned and saw, in quick flashes, a perfectly-formed boy, beautiful beyond telling, but blazing with such inner heat that Sanjay felt it pressing against his face like fingers. When Sanjay turned back, the doctor pointed towards Gul Jahaan, and now she trembled as if in a fit of ague, all the cold damp cloths pressed against her were useless, and she turned her head towards one side, and died. Under the cloth of the tent the heat was ferocious, and Sanjay rushed out, but in all the land there was no relief, the deepest shade breathed an air full of dragging thorns, Sanjay felt each pulse of his heart throb in his head. Walking was cruel but he could not keep still for fear of madness, and so all day he stumbled from tree to building, hating the nameless, dusty town that went drudgingly about its business. All day Sunil walked after him, giving him water and trying to force him to eat, and when it was evening (he could not remember when the day had turned), Sunil led him back to the camp.

'The child is safe, the child is safe,' he was told as soon as they saw him. Indeed, the boy's brilliance was much diminished: it was possible now to look directly at him, and although one could not sustain the gaze for too long it was feasible to touch his skin lightly. The women attending to him with buckets of water and muslin cloth murmured admiringly about the infant's complexion, but Sanjay asked, 'Where is Gul Jahaan?' The doctor, they said, and Sanjay turned and ran, not knowing why but as if there was some urgency, towards the English tent; at the door there was some flurry as if to stop him, but he brushed by it, went in and saw, on a raised wooden table, a flat white figure, arms out and palms up, mouth slightly open. There was a vertical cut that ran from the sternum down to the pudenda, two flaps that opened outwards and raised away to expose the packed and distinct layers of the body, the surprising depth and width of the places where organs had been removed, namely two grey packets and a striped and red-stippled pocket that lay in an orderly row at the edge of the table, and even as Sanjay came in, Sarthey, leaning over and with delicate but sure prongs and scissors, came up with a large yellowish triangle. Sarthey turned his head slowly over his shoulder, still holding it, and in his eyes was the hard glaze of concentration, wide-pupilled, and his arms were wet to his shoulders. Extremely curious, he began, very curious, and then seemed to recognize Sanjay, upon which he straightened, my dear fellow, my dear fellow, but Sanjay was already out of the tent, running, and without pause he caught up the boy to his chest, ignoring the burning; he ran, and fled the camp of the English.

Accompanied by Sunil, Sanjay rode to the east, his son slung to his chest in a thin cloth, and at every step he knew he was mistaken in his reaction, misguided. He had read of medical autopsies, and understood their purpose; he knew well the importance of scientific investigation, the necessity for dispatch and efficiency in the face of inexplicable phenomena; as he rode, Sanjay berated himself for his wholly sentimental and primitive reaction, the crass melodrama of his actions, but as long as his son lay like a huge knot against his heart he was unable to turn back. We will take him to my mother, he told Sunil, and she will look after him; and it was clear that care was essential: every day of riding through the hot dust brought about a cooling of the boy, a small but perceptible lessening of his fierce heat. In every town Sunil found a wet-nurse, but the child grew more ordinary every day, and it was clear to Sanjay that in this case the mundane was deadly, that the slow onslaught of normality was the coming of weakness and death. As the boy's golden eyes slowly became dull and merely human, Sanjay wished and prayed for a resuscitation of the old miracle of hot light, even if that were to mean, for him the father, blistered skin, dazzled eyes and pain.

Sanjay's mother, seeing him, at first cried out and began to weep, but seeing the child she put aside in a moment all her grief and happiness, and set to take care of him with determination and snappy competence. Sanjay's father merely smiled a smile shocking in its absolute toothlessness; both the parents looked alike, he a little heavier and she thinner, so that the years had made them somehow sibling-like, brother and sister in their old age and love. They did not ask Sanjay about the years that had passed, but instead began to feed him enormous quantities of food and tell him stories about neighbours and friends he had forgotten quite completely; so Sanjay sat in his old house, now cracked and conspicuously sagging at the beams, and talked to his old parents, and felt his own cruelty to them like a steel bar in his throat. In this twilight, he remembered his childhood distinctly, with colour and smell and sound, but all the rest of his life seemed without shape and shadowy.

The boy grew colder and close to death; Sanjay knew that when his fever went, if fever it was, he would die. Meanwhile the world was changing every day, the trees were smaller, the town every day seemed to sink a little lower into the mud, the days seemed longer and the boredom inevitable, and a quiet kind of terror drove ordinary people mad in the streets; that this was actually happening, and was not imagined, was so clear to Sanjay that in his letter to Begum Sumroo asking for help and magic he added a cautionary postscript ending: Is there madness in Delhi too? This question the Begum ignored, and answered succinctly only Sanjay's query for strategic advice: if you want to defeat the Englishman's power and save your son, she wrote, burn his books; and she added a flat and unequivocal postscript of her own: Convert; all this is useless; become what I have become; I call myself a Christian, but what I have really become is an English man.

So Sanjay determined to save his child, and taking Sunil, he set out to ambush the foreigner and set fire to his books. The journey to the north was exhausting and long, but to find Sarthey was simple enough: he was camped outside Delhi, surrounded by a jostling crowd of supplicants. They waited until nightfall, and then it took no great skill to evade the two guards, or to cut an opening in the canvas tent, but once in they were overwhelmed by the number of books stacked on folding shelves and crated neatly in wooden boxes.

'Which ones to take?' Sunil whispered.

'She didn't say.' Despite the darkness and the danger outside, Sanjay was battling an overwhelming urge to sit suddenly, to flop down and read and read, randomly and thirstily until he was sickened by surfeit.

'Take as many as you can and let's go,' he said desperately, feeling his self-control waver. They piled books into two thick cotton sheets, made enormous and crude knots, and then stumbled out and staggered through the camp, burdened and clumsy burglars, blessed by some overly-kind thievery-goddess who led them to the perimeter and beyond. By lifting each pack together, by grunting and pushing underneath and using their whole bodies to lift, they managed to get the books onto the waiting horses; the horses blew and stumbled, and as Sanjay walked alongside, a supporting hand on the bulky mass, it seemed that at every moment the tomes grew heavier. Although — scientifically speaking — Sanjay knew this to be impossible, he felt it so strongly that he stopped every half-hour to let the horses rest, against Sunil's advice and increasingly urgent recriminations.

When dawn came they were half-way across a great scrubby plain, ringed by haze and filled by the metallic, unceasing squeaking of crickets. 'Burn it here,' said Sunil. 'Burn it here and let's get done with it. Finish it, and let us go.'

Still, Sanjay hesitated; then, remembering the face of his son, he nodded, and they pushed the books onto the ground. While Sunil struck sparks and made tapers, Sanjay took a few volumes and made a pile; at first the flames seemed barely to move across the jackets and leather-bound spines, and Sunil puffed and blew with obvious kitchen-expertise. Then they got a snapping blaze going, which Sunil judiciously fed with albums and hand-books and manuals; Sanjay sat on a rock and watched quietly, unable to stop himself from reaching out now and then to handle a book, to study its title-page, place of publication, the end-papers, a page or two from the middle, stopping only when Sunil took the piece firmly from his hand and laid it gently on the fire.

Something collapsed in the fire, a noiseless breaking of some leather-bound spine, and with a puffing exhalation the fire blew out a wafting curl of sheets over the ground. As Sanjay darted around the fire, bent over, picking up the pages, he noticed that they were covered with the smallest handwriting he had ever seen, an impossibly fine hand but precise, done with fine nib and green ink in orderly rows stretching from margin to margin without error or smudge.

On the blackened sheet under his thumb, Sanjay read:

I am in Hell. I am in Hell. On my second day at Norgate I thought this repeatedly. Dulwich tipped me out of bed, saying, up, bitch. We were Porter's fags, Byrd and I, puffing at a fire at five in the morning for hot water, for Porter's shave and wash. It was devilish cold, and the buckets pulled out your arms on the long walk back to Porter's room, and what was slopped off through exhaustion had to be made up with another trip. Then back to the long room for a panic-stricken minute or two for your own scrub, then the stairs two and three at a time for morning call at the Rectory, sundry prefects kicking away. I collected a kick on the back of my thigh that left a bruise for seven days, and later I wet my crust and the dab of marmalade was salty. Don't snivel, bitch, said Byrd, here comes Dr Lusk. I am in Hell.

At this Sanjay ran around the fire, kicking at it, shouting, 'Stop, stop.' He batted at the piles of paper, trying to knock out pages to the ground.

'What are you doing?' Sunil said, pulling at him, but Sanjay was now kicking at the blaze, unmindful of the billows of embers which puffed up to sting at him. Pages of the diary — of course it must be that — came out still burning, the threads of narrative disrupted and holed by the conflagration.

'Save these pages,' Sanjay said, still dancing around the fire. 'With the green handwriting.' He noticed then that Sunil had turned away, was facing outward from the fire and paying him no attention at all: they were surrounded by half a dozen horsemen, all dressed in brilliant yellow, bearded lancers who were regarding him with curiosity, in fact as if he were mad. 'Who are you?' Sanjay said.

'We are of Skinner's Horse,' said one of the lancers. 'And you are the thieves we were detailed to catch, but why are you burning your haul? Or are you not? Are you trying to save it?'

Sanjay did not answer, but as the captors stamped out the fire, he managed to push the handful of pages he was holding under his shirt; in the pretence of aiding the soldiers he was able to secure a dozen others, variously burnt and charred. Later, on the way back to Delhi, surrounded by these splendid horsemen, Sanjay had much time to study them; of their skill as scouts and cavalry he had no doubt, since they had appeared soundlessly and suddenly, and in this were the apt followers of their commander Sikander, but it was their costumery that interested him.

'Are you of the unit of Sikander?'

'Yes. We are the riders of the sun.'

'What does this yellow colour signify?'

'That those who wear it embrace death already, and therefore care nothing for death.'

To this splendid Rajput sentiment Sanjay could put no further questions, since all of the lancers so obviously believed in it: they laughed, flashing white teeth against pointed black beards, hitched up their lances and galloped their horses, making wild cries and enjoying the glinting of the sun on their steel helmets and lance-heads, and they were a swaggering bunch who threw their heads back and rode with elegant but careless dash.

'Well,' said Sikander, 'do you like my Yellow Boys?'

He was a little more massive, deeper in the chest like a bull, and heavy with that animal's satisfaction with its power: Skinner's Horse was detailed to police the plains around Delhi, to keep the peace and to put down all miscreants, robbers and banditti, and this morning they had done it with a speed that was likely to add to their growing legend. Sanjay was reluctant to tell him why he had stolen Sarthey's books, because the man in front of him was very respectable and somehow foreign, the kind of person who might laugh at the Begum Sumroo's advice as a joke, or a primitive fairy tale. But then Sikander spoke again: 'This is a bad time to do this, this revenge you wanted. The time is bad. We hear, through pigeon-post and other devices, that the Marathas face the English soon, very soon, maybe today or tomorrow, for the final confrontation. It must come soon, de Boigne's brigades against Wellesley's troops, they are now without the old man, de Boigne is gone but his brigades remain to fight for the Marathas, and perhaps the old Chiria Fauj fights for the last time.'

'Where?'

'Near a village called Assaye.'

'Listen, Sikander,' said Sanjay. 'We have both gotten old, and have gone very far on different roads. But in your letters you are still my brother, and I will speak to that Sikander I see in the letters. What happens in Assaye depends upon what we do here: let me burn those books. Otherwise all is lost.'

'How exactly is that?'

'Never mind, but remember what you saw when you lay shot on the battle-field. Will you deny it now? I have a son, a bright son who will decline if those books are allowed to exist.'

'You are talking magic, Sanjay, and I am concerned now with fact.'

'Do you know who this Sarthey is? Do you remember your mother at all?'

Sikander looked at him without reply, and Sanjay heard how absurd, how insane he sounded in that room: the white walls were bare, there was a brown desk with a white blotter, and the air itself seemed calm and permeated with a rationalism from some other shore.

'Do you remember this?' Sikander said, extracting a plain iron spoon from an inner breast pocket. 'I keep it always. It seems it comforts me somehow.'

'By your mother's memory and last words, I enjoin you to grant me this: I ask for the gift of single combat, and let the victor treat the books as he will.'

Sikander laughed. 'You've really gone crazy. It must be the sun.'

Without a word Sanjay leaped over the table, reaching for Sikander's throat but grabbing only a handful of coat, and despite Sikander's agile weaving he managed to get a hand to his face, disregarding the other's entreaties to stop, stop, and then Sikander shifted his weight slightly and brought an elbow to Sanjay's chest, taking the air out and bending him double, then a tremendous buffet at the base of the neck bringing up the floor and black.

When Sanjay awoke his vision had doubled again; he was in a small, comfortably furnished room, clearly not a cell and yet one which offered no hope of escape. The ventilator, high up on the wall, was barred, and its small white image reproduced itself perfectly, so that Sanjay did not know which was real and which unreal. For a long time he sat on the bed with his head between his hands, rubbing his eyes, but finally he pulled out the blackened mass of paper from his waist-band, stained and made mucilaginous by his sweat, and began to read. They were random sheets from Sarthey's diary, and at first he had to lay them out on the bed to sort them, and while reading there were many gaps, many passages made illegible by fire, others wholly reduced, and so it was a curious, patchwork narrative, all torn apart and shattered, but Sanjay read it as if his life depended on it.

There were four who considered themselves blades, and cut a style with cravats, wide cuffs and a considered and elaborate manner of speech. 'Consider this specimen, gentlemen,' said Bowles (the first time I saw them, all four together and abreast, strolling along the cinder-path), 'what say you regarding this homunculus?' 'A nut-brown baggage, isn't she?' said Bailey. 'Exceedingly brown,' said Hodges. 'One might infer certain inferences.' And Durrell seated himself on a bench by the path, one leg crossed over the other and swinging foot, running a finger over a silver-headed walking stick. 'What's your name?' he said. 'Paul Sarthey, sir.' 'Paul?' he said. 'I think not. You will present yourself at my study post-prep. We shall give you a name. We will have a ceremony and we will give you a name.' I went at night to his rooms.

My father's new house was my new mother's house. We came to it one grey evening in October, and I was cold without cease for four months, until I was sent down to school. Despite fires and coats and blanket upon blanket my teeth shivered and rattled because I knew only the sun of Calcutta. I was cold and always alone. At the dinner table I was silent. Sometimes I was told to go outside and take the air, at which times I circled the house, not straying too far from its grey stone because the country-side was muddy and huge, and full of rough people whose tongues produced accents I could not decipher. Inside the house I was pursued by echoes, but I could be alone and safe. I sought empty rooms in the upper apartments, where there was no sound at all, nobody, and then I would walk in a circle, walk till in a species of trance I was again under a warmer sky, and there was about me the familiar ceaseless chatter of birds, and my friends, and so I would escape the room with its dark furniture, its paintings and wood, all away till a servant came to summon me to supper. 'Don't eat quite so fast, Paul dear, you're gobbling. Use your knife.' She was a large woman with blue eyes, my stepmother.

*   *   *

'You're a nigger.' 'No I'm not.' 'You're a nigger wog.' 'No I'm not.' 'Nigger.' 'I'm not.' 'You're blubbering, nigger bitch. Look at this here. She's blubbering.' 'I'm not. That either.'

The school was day and night, and Durrell had the night and Dr Lusk had the day. At the very beginning I was called into the Doctor's study for an interview, as he wanted to know how much I knew. He questioned me regarding the ancient poets, of which I knew none, of history of which I knew nothing. Finally he said what an atrocious accent you have my boy you must work on it. Your education has been patchy. I can do mathematics I said, and I can engineer anything, a model bridge a working windmill. That's very good, he said, but you are here to learn those things which make you an English gentleman. Character, he said, character. He was massive in his proportions, and in his black robes and with his great head and his measured manner of speech, deep basso voice he frightened me quite wonderfully. Yes sir I said, not knowing at all what he meant. Outside the low grey clouds took me back to the docks on the Hooghly where I had learnt knots. That evening I was to see Durrell.

Am I to understand your people are in trade, said Durrell. I was quiet, for what could I say: my own mother passed to the other side before I could remember, and my father was who he was. Then he married my mother. There was something in him that was attractive to women. On his lecture tours they would flock around him, eager and moist-eyed. In his lectures he would stop, his hands raised up, too stirred to go on as he talked about the great task. I think it was that they loved. My new mother married him against her father's wishes. They waited until he was dead. She was very large, and their money was from candles, and cloth.

Your new name, said Durrell, your name now and forever, is Mary. I kept silent. After that they called me Mary. One takes the names one is given.

Bowles was house captain, and Bailey and Hodges were prefects, and Hodges cricket captain besides, and Durrell was nothing. Nothing official, that is, but he was unmistakably the leader. They all followed him, and undeniably, as soon as I met him, I did too. He was small, or smaller than the rest, with neat, dark hair (After two weeks I parted my hair in the middle, like him), and he looked at you as if he were weighing you, all the time amused. He was completely sure of himself. In trying to think of why we all were his disciples, all I can say even now is that he commanded us because he had a certain <u>moral</u> force, a strength of character that was like steel, which appeared only when he chose to reveal it. For all their pretensions I think there is not one master at Norgate who knew what he really was, who understood his position in the world of the boys, which they knew very imperfectly, if at all. I am sure they all thought of him as nothing more than a middling scholar and a bit of a dandy. He was always impeccable. Even when I was that young, it was clear to me that the others were merely brutes, that their cruelty, even when it was malicious, was only of the canine variety, all slobber and grunting and swagger. Durrell was different. I did not understand him for a long time.

Dr Lusk took a great interest in me, for which I shall always be grateful. I suspect he saw in me a worthy project for his reforming instincts, which I surely was: tempestuous; flighty; emotional rather than analytical, despite my scientific leanings; and given to tears and rages. Whatever the cause or mode of his attention, my conversations with him softened my loneliness, although he terrified me. It was like talking to God: the awe one felt was not sufficient to completely dissipate the enormous reassurance of being noticed. He called me to him often as he walked through the paths of Norgate: Well, Sarthey, I hope you're getting along, eating well. Good morning, young fellow. Sarthey, now I hear you're not applying yourself sufficiently to Horace, and I'm not <u>happy</u> about it. His voice curled itself comfortably about the Norgate stones, so rich and round it was, and it seemed that he must be eternal: I'm not <u>happy</u> about it. He appeared like a black vision in the walks, on the grounds, in the dormitories, and he always knew exactly what was being whispered among the boys, what scandals were brewing, who the culprit was. He was uncanny and fearsome and everywhere.

The occasion of my first switching was an offence observed by Dr Lusk: I secreted a piece of bread from the mess and ate it on the walks outside the classrooms. No bread at school, control your appetites, *young fellow, said Dr Lusk suddenly from behind me, assembly hall Saturday if you please. What's that mean, I asked Byrd. You're in for a flog, old Mary, he said off-handedly, and I thought of nothing for the days after. I woke up thinking about it and slept with it. I suppose I ate and read and did the usual, but not a thing I can remember, and then on Saturday morning there was the Hall. The older fellows got it first. They leaned over a desk, trousers down and shirt pulled over their heads, clutching at the side of the desk. Dr Lusk held out a hand for the switch, a bushy terrible pack of wattles, and I looked away but the sound was like a bowl of water being dashed onto a rock. When it went on I could hardly bear it, and when he finally got to us I could hardly stand, my legs were shaking and I was blubbering. Somebody took me to the desk and they did the belt for me, hauled up my shirt. When it hit me there was a very small moment when it was only a shock against my thighs, and I thought that's all that's all it is, but then it seared me like a fire and I howled. I must admit I couldn't stop it. There was a murmur when I roared — the flogging being the chief entertainment on Saturday mornings, there was a crowd of fellows spectating from the pews and they thought my performance ripping. I got three strokes, and afterwards Byrd said you'll have a fair set o' stripes, one of Lusk's better efforts, close together and nicely grouped. After this I went with Byrd to the Saturday shows. Some of the older chaps took it without a groan. Even watching, I jumped every time I heard it make its thin whistle in the air.*

During the holidays I was always alone. I stumbled about my mother's house, clambered about the grounds. Once my parents had Markline up for dinner, and I suppose he was some class of nobility but he seemed to me a pious bore. He asked me very carefully about my classes, with particular attention to the practical sciences, and wrote down my answers in a little book. And is there anything about Norgate you don't like, he said, looking significant and my father goggling at me over his shoulder. They were both so peculiar that it required me a moment to take their meaning, and when I did I almost laughed. But I said, no, because I was supposed to be very nice to him. That's what my mother said, be very nice to him. It was that he was rich, and better, known to the grandees, so he helped them on their crusades, and he got

me into Norgate. For which I am grateful. But to tell him about Dur-
rell, no. I told nobody about Durrell.

. . . that night Bowles had me to his room. I sat there for a while, on a
hard wooden chair. He had hunting prints on the wall. Then he came
in, and he let on he was drunk, but I think he was putting it on. I mean
he had to act drunk so he could do what he did, which was put me on
the bed. He was cursing and pushing me about, not that I was fighting
him but rather that I was completely passive, even when it hurt. The
candle flickered and he whispered bitch but I didn't shut my eyes, just
bore his weight as if it were far away, and it was. Afterwards I was
very cool and methodical, putting on my pants and buckling up, and it
rather impressed him. The next night it was Hodges, and then Bailey.
So when Durrell called me up, and I went to his digs, and he walked
in, I started to unbutton, and he said sharply, oh stop that, you silly
child. I must have looked puzzled, because he seated himself across
from me, crossed his legs, put an elbow on a knee. You're too sharp for
those simple pleasures, he said. Oh no you're much too keen. I have a
special plan for you. I've been watching you he said.

At first nobody understood what I said because I half-sung my words. I
had a whole new language to learn. Bogs were the privies. When you
were flogged it was a good tunding you got. Not chapel but the gaol
was where we went Sunday mornings for a wailing. Nothing was
good, but it was top.

In mathematics, soon enough, I was at the head of the class. There is
something restful about a theorem when you are far from home and
your heart is like a sore chancre. An angle against another angle is
like all the universe. The question of it is the relief.

Durrell said you have talent. I said what. Look here, he said. What I
want from you is not what they. What I want is you to find a dog for
yourself. D'you see? Bring me somebody you can fuck, and show me
you can, right here in front of me. Now for a moment I had the oddest
feeling. I can't catch it now as I write. It was like an opening up. Like
something had opened then like a seam, as if the evening had ruptured

along its centre and had pressed its warm secret heart to me, revealing itself completely. Like suddenly I understood, like I knew. So I said, but how, but I was nodding yes. Durrell smiled and said, you're a crafty little experimenter, ain't you? Use your imagination.

My father and mother were always talking. In rooms filled with the grey light of piety they talked. But when I walked away from Durrell with my mission I never asked why.

In an attic, one summer, I found an enormous cross. It must have hung in a church, high and life-size. But there had been some accident perhaps, because now there were only the crossed beams, lovely dark wood, and the nails, heavy black iron. The image of Him was gone, perhaps broken and removed for repair and then forgotten, but the thing that was left frightened me terribly. It affected me to a degree that I cannot explain still, because it was only after all a large but perfectly ordinary cross with the nails intact, lying covered with dust. But it was the heaviness of the wood and the thickness of the nails.

I looked around, examined those around me and there were the usual lady lot you find in any school company. I mean there were a few obvious choices, smooth pretty little boys who looked always a little scared because they knew what they were. However none of these interested me, I daresay precisely because it would have been easy or at least plausible. I felt, you see, a certain obligation to perform well, to do something that would gain my mentor's admiration. There had been the note of challenge in what he had said, and the gauntlet being flung I did not think it sporting or manly to take an easy slide. No, he expected great things of me and I wanted to do him proud. So I looked around, and waited, and meanwhile the whisper of the house was that I was Durrell's friend, so naturally I put on side and acted older than my years and took no guff from anyone. He saw all this and I thought I saw a clue of a smile on his face, approving or so I imagined.

Every morning I looked in the mirror hoping the dew, the freshness and the wet would take some of the colour from my skin. I did not like the cold but I became accustomed to it, and after a while I remembered the glare of India and the endless heat plains with horror. But even relief from that terrible sun and the good chill winds of Norgate were never to remove the swarthiness from my skin, and to the last of my stay there were sniggers and cutting remarks, although by the end they learned to be careful. By the end of it nobody called me Mary.

My mother I never knew. I have a very small likeness in a clasped locket, of a thin dark-eyed woman with dark hair. My father's second wife treated me well, and as we came to England and I to Norgate through her money, I am grateful. She was a thick, suety woman, very serious, who had displeased and scandalized her family by following my father out to India and marrying him. A candle and tallow fortune, it was, and then later cloth, but they had hoped higher for her than an indigent missionary. I always thought her charmless and stupid, and as I grew older it was her endless and sentimental kindness that was most annoying to me. When I was rude to her she grew sweaty and fatter with hurt, and even more defenceless, which threw me always into a rage.

It's the Boss, said Durrell, and the lot straightened up, Hodges cupping a cigarette behind his back. Well good morning quoth Dr Lusk, and we chorused back. Except that Durrell drawled Maw'nin, and a look Dr Lusk gave him, but Durrell was ever the cool cove, and gave him back stare for stare. Mr Sarthey you know only the uppers may wear cravats. Take it off and assembly Saturday. You must pay attention to rules, Mr Sarthey, and with that he was off. Six I think for you, laddie, said Hodges. It don't signify, I said and took a wheeze at the smoke. You're growing up, pal, said Durrell. He had somehow realized a perfect treasury of cheap American novels and had taken to a lazy drawling affectation of what he called Yankee speech. He may be the Boss, said I, but he can't do a thing to me. Oh he can't, can he, said Durrell. And I said, just you wait, just you wait. And the others, who knew nothing of our contest, or wager, or call it what you will, looked baffled at us and our friendly chaffing. They had stopped, by now, calling me to their rooms, they had. Couldn't grasp what I was at, and didn't understand their god Durrell's interest in me. He's the Boss, I said, but I'll settle his hash.

We had a fair for Merrie England. The Third Form were peasants. The Fourth tradesmen. Some of the Fifth got to be minstrels, and other diplomats. The Sixth were knights and barons. There were tents on the green, strolling players, theatricals and tableaus. All this was for parents' weekend so Dr Lusk gave a speech on chivalry. What we try to do here is to produce Englishmen he said, and what is it we expect of an English gentlemen? We expect application, but I do not expect my boys to be clever, there is nothing worse than a clever boy who hangs back from his fellows out of pride, who shirks his responsibilities and splits fine hairs over the truth. Were one of my charges to become a cabinet minister but a sophist and an atheist, I should think worse, much worse of him than one who never achieved fame, or wealth, or land, but who told the truth always in a forward manly way, who kept his body unsullied and strong, and who performed his duties as a Christian and a loyal subject of his monarch. We live in a curious wintery age, and although we feel the promise of spring we feel the darkness close around us, for the old times were best, when spears clashed on shields, and hardy knights rode out to give battle to the foe. Here there was honour, and trust, and fellowship, and true faith, a Christianity not weakened and effeminised, but strong and potent, that one might fight the good fight, and bring light to the world. Around you today, as you look at your sons, see not the tender faces of your offspring, but the frank, fearless and forthright visages, loving and stern under plumed helmets, of those who ride by St. George for the cross and the crown.

His voice rose and there was never such a wonderful thing as the flapping of the flags, the colours of the coats of arms and the pages' uniforms, all against the dark sky, and all the boys' faces as they looked at each other with eyes afire, and there was indeed there a band of brothers, and there was not one of us who could have said afterwards that he did not almost weep. All agreed it was the most splendid Parents' Day that had ever been.

The Sixth were doughty knights, and they paid their allegiance to a king, and this was Haliburton, a favourite of Dr Lusk's, a large and lumbering sort of fellow who got red in the face in the games of cricket and through his weight and momentum played a tolerable sort of football. He was good at everything but outstanding in nothing, generally kind to his juniors and sincere in prayers. I liked him, and it was known that Dr Lusk liked him, since he was made the ruler at our revels, and with his height he made a picturesque king. During the speech he sat at Dr Lusk's side and I can see his face plain even now, believing and stirred as all of us. He had fine yellow hair and a trick of holding his head to one side when he smiled, which he did even with his cardboard crown on and his eyes fixed on the doctor. Aye the doctor moved us that afternoon with his vision of what we were, and what we could become, and I believed him as we all did as we must, but the day was not over yet, for I was to find yet the other half. After the speeches and the prizes there was a tea, buns and polite chatter on the lawn in front of Dr Lusk's house; I stood with my parents, feeling shunned. Nobody was about to associate with them, she being scandalous still from the marriage, and he nobody; but them, he and she, exclaimed about the fragrance of the damn buns as if nothing was happening. I suppose they were accustomed to it, or rather judging from their panache they expected it and saw it as a martyrdom. But it was horrid, no introductions for me or them, no invitations to visit, and finally my father decided he had enough and looked around for the doctor. Must thank the doctor, said he, and bustled around, me in tow (she standing alone like Boadicea) until a flunkey told us the doctor had retired, very temporarily, to his study. So what must we do but go thumping into the doctor's house, he had the confidence of the devil, my father; and we proceeded without hesitation into the domain of Dr Lusk, where I had never been, and no mortal boy as far as I know. And a dark place it was, full of enormous heavy furniture hideously carved and ornamented, all stuffed together until you couldn't move without knocking your shins, samplers on the walls and a yellow light about it all. We found the study, murmuring inside, and my father knocked on the door, polite tap-tap-tap, and the wood slid aside, and there was Dr Lusk, sitting still with his arm out, and hunched across from him, the crown on his knee, Haliburton, his shoulders forward and his face serious, stopped in the middle of a sentence. Gratitude, wanted to thank you, said my father, and he and Dr Lusk walked a step or two away to the

parlour to confab, leaving Haliburton and I a-staring at each other.
Now there was something in his countenance so curious, so odd, anger
it was, defiance, and something else, fear, no, terror; and I seeing this
clearly said without thinking, I don't know where it came from —
what were you telling him, Haliburton? At this he sprang up, took two
steps towards me, and said as if he were choking, shut up, shut up. And
now suddenly I had that sensation again, secrets falling warm and
fresh into my hands, barriers parting, I understood it all suddenly, all
symmetry and perfection, and I said, smile on my face and tears of
absolute joy starting to my eyes — Haliburton, you're a bloody sneak.
I mean I comprehended with utter clarity the doctor's omnipotence, his
knowledge; and Haliburton said no, but no, but then back came my
father and the doctor, and we fell to good-byes and thank-you's. Out-
side my mother waited, chewing pensively on a bun, what an appetite
she had, but I was too excited to take offence even at her sticky hug
and her farewell exhortations full of Jesus and prayers. No, I went in
to breakfast the next day and ate the miserable bloody bread and but-
ter in an absolute excitement at the gift I had received; Haliburton I
didn't see all day until he found me after school and suggested a walk.
Now see here, he said, when we were out among the trees, now see
here, I don't know what you thought you were saying yesterday; and he
looked as if he were good for a few more minutes of that sort of pap,
which I think was supposed to frighten me, but I said shortly, Halibur-
ton, let off with that, because you're a bloody sneak. And at the word
sneak he emptied, as if punctured, and I marvelled at this word I hadn't
even known a few weeks before. I had to learn it, and learn that at
Norgate you could be a debauchee, a wastrel, a cheat, a thief, and still
the boys would think nothing of it and certainly there were some who
would think you a fine fellow for it; but if you were revealed to be a
sneak it was the end of your career and your life. You were forever
marked, and you were let known it by word and blow; it was the
furthest insult to schoolboy honour, and so now the word sneak took
the strength from Haliburton like a knife. Now look here, he said, but
pleading-like now, Dr Lusk thinks you're a fine fellow, and I've seen
you looking at him, you know his task, and he needs to know things,
it's very important, you can't run a school if you don't know certain
things, what's going on, d'you see? I see you're a sneak, Haliburton.

There's nothing dishonourable about it, said he, and Dr Lusk said so.
You're a bloody liar and a sneak, Haliburton, gentlemen don't peach on
their friends and fellows. So now he looked stricken and rushed off,
and I let him go; stewing in his predicament, I suppose he was, and he
couldn't tell his mentor, because even if they found a pretext to expel
me I would tell, by crook or hook or spite, and there was the end for
him. The next day at Assembly he looked frightened, as if expecting
the worst, I mean he was walking around looking into everyone's faces
as if trying to conjecture if they knew, and when he saw me he smiled a
pursed little smile, and then I knew I had him. I sidled up to him after
the talk (Dr Lusk in fine fettle about the field of honour) and whispered, see me in your rooms at four. At four I went up, amidst curious
glances, because everybody knew I had been taken up by Durrell, so
what was Haliburton about, but inside he was half-delirious with fear.
As soon as the door shut he said, quavering, you haven't told anyone,
have you, old fellow? He had a spread laid out, toast and marmalade
and tea and fat sausages, and I sat down and took a bite before I
shrugged, no. Have some of this marmalade, he said, and coolly I took
it, and said, listen here, Haliburton. I'm not going to tell anyone. Yes,
he said, yes. He was leaning across the table, holding out a jar, and I
put down my knife and reached across, the devil knows where I got the
confidence, but I reached across and touched his hair, stroked it you
could say, and let my knife-hand knuckle rub across his cheek, and he
went from red to white and back. I won't tell anyone, I said, if you do
what I say. He shut his eyes, trembled, the jar still out to me and
shaking, and eyes still shut he whispered yes. What, said I, what was
that, Haliburton? Yes.

In the afternoon, before dinner, there was a furious game of football,
the fellows of the Upper House and Gartner's against the rest. The
numbers varied but there were always enough for a huge hacking knot,
all elbows and boots and knees, and somewhere the ball. You'd come
out of it scraped and bleeding, panting and red in the face, wrung out
as if you'd been to a battle. You'd lie down on the grass and feel your
chest heave, your team sprawled beside you. Then somebody would
say once more into the breach gentlemen and you'd say your mother
but all the same you'd spring up, and it was glorious.

*   *   *

We do not mollycoddle your sons here said Dr Lusk. We make them on these playing fields into soldiers.

Durrell is dead now these three years, murdered by a berserk native in Hong Kong where he served as a consular official. But Dr Lusk is still alive.

and Haliburton's thighs white under his shirt and Durrell's face half hidden by shadow and pale and perfect. And I said to Haliburton you over there and he bent over the foot of the bed and when I raised up the shirt his face hidden by the sheet which he had bunched up in his fists around his head and his shoulders shaking. Every beat of my heart roaring through my temples but I knelt over him but could do nothing, loosen up, damn you I said loose loose but still I was thwarted, it was not him but me I was too nervous and filled with disgust, and looking up at Durrell's face like marble, eyes hidden, I was filled with shame and springing up I took a riding whip from the mantelpiece and swung. At the first stroke my frenzy passed clean away and I felt instead a keen interest and curiosity, and the second was placed to the best of my ability and with restraint and complete calculation, and at his groan I was complete. But I laid on better and better and his buttocks tightening and flinching away and then giving way and soft and on I went until the room was filled with the sharp slaps and the blood ran black in the light. Then I leaned over her and her head moved limply on the end of her neck in time with me and the blond hair against the white sheet, and I looked at Durrell who leaned forward an elbow on his crossed knee and his eyes like brilliant knife-points in the dark and he said, no, observe, observe. He turned her face to me and we looked together at the half-open mouth and the stained cheeks and now I understood

Hey Sarthey d'you want to come along to town said Byrd. So we walked together, and far ahead of us on the country road were fellows ambling along, capering and talking. The trees hung over the hedges so that we were in a tunnel of shadow but on the golden fields the sun lay brightly. And locking arms we walked.

When Sanjay had finished reading what he had of Sarthey's diary he was overcome by fear, and this was a horror he had never known. It was not the fear of the unknown, nor the apprehension of death, nor the pain of blood and laceration. It was a sensation of flying apart, of falling to pieces inside and vanishing, and every moment of holding on demanded an effort, as if he were on a ladder that slipped eternally from his grasp. It was dark outside, but as Sanjay forced himself to walk in circles around the room he saw and sensed the first light. He made himself think of an immediate problem, which was how to dispose of the pieces of paper on the bed before he had to face Sarthey, as he was certain he must soon in the day. Somehow he felt that he had to hide his knowledge, that it was advantageous to appear ignorant, and so he examined the room carefully but there was no window open, no chink in the wall, no hiding place at all. Finally he stood at the bed again, picked up a tattered piece of paper, trying not to look at the fine script on it, and thrust it into his mouth; it turned into a sticky mass in an instant, elastic and hard to swallow, tasting bitterly of ashes, but despite a quick rush of nausea he persisted and finally forced it down. One by one, one piece after another, walking around the room, sometimes bending over and clutching his stomach, he ate it all, and when he finished he leaned panting on the wall in a cold trembling sweat.

He heard Sikander's voice before the door opened, and so he stood rather formally with his hands behind his back, facing the threshold. 'The Marathas lost at Assaye,' Sikander said as soon as he came in. 'We just received word by relay messenger.' Sanjay said nothing, having known this for a certainty during the night, and now feeling as if all this were inconsequential, since he had already decided what he must do. 'De Boigne's brigades are destroyed. The Chiria Fauj is gone: they fought like lions. They knew they had lost and they went on. It was no pretty battle of manoeuvre, no flying cavalry, no great movements. It was a great slogging business, the brigades standing firmly and the British moving up and firing and firing. Then the brigades closing ranks over the casualties, and it went on through the afternoon until there was nothing left. It is all gone. It was a butcher's business, and the English won.'

He looked again at Sanjay, awaiting a response, but Sanjay saw only the flat light of the morning, and all the images of the Chiria Fauj disappearing into a mess of mud and bone seemed only real, only what must happen — there was no horror in it.

'Mr. Sarthey is here to see you,' said Sikander.

Sanjay waited impatiently, consumed by a sense of mission; he felt now as if something was over — the Brigades of Hindustan were gone — as if something had changed, and something was gone forever, so there was no need for idle talk or recriminations. He awaited Sarthey's abuse with equanimity, and when the Englishman appeared Sanjay looked straight into his eyes with such indifference that the other was taken aback, flabbergasted and silenced.

'What were you thinking?' Sarthey said. 'You, even you?' Then, irritated by Sanjay's silence, 'I suppose I was a fool to anticipate anything else. One couldn't expect anything of a primitive like you, no matter how well you mouth English. Despite the polish you remained after all what you always were: a little unschooled savage.'

Sarthey's contempt made no impression because Sanjay had already dedicated his life to killing him, and though the fear was huge and present he had already learnt how to manage it behind a wall of resolve and logic. He looked at the Englishman's mouth opening and shutting.

'He is mad,' said Sarthey. 'Let him go.'

As soon as Sanjay was released he went to the house of Begum Sumroo, which was a short distance away and famous throughout Delhi. When he left, he had not looked at Sikander, saying only, 'I will come for you,' and at the Begum's house he brushed aside all polite enquiry about his health, and stood very still, staring at a wall until he was allowed in for an audience. Before she could speak he said, 'I wish to speak to you alone.' She sat up at his rudeness, but then settled back slowly, motioning her attendants out of the room.

'I have no time,' he said. 'But you will forgive me. I come to ask a boon.'

'What?' she said.

'Am I your son?'

'I have heard it said.'

'Is it true?'

She shrugged.

'I was once told a story about the first time you saw the man called de Boigne. You said, "Everything will become red." You said something about an idea.'

'I said it, but I do not know what I meant. It was like a dream. I saw him and I said it.'

'It does not matter. Listen. The Brigades of India are gone. The time has changed. I will drive the English from India. But to do this I ask a boon.'

'What?'

'I have heard you know things.'

'I don't believe half those things myself.'

'Nevertheless I ask you to tell me. You know the old books, and so I ask you to tell me.'

'What do you want?'

'I wish to be strong. I wish to be hard. I wish never to die.'

She flinched, and her eyes grew watery and old. 'It is very difficult.'

'I can do it.'

'It is dangerous.'

'I will do it.'

'Do not ask this of me.'

'I must ask you.'

'I am your mother and father and you cannot ask this of me.'

'I am your son and I ask you.'

'Go home, Sanjay!' She stood up and screamed at him. 'Go home to your poor mother and your father and be good to them. Write poetry and have children and live in your own city and die there like a man who is loved and who has a home.'

'I cannot,' he said. 'I was born and my mother held me up and said I was born for vengeance. I cannot flee.'

'You know nothing about freedom,' she said. 'And even less about dharma.'

'Still you must tell me.'

She sank to her knees. 'Go find a mountaintop,' she said. She leaned close to him and beckoned him forward and whispered in his ear for a long time.

'Everything will become red,' he said when she finished. 'I will come back to you when it is finished.'

She shook her head. 'I think I may be gone by the time you are finished.'

He knelt and took a fold of her dress and touched it to his forehead. Thank you, Mother.

'And when Sanjay left the room, walking very quickly, the Begum Sumroo drooped her head onto her knees and wept,' said Sandeep. His voice was cracked a little now from telling the story for so long, and his face was thin. 'Begum Sumroo wept, and after a while her attendants crept back into the room, and one of her favourites scuttled up to her and laid her head on the Begum's knee. Then the Begum began to stroke the girl's head, and the skin on her hand was covered with fine wrinkles. The Begum Sumroo's hair was white, her eyes were deep black, her face was lined and she had lost very many of her teeth. Her house was gold and very beautiful, and the birds flew over it and it was surrounded by mango trees and guava trees. This was the Begum Sumroo.'

'The *wicked* Begum Sumroo,' said the other monks.

'Yes,' said Sandeep. 'And everything will become red.'

When Sanjay left the Begum's house, he found Sunil waiting outside, and together they walked to the north; they went to Hansi, where in the ruins of the town — and it was ruined again — they found, scattered and sitting each alone in meditation, the remnants of Jahaj Jung's unruly army. Sanjay spoke to them in the name of his father, George Thomas, and spoke to them of destiny and revenge; by now these soldiers were naked and bearded and matted, each of them was a monk. But when Sanjay spoke to them their radiant eyes filled with tears, and slowly passion entered their bodies, and anger filled their hearts, and they shook themselves wildly, and they left behind their huge delightful solitudes and said, we will come with you. So Sanjay, accompanied by Sunil and forty-seven ragged soldiers, walked to the hills of the north. They went first from the crowded plains into the abundant wilderness of the terai, and then up onto the slopes, where scattered villages hung precariously on the sharp ridges, but they left even this behind and came to the bare valleys of ice and rock, the crevasses and gorges through which the wind came like a blow. Here they stopped before a nameless peak, knotted and ugly, the sheets of rock coloured black and silver by icy water.

Sunil started up the slope, but Sanjay held his elbow and drew him back, pointing to a dark rift in the side of the mountain.

'It was to be a mountaintop, I thought,' said Sunil.

'A top is too open for what we must do,' said Sanjay. 'We will do it down there.'

It was a cave: the entrance was a narrow slit, which opened into a huge cavern, into depths of darkness so deep that their voices were lost without echo.

'It is here that we will do it,' said Sanjay. 'Sunil, wait outside and guard the door. Cover the entrance with rocks and bushes so that we might not be disturbed. And you, my friends, we are setting off on a great adventure. We will do this ourselves, but also for our compatriots. We will suffer, but for a great cause. In the end, we will triumph and our enemies will vanish from the battle-field. We will be invincible.'

Bowing, Sunil left, and Sanjay and his companions walked a little further into the cave, until they were completely in the dark, in the heart of the hill, their torches unable to dispel the illusion that they were falling endlessly through space.

'Come, my brothers,' said Sanjay. 'Let us start.'

They sat in a circle, and in the middle they lit a small fire with sandalwood they had carried up from the plains. As the fragrant smoke curled up into the darkness they chanted together, 'Death, come to me, come to me, Death.' Then, when they had repeated this a thousand and one times, each of them, without stopping, drew a heavy sabre. Sanjay, his motion reflected around the circle, laid his left hand on the hard stone in front of him, raised the blade, and with a single blow took off his little finger. The shock wrenched him so that he dropped the sabre and faltered in the chanting, but really it never stopped, and when he grew used to the pain Sanjay picked up the little curl of flesh and tossed it into the fire with all the others. The flame flickered for a moment and then began to burn even more fiercely, and the smell of it filled Sanjay's head. He held his hand to his chest and continued to chant. When it was time to take off the ring finger Sanjay managed without difficulty, but when it was the thumb he had to remember every insult he had ever suffered, not only from the English but every small hurt and pain of rejection and lost love that had ever lingered in him, every tiny bit of past misery to be able to bring the metal down on himself again. Now it seemed the fire was roaring inside his head, and through the tears in his eyes he could see dark shapes dancing on the smoke, and when he cut his elbow he shouted his agony and the cave replied with murmurs in a thousand languages and the chanting was shaking his body. Once he saw a face in front of him, one of his companions, one of Jahaj Jung's wild men, now panicked and shouting, this is madness, madness, let us go, but he shook him off and felt on the floor for the sabre, and found only bone and foul rot. There was a spinning whirlwind filling the darkness with laughter and he saw clearly but seemed to be alone in the cave, then he felt faces pressing on him, eyes and tongues and teeth of men and tigers and dogs, all noise and roaring, everything in the world screaming, but he was possessed by an enormous strength and he plucked off his toes one by one laughing and the fire bellowed like a living thing. There was a smell so heavy and wet with rot that he felt it slide up his nostrils. Then he heard a voice, what do you want, what do you want, but he did not reply because he wanted everything, and knew what he had to do for it. So he felt around him blindly, and found the sabre, hefted it in his hand, feeling his own unbelievable power, and then he awkwardly but surely held it to one side of his head, saying death come to me, and moved with such decision and quickness that he thought he had failed until he felt his head bounce on the floor like a ball and his body far away jetting blood.

He was alone. The cave was empty and he was sitting cross-legged, and for a moment he believed he had dreamt it all, but then he saw, where the fire had been, Yama kneeling, his head lowered, bleeding and bruised about his body. Yama raised his great black head, and said, panting, 'You burn the three worlds with your depravities. What is it you want?'

Sanjay was still feeling for his body, which seemed intact to him.

'Yes, it is all there,' said Yama. 'All except the first finger, which was the first horrible offering. I was brought here against my will. What is it you want?'

'So I've beaten you after all,' said Sanjay.

'What is it you want, little man?'

'I wish never to die. I wish to be hard as stone. I wish to be stronger than their machines.'

At this Yama looked at Sanjay, and the anger on his face slowly vanished, and was replaced by a feeling quite unrecognizable.

'Why are you looking at me like that?' said Sanjay.

'Don't do this.'

'Listen, you miserable bag of wind, you creature who call yourself a god. Don't tell me what to do. You have betrayed us. We lose because they are better. We lose because we live in a world of dreams, we lose because we are as women, as children. They win because they understand necessity. But I will beat them. I will surpass them.'

'Don't.'

'Give it to me. I said you must give it to me. Must I do it again?' Sanjay looked for his sword.

'No,' said Yama, his face wet with tears. 'You have it already. You have become it.'

Sanjay rose to his feet, raised his hands above his head.

'But,' said Yama, 'you must give me one last offering, to seal the bargain. You will be everything you want. You will never die. But you must give me, now, the thing that is most holy to you. Think about it carefully. You must give me that about yourself which is most precious to you. If you lie about what it is, your head will burst into a thousand pieces, and you will die now. But if you are able to do it you will have what you want.'

And Sanjay staggered two steps towards Yama, and they could not look away from each other.

'My son,' said Yama. 'My son.'

But Sanjay reached up, opened his mouth and jammed his fist inside, caught his tongue which squirmed away, held it roughly and pulled, tore it out by the roots and flung it at Yama wet with blood. This time the pain was too great and Sanjay fell unconscious to the ground.

He was naked when he came to himself again. He pushed himself up into a more complete darkness than he had ever known, and as he crawled he pushed aside things that clattered aridly. He groped about until he found a small round object, and felt its smooth and dry contours this way and that, traced a hole in it, another one, and then when he touched a regular sharpness that he knew to be teeth, he flung the skull away with a grunt. It was not until he had gone another few feet that the implications of the skull struck him, that he considered the meaning of the other bones that he was pushing through: how long had it been? They could be dead, all of them, but how could they be bones? But now he felt, all over his skin, not a ray of light but an area of lesser darkness, a direction of fresh air, and this trail he followed until he came to a wall of debris, an irregular avalanche of stone and mud. He began to work through it, and noticed with satisfaction that he was picking aside boulders that would have fatigued a team of oxen, and that his fingers were strong enough to find an implacable grip on even the smoothest of rocks.

He came through finally with an enormous blow of his fist that shattered a rock and released a huge diamond-burst of sunlight that blinded him. When he could see again the mountain hurt him with its colours, the sky was unbearable to look at, and he couldn't remember ever the incalculable complexity of the textures of the world. And standing in front of a rude hut, with an expression of terror on his face, was a portly old man who bore a quite startling resemblance to Sunil. Sanjay tried to speak, and made instead a gurgling sound somewhere at the base of his throat, and at this the other's countenance lifted, and joyfully he stepped forward: 'O my Sanjay, it is really you.'

Of course it's me, you fool, Sanjay wanted to say, but instead he opened his mouth and pointed to his tongue, or the absence of it, and as he did so, he noticed for the first time that he had a thick white beard, that his skin was smooth and unblemished as a baby's, that it was whiter than the snow. He touched himself, not believing the beard, frightened and yet pleased at the same time by the resilience of his body, by the weight he felt in his heels, but even these compensations were diminished by the fact he knew already. He turned and looked back into the cave.

'O my poor Sanjay,' said Sunil. 'No one else is coming. The others are all dead. Only one came out, a long time after you had gone in, and he was mad and he said all the rest were dead and worse. He said that and ran and fell down the mountain, and I thought he was dead, but he got up and ran again, screaming. And I thought to follow him but I stayed, and a week later a caravan came up and told me he had died insane that following day. They are all gone. But I have stayed. I had not the slightest doubt that you would come back, that you would achieve the goal you sought.'

Sanjay looked around wildly, then knelt and traced on the rock, 'How long?'

'My friend, my friend,' said Sunil. 'It has been thirty-two years, two months, and three days.'

And Sandeep said, quietly:

HERE ENDS THE FOURTH BOOK,
THE BOOK OF REVENGE AND MADNESS.

NOW BEGINS THE LAST BOOK,
THE BOOK OF THE RETURN.

THE BOOK OF
THE RETURN

. . . now . . .

'HERE YOU GO AGAIN,' Yama said, 'exercising your national talent for fissipariousness.'

There had been an altercation exactly at the centre of the maidan, suppressed sharply by the police but simmering still in the murmurs that swept through the crowd. It had started over seating, over who had the god-given right to occupy a particular small patch of land. Then the shoving-match between two people had taken on party lines. Which, Abhay told me, meant that the affair now had religious, ethnic, caste, class, and socio-economic overtones.

'No need to tell me that,' I wrote back. 'I know.'

'Yes,' Yama said. 'Of course you know.'

I looked at him curiously. There was no sarcasm in his voice, only sadness. Even more curious, I had to dredge up, with no little effort, a bitterness for my retort: 'All the better for you if we fight. More turnover.'

But his head was sunk between his massive shoulders, and he made no reply to me at all.

Saira was standing by the window, looking out, a wistful expression on her face. 'Why do we fight all the time?' she said. Then, when all of us looked at her, she laughed and shrugged. 'Sorry. Stupid question.'

'Listen, young Saira,' I wrote on a note, 'forget about fighting, never mind about tensions and lock-outs and hartals and terrorists and missile treaties, no, let's have a feast. Let's have the biggest feast the world has ever seen. Let's eat and eat and eat until we're merry.'

'A feast, a hog, a festival of food,' she said, her eyes shining, and she straightened up and stood straight. 'A khana all you wanna.'

Abhay laughed suddenly, and when he spoke there was a joy in his voice, simple and small and complete. 'A celebration of appetite,' he said.

'Yes,' Saira said. 'Well, let's get to it.'

'Hold on, hold on,' Mrinalini said. 'There's a dash of story left for tonight, just a bit.'

What Really Happened.

THEN CAME ANOTHER WAVE of invaders. Some of these invaders believed that their purity was lessened by the beliefs of others, and so they destroyed much: theirs was a faith with a sword. They lived as rulers but their children were born in the country, and they became of the country. The faith itself changed, and, as before, the different peoples lived together. But the struggles for power became larger and larger, and the winners gained unprecedented empires. After a great victory, there were emperors in Delhi, and there was peace for a while, but then the struggles started again. Everywhere, there was struggle. Kingdoms fell, and emperors died or became poets. Over the seas, something else stirred, another people, but no one had the ears to listen to that sound, because they believed they lived in the heart of the world. Ignorance is the destroyer.

Then the English came.

. . . now . . .

WE WERE EATING, sitting on the ground in a circle, happy and laughing. Abhay sat on my right, Saira on my left, and Ashok and Mrinalini opposite. Saira's mother and father sat with us too, and all the children, submerged gladly in food and smells and the plenty of it all. Veg. and Non-veg., rajma and parathas, fish and rice, tandoori and fried, North and South and Gujarati and Calcutta curds, we had it all, and Abhay had revealed, suddenly, an unexpected talent for chutney-making. I was savouring his mango chutney, and from outside, over the walls, came the sound of music and the shouts of hawkers, many of them selling toys for toddlers and rare fruit and unusual delicacies. Our maidan, despite everything, was now full of squalling new babies and dreamy-eyed mothers-to-be.

'Where's that Ganesha?' said Hanuman, stretched out lazily on one of the rafters, scratching his belly.

'Supervising in the kitchen,' Yama said. 'Something special, I expect.'

It was something special, all right, but nothing unusual. Rather ordinary, actually. I knew because I had asked for it. I jumped up, motioned to the others to keep eating, and went behind the house, where under the peepul trees three halwais had been cooking non-stop since the early morning. Beside each of the three huge karhais were baskets piled high with glistening, golden but quite ordinary bundi-ka-laddoos.

'Took a while, but they're doing it correctly now,' Ganesha said. The three halwais had red faces and sweaty elbows. They had grown testy at first with Ganesha's instructions, passed to them by me on notes. But now they were staring pridefully at the perfect laddoos. 'A good laddoo,' Ganesha said, 'is not a simple thing.'

So we called everybody out of the house, and I sat by the baskets and handed them all their laddoos. They queued for them in a long snaking line and I gave to them all.

Then Abhay and Saira came and stood in front of me, their laddoos cupped uneaten in their palms.

'Where's yours?' Saira said.

I took one. Hanuman sat on the wall, Ganesha beside me, and Yama leaned against the peepul tree.

'To life,' Abhay said, raising his laddoo.

'And to death,' I mouthed, raising mine, but I don't know if he understood me.

And then we ate our laddoos, watched over by the gods.

Afterwards we sent the leftover laddoos out to be distributed on the maidan. I sat on the roof and watched the sun set over the city, and the jostling crowd below. I could see them all eating, the leafy platters of laddoos passing from hand to hand. I could see all their faces, eager and laughing in that golden light. The birds swirled madly overhead, rising and dipping in dark waves. There was the sound of music from all directions, and under it all, the murmur of voices, as deep and endless as the sea.

'It's time to start,' Abhay said.

I nodded, and started towards the staircase, and then suddenly I grew dizzy and had to sit down again.

'What's wrong?' Abhay said.

I shut my eyes, opened them, and wrote: I am very tired.

He squatted beside me and put a hand on my shoulder. 'Perhaps we could take a break today, a holiday from telling.'

No. Not now. I don't have time. There's not much left.

'I'm sure the judges will let you off for this evening. Considering the circumstances.'

No, that's not what I mean. Stories change you as you tell them, this story could go on forever but I'm no longer frightened of silence. I have told you of how I defeated death. But Yama is no longer my enemy. I must continue, not to keep his noose away but simply to finish. We are almost finished, and we must finish so we can start again. Let's finish. Hurry. I'm tired. I'm alive but my strength is almost gone. Let me tell while I can. Listen . . .

In London, a Battle Between Immortals.

WHEN SANJAY AND SUNIL CAME OFF THE MOUNTAIN, the snows were melting and the rivers crashed along the gorges with a leaping carelessness. Sometimes the whole side of a cliff would tremble and shear away into the boiling water, leaving a brown dust sliding across the surface. Sanjay walked quickly down the slopes, eager for the coming encounter with a new world, but Sunil hung back, wary, it seemed, of a time in which they were suddenly old men. Their lives were gone, vanished, and Sunil told him of everything that had gone over the years: his shining son was dead, faded and silent; his parents were dead, of disappointment and loneliness; the Begum Sumroo was dead, of peaceful old age and a wish for rest after a life too rich to be called happy; Sorkar and Chottun and Kokhun were dead, Sorkar of a fever which left him deliriously and happily speaking a tongue which nobody at his village bedside understood; the Reverend Sarthey and Markline were dead, Sarthey in his sleep with a contented smile on his face, Markline after a bursting vessel jetted blood through his nostrils and flung him about on the floor of a castle in Scotland; Sanjay's two teachers of poetry were dead, both the Pandit and the Englishman killed by heartbreak when Hart was exiled as an undesirable from Lucknow by the English resident; they were all dead.

'It is incredible to me that death takes us all,' said Sunil. 'Really it finishes all of us. I never really understood that. But we are strange and alive.'

But Sanjay walked even more strongly, hearing this chant of death; he laughed at the trees fighting vainly against the wind and the cutting water, at the birds and their tip-headed looks of terror and their constant struggle. He laughed, and he felt completely alone and invincible. He felt purpose and velocity, like an arrow almost at its target.

In Delhi Sanjay sat in Chandni Chowk, and a crowd gathered around him, staring quietly. He was now used to this, it had happened in every village and at every well. They stopped to look at his white skin, which despite all the walking took no sun, at his black eyes, at the certainty which sat on him like a venomous cloud. He does not speak, they whispered to each other. But he had a seriousness which was extraordinary enough, especially as he sat in the bazaar street and watched the English drive by. A carriage came past, full of holiday cheer and picnic baskets, going gaily towards the Red Fort. A few minutes later another rolled by, and this time Sanjay rose and walked after it, the crowd after him. They stopped in front of the Fort. The carriage had gone in through the gate, and now Sanjay looked around for Sunil. But Sunil had anticipated, and was already in conversation with a Marwari bania, a well-dressed man wearing a gold-lined turban and a fine kurta; he held a perfumed kerchief to his lips as he spoke.

'Where are they going?' said Sunil.

'They are going to look at the emperor,' the bania said.

'You mean they are going for an audience with the emperor?'

'No, they are going to look at the emperor.'

'Look?'

'Yes. They walk in, they go to the private apartments. He sits on an ordinary chair. They walk in and look at him, emperor of Hindustan. They smile. He nods at them. They do not bow because they are English. I think he tries to write poetry. They remark upon the ragged state of the curtains, the meanness of his robe. He is called the Emperor of Hindustan but his writ runs not even in his own city.' He paused. 'The Emperor of Hindustan is a tourist attraction. The Emperor of Hindustan is also a fine poet.' He laughed.

The bania turned to look at Sanjay before he walked away, and

Sanjay recognized with surprise a resolution equal to his own, and understood then that all the cuts he had taken in the cave were matched and even bested by the daily insults that others had felt outside. Another carriage passed, and an English lady peered out at Sanjay through a pair of lorgnettes, and Sanjay knew what she would tell at home: an almost naked, pale man with white hair and wild eyes, my dear, a holy man! Sanjay spat after the carriage, and the crowd murmured, grinning, and the guards at the gate of the Fort, leaning on their spears, laughed quietly. Sanjay took a piece of paper from Sunil and wrote.

Sunil held up his hand for silence. He pointed at Sanjay: 'Hear: everything will become red. Everything will become red.'

Sikander and Chotta were still alive. They were famous, and they lived in adjoining houses, mansions, off Chandni Chowk; they were renowned, and there were tales of their exploits. They and their regiment had tamed the country around Delhi, had made it safe for the people. As they had made it safe they had mastered it for their masters the English; and so the yellow horsemen were feared for their speed and their suddenness. Sanjay heard all these stories as he walked to the houses, and it was as if all the dreams of their childhood had somehow become true, and had become bitter in becoming real. As he knew they would, the houses had gardens that backed up against each other, and between the gardens was a high wall, worn down in one place where someone climbed over often. Sanjay stood below looking at the smoothness where the stone had been rubbed black, and as he turned it all seemed so familiar that he looked around for a huge knot, a ball of entanglement beyond unravelling. But there was no knot, and no stories being told under the mango tree, and so he sat and waited.

When it was dusk, when the birds were quiet, a head appeared on the other side of the wall. It paused for a moment, and then a body swung over: it was Chotta. Sanjay recognized the cast of the shoulders, the way the head was held, but everything else had changed. Chotta was a pinched old man who came straight at Sanjay with both fists, and when Sanjay held him away he struggled wildly, his eyes rolling white.

'Chotta, Chotta,' Sunil said. 'Look at who it is, look at us.'

But Chotta heard nothing in his hysteria, and finally Sanjay made a noise in his throat, a sort of grunt, and this sound drifted them through memory, so that suddenly they were boys mock-fighting, the game was combat, but — unbelievably — Sanjay was the stronger.

'You?' said Chotta, his hands held between Sanjay's. 'Is it you?'

Sanjay nodded as Sunil laughed, it is, it is. Now Chotta was turning Sanjay around, trying to see him in the darkness, and Sanjay was overcome with pity: the skin on Chotta's hands was loose, his breath was sour with age, his hair had fallen back from his forehead. They sat on the ground, and Sunil recited Sanjay's journey, told about the cave in the mountains, the great adventure, the benediction won from death; as he talked Sanjay heard the laboriousness of despair in the slow in-and-out of Chotta's breath, the fatigue of years, the accents of bitterness. When Sunil had finished, Chotta laughed: 'Either you are mad, or I am. Things like you don't happen anymore. You are monstrous, or this world is.' He held Sanjay's hands, weighing their strength. Sanjay was feeling the fragility of the old man's bones under his.

'Do you want to know what has become of us?' Chotta said. 'Listen. Listen. The story must begin with Sikander again, as it started at the beginning. I have followed him for a long time, and even now when I tell my own story it is really his. Don't look so surprised, yes, I have been the faithful brother, the dutiful, but did you really think I never thought about this? Don't I know that I am a peripheral player? It has been sufficient for me. I have watched. I have seen a succession of wars, and the English are now the undisputed masters of India. There is no army that can face them. We have helped them become this, Sikander and I. We have served them faithfully, we have put down rebellions, we have caught thieves, we have intimidated opponents. We are very famous, and we are hated. But you have hated us too. Sikander remembers, long ago, that you told him you would come for him. He told me, fear Sanjay's anger above all, and so many beds are made for him every night, and none may know where he sleeps. But you might say, still, you have money, you have land, you are loved by your masters. No. No. Do you know what we are? They are wise, and they tell us there is a new species on this earth. It is not this or that, it belongs not here or there, it is nothing. In the beginning, when we were born, Sanjay, we were just what we were, the sons of our mothers and fathers, but now we are something else. But time has passed and the years have made us a new animal: chi-chi, half-and-half, black-and-white. Do you know what this means, black-and-white? It means that we are white, so according to the English king's law, we cannot own land here. Ah, you are white, you are honoured? No, it seems we are not white enough, we are a little black, so we cannot get certain medals, this appointment is beyond us, that promotion of course cannot be sanctioned. We are this new thing that nobody wants, Sanjay. I have followed my brother for this.

'He, he has patience. He tells me to be content. He tells me we must not demand too much of life. He *cooks,* he makes chutneys, he spends hours looking for a particular taste, a tang. He has become wise. Now he writes books. He has written a survey of the tribes of Hindustan, Sanjay, a book that describes and classifies. Once or twice a year he is invited to a big Englishman's house, and he gets a new uniform made, and takes them gifts. He is very happy when they call him Colonel. What do you think, Sanjay? Should I be happy? But I think I must be unhappy. This is what I thought. I thought, if my brother is happy, and Sanjay gone, at least one of us should cling to unhappiness. I am tired of this happiness, this content. It seems hideous to me, Sanjay, and I cannot tell why. Shouldn't we be angry? Is it time for rage, Sanjay?'

Sanjay wrote: 'Come with me. We will make war. We will expel forever this thing that has come into us, and everything will be as before.'

'But what about *him*?'

'We will ask him to come with us.'

'He'll never do it.'

'Why?'

Chotta smiled. 'Because he's a Rajput.'

Sanjay smiled back at him, and they both laughed, and a sudden and painful wave of emptiness, lifting to Sanjay's throat — Gul Jahaan, Gul Jahaan — caught him by surprise, so that he scrawled fiercely: 'If he is obstinate, we shall know what to do.'

Chotta leaned forward and put a hand on his knee. 'He is my brother. Let me see what I can do. I will talk to him, not telling him you are here, not yet. Let me say this and that, let me ask, let me see what he says. Meanwhile, you stay here. Our spies are everywhere but here.' He got to his feet. 'I will send food.' As he walked away he called over his shoulder: 'He is also yours.'

Sanjay motioned: 'What?'

'Your brother.'

*　　　*　　　*

So Sanjay made his revolution from a garden which was not of his youth; the trees were the same, the sky brilliant beyond, and every evening Chotta came out to sit with him, but nothing was the same. Every day Chotta brought news of Sikander, and Sanjay's curiosity grew slowly stronger. Sikander, it seemed, was now a scholar: he had written a survey of tribes, an academic text which was presented to the English resident. To fulfil his battle-field vow he had built a temple, a mosque and a church, a large church in the centre of Delhi, but it was the image of Sikander bent over a desk, bi-focalled, an erudite quill in hand, which angered Sanjay. What has he become?

'But you've become so strong,' said Chotta. 'Look at that too.' He was now given to asking Sanjay for little exhibitions of strength, which made him giggle. 'Here: this nail.'

Sanjay twisted the thing into a horseshoe, and Chotta laughed with pleasure. Sanjay scratched into the mud: 'Have you talked to him about war?'

'I did,' said Chotta. 'He said: war destroys the victor.'

'Does he want the English here?'

'He says, "I have eaten their salt." '

'Do they not insult him?'

'He says, "I am a Rajput and I have eaten their salt." '

'They betray him every day.'

'He makes pickles, and chutneys. In the mornings vegetable-sellers come to his back door and he buys fruit. He collects recipes. He stirs things in his kitchen. When I talk to him of war he looks surprised, as if I were talking about something new.'

'He's gotten old.'

'Perhaps he has.'

'Does he ever come here?'

'Into the gardens? No, this is my place. I wander here. I have eight wives, Sanjay, and many children, but I come here and I am lonely. When I was a boy and I was lonely I thought, when I am married I will be lonely no more. But now it is so bad with them and with everyone else that it drives me here to be alone. I am lonely so much I cry at night and I don't know who it is that I long for. Why am I lonely, Sanjay?'

'I don't know.'

'Nobody knows. I have the impression that it is incurable, that I caught it long ago.'

'It will pass.'

'I think never.'

Sanjay too felt the loneliness, but he gloried in it; it made him feel like an enormous bird coursing through the skies, glittering and jagged. And all the people who came into the garden, traders and soldiers and maids and ministers, all of them came to him with the kind of awe that one gives to something so strange that one is no longer scared by it. They listened to him while he preached the death of the English, their removal from the soil of Hindustan, their dishonour and their coming disgrace, but it was really him that they were interested in, his enormous strength and the white brilliance of his skin. So in his old age, suspended in a frozen youth, Sanjay achieved a secretive nation-wide fame, and fulfilled, in a manner, his most cherished dream of childhood.

Late one night in summer, Sanjay heard Chotta walking towards the garden; Sanjay could never sleep now and his darkness was filled with plans and calculations. At night, Sanjay noticed no difference except the change in temperature and the lessening of noise, and so he strategised in the darkness; he was trying to bring about a simultaneous taking to arms all over Hindustan, an orchestrated turning to battle, and he knew it would take years, decades, but he was no longer frightened of time. So he was awake when Chotta came to the garden sometime after midnight, but he was unprepared for the questions that were brought to him.

'Tell me again what will happen.'

'Everything will turn red.'

As Sanjay traced the words on Chotta's skin, he noticed the cold sweat on his arm, but the pulse was steady and slow.

'Who will die?'

'All of them.'

'Who?'

'All.'

'All right.'

Chotta rose and walked back towards the house, but on the way he turned back. 'I find it impossible to get angry any more,' he said. 'It must be age, or the time.'

Before Chotta went, Sanjay tried to motion, attempted to say something, but it was very dark, and in any case he did not know what it was he was signing. He sat back, breathed through his nostrils, first the right and then the left, but all night he was unable to continue his planning. There was something that he thought he remembered, and always forgot just as it appeared.

In the morning the sun had just appeared above the roofs when Sanjay heard the first shots. He got up and ran to the house, and even as he ran he congratulated himself on his new speed, but the shots were faster, they came one after another without pause, and yet there was something very deliberate about them. They came like an even drum-roll and Sanjay knew there was murder in it, so that when he ran through the sitting-room at the front of the house and saw a maid-servant leaning against the bloody wall it was only what he expected. In the courtyard in the middle of the house there were three more bodies, there was a cook huddled under the dining table, his cheek-bone shattered, and on the stairs up to the roof a woman lay head downwards, her chunni a long green trail up the steps to the top. The shots were on the roof, and when Sanjay came up out of the stairwell Chotta was feeding bullets into a large black gun.

'Have you seen one of these?' he said. 'Revolver. Six shots without reloading.'

The sun was behind him and he appeared to Sanjay as a silhouette darkened by white light. There was a trail of blood moving slowly through the crevices between the bricks on the roof; it turned a right-angled corner first in one direction and then another.

'Miraculous,' said Chotta. 'Fire and fire and fire.'

Sanjay took the gun from him and in the same sweep pushed him to the wall. He held him easily to the stone, a hand on his throat, and then he felt a blow to the small of his back. He turned, dropping Chotta, and stopped a hand at his face, held it absolutely still. Sikander first struggled to release himself and then blanched with shock.

'You?'

'Yes, it's him,' Chotta said, stepping out from behind Sanjay. He was unbuttoning his coat collar. 'It is him, come back from the mountains of ice with a new strength.' He peeled off his jacket, dropped it to the ground, and began to remove his shirt. 'He didn't do it. I did.'

Sikander was looking at Sanjay, leaning forward, holding his hand where Sanjay's fingers had made white marks on the skin. He looked away slowly, at Chotta, his face expressionless. 'You?'

'Yes.' Chotta was sitting on the ground tugging at his boots. He flung one away and it skittered over the roof.

'Why?'

'Because I am disappointed.'

'With what?'

Chotta was naked now. He sat cross-legged at the edge, above the court-yard.

'In you. I am disappointed with you,' Chotta said. 'Do you remember what we were supposed to be? We were supposed to be princes. You were supposed to be emperor, and I was to follow you. I did. I wanted you to be glorious. I spent my life following you, and now I am angry with what you have made me. I was to be a prince, a Rajput, a soldier. I was sure of myself. Today I am nothing. Do you know how I am nothing? It is because I am an Anglo-Indian, which is that thing that nobody owns. I am free and nothing. I am sometimes a soldier, sometimes a trader, sometimes this and sometimes that. I am everything and nothing. I am nothing and in this, my house full of nothingness, I give birth to nothing. So I killed them all and now I kill myself. Give me the gun.'

'No. No.' Sikander reached down and held Chotta by the scruff of the neck and pulled him to his feet. 'What is this? What's happened to you?'

'You can't fight this, big brother. Even your huge arms can't defeat this.' Chotta leaned against Sikander, and he spoke softly and caressingly. 'Ever since Sanjay came back from the mountains I have been granted clear vision. Before that my life passed in a haze of hope and drunkenness. But Sanjay carries with him the coldness of the mountain air, and all who come near him breathe this in, this frigidity, and I saw with clarity the outside of my house, and its inside. Do you know what I saw there? I saw how it pretended to grandeur but was everywhere peeling, I saw the black of the soot on the ceilings I had never seen before, I saw the old webs in the corners, the dried corpses of the long-dead spiders, I saw how my proudest Made-in-England cutlery was cheap and tawdry, I saw everything I had never seen before. And I saw that my wives were bitter, that their laughter was sharp and unbearably nostalgic, that they smoked their hookahs with greed instead of enjoyment. So I asked them, one by one, why are you bitter? And do you know, not one of them asked me what I meant, they just gave me reasons: I do not have enough woollen shawls; my children are not intelligent enough; I hate the place we live in; I have never been beautiful enough. But all these reasons did not satisfy me, they seemed to me to be evasions, but finally I asked my oldest wife, the one I loved first. She shrugged, and said, because we did not become what we thought we would become, because what are you? What are we? And I looked and saw we were nothing. I asked her, I don't know why, have you ever betrayed me? She said no, hesitated, then she looked into my face and saw, I think, how old I was. She said, yes. I said, with whom? She said, it was not important. Who? A servant. Then I saw how our lives are forever not ours. It was not that I was angry at her: it was because I half-expected it I asked. I was not angry. I loved her. But it was that this is not what I asked my life to become. So I did it. Disappointment is an angry disease.'

Sikander's hands slipped to his sides, and then Chotta sat again, tucking his legs in.

'It is interesting that I could not kill the children. I was going to but I could not.' He held up his hand. 'Give me the gun.'

'No,' said Sikander. 'I will not allow it.'

'Do you still believe in your strength?' said Chotta, laughing. 'Poor brother. You are a child still. But there are things your strength cannot fight. Disappointment is stronger than a thousand of you. Look. They say that virtue and penance give a man power over his own death. But I tell you that disappointment is stronger than anything. In the name of disappointment I call upon death to take me.' He looked at Sanjay. 'Take revenge. Don't disappoint me.' He shut his eyes, and took a deep breath. His body seemed to turn an intense red, and all over there were myriad tiny spots that blazed like coals. Then a burning passed over his skin, a searing fire that was hard to look at, and he toppled slowly back onto the roof. Now the spots faded slowly until his skin was white again. Sikander reached out a hand to him.

'He is dead.'

The blood dripped off the roof and made a shapeless puddle below.

*   *   *

At the funeral, Sanjay handed Sikander a note: 'Come with me.' As Sikander read it, Sanjay wrote another: 'Bring your men; we will finish all this.'

'I can't,' Sikander said. 'I've eaten their salt.'

'That's an old excuse even you don't believe any more.'

'I am bound.'

'Even after this?'

'I cannot see any other way out.'

'Will you oppose us?'

'I suppose I will have to.'

'I will kill you this time.'

Sikander said nothing, and Sanjay turned back to the pyre, which had settled into a red glow. He reached in, feeling the heat not as pain but as a foreign element pressed against the skin, and came up with a handful of black ash. As he walked away, Sikander called to him.

'What happened to you?'

Sanjay pointed at him, meaning: exactly what happened to you.

That evening, as the sun set, Sanjay watched as Sunil cooked eight batches of chappatis, each sprinkled with black ash. The smell of the flour was sharp with memories, but Sanjay pressed them away and gave his instructions: each packet of chappatis was to be sent to one of the cardinal directions. At the first village or town the chappatis were to be delivered to those most filled with anger. They were to eat the chappatis, saving only a tiny piece that was to be crumbled and powdered over the chappatis they prepared themselves, and sent on to their neighbours in the next settlement. So the bitter taste of war would spread, multiplying at every eating, until it was rampant and uncontrollable and the hour was right. Sanjay wrote: 'It cannot be stopped.'

Sandeep said: 'So Sanjay prepared a fire for the English. He moved from town to town, travelling without cease by foot and often exhausting Sunil into collapse. His food appeared in every village from Bengal to Punjab, and since it was dusty, small and common no English ever noticed it, at least not until it was too late. There was always the usual, the petty intrigues of small kings, the obsequiousness of the servants towards their masters, the loyalty of the soldiers to their salt, the constant churning of the ocean of trade, and there was no Englishman who understood that everything had changed, that Sanjay walked the streets of Hindustan, which was India now. Sanjay was pale, he gleamed with a hard lustre like machine steel, his hair was white, he was silent, and he spoke to men and women about their humiliation and their rancour, he told them to think about what they loved. He showed them loss. The country grew quiet and the English thought it was peace.'

Sanjay came back to Delhi because there was one man who knew what he was and what he wanted: Sikander. Sikander knew and fought him at every turn, Sikander gathered intelligence and sent out spies and reported to the English, who never believed him. In Agra, Sanjay set up a cabal of Muslim horse traders, but three months after they began their secret work they were arrested for treason by Sikander and executed; Sanjay asked, who is his best friend? An Englishman's name was the answer, and Sanjay said (with bitterness), kill him. This was done, and in return Sikander caused the arrest of a man who was innocent of the Englishman's death, but who was essential to Sanjay's schemes in Delhi, and this agent, a nobleman, was tried for the murder and vulgarly hanged. At this insult Sanjay could bear it no longer, and he sent a message to Sikander asking for a meeting. It was agreed that they would meet on black Amavas night in Hansi.

They met on the barren field where Jahaj Jung had fought his last battle. Sanjay stood, his hands folded across his chest, watching as a slight breeze kicked up dust against his thighs. Some distance away there was a doorway, an empty arch left from some long-disappeared building, and against this Sunil huddled with his men. Three of them were farmers, there was a small land-owner's younger son from Avadh, and two grain merchants, and the other dozen ex-soldiers of all ages. They were cold, but not frightened, even of the Yellow Boys whom they were meeting, because they had seen Sanjay break a man's neck with one shrug, and they knew his coolness and his delicacy. Sanjay felt their eagerness, and the winter's cold against his bare chest made him keenly alive. He was only afraid that Sikander would not come, that he had in his dotage learnt care and the fear of darkness. Sanjay wanted him to come, and it was not the ruin, the door, that struck him as poignant, but the thought that whatever he and Sikander did would be the finish of a lifetime. This was sadly refreshing. The winter earth was new and wet and full of promise.

Finally Sanjay saw a skirmish line of torches curl up out of the horizon. They came slowly, maintaining a sort of patient discipline, an even distance from each other that Sanjay had never been able to get from his men, despite his appearance and their fear of him. It was a skill he found himself envying even now, this effortless military grace, so that when Sikander reined up his horse Sanjay was already angry.

'Halloa,' Sikander said. 'What a hellish long way for a meeting.'

He strode forward, through the wary lines of their guards, and hugged Sanjay, thumping him on the back twice. Sanjay pulled back, and he could see that he was smiling, that he was sincere in his gladness. But Sanjay had no interest in conversation, and he wrote a note and handed it to him: 'Why do you fight us?' Sikander took the note, but was moving his head from side to side, peering at him through the darkness. Sanjay pointed at the note.

'Can you see in the dark?' Sikander said, with an expression more of horror than amazement. Sanjay snatched a torch and held it above Sikander's head, lighting grey hair, dark skin that looked porous in the red light, a jowled face. Slowly, Sikander lowered his gaze to the piece of paper in his hand. Sanjay saw a bald spot on top of the head before him, and was filled with sudden pity.

They walked a little away, into the field, and they sat next to each other on the earth, and Sanjay held Sikander's arm and traced message after message onto it, all asking the same thing: 'Come with us. Why will you not come with us?' Sikander shrugged. 'Do you understand I will have to kill you?' Sikander nodded. 'Why, why will you die for them?' Sanjay told him about the English, what they were, what they had done already and what they wanted to do. 'It is not only that they steal from us. It is not only that our grandchildren's children will starve because they will bleed us into poverty and weakness. It is not only this. Do you remember a voice I used to hear, the voice of Alexander? They are mad, they want more than land, they want to change the world. They will not stop, not ever, when the English are gone it will be somebody else, they will kill everything in their search for beauty. They are mad. Everything else will cease to exist but their madness. Do you understand? We must fight them now or lose forever. Your brother is dead, and he was my brother. Do you remember your mother? We are all lost.'

Sikander was silent, and so Sanjay thought, no, not this, a change of tactics is necessary. He wrote again.

'What is it? Is it what they have given you? You think they've given you honour and wealth? They've made you into a national monument, Sikander. You've become one of the sights of Delhi. They get here, with their children and their nannies and ayahs and dogs and picnic-baskets, and first they do the Red Fort, ladies and gentlemen, mothers and fathers, babies and babas, here please first be seeing the place where Shah Jahan used to hold court; then they go to the Qutab Minar, aunties and uncles, now we are having here the tallest tower in the world, the wonder of the continent; and then they come here, English lords and ladies, now please look at this man, this black man, this nigger man — here, in human shape and form, a mausoleum! His skin has turned into stone, his bones are timbers, he houses the death of hopes and ambitions, but he makes a serviceable shelter for the great ones of Britain. Once it was thought that an emperor lived here, a ruler who would lead his peoples, but as you can see, that was merely illusion, and what lives here now is a doddering old madman (a lunatic inhabits every tomb in this country), a few rot-odoured vultures. But don't be scared, little ones, the old man won't harm you, come on in, sit at his knee, he'll tell you a story, a fine story of adventure and conquest, he has plenty of those, he's served you well, he's dispatched men all over this land for your fathers. Now he sits waiting eagerly for visitors, hungry for an audience, so he can smile and wag his head and entertain them; see how clownishly he acts out the episode, see how he hops and jumps, like this he rode the horse, like this he swung the sword, oh, be kind, children, ladies, reward him with a smile. And then they leave, saying, so, young Robert, did you like the shrine, wasn't it quite amusing in a quaint provincial Indian way? Little Esther, leave that alone, no, it's part of the mausoleum, no, you can't take a couple of bricks with you. Roger, don't let Rover go in those nice rose bushes, he can do it over there, against the side of the building. Now, now, Edward, don't play in the road, watch where you're going, don't use that sort of language, and especially not concerning those wagons, they're taking cotton to Manchester, and iron ore to Leeds, and gold to the Bank of England. No, Edward, all that doesn't belong to this manor — it's not a manor, but a memorial — it belongs to us, because this monument commemorates surrender, fatigue, cowardice. Look at this plaque — what is this shape, Edward? You know this shape. Can you read the writing? — it says, in large carved letters, that dharma is dead, the king has abdicated. That means, Edward, that they have lost, and we have won. Come on, children, hurry now, we're going to the zoo next, to look at the animals, won't that be nice? Grinning monkeys, and miming apes? They've made you into an animal, Sikander, and somehow you don't even feel the insult.'

Finally, Sikander said: 'Everything you say is true. But I am what I am, and I cannot change that. Even you are what you want to deny: you are already changed. I cannot betray them because I have remained what I always was, my mother's son. And you must fight them because you have become what you are, what you had to become. This is also true.' He paused. 'You say I betrayed you, but I am a Rajput, and I have given of my body. I have never been afraid of death, none of us have. We have laughed at it. But you, you were supposed to be a poet. You were supposed to tell us what we should become, what we were. I would have been a king, I would have been anything if you had shown me how. It is you who have betrayed us. You betrayed yourself because you became something else.'

Sanjay slapped him, and Sikander took the blow without a word, without even flinching.

They fought in a ring of torches, a circle of light surrounded by a huge darkness. An unseasonal rain had begun to fall, an irregular flurrying of moisture that released a deep clayey smell from the ground. Sanjay stood naked in the circle and waited as Sikander stripped off his jacket, shivering. Sikander wiped his face with both his hands and then, without formalities, they began. It was over very quickly. In the first moment Sanjay knew Sikander's enormous skill, his years of science that moved him so artfully that he was impossible to catch but gave no impression of speed. Sikander hit Sanjay a dozen times in the first few seconds, smashed him about the shoulders and head, probed under his

ribs with a horned thumb, found a nerve on the inner thigh, but all of it
made no difference. Sanjay was hard and tireless. The blows made no
difference to him and he was content to wait. Finally he caught Sikander in a hug, his arms around the chest, and he held him as Sikander
looked at him with a puzzled look on his face. Sanjay twisted, turned
and they both fell to the ground. Sanjay held him down, pressed him
close to the earth, down, and he felt Sikander strain against him, enormous bursts of strength that drummed against the ground like thunder,
once, twice, thrice, and then Sikander's body broke. Sanjay saw his grey
eyes widen once and then relax. Sikander was dead.

As Sanjay walked away, not looking back, Sikander's soldiers held up
torches to his face. He understood that they were memorizing his face,
that he had made them enemies, and he met their stares with an expression of pride. This confidence stayed with him as he rode away, and
then as he plunged himself into his work. He moved so fast that Sunil
had to organize two teams, one to guard and work while the other slept,
because Sanjay was always awake. There was no village too small, no
regiment too obscure for him to visit with his chappatis and his midnight conferences. He was tireless, and when Sunil told him, they have
buried Sikander in Hansi, he shrugged and went on with what he was
doing, which was a meeting with the head-men of fourteen villages near
Agra. He told these men, be prepared; make weapons and bury them
below the floors of your houses; gather your fellows, discipline them,
train them, and wait. The time is coming.

'Anger is a prolific seed,' said Sandeep to the monks. 'You can scatter it
carelessly, and it will take root quickly. It will appear in cracks in your
windows, it will spread across roofs, it will burst open paving stones,
suddenly, it is everywhere. Sanjay told men and women: they are trying
to make you something else; and in every village it was known that this
was true. It was true. Then a certain cartridge appeared — you know
this — a new kind of manufacture, and Sanjay said, if you put this in
your mouths, it will make you something else. It defiles all faiths, said
the soldiers to each other, it is unclean in every way. The historians will
tell you that this was untrue, that the new cartridge was greased with
neither beef nor pig fat; but Sanjay said, they want to make you some-

thing else, if you eat this you will become something else. And this was true, it was true then and it is true now. Knowing this, people felt anger, and anger cannot be controlled. Sanjay had a plan, a timetable hideous in its complexity; there were passwords all over Hindustan, cells of dedicated plotters, caches of arms, schools of rebellion, but Sanjay, because he was no longer quite human, had forgotten about rage. He forgot about fury because he no longer felt it; sometimes as his speeches were read he spat and grew red in the face, but it was all a pretence. Sanjay thought that kind of anger was a hindrance, and he put it by, what he felt was a huge determination; he could no longer have felt the other thing if he wanted to. But finally anger overtook all Sanjay's plans and defeated his schedule.'

On a hot afternoon in May, in a town called Ranchipur in Bengal, Sanjay heard shots. He was seated under a tree in the bazaar, on an old rocky pedestal that had been built in a circle around the tree. The shots were not the regular cadenced roll from the nearby cantonment ranges, but quick flurries that could only come from combat. The bursts, like pattering rain, came once, again, then again, and in the silence that followed the whole street stood still, quiet, even the dogs quivering on tiptoes, and when it almost seemed that everything had passed, that nothing more was to happen, there came the small popping of a revolver, two shots, then three on top of one another, phap-phap-phap, and then everyone in the bazaar began to run. The shopkeepers shouted as they threw the doors to, a horse ran from one end of the lane to the other, suddenly there were shoes and chappals lying all over the street, the guns rattled and echoed down over the houses. Sanjay ran, and when Sunil and he reached the lines two bungalows were already cracking apart in flames. There seemed to be small groups of soldiers everywhere, some running to and fro purposefully, others huddled together in agonized conversation.

'What's happened?' Sunil asked. 'What's happening?'

Nobody seemed to hear his question, and he stopped asking it to watch a servant, a man in a white uniform and turban, carrying through the crowd a silver soup bowl full of some white stuff, the ladle still in it, his face wet with tears. Sanjay reached out and caught an infantryman by the throat and held him still.

'What's happened?' Sunil said.

'The Thirty-third were put in chains yesterday in Meerut because they refused to use the new cartridge. They court-martialled men of thirty years' service and stripped them of their buttons and chained them in public and took them to jail tied together. So their friends broke them out and they seized arms and they killed all the English, and they are in Delhi already and the emperor is once more the emperor. The English are dead. They will exist no more in Hindustan. We are avenged.'

Sanjay flung him away, and ran through the crowds, but of all the organization that he had carefully hidden, there was nothing apparent in the milling multitude around him. Sunil asked for certain men, those they had chosen to be leaders, but nobody knew where they were. There were some soldiers who were unable to speak, one who cursed those who were weeping and spat on them, and a huge mass of black smoke darkened the neat fields and roads of the cantonment with a seamless shadow. The firing was now mostly in one quarter, around a small church, and the balls hitting the bell made a strange long blare. Sanjay ran around the perimeter of the graveyard next to the church, pulling soldiers into line and directing their fire at the windows. Soon the bell stopped booming and the fire settled into a regular cracking, and Sanjay led a column into the building from the rear. As they got closer to the church, he felt himself getting heavier, and at each step his feet sank deeper into the ground. But he had a velocity that could not be stopped, and using all his strength he rushed on. There were two shots at them from an upper window, but Sanjay did not pause even to look behind, and he was at a heavy black wooden door, which he took off its hinges with one blow of his lowered right shoulder.

There was a thick grey haze of smoke inside, through which Sanjay saw upended pews, and bodies sprawled across the floor. A man with red hair lay at his feet, his throat ripped away and his face turned to the side. Sanjay took a step forward, feeling his own unbelievable weight, and saw, dimly, a red-uniformed officer raising a hand towards him. Sanjay tried to move, but even his breathing was hard now, as if a weight was pressing down on his chest. The bullet took Sanjay on the left side of the belly, and he felt the knock against his spine before he heard the blast. But he moved forward slowly, took the pistol from the Englishman (who stood, mouth open) and flung it aside, leaving the man for the sabres behind him. The long hall was echoing now with screams, and Sanjay walked down the central passage between two rows of benches, indifferent to the contest around him, each step a test of strength. At the end of the hall, he took the two steps up to the little dais and raised his hands above his head. There was finally a quiet in the building, a deep silence without birds or wind or water, and Sanjay lowered his fisted hands and turned to his men. They were all looking at him, at the blue hole to the right of his navel. He smiled at them, wrote a note for Sunil, and then stood pointing at his neck with a quivering finger, at the black mark that circled his throat like an unremovable bruise.

'Don't worry,' Sunil read in a choked voice. 'I've eaten their metal before.'

Sanjay was outside the church, organizing the men into sections when the women and children were brought to him. They had been hiding in a store-room in the basement of the church, four women and seven children, one an infant in blue.

'I am Mrs Treadwell,' one of the women said. She was hugely pregnant, carrying her belly in front of her like a burden. 'I am visiting my sister. I am not from here.' She had fine blond hair, a white dress with an enormous bustle, and a brooch made of black amber in the shape of a horse. 'Oh, do any of you speak English? Surely somebody must speak English.'

No one spoke to her, and all the men turned their faces away, and finally Sanjay motioned at Sunil to take the English back into the church. Now that he was outside, Sanjay could breathe again freely, and he understood that it was the location, the foreign influence of the building that weighted the metal in his body and dragged down his flesh. It was an alien gravity that held him.

Sanjay had determined already that they were to go to Lucknow, where an English garrison held out against a surrounding force of soldiers. He thought about his prisoners, and reasoned: India must be cleansed. He felt strongly that he must be clean and efficient. As he thought of Lucknow, he felt: India must be cleansed. Sunil read from a piece of paper: 'India must be cleansed.' He used the unfamiliar English word, reading from the tiny script on the page, pronouncing it *Een-deeaa*, and said, it must be clean. What does that mean? the men asked. 'It means,' Sanjay wrote, 'that we must leave no English here.' When this was said the men broke formation and they moved away from the church, muttering among themselves. Sanjay called them back with an angry gesture of his arm. 'What are you?' He asked: 'What are you? Do you not know? How many of ours have died already? Do you doubt that they mean to destroy us? Haven't you seen the corpses of the innocents who stand in their path? The fire? The smoke? None of his soldiers had anything to say, but none of them would do it. There was not a man who would do it.'

They stayed next to the church for three days while Sanjay told his men that India must be cleansed. The first morning when they assembled, a full quarter of the men were gone. The next night he posted sentries, but still eleven men were gone in the morning, including three of the guards. Sanjay understood that the contest of wills he had begun with his men would destroy his war before it had properly started, and so on the afternoon of the third day he sent for men from the bazaars. There were two out-of-work butchers, a pimp, and three nondescript goondas who hired themselves out as guards. They were all drunk when they came out to the camp, and once they were there Sanjay gave them huge balls of opium, which they smoked until late in the evening. Then he sent them into the church. When they came out, panting in the dark, Sanjay put a torch to the dark wood of the door. The red fire made a huge circle in the night. The flames lit their way to Lucknow.

All of Lucknow had suddenly become one. There was nothing besides one single struggle raging around the British Residency, where the English held out against regiments that had been theirs yesterday. It was a small white building on a slight rise, surrounded by trees, hedges and the houses of officials, and the English perimeter wound through clumps of trees, along boundary walls and around a graveyard. The morning Sanjay reached Lucknow, the heat was already unbearable for fighting, but the gunners around the camp were putting an irregular barrage into the English position. Now and then a cloud of white masonry would billow off the walls of the Residency building, and a sleepy cheer would rise from the ranks of the attackers. The disorganization, the haphazardness, the unprofessionalism of the attack threw Sanjay into a rage. The men were strewn about the battle-field in comfortable disarray, some of them sleeping, others sharpening their sabres and many cooking. The regiments were mixed together, and many of the soldiers had discarded their uniforms, or had added colourful touches — scarves, badges from other units, helmets from British cavalry — that made it impossible to tell who they were or where they came from. Sanjay asked: 'Who is commanding this?' Those who were awake shrugged.

The next morning Sanjay organized a charge. During the night he had tried to go into the Residency: his plan was to walk in and kill the Englishmen. He was confident, and felt invulnerable, but when he finally started walking he felt the density of his body increase with each step, so that when he was still a good hundred feet from the English breastworks he could hardly move. Each step took longer than the last one, and finally there was a boom from the trenches in front of him and he felt the added poundage of an English bullet in his left shoulder. He turned then and started back, but by the time he was safely back in his own lines he had four more pieces of metal riding in him. So now he knew that the god had played a trick with his boon of invulnerable strength, and that he had to depend on the uncertain will of his countrymen to finish the task. He therefore set them to a charge, and two regiments of cavalry in line awaited his order. They lined up even, as if on parade, and there was a long edge of glittering steel in the morning sun. The officers clustered around Sanjay. 'Where is the artillery?' one asked. 'Isn't there a covering bombardment?' Another said: 'What is the objective? Are there units for follow-up? What if we break through?' Sanjay listened to all this and wished he had Uday by his side, but Uday was long dead (and Sanjay tried not to think of his student, Sikander). This was a craft he did not have, and there were none of its practitioners available. All the Indians were junior officers, and there were no commanders. The questions continued: 'Where are the medical units?' 'Is there to be no forage for the horses again?' Finally Sanjay scrawled angrily: 'There is your objective; they are few and you are many; take the position, if you are men.' The officers shrugged and went back to their men, and a few minutes later the line started forward at a walk. A cheer rose from the trenches, and a moment later a shout came from the

English positions. As the horses started to trot the first shells burst among them, flicking up trailers of dust. Then the rifles started, and the riders hurdled over fallen bodies, and they pressed home to the first breastworks. For a moment there were pistol shots, and one rider spurred his horse up the wall, but he fell a moment later, and then the horse regiments retreated, still taking fire. Sanjay watched them come back, their spirits still high, but he was trembling with impatience and anger. He had conceded always that soldiering was a business of skill, that strength was needed, and agility, and a good eye. But he found now, and over the next few days, that it was an arcane science, and that all the strength in the world was not enough without experience, that success in battle was as elusive as the taste of good poetry. This hard knowledge made him sometimes so angry that he picked up rocks and hurled them over the maidan into the Residency, astonishing the soldiers and only sharpening his frustration, because he knew instantly that it did no good.

The days passed. There was charge after charge, nights of flashing cannon and explosions, there was enormous courage but no one had knowledge enough to break the defences. Finally the besiegers started to run out of bullets and cannon-balls, and so they loaded their guns with any metal thing they could find. They shot, over and into the walls of the Residency, nails, tie-pins, horseshoes, crowbars, pieces of bedsteads, knives, forks and spoons, and one afternoon Sanjay saw a whole bronze statue of a horse flying overhead. He was walking around the perimeter of the camp, looking for breaks, areas of weakness. Even though he looked, he knew he had no talent for it, he knew that a real soldier would see, instantly, dead ground where he only saw a rolling meadow, lines of fire where he saw bunches of wild flowers. But still he looked, and now he watched the horse become smaller and smaller until it disappeared over the broken roofs.

'It came out of him. Look, it did.'

Sanjay turned. There were two small boys, sweaty and dark, carrying cloth sacks full of pieces of the shells fired by the British. They were two of the many who roamed the lines and into no-man's-land, collecting the strange ordnance that was now used to kill. One of them was holding up a metal letter, an *x* in a typeface that looked strangely familiar.

Sanjay stepped up to him and took the letter and rubbed it between his fingers. It was hot and its surface was dulled.

'It dropped out of his arm,' said one boy to the other. 'I swear.'

Sanjay looked at his left arm, where above the wrist a small flap of white skin hung loose. He touched it and the skin flaked away and floated to the ground. Next to the elbow there was a bump, a regular hardness that ridged the skin into a shape he knew. He rubbed at the skin with a nail, and it curled away like a wood shaving, and a Y dropped out of him and clinked onto the ground. The boys whooped and scooped it up.

'Make more,' they said. 'Make more.'

So that summer little fragments of English whistled into the English camp and killed them, killed clergymen, district collectors, wives, tow-headed sons, ambitious young men and their fiancées with fortunes of five thousand. Language crashed down on roofs and crushed babies underneath. Its fire made a smoking shell of the Residency, and all of Lucknow smelt of death.

As the metal fell away from Sanjay's body, he felt himself get lighter. He found that he could get closer and closer to the Residency without being paralysed, and now he knew that in a few days he would be able to go in and finish them all off. But now a terrible thing happened: as he shed the iron, his whole world turned grey. His sharp resolve dulled into endless ambiguities, especially very early in the morning: Is this necessary? Should they all die? In the morning fat Sorkar's voice haunted him with its Shakespearean rags, and little pieces of lyric seemed to flit about over the Lucknow stones. He had noticed his men lose their headlong fury bit by bit, and now they were given to sitting about their cannon smoking and sleeping. They began to desert again at night, and he retaliated with fiery speeches and summary hangings. And then he felt it within himself, this loss of definition, this confusion, this mixing of good and evil, black and white. He tied bandages around his torso and legs so that the letters would stay in his body, but the metal just worked into the cloth and hung there, so that he clinked when he walked. He also saw that the bruise around his neck was fading, which he knew must mean that he was becoming merely human again.

*   *   *

'I wanted to cook.'

It was Sunil. As Sanjay turned to him, he squatted slowly, resting a hand on his thigh. He had lost the ruddy health of the mountains to the war, and now he was a frail old man whose body shook constantly. Sanjay was as usual watching the Residency, but he was glad of the company, because it distracted him from the fact that his body was losing its strength. Now his throws plummeted into no-man's-land, and he had stopped trying because of the effect on the morale of the men he led. He had of late, after many years, begun to feel the need for sleep, but was afraid to shut his eyes because the one time he had drowsed he had dreamt of a church, and had awoken shaking.

'I wanted to cook but I followed you,' Sunil said. 'I waited for you on a mountain after I was certain you were dead.'

Sanjay nodded.

'I wanted to tell you that I am going. I am going to my village. There is something wrong here. There is something wrong with the taste of it. It isn't as I thought it was going to be. Even if we win here it will have been wrong. I have thought about this a long time and now I am convinced it is wrong. I am going. I wanted not to betray you, so I am telling you. You can hang me if you want.'

Sanjay reached out and held Sunil's hand. The skin on the palm was rough and blackened with soot. It felt weightless, and had the translucent look of age. Sanjay wanted to tell him, whatever happened, this is the hand of a great artist. Whatever happened. But his own hands shook and he could not make the letters. The pencil made agitated patterns on the paper. Sanjay looked up at the sun and saw a slow circle of birds high, high overhead. There was a ring torn into the earth, furrows dug into the ground, pieces of skin, fragments of machines, metal and wood, splintered stumps of trees, and everything was broken. After a while Sunil drew his hand back slowly and stood up. He turned and walked away.

The English burnt Lucknow. Finally the relieving force fought its way in, and a fire swept over the roof-tops. Those left in the city fought stubbornly, but their time was gone and there was no rescue for them. Sanjay was in a mansion, a palace once owned by a famous courtesan named Nur, in which the ragged few left of the Ranchipur regiment mounted a final defence. Sanjay loaded their muskets, running from one window to another with bags of cartridges. The shots boomed and reverberated and smoke filled the room with heat. There was a pain inside Sanjay's head that pulsed up and robbed him of thought with every heartbeat. The floor was slippery with blood, and as Sanjay fell and got up he discovered the unfamiliar feeling of absolute fatigue. But the firing continued. Sanjay loaded a musket, his fingers sliding on the cartridge and the searing hot metal of the barrel. The man at the window turned and smiled at him, his top-knot swinging behind his head. His face was black with grime, and his eyes were huge and white.

'Red, red,' he laughed. 'Red.'

Then Sanjay spun across the floor and the window and the wall blew inward and vanished in a cloud of gravel and smoke, and Sanjay saw the roof collapsing gracefully downwards, he felt himself dropping and he knew it was over but the sound that filled his head was not an explosion but a rushing river, water full and heavy and endless.

When Sanjay awoke it was night. His legs were buried beneath rubble, and he scraped against the huge weight on him for hours until he could pull himself free. As he stood swaying he could see fires still burning, and all around him Lucknow was reduced to dust. He began to stumble over the ruins, and the bodies were everywhere. Something moved away from him with a curious rushing sound, and in the glow from the conflagration he saw black vultures swollen with eating, too heavy to fly and hopping clumsily against each other in a moving swarm. The smell from their wings was dank and full and it stayed with him as he tried to find a way out. But the city was gone and he could not tell which direction led away. He knew he was walking in circles, the dark smoke above and the glowing coals on the ground whirled about him, there was a scream in him but he had no tongue for it and Sanjay walked through burning Lucknow, silent.

At dawn Sanjay walked on the banks of the Gomti. Somehow he had left the city behind, but now in the country-side he found the farms abandoned, the villages empty and smoking. He saw a huge banyan tree, its branches firmly planted in the ground, that looked somehow unchanged and complete, in spite of the war that had raged around it. He stood in its shade, and saw the shadows move across the fields. He stood still because he had nothing inside him, no movement, no idea of the future, no memory of the past. The sky seemed to glow in its aridity. The only sound was the harsh cracking of the crickets. When he heard the horses he knew they were bringing his death, but he was eager for it, because the stillness was unbearable.

The horsemen, mostly English, had haltered a dozen ragged men on a black rope. These walked hands tied firmly behind their backs, stumbling a little as the rope pulled at their necks.

'Here's another one.'

'Put him up.' This was a thin, bald man in a pale suit, dirty and stained with patches of brown. There were two men, Indians, standing in front of him, and Sanjay looked at them blankly for a long time before he realized that their tunics were yellow.

'Do you remember us?' one of them whispered. 'God is very good. You must remember us.'

Sanjay nodded. They were two of the men who had stared at his face the night he fought Sikander.

'Because of you,' the man said, 'we stayed loyal to the English. Now it's finished. You'll pay for Sikander.'

The Englishman shouted: 'Get on with it.'

Sanjay felt wire on his wrists, and his shoulders ached as he was pulled below a branch. There were ropes already thrown over the wood. A noose dropped over his head.

'It'll be a good wheat crop this year.' The man next to Sanjay was old, and his neck was veined and creased on the rope. He was speaking to the soldier next in line to him, a Muslim subedar with a pointed and elegant beard and black-rimmed eyes. His uniform was torn and dirty, and a cut on his cheek slowly dripped blood. He was standing erect, his shoulders thrown back, wearing the noose with the dash of a fine scarf.

'The rains are late.'

'But full.'

'Yes. But this area is not especially good for wheat. This and the next five villages are in a low turn of the river. The ground is brackish.'

'Oh? My village is to the north of Delhi. Best land for wheat in all of Hindustan. Twenty-four quintals an acre. Never less.'

The Englishman in the suit was walking up and down the line. His face was working, and his eyes were squinted.

'What does he want?' the subedar said.

'I think he wants us to be scared.'

They laughed, and the Englishman turned away, the angle of his head tight and vicious. Sanjay noticed that he had his hands clasped behind his back, and that in one of them he held a book.

'Good land,' said the subedar. Then his voice choked as an English soldier behind him pulled on the rope looped over the branch. His face turned to the side as he was lifted into the air, legs kicking.

Sanjay felt a pull at his shoulders, the balls of his feet scraping across the ground, and then something like a plane of light moved across his chest, crushing it and blinding him. Time moves, and he sees the world break up into fragments, spinning, the waving fields in the distance, feet kicking next to him, the sun whirling around him, the thunder of hooves, lances, yellow, a tide of red in his eyes, he rises, silence.

When Sanjay realized that he was dead, but that he was still not delivered from memory and from experience, he raged; because he could not speak, he raged silently at Yama, cursed him for the pettiness of his revenge, for his unforgiving vindictiveness, for making him still twist on the end of a rope, cold, lifelessly, undoubtedly dead, and yet alive; and it was certain that he was alive, because as he spun slowly, he saw the plants turning colours and the crop gaining weight on the stalks, he saw the corpses on the branch rot and he saw the birds perching familiarly on the shoulders of the subedar and taking gouges out of the neck that was now dead. But he was dead and yet not dead, because he saw the English ride across the land, he saw them lead long columns of captured peasants and farmers and small tradesmen (there were never so many rebels) to batteries of cannon, across whose muzzles they were strapped one by one; when the guns fired he saw the bodies explode and the entrails spray across the ground and the heads fly turning end over end higher than the top of the banyan tree. He spun slowly on the rope and the birds fluttered around him, but none came close, and in the impenetrable black of their gaze he saw himself defeated, vanquished not just in battle (which was after all not so important) but in the heart, because in refusing to become something else he had changed entirely, because in anger he had lost not only his country but himself. I am not myself, he said to himself, and the rope snapped with a crackle and he fell back to the earth, and somehow the motion was familiar, so that he welcomed the drop even as the ground came up hard and unforgiving; when he hit there was no pain, just a dull shock. He rolled over, writhing against the bonds that held his hands, and finally one of his hands slipped through, tearing the skin, and he felt his face, the hair stiff as straw, and he sat up to look at his naked body, cold and white, and there was something child-like about it, he felt small and weak, the limbs curiously new and half-formed, and he wept: let me go, let me go, I want no more of it, just let me go.

'I'm not holding you.' It was Yama, and he was leaning elegantly against the tree, dressed in a cut-away black tail-coat, spats, a grey bow-tie, a glistening and tall top-hat, twirling an ivory-handled walking-stick from hand to slim hand. 'Really I'm not.'

'What is?'

'Why, you are. You're the one who doesn't want to.'

It seemed to Sanjay that Yama had a twist on his lip, a smug smirk that made his own defeat all the more unbearable and complete, and a dark mass of bitterness and resentment collected in his stomach; damn you, damn you, and damning Yama he struggled to his feet and stumbled away, not having anywhere to go but impelled to move. But Yama walked beside him, lightly and easily, spinning the stick in a shining circle, placing his feet delicately.

'Really. You're the one who has unfinished business.'

Sanjay stopped and groped about for some way to puncture Yama's huge self-satisfaction, and finally flung a feeble dart: 'Why are you dressed like a clown?'

'Why, don't you know? The whole map is red now. Everything is red. Victoria will declare herself Empress of India. Everyone is an English-man now. Including you, but you've been something like that for some time now. And some of them have been something like you. Old chap.'

The stick whistled through the air and Sanjay saw the curving black motion of Sarthey's belt in the moonlight and then the sharp crack, and suddenly every joint in his body seemed to ache.

'Yes,' said Yama softly, 'it seems there's somebody else alive still. A friend of yours.'

'London,' said Sanjay, 'London. It's not over yet. I have to go to London.'

Yama nodded, and before he disappeared into the heat shimmering over the ground, he whispered: 'Sanjay, you've been going to London all your life.'

So Sanjay, who had nothing, set out for London; he was naked, he had no speech, he had no resources, but he could walk and he had no end to time, and a tireless man who has nothing to fear from death can get to London, even if it takes him years and decades. In the Punjab, on the banks of the Ravi, Sanjay was assaulted by robbers (who cared little that he had nothing to rob), and was left for dead in the water, but he recovered and walked on, a little more scarred; near Kabul he was kidnapped by a minor chieftain and enslaved for thirteen years in a barren village near Herat, but eventually the chief died, and in the confusion of the funeral and the struggle over succession, Sanjay walked out of the camp and escaped to the west; he was now wearing an old white smock, and in Persia he was left alone because it was thought he was a holy man journeying to Mecca, and for a while a flock of pilgrims followed him, but they could not keep up with his pace and finally left him with expressions of wonder; in Basra he was given a place on the deck of a ship sailing to Cairo, but the vessel was driven off-course by a storm and capsized on a jagged shore, and so Sanjay found himself covered with salt and naked on a sandy shore; picking himself up, he walked into a sandy wilderness that seemed endless, and the Bedouins who found him kept a fearful distance because his skin stayed a pale white despite the sun; he left them behind when he entered a rocky stretch of desert so terrible that no one had entered it in memory, but when he emerged in Jerusalem he was detained as a madman in a squalid prison that killed its patients with heat and crowding; he did not die, outlived two prison wardens, and escaped by jumping a wall so high that nobody had ever survived the leap; all this time he communicated with nobody, wrote nothing and accepted everything that came with a sense that it was all familiar and unimportant, he had seen it all before, he was driven always by the lure of the end, eager to find completeness; so when on the outskirts of Jaffa he found an open window in a merchant's house, he entered and took bags of silver and gold with a feeling not of triumph, but of necessity, that it was inevitable; then a passage to Crete and on to Otranto was simple, and then the walk up the long length of Italy to Rome was really nothing but easy; here, he purchased a frock-coat, dark trousers and papers identifying him as a Sardinian officer, and as the forger stamped a red visa for England, Sanjay saw his own clouded image in the dusty glass of a cupboard filled with old books, and he thought suddenly, we are not born to be happy.

London swam up on the port bow under a deep red sky, and as Sanjay watched from the rail he had to cover his nose, because a close odour rose from the river; the water was black and viscous, and the smell surprised him because he could hardly remember being affected by his body, he had learnt to ignore the flesh, but now the reek made him gag and his eyes stream. It was a smell he had never encountered before, and he knew it was not human, it was the city, huge and electrified and gassed and geared, the apparatus itself that emptied itself out into the water-course; the roof-tops were endless and black to the horizon, and as the ship moved slowly to the dock, the water surged slowly against the stones like oil, and Sanjay felt as if he were being drawn into a mouth. As he stepped ashore, his handkerchief still against his face, the sailors who leaned near the landing-plank stared at him with interest he knew was caused by his reaction; he had been left alone on the voyage, and he knew it was because of his pallor, the whiteness of his skin, the coldness of his handshake, the black opacity of his eyes, he made them uneasy and they shied away from him, but now he quailed under the weight of London and he thought, I must seem ordinary to them now, I must seem merely human.

'You'll get used to the smell,' said the man flipping through his passport. 'Enjoy it after a while, actually. Once you've been to London, can't live anywhere else. Here long?' Sanjay pointed to his throat and shook his head, and then wrote with a pencil on the man's blotter, and he nodded. 'Officer? War wound? Well, you'll get by. There's some that can speak, but can't speak the language. You've a good hand. Welcome to London.'

The streets were filled with people, but they walked with a furtive quickness that was strange to Sanjay, glancing over their shoulders and jostling each other; it grew dark very quickly and suddenly the lanes were empty, and Sanjay wandered through the streets with no plan, not knowing where he was going and why he was there, he had started so long ago that he no longer remembered why he came. There was a strange feeling pressing at his heart, something so unfamiliar that he no longer knew what to call it — melancholy? sadness? — but it made him unbearably lonely, the wish for a friend, a mother, a father, a need so like a cracking thirst that when the lantern flashed in his eyes he welcomed it and the voice behind it.

'What's your business here? Where are you going to?' It was a policeman wearing a tall black helmet and a cape, and when Sanjay motioned his dumbness the man gripped him firmly by the elbow and played the ray from the dark lantern about his face; a moment later he was blasting shrill calls from a whistle into the fog. In a few moments a jostling multitude of policemen gathered around Sanjay; they ran him off down the alleys, and up the stairs of a police station, through a crowd of angry faces which hurled curses at him: damn foreigner, hang him. Inside, he was seated at a bare wooden table, onto which he emptied his pockets; finally, he was able to scribble a query: 'What is this? What do you want of me?' The young policeman who had brought him in, who answered, it seemed, to the name of Bolton, leaned against a wall and watched as two other men questioned Sanjay: What is your name? What are you doing in London? When did you arrive here? Where were you on the night of 30 September? Sanjay held up his passport, and finally the questions subsided; they took his papers and left, he assumed to check with the crew of his ship, and he waited in the small bare room, with its shelves of files and cosy smell of tea and butter. The policeman Bolton stared at him for a while, and then spoke confidentially, 'If you don't mind me saying so, sir, I'd get a haircut if I were you. And I'd keep off the streets at night. This isn't a good time for people who don't quite look regular, you see, foreign-like, as it were.'

Sanjay wrote a note and held it out: 'Why?'

'You don't know?' Bolton laughed, then sat down across the table from Sanjay. 'There's a madman out there, sir. A bloody murderer.'

The sun was up when Sanjay finally emerged from the station, and the people on the street were buying and reading newspapers with a kind of terrified eagerness, passing each page from hand to hand and talking unceasingly only about one matter. Sanjay bought a rusk from a street vendor and chewed on it as he walked down the street; of late he had started to feel hungry again, and there was no doubt that now he was tired and sleepy, and that he was confused and a little dizzy. He stood on a street corner, unsure of which way to go, when a torn piece of paper on a nearby wall flapped in the wind and caught his eye, and as he peered at it the blood beat in his chest like blows, and it was not the printed headline, 'Fac-simile of Letter and Post Card received by Central News Agency' that roared in his head, but the scripted lettering underneath, the neat precise letters that made their way across the fragmented page:

> *I was not codding dear old Boss when I gave you the tip . . . double*
> *event this time number one squealed a bit couldn't finish straight off*
> *had not time to get ears for police thanks for keeping last letter back*
> *till I got to work again.*

Sanjay looked away carefully from the wall, and two blond children with matted hair and dirty faces were sitting on the pavement, picking at a bone, and above them a large white sign proclaimed 'Estebury's Stationery,' and in the street a large green carriage passed, labelled (on the rear) 'Omnibus' in gold letters, and two young women in black hats walked by, there was a man carrying a pick-axe, the street smelt of horse dung, but when Sanjay turned back to the poster the writing was still there:

> *My knife is nice and sharp I want to get to work right away if I get a*
> *chance.*

Sanjay ripped the poster off the wall and ran, and then as people turned and women shrank away from him he forced himself to walk, holding the scroll of paper firmly against his chest, and he could feel his heart beating against his fingers. At the police station he asked for Bolton, and when the policeman appeared he motioned him to the side of the long hallway and laid the poster on a bench; he pointed at the bottom: 'Any person recognizing the handwriting is requested to communicate with the nearest Police Station.'

'What is it, mate? I'm finished now with my shift and off to home.'

Sanjay wrote across the bottom of the poster: 'I know this man. I have had occasion to study his penmanship. He was my friend. I am certain.'

'Well, out with it. What's the name of this friend of yours?' Bolton was bored now, and he tiredly rubbed the corners of his blue eyes, and Sanjay wondered, don't you want to catch him? but instead he wrote: 'His name is Paul Sarthey. He is a doctor. I knew him once.'

Bolton laughed explosively, and then as Sanjay stared he leaned back against the wall and opened the collar on his dark coat. 'Sorry. But half of London's been here in the last few days, saying their brother-in-law's the one, the man down the street is the killer. And now you. Doctor Sarthey's a friend of yours, is he? Where would a man like that know you?'

Sanjay wrote, 'in India, where I served in a native army,' but it was clear to him that Sarthey was absolved already because of what he had become; according to Bolton he was a renowned Orientalist, a travel-writer of distinction, a trusted advisor to India House on the Eastern possessions, a physician whose practice had included the highest in the land, including the queen's late mother, he was a man of some property, and above all, he had married well, to the sister of a contemporary from Norgate, a Lady Adelia May Haliburton, and their marriage had been famous in all England.

'Besides, Sarthey's old now, must be all of a century. This murderer's so quick he slips away from a hundred of us while the body's still warm. He kills two steps away from a street full of people, and nobody ever sees him. Do you believe a pensioner so fleet that he skips by all of us? You're tired, fellow. Get a bed and a bit of sleep.'

Sanjay wanted to say, the writing's in me, I know it too well to mis-take it, but Bolton walked away, his step weary, and so Sanjay left, the poster folded away into his coat pocket; there was nothing for it, he told himself, but to do it alone, I must stop him, I must. He hurried off to a barber-shop down the street; as a shining razor took the beard off his cheeks, he regarded the face that came up underneath, and certainly, it was not old, but it wasn't young, it was frozen into some indeterminate imitation of life, and when the dresser poured some greasy dark stuff onto Sanjay's temples and rubbed it into his clipped hair, a visage ap-peared in the mirror that was startling in its stark contrasts: the eyes sat like black opals against the matte white of his skin, the hair curved in lustrous black sweeps past reddened lips. A few streets away Sanjay found a haberdasher who provided silk shirts, crimson bow-ties, black coats, grey trousers, polished soft boots, a curious walking stick with a monk's head as the handle and a long slim hidden blade below, and Sanjay thought as he straightened his collar, damn, I could pass for an Englishman.

'Could I have these packages delivered, sir?'

'That will not be necessary.' Sanjay started so violently that he knocked over a stack of grey gloves onto the ground, and as the attendant bent over them Sanjay stumbled backwards, his hand over his mouth; the voice had come from his mouth — of that there was no doubt, but it seemed flat and disembodied, and of how it was happening he had no idea, because he could feel no tongue.

'Are you sure of that, sir? It's rather a lot and it'd be our pleasure.'

Sanjay turned away (mustn't let him see the stump) and spoke through clenched teeth (watch the accent): 'I would prefer not.' There it was again, strange inflections for an Englishman, a little sing-song, but the drawl was about right, and it was undeniably and concretely a voice; he took up his packages and fled the stares of the shop-keepers, and outside, in a hansom he tried it again: 'Do you know a good hotel, please?' It seemed to be coming from his stomach and lower, from the bones of his thighs and the soles of his feet, and the driver's answer was lost in the tears in Sanjay's eyes, and the thought that after all the vernacular is not a matter of the tongue alone, that in this strange new world a man had to die and leave behind his native earth to speak a new language.

That night Sanjay left his hotel and walked the streets of London as an Englishman; he found that if he strode confidently he was stared at but left alone, and he had confidence because he had the clothes of a gentleman, and furthermore he had the sword-stick, and a cosh (purchased that afternoon at a sporting store) in his coat pocket. Besides weapons, he had information: Dr Sarthey, he had been informed by a long entry in Debrett's, lived now in seclusion after a long period of service to the Empire; his wife had died after thirty-four years of marriage without issue, so the mansion in the West End was managed by servants; Dr Sarthey's honours were many, including the C.B.E. and the thanks of the crown on more than one occasion; his publications were numerous and essential to the body of knowledge. Sanjay also knew that Sarthey did not entertain visitors, because that evening he had been turned away by a rotund butler who had refused to even enquire with the master, stating instead that the good doctor saw nobody, at all and ever, and no cards or letters either; Sanjay had thought a warning would suffice to prevent further outrages, that the fact that somebody knew would keep him away, and he had even said this to the butler: 'Tell him I know it's him,' but at this the door had clicked shut firmly, and as he had lingered outside a high garden wall a policeman had appeared down the road, and Sanjay understood that Sarthey's home was truly a castle, and so now he waited in the streets for the man.

The air seemed to be dense and heavy, so that the yellow lights threw a glowing, blurred haze onto the black walls; a blank window-front gleamed, and Sanjay thought, is it madness, why is he doing this? He tried to remember the woman's name, the face that he had sentenced to death, somebody's sister, and he shook in the darkness and had to lean against a cold wall and breathe long gulps of reeking air; no, it is not madness, not that at all, what did I think of in that moment, the pros of this and the cons of that, it is a clarity, a weighing of the advantages and the costs, yes, costs, it's that, it's a logic so sharp and inevitable that it cannot be stopped, it's reason triumphant after all. When his fit of trembling passed Sanjay pushed himself up, steadied his grip on his sword-stick (remembering suddenly his uncle's tale about a huge knot) and whispered, after a very long time, a little prayer for help to his gods, be with me now, and then he walked on.

He saw, now and then, women in the street, and he wondered at the poverty that drove them there in the midst of this terror, and of course it was more than hunger, it was the resplendent belief that life has in itself, the certainty that death could be real for everyone else, for you, but not for me; he spoke to these women, and he showed them a plate taken from a book about eminent men, a collection of laudatory essays (the one on the doctor entitled 'The Discovery of Order') intended to be inspirational; therefore the photograph pictured Sarthey with his chin uptilted, one hand laid across the chest with palm on the heart, there were deep wrinkles etched down from the lips and the hair was now a fine white cloud. Have you seen this man, Sanjay asked, think carefully, have you seen him, but they hadn't, and when Sanjay said, stay away from him, you must stay away from him, they retreated instead from him — he was unable to keep the urgency from his voice, and he sup-

posed the expression on his face was enough to frighten anyone in the
dark, on one of these London nights. But he kept on, from lane to lane
until he was faint with exhaustion, his thighs ached and his fingers
cramped on the sword-stick; he paused finally by an empty cistern,
leaning against a wall with a hand on a thigh, and the complete darkness seemed to reverberate with the harsh rustle of his breathing.

'Well, is it you?'

The shadow by Sanjay's right was leaning against the wall in exactly
the same attitude as him, left arm on left thigh in mirror likeness, and
then Sanjay flung himself away, stumbling on the cobble-stones and
falling to the other side of the lane, when he looked up the figure was
tall and dark against the sky.

'One of the little harlots told me somebody was looking for my father, an interesting somebody. So interesting I had to leave her alone,
lucky thing, and come looking for you. I knew it must be you. My
father. Imagine.' There was a rich laugh under the words, and when the
face came forward into a flat sliver of moonlight the teeth were perfect
and white, shiny, and the eyes above sparkling in young skin, youthful
beyond all dreams, the jawline tight and elegant, the cheeks firm and
red and handsome, the step was jaunty, and Sanjay felt the nausea bubble at the blossoming health of it, and he crouched over and vomited
into the stones.

'Come, come. And I was so glad to see you. At last, somebody to talk
to. Somebody who *understands*.'

Sanjay scrabbled in the dirt and his hands found the rigidity of the
stick, and in a single motion he drew and lunged, the sword sweeping
across the other's shoulder and chest, but Sarthey wasn't there, the steel
cut across stone showering blue sparks, and then Sanjay backed up the
lane, the point swinging from one side to the other, searching for him,
but the lane was empty, Sanjay's eyes still saw the sparks in the darkness, and nothing else.

'Tut. Such vulgarity.' The voice was from above, and when Sanjay
tilted his head back, Sarthey was sitting on top of the wall, one leg
crooked over the other, ankle swinging. 'Of course you want to know
how. How one can leap. Which is mundane, what is of the essence is
why. Why one becomes free of the earth, boing-boing-boing, spring-
heeled as it were, leaping away into the firmament. There was another

cutter before this one, did you know that?' He rose lightly to his feet, and tiptoed along the top of the wall, arms held lightly away from the body. 'I'm being rude. I should've asked, how did you come out of it, I mean, why aren't you dead? But no matter, I have no doubt that it was something like me. Do you know, from this height, what is most prominent about London is filth? It sprawls about in the most annoying way. In the heart of civilisation there are eighty thousand whores. Rut, rut, rut. I've examined it very carefully.' He twisted his face to one side. 'O, o have you seen the devul with his mikerscope and scalpul alookin at a kidney with a slide cocked up? O, o, o.' He laughed. 'Scientific examination, that's the secret.'

Sanjay collected himself, took a running jump at a low wall, scrambled atop, then unleashed a huge back-handed sweep at Sarthey's legs, and the unchecked momentum of the swing toppled him over to the ground, and this time he saw Sarthey soar effortlessly upwards and over, his coat spreading against the night.

'Don't be *silly*. I told you: I'm spring-heeled, I'm light, I'm airy, I'm free. But I remember now, you and your here-to-there stories. You want it explained. All right, I'll tell you. Start, start from the beginning. Now be still and listen. I'm starting from the beginning. I came back. Was that the beginning? We'll say it was.' He was walking lightly on the top of roofs, on window-sills, dancing across walls, and Sanjay had to hurry to keep up with him; he still had the sword-stick, but Sarthey was always a little out of reach, a little too far. 'I came back to England shortly after I saw you in Delhi. That trick you played was underhanded, but really I got all my material back, I had enough for my book. Did you hear about my book? *A Scientific Survey of India and Her People, Her Fauna and Flora*? It set me up, my dear fellow, and it is a great thing to be set up as a literary and scientific lion when one is young, quite apart from dinner invitations; suddenly whatever one does acquires a sort of style. One gets a sort of glow, money puts a glitter around you, not money only, success, a hard halo of beauty, I could see it in my mirror, and yet of course it wasn't only that. It was quite something else, something I hadn't told anyone, a secret you could say. I put everything I saw in India in my book, except for one thing, can you see what it was? Of course you know: it was the matter of the child. That child who glared, who glowed. How could I believe it? For a time I thought I had gone crazy from the heat, that I had dreamt it out of sunstroke, but then I still had my notes, and I could see my writing was steady, reasoned, no question of it, and so one had to conclude that it had really happened. There was no unbelieving it, and yet I had to leave it out, who would have credited it here, they would have thought me insane, me. So I put it aside and went on with my work, doctoring and surgeoning away, and more to the point, paying attention to the pains of those who mattered, it's no small matter to manage the social niceties, a properly-concerned look and a skill at dancing will make you more money and fame than knowing how to cure malaria. I was the favourite among certain old ladies for my quick wit, my sallies at the reigning dames of the day, delivered behind the raised wine glass, barely out of hearing of the poor victim, who is grandly unaware that she is being cut to the quick; I loved those balls, the high colour of the military coats, the sparkling jewels, the dancers sweeping across the floor, but in the carriage afterwards, outside the window there was always a glimpse of something, a face, a ragged-fingered figure shivering in a doorway, and always this wrenched me down, creating a feeling so dolorous that I trembled in anger, the unsightliness of it, the mess so oppressive in itself that I would lean back in my carriage and cover my eyes with my hands. I loved the city, its wide, straight boulevards so filled with light, but always, at unexpected moments, there was the hideous bubbling of the underneath seeping through, street Apaches with their snot-covered faces, the smell, the horse droppings on the streets. I was doomed to be dragged down, but I had another secret, a secret inside a secret, and this rescued me; do you know what it was? Can you conjecture? Do you imagine? You cannot. What delivered me was the edge, the blade, the cutting through, when I sliced through the last wall and the child gleamed through I had it, the first cause, the beginning at the beginning and the answer at the end, the straight line through, the arc, and the universe shivered and for a moment flew into place, it was there and no need to speak of God or gods, I understood. Do you understand? You cannot. But no matter. You need to know what I found out later that afternoon, after you rushed in and fled with the child, no, not in the cadaver but about myself, in myself, it was this: I had become pure spirit, a principle free of this earth, I could fly. I took a walk in the evening, and as it grew dark I turned back to camp, and from the bottom of a river bed I started towards the top, and I stepped lightly over the rocks, jumping from one to another, the water seeping below, and at the last one I looked at the dark edge of the bank above, and jumped, and found myself standing on it, the gleam of the water far behind me. I couldn't understand it, the distance was great, some thirty feet, and finally I thought that I was sick, fevered, and so I took myself home and to sleep, but the next morning I tried it again and found I could leap — from standing still — a good five yards straight up. Now of course I told nobody, but every chance at privacy afforded me glee in this incredible change, this gift, but soon I discovered it was being taken back from me, every day I grew less remarkable, so that by the time I reached Calcutta I was back to my earth-bound existence, dragging my feet like anyone else. It would have been madness to tell anyone, the destruction of a career if nothing else, and so the months passed and I grew to regard the thing as a passing lunacy, a trick of the imagination, an extended aberration of a mind far from home; I was, after all, I told myself often, a scientist.

'At home once again, I devoted myself to my work, I married, in the hurly-burly of everyday affairs and an increasing fame I forgot all about my momentary experience of the mysterious, and when people talked of the supernatural in my presence I scoffed at them, and made a great show of myself as a rationalist of the steeliest order, and I am sure I offended not a few fantasists of the type who like to make each other shiver by tales of monkish ghosts in country houses. But I felt secretly as if I had now a few ghosts of my own: I was given to moodiness, sudden twitches of sentiment that I was unable to comprehend myself, flashes of anger and long periods of the blackest depression, when everything around me seemed as flat as paper and as unsolid, when I fell into a numb silence in which there was nothing except the boredom and nothingness of life; I never understood why this happened, I grew to accept it as the price of intelligence, perhaps, or awareness. It used to take me unexpectedly, I could go from the gaiety of a celebration to this wilderness so quickly and so invisibly that the person I was with, a loved one perhaps, would never know, and they would go on talking, laughing, while I stared at the sickening pink of their gullets and the coarse roughness of their tongue and hated them; it used to happen to me, and it happened to me one evening at dinner, we were supping with friends to celebrate an achievement, a grand success, I had been awarded the Gold Medal by the Society for Scientific Achievement, and we were eating turtle soup and cuts and there was a bottle of Madeira open on the table in front of me, I was happy, when I looked down at the breadth of my shirt front it seemed to me well-filled and solid, and the people I was with were well to know, there was even a duke at the end of the table, and it was all fine, but then as I lifted the bottle to my glass somebody laughed, as I poured and held my silver knife with the other, it was my friend Haliburton, and the sound of it struck me as brutish, no doubt it was not so, because he was a very bred young man, and his laugh must have been handsome, as he was, but it pushed itself against me like some loathsome wet animal, small and leathery-skinned, and suddenly the light howled around me and I was alone by myself in some eternity, I could not bear them anymore, not the table laden with food or the witty talk that flashed, not any of it, I was back in the sweaty hell of Calcutta surrounded by grinning black faces. It was so bad that I pushed myself away from the table, and holding the cloth between my fingers I said, I fear I must leave you momentarily, and before anyone could speak I plunged out of the room, leaving them hubbub-ing, and I was out on the street walking, far, far, very quickly, and suddenly it was dusk; when I took stock I was in some broken-down place I had never been, in a rubbishy yard under a brown house, and so I wiped my face and turned, and trudged down the lane, wanting to find my way back, but then I turned a corner, it was a splintered wooden fence, and leaning against it, face to it, was a woman, and behind her, bent over her back, was a man, heaving back and forth, I stopped, as if in a daze, the man saw me, stumbled back, holding his pants at the waist, fled down the lane, stopping to pick up the cheap bowler hat which fell to the ground, he must have been a clerk or a secretary, but the woman cocked her head at me, still leaning against the wall, not a bit abashed, then she straightened up slowly and as she turned and her skirt fell back for a moment under her there was the darkness, the darkness of creation and pestilential multiplication and I tried to think, think, but she was coming towards me, what'll it be, darlin', coom down for a bit o' slummin', eh, and she reached up to touch my cheek and there was on her fingers the smell of it, the reek of matter its filthy existence and I shoved her aside pushed it away the atrocity and she fell, cursing and crawling away and the knife was still in my right hand and I bent over and cut a line through the right leg the cloth flew apart and the yellow flesh underneath and she screamed, screamed again, I was still, not moving because it was clear to me now, that intelligence is investigative, I was calm now, I felt strength flooding into me as if somewhere a sluice had unplugged, I knew my purpose was to understand, men came pounding down the street, angry and raising sticks, but I was calm, and I looked at them unafraid, they rushed, and I did not attack, I did not flee, I merely took a step forward, and flew.

'You might say then that I had the bare facts of it, as I soared over their terrified faces in their pigsty below I knew what I had to do to fly, that it was the uncovering that freed me from the stupidity of gravity, you may understand it as you will, but I knew that discovery liberates those who dare to attempt the quest, I had been doing it all along in surgical procedures and post-mortem assists but it took the shock to free the power, pure intellect does it for no reason other than to know. I was to go on a trip to Yorkshire the next day, and I went, and explored further on the downs, at night, amongst farms: I stalked by sheep-pens and pig-wallows, I waited, I waited, bulky figure coming in darkness, moving from side to side in the walk, I whistle down behind and swift and sure movement of the wrist and it is done, screechings and wailings as they turn to look at me, holding their bum, but I am away with a laugh debonair, you know, I chuckled and whispered to myself as I winged through the air, happy and sure.

'So now you know, know it's me and what I'm after, yes you do know, I'm not about to give it all to you, after all we feel a certain bond, you and I, and I know you must understand it, feel it as it were. It is lonely if nobody knows, you see, so I wrote those notes to amuse myself, it gives a hint you see, but it's getting a bit light now, I must shove off. Look for me now. Look for me tomorrow, and tomorrow, and the day after, yes, you'll figure out what I'm doing now, what I want. Isn't it lovely to be young and alive? You're still puzzling it out, I'll give you a hint: logic is forever, it does not decay, it is universal, it is the same everywhere, it is infinite.'

With a flap, Sarthey jumped and suddenly he wasn't there, and to Sanjay it seemed as if the cloak had folded in over itself and vanished, collapsing itself into nothingness; he picked up the sword-stick, and he realized now that it had always been useless, but it was something, and he started back towards his hotel, going there because he had no other place to go. He was frightened because he had no idea what he was going to do next, how he was going to stop Sarthey, who was faster, and stronger and invulnerable; he knew also that he could not flee, that he had no choice but to stay and fight, he said it to himself aloud, the voice strange and foreign in the morning: all the world is one now, there is nowhere to run to.

Sanjay's body was tired, but he couldn't sleep, and so he spent his time at the British Museum reading room, leafing page by page through each of Sarthey's books; in the book of Indian travels, he read about: 'Sanjay, a native I thought of some promise, chiefly in consequence of his smattering of education, which he had acquired willy-nilly; however I was to be predictably disappointed, since this man, in a characteristic turn of emotion, for no particular reason, conceived a hatred of me and attempted to steal my books and notes, in which project he was thwarted. He was apprehended by our native forces, but I thought better than to bring him before the courts, as he was so obviously unbalanced; once I had my all-important material back, I let him go.' In the next sentence Sarthey turned back to a discussion of the Indian leopard, and so this was all the notice that Sanjay ever received from Sarthey in his writings, but yet, as he read it, in an immense room crossed by shafts of yellow light, Sanjay felt the unfamiliar shape of a smile form on his countenance, and he laughed quietly, raising the book in front of his face. The other books were more or less technical, on subjects as various as the treatment of prisoners in Her Majesty's prisons, and rock formations in Wales; occasionally, there was an expression of pride, of belief in the future. Sarthey wrote of a bridge in New York City: 'As I looked up at the exquisite geometry of the construction, the shape of it as beautiful as anything ever crafted by the sculptors of classical Greece, I was taken by a dream of a world rescued by the investigations of science, a world delivered from poverty, hunger, disease, war and superstition, by the rational decisions of a polity governed not by emotion, but by scientific principle; the task is before us, we must not quaver. It will be done. It is being done.' Sanjay read till dusk, and then emerged into the streets, and walked into the darkness, craning his head backwards to search the roof-tops, the balconies, the dark sky beyond; Sanjay walked all night trying to think of what he was going to do when Sarthey appeared, because he had no faith anymore in bullets or blades, and he felt weak besides, but Sarthey did not come. Sanjay waited until he saw a vague pale greyness show at the tops of the walls, and then he went back to the library, where he carried on with his reading of Sarthey's work; the later books were increasingly technical, and Sanjay grew lightheaded among abstractions that became ethereal even as they multiplied. That evening, as he walked towards the East End on a street called Bishops-gate, he saw the policeman Bolton; walking up behind him, Sanjay said, 'Do you agree yet it's Sarthey?'

Bolton turned and peered at him. 'What was that?'

Sanjay repeated himself, wondering why Bolton was staring at him so, and then he realized that the last time he had spoken to Bolton he had been a foreigner without a voice, and now he was an Englishman with a clipped accent from between clenched teeth — the man had no idea who he was.

'You'd better come with me,' said Bolton. 'You're not the first one who has taken that name. I expect the inspector would want to hear your story.'

The inspector was a burly man with huge mutton-chop whiskers and the dependable name of Abberline, and he seated Sanjay and launched unceremoniously into questioning: Who are you? How do you know this man Sarthey? What reasons have you for believing it is he? Sanjay told the truth about the details but lied easily about himself, pretending he was a writer, a man who had spent time in India, where he had come upon actual specimens of Sarthey's writing, which he now recognized; he found that it was easy to invent an English name for himself (Jones) and an English life (service in the army, deceased parents), that all the novels and out-of-date newspapers he had read in a long-ago library now became a ready source for this necessary fiction. Finally, Abberline leaned back in his chair and said: 'For our own reasons, we have visited the man's house and seen him; he is old, but that is neither here nor there. We have observed his house, front and back, for several nights running, and nobody comes out, nobody goes in. Supposing he is the one, how do you suppose he does it?'

Sanjay took a deep breath. 'He flies.'

Abberline and Bolton burst out laughing; the inspector sat forward, and his boots thumped on the floor. 'He flies! Of course. Why didn't we think of it?'

Sanjay shrugged and rose to his feet, picked up the sword-stick. 'You have no conception of what you are dealing with.'

'No doubt, no doubt,' said Abberline. 'I don't mind telling you that somebody else told us that not so long ago. A certain mystic, a medium I believe it is called, led us to his house, which he had seen in a trance. We saw Doctor Sarthey, the poor old fellow, he's so feeble he can't stand the light, and he lies in a dark room with the drapes pulled. When we left the house without making an arrest the mystic gentleman made the same observation. Are you also a vision-seer?'

Sanjay was already on his way out, and through a window he saw the night sky black and without end, and without turning he said, 'You will see. You'll see one day.' As he swung a door shut behind him, he heard Bolton's voice trail off, I wonder why the good doctor attracts all the crazy ones, and then Sanjay was in the streets, hurrying, almost running towards the stinking lanes where Sarthey was to be found, and as he went he thought, silence is easier than speech, lies are more believable than the truth. He wandered back and forth through the streets, which he was starting to know, and he thought this again and again, it ran like a rhythm through him, now all that will remain is lies; he was thinking this when he felt a clamp over his left shoulder, and then the street receded below him, the rough texture of the stones shining in the light became a line far below, the lights shrank into points and became a pattern, and Sarthey spoke close to Sanjay's head, whispering into his ear, 'You'll never catch me if you don't think like me. What do I want?' His breath was heavy and sweet, like incense, and Sanjay choked, and Sarthey laughed quietly as he struggled: 'I've found that I can float up here for hours. If you achieve a kind of repose it is really quite beautiful, all that down there, from far away. But then coming down becomes harder and harder. The longer you stay up the harder it is to come down. Some nights I feel like an angel. The moonlight sings to me. I am transformed. Transmuted, really. Not that pathetic child who once was. Not like you. I wrote to Doctor Lusk, you know. One way or another I've told them all. I've even let them see. After one of the events I heard voices and I walked out into the street and there were two policemen, I stumbled artistically and one of them said, sir, are you all right? I said rather. He talked to me, it's cold he said. And then I walked on. A minute later they found the work. But I was gone. A bit of a thrill it was but they're so stupid, you lay it out for them but they can't see it. I've told you most, because I feel you understand. Do you? Answer me. What do I want?'

Sanjay gagged, and then vomited up some white liquid that fell soundlessly back to earth; Sarthey shook him violently, so that his limbs flew about like a puppet's and his head snapped back and forth. 'What do I want?'

And Sanjay said in his beautiful and hollow British accent, 'You want never to die.'

Sarthey screamed, a wild bellow of satisfaction that rolled out over the city, 'Life life life,' and Sanjay felt the grip on his shoulder release and he was dropping, and Sarthey's voice was in his head as the ground rotated underneath him: 'I wish to report my conclusions: I noticed in myself an ability to fly, to cut myself away from the bonds of earth, but still, I grew old. I was free of gravity but not from the dreadful iniquity of entropy. Decay is not fair, it just ain't. I wanted to be pure and incorruptible, the first thing, the cause itself, free like a blade of fire in the dark. I couldn't reason it out, there was no answer. Every time I wielded my scalpel I grew stronger but I still aged slowly, wrinkled and dropped, stunk and pissed. The ageing was retarded, slowed, but it still happened. Damned unfair. But I applied myself, I gave it a try for the old school. Observe, observe. Think it through.' Now the ground is rushing up and Sanjay watches buildings expand and lights are flashing up and he calls Sikander my brother and it is too late. 'Apply logic. Go back to beginnings. Then I got the answer. Go back to the beginning, what everything starts with. That beginning is what I've been looking for. It's filthy but it's what I need. In the beginning is the heat. Tonight I'll get what I want. Or tomorrow. But you can't. You're dead.'

But Sanjay wasn't dead, because he wasn't yet ready to give up life, or life was not willing to give him up, he could no longer tell; he lay on a roof-top, not dead, but every time he tried to move he felt the broken bones all through his body grate against each other, and the sun moved in a grinding arc across the sky, and he saw his father and mother walking through a garden; a tiger painted by gold light on a green forest floor; a burning building and gears turning in circles; a cannon-ball bouncing in the air; a royal lady named Janvi throwing dice on a chaurasa board, laughing, and covering her mouth with her hand; an elephant dancing along a road lit by moonlight; a Calcutta road inhabited only by sweet-sellers and wine-merchants; a boat drifting down the Gomti and a voice singing, *Jaane na jaane gul na jaane, baag to saara jaane hai;* a regiment of cavalry speeding to a gallop and lance-points lowered; his uncle's dragging walk and soft querulous body and his voice whispering, the world is endless and the road is long, sing, my friend, sing, everything that dies must be born. Sanjay was not dead but he knew he had broken, and the pain flew along his limbs, but he felt the fragments knitting together, the pieces pulling together, and though he wept from the ache and his hands twisted and grabbed at the brick underneath, he became alive and whole again; when he was able to push up to a sitting position it was night and he cursed at the fatigue in his bones, he felt old, shaky, and afraid.

He came down to the street by dropping down the wall, skinning his palms as he clawed at the masonry; he had found the sword-stick on the roof, and now he used it as a walking-stick as he hurried towards the station. He knew now what Sarthey was looking for, and how he knew this he did not know, it had come to him when he lay on the roof, and once he knew, it was so obvious that it seemed like he had always known it, but he could do nothing without Bolton or Abberline. He knew what it was but they might know where to find it, and so he stumbled along, wondering whether it was too late, whether Sarthey had already completed his quest; at the station there was no sign of Bolton, and the sergeant on duty was openly suspicious of Sanjay's attire, which by virtue of being covered with dust and ripped in several places was now far from gentlemanly. But when Sanjay asked after Abberline, insisting that he had the most urgent information to convey, the gravity of his tone was apparently persuasive, because he was ushered into Abberline's office.

'Jones, is it?' said Abberline. 'What the hell happened to you?'

'Never mind,' said Sanjay. 'I know what he wants.'

'Jones, if you don't go home immediately I am going to arrest you on suspicion and I am going to sling you into the bloody gaol and I'm going to keep you there.'

'I don't care if you stand me against a wall and shoot me. But listen to me. Was there a murder last night? No? Then there will be one tonight. If you listen to me we can stop him.' Abberline reached out towards the bell on his desk. 'Did one of you constables not see a man a minute or two before a body was found? A youngish man, who looks to be about thirty? A very pale complexion? White tapering hands?' Abberline paused with his hand on the bell. 'His eyes. The most striking thing about him is his eyes. They glow in the dark, they are luminous and unnatural. They talked about the cold.'

'How do you know this?'

'I met the man and he told me.' He motioned at himself, at his clothes. 'He did this to me. You will not believe me, but will you believe me if you see it?'

Abberline drew his hand back from the bell, and now there was a troubled look on his face. 'See what?'

Sanjay said: 'Do you believe that I am speaking to you?'

'Yes, of course you're speaking to me.'

'But look. I have no tongue.' Sanjay opened his mouth wide and stepped up to Abberline, who laughed and then despite himself looked, and then threw himself back, knocking the chair over, and backed up to the wall. Sanjay edged closer to him, pointing at his mouth. 'I have no tongue, and yet I speak. I tell you again, you have no idea what there is on your streets.'

Abberline was silent for a long moment. 'If what you say is true, why is he doing this?'

'He is looking for something.'

'What?'

Sanjay leaned forward. 'Is there a woman in these streets, of the streets, who is with child?'

Abberline took Sanjay back on the streets, where they talked to pa-trolling policemen, to plain-clothes constables, and others, informers, whom the inspector knocked up out of their dark houses and to whom he posed the same question, but nobody had an answer; the night passed, and Sanjay felt fear, once he heard a quavering cry and he and the inspector started and bumped into each other, then stared trembling into the dark until Abberline said curtly, 'Cat.' Sanjay felt the weight of Abberline's curiosity, he knew the other wanted to know about his connection to Sarthey, but this was no time for talk, and so they hurried from alley to alley, always with the same question, which the inspector hid among half a dozen others, have you seen anyone suspicious, have you heard any noises; Sanjay understood that the Englishman was doing this despite himself, that he could not believe and yet believed, and so he waited impatiently, shifting from one painful leg to another, until always the question: A woman with child?

It was very late, past three, when a little policeman named Rollow, a sturdy small man standing straight for Abberline, answered crisply why yes, and then stepped back as Sanjay came forward, mouth working, and Abberline asked who, tell us, man.

'Her name is Mary Kelly.'

'Where?' said Sanjay, 'Where?'

Rollow glanced back and forth from Sanjay to Abberline, then cleared his throat. 'She dosses, sir, in a room at Miller's Court.'

Number 26, Dorset Street, was in darkness as Sanjay and the inspector stepped carefully around the house; each breath cost Sanjay an effort and robbed him of hearing, his pulse beat so loudly that finally he stood still, absolutely still, and Abberline's face was sweaty in the flickering light from a lamp overhead, they looked at each other and they could hear nothing but Sanjay's hands were shaking, he turned his head carefully, something small buzzed through the light and its shadow magnified spun like a wheel on the walls of Miller's Court, Sanjay turned his head carefully, not knowing what to look for but examining every brick, the irregular paving stones, the long pipe running up on the wall, and level with his heart there was a small diamond of light, so tiny that it disappeared when he looked directly at it, but when he turned away it appeared again, a point of light in the wall. He stepped up to the wall, one two three, settling his feet on the ground slowly like an embrace, and his outstretched hand found a sheet of glass, a window, and cloth, a window with one pane broken in it, the gap stuffed with rags and letting through just one burst of light, Sanjay bent his face down (feeling a sensation of falling) and leaned close to the glass, pulled softly at the cloth with his forefinger, and the edge of glass stands sharply in his vision and what is beyond is indistinct for a moment but then it swims and clears into a black bag, a square black leather bag which is open and from which protrudes a steel handle, and beyond that on the floor is a pool of blood, there is a bed, on the bed there is a person, a woman but her face has been cut away, the body has been blasted the flesh peeled from the thighs to the bone, and Sarthey is leaning over her in his shirtsleeves, rolled up, he is concentrated and the light shines on his temples and the long forehead, he picks up her hand and places it slowly and surely in her stomach, in the red cavity where her stomach used to be, the room is red, he places her hand in herself, he is speaking, his voice is steady and calm and low, Sanjay can hear each word clearly, Sarthey says: 'See. See. See, India, this is your womb. This is your heart. This is your bone.'

Sanjay turned, brushing past Abberline, and was at the door pulling at the knob, which would not turn. He held it with both hands and then it suddenly gave way, and he fell forward into the room, past Abberline's arm which came in through the window, he had reached in and pulled back the bolt, and Sarthey was still intent on what he was doing. Sanjay had the sword-stick out and was thrusting but Sarthey turned and took it from him easily, plucked it from the air and twisted it away, reversed it, Sanjay scrambled back but Sarthey fixed him easily with a stab that caught him through the middle, he sat down suddenly, the blade through him. Sarthey raised a finger at him, admonishing, and Abberline was behind him, swinging a cosh, which made a solid thumping noise on Sarthey's head, who turned and lifted the inspector off his feet with a swing of his arm and bounced him off the wall to collapse slowly. Sarthey stepped over his shins, to the door, which he shut quietly, when he turned Sanjay saw his eyes, brilliant and calm, and Sarthey stepped back to the bed, from his bag he lifted an implement, a long knife that Sanjay remembered. Sarthey bent over and worked, Sanjay heard small shifting liquid sounds, then Sarthey lifted something up, holding it in both cupped hands, and Sanjay shut his eyes but the image remained and it was useless, he opened them and Sarthey was staring at the thing in his hand (a piece of somebody, somebody, Sanjay thought), a wet knot of tissue and blood and fluids, Sarthey was muttering, 'Heat, heat, heat,' an expression of exultation and joy on his face, then what was in his hands began to glow, to burn not with flame but an inner radiance brighter than a thousand suns, it seared the room white and Sarthey flung it away into the fireplace and clutched at his eyes, smoke between his fingers, and yet the radiance grew brighter and then it was unbearable to look at and Sanjay turned his face away. When he looked again there was nothing in the fireplace but a blackened and melted utensil of some kind, and Sarthey was kneeling near the bed, his head in his hands, he raised his head slowly and his eyes had become black craters, burnt and bleeding, but it was the skin on his hands that Sanjay watched with horror, because it was spotting, where it had been hard and uncreased it now grew wrinkled, it loosened and grew old. Across the room Abberline was watching, his mouth working, pressed against the wall, and now Sarthey's face was changing, his hair was vanishing, his cheeks fell, sores appeared on his neck, and his shoulders lost their bulk and he grew old. Finally he slumped to the floor and lay twisted, his clothes puddling around the shape of the thin limbs, and his face, with its charred holes, gazed straight upwards with a look of insulted and indignant surprise.

Sanjay pushed himself to his feet, and worked at the sword-stick until it fell to the ground, and the clatter it made seemed to start Abberline from a daze: he jumped up, scooped up the weapon, and brought it down in a huge overhead sweep onto Sarthey, and the blade passed through Sarthey's neck with a dry rustle, easily, and the head rolled to one side, there was no blood, only a little arid exhalation of wind, the fingers on the hand that Sanjay could see crumbled, and collapsed into a fine dust, the body disappeared and the white shirt lay flat on the ground, the fine leather boots lay empty, and still the lips on the head worked, the creased skin jumped back and forth, the nostrils expanded and contracted, and the eyes yet seemed to be staring blindly.

Abberline covered his face with his forearm, and wept: 'What is this? What is this?'

Sanjay shook his head. 'He cannot die.'

'Why?'

'He has found what he wished for.'

'What? What was that?'

'Eternal life.'

The cold air rushing down Sanjay's neck made his new wound ache, but he felt as if its frigid flow were the only thing holding him back from the black precipice of exhaustion; they were in a dog cart speeding towards the edges of the city, with Abberline driving, and the black bag under the seat with its unspeakable burden, next to a shovel. After what had happened, it seemed to Sanjay that Abberline's return to practicality was quick to the extreme and therefore hugely admirable: he had muttered under his breath, wiped his face a couple of times, and then he was suddenly walking about the room taking charge; he had stuffed the rags back into the broken window, he had gathered up the sword-stick and its sheath, he had opened the bag and swept up all of Sarthey's instruments into it, he had lifted the clothes on the floor without flinching, and finally he had brought himself to nudge the head into the open bag, which he then clicked shut. All this time Sanjay had stood with his face to the wall, trying not to look at the woman on the bed, shaking, and when Abberline had tapped him on the shoulder he burst out, 'Who is she?'

'Mary Kelly, I presume.'

'Yes, but who is Mary Kelly?'

'I don't know.'

'I'm sorry.'

'Yes. We must be out of here.'

'I'm sorry.'

'Yes. Are you hurt badly?'

'I will be all right. But I'm sorry.'

'I understand. Come.'

'I'm sorry.'

'Will you shut your mouth and come?'

Sanjay let himself be led out; Abberline picked up a key from the table and locked the door behind them, and then they were fleeing, and Sanjay said nothing more but the same words repeated themselves endlessly in his mind: I'm sorry. Now they were on a dark road, with Abberline going recklessly fast, and Sanjay heard another whisper, a succession of words, and he couldn't tell if it was real, or if his mind was conjuring it up out of the drumming of the wheels, clean, it said, the world must be clean, clean, clean; Sanjay was tired of listening, and thinking, and he wanted to sleep, but he knew it wouldn't come yet.

They stopped next to an enormous iron gate, and Abberline led the way over a fence; once on the other side Sanjay could feel grass underneath his feet.

'What is that smell?' he said.

'It's a cemetery.'

The odour lay over the ground thickly so that there was no escape from it; when Sanjay covered his nose he could feel it burning in his throat, and it was the effluvia of flesh rotting away, the slow dissolution of the tissues and muscles, of the ground permeated by the gasses from human bowels; it made Sanjay's eyes stream and his stomach clench. They emerged from the bushes, and Sanjay saw the darker shape of a church against the dark sky, its steeple and the soaring reach of the towers; finally Abberline stopped, next to a large mausoleum, and began to dig close to one of its walls, and Sanjay stood looking at the elegant outline of the church, tracing it from one end to another, anything to keep back the memory of the room at Miller's Court, and he kept his hand over his nose, but all his attempts were useless, and his mind skittered along the edge of madness and rot.

'Help me,' Abberline said. He had the bag at the bottom of the hole, and now they pushed the earth back in, and tamped it down, and yet Sanjay heard the voice whispering, clean, clean, clean, but he knew now that he was dreaming it, because the thing in the bag was buried, and that he wanted nothing more than to be away. Finally Abberline finished, and they hurried away, and the horse was shivering against the fence; as they got in Abberline caught Sanjay by the elbow. 'Is it finished.'

'It is.'

'I saw the blade go through you, and yet you are not dead. What are you? What was he?'

'We were, we were just ordinary people. We were changed by something.'

'What?'

'It was distance, I think, and a kind of dream.'

'Magic? Do you mean to say, over there? In India?'

'Yes, it was magic all right. But it was never Indian.'

Abberline turned his head away. 'I must be insane.'

They were jolting along now, and Sanjay had to call over the wind to Abberline. 'Is there no chance of it being uncovered over there?'

'No. They won't dig up that patch. Under that mausoleum, I mean. There's a member of the royal family buried there.'

When they reached the city it was early morning, and Abberline left Sanjay at the hotel, telling him to wait, to go nowhere, and went back to the station to await the discovery of the body; Sanjay spent the day lying on the bed, always a step away from sleep, his eyes on the white ceiling; he felt as if something was over, as if a curtain had come down, but he had no strength to draw a moral, and so he examined the plaster minutely, understood the intricate tracery of the cracks, the patterns of the trowel-strokes that were still apparent. Finally he could bear the stuffiness of the room no more, and he went out and walked the streets till evening; the noise was enough to distract him, and he paid no attention to where he was going, and when dusk came he found himself in front of a large palace, next to a huge gate guarded by tall soldiers. A number of carriages rolled through the gate, which closed behind them and a crowd of onlookers cheered; the man next to Sanjay turned to him: 'That was the queen. Queen-Empress Victoria herself.'

Sanjay turned and looked, and the man whose face was sparkling with a huge, excited smile was a very small Indian, a slight man with small shoulders who was wearing a dark evening suit and a tall chimney-pot hat; his English was careful and controlled, and for all his efforts had a Gujarati lilt under it; and he was very young, maybe seventeen or eighteen.

'Yes,' said Sanjay, and he found himself smiling. He pointed at the book the other carried beneath his arm. 'Are you a student?'

'Yes,' the man said, holding the book up; it was Bell's *Standard Elocutionist*. 'I am trying to teach myself proper English.' There was something trusting about his face, something innocent and straightforward, despite the stylish suit and the air of attempted dandyism and the huge hat, too large for the head, and impulsively Sanjay reached out and shook his hand, and felt a rush of wonder at the fragility of the bones, the thinness of the hand.

'Good luck,' Sanjay said. 'I am quite sure you will do well.' He paused, still holding the little hand, and he felt a welling of tenderness that brought tears. 'May the gods bless you.'

'Thank you.' In the gathering darkness the man's eyes were almost lost, but Sanjay could see they were surprised, and pleased, and that they were liquid and brown, almost black. 'Thank you. I must go home to dinner now. Good evening.'

'Good evening.' As the diminutive figure walked away, Sanjay said, 'By the way, what is your name?'

But the young man was already lost in the crowd.

Abberline was waiting for him in the lobby of the hotel, and when Sanjay walked in they nodded to each other and walked up the stairs without a word.

'I must go back to India,' Sanjay said to Abberline as soon as the door to his room was closed. 'I must go back and I have no papers. Or no papers that will suffice now.'

'Why not? I thought you had travelled extensively.'

Sanjay shook his head. 'I'm not who you think I am.'

'Not Jones?'

'My name is Parasher.'

'You're not English?'

'I am. But I am Indian.'

'How can you be English if you're an Indian?'

'It is precisely because I'm an Indian that I'm English.'

Abberline threw up his hands. 'These riddles and paradoxes are too much for me. I want you away. What has happened here in the past few weeks, that thing in the cemetery, all this has no place in my city. D'you understand? I'm a policeman, a detective, I can't believe I'm here talking to you. I don't know who you are or what you are, but I'll get you the papers and I want you away from my city. Is that clear?'

Sanjay wanted to say, but all this *is* your city, your London, but he only nodded; he saw curiosity on Abberline's face, and, stronger, fear, and he understood that the man wanted to ask him questions, but that he was afraid of the answers, and he was glad, because to answer he would have to look back at his whole life, and of this he was afraid. So they said no more to each other that evening, nor the next morning when Abberline brought him a passport and a ticket, or when he saw him through customs at Southampton, walked him to the ship and bid good-bye to him with a nod; they said nothing to each other except farewell.

On the ship Sanjay closed himself in his room and waited out the days; he did not even look out of the port-hole as England vanished, and he paid no attention to the activities on the vessel, or to the people who passed away the time with games of shuffle-board and walks around the deck; he sat on his bunk cross-legged with half-closed eyes and waited. But one day, shortly after they had passed through the Suez Canal, the vibration from the engines ceased and the ship slowed to a halt, and a hush descended, stilling even the holiday-makers, piercing through Sanjay's careful detachment: it was the silence of death. He went up to the deck, and saw that the sea was flat but always moving with number-less sparks, and a crowd of people was gathered about the stern; when he came up they parted to make way, because there was a mystery about him, the man alone in his cabin, he was pale, and now his hair was losing the dye of London and was whitening again. There was a body stitched in canvas on the deck, and the captain was reading from the Bible; Sanjay asked who it was, and an officer leaned over to his ear and began to whisper: 'He was a seaman, the oldest seaman. Perhaps the oldest sea-man who ever lived. A peculiar fellow. He was on ships all of his life. Literally, that is. He would take service only on liners from India to England, and back again, and only those. But in port, in Bombay or Dover, he never went ashore, he would remain on the boat, waiting until it took to sea again. He was old on this vessel when I came aboard twenty years ago, and there were old men who remembered him on other ships thirty years before. He spent his life on the water. Between here and there.'

'What was his name?' Sanjay asked.

'John Skinner.'

'John *Hercules* Skinner?'

'You knew him?'

Sanjay nodded, trying to recall a vague memory of Sikander's older brother, the brother who had gone to be a sailor, who had never been heard from since, who had vanished into the great sea. Now the officer had hurried over to the captain and they were talking in hushed tones, and then both of them took Sanjay aside.

'You know this man?'

'He is my brother.'

They exclaimed in wonder, and agreed eagerly when Sanjay asked if he could see the body; the group of passengers watching buzzed with excitement as the ship's carpenter cut away the stitching on the shroud and peeled it back. The hair was white, the face was long and angular, and Sanjay had no recollection of it at all, but he could see the resemblance to Sikander, and Chotta, and the captain exclaimed, 'He looks like you.' As Sanjay watched he grew aware that something strange was happening to the body, that its outlines were flickering, that the cheekbones were growing translucent, that he could see through the eyelids, that the corpse, in fact, was becoming invisible; the captain must have seen the same thing, because he blanched, shook his head irately, like a man with a headache, and said, 'We must go on with the ceremony, sir.' Sanjay drew the shroud over the face, and they closed it up again, and he stayed next to it through the prayers; when they finally let it overboard it barely made a splash in the calm golden sea, and Sanjay turned and walked back below decks, and by the time he was back in his cabin the engines had started again and the ship was making headway.

The sea at Bombay Harbour was choppy, and Sanjay came to the quay in a launch; it was raining, and whole sheets of water seemed to be falling from the sky to explode against the buildings. Sanjay made his way out of the dock-yard as quickly as possible, leaving his luggage behind, and after making his way through the pack of shivering tanga-wallahs at the gate, he walked down the flooded streets. The shops were shuttered, and there was no one on the roads, so that when Sanjay took off his coat and dropped it into the swiftly-flowing gutter there was nobody to notice, not even when he took off his shoes, his pants, and everything else; finally he walked naked through the city. He walked all night, and the next morning he was in the country-side; the rain had washed away the last vestiges of black from his hair, and when the few villagers out at their fields saw him they assumed he was a sadhu, who else would be walking naked in a monsoon storm. Sanjay walked on, and the rain continued unabated, and then he became aware that somebody was walking beside him; it was a farmer in a white turban, a thin man with wiry muscles drawn like cord, skin blackened by a lifetime in the sun, a face grown patient from a thousand seasons of planting and cropping.

'You again,' Sanjay said. 'Yama, I despise you still.'

'I am your friend.'

'You are nobody's friend.'

'I am yours.'

'I don't need you.'

'But we meet again and again.'

'Yes,' Sanjay said. 'I know I will be reborn, that there is no escape from you. I know my life well and I know that I have not found liberation. I will have to come back to you. But remember, when I die, I do not give up to you, I renounce this world. This world in which nothing is clear, where there is horror at every turn, I am sick of it. I know I will be reborn into it. Since you say you are my friend, I will ask you a question. Does it get better?'

'The world is the world. It is you that makes the horror.'

'A fine way of saying that it gets worse. All right, I ask you another question. If I must be reborn, I prefer not to be aware, to be always divided against myself, to be a monster; I have no doubt cursed myself through my actions, but have I done enough so that I will be reborn as an animal?'

'Why do you think life as an animal is a curse? It is rather a privilege.'

Sanjay stopped short. 'I am to be a human again?'

Yama shrugged, and a gust of moisture splashed across Sanjay's face.

'Listen,' he said. 'You have called me a friend of your own will, from your own mouth. By your tongue you owe me a favour. I ask that I be reborn not as a human. I demand that I be an animal. God, for the first time I ask you for something, and you cannot refuse.'

'I cannot,' Yama said. 'You shall be what you choose.'

They walked on, and now they were among mountains, among steep black cliffs of rock, and there was a river ahead, a stream that was swelled by the rains into a roaring current.

'I leave you now,' Yama said. 'We will meet again.'

'I have no doubt of it,' Sanjay said. When he looked back all he could see were thick banks of mist, and so he walked on alone; he followed the sound of the river until he found a flat rock poised above the gorge, and there was a tree that grew over the rock, its branches hanging in space. Sanjay sat there, cross-legged, and the rain fell on him and the water fell on him from the leaves above, and as he took breath in and out the sound of the water grew so loud in his ears that it receded into a kind of silence, and in this pool of silence he gazed until he saw his childhood, his friends, his parents, and then he saw his youth, how he knew passion, and he saw all this and then he gave it, he let it go, and he felt it leave like a spark from the top of his head; and then he thought about his enemies, the ones he hated, and how he despised them, and he gave that too and it flew away from him; he remembered his crimes, the people he had murdered, and his offences clung to him but finally with a sigh he let it all go; and one by one all the things that tied him to life dissolved and vanished and he felt his soul floating unfettered and close to the white frontier of death but still there was something, it held him back like a thin chain; and suddenly he remembered the student's face from London, the thin boy whose name he had asked, and he cried into the water, you children of the future, you young men and women who will set us free, may you be happy, may you be faultless, may you be as soft as a rose petal, and as hard as thunder, may you be fearless, may you be forgiving, may you be clever and may you have unmoved faith, may you be Hindustani and Indian and English and everything else at the same time, may you be neither this nor that, may you be better than us, I bless you, may you be happy; and then he felt the last cord break, the last spark of desire leaving him, it was the hardest but the bond of pride then vanished and he was free.

The pale body under the tree leaned forward, and then it slipped to the side and toppled down the slope into the spray of the river, and the water took it speedily down the curving course, and it turned over once and then it was gone.

Sandeep paused and looked around at the monks, at Shanker who sat listening with his chin on a knee. Then he continued:

'In the forest my teacher told me this story. She looked into her cupped hands and told me this tale. When she finished she looked up at me, laughed, and threw the water over her face and shoulders.

' "It is time to go," she said.

' "Where?"

' "Home."

' "Into the world?"

' "Yes," she said. "Where there are more stories. Farewell. And thank you."

' "Thank you," I called to her, but she had picked up her deer-skin and was gone, and I waited in the forest for a while but I never saw her again. I believe she went home. So I have come from the forest, and I have told you this story.'

Shanker rose to his feet, and all the sadhus followed him, and they all bowed to Sandeep. He pressed his hands together in humility, and he said, 'Thank you for listening to me. This was the story of Sikander and Sanjay, and those who listen to it attentively and with faith will be delivered from doubt, and after they have heard it they will be changed forever, they will be something else.' He shook hands with Shanker. 'I will go now.'

'Where will you go?' Shanker said.

'I will go into the mountains,' he said. 'And I will meditate, and I will listen. This was after all only part of the story. Perhaps the rest will come to me.'

So Sandeep walked away from Shanker's ashram, into the green terai, and the sadhus watched until he was only a little dot of white against the mountain, and then evening came, and the fires were lit.

HERE ENDS
THE BOOK OF THE RETURN,
THE LAST BOOK.

THE STORY OF SIKANDER AND SANJAY IS OVER.

. . . now . . .

WHEN I FINISHED I leaned back from the keyboard and lay back on the bed and I was feeling tired, but calm and somehow clean, as if I had been absolved of something; Saira sat cross-legged next to me, a hand on my shoulder. It was strange, but I was not afraid anymore, and when Abhay started to speak the vehemence in his voice startled me.

'What, that's it? Get up. There's more you have to tell us. Go on.'

I shook my head, and held up a hand: no more.

'Are you afraid? Have you given up?' He came close and squatted next to me, his eyes angry. 'Do you want that fool Yama to win after all? You're a story-teller. Have you grown weak? Has your imagination run dry? The Book of the Return is *not* over. Get up and do your duty.'

Hanuman looked on from a rafter, and then he swung down easily to land next to Ganesha, who sat in a corner cross-legged, swinging his trunk to and fro.

'Very strange,' said Hanuman.

'Yes,' Ganesha said. 'It seems he loves you after all.'

'He's forgotten his fear of madness.'

'Which was madness, and which is sane?' And then they both laughed together, and Hanuman rolled over and over, and Ganesha's paunch shook mightily. But I couldn't see Yama, and when I looked over to my left, his throne was gone, and he was nowhere to be seen. Then when I lay back, my head on a pillow, I saw that there was someone sitting behind me, behind the pillow: it was an old man with fine white hair and golden eyes, dressed in white with his right shoulder bare, and there was a smile on his lips as he gazed down at me.

'Who are you?' I said.

'You still do not know your friends?'

His eyes never blinked, they were as still as pools of water, and in them I saw reflected a thousand red and white pennants, the glint of lances, the sweating shoulders of horses and the proud riders, I saw the sun flash and a wind blew across the plains, and I saw myself, my monkey-face and the other one besides, translucent and mixed up, the scars of one appearing in another, and as I looked at myself there were a thousand others who seemed to float behind: de Boigne, George Thomas, Begum Sumroo, Ram Mohan, Arun, Shanti Devi, Janvi, Hercules Skinner, Sorkar, Markline, a host of others, even the mad Greek Alexander, they were all there.

'Yes, I know who you are,' I said. 'At last I know you: you are Dharma, who is the friend of men and women. You are forever with us, even when we do not know you, you walk with us in our streets and finally we return to you. You are Yammam-Dharmam, and you are our father.'

He smiled at me, and put his hand on my shoulder. His touch was cool. Then there was a sudden shouting outside, a flaring of angry voices. Ashok hurried out, and when he came back a few minutes later his face was full of worry and grief.

'Three groups were fighting,' he said. 'The police stopped it.' There was no more shouting now, on the maidan, only the buzz of thousands of voices.

'About what?' Mrinalini said.

'Who knows?' Ashok said. 'But now it's become politics.'

'Hurry, Sanjay,' Abhay said. 'You must go on. Continue, and they'll listen.'

So I got up slowly, and went back to the machine, and then I typed all this, and then: 'Abhay, the contract said that a story must be told. You have your part today left to tell, so you must tell it. There was an invitation to a cricket match, was there not? Tell the story. But I am done. Saira, and you, my friends, I thank you. Do not be afraid, there is nothing to fear. Do not grieve, because tragedy is an illusion. We are free, and we are happy, and together we are complete. Abhay, when I have finished, I shall lay my head in the lap of Yama and I shall listen to your story, and the story will never end, in its maya we will play, and we will find endless delight.'

Now I speak no more. Saira is sitting beside me, quiet, holding my hand tightly between both of hers, and she is weeping.

The Game of Cricket.

I HAD NOT PLAYED CRICKET for so long that I had forgotten it. I mean not just how to play, but that I had forgotten the linseed smell of the bat, the smooth heft of the ball and the comfort of its seam, the good green of the grass, the hollow *pok* of a good drive that is the best sound in the world, and distant figures in white, and a glass of ale in the pavilion, the chattering clapping for a particularly elegant cut, fellowship and sportsmanship and well-being. I had borrowed whites from William James, and I had to roll up the bottoms of the trousers, the shirt fell loosely over my shoulders and bunched at my waist, I must have looked ridiculous but I was remembering cricket under a desert sun and so I didn't care, I was remembering Lord Mayo and the mountain Madar overhead, fiercely-fought house-matches, buckling on pads, all of us staring open-mouthed as some schoolboy legend passed by, a school First Eleven cricketer with a double century in the last inter-school match, and school colors in six sports.

I was remembering all this and I suppose the childhood must have shown in my face, because Amanda said, "Why d'you want to do this?" She was lounging in a deck chair, drinking a vodka and tonic, and she was already bored and unhappy.

"Dear, as they say, it's the only game in town."

"You sound funny."

"No doubt."

"I hate this place." We were on the deck of the Regents clubhouse, which was a huge square black building with classical pillars and scrolled cornices. It looked more like a government ministry than a cricket pavilion to me, but then my notion of a sporting building had been formed by the delicate red sandstone fantasy of a pavilion at Mayo, and in any case there was the field in front with the players tossing the ball back and forth, and the pitch really was glorious, smooth and even and hard as a billiard table. So I paid no attention to Amanda, who had just been brought another drink by a dark-skinned waiter in a white coat.

The glass door to the clubhouse opened, letting out a rush of cold air, and William James emerged, followed by a stream of other players. He was tall, and, I noticed, very broad-shouldered, and as he talked to me he slipped a ball from one hand to another, and the bulk of his forearms was really remarkable. He looked ruddy and strong, and clean.

"You'll play for the Coasters," he said, meaning the other team. He was the captain of the Regents. He looked out at the field, and said, "It's a friendly match."

He introduced me to the captain of the Coasters, a fiftyish Englishman named Ballard, and then they walked down to make the toss, which Ballard won. He chose to bat first, and so I sat on the steps and talked to the Coasters, who were a motley collection of Australians, Indians, and Pakistanis, and a couple of West Indians. The Regents team was mostly older men, six Americans, more than I had expected, an Irishman, two Australians, and, strangely, a Japanese. We clapped for the first two batsmen in, and then William James began to bowl. He was a pretty useful pace bowler, medium-fast most of the time but trying for the really whizzing ball, and when he tried to snap it he tended to lose control of the length, but every once in a while he'd get one right on the sweet spot and it would whistle by the batsman. In his third over he clean-bowled one of our openers, and the middle stump cartwheeled end over end for a good six feet and the wicket-keeper caught one of the bails.

I looked around for Amanda and she had disappeared, so I got to my feet and told Ballard that I'd be right back, and went into the clubhouse. The air conditioning was so hard and complete it felt vicious, and I could feel the rivulets of sweat on my back vanishing instantly. Inside, the ceiling was high and everything seemed to be green, the carpets and the wall, and there were huge chandeliers overhead. I wandered around from room to room, and then I found the waiter who had served us.

"Miss Amanda?" he said. "I don't know. Maybe she's on the roof."

"The roof?"

"With her mother at the pool."

"There's a pool on the roof?"

"Yes," he said, smiling. He was an old man with peppery hair, and now I could catch, faintly, the Jamaican in his speech. "Go to the left to the stairs there. Go take a look, young man. It is something to look at."

I didn't think I'd find Amanda with her mother, but I wanted to see this rooftop pool, and so up I went, and emerged into sunlight so blinding that I stumbled for a few seconds, hand over my eyes, in a bright haze, and when I could finally focus I saw a brilliant sheet of perfect blue, blue water, so flawless that it didn't look real. Next to it was Amanda's mother, and when I saw her my heart dropped out of my body and whirled off somewhere into space. Candy, I whispered. She waved at me, and as I went closer I lost sense of myself, me and my body I mean, it was as if I was floating across the surface of the earth, and in the distance, the tops of trees. She was lying flat on her stomach in a gold bikini, a book in front of her, and her body was smooth and long and perfect, she had the string on the top untied, the length of her back burnished and shining, I could see the sides of her breasts as she leaned on her elbows. Something happened to me but it wasn't arousal, you shouldn't think that, it felt deep and hollow and empty, it was bad if it was anything. It made me crazy. It wasn't arousal at all but it was attraction.

I sat down cross-legged next to her and she turned her head (slowly, slowly) and the hair was almost white in the sun, and in her dark glasses I could see myself, eyes wide and flicking.

"How are you, Abhay?" she said.

I shrugged. I couldn't have spoken if I had wanted to, and I didn't want to. I wanted to sit there and look forever, vaguely frightened and on the edge of some precipice. A young waiter came through the door, he looked like a nephew or son of the old man downstairs, and he had his face composed and stiff but as he looked at her I saw the same aching.

"Jamie, take this away, will you?" she said. There was a plate of fruit by her side, barely touched, and she picked it up and held it to him. The cloth moved away from her as her arm stretched and then I saw, under her arm, almost invisible, almost not there but there, a scar. It was a little pucker of flesh, a tiny crease, it was nothing but I was so fixed on it she saw, and very casually, not hurrying, she gathered her bikini top back to her breast. I suddenly flashed on a scalpel cutting, a thin steel blade going into the soft flesh and I felt sick.

"I do hate a mess, don't you?" she said brightly.

I nodded, and she smiled at me, and it occurred to me that this was a woman who went through life accustomed to silences, who had grown accustomed to one-sided conversations. I nodded again.

"In honor of you, I went and got something," she said. "I've always been interested in your country. It's just so, you know, mysterious." I nodded. "So I thought I'd read something about you. About India I mean." When she said *India* she stretched the word so that it sounded weird and wonderful, somehow, *Eeen-dee-yaa.* "So I went to the library." With a friendly smile (I felt my dazzled senses reel even further) she held up the book: it was *The Far Pavilions.* I could hardly see past the golden descent of her chest, but there was another book on the left of her, *Kim,* and one on the right, *A Passage to India.*

"I had better go," I said. "I'm on the batting side."

"You better." She smiled again, and I fled, searching for the door with scrabbling hands, for a last moment I could see the water like a sheet of some amazing new synthetic, and again the air conditioning chill rode up and down my spine, by the time I reached the bottom of the stairs I was moving slowly, like a man stricken by some disease of the bone. As I went out onto the patio the old waiter caught my eye and smiled, and his face looked almost naughty, as if we had shared some secret.

Out on the field William James had been taking wickets, and as I came out he took another with a bouncer that got the batsman slashing wildly and caught easily in the slips.

"Are you a heroic batsman?" said Ballard hopefully.

"Not in the least," I said. "Can I go last? But I do an okay off-break."

We scored twelve more runs and they got another couple of wickets, with William James adding one to his bag, and then, all of a sudden, I was in. As I walked out to the wicket, pulling on the gloves, the smell from them, slightly sweaty, leather, calmed me, and as I adjusted my cap and took my stance I was actually smiling. William James was a good ten yards beyond the bowler's wicket, tossing the ball up and down, and even at that distance I could see his blue eyes. The umpire lowered his hand and William James ran in, his feet making hardly a sound on the grass, and I saw his arm come round, it was one of his fast ones, a little short of a length, and I stepped out to meet it and it reared up wickedly at me, I saw it coming and twisted my body aside but it caught me stinging on the side of the neck and dropped me back to my knees. They crowded round as I straightened up rubbing at my collarbone, it really wasn't bad, thank you, just a snick, and we went on, but there was a red smudge on my shirt. William James was taking his long walk back to his mark, and I could feel my pulse thumping at the back of my head, he came in again running fast, and when he released the ball he made a loud sound, an explosive grunt with the effort of it, and I flinched and never even saw the ball, I held the bat out defensively but never found it, and he took my off stump out of the ground. We were all out for seventy-two, and as we walked back to the pavilion William James came over and patted me on the back.

"Good effort," he said, smiling.

And then he walked ahead of me, there was a large damp spot between his shoulder blades, and his shirt was stretched tight over his back, and he was laughing, he was confident and a little swaggering and very handsome.

Lunch was delicious, cold cuts and potato salad around a buffet table. I looked around for Amanda, but she was nowhere to be seen, and Jamie the waiter hadn't seen her either, so I decided she had bailed out, maybe she was with Tom and Kyrie. I walked down the table piling my plate high — I felt limber and hungry. William James's voice boomed through the room. He was laughing at something Ballard said as they went from plate to plate. I sat at a table with a white tablecloth and began to eat.

"Here, son," said William James. "Try some of these. Prime." He was talking to Swaminathan, one of the Coasters, and he was holding out a plate of ribs. I had one in my hand, and they were good, but Swaminathan, who was thin and dark and very short, shook his head.

"No, thank you," he said. When we had been sitting out on the pavilion steps earlier that day, he'd told me that he'd just graduated from IIT Madras, and was now in the microbiology department at Rice. He had been in the States for maybe two weeks.

"You sure? They're good, good, good!"

"Yes."

"You're a vegetarian?"

"Yes."

"Oh."

William James shrugged and put down the plate, and he and Ballard walked past my table to one at the center of the room. As they went William James inclined his head to Ballard, and I heard him whisper, not too quiet, "No wonder you fellows thrashed them about for two hundred years."

"We got them out after all." My voice was loud and it stilled all conversation in the room. My face was burning, and I had surprised myself more than the others. I mean I don't know where it came from.

"Well, yes, maybe you did, maybe you shouldn't have," William James said, settling into a chair and putting one leg over another.

"Meaning?"

"Meaning look what it's reverting to after the British left, the country."

"Which is what?"

"Well, chaos, isn't it?"

I was so angry now I couldn't speak for a minute, and to tell the truth I didn't know what to say, but I felt like I wanted to scream. But finally I spoke, and my voice was ugly and slow, "You don't know anything about it." I enunciated each word, and as soon as I said it it was inadequate, it felt like I had said nothing.

"Come on, chaps," Ballard said. "No politics in the mess." He took William James by the shoulder and turned him, and William James let himself be turned and he took up his fork, and as they began to eat there was a small smile on his lips.

Swaminathan came and sat down next to me. The fork was shaking in my hand, and as I put it down on my plate it made a small clatter. Under the table Swaminathan put a hand on my forearm, and he held on until I stopped trembling, but even then I was unable to eat.

*   *   *

After lunch William James sent out the Japanese as one of the openers, and the other was the youngest of the Americans, a friend of William James who had only just taken up cricket. It was pretty clear they didn't take the possibility of losing very seriously, and were sending out their fledglings, for practice I suppose. We began to play, and the main bowler on our side was an Australian who roughed up the ball quickly, while the Japanese fellow pushed forward with a straight defensive bat and the American drove into the covers. I was fielding deep-leg, and from where I was standing I could see William James lounging back in an armchair with a drink in his hand. He looked comfortable and re-laxed. They scored twenty runs, and then Ballard gave the ball to Swaminathan, and Swaminathan walked over to the crease, rubbing the ball on his pants. His run-up was four steps, taken slowly, but the ball was a mean off-break that spun in viciously and took the middle stump from the Japanese. I ran over and thumped Swaminathan on the back, and he smiled a little shy smile and said, "Good pitch." With the last ball of his over he had the new batsman swinging wildly at one that looped lazily in the air, bounced and turned, and careened off to the slips, with just enough of a snick from the bat's edge to send the man back to the pavilion with a big fat duck.

"Well done, Swami," I said. "Good show."

"Indeed," said Ballard. "Let's see that off-break of yours." And with that he tossed the ball to me.

So I took the ball and walked up to the wicket, swinging my arm over, and the action was unfamiliar and stiff. I marked out a run, and the ground was edged by trees, and I thought, I've been away a long time. But I steadied myself, and the umpire lowered his arm, and I trotted up and tried it, but the ball was wide and the batsman (one of William James's friends, a banker I believe) drove it confidently past me, to the boundary at mid-on for a four. He was pretty damn elegant about it too.

"Never mind, yaar," said Swami. "Get the length."

I did, too. I gave away another four runs at the end of that over, and then two or three more in the next, but after that I began to settle and I found that I could turn the ball, and I began to enjoy the effort, and it was nothing spectacular but I began to bother them a little. But Swami, he was performing wonders, he hung the ball so long in the air that it seemed to be gliding, reluctant to come down, and it floated and it dipped and it swerved along, and sometimes on the bounce he would spin it, turning it to leg and sometimes he would flip it with top-spin, and the wickets tumbled. In his third over he took one more, and in the next he got two. I just pegged down the batsmen from one end, and from the other he went through them like an executioner, all with a downward-looking smile and shy little shakes of his head. I could see William James standing on the patio now, shading his eyes, and when the next batsman came out he walked with him a little way into the field, talking into his ear urgently.

So we went on, and they got runs, mostly from me, but their middle-order batting pretty much collapsed, and we had them at sixty-nine for seven. William James still didn't come in, I could see his point, he wasn't going to be bothered to put on the pads for the likes of us, and they were only four runs away from victory anyway. The next batsman came in, looking grave, and as he marked his guard I tossed the ball to Swaminathan and chanted, "Bedi, Bedi, Bedi." By now I loved the man, and I was calling him by the names of the heroes of my childhood. Bedi had been one of a trio of spinners, a heavy-set Sikh who bowled devious leg-spin that charmed the batsmen into error.

But William James's teammates were scared of Swaminathan now, and they were sticking to the crease, playing defensive strokes and re-fusing steadfastly to swing at the delicious-looking lobs he floated down the pitch. On the fifth ball of the over he bounced it a little short, and the batsman stepped out to drive but it rose suddenly, took the splice of his bat and went sweetly right back into Swaminathan's hands. The next fellow who came in was young, sweating, and red in the face, and when I called to Swaminathan, "Prassana, Prassana, Prassana," he looked at us suspiciously, as if we were plotting something unfair and probably unconstitutional. Prassana was a fat off-spinner, you remem-ber, a South Indian who looked sleepy and harmless until his break caught you flat-footed and stupid. Swaminathan bowled, the hero at the crease stepped up to it quickly and let fly with a tremendous swing, he was tense and he wanted to catch it before it bounced and he was seeing visions of a triumphant sixer and strawberries in the pavilion, but it was moving in the air, it was zigging and zagging and performing myste-rious perambulations, and with all his strength and his probably good eye he caught it only a glancing snick and it squirted to square-leg, where Ballard sprinted for it, but both batsmen were nearly half-way down the pitch and they decided to dash for it, the runner was safe but the other batsman was still a good two feet from the crease when Ballard tumbled the stumps with a clean and fast throw.

So we had them, almost. Four more runs to make and one more batsman left, and it was of course William James. I could see him standing on the grass near the pavilion, his hands on his hips, and he still didn't have his pads on. Behind him I could see his wife, the cool blond hair above a white dress. He turned around quickly, and I could feel his anger, and then we had to wait while he put on his pads. Swaminathan walked over and gave me the ball, and then he massaged my shoulders. He didn't, of course, have to say that it all depended on me.

William James came in, settling a blue cap on his head, it had a Confederate flag on it. As he went by us Swaminathan thumped me on the back, walked away, and then called back to me, "Chandrashekhar." William James looked up, and his gaze was clear and icy, he looked from me to Swaminathan, and he was furious but collected.

"Chandrashekhar," I said, and William James glared at me, and I laughed. I mean he probably thought we were speaking to each other in some foreign language, or maybe practicing some kind of dark Oriental magic, because Swaminathan was now chanting, Chandrashekhar, Chandrashekhar.

Chandrashekhar was my favorite of the spinning triad, the three gods of the slow ball. He was thin to the point of weakness, and as a child he had suffered polio, which had deformed his right arm, twisted it inwards, and so with it he practiced the art of deception, he bowled googlies, off-breaking with a leg-break action, and I remembered batsmen who watched his arm come round, and who confidently unleashed cover drives, only to find they had been fooled, what had looked like one thing had really been another, that Chandrashekhar's thin twisted arm was capable of lying. But now William James was flexing his wrists at the crease, he meant to hit my delivery straight to the boundary, and Swaminathan was whispering, Chandrashekhar, Chandrashekhar, but I had never bowled a googly in a match, I didn't have the crippled arm, and William James was watching the ball, his eyes were fixed on my hand, my grip on the seam, he was coolly analytical, he was going to know what I was doing as soon as I did it, before even, he had me down his eyes were telling me, he was going to count me and calculate me and predict me and knock me out of the park. He was shifting his weight on the balls of his feet and he wasn't worried, no, not at all. So I took the ball and started my run, holding it behind my back, and I was saying as I ran, Chandrashekhar, Chandrashekhar, my arm came over and William James was watching, and instead of releasing the ball I dropped my wrist and held on and when I let the ball go my arm was turned, I could feel the wrench in my shoulder, the back of my hand was facing the ground, and it wasn't much of a ball, William James came out to it hungrily, he was glad and happy and I could feel it, it dropped desultorily and he set himself for it and he swung, he was going to drive it over my head for a flight to the moon, he was going to murder it, but the ball hit the ground and he knew it was going to break to leg but it didn't, it turned the other way and he swung through empty air and then he was looking around curiously above my head. He wanted to know where the ball had gone.

"Chandrashekhar," Swaminathan screamed, and there was a great shout of laughter, and William James looked around slowly and his middle stump was out of the ground and lying flat. After that I was surrounded by players patting me and hugging, and when I finally struggled my way through them William James was still staring at his stumps, he turned and looked at me with clear hatred. He pivoted on his heel even as I walked toward him, holding out my hand, and he stalked back toward the pavilion without a word.

"Doesn't like to lose," Ballard said. As we walked off the field, me holding my arm, which was starting to ache, he went on, "Around these parts he's known as a bit of a hanging judge. But he'll come around."

I shrugged. I didn't care whether he came around or not.

Back in the building I shivered again under the cool rush of air, and I went looking for Amanda. This time I noticed a heavy brown door across from the dining room, and when I leaned on it it slid back smoothly into the wall. It was the library, dark and huge, with shelves rising two stories to the ceiling, and ladders here and there. There was a thick carpet underneath, and when I went in the backs of books glinted gold all around. I stood for a while, my hand on the back of a soft upholstered chair, and when I turned back to the door I saw Amanda, lying curled on a long couch, looking very small. I squatted down beside her and touched her cheek, and then I whispered, "Amanda, Amanda." But she slept on, and when I leaned closer her breath was sour with alcohol, and her hands were holding each other in front of her face. I put a hand on her shoulder and shook her, but her head moved loosely on the couch and after a while I left her alone.

Outside, as I was shutting the door to the library, I saw William James, and Candy behind him. He had changed into a dark blazer, and as he strode over to me the brass buttons shone in the light from the chandeliers. He reached forward and took my hand.

"Good game, young fellow." He was smiling, but his hand was tight on mine, and I could swear I heard a bone crack. When he let go the back of my hand was throbbing, and I put it behind and held on to my shirt to keep from rubbing it.

"Yes," I said. "Very."

"We're going home."

"Amanda and I were planning to meet some friends for dinner."

"I see." He gave me a long look and then he walked away. Candy waved good-bye from across the room, and I raised my good hand and waved back. I said good-bye then to Swaminathan and the others, and after a while I went outside, where it was getting dark, and I walked out to the pitch. My right arm was aching from the shoulder to the fingertips. It wasn't that, though, that made my heart afraid, and I stayed outside because there was a breeze and it was soothing.

"Hallo."

It was Ballard. He walked out to me and we stood together for a while. Then he held out something to me, and said, "Do you smoke?"

"No," I said, but I reached out anyway and took the cigar. He passed me a lighter, and after a while I got the thing lit and we watched the glow on each other's faces.

"Thanks," I said.

"Pleasure. Glad you played."

"Yes."

"You know," he said, "I was born in India."

"Really? Where?"

"Lucknow. We left when I was very young, maybe five or six. I don't remember very much."

"Yes."

"But I remember a little."

So we stood out there for a long time and smoked, and our cigars kept going out so we passed each other the lighter, it was very quiet but for the crickets and far away, the birds, the wind smelled sweetly of some flower I didn't know, and the moon came up suddenly and covered the field in a silver light.

Later that night Amanda and I drove into the city and we found Tom and Kyrie, and with them White Eagle, they were sitting side by side on lawn chairs in front of the Hokaido, in the rock garden, drinking beer out of cans. Amanda had been quiet and dazed, she had shuddered at the darkness when we had come out of the clubhouse, saying, "But it was just light!" but now she sat cross-legged on the rocks and popped open a beer and started to look less dislocated.

"We were going to go to NASA," Tom said. "We were thinking about it."

"Why NASA?" I said.

"Shuttle takeoff tonight," Kyrie said. "We wanted to see it."

"There are no takeoffs from Houston," Amanda said.

"It's a party," Kyrie said. "They're launching tonight from Cape Canaveral, and so there's a party out near NASA." She held up an orange piece of paper with a hand-drawn map on it. "When they launch the real shuttle, everyone at the party will shoot off their own rockets. Sort of in sync, see?"

I didn't really see. I shrugged.

"You don't want to go see the rockets?" Amanda said. Her hair was tousled from the couch, and she looked about ten years old.

"It's something everybody should see once," White Eagle said.

"Really?" I was sick at having to think of him as White Eagle, I mean his name was really Bob or Ted or something like that. "You think so?"

"Really," he said, sipping from his can and quite unaffected by my sarcasm.

Finally I had to go, they all seemed intent on it and my other choice was to sit at the Hokaido alone, and I wasn't interested in the damn shuttle or rockets but I couldn't face that, so we got into the car, five of us, and we went to NASA. After we got off the freeway we circled around in the dark, stopping at all-night convenience stores, until finally we found a field with other cars scattered about and a lot of people gathered in little circles. They were all working on rockets. There were kegs of beer here and there, but basically everyone had a rocket. Some of them had the little fizzy kind, firecrackers, others had actual working models with decals and everything, there was one group that had a big shiny shuttle that looked about six feet long. We got out, and I walked out into the field to a fence, and Tom followed me, and we stood side by side and pissed, and he said, "How are you?"

"Feeling pretty weird. And you?" I said.

"Good."

"Good? What's going on?"

"With Kyrie?" He smiled. "Nothing. I mean I don't know. I mean it's good."

"Are you ready to go back?"

"To school? No. Are you?"

"I think so."

"Too bad we didn't find heaven."

"Maybe we did."

"Yeah? Where?"

I shook my head and we walked back to the car. I couldn't have explained it to him but I felt like something was over. We sat on the hood of the car and after a while Kyrie and Tom and Amanda wandered off into the darkness, holding hands all of them, they said they were going to look around. As they walked away I called, "Amanda, we won."

"Won what?"

"The game."

"Oh," she said over her shoulder. "That's good."

There was a radio somewhere, a news-reader's voice in the distance. The whole day was in my bones now, and my arm was aching in sweeps from the collarbone, and I waved them away and lay back on the hood. I knew it was too late to sleep but it felt nice to be looking up at the sky, which was sheets of cloud spilling across the moon.

"What kind of game was it?"

I started, and nearly slid off the car. It was White Eagle, and he was sitting in the driver's seat, his head out of the window.

"Cricket," I said.

"Ah."

"Listen, what is your name really?" He just looked at me, his hands on the steering wheel. "I'm going to call you Ed," I said finally, and I lay back and wriggled around until I found comfort. The metal felt good on my back. After a while he began to talk, and I didn't really want to listen but I was too settled to move, and it was sort of nice, to hear a voice telling a story above my head.

"Listen," he said. "I tell the story of Coyote and Wolf, who lived a long time ago in a valley. The valley was full of game, and Wolf lived happily, and Coyote too, around the edges. Then one day Coyote saw a wagon coming into the valley, drawn by huge horses, and he hid and watched them. There was a family of humans in the wagon, and they camped in the bottom of the valley, near a stream, and the next day they began to cut trees. They cleared a meadow and they built a house. Wolf came down from the ridges right to the edge of the meadow, and he stood watching them, and one of the men raised a rifle, and Wolf faced him, unafraid, and then the man laughed and dropped his barrel. Wolf turned and went back to the timberline, and as he went he saw Coyote hiding behind a rock, and he sneered, showing his fearsome curved teeth. So Wolf and Coyote lived in the valley, and Wolf hunted everywhere except down at the bottom of the valley, but then it seemed that the game became scarce, and Wolf had to go hungry for long weeks. Sometimes he saw people in the forest, and seeing him they would stop, and then slowly they would retreat. Meanwhile Coyote stole chickens from the settlement, and he rooted around in their garbage, and they came out of the houses and shouted at him, often they fired at him with shotguns, once a bullet cut open his left flank in a long thin line, but he scrambled away and lived. Now one day Wolf chased a deer, it was an old, scrawny buck, and Wolf chased him down from the side of the mountain, and the deer fled into the town, a town it was now, with roads and poles and lights, and Wolf went right after him, and the deer was running down the middle of a street when he was hit by a machine, a fast-moving machine, and the deer tumbled over and came down dead. Some people got out of the machine, and Wolf looked at them, and they looked at him, but he was hungry, and he was angry, so he ran forward for his deer, he had been stalking it all afternoon, and there was a bang, and the first shot took off his right foot, and he howled and kept going, smearing the street with his blood, and the second shot dropped him short. The people gathered about the body, and poked it with the gun, and Coyote saw all this, because he was inside a dumpster down the street with his nose barely out of the trash. So he sneaked away, and somebody skinned Wolf, and somebody else got the deer, and the next night Coyote took a little of the deer, he broke into a shed and tore off a leg, and the dogs chased him but he got away. Coyote lived long and grew old, he survived poison, and bullets, and gas, and disease, and one winter he was down in the town again, and he saw something that made him laugh, he rolled over and over in the snow and laughed, because at the middle of the town, near the river, the people had put up a statue of Wolf, and it showed him snarling, with one leg raised, very proud and wild and free."

There was something about his voice, not the sense of it but the texture, I wasn't listening to him at all, but there was something about lying down and having my eyes closed and a story in the air that made me small again, I was smelling a gobar fire, the smell of the cow-dung fresh and pure, a delicious wind taking the heat from my skin as we slept in the veranda on a hot summer night, the rustling of the grass, the cool smell of the water, and a hand on my forehead. I jerked up, pushed myself away from the car, and stumbled off, walking quickly, trying to get the image of my grandfather out of my head. He was dead, and it seemed like a long time since I had thought of him, since the phone call that had brought me news of his death, it seemed like centuries, but now his memory hurt in my chest, he was a thin man, a practitioner of a medicine I thought useless, little homeopathic pills that were nothing but sweetness, I had grown up to think him ineffectual. I was walking in darkness now but it seemed to me that I was walking into his house: you went down the narrow paved lane, dusty and dirty, and through a little gate inset into the huge gate, into a garden, a scattering of trees and bushes really, no order, cows chewing placidly in the manger, and you went into the house, past the little sitting room with its ancient furniture and shelves of knickknacks, into the inner veranda, which always smelled of food, and then into the large room with chatais on the floor where we all eat, and there is a cabinet full of old books and vials of medicine, and on the wall, you see two photographs, one is my grandfather, very young, the frame on the picture is cracked and the glass seems to have yellowed with age, but you can see him smiling, he is wearing white trousers, a blue blazer, a straw boater tilted forward over his eyes, he has one hand in his pocket and the other holds forward a ball, the seams clearly visible, and to the right of this photograph is another one, taken thirty-odd years later, his son sits with a group of young men, to your eyes they all look innocent to a degree that is almost pathetic, they are all debonair and confident, there are silver cups and shields strewn before them, and the legend on top of the picture informs you that this is the B.H.U. College of Humanities Cricket Team, 1947.

I sat down in the grass, and I wept for my grandfather, for his death and missing him. I sat for a long time and thought about him.

"There you are." Amanda came running up and sat down in my lap. "I was looking for you."

"I was thinking about my grandfather. And Kate and a guy called Katiyar. He was my school captain and my cricket captain."

She felt my face and then kissed my eyes, and held to me very tight. After a while we got up and started to walk back, she a little behind me, and suddenly she put her arms over my shoulders and hopped up, piggyback, and I carried her for a bit while she giggled into my neck. I was laughing.

"Now your turn," she said. And so she carried me for a while, she was strong, and we were laughing so much we both collapsed to the ground, but we carried each other all over that field. She was singing something into my ear when we went over a grassy rise, and then she said, "Oops." On the other side of the rise, in a little hollow, I could see Tom and Kyrie, their two heads gleaming in the moonlight close together, they were making love, and so I turned. As I turned there was a cheer, and then a succession of pops, rumblings, all melting into a roar, and then a hundred trails streaked into the sky, slivers of light throwing themselves up, unstoppable and prodigious flight, the sky turned to fire as they went keenly up, so bright I turned my face away, and below us I saw silhouetted the car, its elegant shape, and White Eagle sitting cross-legged, still as a rock, on its roof.

Amanda and I left for California the next day. Tom said he was going to stay behind, and I wanted to argue but I suppose I could see why, so I said nothing. We all waited in a coffee shop while Amanda drove home to say good-bye to her parents, and when she asked me if I would come with her I said I had better not. So we drank coffee, and Kyrie fed coins into the jukebox, and W. E., that was what I was calling him now, he shuffled over to the counter and brought back a battered chessboard.

"Do you play?" he said.

"I'll thrash you, W. E.," I said, and so we laid out the pieces, and there was a white bishop missing so I looked around and finally put a shiny quarter on the black square. I led off, but by the time Amanda was back he had me down three games to nothing. After all that he didn't even smile, just looked old, and then we saw the Jaguar pull in, so we went outside. There didn't seem to be anything much to say, so we shook hands, all of us, and Kyrie hugged Amanda and me.

"Call me," I said to Tom.

"I will."

We pulled away quickly and seemed to be on a freeway instantly. He never called, so I have no idea where they are now, or whether they are all together or what. I imagine them in a dusty rental car, red or black, driving across a Texas plain, and Elvis quavering "Heartbreak Hotel," and then they're gone. Amanda and I, we seemed to be back at Pomona almost instantly, it was too quick, and I felt tired almost all the time, walking around the campus. But anyway nobody seemed to have noticed that we had been gone, and I got back into classes and all the rest of it, and the months passed quickly and I graduated. I was with Amanda almost all the time, but we had never talked about what we would do after I was finished, I didn't know either, but on the day that I gave my last exam I looked up and saw the clouds on a distant mountain and knew I wanted to go home. I told Amanda this, and she nodded, looked down. Do you want to come with me? I said. She nodded, still looking down, with her hands behind her back, but when I hugged her she clung to me tightly and trembled.

So I told the college to mail my degree to me, I printed out my father's address in block letters on a card, and we flew out two days before graduation. My mother, I knew, would want a picture of me in a cap and gown, holding my anthropology degree across my chest, but the idea of it annoyed me and I got us on the first flight that had seats. Amanda seemed happy, she skipped around the airport and brought me a chocolate ice cream bar that we shared, and with chocolate smeared around her lips we kissed, and she said, "I'm so happy we're getting out of here," with a sweep of the arm that took in the whole airport and the sky outside. On the plane she put her head on my shoulder, held my arm with both hands and closed her eyes.

"Do you know how I imagine it?" she said, eyes still closed. "Big sky. Green, everything green. Blue water and women in gold saris walking slowly. Everything slow. Birds in the trees, parrots. An elephant in the distance, waving its trunk. Unbelievable sunsets."

"Don't imagine too much," I said.

"Oh, shut up, spoilsport," she said. Then she slept with a smile on her face, and her breath was warm on my skin. But later, in Bombay, when we were waiting in a long underground corridor to go through immigration, she began to look unhappy. I noticed this and looked around, and there were long lines of people waiting, everyone tired from the trip, but smiling a little, patient.

'Relax,' I said, rubbing her arm. She nodded. Then we went through the check, and descended into the swirling crowd around the luggage, and then again we went through the line at customs. Outside, it was still dark, but there was the ever-present gang of boys who wanted to carry our things, and I shooed them off and we got into a taxi. I had no idea what we were going to do, I wasn't ready to go home to my parents yet, and so I gave the driver the name of a hotel in Colaba.

When we stopped at a red light I turned to Amanda again, and she was looking out of the window with a kind of dazed expression on her face. The birds were exploding out of the trees with their usual dawn clamor, and so I leaned close to her and said, 'This is Bombay. It's not all like this.' I meant the long line of slums, the cardboard shacks that stretched away from the road.

Amanda turned to me, and she shook her head a little before she spoke. 'No. You know, there are no straight lines anywhere.'

I looked around, and I had never noticed it before, but there were really no straight lines. By the time we got to Haji Ali, I had made up my mind, and I said to the driver, 'Bhai, take us to Bombay Central instead.' The streets were already crowded, and I could tell, looking at her face, that Bombay was too much, and I remembered after summer holidays, back at Mayo, the Bombay fellows would always talk about Matheran.

'Amanda,' I said decisively. 'We'll go to Matheran. It's a hill station. It's beautiful.'

So we caught a train that swept us up the Ghats, and then a little minia-ture train, a mountain version, that took us up a dizzying hill to Ma-theran. The clouds were dark and low above the wooded hill-tops, there were the long ridges, the familiar motion of the train made me happy, I could smell the rain in the air, and I couldn't stop smiling, the other people in the compartment stared frankly at us and me and my face, and I finally announced, 'Just came back to India after years.' So then of course they wanted to know about my father and mother, what I had studied, where, did I have a job yet, and the trip passed in the conversa-tion, and the children, there were many of them bumping our knees, fascinated by Amanda's hair.

In Matheran we found the Rugby Hotel, which was a dozen cottages scattered over a knoll, around a large garden. It was raining by the time we got to our room, which had two enormous, canopied beds, and a heavy, teak-lined mirror in the dressing room. I liked it instantly, and I liked it even more when a waiter brought me hot toast, marmalade and tea, so that I could sit out on the porch in a cane chair and watch the rain, scalding my tongue and feeling the water splash on the soles of my feet. Amanda emerged from the room drying her hair with a towel. A man had brought a bucket of hot water to the door at the back of the bathroom, and I had to explain to her that you mixed the hot water with the cold water from the tap, and she had exclaimed, Wow.

Now she said: 'Everything's damp.' She held out the towel.

'It's the monsoon, you know.' She didn't seem satisfied with that, but she sat next to me and we had our tea, and after that I sat there and watched it rain till darkness, the trees bending with the wind, the slope of the mountain beyond, and I felt lazy and content. We had dinner in a long, dark dining room filled with round tables, chandeliers above and paintings of English landscapes on the wall. The food, though, was Gujarati, spicy and hot and delicious, and I ate thankfully. The only other people in the room were a small family, parents whom I recog-nized as army across the room and their two teenage daughters. The Colonel — that's what he was — introduced himself as Amanda and I walked towards the door after we had finished. He was from a Poona cavalry regiment, and he had a magnificient grey handle-bar moustache, pointed and upturned at the ends. His wife had a long, elegant nose, a short bob, and pale shoulders wrapped in a pink sari. The two daughters — Tina and Nita, thirteen and fourteen — were pretty in black T-shirts, and they smiled delightedly when I introduced Amanda. 'This is my girlfriend, Amanda,' I said, and they thought it was delicious, I could see the romance novels in their eyes, but after I had turned away I felt the Colonel's raised eyebrow on my back. I didn't care, outside the air was cool, and I had eaten well, and I was pleasantly tired.

In the room I pulled the sheets up to my nose and looked at the canopy of the bed, and I had a feeling of well-being, cosiness I suppose it was, with the wind picking up outside and the shutters creaking and rattling. When Amanda got into bed she screwed up her nose, and I didn't know what it was until I asked: I had smelt the slight damp mustiness of the sheets, and after she told me about it I could see that it might be unpleasant, but to me it was a smell of childhood, of rain and the ground suddenly turning green, holidays when the streets flooded, at one time in the year it was just there. 'Sorry,' I said, though, and I touched her cheek, but then I was asleep, deep in the softness of the bed and the sound of the shower on the roof.

When I awoke I felt Amanda shifting restlessly beside me, turning from side to side. The hands on my watch said nine but it was still dark.

'Hey,' I said, nuzzling into her back. 'Did you sleep all right?'

'No,' she said.

'What?' I said. 'Was it the noise? The shutters? Or the sheets?'

'No, it's this place.'

'The place?'

'It's just, I don't know, so gloomy. All those clouds pressing down. And this stuff in here. It looks like it's been here forever.'

I looked around. The bed was pretty old, and you could see where they had filled in a crack in the canopy.

'Well, a century or maybe two,' I said. 'But it works, more or less.'

She shook her head, then looked intently at me. 'This sounds crazy. Do you think there are ghosts here?'

'Did you hear something?'

'No. I just feel it. It's like just the density of this place. I feel them right here.' She pointed to the middle of her chest. I knew what she meant. There was something in the place, about the sighing of the wind between the cottages, the age of the bricks, there were memories waiting behind every door. I had felt it in the dining room, holding an old fork in my hand, and I felt it in the dressing room, looking in the mirror, I mean it wasn't hard to imagine some Englishman doing the same a hundred years ago.

'Do you feel it too?' Amanda said.

'Sure,' I said. 'You're not crazy. They're probably here, all over the place. Dozens of ghosts. But it makes the place more homey, don't you think? It's kind of a nice feeling.' I was serious, but she burst out laughing, put her hands over her face and collapsed into my chest. We held each other, and it was the first time we had laughed together since the plane had landed. 'Come on now. It's just this rain. It'll clear up and the sun will come out and everything will look better. Let's eat something.' She nodded, and I kissed her, but she still looked tired and wan.

The bearer brought us tea, and I told him to put it on the porch, and then I ran through a slight drizzle to the Colonel's cottage next door to borrow his newspaper. He was wearing a tweed jacket and an ascot, and we were just exchanging good mornings when I heard a loud scream from behind me. I turned and ran back to the cottage, and the Colonel followed, and when we came up the steps Amanda was standing in the doorway, backing away from a large red monkey, which was sitting on the table, its tail curled over the teapot, eating a piece of toast.

'Don't worry, my dear,' said the Colonel. We both gestured and shooed at the monkey, and he watched us impassively, taking quick little bites from his toast. I picked up a chair and stepped forward, and then, very slowly, he turned and hopped onto the railing, then down to the ground, where a dozen others of his family waited. 'Rascals, rascals. You have to watch out for these chaps. When the rain lets up they come out in full force. They'll steal your food if you look away for a second. But really nothing to be frightened of. You'll get used to them.' He smiled at Amanda, and she nodded, and then he thumped me on the back and marched off to his house. 'Watch the flanks,' he called back to me.

I waved to him, and I growled at the monkeys, who watched us for a while and finally moved away, but it was a long time before I could get Amanda to eat anything. It was a shock for her, I guess. The day passed slowly, and again I sat on the porch and watched the rain, but Amanda was restless, and so in the evening, when the showers paused, I proposed a walk. We strolled along a muddy path between dense patches of trees, and we walked past cottages with names like 'Mount Prospect' and 'Clearview,' most of them boarded up. The path curled around the ridge, and we could see the clouds far below, drifting against the mountain, but there were too many mosquitoes to stop and look, they droned in thick clouds around our faces and hands as soon as we paused. So we walked on, and when we came around a corner, and there was a family of monkeys scattered across the path, Amanda pulled back at my hand.

'Really, they won't do anything. Look.' I touched her shoulder, and walked through the monkeys, they barely moved to give me way on the path, and then I walked back again through them. 'See?'

Amanda shook her head. It was getting dark. As we walked, the path widened into a little clearing, and on the edge of the path, over a cliff, there was a rock, a black rock which curved out into a smooth shining curve, and somebody had put a smear of red turmeric, many years of it, onto the shape. There were piles of flowers at the foot of the rock, I could smell the sweetness, and above it a tree sighed as the wind moved through the branches. I felt a stir along my spine, a vague shifting.

'What is it?' Amanda asked.

'A shrine.'

'To what?'

'I don't know.'

She was looking away from it uneasily, away from the red as we lost it in the gathering darkness. So I turned her around and we went back to the hotel, and again the dinner in the cavernous dining room was delicious. I slept as soon as I was in the bed, and my sleep was deep and long.

The next morning when I awoke Amanda had her eyes closed, but I couldn't really tell if she was asleep or not, her eyes moved under the lids nervously. I crept out of bed and dressed, and went outside and walked the path. The air was brilliantly clear, and the slope fell away sheerly for thousands of feet to the plain. The horizon was hundreds of miles away, and the freshness made me walk briskly, enjoying the snap of grass under my feet and the birds curving out of the trees. I found a stone seat on a promontory, and sat on it to watch the sun rise, the serried gradients illuminated one by one. Below me, a herdsman took his cattle down the slope. Near the seat there was a rock with a carved legend in it: 'Louisa's Point.' The rock had cracked straight through the middle, and there was the shoot of a plant growing through it, but the writing was still clear. I wondered what Louisa had seen from this mountain. I squinted my eyes against the sun; if it was blurred, if it was veiled, Louisa could have thought it was the Sussex Downs, maybe, the dark line of an English wood, and perhaps for a minute or two she was at home.

When I got to the hotel the Colonel and his family waved to me from his cottage, and I sat on my porch and waited for the bearer to bring me my tea. I was drinking it when Amanda came out.

'Look,' I said as she sat down. 'The sun's out.'

She smiled, and it only made her look more tired and pale.

'Hey, cheer up.' I was irritated, and I suppose there was anger in my voice. She flinched and rubbed her chin.

'But maybe I should go home,' she said.

'Home?' I put down my cup, and at the sound she drew up her legs into the chair and put her arms around her knees.

'I'm sorry,' she said.

Her voice was so small that I barely heard her, and she looked so unhappy that my heart turned, and I got up from my chair and walked behind hers, I squatted and put my arms over hers, my head on her shoulder, and I kissed her cheek, I meant to say, it's all right, but looking over her shoulder something strange happened to me, the world tilted on some axis that I had never known existed, suddenly the trilling voices of the Colonel's daughters, happily dipping in and out of Hindi and English and two other languages, suddenly they became a babel, a multiple confusion and harsh, lost in the ceaseless chattering of the birds, the tinkling of cow-bells tinny and hurtful in the noise, the cottages and their endless memories were heavy and decaying, the trees were huge and unarranged, they seemed to loom over the mad stupefaction of the garden, the uncontrolled profusion, the sky was bright and hard with sunlight, I felt nausea, loneliness, my self was a hard little point, a unitary ball spinning and yawing in a hugeness of dark where there was no beginning, no middle, no end: no meaning. And through my terror I saw the monkeys watching me, their reddish pelts glowing in the sun, their eyes expressionless.

When I was able to get up, I slowly went back to my chair, sat down and tried to breathe. I felt tears in my eyes, so I had my face turned away. The Rugby Hotel was itself again, back to the shape that comforted me, and in the valley clouds were forming, it was going to be another afternoon of rain, I could feel it on my face. I had to swallow again and again before I could speak, and when I did I had no anger left, only sadness.

'Yes,' I said. 'Maybe you're right. Maybe you should go home.'

When I said good-bye to Amanda in Bombay she said, I'll see you soon, in a few months, and I said yes. But I really didn't know, I felt lost, all I knew was that I had to go home too. We had come down from Matheran with an awkwardness between us, and in the taxi on the way to the airport we had talked about movies. Now as we stood in the airport I was telling her that I would come back to the States, that we would be together again.

'I'll see you soon,' I said.

'Are you angry with me?'

'No.' I truly wasn't, not with her, and as we hugged, and as she walked away through the immigration gates I felt a huge sadness, and, I suppose, anger, but it was never at her. Later that day I got onto a slow train going north, it was the only train on which I could get a reservation, and then I was very angry with the slowness of the train, at how it stopped at every little town, I was angry at the crowds of people who got on and off at every station. I watched the landscape change slowly as the train scraped interminably up the country, and I was angry at lots of things. There was an unreasonable sadness inside me, a bitterness I could find no focus for, but I could taste it in the grit inside my mouth, it seemed to go right through me.

There was the house I remembered, the little white house on the edge of the maidan, and when the door opened my mother put her hand to her mouth and screamed, and then she hugged me. My father hurried up and hugged me and then insisted on carrying my bags in. We talked while my mother fed me, and she scolded me because she didn't have my favorite vegetables in the house. That night, I wasn't able to sleep, I turned and tossed till early in the morning, and then I fell into a doze that seemed to give me a headache. I woke up with my head hurting, and of course when I tried to shower there was no water. I was sweating, it was hot. While I ate I looked up and saw a white-faced monkey on the roof, I knew him well, he had been stealing things from my parents for years. Later that afternoon I sat with them and tried to tell them about America, my mother kept asking, but what is it like? I tried to tell her, but it all seemed hollow, as if I was saying nothing. Then I saw the monkey again, on the roof. He was pulling my jeans from the line. By the time I got up to the roof, he was in a tree, and I bounced a piece of brick off his behind, and he went off across the tree-tops, taking my jeans. I came down from the roof, and I knew I had to do something. Through that day I had this sensation that if I didn't do something the heat and the anger, the burning would burst my head apart. So I sat in the darkness and waited for him. I thought of machines, of rockets powering upwards, and the house I was in seemed small and defenceless, somehow primitive. In my lap I had a rifle, and I worked its bolt back and forth. The metal was good and smooth to touch. Snick-CLACK. I sat and waited for the monkey. I knew he would come.

After . . .

I AM SITTING in a church. The roof curves high above, and the light is clear, the names — Indian and English — of men gleam from the walls in gold. This is the St. James Church in Delhi. It is very quiet, and the rush of the cars and trucks on the road outside is stilled. In front of the altar, even with the ground, is a great stone slab, marked:

HERE REST THE
REMAINS OF THE LATE
COLONEL JAMES SKINNER C.B.
WHO DEPARTED THIS LIFE,
AT HANSI
4th DECEMBER 1841
THE BODY WAS DISINTERRED,
REMOVED FROM HANSI AND BURIED UNDER
THIS ON THE 19th JANUARY 1842

I don't know why they moved him. When I walk around the church, on the wall I find the reason.

THIS CHURCH WAS ERECTED AT THE
SOLE EXPENSE OF THE LATE
COLONEL JAMES SKINNER C.B.
IN FULFILMENT OF A VOW
MADE WHILE LYING WOUNDED
ON THE FIELD OF BATTLE
IN GRATEFUL ACKNOWLEDGEMENT

OF THE MEMORY OF DIVINE PROVIDENCE
AND IS TESTIMONY
OF HIS SINCERE FAITH IN THE TRUTH
OF THE CHRISTIAN RELIGION

I say to Sikander, my name is Abhay, I knew someone who knew you, and I ask, where are your mosque and your temple, but he cannot reply from under his stone. I try to pray, but I cannot, and I walk outside into the bright sunlight. I don't know why I came, to this church, to this place, but somehow I had to come, to greet what lies buried there and everywhere. I am also asking for help, I suppose, because my friend Saira is wounded and near death.

When I had finished telling my story of returning from foreign lands, the noise was rising outside. There were shouts and calls, loud arguments, the frightening roar of crowds, of conflict. Since then I have tried to find out what the fight was about, and I have discovered that there were dozens of factions, a hundred ideologies, all struggling with each other, there were politics old and deep, alliances and betrayals, defeats and triumphs, revenge and friendship, the old story, you've heard it before, but there was one new thing, one new idea that overwhelmed everything else, and this was simply that there should be only one idea, one voice, one thing, one, one, one. So as I finished my story, and as Sanjay lay with his head in Yama's lap, a fight broke out, we heard the clamour from inside. Saira was holding Sanjay's hand, and when it began he started, a look of pain on his face, and without a pause Saira leapt off the bed and ran outside. I sprinted after her but she was fast, and not hesitating she ran into the roiling crowd, amongst the men and women pushing and beating at each other, and she called, 'Stop! Stop it. Stop it right now.' There was a light about her, an energy that stilled those who saw her, and as she ran into the middle of the maidan the crowd cleared around her and I think she would have succeeded, she would have stopped it all, but dropping out of the sky there was already a black point, a singularity, a bomb. Nobody knows whose it was, what party affiliations it had, whether it believed in this or that, but it came down, perfect and sleek and technologically advanced and clicking, and when it burst it did what no one has been able to do ever, it stilled every voice and its roar became the owner of the world. Saira was still running and I don't believe she ever saw it. It wounded her, only her, it hurt her in ways I can't bring myself to describe. She is alive but she is wounded.

We took her to hospital, and the good doctors struggled to save her. Finally it was decided that she should be taken to Delhi, to the All-India Medical Institute, and before we left I came back to my house, her blood still on my clothes. I found my father and mother still sitting with Sanjay, whose chest heaved up and down, his eyes were almost closed. He had been waiting, I think, only for news of her. He had said he would not speak again, but when I told him he broke his vow and told me something. I whispered to him, and then he put his hand in mine, and with a trembling, feathery finger he traced the words on my wrist, Help her.

'How?' I said.

He said: 'Tell a story.'

Why, how, my questions were still bursting out when his finger shook one last time on my wrist, and I may have imagined the word that it wrote on my pulse, I cannot be sure, but he said, Brother, and then he died. I held his body, small it was, in my arms and I wept. Then I asked my father, what does one do with the body of this animal? He shook his head. Finally we walked through the dark streets of the town, through the curfew, unseen, and then into the country. We found a river — its name I do not know, I could not find it again — and I lowered Sanjay into the water, and the steady current beating against my thighs carried him away quietly.

I am now in the hospital room, watching Saira. My parents and hers keep anxious vigil, and the serious young doctors of the Institute are fighting hard to save her. I trust them, and I like them, but I remember what Sanjay told me, and I know there is more to be done. Her little face is framed by bandages, and her hands lie still on top of the sheets. I tell my elders that I will be back, and then I walk out, out of the room and out of the building, into the street. There are people walking about the gates, cars and scooters passing by. I take a deep breath. I am mad, perhaps I will be arrested. Will I wander barefoot in the streets of Delhi, will you exile me from this city I love? Will you listen to me? Will you stone me, will you imprison me? I cannot care, I must tell a story. Listen. I am about to tell a story. I will tell you about wives, and good doctors, soldiers, poets, tribesmen, loafers and goondas, untrustworthy characters, loan-takers, dashing pilots, fast horses, card-players, social-ites, actresses, politicians, I will tell you about underground deals, black money, great loves, cross-country runs, farmers and their crops, fish-eries and city councils, religious leaders and, of course, cavalrymen. I will tell you a story that will grow like a lotus vine, that will twist in on itself and expand ceaselessly, till all of you are a part of it, and the gods come to listen, till we are all talking in a musical hubbub that contains the past, every moment of the present, and all the future. And the great music of that primeval sound will reach Saira's ears, and she will rise from her bed, she will shake off her bandages and she will jump down to stand with her hands on her hips, and she will say, laughing, what's the matter, yaar, why so long-face, want to play a game of cricket? And we will all walk to the maidan holding hands, and as we walk you and I will look from side to side and we will see them all, we will see that everyone is there, all our fathers and mothers and their enemies, all together now, and in the crowd a bottomless basket of laddoos will pass around, and we will all eat our fill. We will play till the sun sets, feeling fine and free and running about. Then we will sit in circles and circles, saying, bless us, Ganesha; be with us, friend Hanuman; Yama, you old fraud, you can listen if you want; and saying this we will start all over again.